IBERIAN AND LATIN AMERICAN STUDIES

Theatre Censorship in Spain, 1931–1985

Series Editors

Professor David George (Swansea University)
Professor Paul Garner (University of Leeds)

Editorial Board

Samuel Amago (University of Virginia)
Roger Bartra (Universidad Autónoma de México)
Paul Castro (University of Glasgow)
Richard Cleminson (University of Leeds)
Catherine Davies (University of London)
Lloyd H. Davies (Swansea University)
Luisa-Elena Delgado (University of Illinois)
Maria Delgado (Central School of Speech and Drama, London)
Will Fowler (University of St Andrews)
David Gies (University of Virginia)
Gareth Walters (Swansea University)
Duncan Wheeler (University of Leeds)

Other titles in the series

Doña Bárbara Unleashed: From Venezuelan Plains to International Screen
Jenni M. Lehtinen

Fantastic Short Stories by Women Authors from Spain and Latin America: A Critical Anthology
Patricia Gracía and Teresa López-Pellisa

Carmen Martín Gaite: Poetics, Visual Elements and Space
Ester Bautista Botello

The Spanish Anarchists of Northern Australia: Revolution in the Sugar Cane Fields
Robert Mason

Paulo Emilio Salles Gomes: On Brazil and Global Cinema
Maite Conde and Stephanie Dennison

The Tlatelolco Massacre, Mexico 1968, and the Emotional Triangle of Anger, Grief and Shame: iscourses of Truth(s)
Victoria Carpenter

The Darkening Nation: Race, Neoliberalism and Crisis in Argentina
Ignacio Aguiló

Catalan Culture: Experimentation, creative imagination and therelationship with Spain
Lloyd Hughes Davies, J. B. Hall and D. Gareth Walters

Madness and Irrationality in Spanish and Latin American Literature and Culture
Lloyd Hughes Davies

IBERIAN AND LATIN AMERICAN STUDIES

Theatre Censorship in Spain, 1931–1985

CATHERINE O'LEARY AND MICHAEL THOMPSON

UNIVERSITY OF WALES PRESS
2023

© Catherine O'Leary and Michael Thompson, 2023
Reprinted 2024

All rights reserved. No part of this book may be reproduced in any material form (including photocopying or storing it in any medium by electronic means and whether or not transiently or incidentally to some other use of this publication) without the written permission of the copyright owner. Applications for the copyright owner's written permission to reproduce any part of this publication should be addressed to the University of Wales Press, University Registry, King Edward VII Avenue, Cardiff CF10 3NS.

www.uwp.co.uk

British Library CIP
A catalogue record for this book is available from the British Library.

ISBN   978-1-78683-982-4
e-ISBN   978-1-78683-983-1

The rights of Catherine O'Leary and Michael Thompson to be identified as authors of this work have been asserted in accordance with sections 77 and 79 of the Copyright, Designs and Patents Act 1988.

Typeset by Geethik Technologies
Printed on demand by CPI Group (UK) Ltd, Croydon, CR0 4YY

To all the theatremakers who struggled against Francoist censorship
To Lisa, Alex, Liam and Oscar

Contents

Series Editors' Foreword	ix
Acknowledgements	xi
List of illustrations	xiii
List of abbreviations	xvii
Introduction	xxi

1. The Evolution of Theatre Censorship in Spain from the 1830s to the 1930s — 1
2. *Un teatro de ida y vuelta*: All Change and No Change in the Second Republic and the Civil War — 38
   Case study: *Santa Teresita del Niño Jesús*, by Vicente Mena Pérez — 78
3. The Franco Dictatorship: Censorship as 'Propaganda', 'Education' and 'Information' — 87
   Case study: *La casa de Bernarda Alba*, by Federico García Lorca — 142
4. The Pervasiveness of Censorship during the Dictatorship: Right-Wing Triumphalism, Commercial Theatre, *Revistas* and Catalan Theatre — 155
   Case study: *La Infanzona*, by Jacinto Benavente — 199
5. The Realist Generation: A Spotlight on the Margins of Society — 207
   Case study: *Escuadra hacia la muerte*, by Alfonso Sastre — 254

6 Experimental, Avant-Garde and Independent Theatre:
   Pushing the Boundaries   265
   **Case study: *Castañuela 70*, by Tábano and Las Madres
   del Cordero**   316
7 The Censorship of Foreign Theatre: From Taming the
   Text to Disruptive Drama   326
   Case study: *El círculo de tiza caucasiano*, by Bertolt Brecht 370
8 Dénouement: Dismantling the Apparatus during the
   Transition to Democracy   380
   Case study: *La torna*, by Els Joglars/Albert Boadella   402

Conclusion   406

Bibliography   427

    Archival sources   428

    Legislation   448

    Other sources   457

Index   499

Series Editors' Foreword

Over recent decades the traditional 'languages and literatures' model in Spanish departments in universities in the United Kingdom has been superseded by a contextual, interdisciplinary and 'area studies' approach to the study of the culture, history, society and politics of the Hispanic and Lusophone worlds – categories that extend far beyond the confines of the Iberian Peninsula, not only in Latin America but also to Spanish-speaking and Lusophone Africa.

In response to these dynamic trends in research priorities and curriculum development, this series is designed to present both disciplinary and interdisciplinary research within the general field of Iberian and Latin American Studies, particularly studies that explore all aspects of Cultural Production (inter alia literature, film, music, dance, sport) in Spanish, Portuguese, Basque, Catalan, Galician and indigenous languages of Latin America. The series also aims to publish research in the History and Politics of the Hispanic and Lusophone worlds, at the level of both the region and the nation-state, as well as on Cultural Studies that explore the shifting terrains of gender, sexual, racial and postcolonial identities in those same regions.

Acknowledgements

We wish to thank the institutions that made the Theatre Censorship in Spain project possible: the British Academy, which funded some of the preparatory work, and the Arts and Humanities Research Council, which funded the main period of research between 2008 and 2011. We are also grateful for the support provided over the years by the School of Modern Languages and Cultures at Durham University, the School of Modern Languages, Literatures and Cultures at Maynooth University and the School of Modern Languages at the University of St Andrews, and by colleagues in all those places. Institutions in Spain and the staff who work in them have been enormously helpful: the Archivo General de la Administración (AGA) in Alcalá de Henares, the Arxiu Nacional de Catalunya in Sant Cugat del Vallès, the Biblioteca Nacional de España, the Centro Documental de la Memoria Histórica in Salamanca, the Ministerio de Cultura y Deporte, the Archivo Regional de la Comunidad de Madrid and the Centro de Documentación Teatral. Thanks are also due to the AGA and the Comunidad de Madrid for granting permission for the reproduction of images from their collections.

Our findings have been enriched by the memories of the authors, directors and actors who talked or wrote to us about their experience of censorship. Our heartfelt thanks go to José Luis Alonso de Santos, Fernando Arrabal, Josep Maria Benet i Jornet, Fermín Cabal, Jesús Campos, Josep Anton Codina, Teresa del Olmo, Antonio Díaz Zamora, Mayca Estévez, Ángel Facio, Alfonso Guerra, Jerónimo López Mozo, José Monleón, Francisco Nieva, Josep Maria Pou and José María Rodríguez Méndez. We wish to pay tribute to Pat O'Connor, whose pioneering work laid the foundations for our own investigations, as well as to Berta Muñoz Cáliz and to

Raquel Merino Álvarez (and the TRACE project), who have done much to highlight the importance of theatre censorship in Spain.

We are grateful to our post-doctoral research associate, Diego Santos Sánchez, for his diligent archival work and skilful interviewing, and to Mary Bradshaw for her careful proofreading and transcription work, as well as to Lisa Goldman, Théâtre Sans Frontières in Hexham and the Cervantes Theatre in London for their enthusiastic collaboration with follow-up activities building on the Theatre Censorship in Spain project.

Some of the material in Chapter 2 was previously published in Spanish in Catherine O'Leary, *La censura del teatro durante la guerra civil española* (Madrid: Guillermo Escolar, 2020) as part of a Spanish government-funded project on civil war culture, directed by Emilio Peral Vega.

We are indebted to our friends and families for their support and encouragement throughout, and to Sarah Lewis at University of Wales Press for her flexibility and helpful advice. And finally, our profound thanks go to Gustavo and Jenn, whose loving patience has sustained us through the long gestation of this work.

List of illustrations

All illustrations apart from Figure 13 are courtesy of Ministerio de Cultura y Deporte (Spain), Archivo General de la Administración (AGA).

Figure 1: Report on the premiere of *Mariana Pineda* by Federico García Lorca (Madrid, 13 October 1927) (2 pages) (AGA: IDD (03)036.000, Caja 21/5822, Legajo 07398). 10

Figure 2: Cover of a copy of the typescript of *La Santa Hermandad* by Eduardo Marquina submitted for censorship (1939) (AGA: IDD (03)046.000, Caja 73/8179, Expediente 464/39). 36

Figure 3: Authorisation certificate for *Y el Imperio volvía* by Ramón Cué (31 January 1939) (AGA: IDD (03)046.000, Caja 73/08147, Expediente 6/39). 77

Figure 4: Report by an inspector from the Dirección General de Seguridad on the second performance of *Santa Teresita del Niño Jesús* by Vicente Mena Pérez (Madrid, 30 June 1933) (pages 1 and 4) (AGA: IDD (03)036.000, Caja 21/0646, Expediente 6192). 83

Figure 5: Letter signed by F. G. de Canales (Delegado Nacional de Propaganda), sent to the head of the Sección de Cinematografía y Teatro, setting out criteria for theatre

censorship (6 July 1943) (AGA: IDD
(03)049.000, Caja 21/0646). 107

Figure 6: Page from Act 2 of the typescript of *La casa de Bernarda Alba* by Federico García Lorca, showing a cut recommended by a censor (AGA: IDD (03)046.000, Caja 73/08489, Expediente 193/43). 149

Figure 7: Censor's report by Gumersindo Montes Agudo on *El gran Galeoto* by José Echegaray (11 November 1943) (2 pages) (AGA: IDD (03)046.000, Caja 73/08163, Expediente 205/39). 171

Figure 8: Censorship certificate authorising *Cinco minutos nada menos* by José Muñoz Román (13 November 1946) (2 pages) (AGA: IDD (03)046.000, Caja 73/08552, Expediente 25/44). 183

Figure 9: Letter from General Carlos Asensio (Alto Estado Mayor) to the Director General de Cinematografía y Teatro recommending the prohibition of *Escuadra hacia la muerte* by Alfonso Sastre (16 January 1956) (2 pages) (AGA: IDD (03)046.000, Caja 73/09057, Expediente 94/53). 259

Figure 10: Notification of the prohibition of *Escuadra hacia la muerte* (27 January 1956) (AGA: IDD (03)046.000, Caja 73/09057, Expediente 94/53). 260

Figure 11: Letter from Commander Juan Guerra y Romero (Alto Estado Mayor) to the Director General de Cinematografía y Teatro recommending authorisation of *Escuadra hacia la muerte* (19 November 1962) (AGA: IDD (03)046.000, Caja 73/09057, Expediente 94/53). 261

Figure 12: Notification of the prohibition of *Espectáculo collage* by Alberto Miralles (26 November 1971)

(AGA: IDD (03)046.000, Caja 73/09899, Expediente 631/71).	305

Figure 13: Photograph by Martín Santos Yubero of a performance of *Castañuela 70* by Tábano (1970), Teatro de la Comedia (Madrid) (Archivo Regional de la Comunidad de Madrid: Fondo Martín Santos Yubero, Código de referencia 27404/85). 321

Figure 14: Censor's report by Andrés Avelino Esteban Romero on *La última cinta de Krapp* by Samuel Beckett (13 December 1959) (AGA: IDD (03)046.000, Caja 73/09314, Expediente 374/59). 357

Figure 15: Inspector's report by Rafael Salazar Ruiz on the first performance of *El círculo de tiza caucasiano* by Bertolt Brecht (30 March 1965) (AGA: IDD (03)046.000, Caja 73/09492, Expediente 13/65). 375

Figure 16: Censor's report by Antonio Albizu on *No hablaré en clase* by Joan Ollé y Josep Parramon (September 1976) (2 pages) (AGA: IDD (03)046.000, Caja 73/10175, Expediente 1138/76). 386

List of abbreviations

ACNP	Asociación Católica Nacional de Propagandistas (influential lay Catholic organisation)
ADB	Agrupació Dramàtica de Barcelona (amateur theatre group)
AGA	Archivo General de la Administración (state archive)
AHMD	Aula d'Història i Memòria de la Universitat de València (research group on historical memory)
ANC	Arxiu Nacional de Catalunya (Catalan national archive)
BOE	*Boletín Oficial del Estado* (official gazette in which legislation is published)
CCT	Consejo Central del Teatro (Republican theatre council)
CET	Comité Económico del Teatro/Comité Econòmic del Teatre (CNT-affiliated organisation controlling theatre in Catalonia during the civil war)
CDMAE	Centre de Documentació i Museu de les Artes Escèniques (archive of the Theatre Institute in Barcelona)
CDMH	Centro Documental de la Memoria Histórica (government archive of civil war and post-war documents)
CDT	Centro de Documentación Teatral (now Centro de Documentación de las Artes Escénicas y de la Música) (state archive of theatre documents, photographs and videos)

CEDA	Confederación Española de Derechas Autónomas (right-wing Catholic party during the Republic)
CNT	Confederación Nacional del Trabajo (anarchist trade union)
CST	Consejo Superior del Teatro (Francoist theatre council)
DEPP	Delegación del Estado para Prensa y Propaganda (Nationalist propaganda office during the civil war)
EADAG	Escola d'Art Dramàtic Adrià Gual (theatre school in Barcelona)
FESTA	Foment de l'Espectacle Selecte i Teatre Associació (Catalan amateur theatre association)
FET y de las JONS	Falange Española Tradicionalista y de las Juntas de Ofensiva Nacional Sindicalista (Francoist organisation based on the pre-civil war Falange party)
GTR	Grupo de Teatro Realista (campaigning theatre group founded by Alfonso Sastre and José María de Quinto in 1960)
INAEM	Instituto de las Artes Escénicas y de la Música (government department responsible for theatre and music)
JDN	Junta de Defensa Nacional (the first provisional military government established by the leaders of the uprising in July 1936)
MIT	Ministerio de Información y Turismo (the ministry responsible for the promotion and censorship of theatre between 1951 and 1977)
PCE	Partido Comunista de España (Spanish Communist Party)
PSOE	Partido Socialista Obrero Español (Spanish Socialist Workers' Party)
SEU	Sindicato Español Universitario (official students' union controlled by the Falange)
SGAE	Sociedad General de Autores de España (body defending the rights and interests of playwrights, composers and songwriters;

	since 1995, Sociedad General de Autores y Editores)
SIE	Sindicato de la Industria del Espectáculo/ Sindicat de l'Industria de l'Espectacle (successor to the SUEP)
SUEP	Sindicato Único de Espectáculos Públicos/ Sindicat Únic d'Espectacles Públics (wartime entertainment industry trade union in Catalonia, affiliated to the CNT)
TAC	Teatro Ambulante de Campaña (war-time theatre group sponsored by the Nationalist army)
TAS	Teatro de Agitación Social (campaigning theatre group founded by Alfonso Sastre and José María de Quinto in 1950)
TEI	Teatro Español Independiente (theatre group founded by Miguel Alcobendas in 1960, or the independent theatre movement of the 1960s and 1970s in general)
TEM	Teatro Estudio de Madrid (independent theatre company and school founded by William Layton and Miguel Narros in 1960)
TEU	Teatro Español Universitario (network of student theatre groups established by the SEU)
TNCE	Teatro Nacional de Cámara y Ensayo (state-sponsored company intended to promote new, experimental or fringe theatre)
TNU	Teatro Nacional Universitario (student theatre company founded in Madrid in 1962)
UGT	Unión General de Trabajadores (trade union affiliated with the PSOE)

Introduction

This book explores the history and practice of theatre censorship in Spain in the twentieth century. It aims to understand Spanish culture and cultural policy during this period through the analysis of the work of a range of playwrights and companies, and the changing circumstances in which theatre was produced. While focusing primarily on theatrical activity in Spain, the book also addresses more general questions about the nature of censorship, its role in the relationship between cultural production and the state, and its effect on the formation and policing of artistic canons. It is the product of a collaborative research project that was funded by the UK Arts and Humanities Research Council and represents the first substantial study of Spanish theatre censorship published in English, and the first in any language to cover the whole period from the Second Republic to the transition to democracy.

The objective of the book is, first, to investigate the mechanisms of theatre censorship throughout much of twentieth-century Spain. Drawing on extensive archival evidence, vivid personal testimonies and in-depth analysis of legislation, the book documents the different kinds of theatre censorship practised during the Second Republic (1931–6), the civil war (1936–9), the Franco dictatorship (1939–75) and the transition to democracy (1975–85).

The second objective is to consider how censorship and creative responses to it adapted and developed over time as political circumstances changed and new theatrical trends emerged. Our study of the interaction between the highly variable interpretations of the censors and the strategies adopted by writers, directors and producers in response to the constraints will lead to more complete and fully contextualised readings of the dramatic texts discussed. Changes in criteria, administrative structures and personnel are traced in relation to wider political, social and cultural developments, and the responses of playwrights, directors and companies are explored.

Thirdly, the book considers the impact of censorship across a variety of theatrical genres. Our focus on censorship casts new light on particular theatremakers and their work, on the conditions in which all kinds of plays were produced and on the construction of genres and canons. Analysis of detailed case studies provides not only evidence on the day-to-day realities of the functioning of the system, but also new insights into the creative and interpretative processes.

Finally, the book considers how our understanding of cultural production and power is enhanced by gauging the impact of censorship on Spain's theatrical and cultural scene both at the time and in terms of legacy. The archival documents are analysed in relation to a range of contextual evidence on cultural policies and structures, legislation and theatrical practice, together with views expressed by participants at the time and in retrospect.

Theatre in Spain

While the mainstream theatre at the start of the twentieth century provided entertainment for a largely middle-class public, the early decades also saw the development of a minority avant-garde theatre in the 1920s and a politicised theatre in the 1930s, both of which were influenced by international trends. Although the impact of avant-garde groups was limited and their existence short-lived, they served as a useful platform for experimentation among authors and directors, some of whom, such as Ramón del Valle-Inclán and Cipriano de Rivas Cherif, would later bring their work to a wider public. The political theatre that emerged in the 1930s was both a reflection of new ideas about the proletariat and an enactment of the social and revolutionary change that many at the time saw as necessary. It was deliberately harnessed as an identity-building tool by a Republican government that sought to inculcate in the largely uneducated masses an acceptance of their political project. Although the cultural output from the left dominated, the growth of a right-wing theatre embracing religious, folkloric and other elements as a reflection of a newly envisioned traditionalist state is also considered.

During the civil war, left-wing political theatre underwent a shift from an internationalist view to a local one, often employing new techniques of agitation propaganda to great effect in its efforts to convince, enthuse and rally the political faithful, while demonising the enemy. The theatre was used as a weapon by both sides during the civil war and was employed by figures who were significant cultural and political actors in the conflict and in the dictatorship that followed.

In the aftermath of the war, the victors did not easily forget the power of culture to convince, and immediately set about legislating for its control. The fascist-inspired Falange Party (Falange Española Tradicionalista y de las Juntas de Ofensiva Nacional Sindicalista: FET y de las JONS) was initially in charge of censorship, and the influence of the intellectual and culturally sophisticated – but politically reactionary – clique surrounding Dionisio Ridruejo shaped its practice in the early years of the dictatorship. Like the Republican leadership of the 1930s, they recognised the usefulness of culture, and the theatre in particular, in the consolidation of their victory and in the embedding of their values within people's experiences and everyday lives. Before long, however, the emphasis moved increasingly towards a depoliticisation of the theatre. The aim of the authorities was to prevent its use as an instrument of social change and to encourage or force society to conform to a particular set of political and moral values.

Theatrical performance is live and therefore difficult to control. The people who work in the theatre often wish to challenge rules and traditions and embrace the opportunities for playing out the alternatives that it offers. Unlike other fixed cultural forms, such as a novel or a film, a play can be adapted to circumstances at the moment of delivery. There is no guarantee that what is on the page will be performed in a specific way and this can make those in power nervous. The influential critic José Monleón suggested in an interview for this project that the theatre under the dictatorship became one of the 'espacios fundamentales para articular la crítica al régimen' ('fundamental spaces for the articulation of criticism of the regime') (2011). Its power, he argued, was a creative one: 'Es abrirse imaginativamente a una serie de posibilidades que el orden las considera inoportunas' ('It means opening oneself up in the realm of the imagination to a series of possibilities that the authorities consider inopportune').

The theatre, moreover, gathers the public together in a shared space. In the context of the dictatorship, when protests against the regime were outlawed, the theatre could offer an opportunity not only to view and share reactions to plays that contained or enacted social and political messages about the need for change, but sometimes even suggested a desired collective response. Alfonso Guerra, former student theatre director and later one of the most influential politicians of the early post-Franco period, speaking of his days in student theatre, noted in an interview for this project how in tune they were with their public, as the latter was anti-Francoist and seeking a political message: 'Era una comunión total' ('It was total communion') (2010).

Theatre censorship

Our approach to the study of theatre censorship in Spain is to acknowledge its complexity in terms of its various goals and applications, from protecting valuable relationships and avoiding giving offence, to silencing alternative political views and reinforcing particular moral values. Studies by Richard Burt (1998), Judith Butler (1998) and Helen Freshwater (2009), among others, have informed our view of censorship in Spain as a continuum involving legally determined state repression and less obvious persecution and humiliation of dramatists and practitioners, but also the notion of a constitutive censorship that led many to normalise compliance, internalise the rules and neuter their own creative voice.

Ideas such as those put forward by Louis Althusser (1971) and Michel Foucault (1978; 1979; 1980) have been useful in framing our understanding.[1] They explore how censorship, rather than a straightforward imposition of state repression, can be seen as a productive force in society, in the sense that it defines acceptable discourse and contributes to the formation of model citizens. Susan Curry Jansen (1988), Pierre Bourdieu (1992), Judith Butler (1997) and Robert C. Post (1998) have also enhanced our view of censorship and cultural control, both regulative and productive. Bourdieu, for example, suggests that 'censorship is never quite so perfect or as invisible as when each agent has nothing to say apart from what he is objectively authorized to say', an idea reflected in the atmosphere of fear created by the regime and the resulting impossible-to-measure self-censorship that pertained in Spain under Franco (1992: 138). In addition, the types of restriction imposed on production runs and locations can be understood in terms of Richard Burt's notions of censorship operating as 'dispersal and displacement', rather than 'removal and replacement' (1998: 17). Also valuable is Jacques Rancière's discussion of the difference between 'politics as police' and 'disruptive politics', which we have found useful when exploring the threat that the theatre posed to the regime's attempts to control public discourse and the ongoing struggle played out at the level of censorship (2006). While the former type of politics engaged in the 'distribution of the sensible', determining what was visible and sayable in society, aesthetic and artistic practices, which he relates to the latter, offered an unsettling counterpoint.

In our exploration of censorship, we have also considered the regime's own justifications for cultural control. This is seen in the legislation produced at various stages, which is discussed in detail in Chapters 1 and 3, but also in the more theoretical discussions expounded in the *Textos de doctrina y política española de la información*, published by the first Minister for Information and Tourism, the conservative Catholic, Gabriel Arias-Salgado (1960); the memoirs of the liberal Director General José María García Escudero (1978a); and those of the influential Minister for Information and Tourism, Manuel Fraga Iribarne (1980). In fact, Fraga agreed to be interviewed for the book but terminated the conversation after the following brief statement. His retrospective view justified the regime's censorship as necessary in what he described as a transition from war-time legislation to the freedom enjoyed by practitioners in the democratic period:

> Se trataba de hacer una transición muy delicada, que ha salido de un régimen regido por la ley del 38, que era una ley de Guerra ... se pasó a la situación actual en que hoy hay absoluta libertad en todos los terrenos, desde la prensa hasta el teatro. Entonces, lo único que hacíamos desde el Ministerio de Información [y Turismo] era controlar que nadie se pasara de velocidad, porque eso podría haber dado lugar a un retroceso mucho mayor. Y la censura del teatro, o la del cine y otras varias, tuvieron cuidado de que nadie se creyera más listo que los demás y diese pasos más rápidos. Y el resultado es que hemos conseguido nuestro objetivo, porque se ha pasado de una censura absolutamente cerrada al sistema actual, que es comparable a cualquiera del mundo. No tengo más que decir. (Fraga 2010)

It was about a delicate transition, which came out of a regime governed by the 1938 law, which was wartime legislation ... we moved to the current situation in which today there is absolute freedom in all areas, from the press to the theatre. Back then the only thing we did from the Ministry of Information [and Tourism] was to keep control to ensure that nobody moved too fast because that would have led to a much worse regression. And theatre censorship, or cinema censorship or the various other types, took care to ensure that nobody considered themselves smarter than the rest and took faster steps. And the result is that we have achieved our goal because we have moved from an absolutely closed censorship to the current system, which is comparable to any in the world. I have no more to say.

When censorship was in operation, however, justifications related more to the protection of the common good or of the weaker members of society, and the protection of a set of core values associated with Spain's political and religious rulers. Minister Arias-Salgado, for example, defined the common good as 'un bien material y moral a la vez' ('both a material and a moral good') and argued that censorship allowed 'toda la libertad para la verdad; ninguna libertad para el error' ('total freedom for truth; no freedom for error') (1960: 7–8, 35). The regime declared itself the holder of the truth and defender of the common good and employed censorship as a tool to fulfil these self-assigned roles. García Escudero argued in a similar vein that 'la censura no tiene por qué verse como un antipático adoctrinamiento, sino como la defensa de una serie de libertades, y esencialmente de la libertad de ser lo que somos, y de unos valores más altos que los mismos valores estéticos' ('censorship should not be seen as unpleasant indoctrination, but rather as the defence of a series of freedoms, and essentially of the freedom to be who we are, and [the defence] of a set of values that are greater than aesthetic values themselves') (1952: 181).

Both within the legislation and the censors' comments in their reports, we see the importance that the regime placed on the moral and educational influence of the theatre. During the Republican period and the civil war, the theatre became a testing ground for new ideas and a propaganda tool for inculcating them; during the dictatorship, it was employed variously as a distraction from reality and as a tool for the reinforcement of the regime's values. The authorities were understandably made uneasy by the mid-century realists' criticism of the status quo and their representation and enactment of alternatives to it, and by the later experimental practices that upended the very format and established rules of the theatre.

Unlike some other authoritarian states (especially communist ones), the Franco regime did not hide its censorship practices but claimed them instead as positive and protective acts. The regulatory framework built by the regime was intended to be exhaustive in its coverage of possibilities but, of course, the laws, like the plays themselves, remained open to human interpretation. Indeed, there is an ironic parallel in the power of the theatre to influence and shape collective responses to particular issues and the functioning of the censorship boards, in which the verdicts of some censors were manifestly influenced and shaped by the opinions or anticipated responses of other board members.

Beyond the legislation and censorship boards, secondary forms of censorship operated in the decisions made by theatre managers and directors about the choice of play to stage (either ones that would be unproblematic or those chosen to cause a stir); in media and academic reviews; in the Church's own form of censorship; in granting or withholding permission to participate in national or international festivals or productions; and in the promotion of certain works through prizes. We see this in the debates about what plays should be staged during the civil war; in the promotion of certain acceptable authors in its aftermath; in the exclusion from the theatre and the press of signatories of protest letters in the 1960s; and in the legal trials and negative press campaigns faced by some experimental and independent dramatists.

Theatre censorship as applied in Spain affected more than the approval of a playscript but also had implications for script development, live performance and publication. The existence of systematic state censorship under an authoritarian regime, combined with more insidious forms of control, led, on the one hand, to the development of certain modes of theatre, and on the other hand, the failure of other modes to emerge or evolve. One of the most damaging effects was self-censorship, both conscious and unconscious. In his analysis of Spanish censorship published at the end of the dictatorship, Antonio Beneyto, the author of a study on censorship and politics, concludes: 'El verdadero poder de la censura: el de convertir a muchos escritores en censores de sí mismos' ('The true power of censorship: that of converting many authors into self-censors') (1979: 158). A 1974 survey of ninety-five Spanish authors carried out by Manuel Abellán, one of the first scholars to study Francoist censorship and its effects, found that while just under a third of them claimed that they had never engaged in self-censorship, a little over two-thirds of them divulged that they had (1987: 20). Given the unconscious nature of much self-censorship, it is impossible to come to any accurate conclusion about how widespread it was, although the very fact that so many surveyed admitted to it suggests that it was a very common practice.[2]

The focus of this book is on performance, rather than publication. It investigates a complex form of censorship, involving a playscript in addition to performance and a variety of players, from author and director to actors, producers, designers, translators, spectators and critics. Indeed, the legislation relating to censorship of performance, which is much more detailed than that for publications, is indicative of the threat that the regime perceived in live performance. As José Monleón stressed in his interview with us, the theatre could question the 'camino recto' ('correct path') and 'orden mítico' ('mythical order') that the official doctrines of Church and politicians proposed, and instead present alternative pathways and undermine myths (2011).

In practice, theatre censorship involved pre-production scrutiny of the script, as well as consideration of the dramatist, theatre company, director, actors, and the impact on spectators of the location and production run. Political circumstances were also taken into account, so each separate production was considered in its own right; it was not simply the case that the play was or was not authorised for good. During the production, official monitoring continued, and it was common to have an inspection of the dress rehearsal to ensure that costume, delivery of lines, set design, and so on, complied with what was allowed. Inspectors could also be sent to the performance itself and this could also lead to further censorship or even the withdrawal of a work.

It is also important to recognise that those who were on the receiving end of censorship did not all react in the same way, and we can discern varied and often sophisticated responses among authors, practitioners and spectators. Some, like Antonio Buero Vallejo, were willing to compromise and negotiate with censors to gain authorisation for their work; others chose to write and stage non-political works; while others employed foreign drama to say

Introduction xxix

the unsayable. In terms of spectators, there were some who were determined to be entertained, while others resolved to find a political interpretation in whatever they viewed. Nor can we consider all censors as being in the same mould. Some were employees of the state, conscientious in their interpretation and application of the rules; others were literary critics or authors themselves and focused more on ideas of artistic quality; still others represented the Church and its moral values. As time progressed and the regime adapted to new internal and external circumstances, so too did the censors; their work, just as much as the plays they scrutinised, can be seen as a reflection of the changing times.

Source materials and the structure of the book

This study encompasses historical research in archives, analysis of legislation, an investigation of the theory and practice of censorship and a consideration of theatre as both creative and political practice. In our analysis, we have incorporated primary documentary evidence from several archives: the Archivo General de la Administración (AGA); the Arxiu Nacional de Catalunya (ANC); and Centro Documental de la Memoria Histórica (CDMH). The AGA is the most significant of these in terms of the overall study, as it contains the official state censorship files from the government ministries that oversaw its implementation. Some materials relating to censorship are also held in regional archives and we have looked at several of these, although, as the system in Spain was highly centralised, provincial delegates were required to inform the authorities in Madrid of their activities and the AGA contains copious correspondence between the centre and the regions in matters relating to local controls. The material in the files is organised by play and contains information relating to specific productions, including the application paperwork, copies of the playscript (though not in all cases), individual censors' reports, internal correspondence and correspondence with directors and playwrights, and records of plenary meetings of censorship boards. The ANC contains materials specific to cultural activities in Catalonia, including notifications sent to the local censorship office from Madrid (organised by year rather than by play, offering a different perspective from the AGA files). The CDMH has holdings relating to many aspects of the civil war period, including data collected by Francoist investigators to be used as allegedly criminal evidence of Republican sympathies, which becomes a rich source of documentation relating to the organisation and control of cultural activity.

Personal testimony from published memoirs and interviews with directors, playwrights and actors have been used to complement the state files and to create a fuller picture of the relationship between cultural practitioners and the state. We have also made extensive use of newspaper archives for performance reviews and reactions to state interventions in the cultural sphere (in particular *hemeroteca.abc.es*; *prensahistorica.mcu.es*; *teatro.es/contenidos/documentosParaLaHistoria*; *hemeroteadigital.bne.es*). We consulted the relevant legislation in the *Boletín Oficial del Estado* and the earlier *Gaceta de Madrid*, *Gaceta de la República* and *Boletín Oficial de la Junta de Defensa Nacional*, and examined theatre archives, such as those held at the Instituto Nacional de las Artes Escénicas y de la Música, and its Centro de Documentación de las Artes Escénicas y de la Música for other key information about theatrical trends and influential figures within the Spanish theatre world. Materials on the various theories of censorship and general information about the theatre were located in the Biblioteca Nacional de España, the British Library and a number of university libraries. We also drew on important studies about Spanish theatre censorship by Abellán (1978, 1980, 1984, 1987, 1989), Díez (2007, 2008, 2009), Gallén (1996), García Ruiz (1996, 1997, 2000, 2013), Merino Álvarez (1994, 2007, 2016), Muñoz Cáliz (2005, 2006, 2010) and O'Connor (1973, 1976).

The book is structured chronologically and by genre. It provides both a broad survey of the theatrical landscape and its interactions with the state and individual case studies that allow us to explore key works and influential figures in depth. The case studies at the end of the thematically focused chapters have been selected to provide detailed explorations of plays that, either in terms of content or reception, captured the *zeitgeist*. Overall, in determining our selection, we have focused on case studies that highlight a variety of censorship practices from prior censorship to inspectors' reports on performances, behind-the-scenes negotiations with censors, state responses to political circumstances, and a variety of outcomes, from authorisation to limited approval, withdrawal or prohibition. We also consider a broad range of genres, including religious drama, mainstream commercial productions, student productions, experimental performance, political and foreign drama. With these case studies, we reflect on a variety of periods and theatrical trends in order to give an overview of a complex and ever-changing system and the place of the playwright, practitioner, censor, critic and spectator within it. The book also contains a detailed bibliography both of theatre in Spain in the twentieth century and of censorship.

Chapter 1 summarises how theatre censorship developed and was practised in Spain in the nineteenth century and up to 1931, as well as developments during the Second Republic (1931–6) and the civil war (1936–9). This survey, tracing legislation and changes in political structures, shows how the modern theatre industry was formed and provides context for the study that follows. Features that would re-emerge in the post-civil war period, such as ecclesiastical censorship and the banning of performances in Catalan, are highlighted. An account is then given of developments during the Second Republic and the civil war. Republican censorship before the war was directed principally at defending the legitimacy of the Republic itself and restraining extremism on the right and left. It became fragmented and explicitly politicised in war time as particular factions on both sides took over propaganda and morale-building activities.

Chapter 2, focusing in detail on examples of theatre censorship during the Second Republic and the civil war, covers a period in which conservative values were under threat and new left-wing and right-wing ideas were doing battle in society and on stage. It summarises the established context of entertaining bourgeois fare, the diagnosis of a cultural crisis and attempts to reform the Spanish stage, in order to contextualise the emergence of left and right-wing theatre. In this period, many key figures used their works to comment on politics. While official reaction shows some moralising disapproval of popular *revistas* ('musical comedies'), the response during the Second Republic to new forms of politicised theatre that questioned traditional structures and moral absolutes ranged from tolerance between 1931 and 1934, coupled with nervousness about fomenting of unrest and a desire to defend constitutional legitimacy, to outright hostility during the *bienio negro* ('black biennium') of conservative Republican rule from 1934. The civil war saw a rise in agitprop productions on both sides of the divide. The theatre industry was collectivised and controlled by multiple bodies, including unions, in the Republican zone; in the Nationalist sector, the Falange consolidated its role as the centralised instrument of ideological and cultural control. Both sides employed censorship and propaganda to protect their values and the impact of this will be explored. The case study for this chapter is Vicente Mena's *Santa Teresita del Niño Jesús* ('Saint Therese of the Child Jesus'), an example of the trend in religious plays that, despite its relative unimportance in dramaturgical terms, led to a protest in the theatre and a press scandal involving some of the biggest names in left and right-wing theatre.

Chapter 3 presents a chronological account of political and legislative developments during the Franco dictatorship (1939–75) and the beginning of the transition to democracy in 1976. Changes in the censorship apparatus and criteria are related to ideological shifts in the regime, the involvement of particular ministers and censors, and wider social and cultural processes. We show how war-time politicisation was institutionalised by the dictatorship and built into an alliance between the competing factions within the regime; how shifts in the balance of power between those groups were reflected in changes in the exercise of censorship; and how limited such changes were in comparison to the deadening continuity of personnel and underlying ideological assumptions over four decades. The case study for this chapter is Federico García Lorca's *La casa de Bernarda Alba* (*The House of Bernarda Alba*). This play, completed in 1936 just before the outbreak of war, was repeatedly banned during the dictatorship due not only to features of the text but also to general political unease about Lorca himself, until it was finally approved in 1963. The often-frustrated production history of the play in Spain highlights the continuing importance of Lorca as a focus for political dissent and countercultural experimentation.

Chapter 4 examines how the victory of the Nationalists was accompanied by an intense propaganda campaign aimed at legitimising the new regime and erasing the ideological and cultural legacy of the Republic. In the early post-war years there were attempts to create a right-wing national-Catholic theatrical culture, but they received little support from the government, the theatre industry or the public. This chapter reveals that far from encouraging this movement, the censors obstructed it, showing nervousness about excessive triumphalism and promotion of the revolutionary spirit of Falangism. The regime's aim was the depoliticisation of art, and the main feature of the theatrical landscape in the postwar period was the restoration of the kinds of commercial theatre that had prospered before the war. We discuss the attention paid by censors to the work of well-established dramatists such as Benavente, popular comedies and *revistas*, and classics of the Golden Age and the nineteenth century. The chapter also pays substantial attention to Catalan theatre, drawing on evidence from archives in Barcelona. Our case study for this chapter is Jacinto Benavente's *La Infanzona* ('The Gentlewoman'), an unusually dark play by the dramatist, performed in January 1947. The file provides evidence of the censors' concern about the morality of the piece and of internal wrangling among the various agents of censorship who attempted to influence the process.

The focus of Chapter 5 is the so-called 'Realist Generation' of dramatists, which emerged in the late 1940s and 1950s, and had a continued, if curtailed, presence in Spanish theatre for much of the 1960s and beyond. Following a brief description of the political and theatrical context in which this generation emerged, the chapter surveys the main authors (Antonio Buero Vallejo, Alfonso Sastre, Lauro Olmo, José María Rodríguez Méndez, José Martín Recuerda and Carlos Muñiz) and the effects of censorship on their most important works. Detailed analysis of censorship reports and negotiations with the censors illuminates the strategies used by these dramatists to evade censorship while denouncing the injustices of society and, by extension, the dictatorship. We show how they employed humour, allegory, myth and history in their attempts to evade censorship and to say the unsayable. In order to reach bigger audiences, some of them also incorporated popular cultural forms and everyday language into their socially engaged works. How the authorities responded to this challenge depended on the political circumstances of the day and the reputation of the dramatist. Our case study is Alfonso Sastre's *Escuadra hacia la muerte* (*Condemned Squad*), which was staged by a student group in March 1953. The play was withdrawn following military intervention and was later banned. The impact of the prohibition was significant, we argue, not only for the dramatist, but for the realist trend as a whole.

Chapter 6 explores experimental, avant-garde and independent theatre. One of the major cultural consequences of the victory of the Nationalists in the civil war was the stifling of the wave of theatrical experimentation of the 1920s and 1930s. By April 1939 most of the prominent avant-garde playwrights and directors had died, been killed or gone into exile. The new regime was generally hostile to modernism and particularly to the work of writers associated with the Republic, and the theatrical establishment had little interest in reviving their legacy in the 1940s and 1950s. By the mid-1960s, however, interest in the pre-war avant-garde was booming and helping to shape a new postmodernist avant-garde. This was a broader, more varied tendency than the realist movement, with stronger links to theatrical developments outside Spain. In addition to the playwrights of the New Spanish Theatre, the discussion will focus on festivals and on fringe groups developing collective modes of theatremaking and seeking new audiences (especially in Catalonia). We analyse the censors' wary responses to unconventional scripts, and the challenges posed to censorship by symbolism and new modes of performance emphasising improvisation, the visual and the physical. As it was for the realists, the distinction between authorisation for commercial productions and for *cámara* ('studio or club theatres') is a crucial factor here, and the argument that censorship paradoxically stimulated creativity is examined with particular attention to the Catalan *teatre independent*. The case study is Alonso and Margallo's *Castañuela 70* ('Castanets '70'). This satirical musical, developed by the collective Tábano, was the subject of a celebrated running battle with the censors in 1970.

Chapter 7 examines the extent to which foreign plays and those written by Spanish dramatists were treated differently by the regime's censors. This chapter considers the relationship between censorship and translation or adaptation, and the influence of the dramatists and directors who created versions of foreign dramas for a Spanish public. By highlighting both the strategies employed by translators and adaptors to evade censorship and convey a political message or defy taboos, and those employed by the censors to minimise the impact of challenging foreign ideas on the Spanish public and to protect its reputation, we give a comprehensive view of the constant negotiation involved in staging foreign theatre under the dictatorship. We chart the shift over time from foreign drama used to support the regime, through domestication of foreign drama to what was tolerable in Spain, to its use with disruptive, political intent. Using examples of the staging and reception of foreign plays by dramatists such as Shakespeare, Miller, Sartre, Brecht and Beckett, we trace the political use of foreign drama in Spain and show what it allowed in by the back door. In the case study for this chapter, we look at a student production of Bertolt Brecht's *El círculo de tiza caucasiano* (*The Caucasian Chalk Circle*) in March 1965. Student groups had long been an important and innovative feature of the theatre scene, but now an increasingly vocal student opposition was employing theatre and other forms of cultural activism as weapons in its attacks on the regime. This fact, combined with the notoriety of the dramatist, made this a production to watch.

The eighth and final chapter reviews the winding-up of theatre censorship during the transition to democracy. Rapid changes in political circumstances were echoed in a confused and confusing censorship that gradually gave way to increased tolerance and the eventual disappearance of Francoist practices. Increased freedom of expression led to a testing of limits in the cultural sphere and, for a while, the excesses of the *destape* (uncovering), described by Alfonso Guerra as 'una reacción infantil a una represión absurda' ('a puerile reaction to an absurd repression') (2010), threatened to overshadow all other change. Great expectations for a new golden age of theatre, inspired by previously silenced dramatists and censored works were largely misplaced and the cultural focus, like the political one, turned towards shaping Spain's future. In the case study, we examine an iconic episode of the transition: the scandal surrounding the staging of Els Joglars' *La torna* ('The Rounding-Up'). The play was authorised in September 1977, only a few months before the abolition of censorship, but then banned after forty performances by the military authorities. Members of the company were arrested and tried by a military court, which provoked public protests and strikes by actors.

The conclusion considers the impact and longer-term legacy of censorship on playwrights, companies, audiences, cultural policies and institutions, and on theatrical culture in general.

Overall, this book aims to show how theatre censorship throughout the period under investigation was complex and multifaceted, involving political, moral, religious, aesthetic and commercial dimensions. Duncan Wheeler has argued that archive material in this field has often been used in a simplistic manner, producing scholarship that is over-reliant on a single source (the AGA) and 'alternates between two dominant visions of the Francoist censor: the ubiquitous and draconian fascist oppressor, and the easily hoodwinked bureaucratic buffoon' (2020: 90). We have been careful to weigh the evidence from several archives against data from various other sources (newspaper reviews and reports, legislative documents, first-hand testimony, critical studies), and to look beyond the obvious cases of dissident dramatists, covering a wide range of theatrical forms and political standpoints. The picture that emerges takes full account of 'the complex and frequently contradictory dynamics at play' (Wheeler 2020: 99).

We examine the extent to which censorship conditioned the formation of the theatrical canon and consider how dramatists, theatre practitioners and the public responded. This book, therefore, traces the changes in censorship and theatre practice that moved in parallel both with political and social change and with internal cultural shifts and outside influences. Yet we do not lose sight of how the theatre, including works that were not openly dissident, could act as a challenge to the stability and validity of the regime's manufactured consent and discursive order. It is our belief that the history of the theatre in Spain cannot be understood without an appreciation of the censorship that helped to shape it.

Notes
1 For a more detailed discussion of theories of censorship, see the introduction to our study, *Global Insights on Theatre Censorship* (O'Leary, Santos Sánchez and Thompson, 2015, pp. 1–24).
2 Self-censorship is discussed further in the Conclusion.

Chapter 1

The Evolution of Theatre Censorship in Spain from the 1830s to the 1930s

Much of this book will focus on a particular manifestation of theatre censorship – the coercive system set up in Spain by the right-wing Nationalist forces during the civil war of 1936–9, maintained and honed by General Franco's dictatorship until his death in 1975, then gradually dismantled during the transition to democracy. This was an especially draconian apparatus of authoritarian cultural control, yet it is important to appreciate that it was not unprecedented or innovative but the product of a lengthy historical process in which theatre censorship took a variety of forms and was exercised with varying degrees of severity. The survey offered in this chapter begins in the early nineteenth century and traces state control of the theatre through the reign of Isabel II (1833–68), the provisional government that followed it (1868–71), the brief reign of Amadeo (1871–3), the First Republic (1873–4), the Restoration (1875–1931), the Primo de Rivera/Berenguer dictatorship (1923–31), the Second Republic up to the outbreak of the civil war (1931–6), and the war period (1936–9). It will show censorship forming part of various inter-related processes: public-order policing, the enforcement of literary copyright, the regulation of the entertainment market, the definition of theatrical genres, shifts in the relationship between central and provincial government, the defence of moral and religious values and institutions, the stifling of expressions of political dissent, propaganda and morale-boosting, and revolutionary restructuring of the industry.

Historical backdrop: monarchy and liberalism up to 1923

The emergence and consolidation of the modern theatre industry over the course of the nineteenth century was conditioned by a complex series of shifts between authoritarian interventionism and enlightened liberalism. Varying degrees of state censorship of the content of dramatic texts and the nature of productions went hand in hand with negotiations over the regulation of the market, the consolidation of copyright law, and measures to control the behaviour of performers and spectators. When Fernando VII was restored to the Spanish throne in 1814 after the War of Independence, 'the theatre suffered from the same fierce censorship which stifled the free exchange of ideas in every part of Spanish society' (Gies 1994: 8). The institutions had been in place since the seventeenth century. The *Juez protector de los teatros del reino* ('Judicial Protector of Theatres of the Realm'), responsible for overseeing all aspects of theatrical activity nationwide, was appointed directly by the king and in turn appointed the *Censor político de los teatros de la corte* ('Political Censor of Theatres in the Capital'). The Church also exerted a powerful influence, especially outside Madrid (Sala Valldaura 2012: 137).[1]

Fernando died in September 1833 and was succeeded by his two-year-old daughter Isabel. The regency of the queen mother, María Cristina de Borbón-Dos Sicilias, brought a significant degree of liberalisation in cultural policy. The office of *Juez protector de los teatros del reino* was abolished in March 1834, its functions transferred to the provincial delegates of the Ministerio de Fomento ('Ministry of Development') (Gaceta de Madrid 1834b). The office of *Censor político de los teatros* was also abolished in October of that year (Gaceta de Madrid 1834c), though censorship was soon reintroduced, administered by the new Ministerio de la Gobernación ('Ministry of the Interior'). Alongside these steps to take the management of censorship out of the purview of the Crown and into the routine business of constitutional government, the power of the Church to impose its own controls was curtailed. An attempt by the Archbishop of Sevilla to prevent a touring company from performing in Carmona – despite the production having been licensed – led to a decree ordering that theatrical performances were to be allowed in all parts of the kingdom (Gaceta de Madrid 1834a). Further measures were taken in 1835 to deprive the clergy of an official role in censorship, 'although naturally the Church never relinquished its self-defined right to guard the morality of society by trying to regulate its spectacles, putting constant pressure on the civil authorities to ban works which were disrespectful of the Church or its teachings' (Gies 1994: 13).

A new Constitution introduced in 1837 guaranteed a general right to freedom of expression in print without prior censorship (Gaceta de Madrid 1837: 1). However, this did not prevent the authorities from continuing to apply pre-performance and post-performance censorship to theatre and other forms of public entertainment. Their power to do so was modified several times over the following 100 years in a series of laws governing theatres, including five comprehensive sets of regulations in 1847, 1849, 1852, 1886 and 1913. The theatre was being transformed over the course of the nineteenth century from an activity directly managed by the government as part of 'a system of self-promotion and social welfare' into 'a commercialised industry run by private individuals' (Surwillo 2012: 244), and this process of privatisation demanded a renegotiation of the relationship between business management, artistic direction and public-order policing.

The Royal Decree of 30 August 1847 was the first attempt to draw up a set of regulations for the management of the theatre industry. Article 6 empowered the government to suspend performances of plays that 'perjudiquen a las buenas costumbres, o contengan alusiones que puedan comprometer el orden público, o más o menos directamente contrarien las instituciones y los actos del Gobierno establecido, o zahieran a determinadas autoridades o personas' ('undermine common standards of decency, contain statements liable to threaten public order, directly or indirectly oppose the institutions and acts of the established government, or cause offence to particular individuals or figures of authority'). Article 8 granted ample powers to *Jefes políticos* (the government's representative in each province, later known as *Gobernador Civil* ('Civil Governor')), and in smaller towns to the mayor, to maintain public order and propriety during performances, while article 9 made *Jefes políticos* responsible for correcting 'los abusos y faltas de los actores en el ejercicio de su profesión' ('the abuses and failings of actors in the exercise of their profession') (Gaceta de Madrid 1847: 1).

At the same time, policing of the theatre was focusing more on play texts, which were becoming an increasingly valuable commodity. Playwrights lobbied energetically to protect their intellectual property and ensure that they were paid for performances of their plays. Measures passed in the 1830s noted that plays were frequently being performed without the author's permission and asserted repeatedly that copyright law applied to both the printing and staging of play texts. The principle was confirmed by the 1847 legislation, which made permission to perform a play subject to the payment of royalties and prohibited theatre companies from altering play texts (Gaceta de Madrid 1847: 2). The effect of these developments is described by Surwillo as 'fusing censorship and copyright through regulation of a fixed text' (2012: 247).[2]

The 1847 decree also set up a two-tier arrangement for the prior vetting of play scripts, closely linked to regulations designed to limit the number of theatres and prescribe their repertoires. There was to be a central *junta de censura* ('censorship board') specifically for the Teatro Real and the second-ranking Madrid theatre, and a local *junta* in each province presided over by the *Jefe político*. Each theatre was required to have a *junta de lectura* ('commissioning board') that would select plays for performance and submit them for authorisation. Censors were expected to assess the suitability of each work for the prescribed repertoire of the venue in which it was to be performed, and to apply aesthetic, moral and political criteria (Gaceta de Madrid 1847: 1).

Censors were required to submit their report on each play within eight days to the *Jefe político*, who decided whether to award a licence for performance. Generally, it was assumed that a licence issued for a Madrid theatre would be valid for productions in other parts of the country, but censorship boards were expected to consider whether local circumstances might make a play unsuitable for staging in a particular place, and *Jefes políticos* were empowered to ban plays that might cause specific difficulties in their province (Gaceta de Madrid 1847: 1). Conflict between central and local jurisdiction (and between secular and ecclesiastical authority) was an issue that would continue to arise from time to time over the next 130 years.

The extent to which the 1847 law sought to over-regulate all aspects of the industry provoked a storm of protest from various quarters, which led to new sets of regulations in 1849 and 1852. The main change made in these laws was a greater centralisation of theatre censorship. The board of censors at the Ministerio de la

Gobernación in Madrid was now responsible for vetting scripts for productions in all theatres in Spain, while local censors appointed by *Jefes políticos* were charged with ensuring that no unlicensed plays were staged and checking that texts were performed as authorised. A further centralising measure was taken in 1857, when the national *Junta de censura* was replaced by a single salaried censor on the grounds that the existing arrangement of four censors acting independently did not provide sufficient consistency (Gaceta de Madrid 1857: 1).

Modifications were also made to the process and criteria for pre-performance censorship of texts. The time limit for the issuing of licences was extended from eight days to fifteen days in 1849, then to one month in 1852. Article 10 of the 1849 law announced the abandonment of the assumption that censors were expected to apply aesthetic criteria: 'La Junta en sus calificaciones prescindirá del mérito literario de las obras, y se concretará exclusivamente a la parte moral y política' ('The Board's assessments shall take no account of the literary merit of plays and shall focus exclusively on moral and political considerations') (Gaceta de Madrid 1849: 1). While these changes amounted to a tightening of centralised moral and political control, in other respects the legislation of 1849 and 1852 represented a retreat from the extreme interventionism of 1847. Article 96 of the 1849 decree limited the role of officials presiding over performances, specifying that they were not to interfere with the business on stage unless obliged to do so by a clear threat to public order. The 1852 law reduced the extent to which *Jefes políticos* were expected to micro-manage the theatre industry and relaxed the constraints on numbers of theatres and allocation of venues to particular genres.

Another development worth highlighting from this period is a short-lived attempt to cut off the flowering of Catalan theatre that was gathering pace in the 1860s, anticipating one of the most draconian features of Francoist censorship seventy years later. Several companies in Barcelona and Valencia began to specialise in Catalan-language productions, which prompted the government to issue a decree on 15 January 1867 declaring that plays written entirely in any of the 'provincial dialects' of Spain would no longer be approved by the censors. Although the ban may have been motivated partly by commercial interests, the measure shows the central government's concern about the links between cultural renaissance and political separatism: 'Esta novedad ha de contribuir forzosamente a fomentar el espíritu autonómico de las mismas [provincias]' ('This new tendency will inevitably contribute to the growth of demands for autonomy in those provinces') (Boletín Oficial de la Provincia de Barcelona 1867). Cultural institutions, writers and impresarios in Barcelona lobbied against the 1867 order, while the authority of the government was draining away. By the time the law was repealed on 23 September 1868, the liberal 'Glorious Revolution' was under way, leading to the exile of Queen Isabel II. The order of 23 September ruled that plays in any of the 'dialects' of Spain could be performed and would be vetted by censors in the relevant provinces. Central oversight was maintained, though: a copy of each work approved, together with a translation into Castilian, had to be sent to the government censor in Madrid, subjecting productions in Catalan, Basque or Galician to an additional layer of bureaucracy (Gaceta de Madrid 1868: 2).

The leaders of the 1868 revolution announced a new era of freedom, and impresarios rushed to stage a number of previously banned plays. A decree of 16 January 1869 proclaimed 'en su más lata expresión, la libertad de teatros' ('in its broadest sense, the freedom of theatres') (Gaceta de Madrid 1869: 1). Although this referred primarily to the liberalisation of the theatre market by removing any remaining controls that gave specific theatres exclusive rights to the performance of particular genres, the phrase 'en su más lata expresión' sent a clear signal that a more permissive attitude would also be taken towards freedom of expression. Article 17 of the new liberal Constitution promulgated in June 1869 guaranteed the freedom to express ideas and opinions, and article 22 prohibited censorship, albeit in a way that seemed to refer only to publications (Gaceta de Madrid 1869: 1). Censorship did not, however, disappear altogether as a result of the revolution. Prior vetting of texts was largely abandoned, but censors continued to monitor performances and could still suspend productions and demand textual cuts.

Following the restoration of the monarchy in 1875, the right to freedom of speech was confirmed in article 13 of the 1876 Constitution, which made clear that the prohibition of prior censorship applied to all forms of expression (Gaceta de Madrid 1876). Nevertheless, uncertainty about how censorship should be applied to theatrical productions persisted. A law of 26 February 1881 declared: 'Se ejerce hoy, respecto de las obras dramáticas, una censura previa que [. . .] carece de fundamento legítimo en que apoyarse' ('Prior censorship of dramatic works is being exercised without any legal foundation') (Gaceta de Madrid 1881). Civil Governors were reminded that they had the power to prevent offences from being committed on stage and to report offenders to the courts, but pre-performance vetting of texts was illegal. All that impresarios were required to do was to notify the authorities of the title of any new work three days before the first performance.

A detailed *Reglamento de Policía de Espectáculos* ('Regulations for the Policing of Public Spectacles') was issued in 1886. It contained no provisions for pre-performance censorship, other than general powers for the government to suspend all public spectacles for reasons of public order or in the event of national mourning or epidemic (Gaceta de Madrid 1886: 369). There was a requirement for two copies of the script to be submitted to the authorities, but this did not have to be done any earlier than the start of the first performance, leaving no time for any prior vetting of the text. Article 32 consolidated the assumption that performances could only be censored by judicial action: 'Cuando a juicio de la Autoridad gubernativa se cometiere en la representación de una obra dramática alguno de los delitos comprendidos en el Código penal, lo pondrá en el acto en conocimiento del Juzgado correspondiente' ('When the representative of the authorities judges that an offence against the Penal Code has been committed in the course of a dramatic performance, he shall report it immediately to the relevant court of law') (Gaceta de Madrid 1886: 369). In the meantime, further performances of the offending play could be suspended.

The authorities were also expected to 'impedir que se ponga en caricatura en la escena, en cualquier forma que sea, a persona determinada' ('prevent the caricaturing on stage of particular persons, whatever form it may take') (Gaceta de Madrid 1886: 369). Although they were no longer responsible for assessing the work of performers, they were still charged with monitoring performances. Article 21 forbade performers from addressing the audience directly, and article 35 ruled that if an offence against the Penal Code was committed that consisted of words or actions not indicated in the script but added by actors, the latter would be fined or taken to court. The 1886 regulations therefore established a fairly stable compromise, making pre-performance censorship difficult but giving the authorities various means of suspending or modifying productions once they had opened – now, crucially, subject to judicial oversight. The application of the regulations tended to be less severe under liberal governments than under conservative ones, which 'bristled at even the slightest satirical threat to their power' (Membrez 1992: 100). Membrez gives a few examples of controversial cases of both political and moral censorship from this period, all involving satirical musical comedies (1992: 100).

The *Reglamento de Policía de Espectáculos* was updated in 1913, expanding technical regulations on buildings, health and safety procedures, publicity and ticket sales, and extending its coverage to bullfights, cabarets and the cinema. It clarified which public officials were responsible for implementation: the Director General de Seguridad (head of the department in the Ministerio de la Gobernación responsible for public order and policing) in Madrid, civil governors in provincial capitals, and mayors in smaller towns. The fact that censorship was in the hands of the Dirección General de Seguridad was a clear indication that it was now seen less as moral guidance and more as routine public-order policing. The requirement for copies of the script to be submitted was tightened, and an important adjustment was made to the clause referring to 'caricaturing', now specifying 'cualquiera institución del Estado o a persona determinada' ('any state institution or particular individual') (Gaceta de Madrid 1913: 347–8).

The Primo de Rivera dictatorship

The 1913 legislation remained technically in force until it was replaced by a new *Reglamento de Policía de Espectáculos* in 1935. However, the constraints imposed on the authorities by the prohibition of prior censorship in the 1876 Constitution were swept aside during the military dictatorship led by General Miguel Primo de Rivera (1923–30). Martial law was imposed, the Constitution was suspended and Parliament was closed down. Civil governors and mayors were sacked *en masse* and replaced by army officers, and rigorous censorship of newspapers and other publications was introduced. Primo de Rivera gradually reintroduced civilian involvement in government and public administration but did not allow free elections or reintroduce constitutional guarantees. As part of the process of demilitarisation, an order of 28 May 1924 confirmed that civil governors would regain responsibility for enforcing regulations governing public spectacles, while the military authorities would be responsible for censorship of the press and the maintenance of public order (Gaceta de Madrid 1924: 1013).

No specific legislative or administrative structures were put in place to facilitate more thorough censorship of the theatre. The Dirección General de Seguridad, civil governors and mayors were expected to use the existing apparatus, but without being constrained by constitutional safeguards. The military officer in charge of press censorship, Celedonio de la Iglesia, published a remarkably frank account of his work in which he noted that for action to be taken against a newspaper 'bastaba un informe policiaco procedente acaso de una delación sectaria' ('a police report, possibly resulting from a partisan denunciation, was all that was required') (cited in Ucelay 2007: 150). It is likely that the same approach was applied to theatrical productions. As a result, the censorship carried out during this period was arbitrary, unpredictable and unaccountable. Some productions were banned in advance or suffered cuts, others were closed down after the dress rehearsal or the premiere, and impresarios generally became extremely cautious in their programming decisions.

There are very few theatre censorship files from this period in the Spanish government archive (AGA), so documentary evidence for particular cases is scarce. However, some files relating to applications during the Republic or the Franco period contain earlier documents. For example, a file on Federico García Lorca's *Mariana Pineda* contains two documents referring to the production at the Teatro Fontalba in Madrid in October 1927. There is a handwritten authorisation dated 12 October: 'No hay inconveniente alguno a juicio del funcionario que informa en autorizar el estreno, que se anuncia para hoy en el teatro Fontalba, del romance popular titulado "Mariana Pineda"' ('In my view there is no obstacle to the licensing of the "popular ballad" entitled *Mariana Pineda*, which is scheduled to open this evening at the Teatro Fontalba') (AGA 21/5822a). This provides useful evidence of the functioning of the censorship apparatus at this time, showing that at least some plays were subject to prior censorship but that this was carried out in a cursory way.[3] There is also a report on the opening night, dated 13 October, by José M. Ortiz, chief inspector of the central Madrid police district, and addressed to the Jefe Superior de la Policía Gubernativa (head of the Madrid police force) in the Dirección General de Seguridad (Fig. 1).[4] It indicates slight concern about the impact on the audience of the play's political content, but no action was taken: 'A juicio del que suscribe no contiene concepto alguno contra la moral ni delictivo. La obra fue aplaudida repetidamente, y señaladamente en algunos pasajes de ella, a mi juicio, más que por la labor literaria en sí, por las ideas que parece defender' ('My judgement is that it contains nothing that constitutes an offence against morality or the law. The work received repeated applause, which was particularly noticeable in certain passages, in my view more on account of the ideas that it appears to advocate than for any literary merit') (AGA 21/5822a).

The prohibition in 1929 of Lorca's tragicomic farce *Amor de don Perlimplín con Belisa en su jardín* (*Love of Don Perlimplín for Belisa in His Garden*), apparently on the grounds that it was judged to be pornographic, provides more evidence of the arbitrariness of theatre censorship under the dictatorship. There is no record of the ban in the AGA files, but vivid accounts of the episode drawing on first-hand testimony are given by Margarita Ucelay (2007: 140–53) and Ian Gibson (1985: 590–2). A single performance by

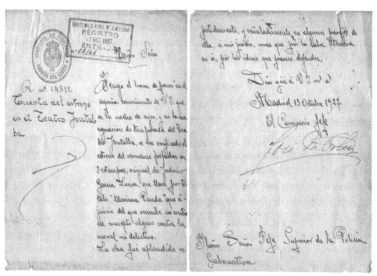

Figure 1: Report on the premiere of *Mariana Pineda* (1927)

the group El Caracol in its studio theatre in Madrid was scheduled for 5 February 1929, then postponed until the next day. The Queen Mother (María Cristina of Austria) died in the early hours of 6 February, resulting in the closure of all theatres in Madrid as a mark of respect. El Caracol placed an advertisement in the newspaper *ABC* on 7 February announcing that the performance would be given on that day (ABC 1929: 39). However, during a rehearsal on the evening of 6 February, the police raided the theatre, confiscated copies of the script and banned the production. The Chief of Police, General Marzo, arrived just in time to witness the scene in which Perlimplín appears in bed sporting an enormous pair of cuckold's horns. In one of the copies of the script later recovered from the Dirección General de Seguridad, the reference to horns in the stage direction is crossed out, presumably by a censor, as is the subtitle, *Aleluya erótica* ('erotic lampoon') (Ucelay's note in García Lorca 2007: 269).

Vilches de Frutos and Dougherty highlight the prohibition of Jacinto Benavente's *Para el cielo y los altares* ('For Heaven and Altars') as the most well-known – and most counter-productive – case of theatre censorship during the dictatorship. The work was regarded as anti-clerical and anti-monarchical, and was banned shortly before its premiere in November 1928. The ban provoked widespread protests, homages to Benavente and performances of many of his other works in Madrid theatres, at which he received rapturous applause (Kany 1930). The government ended up issuing a statement justifying its decision in which it expressed its fear that the public would be stirred up by the drama, 'transformando el teatro en permanente mitin, con riesgo seguro de la paz espiritual y del orden público' ('turning the theatre into a permanent political meeting and putting spiritual peace and social order at risk') (Vilches de Frutos and Dougherty 1997: 46). The fear of theatrical performances being turned into *mítines* would be expressed repeatedly during the Republic and in reports written by Franco's censors.

It was not only serious treatments of religious and political themes that attracted the attention of the censors in this period. Popular comedies, musicals, farces and revues also suffered bans and bowdlerisation due to sexual content and satirical references to current issues, and general pressure was brought to bear on impresarios and companies to tone down the sauciness and mild subversiveness to which these hugely popular forms of entertainment were often inclined. Vilches de Frutos and Dougherty mention several examples of prohibitions from 1928: *La Cascada (Balneario de Moda)* ('The Cascade: Spa à la Mode') by Carlos Jaquotot, *¡Abajo las coquetas!* ('Down with Coquettes!') by Antonio Paso; and *El candil del rey* ('The King's Lamp') by Manuel Fernández Palomero.

By the beginning of 1930, Primo de Rivera's power was draining away. He resigned on 28 January and was replaced by a fellow general, Dámaso Berenguer, who called a general election for March 1931 and promised a restoration of civil liberties. Although censorship was being eased only slowly, the theatre industry was becoming bolder about challenging it. Protests about the banning of *Los mesianistas* (Horacio de Castro's translation of Maxwell Anderson and Harold Hickerson's 1928 play *Gods of the Lightning*) led to Berenguer agreeing to meet representatives of the company on 22 April. They argued that the new government, 'puesto que representaba una tendencia enteramente opuesta a la del anterior régimen, debía autorizar la representación ya que no se trata de una obra disolvente' ('since it represented a tendency entirely different from the previous regime, should authorise the production as the work is not subversive'); the General is reported as promising to order the Ministro de la Gobernación to look into the matter (ABC 1930: 17). This was followed by a letter to Berenguer published in the press on 26 April signed by thirty-two prominent writers, politicians and journalists, which argued that the draconian approach taken by the dictatorship had discredited Spanish culture in the eyes of the world, and expressed confidence that the situation had changed and that a play performed to acclaim around the world would now be allowed to be seen in Spain (Vilches de Frutos and Dougherty 1997: 43–4).

That same day saw the premiere in Madrid of a *revista* (risqué musical comedy) entitled *Las pantorrillas* ('Legs'), which staged a bawdy parody of censorship. The puritanical attitude of the protagonist, who is president of a League Against Pornography, is shown as hypocritical, giving rise to a musical 'número de la censura' ('censorship number'). The painted backdrop displayed a collection of erotic images from films and magazines covered by a huge red cross, and the chorus girls' skimpy costumes incorporated chastity belts and huge red pencils attached to their backs (Montijano 2009: 402–3).

Despite Berenguer's efforts to slow down the pace of change, the momentum of feeling against Primo's legacy, against the king and for a republic was now unstoppable. Berenguer and his cabinet resigned, republican parties won massive support in urban areas in local elections on 12 April 1931, Alfonso XIII left the country, and the Second Republic was declared on 14 April. Primo's dictatorship would have been little more than a brief and exceptional parenthesis in the history of Spain if it had not laid the foundations – nationalist, authoritarian, Catholic, propagandist – for the much more ruthless and durable dictatorship that followed the destruction of the Republic: 'Francoism was constructed using many of the same ideological postulations which had previously been developed by *primorriverismo*' (Quiroga 2012: 52). In April 1931, though, freedom was in the air. Theatremakers were keen to explore new possibilities for political and social drama, avant-garde experimentation and erotic musical comedy liberated from the heavy hand of the Dirección General de Seguridad.

The Second Republic

The leaders of the Republic established in April 1931 were acutely aware of its fragility. The success of republican parties in the municipal elections had been overwhelming in Barcelona and Madrid and clear in most other provincial capitals, but they had not won the largest share of the overall vote or a majority of council seats (Carreras and Tafunell (2005: 1098). The monarchist cause retained significant support and the Church, generals and landowners became increasingly alienated by the programme of religious, educational, military, agrarian, economic and constitutional reform embarked on in the first two years. There was also opposition from organisations on the left, frustrated that the reforms were not going far enough.

The provisional government in power up to December proceeded swiftly to declare the re-establishment of the rule of law and hold elections for a constitutive assembly. However, its nervousness about the instability of the situation can be seen in the wide-ranging emergency powers with which it equipped itself. The law of 21 October 1931 known as the *Ley de Defensa de la República* ('Defence of the Republic Act') defined a wide range of activities as acts of aggression against the Republic, including the dissemination of news likely to damage public confidence or disturb public order; 'toda acción o expresión que redunde en menosprecio de las Instituciones u organismos del Estado' ('any action or statement fomenting contempt for the institutions or organs of the State'); and any defence of the monarchy or use of monarchist emblems (Gaceta de Madrid 1931a: 420). The law was mainly aimed at political activity and publications, but these provisions were clearly also applicable to creative expression, including theatrical performances. The head of the Provisional Government, Manuel Azaña, had argued in Parliament that exceptional powers were justified by the gravity of the threats faced by the Republic and the need to demonstrate that it was capable of maintaining order in the face of reactionary efforts to undermine its legitimacy (Gómez-Reino y Carnota 1981–2: 177).

The *Ley de Defensa* remained in force alongside the liberal Constitution adopted in December 1931 until it was replaced by a new *Ley de Orden Público* ('Public Order Act') in July 1933, a contradiction that reflected the inevitable duality of a generally progressive regime frequently resorting to repressive behaviour in order to be seen to be capable of defending its legitimacy. The key provision of the 1931 Constitution with regard to censorship is article 34: 'Toda persona tiene derecho a emitir libremente sus ideas y opiniones, valiéndose de cualquier medio de difusión, sin sujetarse a la previa censura' ('Every person has the right to express their ideas and opinions freely, making use of any medium of communication, without being subject to prior censorship') (Gaceta de Madrid 1931b: 1581). Article 42 declares that freedom of expression and other rights may be suspended for urgent reasons of national security, but the *Ley de Defensa* effectively gave the government *carte blanche* to override civil rights. This situation of open-ended exceptionalism was brought to an end by the new *Ley de Orden Público*, which set out detailed definitions of powers, offences and sanctions. It defined three levels of states of emergency: *prevención* ('precaution'), *alarma* ('alarm') and *guerra* ('war'), the second and third of which entailed the suspension of article 34 of the Constitution. One or other of these states of emergency would be in force in at least parts of the country almost continuously from December 1933 to the outbreak of war in July 1936.

In practice, these exceptional powers do not seem to have been used to censor theatrical performances. The 1913 *Reglamento de Policía de Espectáculos* remained in force during the first four years of the Republic, administered as before by the Dirección General de Seguridad (part of the Ministerio de la Gobernación), and outside Madrid by civil governors and mayors. As noted earlier, there was no specific legal basis for prior censorship of scripts, which needed to be submitted to the authorities no later than the start of the first performance so that they could be referred to if any official action was taken. In principle, a production could only be closed down on the grounds of a specific criminal offence, on the orders of a judge. Various offences listed in the Penal Code (revised in 1932) might be committed in the course of theatrical performances: insulting the head of state, members of Parliament or government ministers (articles 149, 161 and 165); advocating a change in the form of government (article 168); denigrating the teachings or rites of any religion (article 235); insulting or threatening government officials (article 265); causing disorder in a public building or during a performance (articles 266 and 564); calling for rebellion or sedition in a public place, or displaying slogans or banners that provoke disorder (article 268); offending against decency and public morality (articles 433 and 562); slander and libel (articles 451–56); organising meetings or performances without the required licence, or breaching the terms of such a licence (article 573) (Gaceta de Madrid 1932).

The authorities also had a broader power to prevent the lampooning of individuals or institutions and a general responsibility to maintain public order during performances, and there is evidence of a small number of productions being banned in advance of the premiere or having lines cut. The scarcity (or cursoriness) of prior vetting of texts is confirmed by the contents of censorship files for the first four years of the Republic held in the Spanish government archive (AGA): there are very few reports on texts or clear records of an explicit decision having been made to allow or prohibit a production in advance. In most cases, it was the first performance on which a report was produced by a police inspector. This usually offered a brief synopsis of the play and reported on the response of the audience, any political or moral issues, controversial references to institutions or individuals, and any unusual features of the event (e.g., disturbances in the audience or the involvement of performers under the age of eighteen).

In Chapter 2, archival evidence relating to particular productions will be analysed in order to show in more detail how the censorship apparatus was being used in this period and how rigorously. It is difficult to obtain a global picture of the operation of theatre censorship during the Second Republic since the files from this period refer only to productions in Madrid, that is, under the jurisdiction of the Dirección General de Seguridad. Documents relating to productions in other cities and towns were not collected centrally, and we have been unable to locate any in provincial archives. For the moment, though, it is safe to say that in general the advent of the Republic meant a significant loosening of theatre censorship with regard to political, religious and moral issues. Within the first few months, shows that would not have reached the stage during the Primo de Rivera dictatorship were attracting large audiences and making headlines. The revolutionary political dramas *Rosas de sangre o El poema de la República* ('Roses of Blood, or The Poem of the Republic') by Álvaro de Orriols (premiered on 3 May) and *Fermín Galán* by Rafael Alberti (1 June) were greeted with a mixture of acclaim and consternation. There was a riot at the premiere on 6 November of *A.M.D.G.*, Cipriano Rivas Cherif's adaptation of Ramón Pérez de Ayala's anti-Jesuit novel of 1910, resulting in the intervention of armed police. Ramón del Valle-Inclán's satirical *Farsa y licencia de la reina castiza* ('Farce of the True-Blue Queen') (3 June), banned throughout the 1920s, was another controversial hit of 1931 in spite of its subject matter – the wayward behaviour of Queen Isabel II – having become rather dated. Other works censored under the dictatorship were now performed, notably Lorca's *Amor de don Perlimplín* (5 April 1933).

The popular genre of the *revista* (musical comedy) soon took advantage of the more liberal political and social climate, engaging playfully with topical issues such as divorce and political reform, and pushing sexual innuendo and the display of female flesh to new extremes in shows such as the immensely successful *Las leandras* ('Leandro's Girls') by González del Castillo and Muñoz Román (12 November 1931) and *La pipa de oro* ('The Golden Pipe') by Paradas and Jiménez (14 May 1932). The latter made its mark by being the first production to feature bare-breasted chorus girls, celebrated in the magazine *Crónica* as a 'signo inequívoco del avance de los tiempos' ('unmistakable sign of the advances of the times') (Montijano Ruiz 2010: 96–7).

The exhilaration did not last long. The coalition of Socialists and left-wing Republicans which had been in power since December 1931 under the leadership of Manuel Azaña collapsed in September 1933. In the general elections held in November, a conservative-Catholic coalition benefited from the fragmentation of the left-wing vote, resulting in a government led by the Partido Republicano Radical (PRR – 'Radical Republican Party') with the support of the conservative Confederación Española de Derechas Autónomas (CEDA – 'Spanish Confederation of Autonomous Right-Wing Parties'). The PRR and CEDA had opposed many of the reforms set in motion in the first two years of the Republic, and the coalition government, led by several different prime ministers between November 1933 and February 1936, set about reversing or slowing down most of them.

Theatre censors had sometimes felt frustrated by the constraints imposed on them by the 1913 regulations. In a report of August 1934 on the play *El confidente* ('The Confidant') by Manuel García Adanero, one of them complained that 'por no existir censura no puede procederse a tachar el texto de una obra teatral, ni dispone nada respecto del caso la Ley de orden público' ('as there is no censorship we are not able to impose cuts on a theatrical text, and the Public Order Act does not offer any guidance on this kind of case') (AGA R6565).[5] The complaint is a clear indication that officials in charge of censorship regarded the 1913 regulations as inadequate. After November 1933, they were working for a government that was more conservative than its predecessor, more insecure and inclined towards authoritarianism, and more concerned to protect the interests of the Church, the army, landowners and employers.

A new *Reglamento de Policía de Espectáculos públicos y de construcción y reparación de los edificios destinados a los mismos* ('Regulations for the policing of public spectacles and for the construction and maintenance of premises intended to be used for such spectacles') was introduced in May 1935. As its title indicates, the new statute was largely concerned with bringing technical and safety standards up to date. However, it was also intended to strengthen the authorities' powers of censorship. Three new clauses added powers and responsibilities that were much broader and less constrained by legal protocols.

Article 27 expanded the list of problems that officials were empowered to resolve on the spot by adding: 'En caso de tumulto o de desórdenes o de peligro para el público o de ofensa a la moral, el Delegado de la Autoridad podrá disponer la suspensión de un espectáculo y, si hubiere lugar, el desalojamiento del local' ('In the case of tumult, disturbance, danger to the public or offences against morality, the representative of the authorities may order the suspension of a performance and, if necessary, the evacuation of the premises') (Gaceta de Madrid 1935: 1057). Article 8 declared: 'Quedan prohibidos los espectáculos o diversiones públicas que puedan turbar el orden o que sean contrarias a la moral o a las buenas costumbres' ('Spectacles or public entertainments likely to disturb public order or be offensive to morality or social decorum are prohibited') (Gaceta de Madrid 1935: 1056). And finally, article 21 reproduced the existing wording about caricaturing and added a catch-all clause empowering the authorities to prohibit any performance in which 'se haga la apología de un vicio o de un delito, o que tienda a excitar el odio o la aversión entre las clases sociales, que ofenda al decoro o prestigio de la autoridad o sus Agentes o de la fuerza armada, así como la vida privada de las personas o los principios constitutivos de la familia' ('vice or crime is defended, or which may stir up hatred or aversion between social classes, or which flouts decorum or damages the prestige of the authorities and their agents or the armed forces, or which may prove prejudicial to the private life of individuals or family values') (1935: 1057).

The anxiety about possible threats to public order that had always characterised theatre censorship was heightened by the social and ideological tensions of the Republican period. Plays expressing political views of both the right (such as Muñoz Seca's sardonic satires of Republican reforms or patriotic history plays by Catholic conservatives) and the left (such as Alberti's revolutionary *Fermín Galán*) prompted vehement demonstrations of support and opposition, while the ribald atmosphere created by some *revistas* occasionally threatened to get out of hand. Rather than attempting simply to suppress radical or immoral content, the main aim of Republican censorship was to ensure that it did not provoke or exacerbate public disorder. The regulations introduced in 1935 were designed to strengthen the authorities' ability to anticipate trouble and deal with it firmly.

It was not made explicit in the legislation that pre-performance censorship of texts was required in order to enable the authorities to enforce the new regulations, but there was a clear implication that censors were now expected to take preventive action rather than rely on monitoring performances and referring offences to the judiciary. To facilitate this, article 31 stipulated that two copies of the script must be submitted to the authorities at least twenty-four hours before the first performance of a play. Emeterio Díez underestimates the difference between the 1913 and 1935 *Reglamentos* and the impact of the latter, commenting that they were both based on a combination of prior censorship of texts and inspection of performances (2007: 424–5). In fact, the 1935 legislation brought a significant change of emphasis, and the cases examined in Chapter 2 will show decisively that prior censorship – either banning productions before the first performance or imposing cuts or changes – was not a routine part of the apparatus until after May 1935.[6]

Other minor changes introduced in 1935 contributed to the tightening of controls. Mayors were now required to report their decisions within twenty-four hours to the civil governor of their province, who could overrule them. Article 30 specified that the requirement for submission of texts at least twenty-four hours in advance applied to the lyrics of songs – an important acknowledgement of the success and social impact of the *revista*. The ban on performers directly addressing or interacting with the audience – which had been regularly flouted in popular comedies and *revistas* – was maintained and reinforced by the stipulation that any announcement in a theatre must be authorised by the representative of the authorities.

Officials in the ministry and in civil governors' offices now had the opportunity to check all scripts in advance of the opening night. As they often had only twenty-four hours in which to do so, the job must have been done cursorily in many cases. When there were concerns, a report was written recommending unconditional authorisation, authorisation subject to cuts, or prohibition. As there was not yet a standard printed form to be used by theatre managers when submitting texts, they would enclose a covering letter. Sometimes this would simply declare that the work was to be performed in their theatre on a given date. After May 1935, the notification was usually formulated as an explicit request for approval, using phrases such as 'a fin de que se digne conceder la oportuna autorización' ('in order that the appropriate authorisation may be granted').

In Madrid the process was administered by the Sección de Asuntos Generales ('Department of General Affairs') of the Dirección General de Seguridad, where each script was logged and date-stamped. The cover or first page was marked with a stamp reading 'Pase a informe y propuesta del Letrado Sr. . . . .' ('To be referred for report and recommendation to legal adviser Mr . . .'), and the name of an official in the Asesoría Jurídica ('Legal Support Department') would be handwritten in the blank space. The recommendation made by the censor would then be confirmed by (or on behalf of) the Director General and the decision communicated to the theatre management. Reports on performances were produced by officials of the Comisaría de Vigilancia ('Inspectorate'), addressed to the Jefe Superior de la Policía Gubernativa ('Chief of Police') for Madrid. An example of a production approved in January 1936, Azorín's *La guerrilla* ('Guerrilla Fighters'), shows the typical process in full: the application submitted on 9 January, two days before the opening night; a brief report on the text by the *letrado* dated 10 January, confirming that 'no contiene concepto alguno contrario a las leyes ni a las instituciones, al régimen constituido, las Autoridades o sus Agentes' ('it does not contain any ideas contrary to the law, the institutions, the government, the authorities or their agents') and recommending authorisation; confirmation of approval by an official on behalf of the Director General, also dated 10 January; and finally a report on the first performance on 11 January submitted by a *comisario jefe* rather belatedly on 24 January, summarising the plot and remarking that 'la obra que fue muy aplaudida carece de alusiones políticas y no afecta para nada a la moral' ('the play, which received warm applause, does not contain political allusions, nor does it pose a threat to morality') (AGA R6530).

The fact that prior censorship was carried out by lawyers – either an Abogado del Estado (a senior officer of the Asesoría Jurídica) or one of the *letrados* under his command – is an important detail that marks a sharp contrast with the politically focused approach that would be introduced during the civil war by Franco. Republican censors' primary concern was the defence of the institutional legitimacy of the Republic itself in the face of scepticism or outright hostility from across the ideological spectrum. They appear to have been relatively pragmatic and even-handed in political terms, unprudish about moral and sexual matters, and generally scrupulous about respecting procedures and legal constraints.

The victory of the Frente Popular ('Popular Front') in the general election of February 1936 brought a swing back towards the left that was more pronounced on the streets than in the government. The Partido Socialista Obrero Español ('Spanish Socialist Workers' Party') won the largest number of seats but was unwilling to form a government with the moderate Republican parties under the leadership of Manuel Azaña. Socialists, communists and anarchists campaigned inside and outside Parliament for more radical change and increasingly came into conflict with right-wing groups, especially the Falange. Conservatives were alarmed and generals firmed up their plans for a coup.

The authorities were therefore more anxious than ever to defuse manifestations of extremism from the left and the right. A state of alarm was in force throughout the period from the election to the outbreak of war in July, but the government was careful to avoid resorting to the declaration of a state of war, which would have handed power to the military. The election campaign and the subsequent period of agitation stimulated a wave of politically engaged theatre, and the censors' response was uncertain: 'La crispación política, las huelgas y el terrorismo de izquierdas y de derechas generan durante el primer semestre de 1936 una práctica censora claramente diferenciada, la cual podríamos definir de contradictoria, vacilante, prudente y expeditiva' ('The atmosphere of political tension, the strikes and left-wing and right-wing terrorism in the first half of 1936 prompt a clear shift in the practice of censorship, which becomes contradictory, hesitant, prudent and expeditious') (Díez 2007: 94). The desire to prevent public performances from exacerbating social and ideological conflict was clearer than ever, leading to the imposition of a larger number of bans and cuts than in previous periods.

The civil war

The rebel generals who led the attempted *coup d'état* of 17–18 July 1936 immediately imposed martial law in the areas over which they gained control, while popular resistance and the arming of trade union militias played a crucial role in thwarting the insurrection in most of the large cities and had a profound social, political and economic impact on the areas held by the government. Civil war became an opportunity for social revolution led by the socialist Unión General de Trabajadores (UGT – 'General Workers' Union') and the anarchist Confederación Nacional del Trabajo (CNT – 'National Confederation of Labour'). Committees at various levels, including individual workplaces, set about the socialisation of the economy and the dismantling of traditional social structures.

Most theatres in the big cities were closed for the summer and many companies were on tour in the provinces or Latin America, but the transformation of the economic structure of the industry began almost immediately. In Barcelona the process was dominated by the CNT through its Sindicato Único de Espectáculos Públicos (SUEP – 'Joint Union of Workers in Public Entertainment'), replaced in 1937 by the Sindicato de la Industria del Espectáculo (SIE – 'Union of the Entertainment Industry), which coordinated the collectivisation of almost all the theatre buildings and companies in the city.[7] The Generalitat de Catalunya (the autonomous government created by the 1932 Statute of Autonomy) set up its own Comissaria d'Espectacles on 26 July 1936 to oversee the entertainment industry, and soon after that nationalised two of the largest venues in Barcelona, the Liceu and the Poliorama. However, the legislation establishing the Comissaria made no provision for how it was to fulfil its mission of ensuring the 'normal' functioning of the entertainment industry (BOGC 1936: 785), and in practice, it was the CNT that set the agenda in most parts of Catalonia (Coca 2008: 39).

The SUEP/SIE ran a powerful Comité Económico del Teatro (CET – 'Economic Committee for the Theatre Industry'), which led the process of collectivisation in Catalonia and exercised control over a wide range of activities: the recruitment, payment and working conditions of performers and other staff; the appointment of management committees of venues and companies; the selection of works to be performed and their allocation to particular theatres; casting of shows and monitoring of workers' attendance; promotion, ticket sales and collection of revenues. On 1 September 1937, the executive committee of the SIE wrote to the CET urging it to press ahead with the collectivisation of the industry: 'Os hemos de recordar que el plazo fine el día 15 del presente mes y es indispensable que antes de esta fecha esté todo reglamentado' ('You are reminded that the deadline is the 15th of this month and it is essential that everything should be in order by that date') (CDMH PS-Barcelona 1067, 7, p. 141). The SIE also employed agents to maintain public order in theatres and cinemas. An internal letter from the executive committee of the SIE to the CET in August 1938 authorises two union members to act as *guardias*, to be available at all times to intervene in matters of public order when required (CDMH PS-Barcelona 1067, 7, p. 115).

The situation in the Valencia region was similar to that of Catalonia, albeit benefiting from greater cooperation between the CNT and the UGT. Sirera (2008: 158) notes that the collectivisation of venues and companies was more or less complete by the middle of September 1936, and a joint executive committee (Comité Ejecutivo de Espectáculos Públicos/Comité Executiu d'Espectacles Públics) was set up in October 1936 to oversee the industry, with equal representation from the CNT and the UGT.[8]

In Madrid the UGT was the dominant trade union but did not impel or control the collectivisation of theatres to the same extent as the CNT in Catalonia. The result in the capital was a more varied patchwork of takeovers by different groups of trade unionists and theatre workers, some of them with government support. To begin with, 'groups simply claimed or were offered the theatre of their choice if they were able to command sufficient trade union support for their actions' (McCarthy 1999: 34). The process of socialisation was gradually regularised with the establishment of the Comité de Control de Espectáculos Públicos and a Comité de Incautación y Control ('Confiscation and Control Committee') for the theatre industry, which ensured a degree of cooperation between the UGT and the CNT. The committee set up to run the Teatro Pavón in October 1936, for example, comprised two actors, two stagehands and two front-of-house staff, four of them CNT members and two UGT members (CDMH PS-Madrid 1120, 29).

In contrast, the autonomous government established in the Basque Country (Euzkadi) in October 1936, based in Bilbao until the city fell to Nationalist forces in June 1937, moved quickly to head off collectivisation by the *sindicatos*. By early December 1936 it had established its own version of the traditional structure of state regulation of the theatre and cinema industries. A letter of 9 December from the Sección de Espectáculos of the Departamento de Gobernación, to the management of the Coliseo de Albia theatre in Bilbao calls for their compliance and collaboration:

> Constituida en este Departamento de Gobernación la SECCIÓN DE ESPECTÁCULOS a cuya competencia se somete la vigilancia y normal funcionamiento de los mismos, dentro del territorio de Euzkadi, le participamos que este organismo asumirá todas las funciones que eran peculiares de las extinguidas Juntas Provinciales de Espectáculos. Teniendo esto en cuenta, nos dirigimos a esa Empresa para que en lo sucesivo cuide de cumplir las disposiciones que venían estando en vigor en materia de Policía de Espectáculos. (CDMH Santander-HA, 5, 10)

> Following the establishment in this Department of the Office for Public Spectacles charged with regulating and ensuring the normal functioning of the entertainment industry within the territory of Euzkadi, we hereby inform you that this body will take on all the functions previously assigned to the former Provincial Boards of Public Entertainments. In view of this development, your company is urged to ensure that from now on it complies fully with the regulations previously in force relating to the entertainment industry.

This was followed by a decree issued on 14 December which took all theatres and cinemas in the Basque Country into government ownership. It offered as the primary justification of nationalisation the urgent need to raise funds for the care of war victims, but also articulated a progressive vision of state intervention in cultural production:

> Es la función social que las Empresas, atentas en la mayoría de los casos a su provecho particular, no sabrían atender: función social que en estos momentos de realización de humanas concepciones, las que de entre la catástrofe que la guerra origina crearán una libertad más amplia a los pueblos oprimidos y una mayor justicia social a los hombres, es necesaria para la formación de la conciencia popular; función social que al Gobierno le corresponde obligadamente tutelar. (Diario Oficial del País Vasco 1936: 578)

> The other justification for expropriation is the social function that commercial theatre companies, with their attention mostly focused on profits, would not be in a position to fulfil: a social function that is necessary for the formation of popular consciousness at a time in which humanist concepts are being developed amidst the catastrophes of war with the potential to liberate oppressed peoples and

create social justice for all men. This is a social function that the Government has an obligation to nurture.

The Basque Departamento de Gobernación retained regulatory responsibility for 'cuanto se relacione con la policía de espectáculos, aprobación de programas, determinación del horario de apertura y cierre de los espectáculos, higiene de los locales, etc.' ('all matters related to the regulation of public entertainment, approval of programming, fixing opening and closing times for shows, hygiene in theatre buildings, etc.') (Diario Oficial del País Vasco 1936: 579). Presumably, 'aprobación de programas' included prior censorship of scripts and 'policía de espectáculos' included the maintenance of public order during performances, as required by the 1935 *Reglamento de Policía de Espectáculos públicos*.

The main aims of restructuring in all these areas were to improve working conditions, ensure continuity of employment, democratise management, share profits and make the theatre more accessible to working-class audiences. The various models of socialisation also shared an aspiration to reflect the ideals of popular revolution and create new theatrical forms. A bourgeois-dominated culture of exploitative commercialism, aesthetic stagnation and moral decadence was to be replaced by an authentically popular culture that would find new sources of creativity in collaborative working practices, address new audiences and new issues, and imbue even the most low-brow entertainment with dignity and educational value: 'La cruzada cultural debía eliminar todo aquello que pertenecía a una época caduca e instaurar unas relaciones humanas acordes con los anhelos revolucionarios' ('The cultural crusade aimed to eliminate all that pertained to a bygone era and to create human relationships consonant with the aims of the revolution') (Foguet i Boreu 2002: 45–6)

As the 1936–7 season got under way in mid-August, the CNT-affiliated Sindicato Único de Espectáculos Públicos issued a declaration succinctly linking workers' control with artistic innovation and moral purification:

> No se trata sólo de una renovación técnica, sino que el teatro va a renovarse espiritualmente. De él van a desaparecer toda obscenidad, vulgaridad y grosería. El teatro siente el orgullo de su deber y arrojará de sí a todos los elementos que confundan las tablas de la escena con los mercaderes del mercado o con los prostíbulos. (ABC 1936a: 13)

It is not just a matter of technical renewal: the theatre is going to renew itself spiritually. All obscenity, vulgarity and crudity will disappear from it. The theatre is proudly conscious of its duty and will rid itself of all elements that confuse the boards of the stage with market stalls or brothels.

The socialist-anarchist project to dignify the theatre, cleanse it and rescue it from commercialism is reminiscent of the rhetoric of mid-nineteenth-century legislation: it made a similar claim that control of theatrical production is justified in terms of both social harmony and artistic quality. And like the Enlightenment reformers, the CNT and UGT also aimed to regulate repertoires and limit competition, allocating specific genres to different theatres and fixing ticket prices. Of course, the ideological basis was now radically different: the main point of demarketisation was to achieve a fair, stable distribution of work across the industry, and the rationale for the rejection of obscenity and vulgarity was a feminist argument about gender equality. When music halls and *revistas* resumed performances in late 1936, posters at box offices urged spectators to accord 'el máximo respeto a todas las compañeras que vas a ver en el escenario. Son trabajadoras como tú' ('maximum respect to all the female comrades you see on stage. They are workers just like you') (Mundi Pedret 1987: 44).

The efforts of the various unions and committees to control theatrical activity and encourage performances supportive of the Republican cause clearly constitute a wide-ranging form of censorship, but there is little documentary evidence of decisions to ban productions, or to cut or modify scripts or staging. The Comité de Control de Espectáculos Públicos in Madrid certainly had the power to authorise and prohibit public entertainments, as shown by the programme for a *festival artístico* at the Teatro Metropolitano on 1 October 1936. There are also several examples from October 1936 in the Centro Documental de la Memoria Histórica of requests for authorisation of dance and theatre performances in Catalonia, although these requests are to do with authorising events organised by local committees rather than approving particular works (CDMH PS-Barcelona 584 and 1421). It is also clear that the SIE in Barcelona operated a *comité de lectura* (reading committee) to assess the suitability of works for performance in the venues under its control. There are several letters of complaint about the length of time taken to complete these assessments, and even a sardonic internal memorandum from the head of the accounts section of the CET informing his superiors that some of the people employed for this task were only claiming payment for one script per week: 'Un lector debe leer más de una obra en siete días. O de lo contrario no hace de lector' ('A reader ought to read more than one play in seven days. If not, he shouldn't be working as a reader') (CDMH PS-BARCELONA, 1067, 7, p. 138).

One of the reasons for the delays was that works submitted to the CET were examined by two or three different sets of readers, as shown by the following letter of September 1937 from the Sindicat Únic d'Espectacles Públics in Vilanova i la Geltrú referring to a musical show titled *Barbas de cobre* ('Copperbeard'):

> La Junta del Sindicato de la Industria del Espectáculo C.N.T., de Villanueva y Geltrú ruega al Comité de Actores que imforme esta obra como también ruega al Comité Económico del Teatro que haga justicia reparando el inmerecido olvido que se ha tenido con esta obra y procurar que los Compositores imformen lo más pronto posible. Esperamos que tratándose de compañeros y militantes antiguos de la Comfederación como somos la mayor parte de esta Junta, tomaréis en concideración el presente ruego.
>
> Saludos anárquicos,
> LA JUNTA.
> (CDMH PS-Barcelona, 1067, 7, p. 157 [spelling errors in the original preserved])

> The Executive Committee of the CNT Sindicato de la Industria del Espectáculo in Villanueva y Geltrú requests that the Actors' Committee produce a report on the above work. It also asks the Comité Económico del Teatro to make up for the undeserved neglect suffered by this work by ensuring that the Composers' Committee issues a report as soon as possible. In view of the fact that this request is made by comrades and long-standing militants of the Confederation, which most of the members of this committee are, we trust that you will give it favourable consideration.
>
> Yours anarchically,
> THE EXECUTIVE COMMITTEE.

The committee in Vilanova wrote again a few days later to thank the CET for chasing up the reports (CDMH PS-Barcelona, 1067, 7, p. 162). Two playwrights who wrote to the CET in October 1937 were not so easily satisfied. Salvador Valverde, a successful author of songs, musical comedies and *zarzuelas*, wondered whether he was being blacklisted for being associated with the UGT, as his plays were being accepted for staging in Madrid but not in Barcelona, where he lived (CDMH PS-Barcelona, 1067, 7, pp. 216–17). Another author complained about the lack of accountability of the reading committee and proposed that there should be an appeals process:

> Amparados en una aparente imparcialidad, hoy pueden ser eliminadas obras y autores, mientras otros de inferior capacidad sigan estrenando mediocridades y refritos con acordes de la marcha real, como ocurrió en un teatro de Barcelona. Para que nuestros teatros no se conviertan en un feudo exclusivo de unos cuantos señores, precisa conceder a los futuros autores, un margen para su defensa. (CDMH PS-Barcelona, 1067, 7, p. 221)
>
> Behind a façade of apparent impartiality, plays and playwrights can currently be eliminated, while others of inferior talent continue to stage mediocre, rehashed works with echoes of the monarchist national anthem, as has occurred in a theatre in Barcelona. If our theatres are not to become the exclusive fiefdom of a privileged clique, it is essential that emerging authors are given a means of defending themselves.

The evidence from Barcelona points, therefore, to a complicated situation in which it is difficult to distinguish between coercive censorship and the variable effects of circumstances and ideology on routine decisions about programming and production. Censorship – or self-censorship – was built into the creative and management processes even if it was not being directly imposed by external forces.

In practice, the campaign for revolutionary renewal had a limited impact on the artistic output of the theatre industry. A few of the theatres taken over by workers' committees were used by collectives performing new agitprop pieces alongside versions of classics, poetry readings and translations of left-wing foreign plays, but the majority – in both Madrid and Barcelona – continued to offer a fairly conventional commercial repertoire, including variety shows and *revistas*. The assumption that a revolutionary theatre was the logical result of a social revolution and that 'a revolutionary audience would automatically present itself if it were offered a revolutionary theatre' proved to be ill-founded (McCarthy 1999: 39).

In the midst of all this upheaval, the official censorship apparatus administered by the Dirección General de Seguridad continued to operate to some degree in Madrid until the theatres there closed in November 1936 as a result of the siege by Nationalist forces. There is a file in the AGA containing documents relating to a triple bill at the Teatro Español on 20 October – Ramón Sender's *La llave* ('The Key'), Rafael Dieste's *Al amanecer* ('At Dawn') and Rafael Alberti's *Los salvadores de España* ('The Saviours of Spain') – which show all the normal procedures being followed. There are the two copies of each script and the fire safety certificate as required by the 1935 *Reglamento*, together with a covering letter addressed to the Director General de Seguridad, dated 19 October. There are also records of the texts being passed to the Asesoría Jurídica and a brief report on each one signed by the Abogado del Estado on 20 October (AGA 21/5804).[9] Díez comments that very few censorship files were processed after the uprising of 18 July (2007: 97), mentioning four other examples from August–September 1936. It may be that only relatively high-profile productions were accorded the full prior-censorship treatment at this time: Sender, Dieste and Alberti were all prominent writers and the company, Nueva Escena, was part of the Alianza de Intelectuales Antifascistas ('Alliance of Anti-Fascist Intellectuals').

The Dirección General de Seguridad probably ceased to carry out prior censorship of theatre in the capital in November 1936, though it may have continued to inspect first-night performances of commercial productions. With Nationalist forces closing in, the government of the Republic moved to Valencia on 6 November and set up the Junta de Defensa de Madrid ('Council for the Defence of Madrid'), to which it delegated full civil and military powers to defend the city. This body (relabelled as the Junta Delegada de la Defensa de Madrid on 1 December) set out to re-establish official control over cultural activities. After the reopening of theatres in Madrid in January 1937, it created a Junta de Espectáculos ('Public Entertainments Board') comprising representatives of the UGT and the CNT under the presidency of José Carreño España. This body's role was summed up in a newspaper report of 24 January as 'una labor depuradora sobre los repertorios y una fiscalización de ingresos y gastos' ('purification of repertoires and tightening of financial control over revenues and costs') (ABC 1937a: 9). It first met on 16 February and began a process of assuming administrative and financial control of all the theatres in the capital.

As before, though, the impact on the output of the industry appears to have been limited, both in terms of artistic quality and of ideological conformity. An article of 8 April expressed surprise that a recent production was allowed to use a backdrop featuring a red band across a yellow background (the colours of the traditional flag used by the Nationalists, which the Republic had replaced with a tricolour of purple, red and yellow), and lamented the almost complete absence of works reflecting the revolutionary spirit of the time: 'Diecisiete locales brindan, en sus tabladillos, los más diversos géneros a la curiosidad recreativa del espectador. De ellos, dieciséis se consagran a las mismas puerilidades ñoñas y anodinas anteriores al 19 de julio' ('There are seventeen establishments offering on their stages the most diverse range of entertainments for the delectation of spectators. Of these, sixteen are devoted to the same puerile, anodyne drivel as used to be peddled before the 19th of July') (SAM 1937a: 14).

Carreño España issued a statement insisting that the Junta, having been hampered by administrative delays and a shortage of suitable works by Spanish authors, was now making a difference. He proudly reported that a number of counter-revolutionary films had been banned, as well as the entire oeuvre of Antonio Quintero and Pascual Guillén, exiled writers of hugely popular musical comedies based on a clichéd vision of Andalusian culture. He also reassured his readers that the Junta was about to set up a reading committee to evaluate all works to be premiered (SAM 1937b: 14). However, the extent to which the Junta de Espectáculos managed to exercise effective censorship in this period seems to have been limited, and all these developments in Madrid were interrupted by the government's decision to abolish the Junta Delegada on 22 April 1937 and re-establish separate structures for civilian and military administration. On 26 April, Carreño España ruefully summed up his brief term of office as a struggle to balance the conflicting demands of the various Republican factions and to impose some degree of ideological and economic control over a chaotic theatre industry:

> Los cines y teatros eran constantemente incautados por los organismos políticos y sindicales, que los explotaban sin previa autorización del Orden público, sin pagar las contribuciones, deber elemental de

la ciudadanía, y que alardeaban con símbolos y banderas de estar sometidos a las organizaciones políticas y sindicales y de no estarlo a la autoridad del Estado. (ABC 1937b: 11)

The cinemas and theatres were constantly being taken over by political organisations and trade unions, which ran them without any official authorisation and without fulfilling the fundamental civic duty of contributing to the public purse. The symbols and flags that adorned the venues made it very clear that they were under the control of the parties and unions, and not of the state.

The re-establishment of central government authority in Madrid (increasingly influenced by the Communist Party) was followed by a more determined effort to gain control over the theatre industry. The reading committee set up by the Madrid Junta de Espectáculos continued to operate after April 1937, but it attracted increasing criticism for particular decisions and for the ambiguity of its role. Like the CNT committee in Barcelona, it acted both as a censorship board and as a programming committee for all the theatres in Madrid, selecting plays considered suitable for a popular, state-run, revolutionary entertainment industry. A newspaper article of 10 October 1937 argued that it should be limited to political vetting of works chosen by artistic directors (García Iniesta 1937).

In the meantime, a national Consejo Central del Teatro (CCT – 'Central Theatre Council') was created in August 1937. The declared aim was to 'redimir el teatro español de su carácter exclusivista mercantil, evitando que sea una actividad de lucro, para convertirla en manifestación cultural y educadora' ('redeem Spanish theatre from commercialism, preventing it from being a purely profit-making activity, in order to turn it into a public service of cultural and educational benefit'), and to ensure that the theatre functioned effectively as an instrument of propaganda at the service of the Popular Front in order to win the war (Gaceta de la República 1937a: 769). The law creating the CCT gave it remarkably broad responsibilities for encouraging and overseeing theatrical activities, supporting performance groups, establishing drama schools, taking over the management of venues, and setting up commissions to liaise with the unions over employment matters. Article 3 also gave the CCT specific responsibility for censorship, especially of political material: 'El Consejo Central del Teatro ejercerá la censura de los espectáculos en su aspecto artístico-cultural, velando también por que el contenido de los espectáculos teatrales no sea contrario a la línea de la República y del Frente Popular' ('The Central Theatre Council shall exercise censorship with regard to the artistic and cultural dimension of public entertainments, and shall ensure that the content of theatrical performances does not conflict with the strategic line taken by the Republic and the Popular Front') (Gaceta de la República 1937a: 769).

The Madrid Junta de Espectáculos was finally relieved of its censorship role in October 1937. It was restructured by a law of 28 October 1937 subordinating it to national bodies, especially the CCT, which was now established as the organisation responsible for all theatre programming and censorship, at least in Madrid and Valencia (Gaceta de la República 1937c). On 5 December 1938, the CCT issued a statement declaring that it generally wished to allow freedom of expression and that its censorship activity would be limited to reporting to the authorities anything that was judged to be harmful to the work of defending the Republic, either for political reasons or on account of crudity of expression (El Sol 1937). The Council's vice president, the writer and director María Teresa León, declared in an interview that it had authorised almost everything that had been submitted and that the only work to have been banned outright was *Currito de la Cruz*, a *zarzuela* of 1931 by José Silva Aramburu based on Alejandro Pérez Lugín's novel, which was seen as representing 'the other Spain', all bullfighters, Andalusian Holy Week traditions and superstitious Catholicism. She asked 'Pero ¿piensa nadie que esto se pueda permitir en los momentos presentes, cuando hay un millón de muertos producido por la guerra?' ('But does anyone really think that this sort of thing can be allowed at the present time, when a million people have been killed in the war?') (Laertes 1937).

At the same time, the government speeded up the process of formally taking economic and administrative control of the entertainment industry. A law of 27 December 1937, noting the 'abnormal' state of the industry in Alicante, ordered the Ministerio de Hacienda y Economía ('Ministry of Finance and the Economy') to take all theatres in that city into provisional state ownership, and to appoint an administrator to decide which ones should be run directly by the ministry and which could be allowed to manage themselves (Gaceta de la República 1937d). Similar orders were enacted in 1938 with reference to Valencia, Madrid and other parts of what remained of the Republican zone. The order relating to Madrid specified that the government-appointed administrator would work with the Junta de Espectáculos 'a fin de coordinar la intervención económica con las facultades que a la Junta corresponden en los aspectos artístico y cultural del espectáculo' ('in order to coordinate economic intervention with the Junta's functions in relation to the artistic and cultural aspects of the entertainment industry') (Gaceta de la República 1938a). From 8 May 1938 until 28 March 1939, theatre listings for Madrid in *ABC* and other newspapers bore the subheading 'Industria intervenida por el Estado' ('Industry under State control').

There is clear evidence of the reimposition of the traditional structure of official censorship (presided over by the Ministerio de la Gobernación) in Valencia. A meeting of the Junta Consultiva e Inspectora de Teatros ('Theatre Supervision and Inspection Board') for the province of Valencia on 24 September 1938, chaired by the Civil Governor, declared that this body was now functioning again and resolved to instruct the CNT and UGT to give its inspectors access to theatres in order to ensure full compliance with the 1935 regulations. This referred primarily to health and safety matters, but the minutes also note that government inspectors would work with the members of the Junta to prevent 'cuantas anormalidades se pudieran observar' ('whatever abnormal situations might arise') (CDMH PS Barcelona 821, 1), which seems to be a reference to public-order policing in theatres. At least one work soon fell foul of the restored censorship regime: a *revista* entitled *Casos y coses del món que pasen i pasaran* ('Stuff that Happens and Will Go on Happening') was banned after opening at the Teatro Apolo in Valencia on the grounds that it fomented defeatism, a decision ratified by the Ministro de la Gobernación himself.[10]

The CCT exercised little control over theatre in Catalonia, despite the fact that the government of the shrinking Republican zone had moved to Barcelona in November 1937. As the balance of power there shifted away from the anarchists towards the communists and socialists, the Generalitat was making its own arrangements from late 1937 for taking over theatre businesses and limiting the role of the UGT and CNT to pure labour relations. A law of 19 January 1938 decreed the takeover by the state of all theatres and cinemas in Catalonia except for those that had already been taken over by city councils, 'amb l'objecte d'assegurar-ne l'existència i aconseguir el màxim d'avantatges econòmics' ('with the aim of assuring their survival and maximising the economic benefits obtained') (Diari Oficial de la Generalitat de Catalunya 1938: 274). A Comissió Interventora ('Expropriation Commission') was created within the Consell d'Economia (the Generalitat's economic ministry) in order to carry out the process and oversee the management of the industry; the Comité Económico del Teatro was abolished and all its functions absorbed by the new commission; and a joint advisory committee of UGT and CNT representatives was created to work alongside the commission. Xavier Diez asserts that these changes, together with central government taking over control over public order in Catalonia, meant a return to authoritarianism and the imposition of draconian censorship (Diez 2008: 33). However, we have not found any direct evidence of the imposition of state control resulting in a tightening of censorship.

In any case, the CCT was never afforded sufficient resources to fulfil its ambitious remit. Its membership had not been confirmed until October 1937 (Gaceta de la República 1937b), and a civil servant was not appointed to administer it until February 1938 (Gaceta de la República 1938b: 893). A law of 2 March ordered that its functions should be reduced to the work of the *comisión de lectura* and the development of the Guerrillas del Teatro and Guiñol groups: 'Las restantes atenciones o compromisos que a la fecha tenga contraídos el Consejo Central del Teatro tratarán, por ahora, de reducirse a lo imprescindible' ('Any other initiatives or undertakings to which the Council is committed shall for the time being be limited to what is strictly essential') (Gaceta de la República 1938c: 1379). There is evidence of one or two plays being banned in Madrid during 1938, but in general the number of proposed productions blocked by the CCT seems to have been low.

Since it was seeking, like the Junta de Espectáculos and other bodies that preceded it, both to create a new repertoire and police the existing one, it is difficult to gauge to what extent the CCT was exercising censorship by excluding from consideration certain kinds of theatre or the work of certain authors. There was heated debate in the press in 1937 and 1938 over whether the work of successful playwrights who were known to be supporters of the Nationalists (such as José María Pemán, Eduardo Marquina and Pedro Muñoz Seca) should be banned on principle, regardless of the ideological content of particular plays. A decision to do so must have been taken by 14 September 1938, for a memo was issued on that date by the Ministro de la Gobernación ordering the Director General de Seguridad to ban performances of a *revista* from 1932 by Antonio Paso Cano entitled *Las tentaciones* ('Temptations') 'en atención a ser el autor elemento faccioso' ('on account of the author being a rebel sympathiser') (CDMH PS-Barcelona 821, 1). An article of 1 December, lamenting the fact that companies were forced by a lack of new material to rely on established hits by authors who had become politically undesirable, noted that the theatre censors had removed more than a hundred titles from the repertoire (Valdés 1938). The author does not reject the principle but argues that such indiscriminate blacklisting is not in anyone's interests. He suggests a compromise: 'Represéntense las obras de autores fascistas, si tienen méritos para ello y no atacan al régimen, pero los derechos de autor que sean ingresados en la Caja de Reparaciones' ('Let plays by fascist authors be performed, as long as they are fit for the stage and do not attack the Republic, but the royalties should be paid into the official war reparations fund') (Valdés 1938).

An article of January 1939 rehearses the arguments for and against the blacklisting of 'fascist' playwrights and supports Valdés's proposal. It concludes optimistically: 'En cuanto a mi opinión, para después de la guerra no puede ser más clara y terminante: Libertad, Libertad y Libertad. La razón humana no puede ni debe vivir entre tinieblas' ('As for my opinion on this, it could not be clearer or firmer as regards the approach that must be taken once the war is over: Freedom, Freedom and Freedom. Human reason cannot and must not live in darkness') (Zozaya 1939: 176). The shadows of authoritarianism, however, were already closing in. Barcelona was occupied by Nationalist forces on 26 January, Madrid was taken on 28 March, and General Franco declared total victory on 1 April. It was already clear from the rhetoric and actions of the Nationalists that their patriotic 'Crusade' would not end with military victory. They aimed to eradicate the cultural and ideological legacy of the Republic, punish its supporters and remake the nation in a traditionalist Catholic mould.

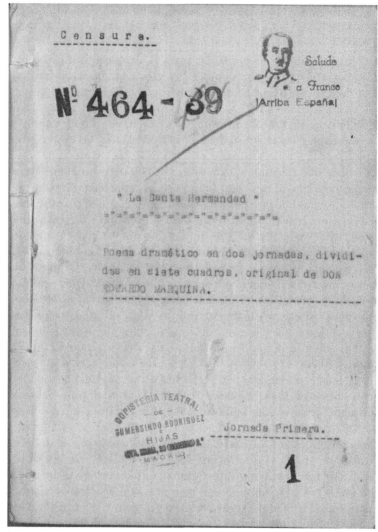

Figure 2: Cover of the typescript of *La Santa Hermandad* submitted for censorship (1939)

Notes
1 For details of Spanish legislation referring to the theatre between 1534 and 1839, together with extracts from publications discussing its moral legitimacy, see Cotarelo y Mori (1904).

2 See also Surwillo (2007).
3 Santos Sánchez (2011) discusses the censorship and reception of *Mariana Pineda* from 1924 to 1967, emphasising Lorca's own statements insisting on the non-political nature of his intentions.
4 José María Ortiz Martínez will feature prominently in Chapter 3 as the key administrator of theatre censorship for most of the Franco dictatorship and beyond (1941–78). It seems unlikely that he was already working as a police inspector in 1927; perhaps this Ortiz was his father.
5 The file on *El confidente* is discussed in more detail in Chapter 2.
6 Díez asserts that between 1931 and 1936 the Second Republic operated a system of censorship that allowed the executive to control the theatre 'sin someter sus posibles abusos al poder judicial' ('without being accountable to the judiciary for any abuses') (2007: 438–9). The evidence from the files, especially the comment relating to *El confidente*, suggests that this was not the case.
7 These CNT bodies also operated under titles in Catalan, but their letterheads, logos, stamps and correspondence were printed mostly in Castilian (as evidenced by documents from 1937 in CDMH PS-Barcelona 1067, 7).
8 There is a copy of the minutes of the meeting at which the CEEP was established in CDMH PS-Barcelona 1421, 9.
9 This case is discussed in more detail in Chapter 2.
10 This case is discussed in Chapter 2.

Chapter 2

Un teatro de ida y vuelta: All Change and No Change in the Second Republic and the Civil War

This chapter explores the emergence of a politicised stage against a backdrop of a so-called 'theatre crisis' and traces the shifting theatrical trends during almost a decade of social and political conflict that included the Second Republic (1931–6) and the civil war (1936–9). In terms of censorship, an initial focus on public disorder in the early part of the Second Republic gave way to more ideological concerns in the late republican and civil war periods. The censorship files are, unsurprisingly, incomplete due to political upheaval, shifts in censorship practice and the loss of documentation during the war. In addition, instances of *teatro de circunstancias*, short pieces created in response to current events, were often not submitted to censorship or published. Nonetheless, the information gathered from state archives, newspapers and memoirs reveals the role of the theatre in social change and conflict, as entertainment, fundraising tool and didactic instrument for identity formation.

Theatre during the Second Republic

A complex picture emerges during the Republican period. On the one hand, the declaration of the Republic seemed to offer new opportunities for experimentation and reform and for the creation of a politicised proletarian theatre (Vilches de Frutos 1999); on the other hand, however, traditional and conservative drama continued to dominate the stage and to inspire talk of a theatre in crisis (Araquistáin 1930; Díaz Fernández 1930; Dougherty and Anderson 2012; Mainer 2010; McGaha 1979).

Although the theatres were closed briefly following the declaration of the Republic on 14 April, they soon reopened. Much of the theatrical offering was the same as before but several playhouses in Madrid underwent name changes, such as from 'Teatro Reina [Queen] Victoria' to 'Teatro Victoria' and 'Teatro Infanta [Princess] Beatriz' to 'Teatro Beatriz', to reflect the shift from Monarchy to Republic (Vilches de Frutos 1999: 257). The early days also saw the staging of a new 'Republican' theatre, including Álvaro Orriols's *Rosas de sangre o El poema de la República* ('Roses of Blood, or The Poem of the Republic') at the Teatro Fuencarral, on 2 May 1931. This play, which depicts class conflict and a series of historical clashes culminating in the end of the monarchy, can be read as an ode to Republicanism (Espejo Trenas 2009). Orriols himself recalled his success in the days following the declaration of the Republic, when after the premiere, the enthusiastic public 'asaltó el escenario al final de la representación para llevarme en hombros hasta la Puerta del Sol, en una espontánea manifestación republicana' ('invaded the stage at the end of the performance to carry me on their shoulders to the Puerta del Sol, in a spontaneous demonstration of republicanism) (2000: 152).

Alberti's *Fermín Galán*, which was premiered at the Teatro Español on 1 June 1931 and re-staged in December, represented in scenic ballad form the life and death of the infantry captain, one of the so-called 'martyrs' of the Republic, who was shot, along with Captain Ángel García Hernández, for their part in the Jaca uprising of 1930 that sought to overthrow the monarchy (Popkin 1975: 63–78; Ramiro de la Mata 2018).

The first Republican government invested in the theatre as part of its ambulatory cultural programme the Misiones Pedagógicas, which had the laudable objective of bringing the culture enjoyed by those in urban centres to the masses in towns and villages throughout Spain (Gaceta de Madrid 1931a). The Misiones Pedagógicas were also employed by the new government in their efforts to build a cohesive and convincing Republican identity 'by incorporating traditional Spanish culture into the nation-building process' (Rodríguez Solás 2013: 786). In addition to a mobile museum, a literacy programme, cinema and musical concerts, the Misiones included two theatre groups: the Teatro del Pueblo, directed by Alejandro Casona, and a puppet theatre with Rafael Dieste at the helm (Aznar Soler 1997: 46–7; Rey Faraldos 1992). The theatre group La Barraca, led by Federico García Lorca and Eduardo Ugarte, would also collaborate with the Misiones Pedagógicas from 1932 (Diez Caneda 1968; Oliva 2013). Government support also allowed Cipriano de Rivas Cherif to establish the Teatro Escuela de Arte at the María Guerrero theatre in 1933 (Mainer 2010: 209), another initiative that can be read as politically motivated.[1]

Republican censorship

Despite the near-constant political upheaval of the Second Republic, the mainstream theatre, including drama, classics, comic theatre and *revistas*, continued much as before. With regard to serious drama, works lamenting the loss of traditional values and the diminished status of the Roman Catholic Church occasionally raised an eyebrow among the censors but it was the comic theatre and *revistas*, with their more overt mockery of the new regime, that tended to generate disapproval.

The files show that in the early days of the Second Republic the censors did not have much to say about works by conventional dramatists such as Jacinto Benavente – considered apolitical and unlikely to cause public order offences – who were consequently largely untroubled by censorship.[2] The tightening of restrictions during the period of conservative governance, while it did have some impact on the commercial stage, left many such established authors unaffected.[3] Moreover, stalwarts of the mainstream theatre like Eduardo Marquina, best known for his commercially successful historical and poetic dramas, were seen as commendable and their works were easily approved.[4] Files on the most successful female dramatist of the Republican period, Pilar Millán-Astray (the sister of General José Millán-Astray, founder of the Spanish Legion), who wrote *sainetes* and *costumbrista* dramas, show that her works were deemed uncontroversial, particularly in the conservative period. However, there is an interesting letter in the file relating to her 1932 play, *Las andanzas de Ginesillo* ('The Adventures of

Ginesillo') (AGA R5993), in which she is accused by a member of the public of attacking and insulting the Republican government (Nieva de la Paz 1994: 129–39; Santos Sánchez 2013).

More notable is the case of José María Pemán, who cast himself as the voice of conservative resistance to change, and whose works became associated in the public mind with condemnation of the left and support for the reactionary forces in society (García Ruiz 2013). He was an ardent monarchist, a member of the CEDA government, and later supporter of the Nationalist uprising and of Franco. Best known in the Republican period for a series of historical dramas, there are files on three of his plays from this period, *El divino impaciente* (*A Saint in a Hurry*, 1933), *Cuando las Cortes de Cádiz* ('When Parliament Sat in Cadiz', 1934) and *Cisneros* (1934), considered among his most important works. *El divino impaciente* was premiered on 27 September 1933 at the Teatro Beatriz and the files contain no reports – just the playscript with some marks, but no indication of censorship (AGA R6211). The censors from the left-wing period seem not to have been overly troubled by what could be interpreted as a response to the Republican government's decision to disband the Jesuit Order in Spain in January 1932. The focus of censorship at this stage is evidently still on public disorder, rather than political content.

Pemán's other two plays were authorised without difficulty and premiered during the conservative period, both in the Teatro Victoria. *Cuando las Cortes de Cádiz* (27 September 1934), described by Vilches de Frutos as 'una diatriba contra la Junta de Cádiz y los valores de la Constitución con constantes alusiones a la situación del momento' ('a diatribe against the Cádiz Junta and the values of the constitution with constant allusions to the current situation') was approved by censors (AGA R6243) and well received by a conservative public (1999: 262). More interesting is the case of *Cisneros* (15 December 1934), a historical drama based on the life of the influential Cardinal and statesman. The file gives us insight into the public and official reception of Pemán's theatre. Two months after the October revolution in Asturias and its brutal repression, the report by the Comisario Jefe ('Chief Commissioner') demonstrates how the play was received as a political act. In his report, he noted that after the performance the dramatist thanked the actor and addressed the public, making an explicit link between the historical action of the play and the contemporary political circumstance and suggesting that 'exemplary rulers' like Cardinal Cisneros were needed once again:

> Lo que se echa de menos, son hombres viejos como el cardenal Cisneros, que tenía la flexibilidad del timonel, que lleva el timón, sorteando las olas y la rigidez de la brújula, que marca al navegante el Norte. Al terminar el Sr Pemán, fué objeto de grandes ovaciones teniendo que levantar varias veces el telón de boca. (AGA R6279)

> What is needed are old men like Cardinal Cisneros, who had the flexibility of the helmsman, who take the helm, handling with great skill both the waves and the rigidity of the compass that orientates the navigator. When he had finished, Mr Peman received great applause and several curtain calls.

The success of the play demonstrates support for conservative views and clear opposition to the secularising and modernising initiatives of the first Republican government.

Classical dramas caused very few problems and their reception was generally positive. The file on Lope de Vega's *Fuente Ovejuna*, at the Teatro Español on 29 May 1932, for example, shows how the classics were generally not perceived by the censors as political works and, moreover, were considered morally acceptable, if not superior to, other more contemporary plays (AGA R5907). Those who staged them also tended to stress their apolitical nature, although, as Dougherty (2013) and Rodríguez-Solás (2014) show, they were sometimes used politically, albeit less obviously than some other types of theatre.

By late 1935 and early 1936 there is evidence in the censors' reports of their reaction to increasing political tensions and even works by 'right-thinking' authors were carefully scrutinised for the offence they might cause. In the wake of recent financial scandals, such as the so-called 'Straperlo' affair in October that brought down the Prime Minister and leader of the Radical Republicans, Alejandro Lerroux, and destroyed the reputation of the party, the censors were particularly sensitive to allegations of corruption (Townson 2000b; Brenan 2012, 479).

In this context, Vicente Castro Les, the popular author of *costumbrista* dramas, fell foul of the censors with ¡La bolsa o la vida! ('Your Money or Your Life!'). The play premiered on 17 November 1935 at an event organised by the Comisión de las Escuelas Laicas de Francisco Mora, only after the removal of language that reflected 'desprestigio de las Autoridades' ('disparagement of the authorities'), highlighted in the censor's report. These cuts included the suggestion that those engaged in a form of theft could be 'un personaje o a lo menos Concejal' ('a well-known person or at least a Councillor'), and one innuendo relating to ministers and theft:

> Hay quien va a la cárcel la primera vez que 'afana' un panecillo, y otros en cambio a fuerza de robar millones cobran fama de hombres de talento y llegan a ministros. De modo que el toque no está en echarse a ladrón, sino en saber robar con capa de hombre de bien. (AGA R6444)

> There are those who go to prison for the first time for 'swiping' a bread roll and there are those, on the other hand, who as a result of robbing millions are famed for their talent and become ministers. So, the point is not becoming a thief but rather knowing how to rob in the guise of an honest man.

The initial censor anticipated trouble from the public and suggested cuts, or a ban, to avoid this, but the performance went ahead once the cuts were made.

Another play to suffer cuts relating to criticism of corruption was Honorio Maura's *Un negociante excelente* ('An Excellent Salesman'). A monarchist politician, journalist and dramatist, his name and political pedigree carried a certain weight: he was the son of Antonio Maura, who had been Prime Minister under Alfonso XIII, and brother of the Monarchist politician, Gabriel, and the Republican politician, Miguel (BNE 2016). The play premiered in December 1935, but not before several cuts were implemented, including a pejorative reference to a government minister: 'Fué uno de los que más viajaron en los tranvías sin pagar. Desde entonces, personaje . . . Y hoy, ya lo ves, Ministro del Tesoro' ('He was one of those who travelled most on the trams without paying. Since then, a VIP . . . and these days, don't you know, Minister for the Treasury') (AGA 21/5849). This seems to be a reference to Joaquín Chapaprieta Torregrosa, whose attempt at economic reforms ensured that the right-wing elites despised him almost as much as the left did (García Escudero 1978b: 32–41). Several more examples of negative references to social and political change are indicated on the censor's copy of the playtext, on nine pages in total.

Overall, it is evident that the mainstream commercial theatre posed few problems for the censors. Even where the plays contained mild political comment, this was easily dealt with. The cases of Pemán and Maura, however, show how the theatre was already being used politically by conservative forces in defence of certain 'essential' values.

The censorship of comic theatre varied in severity. The work of the (now) respected Spanish absurdist, Enrique Jardiel Poncela, was considered apolitical and plays such as *Usted tiene ojos de mujer fatal* (*You Have the Eyes of a Femme Fatale*, premiered at the Teatro Cervantes on 30 August 1933) and *Un adulterio decente* ('Respectable Adultery', premiered at the Teatro María Isabel on 2 May 1935), deemed 'de moral atrevida y mundana' ('of daring and fashionable morality') although 'completamente apolítica' ('completely apolitical') and were staged without difficulties (AGA R6208 and AGA R6264). Other, more popular comic authors found themselves in greater trouble, as they mocked the new social structures and those eager to embrace them. The tightening of restrictions during the conservative period was evident even before the introduction of new legislation in 1935. Carlos Arniches, for example, ran into trouble with his comic piece, *Peccata Mundi*, co-authored with Antonio Estremera with music by Jacinto Guerrero (Teatro Martín, 25 May 1934). Arniches specialised in the genre of the *sainete* – popular comedies, sometimes with songs, set in rural or urban working-class environments, featuring spirited stereotyped characters, lively colloquial dialogue and often farcical plots. *Peccata Mundi* appears to have been a calculated attempt to cash in on the boom of the *revista* in the early years of the Republic.

This light-hearted piece centred on a rich American woman who decides that having only seven capital sins is boringly *passé* and announces a prize of $5 million for the first person to invent a new one. Satan himself enters the competition, complaining that times are hard in the underworld, but the cash is finally awarded to a character who prides himself on never having done anything in his life. While it made it to the stage without any interference, it suffered a cut following the premiere, as the inspector noted a political jibe (a suggestion that Parliament was full of scoundrels) that was not to his liking, and an interaction involving an audience member (Miss Castillo came down off the stage while singing and gave a kiss to a gentleman in the second row of the stalls), which he clearly considered to be in poor taste (AGA R6214). While the contact with the audience member breached article 70 of the 1913 legislation, forbidding direct contact with the audience, it did not seem to overly concern the censors (Gaceta de Madrid 1913: 350). The political reference, which went against article 12 by mocking a state institution, on the other hand, led to a cut (Gaceta de Madrid 1913: 347–8). A handwritten note of 30 May records: 'Se le ha dicho al comisario de orden del Sr Jefe Superior haga gestión particular para que desaparezca lo de "Los hay mayores" etc.' ('On the orders of the Chief of Police, the inspector has been instructed to deal privately with the theatre so that the reference to "there are bigger scoundrels" etc. is removed').[5] Despite this, the show was a big hit in Madrid throughout June 1934, was revived in September and November, and transferred successfully to Barcelona.

One of the most striking examples of how this kind of theatre skirted and sometimes broke the rules is the work of Pedro Muñoz Seca. A monarchist and prolific author of comic theatre, his plays dominated the Spanish stage in the 1930s, along with those of Arniches and the Quintero brothers. His theatre, often the fruit of collaborations with others, such as Pedro Pérez Fernández (1885–1956), was sometimes cut during the early left-wing period, as he often inserted political jokes attacking republican politics into his plays. According to Luis M. González, his Republican-era plays were defined by 'la parodia, el chiste, la caricatura y la sátira política antirrepublicana como instrumento para complacer a un público mayoritariamente conservador que acudía a ver sus estrenos' ('parody, jokes, caricature and anti-republican political satire, used as an instrument to please the largely conservative public that attended his shows') (2007: 72; see also Villamil-Acera 2014). Several of his works were also cut during the conservative period of government, but this was mostly for reasons of decorum.

Some of his most successful dramas attacked the new values of the Republic, most notoriously *La Oca*, premiered on Christmas Eve 1931. The title is an acronym for 'Libre Asociación de Obreros Cansados y Aburridos' ('Free Association of Tired and Bored Workers'), a swipe at the proletariat. Mata Induráin describes it as 'un burdo ataque que trata de ridiculizar a los obreros y sus intentos asociacionistas' ('a crude attack that ridicules workers and their attempts at collective action') and the review in *Blanco y Negro* described the play as a caricature focusing on the seizure of property and redistribution of land, as well as 'el fácil traspaso de las mujeres' ('the easy transfer of women'), presumably a reference to the new divorce laws (Mata Induráin 1995: 73; Blanco y Negro 1932: 133).

While *La Oca* proved a success in Madrid, it was the cause of some scandal when staged in Malaga. The CDMH files contain a carbon copy of a handwritten document from January 1932 citing an incident in the Teatro Cervantes in Málaga during a performance of *La Oca*, which is described in the report as a reactionary play. Members of the audience protested at the 'franca e impúdica agresión que al ideal republicano se hace' ('frank and shameless aggression of the play towards the Republican ideal'); several people, including some local public figures, were arrested and manhandled 'por el delito de defender sus convicciones republicanas' ('for the crime of defending their republican convictions'), and brought a formal complaint against the sergeant who had hit some of them (CDMH PS-Madrid 1120, 27). There is no indication in the files of how this was finally resolved but it is clear that reactions to the play echoed local political conflicts.

Muñoz Seca's *Anacleto se divorcia* ('Anacleto's Getting Divorced'), which premiered in Madrid on 2 May 1932, openly mocks the new divorce laws and social mores and, like *La Oca*, was a resounding success:

JUNCOSA.– Ya no es como antes. Ahora somos laicos.
MANOLITA.– ¿Y eso qué es?
JUNCOSA.– Chiquilla, laicos: que antes se entraba en la Iglesia y ahora se pasa por el lao na más: ¡laicos! (AGA 352/39)[6]

JUNCOSA – It's not like before. Now we're secular.
MANOLITA – What's that?
JUNCOSA – Dearie, 'secular': before you went into the church and now you pass it by in a sec, that's all: 'secular!'

Unfortunately, there is little detail in the files on these plays and, although they denounced Republican values, it is not clear that the censors were particularly minded to act. At this point, they seem to have been quite tolerant of both political comment and moral laxity.

During the conservative period, however, despite his political leanings, Muñoz Seca had several brushes with moralising censors. Alba Peinado cites several cuts to his 1934 play, ¡Soy un sinvergüenza! ('I'm Shameless') and *Ciudadano de honor* ('Citizen of Honour', Teatro Benavente, March 1935), also ran into trouble (2009: 171–2). The official report on the latter criticised the many direct allusions and crude references to the Republic and its praise for the monarchy, which, the censor feared, might create protests and counter-protests. It is interesting that he also noted the importance of the author, with 'sus simpatizantes y seguidores' ('his sympathisers and followers') (AGA R6333). Such a following suggests that performances of his theatre had the potential to become political rallying points and therefore raised public order concerns. Although several cuts were insisted upon, the dramatist himself was suspected of political mischief and the Director General prohibited the play.

A modified version with a new title, *El gran ciudadano* ('The Great Citizen') was authorised on 9 March. The plot thickens, however, as the dramatist was accused in a subsequent report of failing to comply with the agreed alterations and demonstrating scant regard for the authorities. The play was again prohibited. A public order notice announcing the ban on the work is contained in the file. Negotiations continued and an acceptable version was finally authorised for staging on 13 March. A report on the premiere confirmed that the banned phrases had been excluded and that the performance had been unproblematic.

A year later Muñoz Seca was in trouble again. *Bronca en el ocho* ('A Row in Row 8') premiered on 4 July 1936 at the Teatro Cómico, Madrid. By now the Frente Popular government was in place; state censors sought to protect a more radical left-wing government while not alienating moderates. Muñoz Seca was not inclined towards moderation and cuts were made to sections of dialogue that disparaged the current situation with mocking references to political groups. On page 9, Luisa mocks the sudden popularity of socialist politics in the south of Spain: 'Hay que ver cómo está de moda lo del pañolito [rojo]' ('You should see how popular the red kerchief is'). On page 24, Pepe's comment about 'cierto miedo en la "zeda"' ('some fear in the "zeda"') is presumably a swipe at the CEDA. The inspector's report certainly suggests that this is how it was interpreted; Luisa's comment was omitted and the reference to 'zeda' replaced by a more neutral phrase (AGA R6669). It was decided that in the febrile political climate of the time, such provocation was best avoided. Although not cited in the report, the legislation outlawed anything perceived as incitement to hatred of the authorities or aversion between social classes (Gaceta 1935: 1056)

Muñoz Seca had long thrived in the theatre without allowing censorship legislation to concern him much, but the tolerance that had been shown him and his inflammatory and entertaining theatre heretofore would not last. He was executed by Republican forces on 28 November 1936 during the Paracuellos massacres in Madrid, 'por fascista, monárquico y enemigo de la República' ('for being a Fascist, a monarchist and an enemy of the Republic') (Amorós 2006). Just as Lorca's execution became a symbol of Republican victimhood, the killing of Muñoz Seca turned him into a martyr of Nationalism, albeit on a national, rather than international stage, and his memory and plays were used politically by the Franco regime for many decades following the end of the civil war, as will be discussed in Chapter 4.

Another form of theatre that occasionally disturbed the censors was the popular *revista*. The problems usually arose because of their displays of semi-clad actresses, blue-tinged jokes and 'inappropriate' interactions with the public. Sometimes such works also engaged with politics and social change, although generally on a superficial, satirical level. The liberal mores of the early Republic meant that aside from noting some jokes and nudity, little action was taken.

Occasionally, however, the playwrights went too far for the censors, as with Ramos de Castro's *Las del Beni* ('Beni's Girls'), staged on 28 May 1932 in the Teatro Eslava, which was cut to eliminate negative references to political figures. The Comisario Jefe's report noted the positive response from the spectators, who sang along to most of the musical numbers, but also commented on the need to suppress certain – but not all – political comments:

> En varios cuadros hay alusiones sin importancia al Excmo Sr. Presidente del Consejo, Ministro de Justicia Sr. Albornoz, Alcalde y varios políticos más, excepto en el cuadro quinto en donde se alude a Alejandro, Marcelino e Indalecio que por considerarse un poco duras, indicó al Empresario, el Comisario Sr. Galón, la conveniencia de suprimirlas, habiéndose suprimido radicalmente. (AGA R5971)

In several scenes, there are insignificant allusions to his Excellency the President of the Council, Minister for Justice, Mr Albornoz, the Mayor and various other politicians, except in the fifth scene where allusions are made to Alejandro, Marcelino e Indalecio. As these were considered a bit harsh, the Commissioner Mr Galón indicated to the theatre owner the advisability of suppressing them and this was carried out fully.

This is presumably a reference to Alejandro Lerroux, leader of the Partido Republicano Radical, briefly Minister of State under Azaña (April–December 1931), who would later serve as Prime Minister on three occasions from 1933 to 1935; Marcelino Domingo, founder of the Partido Republicano Radical Socialista, who held various ministerial posts; and Indalecio Prieto, a member of the executive of the Partido Socialista Obrero Español (PSOE – 'Spanish Socialist Workers' Party'), who also served as minister several times.

Chungonia ('Lampoonia'), by Antonio Paso (hijo) and Federico López de Saá, with music by Soriano and Azagra, described as a 'farsa caricaturesca' ('satirical farce') (ABC 1932: 35), had a similar experience of censorship. It was due to premiere at the Teatro de la Comedia, Madrid on 5 August 1932 but, in an unusual show of political unease, negative references to the socialists led to its suspension on the opening night (La Prensa 1932: 2). The ban was confirmed on 7 August. Although the reports themselves are missing, the files do contain correspondence relating to the ban, and also the text itself, which shows many cuts. These give an indication of the nature of the mockery involved. One character states, for example, 'Como son [de] izquierdas no hacen nada a derechas' ('As they're from the left, they never do anything right'), and declares, '¡Ah! Socialistas (de esos también los hay): aquí los llamamos de otro modo' ('Ah, Socialists, there are some of them too. We call them something else here') (AGA R6005). The scandal did not harm Paso's reputation, however, and may even have enhanced it, and he remained one of the most sucessful dramatists of the period.

During the conservative period (1933–5), stricter censorship reflected the Catholic-led government coalition's concerns about the immorality on display in some theatres. *La Colasa de Pavón*, a heady mix of sex and politics by Francisco Ramos de Castro and José L. Mayral, with music by Pablo Luna, was criticised by the censors, but nonetheless authorised for staging on 30 November 1935 at the

Teatro Pavón. The play was clearly in contravention of article 8 of the 1935 legislation, which prohibited works that disturbed public order or went against morals or good taste, and before it could be staged several cuts had already been made, including a negative allusion to the Minister of War, the Catholic politician and founder of the CEDA, José María Gil-Robles (Gaceta 1935: 1056–7). The initial report on the performance was scathing in its criticism of the genre and its frivolity and suggested (perhaps wishfully) that the public was unimpressed. The Comisario Jefe commented that there was an abundance of jokes and examples of poor taste, which were received with a combination of applause and protest. The day after the premiere the company was instructed to make further cuts, including the words (presumably juxtaposed) 'ladrón' (thief) and 'Partido Radical' ('Radical Party'), another reference to the financial scandals involving the party (AGA R6465).

Further trouble ensued and the inspector, Luis Colmenar, reported that during the scene in which 'la vedette Srta. Pinillos, ofrece como premio un beso al espectador que acierte el nombre puesto en una banderola, se produjo un gran escándalo' ('the starlet, Miss Pinillos, offers a kiss as a prize to the spectator who correctly guesses the name on a little flag, causing a great commotion'), several spectators clambered onto the stage to claim the prize and mayhem ensued. This blatantly contravened article 95 of the legislation, which forbade interaction with the public. The Inspector ordered a halt to the performance. A further bawdy scene involving a conscript and a servant on a public bench, which included lewd comments and gestures, had been removed earlier, but the company had reinstated it, arguing that it had not been officially prohibited and claiming that the author had threatened to withdraw the play if the scene was cut. The Director General then intervened, banning the scene with Ms Pinillos and insisting on changes to the other scene on the bench.

Despite all of this, the play was a success. The review in *ABC*, which describes it as a 'fantasía cómico-lírica' ('comical-lyrical fantasy'), probably explains why. As well as outlining the rather light plot, it asks the reader to imagine 'las veces que tendrán que vestirse y desvestirse las chicas del conjunto y los bailables que tendrán que ejecutar Laura Pinillos, Amparito Sara, Concha Rey, Isabelita Hernández y demás preciosidades de Pavón ('the number of times the chorus girls will have to dress and undress and the number of dance numbers that Laura Pinillos, Amparito Sara, Concha Rey, Isabelita Hernández and the other beauties of the Pavón will have to perform') (Carmona 1935: 61). One might assume that the public did not attend the Teatro Pavón in search of political enlightenment.

One of the unforeseen and intriguing consequences of the declaration of a secular Republic was the rise in productions of theatre with a religious theme, some mainstream and others staged in non-commercial venues. While few files in this area remain, those that do show the unease of the Republican censors when considering plays that encompassed opposition to the new – and reduced – role of the Church.

De muy buen barro ('Made of the Finest Clay') by Manuel de Jesús Moreno, was staged at the Institución del Divino Maestro on 31 December 1932, with an audience of 350, but was banned the following day because of the phrase, 'Al pobre cura le van a quitar la paga y tendrá que pedir limosna' ('they're going to take away the poor priest's pay and he'll have to beg'), and for criticism of the separation of Church and State (AGA 6077). Despite the fact that the play was clearly aimed at an audience that the government was not going to persuade, it could not tolerate the play's presentation of the victimisation of the clergy and its criticism of the secular state.

One of the most striking cases from the period was Fr Vicente Mena's mystical drama, *Santa Teresita del Niño Jesús* ('Saint Therese of the Child Jesus'), which premiered at the Teatro Beatriz on 29 June 1933 and, despite being described in the inspector's report as without political allusions, caused a scandal that played out in the press. As we shall see in the case study at the end of this chapter, this involved some of the most influential cultural figures on both left and right of the cultural divide. The seemingly innocuous play in question and the reaction that it provoked show how the theatre had become a forum for political statement and protest.

Even theatre aimed at children was subject to censorship and Manuel Soler Chamizo's *Los dientes de un lobo* ('Wolf's Teeth') was cut in 1935 for moral reasons, although the censors seemed to struggle to find justification in the legislation for their action. The official report on the play the day before staging recommended that performance should not be approved unless a cut was made to the text. The reason given was that 'no pueden considerarse obras aptas para niños aquellas en que uno de los personajes pretende abusar, prevaliéndose de la fortuna que posee, de la honestidad de una joven' ('works in which one of the characters, taking advantage of the fortune he possesses, intends to abuse the honesty of a young girl cannot be deemed suitable for children'). The report noted that this defect did not justify banning the work, as it did not attack classes, authorities or state employees. A cut was made, however, to the dialogue in which a state surveillance agent shouts: 'No trate de escaparse pues entonces nos hará tratarle con violencia y tal vez perdiera Vd. la vida' ('Don't try to escape or we'll have to use violence and you might lose your life') (AGA R6446).

In December 1935, the children's play, *Hambre atrasada* ('Never-Ending Hunger', written in 1910), by Nonato Ovejuna Inia (the pen name of Antonio Juan Onieva), was censored to remove references to the King and the national anthem, the 'Marcha Real' (AGA R6497). This example of moral theatre aimed at children and from the pre-Republican period was pruned to fit the circumstances of the day, eliminating monarchical touches. It again shows how the theatre was considered important in the political and moral education of citizens.

Several avant-garde theatre groups established before 1931 continued their work under the Republic. One of the most important and successful developments, which began in 1930, involved a collaboration between the director and playwright Cipriano Rivas Cherif and the actor and impresario Margarita Xirgu. Together, they brought a new artistic and aesthetic vision to the Spanish commercial stage until their progress was halted in 1935 by the right-wing Patronato ('Board of Trustees') that was appointed to run the theatre.[7] They introduced plays by dramatists such as Ramón del Valle-Inclán, Federico Oliver, Federico García Lorca and Rafael Alberti, and challenging drama from abroad (including works by Wilde, Gorky, Chekhov and Lenormand) and staged important premieres in Barcelona, enhancing the often fraught cultural links between the major theatre centres of Madrid and Barcelona.[8] They achieved commercial success by balancing radical works with more familiar popular ones by authors such as Benavente, Millán-Astray and Marquina, and classics by Tirso de Molina, Lope de Vega and Calderón de la Barca.

It was also in avant-garde circles that the most interesting foreign drama was presented, as they looked beyond Spain's borders for inspiration and imported foreign ideas, forms and techniques to bring to the stage in an effort to change it. Indeed, the visit of the Moscow Art Theatre to Madrid in 1932 and its staging of works at the Teatro Español in February and March is indicative of an increased openness to radical foreign productions at the time. This was also to have an impact on the development of revolutionary home-grown theatre.

The fact that the avant-garde theatre tended to serve minority audiences or was seen as artistic, rather than political, meant that it had few problems with the censors. Works such as Unamuno's *El otro* (*The Other*), premiered at the Teatro Español on 14 December 1932, were authorised by the censors without any difficulty (AGA R6061). Similarly, Valle-Inclán's *Divinas palabras* (*Divine Words*), which one might expect to have caused some upset, was authorised and premiered there on 16 November 1933 (AGA R6125). Alejandro Casona's *La sirena varada* (*The Stranded Mermaid*) winner of the Lope de Vega theatre prize and seen as a game-changer in the Spanish theatre at the time, was authorised without difficulty and put on at the Español in March 1934, with Margarita Xirgu in the main role (AGA R6177).

Lorca's *Yerma*, which was premiered in the Teatro Español on 29 December 1934 in a production by the Margarita Xirgu-Enrique Borrás company, caused a minor upset during the premiere.[9] While the censors found nothing to object to and it is noted in the report dated 30 December that the play was generally well received, it seems that not everyone considered the work to be unproblematic. The Chief Inspector's report, while noting 'alguna crudeza en el lenguaje y escena' ('some crudeness in the language and staging'), stated that there was no immorality or politics in the piece (AGA R6293). Nonetheless, there was a public order disturbance in the theatre and some young right-wing protesters, who objected to the republicanism of both Lorca and Xirgu, were arrested (Edwards 1999: 435–6). In *El Heraldo de Madrid*, Alfredo Muñiz wrote of 'un triunfo clamoroso' ('a resounding success') (1934: 4), and Miguel Pérez Ferrero dismissed the protest as 'tan débil, tan pequeñita, tan triste' ('so weak, so small, so sad') (1934: 4). The unproblematic reception by the authorities of Lorca is interesting when one considers how severely his work was censored under the dictatorship, when he was seen as a symbol of the defeated Republic (see Chapters 3 and 6).

Overall, avant-garde works were not perceived as challenging the censorship legislation of the day in a serious way. Many of the plays were considered apolitical, or sufficiently distanced from Spain, and if there was some question about their morality, this did not bother the early Republican censors, who were quite forgiving when it came to issues of sexual morality and the family. Towards the end of Republican period, however, the censorship records highlight the government's awareness of rising tensions and their attempts to mitigate them by censoring some works that might earlier have been authorised. Concern about politics is obvious in the reports, even when dealing with works that were not deliberately provocative, but that reflected the changing social dynamic. By this point too, political positioning takes precedence over artistic qualities when works are considered by some censors and critics.

Perhaps the most prominent example of this is Alejandro Casona's *Nuestra Natacha* (*Our Natasha*), with its portrait of a new generation of engaged youth, which was premiered in Barcelona on 13 November 1935 and at the Teatro Victoria in Madrid on 6 February 1936. This is much less experimental in form than his other work, but the timing of its Madrid premiere – a few days before the elections that would bring the Frente Popular to power – and its clear identification with the cause of the left, meant that it was interpreted as a political work, although more in the press than by the censors. The critic in the *Heraldo de Madrid* noted its reflection on current concerns and social transformation and suggested that with this work, Casona 'entra en combate' ('enters the fray') (Heraldo de Madrid 1936: 8).[10] The play was authorised the day before, 'por no contener la misma, alusiones intolerables ni frases violentas para Instituciones del Estado, idearios ni personas determinadas' ('as it did not contain intolerable allusions to or violent discourse directed at the Institutions of the State, ideologies or specific people'). The report on the first night by the Comisario-Jefe noted its particular social setting but concluded that it did not attack the authorities, was completely moral and was well received (AGA R6554). The right-wing press were predictably less positive about the play. For example, the reviewer in *Gracia y Justicia* stated:

> El señor Casona no es comunista; pero pertenece a 'los amigos de los soviets' [. . .] 'Nuestra Natacha', moralmente, es un engendro de falsedades, hipocresías y groserías repugnantes sin paliativos, y así

hay que afirmarlo, sin echar piropos al ropaje, que resulta envilecido con el uso que se le da [. . .] Si una obra es inmoral y está mal escrita, malo; si está bien escrita, peor. (Gracia y Justicia 1936: 14)

> Mr Casona is not a communist; but he belongs to the 'friends of the Soviets' [. . .] *Nuestra Natacha*, morally, is a source of unmitigated untruths, hypocrisies and repugnant vulgarities, and it must be stated baldly, without flattering its embellishments, with which it debases literature [. . .] If a work is immoral and badly written, that is bad; if it is well written, it is worse.

The Falangist intellectual, playwright and critic, Gonzalo Torrente Ballester, described Casona's *Nuestra Natacha* as 'el más importante de sus fracasos estéticos, la más honda de sus caídas' ('the most important of his aesthetic failures, the lowest he has fallen') (1957: 207). The divided reception of this play in the left and right-wing press neatly summarises the increasing politicisation of theatre as a reflection of society.

Such use of the theatre as a site of ideological battle was nowhere more obvious than in the emergence of agitation-propaganda (agitprop) theatre of the left, allied to an attempt to establish a new social and political order. This often didactic theatre was anti-capitalist and consciousness-raising and was employed as a tool of ideological inculcation. In form, as well as content, it aimed to challenge tradition and convention. Those involved included César and Irene Falcón, directors of the Nosotros theatre group, Ramón J. Sender, who published *El teatro de masas* in 1931, Miguel Prieto, director of the puppet groups Guiñol Octubre and La Tarumba, and Rafael Alberti and María Teresa León, who used their journal, *Octubre*, to encourage revolutionary theatre.[11] As we shall see in Chapter 7, the use of foreign drama to deliver a political message was a trend, in particular among agitprop groups, who sought to connect Spain to international political movements that were emergent on a world stage.

Aimed at a non-traditional public and staged in non-commercial venues, programmes often included a combination of comic sketches, short didactic plays and political statements and songs, the latter to encourage an uneducated public's participation and identification with the ideological message. The dramas themselves were simple in plot and structure, and frequently employed a basic set design that could be improvised in factories, *Casas del*

Pueblo (trade union or socialist party (PSOE) branch offices where cultural activities would take place) and public squares (Vicente Hernando 1999: 136–7). The removal of the fourth wall created an intimacy with the spectator that heightened the emotional impact of the message.

Not all political theatre was earnestly didactic, however. Some, such as Hilario Torres's *Por triunfar* ('Through Triumph'), performed at the Sindicato de Trabajadores de Banca y Bolsa del Centro de España on 27 October 1935, which revolved around 'los esfuerzos de un obrero inteligente y poeta para sustituir en el cariño de una mujer al señorito a quien ella prefiere' ('the efforts of an intelligent worker-poet to usurp the place of her preferred gentleman in the affections of a woman'), relied on farce to convey a message heralding the dawning of the day of the proletariat (AGA R6439).

Much of this political theatre of the Republican period was considered unproblematic by censors. For example, in March 1933, *No hay novedad en el frente* ('No News from the Front') by Emilio Gómez de Miguel and Eduardo Borrás, was deemed apolitical, morally correct and a crowd-pleaser (AGA R6158). Other plays, such as Julio G. Miranda's *Pinitos fascistas* ('First Steps of a Fascist'), staged by the Grupo Teatral Independiente at the Teatro Social y Proletario on 22 October 1933 were in much the same vein and, under the left-wing government, caused little upset (AGA R6222). Yet other works were more problematic because of what they said about the political authorities of the day. José Martín Villapecellín's 1933 'drama político social' ('socio-political drama'), *República Inmoral* ('Immoral Republic'), for example, was prohibited by the left-wing government for obvious political reasons, indicated by the slur in its title (AGA R6078).

Unsurprisingly, political theatre suffered a little more at the hands of the conservative-era censors, whose new legislation targeted some of the elements of agitprop theatre, such as the use of caricature, the encouragement of class war (article 21), and audience participation (article 95). For example, in December 1935, Manuel García's poetic dialogue between a grandfather and grandson, *Guerra a la guerra* ('War on War') was prohibited for its crude attack on 'la idea de la patria y el sentimiento patrio' ('the idea of the fatherland and patriotic sentiment'). The censors deemed it 'de un marcado y declarado sabor comunista, incompatible con las actuales instituciones' ('of marked and overt communist flavour, incompatible with our institutions') (AGA R6467).

In the lead-up to the 1936 elections, *La obrera del tejar* ('The Woman from the Roof-Tile Factory'), by Julio Sánchez Godínez and Florencio Domínguez, was condemned as a socialist play that exaggerated a conflict between an employer and his workers. Despite this, the censors struggled to find a legal basis for prohibition, suggesting that they were not as familiar with the legislation as they ought to have been. It was authorised for staging by the Círculo Socialista Latina-Inclusa on 9 February 1936 (AGA R6562).

Los hombres grises ('The Grey Men'), submitted to the censors in February 1936, was a translation of the US play *The Criminal Code* (1929) by Martin Flavin. The play would have been familiar to many spectators, as it had already been turned into a successful Hollywood film, directed by Howard Hawks (1930), and a Spanish version, *El código penal*, starring well-known Spanish actors, had been filmed in México for Columbia pictures in 1931. The play is critical of the corrupt penal system and in the context of the Frente Popular's election victory on 16 February and ongoing political unrest, the censor's report expresses concern about its negative impact and defers to his superiors for a verdict on the wisdom of staging it now, 'dadas las actuales circunstancias de febril actividad política, propicias a la excitación de las pasiones del público' ('given the current circumstances of feverish political activity, conducive to the excitement of the passions of the public') (AGA R6546). As Emeterio Díez notes, this is a reference to the Frente Popular's election promise to grant amnesty to those imprisoned for their role in the October Revolution of 1934 (2007: 435). The Director General, in turn, consulted his superiors and, in the end, the play was banned.

There is significant evidence that plays likely to incite violence in what was a volatile time in politics were treated with caution. So, even after the Frente Popular victory, there was some nervousness on the part of censors who seemed disinclined to fuel conflict. Arturo González Verdú's *¡Comunista!* ('Communist!'), which was due to be staged in a *Casa del Pueblo* (workers' cultural centre) on 9 May 1936, was prohibited the previous day. The report stressed that no fault was found with its Communist ideology, but rather with its incitement to revolutionary violence:

> En sí la obra es una constante excitación a la rebelión que queda coronada con uno de los últimos párrafos en prosa de la misma,

> donde incita a imitar el movimiento de Asturias, dedicándose a continuación unos versos en recuerdo a los que denomina 'bravos asturianos', invitando por último a los comunistas de acción porque luchan todos por la revolución. (AGA R6633)

> In itself, the work is a constant incitement to rebellion that culminates in one of the last prose paragraphs, which advocates the imitation of the events of Asturias, going on to dedicate some verses in memory of what he calls 'brave Asturians', and finally calling on the communists because they all fight for the revolution.

The play refers to the miners' political uprising in Asturias in October 1934, which was brutally repressed by government forces led by a young General Franco. The censors also denounced the portrayal of certain institutions of the state, the police and prison services, the former portrayed as puppets of the Jesuits, and the latter as thugs. It is worth noting that the play was staged later, during the war, in the Teatro Popular in January 1937, when the political situation had clearly changed (Collado 1985: 81).

In the tense atmosphere of the Frente Popular victory, measures were also taken to limit the impact of *Miserias* ('Misfortune') (1934), by Rafael Perpiñán, which was submitted to the office of censors on 6 March 1936. Mata Induráin cites the verdict, which was authorisation but with the stipulation that it only be staged in a *Casa del Pueblo* in order not to offend those who held other values (1995: 80). Interestingly, it had been banned in December 1935 before being revived following the Frente Popular victory.

Manuel García Adanero's *El confidente* ('The Informer') upset both conservative-era censors and those protecting the values of the Frente Popular, due to its lack of respect for the organs of the state. It was first submitted to censorship in August 1934. The censors objected to the representation of class division: 'Que toda la obra está escrita en unos términos que hacen resaltar el odio existente entre patronos y obreros, exaltando repetidamente el momento en que se proclame el comunismo, hablando algunos personajes en comunistas de acción' ('That the entire work is written in terms that highlight the existing hatred between employers and workers, repeatedly exalting the moment when communism is proclaimed, with some characters speaking as active communists') (AGA R6565). The report detailed many problems with the work, including negative references to the police and other agents of the state and, although the censor struggled to find the legal grounds for prohibition, he concluded that it could lead to a public order disturbance. The verdict, handed down on 23 August, was: 'PELIGROSA para el orden público la representación de esta obra' ('The staging of this work is DANGEROUS for public order').

When an application was made to stage it again in March 1936, the verdict was similarly negative. The report concludes that the action of the play, with its anti-state tendencies 'redundarían contra el prestigio, honor y buen nombre de la Policía en el concepto público' ('would work against the prestige, honour and good name of the Police in the public mind'). Moreover, the censor damned the play for its attacks on the legitimate institutions of the state and 'la exaltación del brutal principio de "tomarse la justicia por su mano"' ('exaltation of the brutal principle of taking the law into one's own hands'), thus negating the role of the justice system. It was prohibited once again.

On the whole, we can see a shift in perspective from the early days of Republican censorship that focused on public order disturbances to a more nuanced consideration of the possible impact of plays. This is not surprising, as the theatre increasingly reflected and enacted the polarisation of Spanish society. In the lead-up to war, the censors did not simply protect the ideology of the Frente Popular but, rather, employed censorship to attempt to reduce tensions and avoid conflict. Their actions show that the theatre of the time was perceived as a significant persuader of people who could be manipulted politically.

Civil war theatre

By 1936 censorship plainly reflects the turmoil in society and is, as Emeterio Díez suggests, 'contradictoria, vacilante, prudente y expeditiva' ('contradictory, hesitant, prudent and expeditious') (2007: 94).[12] The upheaval of war and the divisions within the Republican side had a significant impact on theatre censorship, both in Madrid for the duration of the conflict and when the government moved eastwards to Valencia and then Barcelona; in the Nationalist zone, which established its headquarters and alternative government in Burgos, cultural control was also on the agenda even before the end of the war (see Chapter 1).

As the war progressed, the theatre was increasingly viewed as one more weapon in the ongoing ideological battle, and there was a rise in agitprop productions on both sides of the divide. Existing political and proletarian theatre groups, such as Nosotros, served as models for Republican war-time agitprop (McCarthy 2012; O'Leary 2020). Bridging the gap was Cultura Popular, an umbrella group created before the outbreak of war (Dennis and Peral Vega 2009: 63). Several other political theatre groups were established in the early days of conflict, among them el Teatro Popular at the Ateneo de Madrid in May 1936, with Luis Mussot and Santiago Masferrer i Cantó (Plaza Plaza 2010; Gómez Díaz 1993: 521; Mundi 1987: 23). By mid-August, this group was based at the Teatro Fontalba, renamed the Teatro Popular (Dennis and Peral Vega 2009: 58, 60). Miguel Prieto, whose La Tarumba puppet theatre had not operated since the conservative *bienio*, worked with the Subcomisariado de Propaganda del Comisariado General de Guerra, taking his anti-fascist puppets wherever they could help the cause (González Tuñón 499). Works staged by the puppeteers included Lorca's *Retablillo de Don Cristóbal* (*Don Cristóbal's Puppet Play*), the marionette version of Alberti's *Los salvadores de España* ('The Saviours of Spain'), and other works that mocked Queipo de Llano, Hitler and Mussolini (González Tuñón 501). Cabañas Bravo tells us that the revived La Tarumba also staged Sender's *El secreto* (*The Secret*), which was one of the great successes of the time (2011: 368).

A key cultural group to emerge was the Alianza de Intelectuales Antifascistas ('Antifascist Intellectual Alliance'), with Dieste and Sender among its initial members, which operated across a variety of media but had significant impact on the theatre. José Bergamín was the Alianza's director and Alberti its secretary; it was housed in the evacuated mansion of the Marqués de Heredia Spinoza, which had been given to them by the Republican government. The Alianza published its manifesto in *La Voz* on 30 July 1936:

> Contra este monstruoso estallido del fascismo, que tan espantosa evidencia ha logrado ahora en España, nosotros, escritores, artistas, investigadores científicos, hombres de actividad intelectual, en suma, agrupados para defender la cultura en todos sus valores nacionales y universales de tradición y creación constante, declaramos nuestra unión total, nuestra identificación plena y activa con el pueblo, que ahora lucha gloriosamente al lado del Gobierno del Frente Popular,

defendiendo los verdaderos valores de la inteligencia al defender nuestra libertad y dignidad humana, como siempre hizo, abriendo heroicamente paso, con su independencia, a la verdadera continuidad de nuestra cultura, que fué popular siempre, y a todas las posibilidades creadoras de España en el porvenir (*La Voz* 1936: 3).

Against this monstrous outbreak of fascism, of which we now have such appalling evidence in Spain, we – writers, artists, scientific researchers, men of intellectual activity – have come together to defend culture in all of its national and universal values of tradition and constant creation; we declare our total union and our full and active identification with the people, who now fight gloriously alongside the Popular Front Government, defending the true values of intelligence by defending our freedom and human dignity, as they always have done, heroically and independently opening the way to the true continuity of our culture, which was always popular, and to all the creative possibilities of Spain in the future.

Among the signatories were Dieste, Prieto, Cernuda, Altolaguirre, Bergamín, Buñuel and Chacel. Its weekly newssheet, *El mono azul*, was launched at the end of August 1936 and those involved in the publication included León, Bergamín, Dieste and Alberti.

The Alianza attempted to harness the stage for propagandistic purposes. Indeed, according to José Monleón, its goal was a hostile takeover of the theatre genre itself (1979: 185). It created a company, Nueva Escena, housed at the Teatro Español, which had been given over to them temporarily by the government and was under the direction of Altolaguirre. Nueva Escena would be responsible for one of the most important political performances of the early civil war before the closure of the theatres in November 1936 saw its end. When the theatres reopened, the Teatro Español became home to Manuel González and the Grupo García Lorca, whose work, according to Mundi, 'fue siempre elogiada y admirada como ejemplar' ('was praised and admired as exemplary') in both artistic and political terms (25; see also ABC 1937c: 18).

The other main theatrical group was Altavoz del Frente, established by the Peruvian writer, activist, and founder of the Nosotros theatre Group, César Falcón, and operating under the Comisión de Agitación y Propaganda of the Communist Party. For Christopher Cobb, this was the group that was best adapted to the war (1992–3: 246). As with the Alianza, theatre was only one of the sections it contained. It staged propaganda works in Madrid at the

Teatro Lara (renamed Teatro de la Guerra) and, with the ambulatory 'Guerrillas del Teatro', brought drama to where the action was taking place, at the battlefront, in hospitals, and in barracks. The Altavoz's first production in the Teatro de la Guerra was on 22 October 1936 with a programme that contained *El bazar de la providencia* ('The Providence Bazaar') by Rafael Alberti; *La conquista de la prensa* ('The Conquest of the Press') by Irene Falcón; the fourth act of *Asturias*, by César Falcón and *Así empezó*... ('So Began...'), by Luisa Carnés (Peral Vega 2012).

A later development was the PCE-dominated Teatro de Arte y Propaganda, which was established with the support of the Consejo Central del Teatro (CCT) at the Teatro de la Zarzuela in September 1937, with María Teresa León at the helm. In fact, Felipe Lluch Garín, who in June 1939 would propose the creation of a National Fascist theatre, was also involved (García Ruiz 2000). The first performance organised by the group was the premiere of Lorca's *Los títeres de cachiporra* (*The Billy-Club Puppets*); the second, on 16 October, was Vichnievski's *La tragedia optimista* (*An Optimistic Tragedy*). December 1937 saw the performances of both Germán Bleiberg's *Sombras de héroes* ('Shadows of Heroes') and Alberti's adaptation of *Numancia*.[13] The Teatro de Arte y Propaganda ceased operations in April 1938 and the Teatro de la Zarzuela returned to its traditional fare. By early 1938, Alberti and León were focusing their attention on an ambulatory and militant group, the Teatro de Guerrilla, bringing stripped-back agitprop works to the war front.

On the Nationalist side, what might be termed right-wing political theatre was less in evidence than left-wing agitprop but it did exist and several important figures from the theatre and from Falangist circles were involved. The intellectuals of the right, like those of the left, saw in the theatre a tool for ideological inculcation. As Schwartz observes, authors such as Joaquín Calvo Sotelo and José María Pemán discussed the state of the theatre in the pages of the Sevilla-based and nationalist-supporting *ABC*, which had split from the main Madrid-based newspaper at the start of the conflict. Their vision of theatrical renovation, unlike that of the Republicans, was based on notions of past glory (Schwartz 1965: 560). Manuel Machado advocated the revival of Spanish classics, with their catholic universalism (1938: 3). Gonzalo Torrente Ballester outlined his view in *Razón y ser de la dramática futura* ('Rationale and Essence of the Dramaturgy of the Future') published in 1937, arguing for a theatre combining tradition, order and style (García Álvarez, 1990: 198; Gómez Díaz 2006). Dionisio Ridruejo, who would be in charge of the Delegación Nacional de Prensa y Propaganda from 1938 until 1941, also stressed the need for a national theatre (Rodríguez Puértolas 2009: 140). José María Pemán, too, wrote about his ideas for the theatre in an article published in *ABC (Sevilla)*, 8 April 1937. In it, he declared that the theatre was an expression of what is communal and shared by society but also saw the theatre of the day as a political act: '*Ir al teatro* no es una decisión más o menos frívola de una tarde desocupada, sino función honda y casi religiosa, de comunión en los ideales colectivos, de examen de conciencia, de estímulo y fervor' ('Going to the theatre is not the more-or-less frivolous choice of a free afternoon, but a profound and almost religious action, of communion in collective ideals, of examination of conscience, stimulus and fervour') (1937: 11).

While Republican political theatre tended to focus on morale-boosting and didactic works explaining the reasons for the war and the need to keep on fighting, Nationalist works generally represented an imperial past and drew on the religious tradition of *autos sacramentales* (Rodríguez Puértolas 2009; Schwartz 1965; Dennis and Peral Vega 2010). In sum, what the Nationalist renovators proposed drew on religious ceremony and the classics to create a new nationalist-Catholic art.

The Nationalists also borrowed some ideas and techniques from the political theatre of the other side to achieve their goals, in particular with José Antonio Álvarez's TAC (Teatro Ambulante de Campaña), whose methods echoed those of Republican ambulatory theatre groups. Moreover, just as the left had during the identity formation years of the Republic, the right laid claim to Spanish classics. One of the most successful initiatives was the Compañía de Teatro Nacional de FET y de las JONS, established in 1938 and directed by Luis Escobar, who would be one of the most important figures in the post-war theatre (Rodríguez Puértolas 2009: 96).

War-time censorship

Few official files remain from the period. State censorship did not operate normally and even the records that were created did not all survive the war. In fact, the loss of files is referred to within the surviving documentation. For example, a letter (dated 29 May 1937) from the Grupo García Lorca, based at the Teatro Español and affiliated with the UGT (Unión General de Trabajadores), shows that they wished to stage Lorca's *Yerma* and Benito Pérez Galdós's *Tormento* (*Torment*). The applicant, Julián Arenas, wrote to the Director General de Seguridad asking for copies of the playtexts, because he considered the plays 'de máximo interés para llevarlas a la escena' ('of maximum interest for staging'), but could not get copies and wondered if the censors' office might have scripts submitted when the works were previously staged (AGA R6293). There is no record in McGaha of a staging of *Tormento* during the Second Republic, but *Yerma* had been staged by the Margarita Xirgu company at the Teatro Español in December 1934 (1979: 62). Arenas signs off with a commitment 'al servicio de la causa' ('at the service of the cause'). Another example from the same group, this time to stage Lorca's *La zapatera prodigiosa* (*The Shoemaker's Prodigious Wife*), is dated 17 November 1937. Once again, they did not have a copy of the play and were writing to the censors to ask for the copy that would have been submitted by the Margarita Xirgu company when she staged it at the Teatro Español (AGA 21/5822b). There is no trace in the files of a subsequent application to stage the play, or indeed of the earlier Xirgu production, which took place on 3 May 1933. We can only assume that much material was lost in the war.

Most extant files relate to Republican censorship and it is only towards the end of the war that the Nationalists began to formalise alternative structures. Much of what was censored was political theatre but, as Jim McCarthy has suggested, this was also the type of theatre least likely to be found in the formal records: 'Rather than any interest in posterity, current political circumstances were the writers' sole concern' and this, obviously, had an impact on the survival of these works, many of which were never published (1999: 18).

As central control of censorship in the Republican zone moved from the Dirección General de Seguridad to the Junta de Espectáculos, and then to the CCT, records of the process remained patchy. While the legislation from this period gives us a clear indication of how the censorship was intended to be used and the weight it was given in the ideological battle, there is very little trace of actual reports on plays or performances. A later change in personnel in the Ministry from the Communist Jesús Hernández to the anarchist Segundo Blanco González in April 1938 saw a reduction in PCE influence on censorship decisions; by this stage in the war, we have no formal censorship records on the Republican side.

What the files show is that official censors during the early stages of the conflict were worried about plays that could alienate would-be Republican allies or potentially further the Nationalist cause. As the war continued and control of censorship changed hands, the files show a shift in emphasis away from such diplomatic concerns and in April 1937 the Junta de Espectáculos decided to ban the work of 'autores facciosos' ('rebel authors'), a task that was almost impossible to carry out efficiently (O'Leary 2020: 25).

Moral censorship was less of a priority for the Republican state censors, whose focus was on politics. This did not mean that they simply ignored non-political dramas, however, as those most concerned with employing the theatre as an ideological tool were generally against works that distracted from the political message. This led to some confusion about the purpose of censorship under the Junta de Espectáculos. Serafín Adame Martínez (SAM) in *ABC* was critical, for example, of the Comité de Lectura's decision not to read any frivolous works, despite the fact that these were frequently staged (1937b). In fact, the debates about what was appropriate theatre for the times was compounded by the tension between various groups with a vested interest. Certain politicised intellectuals were most concerned with the employment of the theatre as a didactic and propagandistic tool, while the unions were more focused on the provision of labour and adequate pay for theatre workers, even if this meant staging frivolous entertainment or risqué plays.

One of the earliest examples of political censorship during the war period relates to Aurelio González Rendón's *Ya están de pie los esclavos sin pan* ('The Slaves without Bread Are on Their Feet'), performed at the Teatro Español on 13 August 1936. The censor was concerned about offending the members of the military still loyal to the Republic and suggested cutting the line, 'todas las lumias, compañeras de una noche, eran hijas de militares' ('all the easy women, companions for a night, were the daughters of military men') (AGA R6613). An interesting review of the play by SAM in *ABC* damned it as an example of the 'seudorrevolucionarios escénicos' ('pseudo-revolutionary shows') appearing in theatres and capitalising on the politics of the day without any meaningful engagement. He criticised it for its crudeness and blue jokes and compared it unfavourably to reforming works such as those of Lorca, Alberti, Ugarte, Casona and López Rubio (1936: 16).

A more interesting case is that of Luis Mussot, one of the figures most associated with agitprop theatre, co-founder of the Teatro Popular and author of the 'Manifiesto para la creación de un batallón de actores' ('Manifesto for the creation of a Batallion of Actors'). His play, *¡No pasarán!* ('They Shall Not Pass!'), which links class war to the civil war, was submitted to the censors on 22 September 1936 and staged at the Fontalba the following day (Gómez Díaz 1993: 523) (AGA R6678). The play's emblematic characters and simple political message regarding soldiers' duty to the people and their own class, rather than to the demonised political and military leadership, raised some concerns. The negative portrait of the General emphasised the need for class solidarity rather than blind adherence to military leadership. The leadership, after all, justifies the sacrifice of workers' lives not only for the good of the country but also in the interests of 'la sagrada propiedad' ('sacred property') (page 3). The play ends with the enlightened, united worker-soldiers listening to a voice from offstage that delivers the final message of the play:

> VOZ.– Camaradas: Una vez más en la historia, han querido las castas en extraño maridaje sojuzgar al pueblo. Todo lo podrido, la iglesia, el capitalismo y el militarismo, decidieron implantar el Fascio en nuestro país, pero el Gobierno del Frente Popular ha armado al pueblo y al pueblo no hay quien le venza jamás. ¡Viva la República Democrática!

> VOICE – Comrades: Once again in history, the privileged castes in a strange marriage have set out to subdue the people. All that is rotten, the church, capitalism and militarism, decided to implant Fascism in our country, but the Popular Front Government has armed the people and the people will never be defeated. Long live the Democratic Republic!

The soldiers respond in unison with the emotive cry:

> TODOS.– ¡No pasarán! ¡No pasarán! ¡No pasarán! ¡Retrocederán! ¡Retrocederán! ¡Retrocederán!

ALL – They shall not pass! They shall not pass! They shall not pass! They shall retreat! They shall retreat! They shall retreat!

Although praised for its 'propósito muy laudable de exaltar la soberanía del pueblo y el triunfo de la República, del Gobierno legítimo y de la Democracia' ('laudable purpose of exalting the sovereignty of the people and the triumph of the Republic, the legitimate government and democracy'), the censors were uneasy about the play's potential to upset the military and in particular those who had remained loyal and therefore sought to avoid anything that might spark indiscipline among the ranks of soldiers and militia. Despite this, the report concluded, in a rather contradictory fashion, with the wish for more works like this to raise public spirits (AGA R6678).

The information we have about the Teatro Popular also highlights another, unofficial type of censorship that operated during the war as new theatre groups, informed by particular ideologies, selected and excluded works and authors according to their political values. In fact, Mussot declared the Teatro Popular's intention to 'purify the stage' with a theatre geared directly at the masses (Mussot 1936). It remained in operation for just over a month, staging, in addition to Mussot's *¡No pasarán!*, Sender's *El secreto* (*The Secret*) and *El Gil Gil* ('Gil the Gullible') by Alberti before the siege of Madrid caused the closure of theatres. At this point Mussot joined the army and brought ambulatory theatre to the battle front (Gómez Díaz 1993: 525, 527).

A month after Mussot's play was staged, the Alianza's Nueva Escena was in action and on stage for the first time on the evening of 20 October 1936. The short agitprop plays staged, *La llave* ('The Key'), *Al amanecer* ('At Dawn') and *Los salvadores de España* ('The Saviours of Spain'), were authored by three of the most influential writers of the day: Ramón J. Sender, Rafael Dieste and Rafael Alberti.[14] All three had played a role in the politicised theatre of the Republican period and all considered the theatre an important tool in effecting social change (Sender 1931; Pérez-Domenech 1933). Dieste was director of the Teatro Guiñol de las Misiones Pedagógicas (1933–4 and 1936) and at the time of the emergence of Nueva Escena, Alberti and Sender are also listed among the members of the Comisión Central del Patronato de Misiones Pedagógicas (Otero Urtaza and García Alonso 2006: 53–5).

Sender's *La llave* is satirical, mocking the greed of the bourgeoisie, who are contrasted with a group of brave and noble miners. The plot is simple: a group of miners goes to the house of a nasty moneylender and his unpleasant wife to ask for money. The moneylender swallows the rusty key to his safe, rather than help the miners, but dies in convulsions, concerned to the last that they do not open him up to retrieve the key. The plot of Dieste's *Al amanecer*, a 'farsa-reportaje' ('farce-like report') supposedly based on real events from the war, presents a story of betrayal. A man who volunteers to fight for the Republic later murders his superior officer and his fellow *milicianos*. There is hope, however, because the new day brings a reaction from a group of workers, who kill the murderous and cowardly traitor. Alberti's *Los salvadores de España*, described by its author as 'una ensaladilla' ('a macédoine salad'), is set in an Andalusian square and confronts the public with caricatures of a bishop, a group of foreign soldiers (a Moor, an Italian, a German, a Bulgarian and a Portuguese, with stereotypical costumes and character traits), people dressed for the fair, Republican soldiers and General Queipo de Llano, the Nationalist leader, notorious for his cruelty. The soldiers, mockingly referred to as 'los salvadores de España' ('the Saviours of Spain'), receive the encouragement and blessing of the General and the Bishop, before going off to fight for Spain.

Dieste directed all three plays on the night, and Alberti was also present. Sender was not there, as he was fighting at the Guadarrama front. The actors, many of them very well known, included La Brú (María Bru), Francisco Fuentes, (José) Espantaleón, Carmen de los Ríos, Menéndez Arbó, Soto, Armet; sets were by Souto, Ontañón and Miguel Prieto. When it came to censorship, it is no surprise that the Republican censors found little to criticise in *Al amanecer* and *La llave*, both of which were approved without cuts. *Los salvadores de España* was censored, however, and the files reveal the determination of the censors (and political leaders) in the early months of the war not to antagonise foreign leaders or monarchists. The report insists on the amendment of several 'alusiones a varios Jefes de Estados extranjeros, con cuyas Naciones España no ha roto oficialmente sus relaciones diplomáticas' ('allusions to several foreign Heads of States, with whose Nations Spain has not officially broken its diplomatic relations') and, in the interest of public order, the removal or replacement of two songs (AGA R6681). An additional document stated that the play would be authorised once the monarchist 'Marcha Real española' ('Royal Spanish Anthem') was replaced with 'La canción del soldado' ('The Soldier's Song') or another analogous song. This shows that, while the censors were in sympathy with the spirit of these works, which were written in an attempt to defend the new government, they faced great difficulties in terms of negotiating a delicate diplomatic balance in times of great political uncertainty.

The three plays would be staged together eleven times, before the war terminated the production. In the end, the ambitious plans for Nueva Escena were never realised. By the time theatres reopened in Madrid in January 1937, many of those involved had left the capital. Changing circumstances and the desire to reach fighters on the frontlines led to a shift of focus away from theatre-based works. Within the Alianza de los Intelectuales Antifascistas, the attention on Nueva Escena was superseded in 1937 first by el Teatro de Arte y Propaganda at the Zarzuela, and later by the ambulatory group las Guerrillas de Teatro, both also involving León and Alberti. There are no censorship records relating to the work of these groups.

Altolaguirre, head of the theatre section of the Alianza, which had named him director of the Teatro Español, recalled another form of censorship in his memoirs. The morning after Nueva Escena's debut, he witnessed a protest by workers outside the theatre. He interpreted their chants as a direct consequence of the anti-clerical and anti-bourgeois plays staged the night before:

> Un, dos, tres, cuatro,
> que se cierren los teatros.
> Un, dos, tres, cuatro,
> que se cierren los teatros. (2010: 23–4)

> One, two, three, four,
> Theatres need to shut their doors.
> One, two three four,
> Theatres need to shut their doors.

Manuel Aznar, on the other hand, offers a more persuasive argument, that the workers' protests were related to the unions' decisions around the protection of the livelihood of theatre workers, rather than upset at the staging of agitprop works (1997: 55).

The files show how the focus of political censorship changed over the course of the war. From early concerns about diplomatic relations with foreign or non-allied powers, later reports reflect internal structural change. The censorship of José María Acebo's *Bandera de amor* ('Flag of Love'), which premiered at the Calderón on 3 October 1937, coincided with the establishment of the CCT and dismantlement of previous censorship arrangements. The report on the play is atypical in not having a heading, stamp or signature, which may be explained by the transition. The CCT's more ideological focus is evident from the political cuts made. The action takes place in an Andalusian village bombed by Nationalists and about to be occupied. The censor's report describes it as a three-act 'obra antifascista que se refiere a la rebelión militar y se desarrolla durante el año 1937' ('an anti-fascist work that refers to the military rebellion and takes place in the year 1937'). While no cuts are listed in this unusual report, the file also contains two scripts, which suggest that there was some pruning done before this work was approved. One of the scripts contains numerous passages marked with red and blue pencils and a second script shows that the marked passages have been eliminated. The passages in question relate to political issues, including pacifist statements by the liberal teacher, a German soldier and a German officer (who turns out to be Spanish), which may have been regarded as defeatist. These include the following anti-war declaration made by the schoolmaster:

> D. JOSÉ.– Esto no ocurriría si los hubieran enseñado a odiar la guerra, a negarse a ir a ellas, mándelo quien lo mande, dígalo quien lo diga; que no habiendo soldados no habría generales y sin soldados se acabarían las guerras, pues mientras se guerrea no se labra y donde no se labra, pasta la muerte. (AGA 21/5814a)
>
> D. JOSÉ – This would not happen if they had taught them to hate war, to refuse to go to them, no matter who instructs them to, no matter who says it; without soldiers there would be no generals and without soldiers, wars would end, and as long as there is warmongering, the land is not worked and wherever land is not worked, death comes to graze.

Other marked passages include the defence of the local landowner, who is depicted as a protector of the poor, and the Germans, rather than clear enemies for demonisation, turn out to be socialists who ally themselves with the villagers. The cuts reflect an attempt to rectify the ideological confusion of the piece and the resulting second version is much more politically coherent than the first, in line with the CCT's goals of turning the theatre into 'un medio de propaganda al servicio del Frente Popular para ganar la Guerra, evitando a toda costa los casos lamentables en que, seguramente por inconsciencia, se ponen en nuestra escena obras que perjudican a la causa de la República' ('a means of propaganda serving the Popular Front's efforts to win the war, avoiding at all costs the regrettable cases in which, probably unconsciously, works that harm the cause of the Republic are put on the stage') (Gaceta de la República 1937a: 769).

Towards the end of the war, the files show a further shift in censorship focus away from the risk of antagonising foreign allies and towards concern for the morale of their own side, who they needed to keep fighting and supporting the war effort. In Valencia, in January 1939, for example, Josep Peris Celda's *revista, Casos y coses del món que pasen i pasaran* ('Stuff that Happens and Will Go on Happening'), which was on at the Teatro Apolo, caused disquiet, not only because of its 'pobreza, chabacanería y mediano gusto' ('poverty, vulgarity and poor taste') but also because of what was perceived as mockery of the Levantine rearguard and its failure to support actively the goals of the Republican government (CDMH PS-Barcelona 821, 1). The report from the Intelligence Agency, the Servicio de Información Militar (SIM) at the Ministerio de Defensa, concluded that the play had clearly caused some upset and the Head of SIM wrote to the Ministerio de Gobernación requesting a clear verdict regarding its authorisation or prohibition. Yet the report also acknowledged that the intention of the dramatist was not to satirise the Republic. Peris Celda was not an anti-Republican dramatist. In fact, he had earlier written and staged *La bolcheviqui del Carme* ('The Bolshevik Girl from El Carme', 1932) about a Republican feminist who challenges the conservatism of her working-class community and promotes the progressive values of the Republic. Moreover, despite the concerns of the authorities, it seems that the public did not see this as an anti-Republican or defeatist work but, rather, responded to *Casos y coses* with pro-Republican shouts and chants. At this late stage in the war the weakened Republican authorities were clearly very sensitive to works that might discourage or dishearten its followers and the harsh verdict in this case was suspension for 'derrotismo' (defeatism).

Another form of censorship introduced by the Republican side involved fundraising productions. These were commonplace at the start of the war and often took the form of variety shows, with a combination of musical entertainment, didactic plays and comedy. The varied programme allowed the organisers to address their political message to an audience of different ages, interests and education. The shows were initially supported by the unions, although they later banned them. An announcement in *ABC* on 15 September 1936 stated: 'Los Comités de control e incautación de industrias de espectáculos públicos de la U.G.T. y C.N.T. han tomado el acuerdo de no autorizar la celebración de más festivales benéficos' ('The Committees for the control and seizure of public entertainment industries of the U.G.T. and C.N.T. unions have agreed not to authorise the celebration of any more fundraising festivals') (SAM 1936:16).

Despite this 1936 ban on fundraising festivals by the main unions, a common feature of several 1937 reports is a mention of fundraising for those fighting for the Republic. The rule was evidently not being enforced. These plays were also subject to normal censorship but given their pro-Republican content, tended to be authorised without much trouble. For example, Luis Pérez de León's one-act *Noches de bombardeo* ('Nights under Bombardment') was staged in the Teatro Español on 4 January 1937 in support of the Batallón de Retaguardia 'Águilas de la Libertad'. It was authorised without cuts (AGA 21/5814b). José Ricardo Navas's three-act play *Ropa limpia* ('Clean Clothes') was staged in early July 1937, in a benefit performance organised by the workers of a toolmaking company for the Red Cross at the Teatro Barral (AGA R6862).

Although their main concern was to ensure employment and pay for theatre workers, when they took over the theatres, the unions also expressed an interest in the quality and morality of the works being staged. On 15 August 1936, the *ABC* published an announcement from the Confederación Nacional del Trabajo (CNT) theatre branch, the Sindicato Único de Espectáculos Públicos, which announced its vision for the theatre, beginning with the removal of all obscenity, vulgarity and crudeness from the stage (ABC 1936: 13). Although it did not constitute official censorship, the unions also formally requested the respectful treatment of the actresses involved in risqué reviews (as noted in Chapter 1).

The most interesting case we have of moral censorship from the civil war period relates to Alberto Álvarez de Cienfuegos and Manuel Arquelladas's ¡Tatí. . . Tatí!, described by SAM in *ABC* as 'una opereta bufa graciosa y entretenida' ('a funny and entertaining comic operetta'), with plenty of vulgarity, which opened at the Teatro de Maravillas on 14 October 1937 (1937d: 6). Yet in the end, what initally appeared to be a morally inspired scandal was as much about political in-fighting and a battle for control of the theatre, as it was about virtue. The polemic surrounding the production led to the dissolution of the *Comité de lectura* (censorship committee), which had been established by the Junta de Espectáculos and had significant union representation; it was, in other words, a victory for the new CCT, which sought to reduce the power of the unions.

The night of the premiere, General Miaja, the man charged with defending Republican Madrid, saw ¡Tatí. . . Tatí! and was unimpressed by a show that failed to represent Republican goals for the theatre. On 15 October, the *ABC* published a notification of the prohibition of the play: 'Según manifestaciones hechas ayer a los periodistas por el general Miaja, ha prohibido las representaciones de "Tatí, Tatí", por considerarla "inadecuada y subidamente inmoral"' ('According to statements made yesterday to journalists by General Miaja, he has banned performances of "Tatí, Tatí", considering it "inappropriate and highly immoral"') (SAM 1937d). The next day, a further note was published in *ABC*, indicating the far-reaching consequences of the prohibition. Those who had approved the play would be punished for their error:

Suspensión del Comité de Lectura
En el día de hoy, y por orden de la presidencia de la Junta de Espectáculos de Madrid, ha sido suspendido en sus funciones el Comité de Lectura, que venía actuando dentro de la citada Junta, con motivo del incidente producido por la representación de la obra "Tatí, Tatí", en el Teatro Maravillas de esta capital. (SAM 1937e)

Suspension of the Readers' Committee
Today, by order of the presidency of the Entertainment Industry Board in Madrid, the Readers' Committee, which had been acting under the aforementioned Board, has been suspended from its du-

ties, due to the incident produced by the performance of the play 'Tatí, Tatí', at the Maravillas Theatre in this capital city.

This was all taking place against the backdrop of the consolidation of the PCE-influenced CCT's power. The scandal provided an opportunity for the CCT to sideline the anarchist-dominated union and consolidate its control of the theatre. Shortly afterwards the Junta de Espectáculos itself would be formally restructured. The play, on the other hand, survived the scandal and, according to Mundi, the ban was overthrown and performances recommenced ten days later and would last four months (Mundi 1987: 235).

Nor was this the only battle between unions and CCT played out at the level of censorship. Halma Angélico's *Ak y la humanidad* ('Ak and Humanity') adapted from a Russian story, was premiered at the Teatro Español on 26 August 1938. As P. Cataslán observes, the harshest criticism of the piece came from the CNT, of which Angélico was a member. They regarded her and the play as 'contrarrevolucionarias' ('counter-revolutionary'), and later accused her of plagiarism (2008: 172, 183). Angélico defended herself in the press but the outcome was a victory for neither; instead, the CCT imposed censorship on both the play, which was withdrawn from the stage, and *Castilla Libre*, the mouthpiece of the CNT. The internal divisions of Republicanism were once again laid bare.

Nationalist censorship

The progression of the war also saw the emergence of a Nationalist censorship outside Republican Madrid. The few files in the AGA relate to the final stages of the conflict and both reveal the political concerns of that side and anticipate the rigorous system that would be imposed under the dictatorship that followed the end of the conflict.

In terms of morality, there was little produced on the Nationalist side that challenged conservative, Catholic doctrine, although occasionally a play would cause unease due to some unorthodox aspect. This was the case with Gonzalo Torrente Ballester's *El viaje del joven Tobías* ('Young Tobias's Journey', 1938) but also some lesser-known authors and plays. As Janet Pérez noted, Torrente Ballester's conversion play, because it inferred conversion not to the Church but to Falangism, fell foul of ecclesiastical censors and was denounced as heretical (2010: 48).

Antonio Quintero's *El delirio* ('Delirium'), about a businessman who is saved from constant failure by the love of a good woman, was authorised for staging in Zaragoza in March 1939, but only once cuts were made to remove references to inappropriate behaviour on the part of a character, in this case, a child. The cuts included 'A mí me da unos besos cuando me ve' ('he kisses me when he sees me') and 'A muchas les muerde la oreja' ('he bites many women's ears') (AGA 393/39). When the play was staged in Madrid in October, it was a resounding success (Cueva 1939).

In April 1939, the María Fernanda Ladrón de Guevara Company applied to stage the musical comedy *María Magdalena* ('Mary Magdalene') by Valverde, Quiroga and León. According to the censorship file, this was a gypsy comedy inspired by a song, but it was banned, presumably because its combination of superstition and religion did not sit easily with the conservative moral vision of the Nationalist censors, or perhaps because its creators had worked in the Republican zone throughout the war. It was later staged in Barcelona in May and was very successful (Vanguardia 1939c).

As regards overtly political theatre, we know that José María Pemán wrote two plays for the war: *Almoneda* ('Auction', 1937) and *De ellos es el mundo* ('The World Is Theirs', 1938) (García Álvarez: 206). There is no official record of their censorship, although according to García Ruiz, *De ellos es el mundo*, which was conceived as a type of *teatro de urgencia* and presented as an 'obra de ocasión' ('work for the occasion') that aimed at encouraging those fighting for the Nationalist cause, was censored by the dramatist himself after the war and he refused to allow it to be restaged (2013: 2737).

The few existing Nationalist censorship files from the period give us a window onto the politics of that side prior to the end of the conflict. Fr G. de Orizana's (Nazario González Ramos) pro-Nationalist *El Alcázar de Toledo* was censored in Bilbao in January 1939 when an application was made for a private performance at the Colegio Santiago Apóstol in Bilbao. References to Franco's heroism were marked on the script, with an annotation instructing that they be replaced, 'mientras duren las circunstancias' ('in the current circumstances'), by references to General Varela, who was in fact the man who relieved Colonel Moscardó and the besieged Nationalists, although Franco took the public glory (AGA 9/39). Such evidence of discord about the heroism and leadership of Franco is surely why a verdict of prohibition was handed down on 3 February by the Department of Censorship in Burgos, where the Nationalist Government was based.[15] The censors were still cautious about the figure of Franco, although the shift towards triumphalism is already evident. For example, a company in Burgos applied to the nationalist authorities to stage the exultant play, *Y el imperio volvía. . .* ('And the Empire Was Returning'), by the Jesuit Ramón Cué. The verdict explicitly excises references to Franco from the play (AGA 6/39) (see Figure 3).

Once the war ended, things changed rapidly. The political theatre of the left disappeared; theatre ownership was returned to commercial interests or the state; and the Junta Nacional de Teatros y Conciertos took on greater importance in defining the future direction of the Spanish theatre. In newly taken Madrid, *revistas* were put on hold, 'para no solamente adecentar los locales, sino también para que se representen obras con el decoro que el momento español exige' ('not only to clean up the theatres, but also to represent works with the decorum that the Spanish moment demands') (Arriba 1939). The Nationalist press promised a return to past glories, pledging that 'pronto será realidad el sueño, que parecía imposible, de que la patria de Lope y Calderón vuelva a primera fila, como en los años gloriosos de nuestro Siglo de Oro' ('the dream that seemed impossible will soon come true – that the homeland of Lope and Calderón will return to the forefront, just as in the glorious years of our Golden Age') (Ya 1939).

While the nationalist press celebrated their cultural 'martyrs', such as Pedro Muñoz Seca and Honorio Maura, many of those who had been involved in Republican political theatre, but also in avant-garde theatre and other attempts at innovation and reform, were in exile, in prison or dead and not publicly lamented (Serrano Anguita 1939; Informaciones 1939; Obregón 1939b). A new chapter in the history of the Spanish theatre and theatre censorship was about to begin, and the 'Normas para los empresarios de espectáculos públicos' ('Norms for theatrical impresarios'), published a few days after the end of the war, set out the rules for the theatre under the new regime (ABC 1939a: 28).

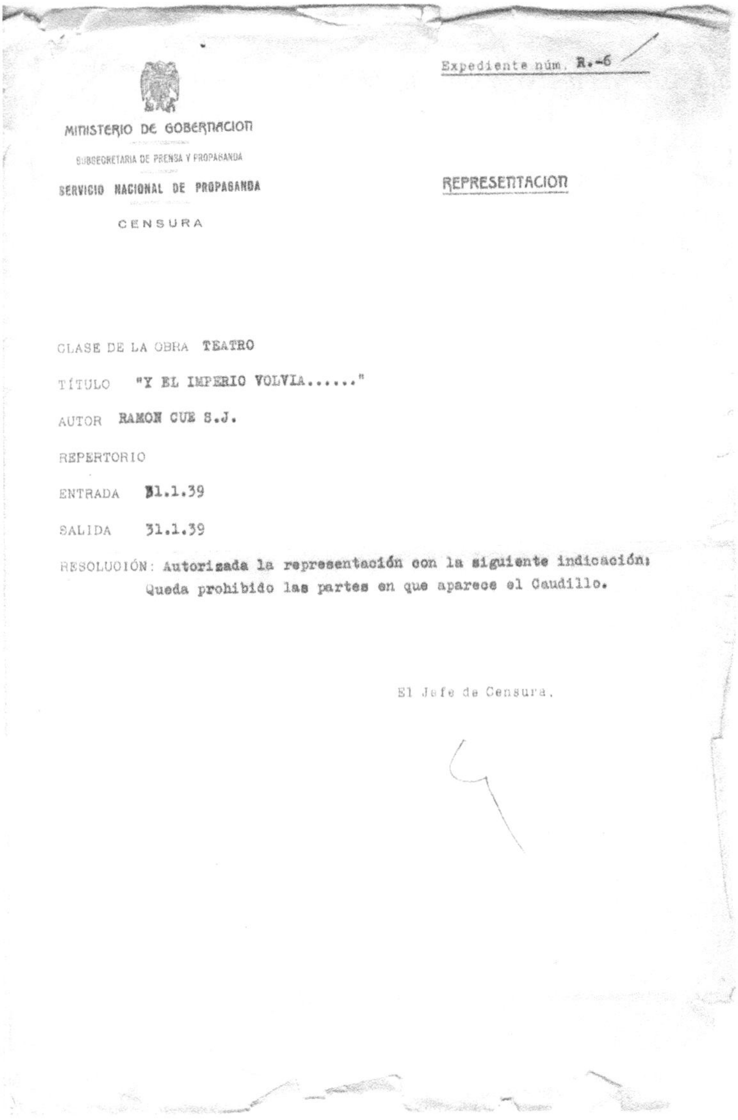

Expediente núm. R.-6

MINISTERIO DE GOBERNACION

SUBSECRETARIA DE PRENSA Y PROPAGANDA

SERVICIO NACIONAL DE PROPAGANDA

CENSURA

REPRESENTACION

CLASE DE LA OBRA TEATRO

TÍTULO "Y EL IMPERIO VOLVIA......"

AUTOR RAMON CUE S.J.

REPERTORIO

ENTRADA 31.1.39

SALIDA 31.1.39

RESOLUCIÓN: Autorizada la representación con la siguiente indicación: Queda prohibido las partes en que aparece el Caudillo.

El Jefe de Censura.

Figure 3: Authorisation certificate for *Y el Imperio volvía* (1939)

Case study

Santa Teresita del Niño Jesús, by Fr Vicente Mena Pérez
Teatro Beatriz (Madrid), 29 June 1933, Compañía Pilar Torres

One of the interesting trends from the Republican period was the increased popularity of theatre with a religious theme. This was not mere coincidence. The performance on the commercial stage of overtly Catholic dramas was in clear opposition to the secularising initiatives of Republic. The Azaña-led government determined that Spain would be a secular state and had introduced legislation to make it so. The *Ley de Confesiones y Congregaciones Religiosas* ('Religious Confessions and Congregations Act') passed in 1933 made education secular and redistributed some of the wealth of the Church. The weakened status of the Catholic Church was opposed by many traditionalists who resolved to see it reversed.

Vicente Mena's *Santa Teresita del Niño Jesús* was staged in Madrid in June 1933 and published in the following year, against the backdrop of the emergence of a strong Catholic political voice. The Confederación Española de Derechas Autónomas (CEDA) had been founded by José María Gil-Robles in March 1933 and, as Mary Vincent observes, it 'saw itself as a defensive organisation, formed to protect the fundamental institutions of traditional Spanish society: religion, family, and property' and Christian civilisation (2011: 202). Gil-Robles, inspired by his visit to the Nuremburg Rallies, brought Nazi-style propaganda to his electioneering and offered a vision of a Catholic state that appealed to many conservatives who were unhappy with the Left's ideas for Spain (Preston 2003: 70–1).

Mena (1896–1954), was a priest and author. His political commitment to the Nationalist side in the war would become clear: in February 1937 he, along with several other priests, joined the ranks of soldier-priests in the 'Regimiento de Farnesio, 10 de caballería' (BOE 1937b: 399). Following the end of the war, he not only continued to write literary and historical works but also had a regular religious programme on national state radio in the 1940s.

One of several successful plays by Mena, *Santa Teresita del Niño Jesús*, a mystical, religious drama, is a lyric poem in three acts. A report in *ABC* describes it as 'obra de ingenua poesía, impregnada de místico fervor' ('a work of innocent poetry, permeated with mystical fervour') (1933: 57). It was premiered at the Teatro Beatriz on 29 June 1933 before moving to the larger venue of the Teatro de la Comedia on 8 July (ABC 1933: 57) The review by A.C. published in *ABC* on 30 June outlines the play as follows:

> Se desarrolla el tema sencillísimo en seis cuadros. Teresita en la paz de su casa, inflamada por su vocación. Teresita ante la Santidad de León XIII, solicitando dispensa de edad para hacer sus votos. Profesión de Teresita. Visión íntima del claustro en el momento en que las monjitas endechan al Niño. Leves tentaciones mundanas de Teresita. Y el tránsito a Dios. (1933: 50)

> The very simple theme is developed over six scenes. Therese in the peace of her house, inflamed by her vocation. Therese before his Holiness Pope Leo XIII, requesting a dispensation in terms of age in order to make her vows. Therese's profession. An intimate view of the cloister at the moment when the nuns mourn the Infant Jesus. Therese's minor worldly temptations. And her passing over to God.

The police report on the first of two performances on the second night (30 June), also gives a detailed outline of the play and notes:

> En todos los entre-cuadros, en lugar del telón corriente, aparece uno de color morado que en su centro, ostenta una cruz de grandes dimensiones, una corona de espinas y un sagrado corazón. La obra es de carácter místico, no teniendo alusiones política[s], habiendo terminado a las 20'40 horas, sin que ocurriese incidente alguno. (AGA R6192)

> Between each scene, instead of the normal curtain, there is a purple one with a large cross, a crown of thorns and a sacred heart in its centre. The work is mystical in character, does not contain political allusions, and ended at 8:40 p.m., without incident.

Although no details are given in the censorship file, the press reviews of the play comment on a protest that took place on the night of the premiere, which led to the removal of an individual from the theatre. This minor incident would, in fact, not only have repercussions for some of the biggest names in the theatre of the day but would also call attention to the increasing politicisation of the theatre.

In A.C.'s review, for *ABC*, he praised the play's poetry, although he found it lacking in dramatic impact and was unimpressed by the fantastical elements introduced in the third act: 'El autor es creyente y poeta también, y supo verter esas mieles en bello panal de poesía, en lindos versos muy sonoros y tersos' ('The author is a believer and a poet too, and he knew how to pour honey to create a beautiful honeycomb of poetry, in beautiful, very sonorous and smooth verses') (A.C. 1933: 49). He went on to say that despite the lack of dramatic conflict, the author managed to create 'admirable', elegant scenes, which he likened to the works of Fray Luis de León and San Juan de la Cruz. He praised the acting and in particular the performance of Pilar García Torres in the role of Teresita and mentioned the positive audience response to both lead actress and author. This favourable review, stressing the aesthetic and acting achievements of what was clearly more a poetic than a dramatic piece, ends with a brief reference to 'un incidente desagradable' ('a disagreeable incident') during the second act, when an individual objected loudly, while others applauded the performance. His protest was such that security was called and he was removed from the theatre. The protester was not named, but more on him presently.

In the conservative *La Época*, Luis Araujo-Costa also praised the play: 'Saludemos en don Vicente Mena a un poeta estimable, y no nos cansemos nunca de dar alientos a estas manifestaciones de teatro religioso' ('Let us hail in Don Vicente Mena an estimable poet, and let us never tire of giving encouragement to these manifestations of religious theatre'). He too referred to the protest of an unnamed 'espectador aislado' ('single spectator'), but gives more detail than A.C. in *ABC*, suggesting that his protest sparked raised voices and flared tempers, until he was removed and the performance could continue. Despite writing of 'espectáculo en el escenario y espectáculo en la sala' ('a spectacle on the stage and a spectacle in the auditorium'), Araujo-Costa noted that people behaved wisely, the interruption was fleeting, and normality soon returned to the theatre (1933: 4).

In his review in *La Voz*, V.T. suggested that the play was boring and undramatic. He mentioned the single voice of protest but, interestingly, implied that the reaction to it was excessive: 'Provocó una contraprotesta de tonos excesivamente airados por parte de algunos miembros del público' ('this provoked a counter-protest of excessively angry tones by some members of the public') (1933: 3).

Events took an interesting turn when the Dirección General de Seguridad issued a statement in the press relating to the incident and naming three prominent right-wing dramatists who had been fined for their part in the events of the night before. The protestor, however, was still not named:

> Esta madrugada la Dirección general de Seguridad facilitó a los informadores de Prensa una nota oficiosa, en la que consta que le ha sido impuesta una multa de 500 pesetas al Sr. Muñoz Seca, a doña Pilar Millán-Astray y a D. Honorio Maura por escándalo en la función celebrada en el teatro Beatriz, anoche, con motivo del estreno de la obra *Santa Teresita de Jesús*. (A.C. 1933: 50)

> This morning the General Directorate of Security provided press informants with an official note, in which it states that a fine of 500 pesetas has been imposed on Mr Muñoz Seca, Ms Pilar Millán-Astray and Mr Honorio Maura for a scandal at the performance held at the Beatriz Theatre, last night, on the occasion of the premiere of the play *Santa Teresita de Jesús*.

An official note was also published in *La Voz* (1933: 3). In this case, the direct involvement of Maura and also Millán-Astray and Muñoz Seca is mentioned. *La Voz* defended the actions of the Director General de Seguridad who, it stated, was obliged to fine them for creating a public order disturbance. Not everyone agreed with the sanction, however. J.G.O. in *El Heraldo de Madrid* described the play as inoffensive and not worth the protest, and expressed unhappiness at the politicisation of the work, declaring that the Director General de Seguridad acted wrongly in fining three well-known playwrights:

> Hay otra interpretación que a mí, republicano, no me place tanto: la que desde su despacho y a poco de tener conocimiento del suceso diera anoche mismo al escándalo el director general de Seguridad: multar a la señora Millán Astray y a los señores Muñoz Seca y Honorio Maura por oponerse a la protesta de un espectador que encontraba cursi la obra que aquéllos parecía de perlas, lo encuentro yo impolítico y contraproducente. (1933: 5)

> There is another interpretation that I, as a Republican, am not so happy about: the interpretation of the scandal made by the Director General of Security from his office and shortly after hearing about the event. Fining Mrs Millán Astray and Messrs Muñoz Seca and Honorio Maura for opposing the protest of a spectator who found the work corny, and which they found charming, is an action I consider politically unwise and counterproductive.

La Época published a letter from Honorio Maura, one of the apparent culprits (1933: 4), which at last provides essential, if partisan, details about the episode. In his letter, he claims to set the record straight for the public and the state's Security Directorate. He describes the public's positive response to the play, with the exception of 'un joven de copiosa cabellera, que hacía alarde de su protesta, en uso de un perfecto derecho, pateando con entusiasmo realmente conmovedor' ('a young man with thick hair, who flaunted his protest, making use of his perfect right, stamping his feet with truly moving enthusiasm'). He states that the protestor later faced the public and in a 'boastful' tone, explained that he was protesting because the work was 'muy malo, muy cursi y una obra de sacristía' ('very bad, very twee and a sacristy play'). According to Maura, a group of spectators surrounded the troublemaker and moved into the aisles, arguing and gesticulating. He insisted that Millán-Astray, Muñoz Seca and he played no part in this first incident.

Maura states that it was after the second act that the protestor made a coarse gesture towards him, as he sat in a box with a friend and some ladies. It was at this point that Maura admits he and his friend went down to confront him, 'indignados y dispuestos a no dejar pasar tal ordinariez' ('outraged and willing not to let such vulgarity go unpunished'), but found that he was already surrounded by people who had witnessed the gesture. Maura then demanded that he be detained and a policeman evicted him from the theatre.

Upon leaving the theatre himself, Maura writes that he was approached by the policeman who enquired if he wished to pursue his complaint against the protestor. He did, and accompanied the policeman to 'do his civic duty'. He insists in the letter that he did not see Muñoz Seca or Millán-Astray at any point. He then expresses his surprise and outrage at the fact that he and other 'innocent' parties were the subject of fines for disturbing the peace, rather than the person who caused the incident. Moreover, he claims that the police officers involved, both there and at the station, supported his actions, rather than those of the impertinent agitator. In a rather theatrical flourish, Maura unveils the true culprit at the end of his letter, naming the protestor as Antonio Sánchez Barbudo.

Sánchez Barbudo, although not from the same generation or circles as the dramatists who were fined, was not some unknown figure but rather a public intellectual of the left, well known as a writer and critic. He wrote for *El Sol* and *La Gaceta Literaria*, among other news and literature publications, and was the founder of *La Hoja Literaria*. He was also a member of the Misiones Pedagógicas and the Alianza de Intelectuales Antifascistas para la Defensa de la Cultura. At the time of his protest, he was working for the Ministerio de Instrucción Pública, which might explain why the authorities chose not to punish him for his actions, instead stirring up controversy by penalising famous figures associated with the opposition.

As a result of the incident on the night of the premiere, the authorities were concerned that the work might become a focus for political protest. The file shows that the authorities were warned of further trouble and sent representatives to both performances on 30 June. The police report from the earlier show noted that Commissioner Alfredo Verdú would attend the later performance 'con todo el personal disponible' ('with all available personnel'). The second report, signed by an inspector from the Dirección General de Seguridad, found nothing contentious in the playtext and noted that the later evening performance was not well attended, and that the spectators were well behaved.

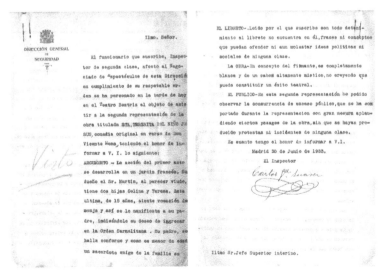

Figure 4: Inspector's report on *Santa Teresita del Niño Jesús* (1933)

This was not the end of it, however, and two days later, *El Sol* published extracts (due, it claimed, to space restrictions) from a letter signed by several well-known left-wing theatre practitioners, in which they expressed solidarity with Sánchez Barbudo and not only disparaged much of the contemporary theatre but also extended their criticism to the entirety of the works of Muñoz Seca, Maura and others. The signatories, a roll-call of left-wing cultural figures, were Arturo Serrano Plaja, Rafael Dieste, A. Rodríguez Luna, Enrique Azcoaga, Alberto Fernández Mezquita, Miguel Prieto, Eugenio Fernández, Gustavo Quevedo, Rafael Alberti, Enrique Climent, R. Suárez Picallo, Mariano Gómez Fernández, Antonio Espina and Raúl Verneuil (1933: 12).

The following day, on 3 July, the newspaper *Luz* also referred to the same signed letter and highlighted the signatories' insistence that 'no había manera de confundir con un gesto grosero la mueca de asco juvenil que hizo contra la obra que se representaba' ('there was no way that the the grimace of youthful disgust he made against the work being performed could be confused with a rude gesture') (1933: 11).

In the end, those involved moved on and, in the context of a constantly shifting political and cultural landscape, the incident was soon forgotten. It is worth remembering now, however, as a manifestation of an ideological conflict about religion and the state that pitted several of the most influential left- and right-wing dramatists and intellectuals of the day against each other in the press. The play itself was generally acknowledged as a well-written lyrical piece, focused on the life and faith of a saint. The events surrounding its staging, however, were entirely political and show how the theatre at the time was being used as a space for displays of ideological affiliation and public protest, which is exactly what Republican censors were worried about. Sánchez Barbudo knew that by protesting at the premiere, which was attended by the leading lights of the conservative theatre world, he would cause a stir, and he did.

Right-wing political parties had already done well in local elections earlier that year and would win the November general election. This play and its staging, therefore, signalled a shift in Spanish society and politics towards the conservative, religious right and away from a secular, progressive Republicanism, for the moment at least. Indeed, the success of right-leaning parties in the

1933 elections would see several CEDA members in government and the rescinding of many of the reforms previously introduced.

As for the protagonists of this minor act, Sánchez Barbudo continued his cultural work for the Republic during the civil war and, in 1937, co-founded one of the most important publications of the period, the monthly magazine *Hora de España*, which contained essays, poetry and criticism 'al servicio de la causa popular' ('in the service of the popular cause'); after the war, he went into exile, first to Mexico, then to the United States, and spent the rest of his professional life teaching at the University of Wisconsin (Kronik 1997).

Honorio Maura and Pedro Muñoz Seca were outspoken cultural figures of the right and both would be assassinated by Republicans in the early days of the war, Maura by the CNT-linked Federación Anarquista Ibérica in April 1936 and Muñoz Seca, as indicated earlier, during the Paracuellos massacres in November the same year (BNE 2016; JMA 1949). Pilar Millán-Astray spent some time in a Republican prison but went on to enjoy a successful theatrical career in the 1940s and 1950s with her conservative, female-focused works. Fr Vicente Mena continued to write and preach, although his theatre never achieved such attention again.

Notes

1 For more information about developments spearheaded by Republican intellectuals, see Vilches de Frutos (1999), Bilbatúa (1976) and Aguilera Sastre (1992).
2 For example, Benavente's *La duquesa gitana* ('The Gypsy Duchess') (AGA R6033).
3 The conservative period saw the reversal of some of the cultural reforms initiated by the first Republican government, including the cutting of funds for the Misiones Pedagógicas (Aznar 1997: 53).
4 A conservative whose sympathies lay with the traditional powers in society, Marquina would later declare his allegiance to the Nationalist side from Argentina (Dennis and Peral Vega 2010: 34). His plays *La Dorotea* (AGA R6306) and *En el nombre del padre* ('In the Name of the Father') (AGA 21/5797) were both staged in 1935.
5 For more on this case, see Dosa (1934a and 1934b).
6 Script in the 1939 censorship file (reproduced in Alba Peinado 2009: 156).
7 For a detailed discussion of the scandal around the creation of the Patronato and its role in the ending of the Cherif-Xirgu years at the Español, see Gil Fombellida (2003: 116–21).

8   For more on the theatrical connections between the two cities and the role of Xirgu in both, see David George (2002).
9   Lorca's *Bodas de sangre* (*Blood Wedding*) had premiered at the Teatro Beatriz on 8 March 1933. As the censors' concerns at this point related to matters of politics and public order, it was seen as unproblematic (AGA R6117).
10 See also Casona (1936: 14) and González Olmedilla (1936: 14).
11 For more on this type of theatre, see Cobb (1985); Cabañas Bravo (2011); Aznar Soler (1993); Fuentes (2006); O'Leary (2017a, 2020).
12 For more on the theatre of this period, see Aznar (1987, 1997); Bilbatúa (1976); Collado (1989); Dennis and Peral Vega (2009, 2010); Gómez Díaz (2006); Marrast (1978, 1986); McCarthy (1999); Monleón (1979); Mundi (1987); O'Leary (2020); Peral Vega (2013); Rodríguez Puértolas (1986, 2006). The special issues of *ADE Teatro* (no. 97, 2003) and *Anthropos* (no. 148, 1993) are also very useful.
13 For an excellent analysis of *Numancia* and its importance at the time, see Gagen (2008).
14 For a detailed analysis of the censorship of *La llave, Al amanecer* and *Los salvadores de España*, see O'Leary (2020: 113–23; 199–201).
15 For a detailed analysis of censorship of *El Alcázar de Toledo*, see O'Leary (2020: 106–8).

Chapter 3

The Franco Dictatorship: Censorship as 'Propaganda', 'Education' and 'Information'

The dominant feature of the 100-year period surveyed in Chapter 1 was a struggle between two tendencies: liberal forces defending freedom of both expression and the theatrical market; and conservative forces seeking to suppress dissent, centralise control, enforce Catholic moral values and tightly regulate the industry. For most of that time, the reactionary tendencies were constrained by constitutional principles and judicial procedures, particularly with regard to the extent of pre-performance censorship. Although the Primo de Rivera dictatorship flouted those principles and procedures, it did not attempt to remove them permanently. The civil war period in the Republican zone also constituted a brief exception, in which cultural control and the theatre industry were radically fragmented and reimagined. Throughout all these periods, there was vigorous and open debate about the necessity for censorship and its impact on society and culture.

The victory of the Nationalists in 1939 brought a decisive swing back to conservative coercion, now part of a ruthless project to discipline Spanish society and impose permanent political and cultural change. The legal framework for theatre censorship set up by the Franco regime was in many ways a throwback to the 1850s. The liberal 1913 model of regulation – decentralised and secular, subject to judicial authority and more reliant on monitoring of performances than prior vetting of texts – had been toughened up but not overturned by the 1935 regulations, which remained technically in force after the civil war. Now, liberal principles were rejected in favour of an authoritarian apparatus that was highly centralised, heavily influenced by the Church and the military, run by political activists as part of a propaganda operation rather than as routine maintenance of public order, and insistent on rigorous prior censorship of all scripts as well as inspection of dress rehearsals and performances.

Three main phases can be identified in the administration of censorship during the dictatorship. The first, from 1938 to 1945, was dominated by the Falange, the radical nationalist movement that before the war had pursued revolutionary aims inspired by Fascism but in 1937 had been forced to merge with the Carlist party Comunión Tradicionalista and become incorporated into the structure of the emerging military regime, forming the core of what was known as the *Movimiento Nacional* ('National Movement').[1] During this period, censorship offices were part of departments devoted primarily to propaganda, first the Ministerio del Interior, then the Ministerio de la Gobernación, and lastly the Secretaría General del Movimiento, the Falange organisation that acted as a ministry with a wide range of social, cultural and ideological functions. The second stage, from 1945 to 1951, can be characterised as the Catholic phase. Responsibility for censorship was transferred to the Ministerio de Educación Nacional ('Ministry of National Education'), which was heavily influenced by Catholic organisations, notably the ACNP.[2] The period from 1951 to the beginning of the transition to democracy following Franco's death in November 1975 was a 'technocratic' phase under the aegis of the Ministerio de Información y Turismo (MIT – 'Ministry of Information and Tourism'), during which the influence of the Church gradually declined and the censorship apparatus was reformed and made more flexible. Finally, the winding-up of censorship, which began with the appointment of Adolfo Suárez as Prime Minister in July 1976, would be overseen by the Ministerio de Cultura ('Ministry of Culture'): this final part of the story will be told in Chapter 8.

Setting up the system: censorship as part of a totalitarian propaganda apparatus (1938–45)

Since the two main centres of theatrical activity – Madrid and Barcelona – had remained in the Republican zone for almost the whole of the war, control of the theatre industry had not been a major concern for the rebel Nationalist forces as they consolidated their hold on the areas occupied in July 1936 and gradually chipped away at the territory held by the government. A few commercial companies that had been touring in the provinces when war broke out operated in the Nationalist zone, performing works from their existing repertoire as well as new plays by ideologically acceptable dramatists such as Joaquín Calvo Sotelo, Agustín de Foxá, Juan Ignacio Luca de Tena, José María Pemán, Antonio Quintero, Adolfo Torrado, and Joaquín and Serafín Álvarez Quintero.[3] The conventional repertoire of light comedies and musicals was supplemented by propagandist pieces about the war, historical dramas and Catholic *autos sacramentales*, some of them performed by companies sponsored by the Nationalist authorities. Like their left-wing counterparts in the Republican zone, some of the authors and directors involved in the Falange's theatrical ventures nurtured dreams of generating heroic new forms of performance inspired by patriotism, Catholicism and the classical tradition. As in the other camp, these visions were under-supported and short-lived.[4]

The Nationalist authorities quickly demonstrated their determination to control all forms of cultural production and overturn Republican culture. Military discipline was offered as the remedy to the chaos that was purported to be the inevitable result of liberalism and democracy. The restoration of traditional Catholic morality would reverse the collapse of moral values allegedly permitted by the Republican authorities. The reimposition of national unity would halt the slide towards territorial and social fragmentation, and conservative social and cultural attitudes were meant to bring stability in place of the uncertainty generated by modernity and experimentation. In the field of cultural production, tough, centralised censorship would replace the laxity and variability of procedures applied in the Republican period, and ensure that the renewal of 'National-Catholic' values was reflected in the press, the theatre, and other arts and mass media.

To begin with, all areas in the Nationalist zone were under martial law. The first provisional government, the Junta de Defensa Nacional, replaced all civil governors with military commanders (Boletín Oficial de la JDN 1936a and 1936b; and BOE 1936). During 1937 and 1938, as the Nationalists extended their area of control, civilian administration was gradually restored and non-military civil governors were appointed, their powers with regard to the maintenance of public order still regulated by the wide-ranging *Ley de Orden Público* of 1933. The social control they were expected to enforce went well beyond the requirements of keeping the peace. A circular from the Minister of the Interior sent to civil governors in July 1938 instructed them to crack down on blasphemy and other 'actos contrarios a la moral y la decencia pública' ('acts contrary to morals and public decency') (BOE 1938d).

In principle, civil governors also continued to have responsibility for theatre censorship. It is difficult to assess how frequently they interfered with theatrical activities in this period, but some evidence is available. Emeterio Díez cites a circular sent in November 1936 by the Civil Governor of Logroño to mayors in his province warning them that films and performances must 'acomodarse al medio ambiente moral y patriótico en que vivimos, hallándose desprovistas de todo lo que pueda ser propaganda de ideas socialistas o comunistas' ('conform to the moral and patriotic environment that we now inhabit and must be devoid of anything that may constitute propaganda for socialist or communist ideas') (2009: 376). The theatre director Luis Escobar recalls in his memoirs that in the autumn of 1938 the Civil Governor of Salamanca attempted to ban his production of José de Valdivieso's *El hospital de los locos* ('The Madhouse'), a religious spectacle produced with government and ecclesiastical support by a Falange-sponsored company. What made this even more surprising was that at the time Escobar was head of the government department responsible for both promoting and censoring theatre (Escobar 2000: 120).

The emerging regime was constructing a centralised mechanism of ideological and cultural control. Censorship of theatre and other media was now incorporated into an explicitly political totalitarian propaganda apparatus. Although the strategy was inspired by the systems developed in Nazi Germany and Fascist Italy, Franco's regime was not able or willing to commit comparable levels of political leadership, resources or personnel. The degree of coordination and control over the German theatre industry established in 1933–4 by Goebbels's Ministry of Public Enlightenment and Propaganda, or Mussolini's personal commitment to shaping theatrical culture, were beyond the wildest dreams of the Falange's amateur propagandists.[5]

As Nationalist forces advanced into Republican areas and constructed a parallel state, its propaganda and censorship apparatus were assembled bit by bit. Between October 1936 and January 1938, responsibility for press and propaganda was given to the Sección de Prensa y Propaganda in the Comisión de Cultura y Enseñanza ('Commission for Culture and Education').[6] In January 1937, this body was given a more central role (now known as the DEPP – 'Delegación del Estado para Prensa y Propaganda') within the Head of State's department (Secretaría General del Jefe del Estado), under the leadership of Vicente Gay Forner, a Falangist and devotee of Nazism (AHMD 2016: 75–80). A network of provincial delegations was established in June. In addition to disseminating propaganda through various media, and 'orienting' the press and radio stations, the Delegation was charged with drawing up guidelines for censorship (BOE 1937a). In the meantime, the Falange ran its own Delegación Nacional de Prensa y Propaganda.

Franco's first civilian government, established in Burgos in January 1938, brought the state and Falange propaganda operations together in the Delegación de Prensa y Propaganda within a new Ministerio del Interior led by Ramón Serrano Suñer, giving the Falange a dominant role. This ministry was then merged with that of Public Order in December 1938 to re-form the Ministerio de la Gobernación, headed by Serrano Suñer, who also held a leading role in the Falange itself. The Subsecretaría de Prensa y Propaganda was divided into three Servicios Nacionales: Prensa, Propaganda and Turismo. The Falangists José Antonio Giménez Arnau and Dionisio Ridruejo were appointed as Directors of Prensa and Propaganda respectively in February–March 1938, and legislation was introduced consolidating the censorship of the press and books. The *Ley de Prensa* ('Press Law') of 22 April declared that the state had a duty to organise and control the press, and that this function included 'la censura mientras no se disponga su supresión' ('censorship, until legislation is passed suspending it') (BOE 1938a: 6938). Another law of 29 April required all books and pamphlets printed in Spain or elsewhere to be authorised by the Servicio Nacional de Propaganda (BOE 1938c).

Although none of this legislation mentioned theatrical activity, the Servicio Nacional de Propaganda was certainly exercising censorship of performances during 1938. In April, Ridruejo appointed Luis Escobar, a relatively liberal monarchist, as head of the

Departamento de Teatro. This body, together with the provincial propaganda offices, was responsible both for promoting theatre and dance and for censorship, as recorded in the Department's report on its activities in 1938:

> Se prepara intensamente la futura legislación sobre Teatro español, en el sentido de orientar la producción teatral profesional a la cual se prestará la ayuda que viene necesitando y en cambio se exigirá la dignificación de sus espectáculos. En este sentido principalmente, se lleva a cabo la censura de las obras teatrales que han de ser estrenadas. (Reproduced in Díez 2009: 385)

> Intensive preparatory work is being carried out on legislation governing the theatre in Spain, focusing on guiding the theatrical profession, which will be offered the support it needs in exchange for a greater degree of dignity in its productions. In pursuit of this aim, the Department carries out censorship of plays proposed for performance.

The report gives a figure of 111 for 'control y censura de obras' ('control and censorship of plays') in the course of 1938 (Díez 2009: 386), which must have included professional productions as well as Falange-sponsored ones. It gives no indication of how many of those productions were banned or subjected to cuts, and there are no archival records of censorship decisions in 1938. Escobar's own account of this work is characteristically flippant:

> En un cierto momento, hasta nos encargaron de la censura. Los autores que tenían obras presentadas tuvieron suerte, porque yo me limitaba a poner el sello de 'aprobado' en cada hoja, sin leerlas siquiera; para ello no tenía ni tiempo ni vocación. Desgraciadamente para los autores, esta situación duró pocos días. Enseguida me aliviaron de tan grato trabajo. (Escobar 2000: 129)

> At one point, they even put us in charge of censorship. The authors whose scripts were submitted for authorisation were lucky, since all I did was to stamp 'approved' on every page without even reading them. I had neither the time nor the inclination to do the job properly. Unfortunately for the playwrights, things didn't stay like that for long. I was soon relieved of such an agreeable task.

Ridruejo too favoured a relatively light touch in the exercise of censorship, but found that his hands were usually tied by the Junta Superior de Censura, a body mostly responsible for vetting films but also monitoring other forms of censorship:

Durante tres años ocupé el cargo del que dependían los servicios de censura de libros, cine y teatro. Pero yo mismo no podía aflojarla ni dirigirla. Una Junta Superior, más o menos secreta y con abundante participación eclesiástica, establecía normas y confeccionaba listas de exclusiones. Eran decisiones inapelables. (Quoted in Díez 2009: 378)

For three years I was in charge of the offices that carried out book, film and theatre censorship. But there was little I could do to loosen or direct it. A Central Committee, more or less secret and packed with Church representatives, laid down guidelines and drew up blacklists. Their decisions were unchallengeable.

Most of the guidelines referred to by Ridruejo were issued during 1938 in memos from Franco's military headquarters. Juan Beneyto, who ran the book censorship office from 1938 to 1941, describes them disparagingly as 'pura casuística' ('pure casuistry') and suggests that between 1938 and 1943 he and his fellow censors managed to maintain a relatively liberal approach. Many of the criteria concerned details of the ideological orthodoxy being imposed by the new regime: how to refer to the military uprising of July 1936 and the roles of different organisations in it; the official status and titles of Franco himself; the interpretation of the aims and 'style' of the Falange; and of course, respect for the Catholic Church and its dogma (Beneyto Pérez 1987: 30–7). Although some of these issues were abstruse and the primary targets were print media rather than theatre, the criteria help to explain certain apparently surprising decisions made by theatre censors in 1939–40 (discussed in Chapter 4).

As the war drew to a close, Franco's regime began to return theatres and theatre companies to their former owners and took steps to ensure the enforcement of censorship in all areas. On 26 January 1939 Nationalist forces occupied Barcelona, where theatres had closed on 22 January. The propaganda office issued the following announcement on 6 February:

A fin de poner en marcha, a la mayor rapidez, todas aquellas actividades que atañen al Teatro, la Música y los espectáculos de análoga naturaleza, el Departamento correspondiente del Servicio Nacional de Propaganda del Ministerio de la Gobernación, convoca con carácter de urgencia a cuantas personas tengan relación e intereses con aquellas actividades, para que se presenten en sus oficinas [. . .]

advirtiendo que cuantas disposiciones y medidas hayan de tomarse sobre el particular, lo serán, naturalmente, con carácter de obligatorias para todos los locales de teatro, música o espectáculos análogos de Barcelona. (Vanguardia 1939a)

In order to set in motion activities associated with the theatre, music and similar public spectacles as rapidly as possible, the Theatre Department of the National Propaganda Service hereby issues an urgent call to all persons intending to engage in such activities to report to its office [. . .] It should be noted that all legal measures introduced in this regard shall apply obligatorily to all theatrical, musical and entertainment venues in Barcelona.

This was not a friendly invitation to theatremakers to resume business as usual but a warning that the industry was going to be subject to strict supervision by a police state. The regime was collecting huge amounts of information about people's activities over the preceding eight years, with the intention of punishing all those who had supported the Republican cause or failed to support the Nationalist one with sufficient enthusiasm. The Delegación del Estado para la Recuperación de Documentos ('State Delegation for the Recovery of Documents') set up in April 1938 was charged with collecting and cataloguing all kinds of documents that provided evidence of 'las actuaciones de los enemigos del Estado' ('the actions of enemies of the State') (BOE 1938b: 6986). The masses of correspondence, lists of union members and jobs in collectivised companies, minutes of meetings, and other similar documents on which Chapter 1 drew for the overview of theatre in Republican Spain during the war, were gathered by this sinister delegation to be used as evidence of opposition to the 'national' cause.

The campaign of retribution was implemented through military tribunals and the far-reaching *Ley de Responsabilidades Políticas* ('Political Responsibilities Act') of February 1939. This measure sought to punish all those who had been involved passively or actively in 'la subversión roja' ('the red subversion') and in obstructing 'el triunfo providencial e históricamente ineludible del Movimiento Nacional' ('the providential, historically inevitable triumph of the National Movement') (BOE 1939a: 824). Several hundred thousand people were indicted by Political Responsibilities tribunals between 1939 and 1945 (Richards 1998: 45 and Preston 2012: 506). Thousands of 'enemies of the State' were killed, imprisoned, fined, or purged from the education system, the civil service and other public-sector jobs. The regime was determined not only to punish Republican sympathisers but to erase their social and cultural influence. The information amassed by the Delegation, the tribunals, military courts and the police was used to blacklist actors and other theatre professionals by denying them membership of the new Falangist trade union, the Sindicato Nacional del Espectáculo, to refuse to license theatre companies, to prevent impresarios or theatre owners from resuming their business, and to prohibit the staging and publication of the work of certain playwrights. Díez gives examples of actors, directors and authors branded as 'Reds' and blacklisted (2009: 373–4), and Muñoz Cáliz (2010) provides details of the police files compiled on prominent exiled dramatists.

The first post-war productions in Barcelona – all in Castilian and advertised in the press with pro-Franco slogans – got hesitantly under way in late February 1939. The authorities must have been disappointed by the response to their summons of 6 February, since on 8 March they issued a more detailed reminder of the requirement for any theatrical activity, including amateur and non-commercial productions, to be officially approved by central government (Vanguardia 1939b). A similar notice referring to Madrid was published in the press on 8 April, a week after the declaration of the end of hostilities and the first day of the new theatrical season. This announcement specified that all works written after 18 July 1936 or performed in the Republican zone during the war must be submitted for authorisation (ABC 1939d). Not many works in these categories were presented for approval in 1939: the new and reconstituted companies and theatre managements generally fell back on safe genres (light comedies, familiar *zarzuelas* and sanitised *revistas*) from safe periods (prior to 1936) and by safe authors (not associated with the Republic).

The Servicio Nacional de Propaganda, including its censorship departments, moved from Burgos to Madrid in April 1939. Escobar became artistic director of the state-run Teatro María Guerrero in September 1939. His successor as Jefe de Censura, probably dealing with publications as well as theatrical and musical performances, was the Falangist writer Samuel Ros, who had been working for the Nationalists as their propaganda representative in Chile until his return to Spain in August 1938. Not long after his appointment as editorial director of the Falangist magazine *Vértice* in January 1940, Ros ceased to run the censorship office, but he was certainly signing censorship documents up to May 1940.[7] His deputy was Santiago Magariños Torres, a Falange activist who at the beginning of the war had been removed by the Republican authorities from his post as professor of law in Madrid and imprisoned, but later released.

To begin with, Ros and Magariños were operating with scarce resources, minimal documentation and no explicit legal mandate. It is not clear who was doing the reading of scripts submitted for approval, and formal written reports do not seem to have been required until 1940. Authorisation certificates were issued on the basis of brief remarks scribbled by Ros and Magariño on the applications themselves. Most decisions about performances in provincial theatres were probably being taken by Delegados Provinciales de Propaganda.

This state of provisionality was brought to an end after the introduction of new legislation establishing a definitive legal framework for censorship of all forms of expression other than periodical publications (which continued to be administered by the Servicio Nacional de Prensa). The law of 15 July 1939 justified censorship as necessary for 'la educación política y moral de los españoles' ('the moral and political education of the Spanish people') (BOE 1939b: 4119). It made provision for a Sección de Censura covering publications, the scripts of theatrical works of all genres, film screenplays, songs and some musical compositions. The act did not go into detail about censorship criteria or procedures. It simply declared that authorisation was required and repealed any previous measures that conflicted with the present law – implicitly scrapping the previous constraints on pre-performance theatre censorship and reversing the devolution to provincial and local authorities that had been built into the 1935 regulations.

Bit by bit, a more organised and centralised theatre censorship apparatus was being assembled. A basic format was established for reports on scripts, which appear in some censorship files from August 1939 onwards, written by Ros or an anonymous censor. Three things are striking about this initial model for *informes*. First, the emphasis placed on evaluating the quality of the text: censors would continue to be invited to express judgements on literary and theatrical quality throughout the dictatorship, but these views rarely made a significant difference to their decisions. Indeed, there are some reports in which censors complained about having to authorise what they regarded as trivial rubbish. Second, there was no explicit requirement to comment on moral or religious issues, indicating that the Church was not yet playing a significant role in the censorship process. The next model, introduced in 1943, would specify religious as well as political implications. Third, the evaluations were typically brief and sometimes surprisingly blunt. An early example of Ros's terse approach is a handwritten report from August 1939 on the musical comedy *Yo quiero divorciarme* ('I Want to Get Divorced') by Pepe Romeu. With little literary value, no documentary value and no political implications, it was judged to be a 'comedia lírica que adolece de muchos defectos en su construcción. Argumento poco original y sin interés. Aprobada' ('musical comedy suffering from numerous defects of construction. Plot unoriginal and without interest. Approved') (AGA 111/39).

The number of applications increased from September, as the autumn theatre season got under way. An announcement in the press in October made clear that censorship was no longer limited to new works: 'A partir del 26 de diciembre, cualquier obra o espectáculo que se represente en el territorio nacional, deberá disponer de la correspondiente hoja de censura, cualquiera que sea su carácter, hecha excepción solamente de las obras consideradas clásicas' ('As from 26 December, any play or other public spectacle to be performed in any part of the country must have been issued with the relevant censorship certificate. This applies to all genres except those works that are considered classics') (ABC 1939i).

As for the criteria to be applied by censors, no specific rules were published in legislation until 1963, though it should be remembered that a number of articles of the Penal Code referred to criminal offences that might be committed during the course of a theatrical performance. The Code, little changed since 1932 except for a few amendments in 1944 to add the offence of blasphemy and afford specific protection to the Catholic Church and the institutions of the *Movimiento Nacional* (BOE 1944), served as an implicit guide to the more serious transgressions that censorship was intended to prevent. The internal censorship instructions that had been circulated in 1938 and 1939 were consolidated in a document sent to all censors in January 1940, which still placed a heavy emphasis on the internal politics of the regime, the legitimacy of its authority, the reputation of particular institutions, and the balance of power within the *Movimiento*. Religion and Catholic morality seem at this stage to have been of secondary importance, lumped together with the revolutionary National-Syndicalist programme of the Falange. Censors were instructed to suppress the following:

> 1º.– Sobre el Alzamiento y la Revolución Nacional. Cuanto pueda desilusionar, lo que se refiera a juicios sobre el Alzamiento o la marcha de la Revolución Nacional y especialmente cuando se trate de valorar de manera desorbitada su sentido unitario en lo militar y en lo político. 2º.– En materia política. Cuanto pudiera molestar a las Instituciones Militares, Civiles, Eclesiásticas o Políticas; lo que vaya contra el actual régimen político, incluso el sentido de la interinidad de los poderes del Caudillo; lo que ataque la constitución social de unidad del pueblo, de clases y de tierras; lo que contradiga el sistema económico de predominio de interés común; lo que pueda dañar a nuestra política internacional. 3º.– En materia de razones doctrinales. Cuanto ofenda al dogma o la moral católicas, lo que contradiga o deforme la Doctrina de los 26 Puntos con sus antecedentes y textos complementarios; toda interpretación no ortodoxa del estilo de la Falange. (AGA 21/1477)

> 1. On the Rising [of July 1936] and the National Revolution: anything that may foment disillusion with regard to assessments of the Rising or the progress of the National Revolution, especially when their sense of military and political unity is presented in a distorted way. 2. In political matters: anything that may offend the Military, Civil, Ecclesiastical or Political Institutions; anything that goes against the current political regime, including the issue of the interim nature of the powers of the *Caudillo*;[8] anything that threatens the social framework guaranteeing the unity of the people, classes and territories [of Spain]; anything that challenges the principle that the economic system is founded upon the public interest; and anything that may damage our international policies. 3. In doctrinal matters: anything that may offend Catholic dogma or morality, or may contradict or distort the Doctrine of the 26 Points, together with its antecedents and complementary texts; and any unorthodox interpretation of the style of the Falange.[9]

By early 1940, then, the theatre censorship apparatus was established as a centralised structure requiring pre-performance authorisation of virtually all theatrical activities. It was administered nationally by the Dirección General de Propaganda in the Ministerio de la Gobernación and locally by the provincial Delegados de Propaganda, and it was generally dominated by the Falange. Francisco Ruiloba Palazuelos was in post as Jefe de Censura by March 1940, with J. Palazón also working as a censor. A total of 438 applications for approval of theatrical productions were considered in 1939, and 1036 in 1940. Not many of these were banned outright, as hardly anyone was attempting to stage politically dissident or morally unacceptable material at this time. However, the censors were imposing cuts and they made some apparently surprising decisions to prohibit the performance of right-wing works (see Chapter 4).

Ridruejo was becoming increasingly disenchanted with Francoism and became one of the casualties of a political realignment in 1941. Serrano Suñer, keen to play a leading role in relations with the Axis powers, had taken over the Ministerio de Asuntos Exteriores ('Ministry of Foreign Affairs') in October 1940. When Franco appointed a new Ministro de Gobernación in May 1941, his choice was the monarchist General Valentín Galarza, who immediately carried out a purge of Falangists in the ministry. Both Ridruejo and his immediate superior Antonio Tovar (Subsecretario de Prensa y Propaganda) were sacked. However, the Falange retained control over press and propaganda, which were transferred into the Secretaría General del Movimiento, the Falange-led organisation that coordinated all kinds of popular mobilisation activity through youth, sporting and women's organisations as well as the state trade union structure. On 20 May 1941 a new Vicesecretaría de Educación Popular was created within the Secretaría General, led by Gabriel Arias-Salgado, the civil governor who had attempted to ban *El hospital de los locos* in 1938. The concept of *educación popular* should not be confused with education proper, which was the preserve of the Ministerio de Educación Nacional. It covered instead a wide range of activities, including propaganda, control of the press, promotion and management of culture, support of youth organisations and popular mobilisation.

The Vicesecretaría comprised the Delegación Nacional de Prensa and the Delegación Nacional de Propaganda. Manuel Torres López was Delegado Nacional de Propaganda from May 1941 to December 1943, succeeded by David Jato Miranda (December 1943 to July 1945), with much of the administrative work being overseen by the Secretario Nacional de Propaganda, Patricio González de Canales. Within the Delegación Nacional, theatre censorship was administered by the Departamento de Teatro, part of the Sección de Cinematografía y Teatro, which was headed first by Antonio Fraguas Saavedra and then by Joaquín Argamasilla. Decisions were administered at the provincial level by new Delegaciones Provinciales de Educación Popular with responsibility for both press and propaganda, created by a law of October 1941 (BOE 1941).

Arias-Salgado, a traditionalist Catholic and member of the ACNP who had joined the Falange during the war, took the view that censorship had been exercised too leniently and haphazardly under Ridruejo's leadership. New censors and local inspectors were employed, and procedures and documentation were tightened up. Each application would from now on require reports from two censors. Despite Arias-Salgado's zeal, however, progress was slow. Administrative documents from 1943 (AGA 21/0646) tell a comical tale of administrative failure and scarcity of resources. Francisco Ortiz Muñoz (a screenwriter who later became the resident censor for Televisión Española), Guillermo Salvador de Reyna Medina (a journalist and civil servant who became Secretario General de Cinematografía y Teatro in 1946) and Antonio Pastor Bela (Falangist and screenwriter who became the head of the Department of Filmology at the CSIC (National Research Council) in the 1950s) were working as readers for both film and theatre censorship. On 22 May, Pastor Bela was replaced by Gumersindo Montes Agudo (veteran Falangist, writer, screenwriter and film critic), alongside Bartolomé Mostaza Rodríguez (journalist, poet and theatre critic who had been a provincial head of press and propaganda in the war).

Documents in the archive show the build-up of substantial backlogs of scripts to be vetted, complaints from officials about the idleness of the readers, and problems with Delegados Provinciales causing delays and failing to follow procedures (AGA 21/0646). A great deal of work clearly remained to be done to establish the nationwide control of theatrical activities that was desired. A new application form for theatre censorship introduced in early 1943 includes guidance advising that applications for authorisation must be submitted either through one of the Delegaciones Provinciales de Educación Popular or directly to the Delegación Nacional in Madrid; that authorisation was needed for all performance genres, including circus and variety shows; that decisions would normally be made within seven working days; and that authors or companies could appeal against censorship decisions. What appears to be a new element in these guidelines is the stipulation that non-professional performances could be licensed locally:

1.º Corresponde autorizar a esta Delegación Nacional de Cinematografía y Teatro todas las representaciones teatrales, de cualquier clase que sean, que se vayan a efectuar por compañías profesionales.
2.º A las Delegaciones Provinciales de Educación Popular compete el autorizar las representaciones teatrales que reúnan las siguientes características: a) realizarse por una compañía **no profesional**; b) ser gratuita, y c) tener lugar las representaciones dentro de un círculo cultural, artístico, etc., y para sus respectivos miembros. (AGA 205/39).[10]

1. The National Delegation for Cinema and Theatre is responsible for the authorisation of all theatrical performances of any kind which are to be given by professional companies.
2. Provincial Delegations of Popular Education are responsible for authorising theatrical performances which: a) are carried out by a **non-professional** company; b) are free, and c) take place in a cultural or artistic club, society, etc., attended by the members of the same.

Provincial authorisation of productions by student, Falange and other amateur groups had sometimes been carried out by mayors, civil governors and Delegados de Propaganda between 1939 and 1942, as noted by Díez (2008: 317–18), but this is the first time that it was set out explicitly as policy. Indeed, the devolution of decision-making at this time went further: a set of guidelines issued in January 1944 by the Delegado Provincial in Huelva to district officials in his province advised them that in the case of performances by local amateur groups, 'podrás censurar tú mismo el libreto' ('you may censor the script yourself') (reproduced in Abellán 1980: 254). District officers also became responsible at this point for the approval and monitoring of *espectáculos de variedades* (variety shows comprising songs, dances, comedy sketches, etc., performed either in a theatre or in a club, dance hall or café). As the 1944 guidelines explained, the content and staging of such shows tended to be so variable that centralised control was impractical.

Approval and continuous monitoring of performances needed to be done at a level as local as possible, including not only scripts but also costumes and sets (Abellán 1980: 258). These arrangements sometimes enabled companies to persuade local officials to turn a blind eye to transgressions but made the censorship of this kind of entertainment highly unpredictable.

The central authorities' lack of confidence in the provincial offices must have persisted, since their role was later curtailed: by the early 1950s, non-professional performances were being censored by the ministry in Madrid, and in 1955 they would come under new procedures for *teatros de cámara o ensayo* (theatre clubs), which will be discussed later in this chapter. Censorship decisions would still occasionally vary according to location, but this would usually be the result of negotiation between Madrid and the Delegado Provincial, with civil governors sometimes making recommendations based on local sensitivities. The responsibility of district or provincial delegates for censoring *variedades*, however, seems to have continued.

The backlog in the processing of applications in 1943 was exacerbated by a drastic policy decision announced by González de Canales on 26 June: 'Quedan sin rigor cuantos certificados de censura de obras teatrales, incluidos todos los géneros, que se han expedido con anterioridad al 1 de marzo de 1942' ('All theatre censorship certificates issued before 1 March 1942 for works of any genre are hereby declared to be invalid') (AGA 21/0646). Arias-Salgado had decided that the work carried out under his predecessors could not be relied on, and companies were now obliged to reapply for authorisation of works that had been unquestioned fixtures in their repertoires for years, many of which were now banned or affected by newly imposed cuts.

Action was finally taken in October 1943 to make the operation more efficient. Priority was given to applications specifying a company and a firm performance date, and tighter procedures were put in place for keeping track of applications and decisions, and checking that textual cuts were marked on scripts. Firmer control was also imposed on Delegados Provinciales. While struggling to get the operation of the creaky apparatus up to speed, Arias-Salgado and González de Canales were also intent on making the criteria to be applied by censors clearer and more rigorous. A memo sent to the Sección de Cinematografía y Teatro on 24 June prescribed surprisingly demanding aesthetic criteria:

Para la aprobación de cualquier obra, se requiere que ésta posea aristas y dignidad mínima, en cuanto se relacione con:

a) .– Que los tipos estén dotados de carácter, es decir, que sean caracteres con vida propia y no fantasmas.
b) .– Que la intención tenga calidad humana, y
c) .– Que el diálogo esté redactado en castellano correcto y conciso, procurando que la construcción sea perfecta. (AGA 21/0646)

For any work to be approved, it must have solidity and a certain degree of dignity in the following respects:

a) the dramatic characters should possess genuine human character, coming across as people with lives of their own, rather than mere phantasms;
b) the theme should deal seriously with human experience;
c) the dialogue should be written in correct, concise Spanish, aiming for perfect construction.

If applied conscientiously, these requirements would have put half of the nation's theatres and playwrights out of business, but the intention was more to do with raising morale among censors and dignifying their labour than with providing practical guidelines. The proposition that censorship was intended to play a constructive role in raising artistic standards was also aired in public forums around this time. An article published in the Catholic newspaper *Ya* in January 1944 celebrated the work of the Departamento de Teatro in 1943 and insisted that the censorship it was exercising was not repressive. On the contrary, its primary purpose was: 'Estimular la producción de excelentes obras escénicas, de buen teatro. Al realizar su misión no se limita a prohibir, sino que pretende orientar a los autores, señalándoles vicios, defectos, tanto de técnica como literarios o morales' ('To stimulate the creation of excellent work for the stage, good theatre. In carrying out its mission it does not confine itself to prohibition, but rather aims to offer guidance to authors, pointing out failings and defects, whether literary, moral or technical') (Alcocer 1944).

This idealised account of the work of the censors is not reflected in the evidence preserved in the censorship files. Reports very rarely offered helpful suggestions, and cuts or amendments were never marked as optional. Moreover, Alcocer undermines his own propaganda by going on to assert that ninety percent of the works authorised in 1943 were not performed, since many of the applications were speculative attempts by inexperienced authors with little expectation of getting their work on stage – which seems to indicate a massive failure of the supposed mission to provide supportive mentoring to playwrights.

The idea of censorship dignifying Spanish theatre and stimulating creativity was also promoted by the theatre critic, dramatist and translator Nicolás González Ruiz, who began work as an adviser to the censorship office around this time. In an article of July 1944, he argues that 'la verdadera misión de esta Censura es creadora; tiene que abrir el camino y despejar el ambiente, tiene que dejar expédita la senda al buen teatro. Sabemos que ésta es la manera como la censura teatral está actualmente entendida [. . .] Su misión no es derribar sino crear' ('the true mission of the Censorship Office is creative; it is meant to show the way and clear the air, opening up the path to high-quality theatre. We know that this is how theatre censorship is currently understood [. . .] Its mission is not to destroy but to create') (González Ruiz 1944). The first battle – already won, according to González Ruiz – was to clean up the *revista*, described with distaste by Alcocer as almost invariably pornographic. González Ruiz's confidence in this small victory is contradicted by an official notice that had been published in the press in January deploring 'la alarmante frecuencia con que los empresarios y artistas del género teatral de revistas intentan montar sus obras sin el requisito previo de la censura' ('the alarming frequency with which impresarios and artists specialising in the theatrical genre of the *revista* are attempting to stage shows without the required censorship approval') (Ya 1944), as well as by evidence from censorship files showing that the authorities continued to have trouble with *revistas* throughout the 1940s and into the 1950s, as will be shown in Chapter 4.

The second and third of González Ruiz's battles involved having the courage to ban inoffensive work on the grounds of poor quality, and showing respect for high-quality scripts even if they presented morally or politically difficult material. Subsequent chapters will show that throughout the dictatorship literary or theatrical quality was sometimes a significant factor in censors' judgements in the positive sense (making allowances for a text seen as important or well written), but judgement of aesthetic quality was rarely decisive in the negative sense (banning a play because it was regarded as worthless). On the contrary, there are many reports in which a censor would condemn a script in the most scathing terms but wearily conclude that there was no reason not to give authorisation. José María Ortiz's judgements could be the most withering. He summed up a *revista* in 1956 as 'un verdadero engendro tanto en el orden literario como en el aspecto escénico. El autor carece de toda noción sobre lo que es una obra de teatro [. . .] Puede autorizarse con los cortes que seguidamente se señalan' ('a veritable monstrosity in both literary and theatrical terms. The author has absolutely no idea of what a stage play is [. . .] It can be authorised with the cuts specified below') (AGA 201/56). Our analysis of particular cases will show that censors' evaluation of quality was often determined by deeply conservative assumptions about established canons and the conventions of theatrical genres. They were not necessarily hostile to innovation but tended to be suspicious of texts that did not conform to expectations. Respect for the canonical status of a text could sometimes work against its chances of being staged or result in restrictions on the creative freedom of adaptors or directors. Some of Valle-Inclán's plays, for example, were full of verbal and visual elements that were considered unacceptable, but some censors argued that the integrity of the texts should not be marred by cuts or amendments and that complete prohibition was preferable (see Chapter 6).

A more pragmatic restatement of censorship criteria was issued by González de Canales on 6 July 1943 (see Figure 5). It marks a clear shift of emphasis away from the political issues of the immediate post-war period towards moral and religious concerns:

En lo sucesivo la censura teatral se ajustará a las siguientes normas:

a) .– En el orden moral se atenderá a la tendencia perniciosa que pueda existir en el fondo de la obra de teatro, prohibiéndola si dicha tendencia existiese.
b) .– En cambio, cuando de la obra pueda desprenderse una beneficiosa ejemplaridad, no se censurarán aspectos parciales, que se hallaren dentro de lo que es común en sociedad y en la vida y todo el mundo lo sabe.
c) .– Se estimarán de ejemplaridad perniciosa las obras de ambiente y diálogo burdo, grosero y ordinario, aunque el asunto fuese de impecable blancura.
d) .– Las obras clásicas nacionales y extranjeras, no podrán ser objeto de intervención parcial de la Censura, pudiendo sólo

prohibirse su representación en el caso extraordinario de que algún superior motivo político lo aconsejase.

e) .– Para las obras que toquen cuestiones religiosas o que aborden a fondo problemas morales propugnando la solución de ellos se solicitará el dictamen de la Censura eclesiástica.

f) .– En general se tenderá a la Censura global de las obras autorizándolas o prohibiéndolas [...]

g) .– El fallo de la Censura de Madrid será válido para toda España, no pudiendo ninguna autoridad provincial o municipal proceder en contra de él. (AGA 21/0646)

Henceforth, theatre censorship shall be governed by the following principles:

a) With regard to moral matters, care must be taken to identify pernicious tendencies underlying a play, which if present should result in prohibition of the production.

b) On the other hand, when the overall moral to be derived from a play is exemplary, censorship should not insist on suppressing particular details that amount to no more than what would generally be recognised as common failings in society and human existence.

c) Works characterised by vulgar, coarse and indecent ambiance and dialogue shall be classed as pernicious, even if the subject matter is entirely innocuous.

d) Classic works, whether Spanish or foreign, shall not be subject to piecemeal censorship, and performances of them should only be banned in exceptional cases if justified by serious political considerations.

e) In the case of plays touching on religious questions or proposing solutions to profound moral dilemmas, the views of the ecclesiastical censors shall be sought.

f) In general, works should be censored in the round and either approved or prohibited [...]

g) Decisions taken by the Censorship Office in Madrid apply nationwide and may not be countermanded by any provincial or municipal authority.

The crucial procedural elements consolidated here are, first, the insistence on the primacy of central government authority in censorship, and second, the embedding of ecclesiastical involvement in the apparatus. There is evidence of the appointment of religious censors as members of the film censorship team in February 1943: the Bishop of Madrid-Alcalá nominated one representative

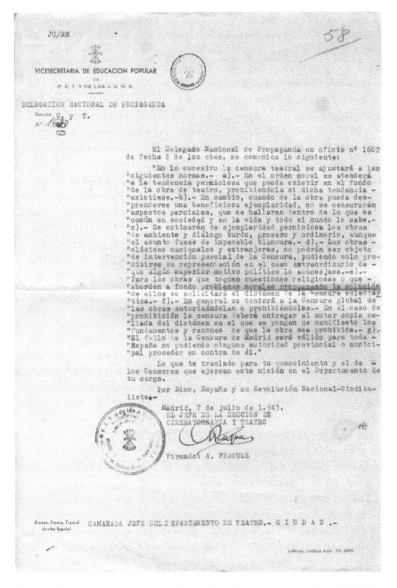

Figure 5: Letter setting out criteria for theatre censorship (1943)

to the Junta Nacional Superior de Censura Cinematográfica and another to the Comisión Nacional de Censura Cinematográfica (AGA 21/0646). We have not come across specific evidence of a similar provision for theatre, but religious censors must have been appointed to the Departmento de Teatro at some point in 1943. By 1944, Constancio de Aldeaseca, a Capuchin friar, was one of the regular readers, joined in 1944 or 1945 by Mauricio de Begoña, also a Capuchin and a poet, essayist and film critic. The convention that the ecclesiastical censors must be consulted on religious or moral issues was generally adhered to, though this could be a very broad category, overlapping with social or political issues and taking in blasphemous language, the representation of the Church and clergy, references to sexual relations, or anything seen as undermining Catholic family values.

Religious organisations had for some time been issuing guides to the moral acceptability of films and plays, such as the one published monthly by the magazine *El Perpetuo Socorro*, which classified them by colour: white for 'acceptable for all audiences'; blue for 'with flaws that can be corrected'; pink for 'only for educated persons'; red for 'dangerous even for educated persons', and the word *No* indicating 'pernicious for all' (García Ruiz 1997: 129).[11] However, the regime had clearly established the primacy of state censorship. The Church was given considerable influence in the system but its representatives were generally careful to remain within their remit. Secular censors would sometimes explicitly refrain from passing judgement on religious and moral elements of scripts, referring them to their ecclesiastical colleagues, who in turn would often refer clearly political matters to the non-religious censors or to 'la Superioridad' (higher authorities, that is, the Delegado Nacional in this period and the Director General in later periods).

The revised criteria and reformed procedures were reflected in the format of a new model for *informes* ('reports') to be completed by censors, introduced in 1943. Censors were now expected to produce a more extensive report and make more specific recommendations with regard to authorisation and the nature of cuts or emendations required. The ambiguous category of 'valor documental' in the previous model was replaced with a question about theatrical qualities, and the increased emphasis on morality and religion was signalled by the addition of an invitation to comment specifically on religious aspects. Censors were asked to complete the following sections:

Breve exposición del argumento:
Tesis:
Valor puramente literario:
[p. 2] Valor teatral:
Matiz político:
Matiz religioso:
Juicio general que merece al censor:
Juicio que merece al censor respecto a la posibilidad de su representación:
Tachaduras páginas:
Correcciones páginas:
[p. 3] Caso de que la obra, tal como se presenta a la censura, no se la considere apta para su representación y se aprecie en ella algunos valores, indique el censor si con algunas modificaciones se podría tornar representable:
En qué lugares de la obra habrían de introducirse esas enmiendas y en qué sentido?
Alguna otra observación que el censor considere pertinente: (AGA 205/39)

Summary of the plot:
The play's message:
Purely literary value:
Theatrical value:
Political implications:
Religious implications:
Overall assessment by the Censor:
The Censor's judgement on whether the work should be licensed for performance:
Deletions on pages:
Corrections on pages:
If the work is not considered suitable for performance in the form in which it has been submitted for censorship but some value can be found in it, the censor is asked to indicate whether it may be made performable with certain modifications:
In which parts of the text should such emendations be effected and in what way?
Any other remarks considered relevant by the censor.

Plot summaries provided by censors were often perfunctory but in some cases they can be very revealing, especially when different readers interpreted the same play in different ways. Cuts were marked, usually in red or blue pencil, on a copy of the script, to be confirmed once the definitive verdict was issued. The last three questions on the form were frequently left blank: censors did not often have the time or the inclination to spell out in detail how a play might be made acceptable.

All these developments in 1943 made this phase in the evolution of censorship a particularly draconian and damaging one. The delays caused serious disruption to theatre companies, and a relatively high proportion of applications were rejected. A memo of 22 November 1943 lists twenty-four applications dealt with in the previous week, nine of which were plays approved before March 1942, now being re-censored. Seven productions were prohibited (29 per cent), four authorised with cuts or alterations (17 per cent), and thirteen authorised without amendment (54 per cent) (AGA 21/0646). This is more or less consistent with archival evidence cited by Emeterio Díez indicating that 799 works were processed in the whole of 1943, of which 191 (24 per cent) were prohibited, 139 (17 per cent) were approved with cuts or changes, and 330 (59 per cent) were approved without changes (2008: 321). Our concluding chapter will offer a tentative estimate of the proportion of plays banned during the whole period from 1939 to 1978, which comes to no more than 8 per cent, indicating that censorship in 1943 was particularly harsh as well as slow.

By the end of 1944, the apparatus was functioning reasonably efficiently, with an expanded *cuerpo de lectores* ('team of readers'). In addition to the two religious censors, the new members were Luis Ortiz Muñoz (brother of Francisco, a journalist and civil servant in the Ministry of Education who would become Subsecretario de Educación Popular in 1946), Virgilio Hernández Rivadulla (journalist, sports presenter and civil servant) and E. Romeu (about whom no sources give any information).[12] The secretary of the Sección de Cinematografía y Teatro, José María Ortiz Martínez, was also acting as a reader when necessary. The structure would soon be affected, however, by wider political changes in Spain and beyond.

Defending Spain's truth: censorship as part of 'national education' (1945–51)

As the war in Europe turned against the Axis powers, Franco's regime had begun to distance itself from them, abandoning some of the trappings of totalitarianism and limiting the influence of the Falange. In July 1945, Franco formed a new government, dismissing José Luis Arrese from the post of Secretario General del Movimiento. A decree of 27 July transferred all the press and propaganda functions of the Vicesecretaría de Educación Popular to the Ministerio de Educación Nacional, on the grounds of their importance to 'la formación espiritual y cultural de los ciudadanos' ('the spiritual and cultural education of the population') (BOE 1945a). The new Subsecretaría de Educación Popular retained the structure and most of the personnel of the old Vicesecretaría until January 1946, when Arias-Salgado was replaced by Luis Ortiz Muñoz as Subsecretario de Educación Popular, and responsibility for theatre and cinema was separated from Propaganda and vested in a new Dirección General de Cinematografía y Teatro. The Director General was Gabriel García Espina, a journalist who had been working as head of the press department in the education ministry and as a theatre critic (ABC 1946a: 8). Theatre now gained the status of a Sección, headed by José María Ortiz Martínez.[13]

Ortiz Muñoz was very different from the Falange propagandists. A journalist and teacher of Greek, he had been Director of the elite Madrid school Instituto Ramiro de Maeztu since 1939, had served as Director General of Secondary and Higher Education and, like his boss Ibáñez Martín, was an influential member of the ACNP (ABC 1946a: 7). This background made him no less committed to the principle that culture should serve the state and needed to be tightly policed. On taking up his post on 15 January 1946 he expressed a determination to defend the regime's 'truth' in the face of pressures from liberalising forces outside Spain:

La Prensa, el cine, la radio, la propaganda no son más que un instrumento que pone el régimen en nuestras manos para defender en esta hora amarga y difícil la verdad de España. Todo el mundo habla y piensa de la libertad. Lo único que nos guiará en nuestro trabajo es la verdad que nos hace libres, la verdad de España. No tenemos otra misión. Que nadie espere más de nosotros. Venimos a servir incondicionalmente al Caudillo y a la verdad de España. (ABC 1946b)

The Press, the cinema, radio and propaganda are nothing more than an instrument placed in our hands by the regime to defend the truth of Spain at this bitter and difficult time. Everywhere people are talking and thinking about liberty. The only thing that will guide us in our work is the truth that makes us free, the truth of Spain. We have no other mission, and no one should expect more of us. We are here to offer unconditional service to the *Caudillo* and to Spain's truth.[14]

The move to Educación Nacional did not result in major changes to the structure of the censorship office or its procedures. Existing readers were retained except for Romeu and Reyna, and several new censors were taken on between 1945 and 1949: Francisco de Narbona González (journalist, director of several Falange newspapers), Emilio Morales de Acevedo (theatre critic for *Arriba* and *Alcázar*, and author of a *zarzuela* and plays for children), Adolfo Carril (a civil servant and scriptwriter for documentary films on art and architecture), Manuel Díez Crespo (poet, editor of the Falange newspaper *FE* during the war and theatre critic for *Arriba*) and Andrés Avelino Esteban Romero (Catholic priest, journalist and author of historical and religious books). Between 1946 and 1949, a number of other people acted as occasional readers for the theatre department: the Falangist José María Conde-Salazar, the *zarzuela* librettist Rafael Fernández-Shaw, the Falangist lawyer Jesús Díaz de la Espina, the technical designer Fermín del Amo y Gilí, the painter Juan Esplandiú Peña, José Luis García Velasco, Francisco Fernández y González and Francisco Alcocer Bárdena (Muñoz Cáliz 2006a, vol. 1: LV–LVI.)

One important policy change took place during this period: the removal of the prohibition of performances in languages of Spain other than Castilian, which had been in force since the end of the civil war. A gradual increase in official tolerance towards cultural production in Catalan, Galician and Basque was one of the products of the move away from totalitarianism after the end of World War II, though any hint of political separatism was still taboo. The blanket ban had had a particularly severe effect on Barcelona, the second most important centre of theatrical activity in Spain after Madrid. The combination of the move of censorship to Educación Nacional and the appointment in August 1945 of Bartolomé Barba Hernández as Civil Governor of Barcelona led to the first authorisations of plays in Catalan in May 1946. Although this made a significant difference to the cultural landscape in Catalonia (discussed in Chapter 4), the regime – and the Madrid-dominated theatre industry – continued to impose a range of constraints on Catalan theatre.[15]

The enforcement across the country of censorship decisions taken in Madrid depended upon the effectiveness of the provincial delegations in ensuring that no performances took place without authorisation and that cuts and other conditions specified on censorship certificates were implemented on stage. The creation in January 1948 of a network of Servicios de Inspección de Espectáculos Públicos ('Inspection Services for Public Entertainments') was designed to make enforcement of film and theatre censorship outside Madrid more reliable. A Servicio de Inspección was set up in each provincial delegation of Educación Popular, reporting to the Dirección General. The new corps of inspectors had a much clearer line of accountability and were given professional training.

The other significant structural change in the Educación Nacional period was the creation of the Consejo Superior del Teatro (CST – 'National Theatre Council') in December 1946. Aspects of the new council's role were supportive of the creative process – awarding prizes, subsidies and grants for training – but it was also intended to be part of the censorship apparatus, providing a court of appeal. Its functions included 'dictaminar y resolver aquellas obras que por entrañar especiales dificultades de censura o por su elevado valor literario, les sean sometidas a su estudio por la Dirección General' ('adjudicating in cases of plays referred to the Council because they pose exceptional difficulties for the censorship process or because they are of especially high literary value'), as well as ruling on appeals submitted by applicants against prohibitions or other restrictions (BOE 1947a).

The link with censorship was cemented by the CST's composition, which included two of the readers employed by the Sección de Teatro and a representative of the Church, whose opinion 'será especialmente digno de respeto en las cuestiones morales, siendo dirimente en aquellos casos graves de moral en los que expresamente haga constar su veto' ('shall be accorded particular respect with regard to questions of morality, and shall be decisive in cases involving serious moral issues on which he expressly asserts his power of veto') (BOE 1947a). The members appointed in December 1946 included the censors Mauricio de Begoña and Emilio Morales de Acevedo, as well as David Jato Miranda (President of the Sindicato Nacional del Espectáculo and former Delegado Nacional de Propaganda) and Luis Escobar (former reluctant censor, now artistic director of the Teatro María Guerrero) (BOE 1947b).

The composition of the CST was modified and slightly expanded in November 1951 so that all the places were allocated to representatives of particular institutions or professions, now including only one member of the *cuerpo de lectores*. Surprisingly, no Church representative was stipulated, though that omission seems to have been an oversight, since an order modifying the membership again in November 1956 – now including a religious adviser – was presented as a 'rectification' of the 1951 law (BOE 1956a). The censorship role prescribed by the 1946 order is not specified in the 1951 revision, which merely refers vaguely to advising on plays referred to it by the Directorate General (BOE 1951b). This function was largely to do with evaluating works submitted for prizes and festivals or for staging by the two national theatres, but it also continued to include adjudicating on appeals against censorship decisions, a task carried out by the CST's Comisión Permanente de Lectura ('Permanent Reading Commission') until the system was reformed in 1963. The censor Bartolomé Mostaza, appointed to the CST in 1951, was a member of this commission, along with González Ruiz and the writer Gonzalo Torrente Ballester.

The two dimensions of the work of the Sección de Teatro – supporting and policing theatrical activity – were therefore inextricably intertwined. The aesthetic evaluation of scripts for subsidies, prizes or performance in state-run theatres was always cross-checked with the censorship process and with security records on the individuals involved in productions, and there was always an overlap of personnel. For example, the jury for a national competition for new dramatists in 1959 included Nicolás González Ruiz and one of the regular religious censors, Andrés Avelino Esteban Romero (BOE 1959a). A number of critics, playwrights and directors who were not officially employed as censors were drawn into the censorship process by their involvement in the CST.

Reform and *apertura*: censorship as part of 'information' (1951–76)

In 1951, the government decided that the remit of the Ministerio de Educación Nacional had become too wide. A decree of July 1951 created the MIT, comprising the former Subsecretaría de Educación Popular – responsible for the press, theatre, cinema and radio – together with the Dirección General de Turismo, transferred from the Ministerio de la Gobernación (BOE 1951a). Theatre censorship remained within this ministry until the end of the dictatorship. The tourism industry was still in its infancy at that time, but there was a realisation that this department's business would have more to do with promotion, brand management and public relations than the traditional Gobernación functions of security, public order and territorial administration. Theatre censorship too would eventually come to be seen increasingly in terms of the management of information and public opinion, rather than as a fascist-style instrument of propaganda or an enforcer of Catholic moral education.

The change of ministry brought the return of Gabriel Arias-Salgado, who was Ministro de Información y Turismo from July 1951 to July 1962. During his tenure there were several Directores Generales de Cinematografía y Teatro: José María García Escudero (1951–2), Joaquín Argamasilla (1952–5), Manuel Torres López (1955–6), José Muñoz Fontán (1956–61) and Jesús Suevos Fernández (1961–2). José María Ortiz remained as head of la Sección de Teatro and most of the *cuerpo de lectores* continued in post, joined later in the 1950s by two new members: José María Cano Lechuga (lawyer and theatre critic, Secretario General de Cinematografía y Teatro from 1955) and Pío García Escudero (engineer and Director General of Technical Education).

The transfer of censorship from Educación to the MIT did not diminish the influence of the Church and the ACNP. Arias-Salgado was a fervent advocate of *nacionalcatolicismo* (the integration of authoritarian nationalism with traditionalist Catholicism) and a religious view of the duty of the Christian state to exercise firm control over cultural production in order to safeguard the 'truth' and protect the public from moral and spiritual threats. His most famous claim was that 'gracias a la censura previa se salvan ahora más almas en España' ('thanks to prior censorship more souls are now being saved in Spain') (cited in Moradiellos 2000: 119). He expressed the doctrine more soberly in a speech of December 1954:

> La libertad de divulgación, pues, está también condicionada por el servicio y la sumisión a la verdad. Toda la libertad para la verdad; ninguna libertad para el error [. . .] Libertad de divulgación, por lo tanto, para lo bueno y verdadero; ninguna libertad para el error y el mal. (Arias-Salgado 1960: 13)

Freedom of expression, then, is also conditioned by service and submission to the truth. Complete freedom for the truth; no freedom for error [. . .] Consequently, freedom of expression should only be granted for what is good and true; no freedom for error and evil.

In the meantime, the Church had been centralising and formalising the various efforts made by Catholic organisations to supplement official film and theatre censorship with their own moral and religious warnings. In 1950 it set up the Oficina Nacional Permanente de Vigilancia de Espectáculos ('Permanent National Office for the Supervision of Cinema and Theatre'). An episcopal commission, in consultation with Acción Católica, had drawn up a new set of *Instrucciones y Normas para la censura moral de espectáculos* ('Instructions and Guidelines for the Moral Censorship of Cinema and Theatre'), replacing the earlier colour-coding system. It prescribed the following categories for theatre, to be applied by the national Oficina de Vigilancia and by diocesan censorship committees outside Madrid: 1 'Infantil, sin reparos' ('suitable for children under fourteen, posing no moral problems'); 1-R 'Infantil, con reparos' ('suitable for children under fourteen but with minor reservations'); 2 'Jóvenes' ('suitable for young people between the ages of fourteen and twenty'); 3 'Mayores' ('for spectators aged twenty-one and over'); 3-R 'Mayores con reparos' ('for spectators aged twenty-one and over, with "a solid moral education"'); and 4 'Gravemente peligrosa' ('gravely dangerous') (Comisión Episcopal de Ortodoxia y Moralidad 1950: 2–3).

The commission formulated a detailed scale of criteria for each of the categories. Films and plays in category 1 could not feature vices or immoral characters; violent or frightening scenes; vampires, robberies or duels; violent death, suicide or murder; or scenes of sensuality. Representations of criminality, immorality, sexuality or violence could be tolerated to some extent in categories 2 and 3, as long as wrongdoing was always seen to be condemned or punished. Category 3 specified that main characters must not be involved in scenes of sexual perversion, prostitution or rape, and ruled out provocative costumes and suggestive dialogue. *Revistas* could be tolerated in this category, 'siempre que se limiten a ligereza de ropa, sin reiterada intención sensual en gestos o ademanes' ('as long as they go no further than skimpiness of clothing, without insistence on sensual intentions in gestures, movements or postures'). Category 4 was for cases in which the problems identified in the other categories reached a level of 'violencia, crudeza o desenfreno' ('violence, crudity or wantonness'). It is only in this category that anticlericalism and the irreverent representation of religion and the clergy are specified.

While the main emphasis in the criteria was on morality and Catholic doctrine, political criteria were blended into categories 2, 3 and 4 in a way characteristic of National-Catholicism: in category 2, 'cualquier idea, tendencia o frase de carácter antipatriótico') ('any idea, tendency or phrase of an antipatriotic character'); in 3, 'ambientes o actos contrarios a la Patria o sus instituciones fundamentales' ('settings or actions contrary to the Fatherland or its fundamental institutions'); and in 4, 'antipatriotismo declarado' ('explicit anti-patriotism') (Comisión Episcopal de Ortodoxia y Moralidad 1950: 4–5). As in the previous period, however, it was made clear that these recommendations were advisory, for the guidance of the public and the clergy. Ecclesiastical representatives could certainly play a decisive role in official censorship, sometimes explicitly applying the criteria set out above, and bishops would often lobby ministers or directors general about plays, films and books of which they disapproved, but clear demarcation lines were maintained. Ultimately, censorship decisions were taken by political appointees.

By the end of the 1950s, hairline cracks were beginning to appear in the previously monolithic edifice of the partnership between Church and state. The support of the ecclesiastical hierarchy, Catholic organisations and parish priests for the regime was no longer unconditional. The hardship created by the introduction of economic reforms from 1957 prompted calls for the Church to do more to support the working class and advocate social justice (Gómez Pérez 1986: 81). For its part, the state was beginning to be more prepared to subordinate the Church's concerns to other political priorities. The case study at the end of this chapter will show evidence from 1961 of a religious censor being persuaded by officials to set aside his moral objections to a play in favour of a more pragmatic tactical assessment of the pros and cons of banning a work by a well-known dramatist.

The most important structural change to the censorship system made in the early years of the MIT phase was the construction of a special regime for the regulation of non-commercial theatre.

The 1950s saw significant growth in the activity of student theatre groups, amateur companies and theatre clubs. The Teatro Nacional de Cámara y Ensayo (National Studio Theatre) was created in 1954 with the aim of stimulating theatrical activity outside the official structure of the two national theatres.[16] This organisation was charged with staging work by Spanish and foreign playwrights unlikely to be taken on by the private sector; awarding prizes for plays by new Spanish authors and staging the selected works; and organising festivals as training grounds for writers, directors and performers (BOE 1954a). In principle, this was a valuable initiative. However, it was underfunded and was also intended as a way of keeping the new wave of theatremaking under state supervision. The artistic director was appointed by the Dirección General, collaborators were vetted by the security services, the evaluation of scripts was always cross-checked with the censorship process, and censors served on juries for prizes.

A law of 1955 set up a scheme that offered other non-commercial or non-professional groups and theatre clubs public subsidies, and at the same time subjected them to new requirements for registration with the Dirección General, including providing lists of members and details of sources of funding. The scope of their activities was restricted by a stipulation that their productions should normally take place in their own premises, with tickets sold only to club members. Permission to perform in other venues could be obtained, but tickets were to be sold only through the club, not at a box office open to the general public (BOE 1955b). Groups needed to meet these requirements both in order to apply for subsidies and to obtain censorship certificates for their productions.[17] Censors already had the option of restricting authorisations to *cámara* (as opposed to *comercial*), but the new legal structure consolidated this distinction and made it an important part of the censorship apparatus from now on. The restrictions on venues and ticket sales were combined with a rule that *cámara* productions would normally be licensed for a single performance; permission needed to be sought for further performances. The assumption that audiences under these conditions would be small and relatively well educated allowed more challenging work to be approved. Sometimes this was presented as an aesthetic judgement, reserving experimental, unconventional theatre for those who were sophisticated enough to appreciate it, but authorisation for *cámara* only was also frequently used for plays that posed moral or political problems.

Arias-Salgado's term of office as minister saw two other minor adjustments to the operation of censorship. In November 1954, the minimum age threshold for films and plays not considered suitable for children, which had varied between fourteen and sixteen years, was set at sixteen. It was confirmed that the classification – either 'Apto para todos los públicos' ('Suitable for all audiences') or 'Autorizado para mayores de dieciséis años' ('Authorised for spectators over the age of sixteen') – must be displayed outside the theatre, and that the Inspection Service would check that it was being enforced (BOE 1954b: 8228). Then in February 1955, revised arrangements for the licensing of *revistas* and similar shows were introduced. The legislation reaffirmed the key requirement that the licensing of *revistas* must pay attention not only to the book but also the score, costumes and staging. Applications for approval needed to include the music and lyrics of songs, as well as sketches of set designs and costumes. The conditions on the back of censorship certificates for *revistas* warned that changes to the approved script, costumes or sets were forbidden and also that authorisation of all aspects of staging was subject to confirmation by the Delegado Provincial, for which purpose a formal inspection of the dress rehearsal (*visado del ensayo general*) was mandatory – and could be followed up with inspections of performances during the show's run. Whereas permission was previously given for performances in specific locations, licences issued from now on would be valid for any town or city with a population of at least 40,000, but subject in each place to the approval of the Delegado Provincial, who could take into account local sensitivities. Furthermore, Delegados Provinciales were empowered to issue formal warnings (*apercibimientos*) when censorship conditions were flouted during the run of a *revista*; a third warning upheld by the Dirección General would automatically result in the withdrawal of a production's licence (BOE 1955a).

Two further elements of tightening-up of the regulations for *revistas* were added at this time. First, the minimum age threshold was raised to eighteen years, and second, a curious new restriction was placed on costume design. Although not specified in the legislation, the following rule is included in the conditions on the back of authorisation certificates (*guías de censura*) used from 1955: 'No se autorizará en ninguna escena o situación hablada –es decir, sin partitura musical correspondiente a número coreográfico– la exhibición de trajes que no se ajusten totalmente a las características de las llamadas de calle o sociedad' ('In spoken scenes or situations, that is, those without a musical score corresponding to a choreographed routine, costumes will not be approved unless they conform entirely to the characteristics of normal everyday dress') (Censorship certificate dated 18 February 1956 in AGA 25/44). Exotic or mildly titillating costumes (usually for female performers) could be tolerated as part of the stylisation expected of musical numbers, while spoken dialogue needed to be treated as drama, with characters who should be dressed realistically and decorously.

This desire to draw a clear line between musical and spoken content was part of a broader tendency in the censorship system to reinforce generic conventions and regulate the distribution of different kinds of audiences. It was noted earlier in this chapter that two different departments of the Delegación Nacional de Propaganda were responsible between 1941 and 1945 for the censorship of theatre and music. While *revistas* (essentially, comedies with songs and choreography) came under Teatro, entertainments that consisted entirely or almost entirely of music and song, including concerts, variety shows and cabaret-type acts, were assigned to Educación Musical. This demarcation was carried over into the Educación Nacional period, but responsibility for the promotion, supervision and censorship of music was not transferred to the MIT in 1951, remaining in Educación under the Dirección General de Bellas Artes (Fine Arts). The February 1955 law confirmed that the Dirección General de Cinematografía y Teatro was responsible for *revistas* and 'espectáculos arrevistados' (a vague label covering a range of entertainments similar to *revistas*), but not for musicals and operettas, including *zarzuelas* (BOE 1955a).

By the early 1960s, the pace of political, economic and social change in Spain was accelerating. Economic 'stabilisation' programmes introduced in the late 1950s by a new cohort of technocratic ministers – most of them associated with the Catholic organisation Opus Dei – had initially resulted in widespread hardship and unemployment. However, modernisation of the economy, together with foreign investment, expanding tourism and earnings sent home by emigrant workers in other parts of Europe, did eventually lead to rapid growth, which encouraged far-reaching social and cultural change in the 1960s and 1970s:

> Mass emigration, both within Spain and beyond, resulted in an exodus from the countryside, that, along with large-scale foreign and domestic investment, transformed rural and urban societies alike not only in class terms but also in terms of their values, mentalities and culture [. . .] The protests of students, intellectuals, progressive clergy, and workers [. . .] did much to erode the legitimacy of the dictatorship while fostering a collective conviction that change was inevitable. Still, the opposition was too weak and too divided to actually overthrow the dictatorship, though a broader, if more inchoate, social and cultural resistance to the regime grew steadily throughout these years. (Townson 2007: 4)

Cultural production was an important part of that growing climate of resistance. Writers, dramatists, filmmakers, visual artists and musicians were becoming increasingly willing to push against the moral, political and aesthetic boundaries that the regime was now struggling to keep in place. Catholic moral values were being eroded by greater social mobility and increased contact with other, more permissive cultures. Public acceptance of the regime's policies was being undermined by dissatisfaction with social conditions and growing popular mobilisation. The challenging of conservative artistic assumptions was boosted both by a reclaiming of Spain's own early twentieth-century avant-garde and by increased contact with foreign innovations. Certain kinds of live performance, particularly concerts by singer-songwriters and experimental productions by the independent theatre movement that developed from the mid-1960s, became closely associated with the burgeoning counterculture of dissidence: 'El vanguardismo, en esta situación, se validaba por sí mismo, pues venía acompañado de una aureola de contestación, de rechazo de la cultura oficial e impuesta' ('Avant-gardism, in these circumstances, tended to self-validate, as it generated around itself a halo of dissidence and of rejection of the official, imposed culture') (Trancón 2006: 44–5).

Some of the protests were specifically directed against censorship and were not voiced exclusively by dissident artists. A public letter addressed in 1960 to the Ministers of Educación Nacional and Información y Turismo was signed by 227 prominent writers, directors, critics, publishers and painters, including some who were (or had been) very close to the regime. The most surprising signatory was the monarchist poet and playwright José María Pemán, whose name headed the list. Also included on the list were individuals who were, had been or would become theatre censors: Juan Emilio Aragonés, Nicolás González Ruiz, Dionisio Ridruejo and Luis Tejedor. The letter is politely expressed but makes telling points about the inconsistency and arbitrariness of censorship, and its damaging impact on creativity and on Spain's international reputation. Assuming that a call for the total abolition of prior censorship would be unrealistic, the letter ends up making a disappointingly tentative demand for the right of appeal against censorship decisions to be strengthened and for the names of censors to be made public (Pemán *et al.* 1960: 17). Moderate as this protest was, it nevertheless constituted an important gesture of rejection that would be followed by many others during the 1960s and 1970s.

The regime's response to resistance was variable. On the one hand, it was in the process of redefining itself as the guarantor of peace and prosperity, a staunch ally of the Western powers against communism, and a uniquely Spanish compromise between dictatorship and democracy, willing to allow limited economic and social change as long as it did not threaten the political and moral foundations. On the other hand, Franco himself and influential members of the military and ecclesiastical hierarchies remained deeply reactionary and liable to panic over the pace of change. The period between the mid-1960s and the end of the dictatorship saw repeated swings from *apertura* ('openness') to authoritarian backlash; from calculations based on a perceived need for a political safety valve and sensitivity to international criticism right over to an obdurate 'bunker' mentality. These tensions can be seen reflected in the censorship process. The examples analysed in subsequent chapters show some of the censors becoming more calculating, increasingly arguing that banning high-profile plays was counterproductive, or making more frequent use of authorisation exclusively for *cámara* as a way of deflecting accusations of stifling innovation. However, there is also ample evidence of their alarm at the rising incidence of morally and politically challenging material and of a determination to hold the line against the tide of change. The most interesting files from the 1960s and 1970s contain multiple reports by censors who disagreed surprisingly starkly over interpretation, tactics and risk assessment.

The most prominent advocate of cautious reform and limited liberalisation was Manuel Fraga Iribarne, who replaced Arias-Salgado as Ministro de Información y Turismo in July 1962. Born in 1922, Fraga represented the second generation of the regime. Franco's governments of 1957–62 and 1962–5 consisted mostly of an old guard of men born between 1889 and 1908, many of whom had played prominent roles in the civil war. The 1962 government was the first to include men too young to have been combatants (Fraga and the technocrat Gregorio López-Bravo). With the appointment of Fraga, the yoking together of *información* and *turismo* in the same ministry made complete sense: both dimensions of the job were about public relations and image management, creating an impression of modernity and openness as a way of deflecting criticism without significantly changing the political structures, and without causing excessive shocks to the armed forces and the Church hierarchy (Pavlović 2011: 14). Censorship played a key role in this project, accepting that political, social and cultural change was unstoppable but attempting to slow it down; making limited concessions but striving to ensure that transgressions were not blatant.

It should not be forgotten that the sphere of *información* still had a darker, more authoritarian dimension. The *Responsabilidades Políticas* process had been largely wound up in 1945, but the regime continued to keep citizens under close surveillance. Not long after Fraga took over the ministry, he reinforced its role in coordinating political intelligence-gathering by setting up the Oficina de Enlace (Liaison Office) in November 1962. As well as receiving information from other government departments, it was charged specifically with investigating communism and other subversive activities (BOE 1962: 17334). This body (also known as the Gabinete de Enlace or Gabinete de Estudios) collected information on the political and private lives of a wide range of individuals living and dead: cultural figures, intellectuals, politicians, clergy and trade unionists. A number of people from the world of theatre feature among the 2,470 personal files in the AGA, including the playwrights Rafael Alberti, Federico García Lorca, Antonio Buero Vallejo, Manuel de Pedrolo, Alfonso Sastre, Alfonso Paso, Carlos Muñiz, Lauro Olmo and even José María Pemán. There are files on actors and directors including José Luis Alonso, Núria Espert and Maria Aurèlia Capmany, and on members of the Junta de

Censura Teatral and senior MIT officials – Federico Muelas, Gabriel Elorriaga, Florentino Soria and Mario Antolín Paz. Even Fraga himself was investigated, along with members of the royal family, Luis Carrero Blanco, Ramón Serrano Suñer and Franco's sister Pilar.[18]

There is little concrete evidence of these records having a direct effect on censorship decisions, but they were certainly available to the committees and officials considering applications for authorisation of productions and licensing of companies, as well as nominations for prizes and programming in state-run theatres. The file relating to one of the most controversial cases of the 1960s, the banning of Buero's *La doble historia del doctor Valmy* (*The Double Case History of Dr Valmy*) in 1964, contains documentary evidence of consultation with the Gabinete de Enlace, which provided details of Buero's work for the Republicans during the civil war and his membership of the Communist Party (AGA 147/64).[19] In general, the knowledge that writers, directors and performers were all subject to surveillance by the state was a powerful component of the intimidatory environment in which theatremakers still had to operate, up to the end of the dictatorship and beyond. Even relatively obscure amateur or semi-professional theatre groups in the provinces were regularly spied on by the police. Mayca Estévez, a member of the Teatro Popular Keyzán in Vigo between 1968 and 1971, remembers *grises* (armed police nicknamed for their grey uniforms) frequently turning up before performances to question members of the cast, and following them through the streets afterwards (Estévez 2018).

Fraga's key collaborator in the project of cultural *apertura* was José María García Escudero, who had served as a censor in the early 1940s and had briefly been Director General de Cinematografía y Teatro in 1951–2, occupying the post again between 1962 and 1967. His account of the period, written as a diary and published during the transition, depicts a long-running battle to nurture innovative film and theatre in the face of scandalised protests about immorality from various reactionary forces in the regime, the Church and wider society. His claim to be a champion of liberalisation and his dismissive attitude towards traditionalist Catholic moral values are reminiscent of the brief period at the end of the civil war in which Escobar and Ridruejo attempted to get away with theatre censorship that was relatively light-touch and secular.[20] García Escudero characterises his approach as a kind of *posibilismo* – making compromises to achieve as much as one can under the prevailing circumstances – comparable to that adopted by many dramatists and filmmakers (as discussed in Chapter 5). The game needed to be played, he argues, 'porque de otra manera tantas obras, tantos nombres, no habrían llegado a nacer' ('because otherwise so many works, so many names, would never have emerged') (1978: 20). The rhetoric is strikingly different from earlier pronouncements about defending absolute truths and protecting the public from contamination.

The main battleground was the cinema, and it is here that García Escudero claims to have had the most impact. He quotes with apparent pride the ditty that circulated in 1963–4:

Con Arias Salgado
todo tapado;
con Fraga,
hasta la braga. (García Escudero 1978a: 128)

With Arias Salgado, everything under wraps; with Fraga, everything off down to the knickers.

Evidence of *apertura* is less abundant with reference to the theatre, but García Escudero offers some telling examples: his resentment at Alfonso Sastre's refusal to give him credit for the lifting of the ban on *Escuadra hacia la muerte* (*Condemned Squad*); his amusement at Admiral Carrero Blanco (Minister of the President's office) storming out of a performance of Ionesco's *Exit the King* in 1964; complaints from the Archbishop of Madrid-Alcalá about an alleged 'ola de pornografía' ('wave of pornography') in Madrid theatres in 1966 (1978: 230); and his satisfaction at clearing the way for a production of Lorca's *Mariana Pineda* in 1967. In response to an accusation from the Sociedad de Autores ('Society of Authors') in 1964 that *apertura* was already being reversed, García Escudero gives figures for the number of works by Spanish playwrights prohibited: fourteen in 1961, nine in 1962 (3.6 per cent of a total of 249), eleven in 1963 (5.5 per cent of a total of 202) and six so far in 1964 (2.9 per cent of a total of 208) (1978: 142 and 190). This rate of prohibition is certainly much lower than that recorded in the 1940s, at a time when fewer playwrights and companies were presenting challenging material, but writers and theatremakers were now much more inclined to protest at cuts and bans.

García Escudero's own account acknowledges, however, that there were limits to his department's tolerance. He notes that, although there were landmark productions by Brecht, Sartre and Weiss, the proportion of works by foreign authors banned in this period (around 14 per cent) was significantly higher than for Spanish authors (1978: 190). An internal report on censorship commissioned by García Escudero in 1964 aimed to defend the Dirección General against accusations of excessive leniency, especially those levelled by the Church. It notes, for example, that while fifteen plays authorised in 1961 had been classified as 'gravely dangerous' by the Church's own censors, in 1963 there were only seven such cases (MIT 1964: 48). It also stresses that *revistas* were being treated more severely than before, and makes a point of arguing that censorship in Spain was still much more restrictive than in other parts of western Europe. The report provides interesting statistical detail for the two years from June 1962 to June 1964: of the total of 614 plays dealt with, fifty-one (8.3 per cent) were prohibited, 207 (33.7 per cent) were approved with cuts, and 356 (58 per cent) were approved without cuts (1964: 46). It argues that 'la censura debe limitarse a prohibir lo gravemente peligroso' ('censorship should confine itself to prohibiting what is gravely dangerous') and emphasises the key *aperturista* argument that excessively severe censorship can be counterproductive: 'Respecto de ciertas obras crudas pero no inmorales, cuya prohibición las habría aureolado de una peligrosa leyenda, ha bastado su autorización para disipar el mito creado en torno a ellas' ('With regard to certain crude but not immoral works, the banning of which would have given them a dangerously glamorous aura, authorisation has been enough to dispel the myth built up around them') (1964: 8). Our analysis in subsequent chapters provides ample evidence of censorship continuing to restrict theatrical creativity in this period.[21]

As well as attempting to make censorship better attuned to a changing society, Fraga and García Escudero sought to render it more efficient, consistent and transparent. While Ortiz remained as head of the Sección de Teatro, a new Junta de Censura Teatral was created on 16 February 1963, replacing most of the membership.[22] The new team, with a reduced presence of Falangists, was for the first time named in the *Boletín Oficial del Estado* on 26 February (BOE 1963c), though many theatremakers seem to have remained ignorant of who was censoring their work during the 1960s. The membership was also listed in the 1964 report, which stressed that they were not all intellectuals and that the religious members were either nominated by the ecclesiastical hierarchy or – in the case of those nominated by the state – had its full support. It also asserted that most of the lay members were mature family men and professionals, 'seglares de plena confianza, caballeros cristianos cien por cien, hombres de alta cultura y de carrera' ('trustworthy laymen, one hundred per cent Christian gentlemen, men of elevated culture and high professional standing') (MIT 1964: 30).

Mostaza was named as Secretary of the Junta, and as full-time *vocales*, José María Artola Barrenechea (Dominican friar, religious writer), Pedro Barceló Roselló (theatre director, journalist, translator), Sebastián Bautista de la Torre (poet, playwright, journalist), Arcadio Baquero Goyanes (playwright, actor, theatre critic), Jorge Blajot Pena (Jesuit priest, director of the Catholic magazine *Razón y Fe*), Florencio Martínez Ruiz (poet, journalist, literary and theatre critic), Adolfo Prego de Oliver (playwright, theatre critic) and José Luis Vázquez Dodero (journalist, literary and art critic). The playwright Carlos Muñiz served as the representative of the playwrights' professional association, the Sociedad General de Autores (SGAE), but was sacked in October 1963 as a result of signing a public letter to protest at the brutal treatment of striking miners in Asturias (Muñoz Cáliz 2005: 136). Marcelo Arroita-Jáuregui Alonso (poet, actor, film critic) and Víctor Aúz Castro (theatre director, theatre critic, head of the Teatro Nacional de Cámara y Ensayo) were appointed as *vocales circunstanciales* (occasional members).

Muñiz was replaced by Claudio de la Torre, former Artistic Director of the Teatro Nacional María Guerrero, and three other censors were recruited: Florentino Soria Heredia (screenwriter, film critic, Subdirector General de Cinematografía y Teatro), Luis González Fierro (Dominican friar, editor of religious programmes for Televisión Española) and Carlos María Staehlin (theologian, film critic for Catholic magazines). They were joined by Juan Emilio Aragonés (poet, playwright, theatre critic) in 1966, and in 1967 by the first female censors, María Luz Morales (theatre critic, member of a Republican commission on children's theatre in 1938) and María Nieves Sunyer Roig (youth organiser in the Sección Femenina of the Falange). Manuel Díez Crespo (poet, theatre critic, director of the Falange newspaper *FE*), Jesús Cea Buján (priest, religious adviser to national radio and television) and Federico

Muelas (poet, playwright, screenwriter), who had acted as censors in the past, rejoined the board in 1967. Carlos Suevos Fernández (TV director and civil servant) and Antonio Pardo also carried out some censorship duties from 1968. Luis Tejedor Pérez (playwright, screenwriter, librettist of *revistas* and *zarzuelas*) became the SGAE representative in 1968.

The overhaul of the theatre censorship apparatus was consolidated in two key pieces of legislation. An order of 9 February 1963 set out the first public statement of censorship criteria ever issued by the dictatorship. These *normas de censura* were designed primarily for cinema but were intended to be applied to theatrical performances as well. They contained no surprises or significant innovations, being essentially a reformulation of the criteria that had been in use for the previous twenty years. However, the wording to some extent reflects the new, more sophisticated *aperturista* understanding of censorship. The preamble discussed the difficult balance between making rules specific enough to be a useful guide for both censors and theatremakers, but not so specific as to create 'un casuismo que nunca abarcaría todos los casos posibles' ('a casuistical, quibbling approach that could never cover all possible cases') (BOE 1963a: 3929). The first seven *normas* are statements of general principles, recommending a degree of flexibility but assuming that clear-cut distinctions can be made between 'el mal' ('evil, wrongdoing') and 'el bien' ('good'). They advised that each work should be judged as a whole, taking account of genre and style, and prohibited altogether in preference to imposing so many cuts that its nature would be substantially changed; and that wrongdoing or unpleasant material may be presented but must ultimately be condemned and outweighed by a positive moral.

The twelve specific *normas de aplicación* can be divided into two categories: political issues; and questions of morality, religion and propriety. The latter were largely defined by Catholic teachings, forbidding the disrespectful representation of religious beliefs or practices and the justification of suicide, mercy killings, revenge, duelling, divorce, adultery, extra-marital sex, prostitution, abortion, contraception, and 'cuanto atente contra la institución matrimonial y contra la familia' ('anything that constitutes an attack on the institution of marriage and the family') (BOE 1963a: 3930). The representation of homosexuality was to be policed particularly strictly (*Norma* 9-1): '[Se prohibirá] La presentación de las perversiones sexuales como eje de la trama y aun con carácter secundario, a menos que en este último caso esté exigida por el desarrollo de la acción y ésta tenga una clara y predominante consecuencia moral' ('The presentation of sexual perversions as the main focus of the plot [is prohibited], as is their presence as a secondary element, unless required by the development of the action and as long as they are shown to have clear and decisive moral consequences') (1963a: 3930).

Other moral criteria are expressed in very broad terms. *Norma* 10 prohibits images and scenes likely to 'provocar bajas pasiones en el espectador normal y las alusiones hechas de tal manera que resulten más sugerentes que la presentación del hecho mismo' ('arouse base passions in a normal spectator, and references made in a way that makes them more suggestive than the depiction of the action itself') (1963a: 3930). The nature of the 'normal spectator' might have been self-evident to censors ten years earlier (Catholic, middle-class and politically, morally and aesthetically conservative), but the notion was now more contestable than ever and censors' discussions would frequently centre on varying assessments of how different kinds of audiences might respond to controversial material. *Norma* 13 is similarly vague, subjective and outdated, prohibiting 'las expresiones coloquiales y las escenas o planos de carácter íntimo que atenten contra las más elementales normas del buen gusto' ('colloquial expressions and scenes or shots of an intimate nature that flout the most fundamental norms of good taste') (1963a: 3930). For the many theatremakers who were coming to regard assaults on bourgeois norms of good taste as an essential part of their artistic mission, such regulations were more likely to be seen as incitements than warnings, and censors would sometimes conclude that it was less troublesome to allow them to get away with it than to take a hard line.

The political criteria focused on protecting the regime's institutions, National-Catholic ideology and legitimacy. *Norma* 14-2 prohibited 'todo lo que atente de alguna manera contra nuestras instituciones o ceremonias, que el recto orden exige sean tratadas respetuosamente' ('anything that constitutes an attack on our institutions and ceremonies, which must be treated with respect') (1963a: 3930). A requirement that it be made clear to spectators how to distinguish between the behaviour of characters and what they represent is also included in this clause, from which it can be inferred that the main point of concern was the depiction of representatives of those institutions – the political hierarchy, the Church, the armed forces. The question of whether audiences would be likely to see such figures as flawed individuals or metonyms for power or repression was the focus of many debates between censors. *Norma* 16 stipulated that works would be banned if they denied citizens' duty to defend the Fatherland and the state's right to require them to do so, and *Norma* 17 specified the primary institutions and values to be protected:

1°   La Iglesia Católica, su dogma, su moral y su culto.
2°   Los principios fundamentales del Estado, la dignidad nacional y la seguridad interior o exterior del país.
3°   La persona del Jefe del Estado. (1963a: 3930)

1.   The Catholic Church, its doctrine, its moral creed and its liturgy.
2.   The fundamental principles of the State, the dignity of the nation and its internal or external security.
3.   The person of the Head of State.

One criterion that might appear surprising in the light of the regime's history of demonising its enemies, glorifying the racial superiority of Spaniards and condemning all forms of liberalism and socialism, is *norma* 15, forbidding the promotion of 'el odio entre pueblos, razas o clases sociales o [. . .] la división y enfrentamiento, en el orden moral y social, de unos hombres con otros' ('hatred between peoples, races or social classes, or division and opposition in moral and social terms between men') (1963a: 3930). One of the central claims of Francoism, borrowed from the revolutionary rhetoric of the Falange, was that it had superseded class struggle and brought permanent social justice. The idea is summed up in an early piece of labour legislation, which asserts that the *Movimiento* 'borra toda lucha de clases, fundiéndolas en un afán nacional común' ('erases all conflict between classes, fusing them together in a common national cause') (BOE 1939d: 6020). Theatrical representations of class divisions or social inequality could therefore be dismissed as outdated and bad for morale.

The last *norma* (number 19) maintained the tension between a suggestion of pragmatic flexibility and a reminder that firm red lines would be maintained. On the one hand, in the case of works aimed at 'minority' audiences (primarily, members of student or *teatro de cámara* clubs), the criteria were to be interpreted with an appropriate degree of latitude, according to the assumed level of sophistication of such audiences. In contrast, the final criterion was uncompromising and far-reaching: 'Las películas blasfemas, pornográficas y subversivas se prohibirán para cualquier público' ('Blasphemous, pornographic and subversive films shall be prohibited for any audience') (BOE 1963a: 3930). The regulations went some way towards meeting the demand made in 1960 by Pemán and others for greater transparency, and they provided the censorship board with an efficient means of validating its decisions: notifications of the refusal of authorisation would from now on usually cite one or more of the *normas*. Nevertheless, they were not specific enough to give theatremakers greater certainty with regard to what was likely to be permissible, and they remained very much open to interpretation by individual censors.

As well as censorship personnel and criteria, the administrative structure was substantially reformed by Fraga and García Escudero. Local authorisation was now ruled out: the law of 16 February 1963 states firmly that the jurisdiction of the Junta de Censura Teatral was nationwide and absolute: 'No pueden existir otros organismos de carácter oficial con funciones iguales o análogas, ya sean nacionales, regionales, provinciales o locales' ('No other official bodies with the same or similar functions may exist, at a national, regional, provincial or local level') (BOE 1963b: 3931). Clearer procedures were also established: applications would be considered by teams of three censors (*comisiones delegadas*), whose decisions would be ratified by the full Junta, which would also consider any appeals. In exceptional cases, the Director General could suspend the process and refer the decision up to the Minister. This amounted to a formalisation of the long-established practice of *silencio administrativo* ('administrative silence'), to which many censorship applications had fallen victim over the years.[23]

The crucial requirement for approval of the text to be subject to a check by local inspectors on the staging is spelled out in article 11 of this law, which states that an inspection of the dress rehearsal (*visado del ensayo general*) will be carried out when considered necessary by the Junta. In practice, this was required for almost all productions, even when approval had been unproblematic and no cuts were required. In controversial cases, the condition was sometimes emphasised as 'vinculante' (binding), and particular details of performance or staging would be specified on the reverse of the authorisation certificate as requiring special attention on the part of the inspectors. Inspections were not usually required for works licensed for *todos los públicos* ('all audiences'), but occasionally even performances clearly aimed at children provoked the suspicion of the censors.

While the dress-rehearsal inspection could, in principle, result in the suspension of a production one or two days before the opening night (with disastrous financial consequences), this was a rare occurrence. Inspectors could usually be satisfied with undertakings to stick to the script and to remove any stage business that had attracted their attention. Interviewed in 2010, the actor Josep Maria Pou could not recall any instances of the *pase de censura* (run-through for censorship) resulting in the outright cancellation of a production, but he commented that negotiations would sometimes take several hours (Pou 2010). Pou also confirmed that shows that went on tour would usually be subject to inspection in each location visited, with the risk of new objections being raised by different inspectors, and explained that companies would often make the *pase de censura* as dull and unexpressive as possible so as not to call attention to intonation, gesture and potential emotional impact.

Detailed specifications for how the Junta de Censura was to operate were provided in a law of 6 February 1964. It would comprise the Director General, the Subdirector General and Secretario General, the head of the Servicio de Teatro as secretary, and at least nine *vocales*, including one nominated by the SGAE (BOE 1964: 2505). Various existing features of the censorship operation were explicitly reaffirmed by this piece of legislation: the exclusive, nationwide jurisdiction of the Junta, covering all forms of theatre, both commercial and *cámara*; the fact that its deliberations were secret; the range of outcomes available (prohibition, authorisation for particular ages and with or without cuts, inspection of the dress rehearsal); and the requirement for sketches of sets and costumes for *revistas*. New requirements included a decision on whether performances could be broadcast on television or radio; written authorisation from the author of the original text for translations of foreign-language plays; a time limit of fifteen days for decisions to be issued; and the justification of decisions by reference to specific criteria in the 1963 *normas*. The appeals process was made more transparent but no longer allowed for review by an independent body: the Junta itself had responsibility for dealing with appeals, and a law of December 1956 had decreed that official decisions on matters to do with the press, radio, cinema and theatre could not be challenged by means of a *recurso contencioso-administrativo* ('administrative appeal against actions of the state') (BOE 1956b: 8147).

If all three members of the *comisión delegada* examining an application recommended the same outcome, the decision would be confirmed automatically. If they differed, additional readers' reports would be obtained and the final decision would be made by majority vote in a full meeting of the Junta, for which all members were required to submit a written recommendation. These arrangements, in line with the spirit of *apertura*, were designed to achieve greater consistency and (internal) transparency, making individual censors more accountable to the Junta as a whole. As examples discussed in subsequent chapters will show, the more frequent involvement of the whole Junta sometimes worked in favour of leniency, allowing hardliners to be outvoted by more moderate members. It could, however, work the other way round: some censors, especially when brought into the discussion after several colleagues had issued detailed reports, tended to be hesitant about making firm recommendations and would play safe by siding with those advocating severity. What becomes more visible than ever in the documentation from the more interesting cases from the mid-1960s onwards is the variability of censors' judgements. The accumulation of multiple reports reveals stark differences of opinion over interpretation of the published criteria, perceptions of immorality, assessments of political risk and predictions of how audiences were likely to respond. Even at the time when Fraga and García Escudero were encouraging liberalisation, individual *vocales* often showed themselves to be nervous about the risk of being seen by their superiors as excessively lenient, sometimes recommending that decisions should be taken out of their hands and referred upwards to *la Superioridad*. The power to overrule the Junta's decisions was explicitly conferred by article 22 of the 1964 law:

> Excepcionalmente, el Presidente podrá dejar en suspenso el acuerdo del Pleno y solicitar del Ministro de Información y Turismo su revisión por una Comisión especial constituida al efecto para cada caso por las personas que el Ministro designe. Éste, por propia

iniciativa, podrá ordenar dicha revisión e incluso, en casos extraordinarios, acordar por sí mismo, en el momento en que especiales circunstancias lo aconsejen, la decisión que considere oportuna en orden a la autorización o prohibición de las obras o a las medidas excepcionales a que se condicione la autorización. (BOE 1964: 2506)

> Exceptionally, the President may suspend the decision of the Junta and request that the Minister of Information and Tourism have it subjected to review by a special ad hoc committee nominated by the Minister himself. The Minister may institute such a review on his own initiative, and in highly exceptional cases may exercise his own judgement, in the light of extraordinary circumstances, with regard to the authorisation or prohibition of productions, or any special conditions to be attached to authorisations.

While this measure constitutes a clear marker of the limited nature of *apertura*, in practice the minister's power to overturn an authorisation was not used frequently. A notorious example of Fraga deciding to ban a play not considered particularly problematic by the Junta – and then relenting after an appeal was lodged – is the case of Lorca's *Mariana Pineda* in December 1966 (examined in Chapter 6). García Escudero wrote to Fraga on 15 February 1967 advising him to withdraw the ban and reminding him of nine other occasions on which he had used the power conferred by article 22 to cut, delay or ban (AGA 334/66).

The legislation of February 1964 confirmed that the criteria for film censorship issued the year before would be applied to theatrical performances, but added an interesting qualification: 'La Junta tendrá en cuenta la mayor amplitud de criterio que respecto del drama y de la comedia permite el carácter más restringido del público de dichos géneros teatrales y su grado de preparación presumible, y más todavía cuando se trate de teatros de cámara o de sesiones especiales' ('The Board shall take into account the greater degree of permissiveness of criteria with respect to drama and comedy justified by the more restricted nature of the audience for these theatrical genres and their presumed level of education, especially when productions are intended for theatre clubs and special sessions' (BOE 1964: 2506)

The encouragement to make more use of authorisations for *cámara* facilitated productions of important plays by problematic foreign authors such as Brecht, Sartre and Beckett, as well as some politically challenging or aesthetically experimental works by Spanish playwrights such as Alfonso Sastre, Lauro Olmo, Fernando Arrabal and Alberto Miralles. The slightly greater degree of freedom afforded by the *cámara* category was of particular importance to the development of independent theatre in Barcelona, especially groups performing in Catalan, where the commercial sector was dominated by Castilian-language transfers from Madrid. The category of 'special sessions' came to include the theatre festivals which, from the late 1960s, began to offer an important route for the emergence of new work by young dramatists and independent groups: the Festival Internacional in Sitges from 1967, the one-off Festival Cero in San Sebastián in 1970, the Semana de Teatro in Badajoz from 1972, and others during the 1970s. Examples discussed in Chapter 6 show, though, that even in these special, officially sponsored environments the promise of leniency could not be relied on.

Many theatre professionals saw the policy of selective authorisation for *cámara* as a cynical strategy allowing the authorities to claim to be promoting challenging work while in practice strictly limiting its circulation. José Monleón argues that 'TEUs y Teatros de Cámara habían nacido como instrumentos idóneos para enclaustrar la cultura considerada peligrosa [. . .] limitándola a especialistas y sectores minoritarios' ('the official student theatre companies and theatre clubs had been created as ideal instruments for confining culture that was considered dangerous, limiting it to specialists and minority sectors') (1988: 7). The director José María de Quinto concludes: 'En el Teatro de Cámara tenía el gobierno una perfecta coartada al poder incorporar en sus balances anuales a nuevos autores nacionales y extranjeros que ofrecían un aire aperturístico' ('The theatre club sector provided the government with a perfect cover story, allowing it to include in its annual statistics new Spanish and foreign authors to give an appearance of liberalisation') (quoted in Muñoz Cáliz 2005: 59).

The high point of Fraga's *apertura* project was the *Ley de Prensa e Imprenta* (Press Law) of March 1966, which proclaimed the right to freedom of expression in writing and abolished prior censorship of publications. This represented an important loosening of the censorship of books, newspapers and other printed material, but post-publication controls and sanctions remained in place. Authors, editors and publishers could be fined or prevented from continuing to publish, and issues or editions could be suspended or destroyed (BOE 1966: 3310). The impact of this law on the theatre industry was minimal. It facilitated the publication of editions of plays but made no difference to the censorship of performances.

García Escudero was working on an ambitious Theatres Bill designed to expand state support for theatrical activities when he was unexpectedly removed from his post. The government had decided that it needed to cut public spending and streamline bureaucracy, and in November 1967 issued a decree abolishing a number of government departments (BOE 1967). The Dirección General de Cinematografía y Teatro was merged with the Dirección General de Información, forming a new Dirección General de Cultura Popular y Espectáculos headed by Carlos Robles Piquer, who had been in charge of Información. The Junta de Censura de Obras Teatrales, alongside the euphemistically named Junta de Censura y Apreciación de Películas Cinematográficas, continued to operate as part of this Dirección General (BOE 1968). In a gesture towards greater public transparency, in April 1969 the MIT began to release to the press lists of plays and films that had been authorised, together with age classifications. However, there was no mention of those that were banned, and the term *censura* was not used: the announcements would state that the decisions had been made by the 'Junta de Apreciación de la Dirección General de Cultura Popular'.[24]

All appearances of *apertura* evaporated over the course of 1969. In response to strikes and student protests, a nationwide state of exception was declared on 25 January, bringing a tightening of censorship which continued beyond the restoration of normality on 25 March. A hard-line view that the regime had been too tolerant of dissent and disorder was gaining prominence, and Fraga was coming to be seen as one of the chief culprits. He was sacked in December and replaced by Alfredo Sánchez Bella, a more orthodox Franco loyalist who had fought in a Falange unit in the civil war and had served as an ambassador since 1957. García Escudero comments that this change represented 'el desahucio definitivo de la política que tan ilusionadamente habíamos acometido en 1962' ('the definitive demolition of the policy that we had launched with such high hopes in 1962'), resulting in more severe censorship, especially of cinema (1978: 262–3). He mentions the banning of Brecht's *The Caucasian Chalk Circle* in 1968 as a telling indicator of the new atmosphere, in which Admiral Carrero Blanco (now Franco's vice president) was playing an increasingly influential role.[25]

Sánchez Bella presided over another restructuring of the ministry in March 1970, which re-elevated Cultura Popular y Espectáculos to the status of directorate general and located the Junta de Censura de Obras Teatrales in the Subdirección General de Teatro. This was followed by a minor reform of the theatre censorship apparatus in October. It seems to have been prompted largely by perceived deficiencies in the work of provincial delegations, since the main change was the creation of three posts of Inspector Nacional, who would be members of the Junta. Their function was to ensure that all conditions attached to authorisations with reference to staging and performance were implemented, and they were given the power to cancel licences already issued when such conditions were not respected (BOE 1970: 18613). The renewed effort to make sure that censorship decisions were implemented consistently nationwide may have been provoked partly by developments since the mid-1960s in Barcelona, where performances by independent groups had been increasingly improvisational and difficult to police, sometimes with the complicity of officials in the Delegación Provincial. The Catalan director Josep Anton Codina, interviewed for this project, commented that inspections of dress rehearsals in the late 1960s and early 1970s seemed to be less rigorous in Barcelona than in Madrid (Codina 2012).

The 1970 legislation was accompanied by an official pamphlet offering a robust defence of censorship. It claimed that the regime had played a positive role in nurturing theatrical work of high aesthetic and moral standards, and that the censorship board had operated reasonably and independently, maintaining a difficult balance between demands for liberalisation and fears of over-permissiveness. However, it asserted that calls for freedom of expression were often no more than an attempt to indulge the basest of human passions and insisted that what could not be allowed was 'abrir las puertas al panfleto subversivo ni al manifiesto pornográfico' ('to open the doors to subversive pamphlets and pornographic manifestos') (quoted in Muñoz Cáliz 2005: 276). The values embodied in the 1963 *Normas de censura* were restated in uncompromising terms:

> No tendrá franquicia cuanto mine las raíces familiares o morales, ni a las lacras, taras o delitos que provoquen sugerencias peligrosas.

Tampoco la gratuita obscenidad ni la crueldad morbosa, ni el mal gusto, ni la falta de respeto a las ideologías y las religiones. Asimismo se descarta cualquier interpretación tendenciosa de nuestro pasado histórico. La defensa del honor patrio, la evitación de manifestaciones de odio entre los pueblos, aquello que despierte sentimientos en los niños –torpes sentimientos–, será mirado con expresa atención. (Muñoz Cáliz 2005: 276)

No latitude will be given to anything that undermines the foundations of family and morality, nor to vices, degeneracy or transgressions liable to act as dangerous examples. Nor will gratuitous obscenity, unnatural cruelty, bad taste or lack of respect for ideologies and religions be tolerated. Tendentious interpretations of our [nation's] history will also be rejected. Particular attention will be paid to the defence of national honour, the prevention of expressions of hatred between peoples, and anything that arouses feelings – crude feelings – in the young.

Against this general background of a backlash against liberalisation, it is surprising that Sánchez Bella introduced an element of public transparency to the censorship process: a list of the members of the Junta de Censura de Obras Teatrales was published in the press in August 1970. The core members named were Cea, Rocamora Valls, Mampaso, García-Cernuda, Sunyer, Tejedor, Bautista de la Torre, Muelas and Díez Crespo; and as occasional members, Artola, Barceló, Martínez Ruiz, Vázquez Dodero, Soria Heredia, Romero Andrés, Zubiaurre and Vasallo Ramos (ABC 1970). Some of these were newly appointed: Pedro Rocamora Valls (lawyer, journalist, member of Opus Dei, former Director General de Propaganda); José María García-Cernuda Calleja (Falangist, lawyer, journalist, Delegado Provincial of MIT for Madrid); Carmelo Romero Andrés (film and TV director and scriptwriter); Antonio de Zubiaurre Martínez (Falangist, poet, journalist, translator); Jesús Vasallo Ramos (journalist, screenwriter, playwright). And between 1970 and 1976, others joined the board: Antonio Albizu Salegui (a Franciscan friar, author of religious and philosophical books); Vicente Amadeo Ruiz Martínez (theatre and TV director); José Guerra Gutiérrez; José Luis Guerra Sánchez (journalist); Fernando Mier and José Moreno Reina.

The final years of the dictatorship saw a marked increase in the visibility and effectiveness of opposition. The regime, with a noticeably ailing leader, was deeply divided between pragmatic reformers and a 'bunker' of hardliners determined to resist change, and was finding it increasingly difficult to contain strikes, protests by workers and students, clandestine political organisation, and terrorist activity by ETA and emerging right-wing extremist groups. Cultural policy lurched back and forth between attempts to respond to social change and fear of losing control. Theatre censorship in this period was presided over by a series of ministers: Sánchez Bella was succeeded by Fernando de Liñán y Zofio (June 1973–January 1974), Pío Cabanillas Gallas (January–October 1974), León Herrera Esteban (October 1974–December 1975) and Adolfo Martín-Gamero (December 1975–July 1976). Cabanillas had been Subsecretario de Información y Turismo under Fraga and represented a brief resurgence of the spirit of *apertura*, but was dismissed as a result of concern about the approval of controversial films. There were also several Directores Generales de Cultura Popular y Espectáculos (just 'Espectáculos' from 1972 to 1976): Robles Piquer was followed by Pedro Segú (1972–4), Manuel María Fraile Clivilles (1974), and the theatre director Mario Antolín Paz (1975–6). The labelling of administrative units became more euphemistic: the Sección de Teatro became the Sección de Promoción Teatral (suggesting promotion or support), and the title of the Junta was changed in January 1975 from Censura to Ordenación de Obras Teatrales (suggesting merely ordering or classifying).

The apparatus of censorship continued to operate, though there are gaps in the documentation, suggesting that the system was beginning to break down to some extent. Many *expedientes* from the early 1970s contain only a copy of the script. This tendency appears to have been overcome by 1975: we have examined 220 files from September to December of that year, almost all of which contain full sets of applications, reports and certificates. Of those 220 productions, 146 were authorised without cuts and forty with cuts (18 per cent); thirty-four were prohibited (15 per cent), though eleven of those were reconsidered and approved over the course of the next two years. The censors seem to have become more nervous around the time of Franco's death: in the last six boxes of files from 1975, covering November and December, fourteen out of sixty-five applications were rejected (21 per cent). Many of the decisions to ban a work cite the vague first *norma de censura*, which stipulates that works should be judged holistically, but others are more specific. For example, Pere Lluís Caminals Girbent's

Tot és possible a Roma ('Anything's Possible in Rome') was banned for allusions to Julius Caesar as a dictator; a variety show for bad taste and suggestions of homosexuality; Emilio Sánchez's *Los que se niegan a ser* ('Those Who Refuse to Be') for expressions of subversion; Francisco Pérez de Echenique's *Renato* for blasphemy; and Francesc Burguet i Ardiaca's *Sobreviure* ('Survival') for references to torture by the police. In several cases, censors recommended cuts or bans on the grounds of 'inoportunidad' – the unsuitability under current circumstances of particular topics, such as social injustice, political prisoners, support for communism, and negative portrayals of the police and the armed forces.

Theatremakers, especially in the non-commercial independent sector that flourished from the late 1960s to the late 1970s, were increasingly willing to challenge censorship in a variety of ways in their work and offstage. Collective creation, improvisation and audience participation were central to the modus operandi of the independent groups, inevitably clashing with the censors' need for fixed scripts and predictable performances. Censors' interventions against the work of these companies provoked attention-grabbing protests. In response to the last-minute banning of two productions in the international festival held in San Sebastián in May 1970 (Festival Cero), members of participating companies and spectators held a protest meeting, occupied the main venue and decided to close down the festival. The Roy Hart Theatre from the United Kingdom was forced off the stage when they refused to take part in the boycott and attempted to perform their show *Language Is Dead, Long Live the Voice*. The group Tábano drew attention to the suppression of one of the songs in its satirical show *Castañuela 70* (our case study at the end of Chapter 6) by replacing the missing lines with 'La, la, la. . .', prompting the audience to shout protests against censorship (Trancón 2006: 109). The student group that performed a collective piece called *Oraciones laicas del siglo XX* ('Secular Prayers for the 20th Century') alongside the first performance of *Castañuela 70* in June 1970 began by reading out the censorship certificate for their show, including the lines that had been cut. And between November 1970 and early 1976, Josep Anton Codina flouted the censorship regulations more radically by staging unauthorised performances of Maria Aurèlia Capmany's political history play *Preguntes i respostes sobre la vida i la mort de Francesc Layret* ('Questions and Answers on the Life and Death of

Francesc Layret') in schools, cultural centres and churches around Catalonia (Codina 2012).[26]

Business carried on more or less as usual in the Dirección General de Espectáculos as Franco succumbed to advanced Parkinson's disease, fell into a coma at the end of October 1975 and was kept on life support until his death on 20 November. A handful of controversial theatrical productions that had been banned or delayed were finally approved around this time, their premieres in Madrid helping to heighten the feverish atmosphere of uncertainty. Nacho Artime and Jaime Azpilicueta's version of Tim Rice and Andrew Lloyd Webber's *Jesus Christ Superstar* had been in the hands of the censors since 1972 without a decision being confirmed. It was approved by the Junta in March 1975 but did not open until 6 November (AGA 31/75).[27] Artime and Azpilicueta also adapted Mart Crowley's *The Boys in the Band* (premiered on 3 September 1975), which had been banned since 1970 for its frank treatment of homosexuality. Artime recalls an eventful inspection of the dress rehearsal and armoured cars outside the doors on the opening night (2013). Satirical representations of arbitrary dictatorial power were also on offer in Madrid in November 1975: Luis Riaza's *El desván de los machos y el sótano de las hembras* ('Males in the Attic, Females in the Basement'), which had originally been approved in 1972 only for the Sitges Festival, and versions of Alfred Jarry's *Ubu Roi* and Bertolt Brecht's *The Resistible Rise of Arturo Ui*.

Despite these signs of the authorities apparently giving way to demands for greater sexual and political freedom on stage, very little changed in the year following Franco's death and the accession of King Juan Carlos. Arias Navarro, confirmed as Prime Minister in December and backed by the reactionary 'bunker', made it clear that his primary aim was the continuation of Francoism. It was obvious that there was massive popular demand for democratisation, but the regime and all its institutions were still firmly in place and showing few signs of flexibility (Preston 1986: 80). There would be no significant change in the operation of theatre censorship until Adolfo Suárez replaced Arias Navarro as Prime Minister on 3 July 1976 and appointed Andrés Reguera Guajardo as Ministro de Información y Turismo. It would take another year and a half for Suárez's government to introduce legislation abolishing theatre censorship, leaving in place a system of age restrictions that would last for a further seven years. That final phase will be analysed in Chapter 8.

Case study

***La casa de Bernarda Alba*, by Federico García Lorca**
Teatro del Parque Móvil de Ministerios (Madrid), 20 March 1950, Teatro de Ensayo La Carátula, directed by José Gordon and José María de Quinto, and Teatro Goya (Madrid), 10 January 1964, Compañía Maritza Caballero, directed by Juan Antonio Bardem

Federico García Lorca haunted the Franco regime. His murder at the hands of Nationalist troops in August 1936 prompted horrified protests within the Republican zone and from sympathisers outside Spain, rapidly giving him iconic status as a martyr of the Republic (ABC 1936b).[28] The Nationalists never acknowledged their responsibility for Lorca's death, which Franco himself dismissed as an accident: 'Los rojos han agitado este nombre como un señuelo de propaganda. Lo cierto es que en los momentos primeros de la revolución en Granada, ese escritor murió mezclado con los revoltosos; son los accidentes naturales de la guerra' ('The Reds have been waving his name like a propaganda banner. The truth is that in the early moments of the [military] revolution in Granada, this writer died among the troublemakers; it was the kind of accident to be expected in wartime') (Franco 1939: 183).

Murdering Lorca and leaving his body in an unmarked grave was not enough. The victors of 1939 were determined to legitimise their cause by condemning their victims as enemies of Spain. Lorca's name appears in an official list, published on 28 February 1940, of people being investigated by the Political Responsibilities Tribunal for Granada (BOE 1940: 1053). The process required a death certificate, which was issued on 21 April, recording misleadingly that Lorca died in August 1936 'a consecuencia de heridas producidas por hecho de guerra' ('as a result of injuries caused by an act of war') (Libertad 2011).

The censorship archive provides fascinating insights into the regime's attitude to Lorca and his work. Confirmation that he was subject to an outright ban for political reasons appears in the file on *Bodas de sangre* (*Blood Wedding*). A commercial production was approved on 20 September 1948 but on the same day, José María Ortiz wrote on the back of the application form: 'Queda en suspenso la tramitación de esta Obra por hallarse vetado por la D. G. de Seguridad el autor' ('Consideration of this work is suspended, as the author is blacklisted by the Directorate General of Security') (AGA 450/48). One censor who disagreed with the policy was Gumersindo Montes Agudo, who in October 1943 had recommended the authorisation of *Doña Rosita la soltera* (*Doña Rosita the Spinster*), arguing that: 'En mi opinión debemos dar sensación de que estamos por encima de pasiones y malos recuerdos y que no confundimos el recelo político con el amargor de una crítica insensata, o la negación sistemática de valores que no fueron nuestros' ('In my opinion, we should give the impression that we have risen above passions and unpleasant memories, and that we do not confuse political reservations with unthinkingly critical rancour or the automatic rejection of values that we did not share' (AGA 284/43).

Lorca had completed the script of *La casa de Bernarda Alba* (*The House of Bernarda Alba*) in June 1936. The first application for authorisation of a production in Spain was made on 11 September 1943.[29] The applicant was Tomás Borrás, head of the Sindicato Nacional del Espectáculo ('National Union of Theatre and Film Industries') from 1939 to early 1943, and artistic director of the Falange-run Teatro Español in 1940–1. Despite Borrás's closeness to the Falange, the production was prohibited on 24 November 'por motivos de orden ético' ('for ethical reasons') (AGA 193/43) – perhaps an oblique way of referring to the political blacklisting of the author. The report by an unnamed censor declared the work to be completely unacceptable for various reasons. One of the objections was moral: 'Rivalidades paternales entre hermanas ansiosas de hombre' ('Family rivalry between sisters desperate for a man'). Another was the presence of class hatred; as was noted earlier in the present chapter, the regime was anxious to promote the idea that the *Movimiento* had made the Marxist notion of class conflict obsolete. Interestingly, there is an even stronger emphasis in this report on aesthetic issues. The language of the text is described as 'descarnado' ('raw'), and the work is condemned for its 'crudeza agria y punzante' ('bitter, piercing crudeness'). The censor also offered the apparently contradictory phrase 'el arte por el arte' ('art for art's sake'), without explaining why this was a problem. He may have been making a Fascist-style objection to *entartete Kunst* ('degenerate art') – modernist aesthetics unredeemed by a positive moral (Christian) message. He concluded: 'Obras de esta crudeza no cabe admitir más que las clásicas atenuadas con el correr de los siglos' ('This degree of crudeness can only be accepted in classic works attenuated by the passage of centuries') (AGA 193/43). It was not uncommon for censors in the 1940s to argue that the historical moment required absolutely unequivocal moral, religious, political, and even aesthetic guidance from the authorities.

While *La casa de Bernarda Alba* remained banned in Spain, it received its world premiere to great acclaim in Buenos Aires in March 1945 and was published there soon afterwards. In September 1948 in a report on *Bodas de sangre*, Montes Agudo made another plea for the regime to abandon a policy that was damaging the country's international reputation, echoing Franco's reference in 1939 to Lorca being used as a banner by the Reds: 'Creemos que ya es hora de que el teatro de Lorca, de proyección universal, sea autorizado en España. Incluso como gesto de gran valor político, al arrebatar una bandera a la oposición' ('We believe that it is high time that Lorca's theatre, now known around the world, was authorised in Spain. In fact, it would be a gesture of considerable political value, a way of snatching a banner out of the hands of the opposition') (AGA 450/48).

In the summer of 1946, Cipriano Rivas Cherif, who had directed several of Lorca's works before the civil war and had been released from prison earlier that year, took over the Teatro Cómico in Madrid and announced a season of plays that was to include *La casa de Bernarda Alba*. There is no record in the censorship file of an application for this production, yet in several written accounts of the episode Rivas Cherif states that it was authorised. It was not the censors who prevented him from staging the play but the García Lorca family, who were worried about the regime using performances of Federico's plays to enhance its international image at a time of diplomatic isolation (Aguilera Sastre 2013: 37–8).

As international interest in *La casa de Bernarda Alba* grew, a small concession was made in March 1948 with the approval of a dramatised reading by the Thule theatre group in Barcelona. A review in the Falange magazine *Solidaridad Nacional* dismissed the play as an inauthentic folkloric cliché, arguing that cultural events like this were designed to please foreigners: 'Se les da una estampa exacta de lo que ellos se figuran y no es. Aquí, nos producen una pequeña náusea' ('They offer them an image of exactly what they imagine [Spain is like] but does not exist. Here, such things just make us slightly nauseous') (quoted in Gallén 2000: 165).

At some point in 1948, the student theatre group La Vaca Flaca (led by Alfonso Sastre and Alfonso Paso) attempted to stage *La casa de Bernarda Alba* but were refused permission (Paco 2019). There is no record of this application in the file, though a report by Mauricio de Begoña from January 1949 probably refers to it. Begoña recommended prohibition, repeating the argument about inappropriateness for the 'new Spain': 'Esa crudeza, que no carece de antecedentes en la literatura española tolerada en los mejores siglos, es inapta en los actuales momentos' ('This crude quality, which is not without antecedents in Spanish literature tolerated in the best centuries, is not suitable for current circumstances') (AGA 193/43).

By the end of the 1940s, the blanket veto on staging Lorca's work had been relaxed, which enabled *La casa de Bernarda Alba* to receive its Spanish premiere on 20 March 1950. It was a single performance in a small Madrid venue by the *teatro de ensayo* group La Carátula, directed by José María de Quinto and José Gordon Paso. Unfortunately, there is no trace of this performance in the censorship file; it may have been approved unofficially. In an interview of 1992, de Quinto recalled the efforts of the Director General de Cinematografía y Teatro, Gabriel García Espina, to suppress reviews, and his fury at the international coverage given by *Time* magazine (Aznar Soler and Oskam 1992: 47–8). Other accounts make clear that the pressure to prevent the premiere, or at least limit its impact, came principally from the Church and Catholic organisations (Quinto 1986, Cornejo Ibares 2007 and Torres Nebrera 2013: 6). García Espina arrived during the performance and warned the critics present to keep their coverage to a minimum, which they duly did (e.g., see Marquerie 1950). In contrast, Piero Saporiti, the *Time* correspondent, was keen to bring out the political and cultural significance of the event:

> When the final curtain fell, applause rang out loud & long. From the spectators a voice called: 'García Lorca!' In response, the curtain rose on an empty stage. Everyone understood, and cheered. Critics rushed out to write their reviews. They were stopped cold by an order already on their desks. It was from Censor García Espina: 'No

reviews permitted, now or in the future, of *La Carátula* shows. Only short news items.' Next morning Da Quinto and Gordon pleaded with the censor. 'This means.' they said, 'a final blow to the theater in Spain.' Shamefaced Censor García Espina shrugged. 'I'm just as sorry as you are,' he said. 'But orders are orders. You think I'm the boss, but I'm just an egg between two stones.' Mumbled Da Quinto: 'The Bernardas of Spain have the last word. The window is closed once more.' (Saporiti 1950)

The relaxation of the blanket ban on Lorca's work is confirmed by a note written by Ortiz in May 1951 recommending approval of a production of *La zapatera prodigiosa* (*The Shoemaker's Prodigious Wife*) 'puesto que se ha resuelto no poner trabas a la producción lorquiana' ('since it has been decided not to block Lorca's work') (AGA 158/51). Two applications for *cámara* productions of *La casa de Bernarda Alba* were considered in 1953. One, for the recently established El Paraíso group in Valencia, was submitted on 27 April but the censors' reports were not filed until 16 and 18 May. Bartolomé Mostaza recommended authorisation for *teatro de ensayo*, and Montes Agudo continued his plucky defence of Lorca's work: '¿Puede, a estas alturas, seguir ausente de la escena española el teatro –universal, ya– de Lorca? Esta es la pregunta a la que debe contestar la superioridad' ('After all this time, can Lorca's theatre – which now has universal stature – really remain absent from Spanish stages. That is the question our superiors must answer'). He returned to the metaphor of Lorca as an emblem of political opposition, arguing that authorisation with cuts would ruin the play and provoke further 'campañas en torno a esta bandera –Lorca– que nosotros debimos arriar hace tiempo' ('campaigns around that banner – Lorca – which we should have pulled down a long time ago' (AGA 193/43).

However, the case was still seen as problematic, even for a small *cámara* production. There was further delay while the Director General (Joaquín Argamasilla) consulted the Civil Governor of Valencia (Diego Salas Pombo), whose reply of 26 May provides interesting evidence of two features of the censorship process. First, he agreed with Argamasilla that restricting or banning artistic activities could sometimes be counterproductive, showing that such awareness of public relations constraints on censorship was already fairly widely shared ten years before Fraga and García Escudero launched their *apertura* project. Second, while noting that El Paraíso had not yet submitted all the documents required for licensing as an association, Salas Pombo's letter provides evidence of the police investigation to which the licensing of theatre clubs was subject: 'Los informes facilitados por la Jefatura Superior de Policía sobre los organizadores de dicha sociedad eran favorables' ('The police reports on the organisers of the association were favourable') (AGA 193/43). El Paraíso became fully licensed but their production of *La casa de Bernarda Alba* never took place.

In the meantime, another application had been submitted for a production by the Tertulia Teatral group in Zaragoza. Argamasilla wrote to the Civil Governor (Juan Junquera Fernández-Carvajal) on 20 May 1953 to ask if there were any local factors that might make a performance (under *cámara* conditions) in Zaragoza inadvisable. The letter offers two arguments in favour of allowing the performance to go ahead: the literary and dramatic qualities of the play, and the need to counteract the negative political circumstances surrounding Lorca, 'al que se ha llegado a considerar como un martir víctima de nuestra guerra de Liberación' ('who has come to be seen as a martyr and victim of our War of Liberation') (AGA 193/43). Junquera replied to say that Tertulia Teatral had not been in touch to pursue their application.

The next attempt to stage *La casa de Bernarda Alba* came in April 1961. This was to be a fully professional, commercial production opening in Madrid and going on tour around the country. The director was the former censor Luis Escobar, who was now running the Teatro Eslava in Madrid and engaging in regular tussles with the censorship office. There must have been concern about the Church's likely reaction to a high-profile production of *La casa de Bernarda Alba*, as all four of the readers' reports written for this application were by ecclesiastical censors. Manuel Villares recommended authorisation but was concerned about the negative portrayal of Bernarda, the figure who represents traditional Catholic values and family authority. He was also anxious to deny any possible relevance to the present, suggesting that 'acaso sea éste un tipo real en muchos pueblos españoles de hace treinta años' ('perhaps this is a stereotype that corresponded to reality in many Spanish villages thirty years ago') (AGA 193/43).

The three other censors were much more hostile towards the play. Avelino Esteban Romero was shocked by a work in which he could see no positive moral value whatsoever: '*La casa de Bernarda*

Alba es el conjunto de todo lo que no debe ser una familia, una madre y unas hijas especialmente' ('*The House of Bernarda Alba* is everything that a family – especially mother and daughters – should not be'). This report is the one that comes closest to identifying the risk of audiences making a political reading of the play, referring obliquely to 'el posible sentido figurado que la obra pueda tener en la intención de García Lorca, o la que sus admiradores puedan darle amparados en el nombre del autor' ('the possible metaphorical meaning of the work which might have been intended by García Lorca, or may be given it by his admirers, exploiting the author's name') (AGA 193/43).

Antonio Garau was particularly alarmed by the play's foregrounding of the expression of female sexual desire: 'Está la sensualidad femenina más encabritada que se refugia en la solitaria complacencia hasta llegar a la pregonada entrega, motivo de envidia para las demás' ('Female sensuality is displayed at its most rampant, taking refuge in solitary satisfaction until it culminates in the long-heralded surrender, which arouses envy in the other daughters'). Garau was also worried about the suicide and dismayed by 'odios clasistas, odios familiares, odios sociales y . . . ¡revolcones!' ('class hatred, family hatred, social hatred and . . . rolling in the hay!'). Once again, Bernarda herself was a problem: instead of embodying positive moral authority to outweigh the depravity of the daughters, she was seen to represent hypocrisy. The report concluded with a vivid expression of apoplexy: 'Pienso que para escribir estas cosas basta tener una cosa: un tintero lleno de cieno y . . . nada más! Entiendo que es elemental deber defender al público de fuentes tan envenenadas' ('In my view all that is needed to write stuff like this is an inkwell full of filth and . . . nothing else! I believe that it is my essential duty to defend the public against sources as poisoned as this') (AGA 193/43).

In a less hysterical tone, Juan Fernández reiterated the points raised by his colleagues: the unhealthiness of the obsessive focus on female sexuality as a force of nature; the failure of Bernarda to offer a redemptive moral example, and the unacceptability of Adela's suicide as the necessary outcome of the drama. Declaring the play to be 'inmoral en el desarrollo de la trama e inmoral en cuanto a la solución o desenlace' ('immoral in the development of the plot and immoral in the solution or dénouement'), Fernández recommended prohibition (AGA 193/43).

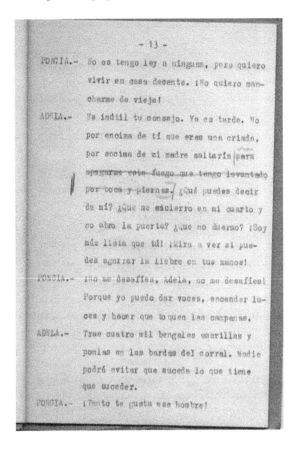

Figure 6: Page from the typescript of *La casa de Bernarda Alba* showing a cut recommended by a censor

The decision to ban the production was not confirmed until 29 May. In the meantime, interesting negotiations appear to have taken place. Fr Esteban issued a carefully worded second report in which he reiterated his moral objections to the play and noted that it was likely to be graded '4' ('gravely dangerous') by the Episcopal Commission. However, in the light of discussions with officials in the department, he was now prepared to accept that it did not pose a danger to public morals from the point of view of the state and could be approved subject to substantial cuts, an age limit of eighteen and restricted circulation (to be performed in large cities only):

Como además es susceptible de suavizarse en determinadas expresiones crudas que pueden resultar ofensivas para los espectadores españoles en general, cabría una autorización limitada de su representación por parte de esa Dirección Gral. habida cuenta cierta ponderación de orden no estrictamente moral, pero que es lícito, por los atenuantes señalados, tener en cuenta por la expresada Dirección y Jefatura del Teatro. (AGA 193/43)

Moreover, as certain crude expressions that may offend the average Spanish spectator can be toned down, it would be appropriate for the Directorate General to issue a limited authorisation, on the grounds of certain considerations that are not strictly moral but may legitimately be taken into account by the said Directorate and Department of Theatre, for the reasons given.

This document shows that, a year before Fraga and García Escudero launched their campaign to loosen the stranglehold of the Church in the name of *apertura*, senior officials were already beginning to feel able to subordinate religious criteria to political priorities, which constitutes an early sign of a crucial shift in the balance of power. Twisting Fr Esteban's arm was not enough to lead to authorisation on this occasion – perhaps higher ecclesiastical authorities intervened to ensure that the prohibition was not overturned.

The next application for licensing of *La casa de Bernarda Alba* was submitted on 6 December 1963 by the Maritza Caballero company for a commercial production directed by the film director Juan Antonio Bardem. Fraga was now Minister, García Escudero was Director General, the *Normas de censura* had been published, and several of the members of the Junta de Censura Teatral – including Villares, Esteban and Fernández – had been replaced. The difference in the tone of the reports and the outcome this time is striking. Three reports were submitted within ten days of receipt of the application, all brief and all recommending authorisation for audiences over eighteen years of age, without cuts. Only one of the three was by a religious censor, José María Artola, newly appointed to the Junta. His report suggested that the tragic gravity of the action was what made an age threshold of eighteen advisable, with no mention of obsessive sexuality or the subversion of family values. Any possible reservations were outweighed by the prestige of the text: 'La calidad literaria de la obra salva ciertos escollos que pudieran señalarse'

('The literary quality of the work overcomes certain problems that might be identified'). Marcelo Arroita-Jáuregui was another new member of the Junta. His report took it for granted that the work was already well known (an edition published in Spain had been available since 1949) and identified no moral problem whatsoever: 'Reina siempre el mayor sentido moral en cuanto se cuenta y en cómo se cuenta' ('An impeccable moral spirit pervades what is recounted and how it is recounted'). And the report by the veteran censor Bartolomé Mostaza, now secretary of the Junta, was even more brisk and insouciant: 'Obra de trágica intención. Un esperpento rural. No ofrece riesgos. Autorizable' ('A play with tragic intent. A rural *esperpento*. It poses no risks. Authorisable') (AGA 191/43). The meeting of the full Junta on 17 December was attended by thirteen *vocales*, three representing the Church. The decision to authorise the production for audiences over eighteen, without cuts and with an inspection of the dress rehearsal, was taken without any sign of dissent. This may look like clear evidence of *apertura* as a decisive change of policy, but it should be borne in mind that Lorca was an exception: there were powerful political reasons for wanting to 'wrest the banner from the opposition'.

Bardem's production opened at the Teatro Goya on 10 January 1964. Despite the apparent ease with which the approval had gone through, certain sections of the regime were still worried about the risk of the premiere becoming a focus for dissent. García Escudero recorded the event in his diary: '*La casa de Bernarda Alba*, con Bardem dirigiendo. El director general de seguridad ha puesto hasta guardias a la puerta del teatro. No ha pasado nada' ('*The House of Bernarda Alba*, directed by Bardem. The Director General of Security even posted police at the doors of the theatre. Nothing happened') (1978: 106). The director's approach to the play, reinforced by Antonio Saura's design, steered clear of Andalusian folklore and period-specific detail, emphasising the work's universality – and implicitly, its applicability to the present.[30] The production was received with enthusiasm by audiences, who paid fervent tribute to the author when the curtains opened on an empty stage after the cast's curtain calls. Reviews in the press were favourable, though not all of them acknowledged the historic importance of the event. The one that did so most explicitly was, surprisingly, Francisco García Pavón's review in *Arriba*, the Falange daily: 'La historia futura de nuestro teatro habrá de señalar con especial énfasis la noche del 10 de enero de 1964, en la que tuvo lugar este acontecimiento' ('The future history of our theatre will mark with particular emphasis the night of 10 January 1964, when this event occurred') (*Arriba* 11 January 1964, cited in ABC 1964).

García Escudero was acutely aware not only of the greatness of Lorca's play but also of its difficult journey to triumph on a Spanish stage, the brutal act of extreme censorship that had been carried out in August 1936, and the regime's ignominious refusal to acknowledge responsibility for the murder: 'Ésta fue realmente, no la mejor, sino la primera del gran teatro que Lorca pudo haber escrito sin el ciego, estúpido tajo que se dio a su vida' ('The truth is that this play was not so much the best of Lorca's work but the first fruit of the great theatre that he could have written if it had not been for the blind, stupid truncation of his life') (1978: 106).

Notes

1. The full title of the merged body, the only political party permitted by Francoism, was Falange Española Tradicionalista y de las Juntas de Ofensiva Nacional Sindicalista (FET y de las JONS). For further information, see Ellwood (1987). The term *Movimiento Nacional* referred to the FET y de las JONS and its associated organisations, as well as the corporatist structure of the regime, its ideology and its origins in the uprising of July 1936.
2. Asociación Católica Nacional de Propagandistas ('National Catholic Association of Propagandists'), founded in 1909: 'A powerful elite lay organization manned mostly by Jesuit-educated members with the objective of influencing public life and infiltrating the labor movement' (Romero Salvadó 2013: 62).
3. See Martínez Cachero (1986) for a survey of theatre in the Nationalist zone.
4. For more detail on these projects, see Linares (1996), Wahnón (1996), Rodríguez Puértolas (2009), and Dennis and Peral Vega (2010).
5. Panse and Mumford (1996) and Pine (2017) offer useful analyses of Nazi theatre censorship. For Fascist Italy, see Bonsaver (2007) and Gaborik (2021).
6. The *comisiones* comprising the Junta Técnica del Estado were effectively ministries, controlled by Franco through the Secretaría General del Jefe del Estado.
7. For further information on Ros, see AHMD 2016: 61–8.

Censorship as Propaganda, Education and Information 153

8   In 1937, Franco declared that while a restoration of the monarchy after the war was possible, he was not willing to be'un poder interino' ('an interim power') (published in the Nationalist edition of *ABC* on 18 July 1937, reproduced in El Español 2017).
9   The Falange's manifesto of 1934 was adopted by Franco's regime without Point 27, which declared that the Falange would not strike deals with other organisations. The 'style' of the Falange was summed up in Point 26: 'Su estilo preferirá lo directo, ardiente y combativo. La vida es milicia y ha de vivirse con espíritu acendrado de servicio y de sacrificio' ('Its style will favour direct, ardent and combative action. Life is military duty and must be lived in a purified spirit of service and sacrifice') (Primo de Rivera 1976).
10 Emphasis in original.
11 The publisher produced a compilation of its lists from 1939 to 1944 (El Perpetuo Socorro 1945).
12 Detailed information about these and later censors is given by Muñoz Cáliz (2006a, vol. 1: LIII–LXIII).
13 Ortiz would remain in post as the linchpin of the operation until censorship was abolished in 1978, and then continued as secretary of the Comisión de Calificación (the body set up to decide age classifications for performances between 1978 and 1985).
14 The biblical echo in the phrase 'la verdad que nos hace libres' was deliberate, part of the regime's strategy of fusing religion and nationalist authoritarianism (*nacionalcatolicismo*). The allusion is to John 8: 32.
15 See Chapter 4, Feldman and Foguet (2016) and Thompson (2018: 47–55).
16 The terms *teatro de cámara* and *teatro de ensayo* are more or less synonymous, both denoting non-mainstream or non-commercial theatre produced in small venues by professional or amateur performers. *Cámara* ('chamber') refers to the kind of space (intimate, studio), while *ensayo* ('test or rehearsal') refers to the approach (workshop theatre).
17 These conditions were similar to those that applied to British theatre clubs until 1968. The crucial difference was that in the United Kingdom the vagueness of the legal parameters meant that the 'private theatre' sector was in practice largely exempt from censorship by the Lord Chamberlain's office and became an important channel for the introduction of new work. See Nicholson (2005: 57, 173 and 299) for details of debates about this.
18 These files, some not yet accessible to reserchers, are stored in the AGA under IDD (03)107.001.
19 A memo from the Gabinete de Enlace to Fraga, referring to consultation with the Dirección General de Seguridad, is reproduced by O'Leary (2005: 296).

20 García Escudero's background was interesting. He had supported the Republic, and at the beginning of the civil war served as assistant to the political commissar in an anarchist brigade before going over to the Nationalist side and enlisting in a Falange unit. See his memoirs (García Escudero 1995) and Lénárt (2009).

21 Important evaluations of the impact of *apertura* on censorship are given in Muñoz Cáliz (2005), and the pioneering accounts written during the dictatorship by O'Connor (1966, 1969 and 1973).

22 The board is also referred to in some documents as the Junta de Censura de Obras Teatrales.

23 *Silencio administrativo* is a formally recognised procedure in Spanish administrative law. It is either *positivo* (the constructive consent of the state is assumed if no response to an application or request is received within the declared time limit), or *negativo* (constructive rejection is assumed), as was the case with censorship decisions (RAE/CGPJ 2016).

24 Several announcements of this kind appeared in *ABC* and *La Vanguardia Española* between April 1969 and November 1970.

25 The censorship of this play is discussed in detail in the Case Study at the end of Chapter 7.

26 This work was authorised in March 1976 after lengthy debate between the censors. See Feldman and Foguet (2016: 194–6) for further details.

27 For details of the censorship of *Jesus Christ Superstar* and other translated musicals, see Merino Álvarez (2015).

28 The most penetrating analysis of Lorca's iconicity and 'afterlives' is offered by Maria Delgado (2008).

29 See Santos Sánchez (2009) for an analysis of the censorship of productions and editions of *La casa de Bernarda Alba*.

30 For detailed analysis of the staging, see Cornago Bernal (2000: 311–14) and Edwards (2000: 705–13).

Chapter 4

The Pervasiveness of Censorship during the Dictatorship: Right-Wing Triumphalism, Commercial Theatre, *Revistas* and Catalan Theatre

The chronological survey provided in Chapter 3 tells a complex story of mutation – censorship institutions, procedures and criteria evolving in response to power shifts between the different 'families' of the regime, changes of personnel and transformation of economic circumstances. Nevertheless, certain features remained constant throughout the period of the dictatorship. Although the balance between them varied from one phase to another, the two primary foci of censorship were always the same: on the one hand, politics (ranging from specific topical concerns to general issues of authority and ideology), and on the other, religion and morality, inextricably intertwined. Another constant was the administrative difficulty of constructing and sustaining a consistent, efficient apparatus that was heavily centralised but capable of extending its tentacles of control into the smallest and most far-flung corners of the theatrical world. And paradoxically, one of the most consistent features of that apparatus was its inherent inconsistency: there were always disagreements within the system over criteria, interpretation of texts, risk assessment and tactics.

156 *Theatre Censorship in Spain, 1931–1985*

The present chapter, focusing mostly on the first half of the dictatorship, covers a broad swathe of theatrical genres that one might assume posed little threat to the regime's hegemony. Pro-Nationalist propaganda spectacles, frivolous musical comedies and commercially successful plays by well-established dramatists turn out to have unexpected implications of concern to the censors for a variety of reasons. Particular additional factors affecting theatre in Catalonia are also examined. In the process, a rich and varied picture of the theatrical life of the period emerges from the archival evidence, marked not only by the deadening influence of censorship but also by spirited gestures of resistance by theatremakers.

Constraints on triumphalism

Between 8 May 1938 and 28 March 1939, the day on which Nationalist forces occupied Madrid, theatre listings in newspapers bore the subheading 'Industria intervenida por el Estado' ('A state-run industry'). From 29 March to 1 April, this was replaced by 'Sindicato de la Industria Cinematográfica y Espectáculos públicos de F.E. de las J.O.N.S.' ('Falange Union of the Cinema and Entertainment Industry'), marking the installation of a new political regime and the liquidation of a cultural experiment. The triumph of the Nationalists was reflected in the theatre industry in various other ways. An article published in *ABC* on 29 March celebrated the work of companies that had been working in the Nationalist zone and noted with satisfaction that they were re-establishing themselves in Madrid and Barcelona, including the celebrated María Guerrero and Fernando Díaz de Mendoza (ABC 1939a).

When the new season got under way on 8 April, the victors' appropriation of theatre to celebrate their triumph was obvious. A revival of Pemán's religious drama *El divino impaciente* was hijacked by the Franco personality cult: 'Al final de la función fue expuesto en el escenario el retrato del Caudillo, y la orquesta del teatro interpretó el himno nacional, que los espectadores escucharon de pie y con el brazo en alto, sonando muchos vivas a España y a Franco' ('At the end of the performance a portrait of the *Caudillo* was displayed on stage and the orchestra played the national anthem, during which the audience stood and saluted with their arm raised, shouting "Long live Spain!" and "Long live Franco!"')

(Araujo-Costa 1939a). A variety show on 22 April was interrupted by an allegedly spontaneous public response to the presence of General Saliquet, one of the leaders of the July 1936 uprising. The audience broke into applause and cheers in favour of Saliquet, Franco and Spain, while the orchestra played the Falange anthem 'Cara al sol' ('Face to the Sun'), to which the public sang along with raised-arm salutes (ABC 1939f).

In this febrile atmosphere of triumphalism, one might expect the state to have put energy and resources into the promotion of theatrical spectacles that would celebrate the victory, help to legitimise the new regime and contribute to a new National-Catholic culture. The two national theatres that grew out of the wartime Teatro Nacional de la Falange represented only a half-hearted step in that direction. Luis Escobar's company at the Teatro María Guerrero – sponsored by the Ministerio de Educación Nacional – focused mainly on classics and works by conservative dramatists not closely aligned with militant Falangism, such as Eduardo Marquina, Jacinto Benavente and José María Pemán. Felipe Lluch, director of the Teatro Español from 1940 to 1941, was much more committed to the project of remoulding theatre along heroic nationalist lines.[1] He had produced visionary proposals for the creation of state structures to promote, purify and supervise a truly national theatre: 'Es preciso, pues, para salvar el teatro, crear otra vez un teatro nacional que sea reflejo exacto de nuestra vida actual, con escrupulosa fidelidad al destino histórico de nuestra patria' ('It is necessary, then, in order to save the theatre, to create once again a national theatre that is an exact reflection of our current way of life, with scrupulous fidelity to the historical destiny of our fatherland') (quoted in García Ruiz 2000: 117). However, the programme offered by the Teatro Español in the early 1940s fell sadly short of these lofty ideals, and Lluch died in 1941. Escobar and Lluch presided over a period of innovation in theatrical technique and design, but 'las tentativas de corte nacionalista en pro de un teatro español-popular en el sentido directamente político no llegaron a nada' ('the nationalist-orientated attempts to create a Spanish people's theatre in a directly political sense came to nothing') (García Ruiz 2003a: 12).[2]

The one spectacle that went some way towards fulfilling the Falangists' ambitions was a theatrical celebration of the first anniversary of the Nationalist victory, developed by Lluch and the

Delegación Nacional de Prensa y Propaganda in 1940. Under the title *Espectáculo de la España Una, Grande y Libre* ('Spain, One, Great and Free'), the show was an allegorical spectacle in a traditional mould made up of scenes from classic plays by Lope de Vega and *autos sacramentales* by Calderón, together with heroic ballads, religious verses and sacred and martial music (including the Falangist anthem 'Cara al sol'), all exalting the unity of Spain, the glories of the Reconquest and the supremacy of Catholicism. Authorisation by the censorship office was applied for on 25 March 1940 and issued without hesitation on the following day (AGA 852/40). The gala performances on 7 April at the Teatro Español and 6 May in Sevilla, then on 18 July and 12 October 1941 at the Español again, did not exactly fulfil the aim of creating a true theatre of the masses or a Nazi-style spectacle of popular mobilisation, since all four audiences were packed with senior members of the military, government and ecclesiastical hierarchies, but the propaganda value was eagerly amplified by the press: 'Eso es teatro, eso es arte, eso es incorporar la nueva España a su espíritu propio nacional manifestado en su fe, en su pensamiento, en su cultura y en el tesoro de su poesía' ('That is theatre, that is art, that is an infusion into the new Spain of its true national spirit manifested in its faith, its thought, its culture and its poetic treasures') (Araujo-Costa 1940).

The favourable reception given to Lluch's work was to be expected. What is surprising is that a number of other triumphalist plays and poetic spectacles celebrating the victory, the *Caudillo*, the Falange and National-Catholic values provoked suspicion or even hostility from the censors. In the final months of the war, Nationalist censors had been anxious to suppress dramatic accounts of the Nationalist victory that gave disproportionate credit to one particular faction or leader, which was identified as a key risk in the censorship criteria circulated in 1940 (AGA 21/1477). Two examples of this were discussed in Chapter 2: the deletion of references to Franco from Ramón Cué's *Y el Imperio volvía...*, and the replacement of Franco's name with that of General Varela in Orizana's *El Alcázar de Toledo*.

José María Cabeza and Luis Felipe Solano would not have expected their verse drama *Por el Imperio hacia Dios* ('Through Empire towards God'), submitted for approval in August 1939, to encounter problems with censorship. The authors were infantry officers, the title was a frequently used slogan of the new regime, and the play was dedicated to the Generalissimo and honoured the triumphs and sacrifices of the Nationalist army. The work was initially authorised without cuts. However, there is an anonymous, undated censor's report which was disparaging about the quality of the text and recommended that authorisation be subject to the removal of 'alusiones a personas destacadas de la situación roja' ('allusions to prominent figures amongst the Reds') (AGA 127/39). As these cuts are not marked on the script, it is difficult to discern the censor's reasoning. It may be that the representation of the enemy was judged to be insufficiently negative. Despite the initial decision to authorise without cuts, the section of the application form to be completed by the Jefe de Censura bears the annotation 'Aprobada con tachaduras' ('Approved with deletions') and is dated 27 October 1939. The two months that had elapsed since the submission of the application coincided with the transfer of responsibility for theatre censorship from Luis Escobar to Samuel Ros, which represented the consolidation of the Falange's control over the apparatus. The process seems to have been affected by tensions between different factions within the regime. Cabeza and Solano had to wait another year and a half to see their work staged: the premiere on 1 April 1941 in Zaragoza and two performances at the state-run Teatro María Guerrero in Madrid were enthusiastically received by both audiences and critics (Checa Puerta 2013: 4).

A genre that was generally acceptable to the censors was the historical play featuring heroes from Spain's imperial past, a genre cultivated with success before and after the war by Eduardo Marquina and José María Pemán. Mariano Tomás's verse drama about Isabel the Catholic, *Santa Isabel de España*, was first performed in September 1934, part of a Catholic backlash against the secularising policies of the first government of the Republic. When the play was revived in October 1939 at the Teatro Español, a new scene was to be added at the end, culminating in an anachronistic tableau of the recovery of Spain's greatness and unity, centred on the Queen on her deathbed 'rodeada de falangistas femeninas que la miran con veneración y curiosidad' ('surrounded by female Falangists gazing at her with veneration and curiosity') (AGA 192/39). Ros approved the production on condition that the new scene was removed. This condition was also attached to the authorisation of productions in 1941 and 1947. No reason was given; it may have been because the Church might be uneasy about over-emphasising an association between an icon of traditionalist Catholicism and the revolutionary – and even potentially feminist – aspirations of the Falange.[3] By 1947, after the transfer of responsibility for censorship to Educación Nacional, the scene looked even more out of place in the context of the regime's efforts to distance itself from Fascism. A report of 16 May by Emilio Morales de Acevedo agreed that it should not be part of the performance: 'Acaso no fuera conveniente en las actuales circunstancias político-mundiales presentar esta apoteosis, merecidísima desde luego y desde luego justa, de nuestra Falange' ('In the current geopolitical circumstances it may not be advisable to present this apotheosis of our Falange, however just and obviously well deserved it is').

Mentions in *Santa Isabel de España* of Don Juan, Isabel's son who died at the age of nineteen, posed the risk of being interpreted as coded references to Don Juan de Borbón, the heir to the Spanish throne since the abdication of Alfonso XIII in 1941, who had issued a manifesto in 1945 calling on Franco to restore the monarchy. Morales recommended the deletion of two lines: '¡Es que Castilla espera al Príncipe Don Juan!' ('Castilla is waiting for Prince Juan!') and 'enfermó la Monarquía / de tristeza por Don Juan!' ('the Monarchy fell ill with grief over Don Juan') (AGA 192/39). These cuts were not imposed in the end. Having passed a Law of Succession in March 1947 giving Franco the power to choose his successor as head of state, the regime was no longer worried about the threat posed by the Count of Barcelona.

Underlying these examples of censorship putting obstacles in the way of dramatic exaltations of the *Movimiento Nacional* was a general wariness about theatre itself as an artistic medium and an industry, and whether it was appropriate for dealing in a dignified way with recent events of historic importance and sacred significance. A review of the musical comedy *Los rojillos* ('Those Mischievous Reds') by Antonio Paso Díaz and collaborators, premiered in June 1939, expressed distaste at the frivolity with which the murderous 'red horde' is depicted: 'Nuestra guerra –guerra teñida de horrenda profanación revolucionaria– es muy seria para ser ofrecida públicamente a broma' ('Our war – a war stained by horrific revolutionary profanation – is too serious a matter to be turned into a joke'). The reviewer asked: 'Nuestra guerra es el espectáculo gigante de los anales que pide el Universo atónito. ¿Por qué encerrar sus posibilidades redentoras en límites de sainete?')

('Our war is the stupendous spectacle of the age which the astonished universe seeks. Why circumscribe its redemptive possibilities within the limits of the *sainete*?') (Arozamena 1939).[4]

A similar argument was made by a censor with reference to a *sainete* by Pilar Millán-Astray entitled *Regina la bien plantá* ('Regina the Well-Favoured'). Set in the immediate post-war period, it features two rivals for the love of honest Regina at the end of the war – an honourable Nationalist doctor and a murderous fugitive who has been a left-wing activist in the Republican zone. Millán-Astray had been a highly successful writer of sentimental, conventional comedies and novels since the early 1920s and was the sister of General José Millán-Astray, which had led to her being imprisoned by the Republicans during the war. She was therefore a figure well respected by the regime. *Regina la bien plantá* was her only attempt at overtly political drama, and it did not go down well. An anonymous censor in August 1940 defined the *matiz político* ('political implications') of the text as an exaltation of the regime and approved of the way in which the play demonstrated the treacherousness of the 'Reds' (AGA 1489/40). Authorisation was given subject to four minor cuts but there is no record of any performances of this play in 1940. Another application must have been made in 1944, since there is a censor's report from that year, but neither the application nor the decision appears in the file. Virgilio Hernández's unenthusiastic report, submitted on 17 September 1944, suggests that censors were getting tired of seeing clumsy attempts to ride the bandwagon of the *Movimiento*, especially by commercial companies:

> Sería conveniente que se aconsejara a los autores que se alejaran lo más posible de estos temas de nuestra guerra; es una cosa muy sagrada para tratarla con el desenfado y tranquilidad con que la tratan, la mayoría de las veces con buena fé y sana intención, pero no siempre con la habilidad necesaria para que sirva de lección y con la agravante de que siempre hay en el fondo un fin lucrativo. (AGA 1489/40)

> It would be a good idea to advise authors to stay as far away as possible from this kind of subject related to our war, which is too sacred to be treated in the casual, nonchalant manner in which they tend to treat it. Most of the time they do so in good faith and with honest intentions, but not always with sufficient skill to give their works real value as lessons, which is made worse by the fact that there is always a profit motive in the background.

Hernández recommended authorisation with one cut and one amendment. The line to be cut was 'Vengan dominguitos y arriba España' ('Let's have a party and long live Spain'), which must have been seen as contributing to the trivialisation of patriotism; and the phrase 'las derechas' ('right-wing people [or parties]') was to be replaced by 'algún otro concepto en el que queden englobados todos los perseguidos por los rojos' ('some other expression that can cover all those who were persecuted by the Reds') (AGA 1489/40). The regime was keen to promote the idea that the *Movimiento* was not a partisan right-wing project but an apolitical, authentically national movement representing the true spirit and destiny of the people. Despite the censors' reluctant approval, there is no record of any performance taking place or of the play being published.[5]

By 1947, some theatrical manifestations of Falangist fervour were regarded as more than inconvenient – they were downright embarrassing. *Arriba España* ('Long Live Spain'), by the Valencian Falange officer Jesús Morante Borrás, must have been first presented for censorship in late 1939, as the file devoted to it is numbered 476/39. There is no application, report or decision from that year, but the play does not appear to have been staged in 1939 or later. Adolfo Carril's report of 30 November 1947 was hostile to both form and political content:

> Se trata de una comedia en donde se pretenden exponer los principios de nuestro Movimiento resultando una <u>farsa grotesca y absurda</u>. Las ideas que se exponen son totalmente de la cosecha propia del autor y su concepción y desarrollo es totalmente inadmisible. Las obras que tratan estos temas para poderlas tomar en serio deben de tener una calidad literaria excepcional y un desarrollo teatral digno y ordenado [. . .] <u>No debe autorizarse la representación</u>. (AGA 476/39)

> The way in which this play sets out to expound the principles of our Movement results in a <u>grotesque and absurd farce</u>. The ideas expressed in it are entirely of the author's own making, and their conception and development is totally unacceptable. If plays that deal with themes like this aim to take them seriously, they need to be of exceptional literary quality and possess a dignified and well-ordered dramatic structure. [. . .] <u>It should not be authorised for performance</u>.

Discussing these examples of right-wing theatre obstructed by censorship, Santos Sánchez speculates that 'political motives may sometimes have hidden a refusal on the grounds of poor quality'

The Pervasiveness of Censorship during the Dictatorship 163

and concludes that censorship worked against the regime's larger agenda in this period (2013c: 1174 and 1176). However, each of the cases analysed above is clearly explicable in relation to an aspect of the complex political context: caution about overplaying the role of particular individuals or organisations in a *Movimiento* that embraced various factions; distrust of theatre as a suitable medium for representing with sufficient dignity the values of National-Catholicism; and a desire to control how and by whom those values were transmitted. The censors did comment on mediocre quality, but in no case is it evident that such aesthetic judgements were the decisive factor.

Further support for a specific rationale behind these apparently surprising decisions can be found in the general censorship criteria circulated in 1938 and 1939. A key factor was the balancing of forces within the regime, both during and after the war: 'Deberían vigilarse los juicios sobre el Alzamiento, evitando una valoración parcial de los distintos elementos que participaron en aquél' ('Judgements on the Uprising were to be scrutinised carefully, avoiding partisan assessments of the contributions of the various participants') (Beneyto Pérez 1987: 30). The regime was anxious to avoid conflict between its competing 'families' and to disseminate a single message about its doctrines and claim to legitimacy. It also sought to maintain strict control over representations of its identity, including its visual iconography.

In the decree of July 1939 setting up the Sección de Censura, the forms of cultural production that would be subject to censorship included the vague category of 'originales y reproducciones de carácter patriótico' ('originals and reproductions of a patriotic character') (BOE 1939b: 4120). The range of materials covered by this broad remit can be seen in files in the AGA referring to the censorship activities of a department responsible for Organización de Actos Públicos y Plástica ('Organisation of Public Events and Visual Arts'). The instructions on the back of the application form specify two categories of material requiring approval. The first comprises official and national flags, emblems, arms, mottos and titles as well as 'representaciones de figuras, episodios, lugares de la Historia de España, de la Guerra y Revolución, fotografías o representaciones de personalidades oficiales, del Régimen o de los Ejércitos' ('representations of figures, episodes and sites of the History of Spain, the War and the [Nationalist] Revolution, photographs or representations of official persons, of the Regime or of the Armed Forces') (AGA 21/0064). Although the main target of this form of censorship was printed matter, the inclusion of *actos públicos* in the name of the department indicates that any kind of public performance involving such representations could be subject to these criteria. The second category includes specific reference to publicity for theatrical productions:

> Los grabados de todo género, portadas de novela, ilustraciones de libros, dibujos litografiados, carteles, pancartas, pasquines, periódicos murales editados con fines propagandísticos por entidades particulares, incluso cines, teatros, salones de bailes y demás espectáculos públicos, cromos, construcciones recortables, dibujos infantiles para iluminar almanaques, tarjetas de felicitación, etc. etc. (AGA 21/0064)

> Engravings of all kinds, covers of novels, book illustrations, lithographs, posters, placards, leaflets, wall newspapers produced for publicity purposes by private bodies, including cinemas, theatres, dance halls and other public spectacles, trading cards, cut-out models, children's drawings to illustrate annuals, greetings cards, etc. etc.

The objects submitted for approval in 1943 included printed advertisements, commercial packaging, collectable cards and stickers featuring film and football stars, book illustrations, humorous postcards, and reproductions of military and Falange emblems. A new logo for the insurance company General Española de Seguros was based on a stylised image of a black eagle, which was approved on condition that the gold halo behind the bird's head was removed so that it was not too similar to the Eagle of Saint John in the new national coat of arms. The producers of La Española sardines and anchovies had been using the royal coat of arms and national flag on their packaging and advertising since 1924 but were now denied permission to use the Francoist national flag and coat of arms (AGA 21/0064). The perceived incongruity between a banal commercial product and the sacred dignity of national emblems is comparable to that between the image of Isabel the Catholic on her deathbed and the squad of eager Sección Femenina girls in *Santa Isabel de España*. The regime's determination to maintain tight control over the iconography of national identity – the protection of the National-Catholic brand – is another key element of the background that explains the censors' reservations about plays which at first sight appear to be entirely in line with hegemonic values.

Business as usual: re-forming the commercial canon

In reality, what the regime, the theatre industry and the majority of its customers wanted most at this time was light entertainment without explicit political messages. The pre-war market based on frivolous comedies, musicals, *zarzuelas*, bourgeois family dramas and Catholic-oriented history plays had not been radically changed by the social and artistic experiments of the war-time Republican zone, nor was it transformed by Francoism's sustained campaign of propaganda and indoctrination. The political plays discussed in the previous section comprised a small and short-lived element of the post-war theatrical landscape, which was dominated by the work of Pedro Muñoz Seca (with twenty-four productions in Madrid between 8 April and the end of 1939), alongside Antonio Paso (father and son, with twenty-eight productions between them) and Antonio Quintero (eight productions).

Another way of quantifying the dominance of certain authors is to track the number of applications for productions of their work throughout Spain in the AGA database that catalogues section (03)46.000 of the archive. In the years 1939 to 1941, the Álvarez Quintero brothers headed this table with seventy works, just ahead of Muñoz Seca with sixty-nine and Carlos Arniches with sixty-seven, followed by Antonio Paso (father and son) with fifty-one and Jacinto Benavente with forty-seven.[6] These playwrights had all been successful before 1936 but had had very few plays staged during the war (except for Benavente). Although the initial policy of the Francoist authorities to censor only works written since July 1936 or staged in the Republican zone during the war was superseded in October 1939 by the decision to subject entire repertoires to censorship, it had a significant impact on programming in the first post-war season as companies looked for safe material. Of 220 professional productions in Madrid between 8 April and 31 December 1939, sixty-two (28 per cent) were new works, and only eight (4 per cent) were works that had been premiered during the war – four of them in Madrid, two in the Nationalist zone and two in South America.

The programming of plays by authors such as these was not without political implications, however. Muñoz Seca's sometimes controversial success in the 1920s and early 1930s, and his death at the hands of Republican militiamen, were discussed in Chapter 2. None of his plays was staged in the Republican zone during the war. As soon as the conflict was over, ardent tributes were paid to him as a martyr of the Nationalist crusade. A production of his play *La tela* ('Folding Stuff'), first staged in 1925, opened the new season at the Teatro de la Comedia on 15 April 1939 in homage to the author and as a protest against 'el brutal crimen que ha privado a la escena española de uno de sus más claros ingenios' ('the brutal crime that has deprived the Spanish stage of one of its most brilliantly ingenious practitioners') (Araujo-Costa 1939b: 24).

Against this background, Muñoz Seca's plays were a good bet for theatre impresarios in the 1940s – not only sure to be popular despite being dated, but officially consecrated. However, these advantages did not guarantee an easy ride through the censorship process. Jurado Latorre records applications for more than a hundred works by Muñoz Seca in the AGA, from the 1940s to the 1970s. Around forty of them were approved without cuts, while the remainder were authorised with cuts, which in some cases were very extensive (2001: 238). Post-war censors suppressed some of the same material as their Republican predecessors had, but for different reasons. Where the Republicans had objected to cynical remarks about democratic political debate, for example, the Francoists simply did not want parties and policies of the early 1930s mentioned at all. Where the author had made scurrilous suggestions about people's reasons for supporting the legalisation of divorce under the Republic, the aim now was simply to remove all mention of divorce. Inevitably, the Francoist censors went much further than the Republican officials, cutting references to trade unions, political parties and voting; flippant remarks about religion, the monarchy or the armed forces; and sexual *double entendres*. They also suppressed moments in which characters express relatively sincere progressive views, such as this line from *La Oca*: 'Estoy de acuerdo con los que protestan contra las injusticias sociales; con los que están ya hartos, aburridos, cansados de ellas' ('I agree with the people who are protesting against social injustices, who are fed up, bored and tired of them') (AGA 1330/40).[7]

The only Muñoz Seca play that was prohibited by Franco's censors was the 1935 hit *Marcelino fue por vino* ('Marcelino Went Out for Wine'). It was staged in June 1939 at the Teatro Chueca in Madrid, though there is no record of an application for this production in the AGA file. An application in July 1940 was approved without cuts, but there is no evidence of this production going ahead. In November 1953, when an application was submitted for a production at the Teatro Maravillas in Madrid, Gumersindo Montes Agudo's report argued that Muñoz Seca's lampooning of republicanism, though courageous at the time, was no longer appropriate:

> Estas obras tuvieron su momento y nada induce hoy a resucitarlas. Viejas querellas sociales, conflictos de orden público, cuestiones de partidos perfectamente definidas entonces, y que hoy dañan, por el recuerdo doloroso que encierran, sin una eficaz lección de ejemplaridad en su caricatura. (AGA 1279/40)

> These plays had their moment and there is no good reason to revive them now. Outdated social issues, problems of public order, party politics – all were sharply relevant at the time but are now harmful, because of the painful reminder they bring without extracting from the caricature any positive lessons.

The impresario was informed that the application had been rejected and was advised that the work might be approved if substantially revised, making the humour less dependent on references to political parties, public figures and social conflicts that were now 'felizmente superadas' ('happily superseded') (AGA 1279/40). What the establishment really wanted was the comic ingenuity of Muñoz Seca stripped of uncomfortable reminders of the existence of republicanism, monarchism, socialism and anti-clericalism. *Marcelino fue por vino* was not performed in 1953, and no further applications were made. By the end of the 1950s, interest in Muñoz Seca's work – except for the historical parody *La venganza de don Mendo* (*Don Mendo's Revenge*), which is still regularly performed – had waned.

Some other playwrights who regained box-office prominence after the war were treated as deserving of reparations for mistreatment at the hands of the Republic. As was noted in Chapter 1, Antonio Quintero Ramírez's plays were banned by the Republican Junta de Espectáculos in early 1937, partly because of the nature of his work – a stereotyped vision of traditional Andalusian culture

– and partly because of his expressions of support for the Nationalists from exile in Argentina. He returned to Nationalist Spain in 1938 via Nazi Germany and established himself in Madrid after the war. The censorship file on his play *El delirio* ('Delirium'), first authorised in March 1939, gives an indication of how much in demand his work was in the post-war period. There were seven applications for commercial productions between November 1939 and November 1944. These applications were all approved, usually within a few days. This was unproblematic entertainment, albeit not of the highest quality. José María Ortiz's report of 11 August 1944 assessed the text as lacking a message, of no literary value, and without political or religious implications: 'Una obra intrascendente del corte y estilo clásico a que nos tiene acostumbrados el autor. Ágilmente dialogada y bien construida en el orden teatral. En el orden moral, no ofrece reparos' ('An insignificant work in the classic form and style to which the author has accustomed us. Made up of agile dialogue and well put together theatrically. In terms of morality, it poses no problems') (AGA 393/39).

The prolific Carlos Arniches did not premiere any new plays in Spain during the civil war, though his *El padre Pitillo* ('Father Pitillo') was first performed in April 1937 in Buenos Aires, where he lived from December 1936 to January 1940. His existing work was regularly staged during the first half of the war but began to go out of favour in 1938 and was not performed in Madrid at all in January–March 1939. He was welcomed back to Spain by the regime and his work again became a staple of the commercial theatrical repertoire through the 1940s and 1950s. As Sotomayor Sáez shows, however, some of his plays from the Republican period encountered difficulties with Francoist censors. References to the political debates and institutions of the time, criticisms of the monarchy and landowners, discussions of social injustice or expressions of sceptical attitudes towards the Church were suppressed from plays such as *Vivir de ilusiones* ('Living on Illusions') and *El padre Pitillo*, and mild sexual references were removed from *La tragedia de Marichu* ('The Tragedy of Marichu') and *La dichosa honradez* ('Bloomin' Honesty'). After the decision to reassess all previous decisions in 1943, two plays – *El pobre Valbuena* ('Poor Valbuena') and *La leyenda del monje* ('The Legend of the Monk') – were prohibited altogether. In the long run, this led to a damaging shift in Arniches's overall reputation. While his most interesting and socially critical texts were blocked or toned down by the censors (or self-censored at their behest) and avoided as risky by companies, he came to be known increasingly as the author of inconsequential or conservative escapist comedy: 'El Arniches que durante este tiempo se ha trasmitido y conocido es un Arniches incompleto, sesgado y censurado' ('The Arniches passed down to us during this period is an incomplete, distorted and censored Arniches') (Sotomayor Sáez 2001: 184).

Another way in which impresarios could find politically safe plays to stage in the post-war period was to turn to dramatists who had died before the advent of the Republic. Although radicals on the left and right regarded him as too closely associated with conservative monarchism and his brand of bourgeois tragic melodrama was generally seen as dated, the Nobel Prize winner José Echegaray held a prestigious place in the theatrical canon, mostly for a single work from 1881, *El gran Galeoto* (*The Great Galeoto*). None of Echegaray's plays was performed in Madrid during the war, though he was not completely excluded from stages in the Republican zone: *El gran Galeoto* was performed in Barcelona in April and September 1938 (Vanguardia 1938). It was also in Barcelona that the reintegration of Echegaray into the post-war repertoire was initiated. *El gran Galeoto*, starring a rapidly rehabilitated Enrique Borrás, was the Guerrero-Mendoza company's first post-war production (8 April 1939, Teatro Poliorama). Performances in Madrid followed in December 1941, November 1942 and October 1943.

The censorship files provide a striking picture of how frequently some of these antiquated plays were being performed around the country in the years following the end of the war. There were forty-eight applications for authorisation of productions of *El gran Galeoto* in the 1940s, nine in the 1950s and three in the 1960s. For *Mancha que limpia* ('A Stain that Cleanses'), there were thirty-four applications in the 1940s, twenty-six in the 1950s and three in the 1960s. *Mancha que limpia* was approved without difficulty on all occasions, though Guillermo de Reyna's report of 13 April 1944 was not enthusiastic about the quality of the text. While crediting it with some literary and theatrical merits, he declared that, like all Echegaray's work, 'la obra resulta un poco pueril y simplista' ('the work is rather puerile and simplistic') (AGA 1687/40). He recommended authorisation, partly out of respect for the author's reputation, but suggested that the company should be required to ensure that the set and costumes were consistent with the period in which the play was written (the 1890s): the piece was to be treated as a quaint historical drama, not as an examination of social or moral issues with relevance to the present. Bourgeois nineteenth-century dilemmas about honour, loyalty and integrity were supposed to have been superseded by the stark certainties of Catholic morality allied with totalitarian patriotism.

Despite the frequency with which it had been performed in the preceding years, *El gran Galeoto*, like all works authorised prior to March 1942, was reassessed by the censors in 1943. Four reports were written in October–December of that year, and one of them contains a major surprise. An anonymous religious censor had mild reservations about the duels that feature in the plot, but as they are not played out onstage and they are condemned by characters in the play, they were deemed acceptable in a period piece.[8] The surprise was sprung by Gumersindo Montes Agudo, who forcefully proposed banning this play, one of the most familiar works of the entire national dramatic canon. He described the language of the play as pretentious and antiquated, and its theatrical impact as facile and overwrought. The real problems he perceived, though, were religious and moral:

> Matiz religioso: Inaceptable. Por su clima moral y por basarse el argumento, en parte, en un duelo. No se reconocen ni virtudes de caridad, ni de amor verdadero. Todo en ella es cruel y amargo.
>
> Juicio general que merece al censor: Obra pesimista, lacerante, sin valor moral. Presenta una lacra de la sociedad –la calumnia– vencedora en la lucha de pasiones que plantea. Por su argumento es deprimente; por su ambientación anticuada; por su desarrollo convencional y muy pesada.
>
> Juicio que merece al censor respecto a la posibilidad de su representación: No autorizar. (AGA 205/39) (See Figure 7)

> Religious implications: Unacceptable. Because of its moral climate and because the plot is based in part on a duel. There is no recognition of virtues of charity, nor of true love. Everything in the script is cruel and bitter.
>
> Overall assessment by the Censor: A pessimistic, harrowing work without positive moral value. It shows a social defect – malicious gossip – emerging triumphant from the conflict of passions portrayed. In its subject matter it is depressing; in its setting it is antiquated; in its dramatic development it is conventional and tedious.
>
> The Censor's judgement on whether the work should be licensed for performance: It should not be authorised.

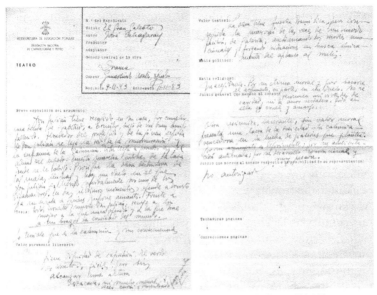

Figure 7: Montes Agudo's report on *El gran Galeoto* (1943)

Montes Agudo's startlingly harsh judgement prompted the head of the Sección de Cinematografía y Teatro, Antonio Fraguas, to commission another report in December 1943 from an ecclesiastical censor, Andrés de Lucas. He agreed that spectators would be left with a bitter aftertaste but did not judge the work to be immoral. He recommended approval, given that the play was so well known and frequently performed, and was so clearly located in the past. *El gran Galeoto* was authorised once more and continued to be staged, mostly by commercial companies on tour around provincial cities, earning mixed reviews in the press, some dismissing it as old-fashioned, melodramatic and contrived, and others expressing surprise that it still retained substantial dramatic power.

Objections to certain Echegaray plays from the point of view of Catholic morality were not unprecedented. In a volume listing morally unacceptable plays published in 1915 by the Franciscan friar Amado de Cristo Burguera y Serrano, four of Echegaray's works had been classified as 'prohibidas por malas' ('prohibited on the grounds of sinfulness'), while *La desequilibrada* ('Not in Her Right Mind') was in the category 'peligrosas por mundanas, sospechosas de inmoralidad o muy libres' ('dangerous on account of their worldliness, suspicions of immorality or excessive freedom') (Burguera y Serrano 1915). In the Church's film and theatre guide, *El gran Galeoto* was given a 'red' classification ('dangerous even for educated persons') (El Perpetuo Socorro 1945). However, it is significant that, even though Montes Agudo's reasons for banning the play were primarily religious, it was the ecclesiastical censors who recommended authorisation.

Even from a political point of view, Echegaray was not entirely to the taste of Francoists and Falangists, as he was too closely associated with nineteenth-century liberalism and the First Republic. Seeking to ingratiate himself with the regime in 1943, the writer Azorín sweepingly dismissed the politics and culture of the previous century as lacking in objectivity and scientific rigour; *El gran Galeoto* is cited as an example, dismissed as 'un drama pueril' ('a puerile drama') (Azorín 1943). In view of other reports written by Montes Agudo, especially his constant defence of Lorca's theatre, it is reasonable to assume that his objection to *El gran Galeoto* in November 1943 was more political than religious – and perhaps more aesthetic than either. It is tempting to think that he was simply tired of seeing this play recycled so frequently and spotted an opportunity to attempt to remove it from the canon.

Spanish theatre's other Nobel laureate, Jacinto Benavente, posed a more complicated challenge for the censors. He had published criticisms of the reformist government of 1931–3, but when war broke out he declared himself to be a loyal supporter of the Republic. He remained in Valencia throughout the war, joined protests against the murder of Lorca, and was appointed to the Consejo Central del Teatro in October 1937. He made a number of statements condemning Fascist brutality and claiming to have always had socialist inclinations (Aznar Soler 2010: 480–515). Although he wrote no new plays during the war, several of his existing works were performed in Madrid, Barcelona and Valencia. As Nationalist troops marched into Valencia on 29 March 1939, he wasted no time in siding with the victors, claiming that he had been forced to collaborate with Red propaganda:

Don Jacinto Benavente, rescatado
Comunican de Valencia que, a la entrada triunfal de las tropas españolas en la ciudad del Turia, una de las primeras personas que estuvieron al lado del glorioso general Aranda, saludando brazo

en alto el paso victorioso del Ejército liberador, fué el ilustre autor dramático D. Jacinto Benavente, cuyo cerebro privilegiado ha permanecido, durante tres años, lamentablemente prisionero de los rojos. (ABC 1939b)

Don Jacinto Benavente, rescued
It is reported from Valencia that, as Spanish troops made their triumphal entrance into the city, one of the first people to stand by the side of the glorious General Aranda, saluting the victorious parade of the Army of liberation with his arm raised, was the illustrious playwright Jacinto Benavente, whose first-rate intellect has, sadly, been held prisoner for three years by the Reds.

The repentant playwright was allowed to return to Madrid and resume his career without serious punishment. It has often been observed that the regime permitted his works to be staged on condition that his name did not appear in publicity and reviews (Rodríguez Puértolas 2008: 497 and Haro Tecglen 2002). In fact, theatre listings for Madrid and Barcelona show that the only period in which Benavente plays were being regularly advertised and reviewed without mentioning the name of the author was in 1943 (e.g., ABC 1943a and 1943b, and Vanguardia 1943). There is no mention in the AGA files of an explicit decision to impose this form of censorship on Benavente. From February 1944, his name again appeared regularly in publicity for his plays, and in October the government awarded him the Grand Cross of the Order of Alfonso X el Sabio.

Throughout the 1940s, Benavente took numerous opportunities to express his support for the regime and the *Caudillo* in speeches, interviews and newspaper articles; telling examples are given by Aznar Soler (2010: 515–24) and Rodríguez Puértolas (2008: 496–8). *Aves y pájaros* ('Birds and Fowl'), written in 1940, was his most blatant attempt to use his dramatic work to distance himself from his pro-Republican past. It contains an author's prologue, delivered by Benavente himself on the opening night, which suggests that the Spanish people, well-meaning but childlike, had been led astray and manipulated by left-wing intellectuals and demagogues. The play offers an 'Aristophanesque' allegory, in which the Republican leadership is caricatured as vicious, unscrupulous vultures, crows and magpies, finally overthrown by noble, patriotic eagles. The premiere took place on 30 October 1940. The review in *ABC* was highly favourable and reported that the audience paid the author a fervent homage, while he, deeply moved, 'dio las gracias y gritó un ¡Arriba España!, que fue contestado con indescriptible entusiasmo' ('thanked them and shouted "Long Live Spain!", which was echoed with indescribable enthusiasm') (Ródenas 1940). Nevertheless, more extreme members of the regime were unconvinced. A scornful critique was published in the Falangist daily *Arriba*, which at this time was generally recognised as a mouthpiece of the government:

> En *Aves y pájaros*, ha equivocado por completo su estrategia, y en cuanto a la comedia, es insuficiente. En lo político, D. Jacinto Benavente nos revela un desconocimiento completo del sentido de nuestro Movimiento [. . .] Lamentamos mucho que cuando ha tratado de escribir un canto a la gran obra nacional ha recurrido a lo fácil. No necesitamos tales alardes demagógicos, y era más nacional haber escrito una buena comedia más sobre el amor o sobre los celos. (Obregón 1940)

> In *Birds and Fowl*, he has completely misjudged his strategy, and as for the play itself, it is inadequate. In political terms, Jacinto Benavente reveals that he totally fails to understand the true sense of our Movement [. . .] It is highly regrettable that, on setting out to write a paean to the great national endeavour, he has resorted to something so facile. We have no need of such demagogic displays, and it would have been more in line with our nationalism to have turned out just another decent play about love or jealousy.

It would be interesting to know what the censors thought of *Aves y pájaros*, but there is no report in the file from 1940. However, the documentation shows that the authorisation was delayed for six months, suggesting that they had reservations. The application was submitted on 15 April 1940 by the López Heredia-Asquerino company, to be performed at the Teatro Lara in Madrid. The decision recorded on 26 April was: 'Suspendida temporalmente su representación' ('Performance temporarily suspended') (AGA 932/40). There is no indication of the reason for this decision apart from extensive cuts marked on the typescript in blue pencil. As the text is generally supportive of the Nationalist cause, it is difficult to interpret the recommendations for suppression. What most of them seem to have in common is that they make the allusions to the war too identifiable with certain factions within the

Nationalist coalition. For example, one line mentions the ignoble birds having killed *el Azor* ('the Goshawk'), which may be a reference to José Antonio Primo de Rivera. Another passage, extending over more than a page, discusses *los señoritos* ('privileged sons of wealthy landowners'), who, having lived a frivolous, carefree, irresponsible existence before the conflict, responded joyously to the call of the eagles and became heroes, redeeming themselves through sacrifice. Primo de Rivera and other Falangists were often characterised as *señoritos*. The problem here seems to be similar to the one encountered in some of the triumphalist spectacles discussed earlier in this chapter: the need to avoid the appearance of giving disproportionate credit for the victory to a particular group. The longest cut, covering more than ten pages of the script, is a piece of dialogue in which *el Ruiseñor* ('the Nightingale') defends his refusal to take sides, insisting that his song transcends worldly affairs and ideological conflict: 'Yo solo sé entrarme por los corazones abiertos de par en par al amor' ('All I know is how to find my way into hearts wide open to love') (AGA 932/40). This may sound innocuous (and may have been intended to reflect the author's own view), but in 1940, such a declaration of mystical neutrality could have been taken as criticism of the Church's zealous support for the Nationalist Crusade.

The López Heredia-Asquerino application was finally approved on 30 August 1940, with a list of twenty-six cuts. The review in *ABC* contains an indication that the cuts marked in the script were imposed: the critic praises Asquerino for being self-assured 'en su breve papel de Ruiseñor' ('in his brief role as Nightingale') (Ródena 1940). A report on *Aves y pájaros* was written by Father Constancio de Aldeaseca in October 1945, after the move of the censorship office to the Ministerio de Educación Nacional. The concerns of 1940 had now disappeared: Aldeaseca had no moral or religious objections and saw no need to maintain the suppressions (AGA 932/40).

Lo increíble ('Hard to Believe'), a non-political drama about the struggle of a married couple of very different ages to overcome malicious gossip and gain social acceptance, was approved more easily than *Aves y pájaros* and immediately became much more popular: applications for ten different productions were submitted between July and November 1940, followed by four in 1941. There is one interesting feature of this case which illustrates a shift in the ideological environment during the 1940s. The licence issued on 7 August 1940 required one speech to be cut. With a witty scepticism typical of the author, a character remarks that fashions and ideas do not really change. He continues:

> Las luchas más enconadas en los pueblos como en las familias, son casi siempre por querer lo mismo. Con distinto nombre o con distinta apariencia. Ya lo hemos visto en la última guerra. Las democracias decían que luchaban por la libertad, y, al emprender la guerra empezaron por suprimir la libertad, con lo que suprimieron para sus defensores y para sus partidarios el único aliciente que podía justificarla. (AGA 1371/40)

> The fiercest struggles between peoples, as in families, are almost always to do with both sides wanting the same thing. With a different name or different appearance. We've seen it in the last war. The democracies said that they were fighting for freedom, yet they began their war effort by suppressing freedom, with the result that they deprived their supporters and allies of the only thing that could justify the fight.

It is unclear whether the conflict referred to is the Spanish civil war or the world war. Cynicism about democracy and the allied powers was not problematic in 1940, but a suggestion that there was no moral or ideological difference between the two sides in the civil war would have been completely unacceptable. The regime's constantly repeated story was that the rebel uprising of July 1936 and the Nationalist victory represented not only the true Spain in opposition to Anti-Spain but also the will of God. When the text was reviewed in January 1944, a positive report by Montes Agudo led to authorisation with no mention of the earlier cut. Someone must have intervened during the first few days of the play's run, since a letter was sent by the Secretario Nacional de Propaganda to the González-Vico-Catalá-Carbonell company on 11 February informing them that the following phrase must be removed from the performance: 'Creería que por segunda vez se había realizado en el Mundo el milagro que solo se realizó una vez para que el Hijo de Dios viniera a la Tierra a redimir al Mundo' ('I'd believe that there had been a second occurrence of the miracle that only happened once so that the Son of God could come down to Earth to redeem Mankind') (AGA 1371/40). This sarcastic remark refers to the pregnancy of the young woman in the play who is married to a much older man. The legitimacy of the regime was no longer an urgent or contentious issue. Religious matters were now being given a higher priority, and such a flippant reference to the virgin birth must have caught the attention of a bishop or a member of a Catholic association.

La Infanzona ('The Gentlewoman') is usually taken to date from 1945, the year in which it was first performed in Buenos Aires. However, the play was written in 1941 and the reason for the Argentinian premiere was that it was banned in Spain. In addition to revealing what lay behind the prohibition and its reversal five years later, the file on *La Infanzona* also provides evidence of an interesting clash between levels of authority within the regime. It will be discussed in detail in the case study at the end of this chapter.

There were few problems with the authorisation of Benavente's pre-war plays. Numerous applications were made in the 1940s and 1950s for the most well-known works: sixty-one for *La malquerida* (*The Misbeloved*) between 1939 and 1967 (AGA 124/39); twenty-four for *Señora ama* (*The Lady of the House*) between 1940 and 1965 (AGA 1431/40), and seventeen for *El nido ajeno* (*Another's Nest*) between 1939 and 1951 (AGA 397/39). *Los intereses creados* (*The Bonds of Interest*) was also perennially popular. A couple of slightly disrespectful remarks about priests were cut from *Señora ama*, as was a suggestion that some Catholics might be ignorant of the Catechism in the case of *Lo cursi* ('The Done Thing') (AGA 1579/40). *Ni al amor ni al mar* ('Neither Love Nor the Sea') was temporarily banned on account of its ambivalent treatment of adultery and divorce, a decision that was reversed in June 1945 after an appeal by the celebrated Spanish-Argentinian actor-impresario Lola Membrives. Cannily, the argument made in the appeal focused not on challenging the censors' judgement but on the prestige of the author and the leading man (Enrique Borrás), both of whom were due to accompany Membrives on a tour of Argentina the following month. She signed off with a veiled threat of bad publicity if the appeal was rejected: 'Haré buen uso de dicha autorización y ello será amplia y favorablemente comentado en todos los círculos' ('I shall make good use of the authorisation, which will be extensively and favourably commented upon in all circles' (AGA 2993/42).

Alfilerazos ('Pinpricks') was the play in which Benavente's mischievous penchant for delivering mild shocks to polite society by having characters expose hypocrisy and sanctimoniousness through the expression of unconventional or revolutionary ideas encountered the strongest hostility from Franco's censors. First staged by Enrique Borrás in Buenos Aires in 1924, the play centres on the frustration experienced by don Remigio, a self-made man from a humble background whose attempts to use his wealth for the benefit of poor families and workers are obstructed by various entrenched interests. An application submitted by Borrás's company on 5 March 1940 was rejected on 24 April – a delay that suggests that there may have been consultation with higher authorities. The report by Palazón acknowledged that Benavente was being characteristically even-handed in his social critique but objected to the fact that 'se defiende la democracia, la huelga, la actitud violenta contra el orden, usando de frases y pensamientos que después de la guerra, nos parecen incongruentes y fuera de lugar' ('democracy, strikes and violent challenges to public order are defended, with the use of language and ideas which, following the war, now strike us as inappropriate and out of place') (AGA 828/40). The prohibition was confirmed in October 1942.

When an application was submitted in August 1945 for a production of *Alfilerazos* in Valencia, however, sharp differences of opinion between censors emerged. Montes Agudo recommended prohibition, judging the play to be of high quality but politically unacceptable and religiously irreverent. He concluded: 'La obra es totalmente contraproducente y negativa en estos momentos' ('The work is totally counterproductive and negative in current circumstances'). The regime was claiming to have given the country political and spiritual certainty through patriotic authoritarianism and traditionalist Catholicism, and anything that threatened to blur those certainties, however jocularly, was regarded as dangerous. Aldeaseca, in contrast, found the text morally unobjectionable, though he was worried that spectators might take the hypocritical attitudes of the religious characters to be representative of the Church's teachings on social issues. He acknowledged that there might be political and circumstantial factors making the play problematic but, as a priest, he left that judgement to his secular colleagues. José María Conde-Salazar recommended prohibition, sharing Aldeaseca's concern about the Catholic point of view being represented by 'unas cuantas beatas equivocadas' ('a bunch of ill-informed god-bothering women') and putting Montes Agudo's political point in more concrete terms: 'Estimamos esta obra difícilmente adaptable a la actualidad, sobre todo en España, donde encontramos nuestra solución Falangista' ('I regard this work as incompatible with current circumstances, especially in Spain, where we have found a solution [to these problems] – the solution offered by the Falange') (AGA 828/40). Benavente's urbane scepticism was incompatible with the official message that the Nationalist Crusade had rendered class conflict and social injustice obsolete.

However, this was the period in which the political centre of gravity was shifting away from the Falange. The censors were now working for the Ministerio de Educación Nacional, and it seems that someone in authority was not happy to let Montes Agudo and Conde-Salazar prevail. A fourth report was obtained from Francisco Narbona González, who argued that the moral-religious problem was not serious and that the political problem could be neutralised by making a few cuts and obliging companies performing the play to inform the audience that the action was set at a time prior to the 'War of Liberation'. In the end, the authorisation that was issued on 26 September did not impose either of these conditions. For the company, however, it was too late: they had planned to perform *Alfilerazos* on 25 August as part of a summer festival. A different company eventually staged the play in July 1947 at the Teatro Calderón in Madrid.

The documentation examined in this section not only reveals the extent to which censorship interfered with the routine business of the Spanish theatre industry by banning, delaying or cutting plays that were far from being politically dissident or posing a serious moral threat. Analysis of the censorship process also casts valuable light on how that industry worked and on the re-formation of the theatrical canon in the first decade of the post-war period. The next section examines another important element of the theatrical landscape that maintained its pre-war popularity and occupied a great deal of the time and attention of Franco's censors: the *revista*.

Taming the *revista*

Despite its reliance before 1939 on political satire, humour based on sexual *double entendres* and the display of female flesh, this genre of musical comedy returned in a less brazen form after the war and continued to be remarkably successful in the 1940s and 1950s. Earlier chapters have shown how the Republican authorities took a relaxed approach to the *revista* until the introduction of stricter regulations in 1935 and the critical reappraisal of the gender politics of this kind of spectacle during the war, and how the Francoist authorities in the early 1940s saw themselves as fighting a battle against a genre regarded as a threat to both public morals and the enforcement of censorship. The head of the Sección de Cinematografía y Teatro commented in an internal memo of October 1942 that he agreed with complaints from members of the public about the immorality of *revistas* and would be in favour of 'anular todas esas modalidades de espectáculos' ('eliminating all such forms of entertainment altogether') but recognised that a total ban would be impractical (AGA 21/0046). The political satire that had been an important part of the appeal in the 1930s was largely eliminated, but the genre continued to defy constraints on verbal and visual indecency. Its habits of improvisation and audience involvement also continued to pose challenges for the censors' aim to make performances conform to fixed scripts.

Many of the *revistas* staged in the 1940s had been first performed during the Republic, which in some cases resulted in censors objecting to outdated political references. *Las de Villadiego* ('The Lasses of Villadiego') by Emilio González del Castillo and José Muñoz Román with music by Francisco Alonso, first staged in 1933, was initially banned in 1940. A censor's report argued that it was not only immoral but also dangerous for its anachronism: 'Elecciones, voto femenino, diputados, república etc. Ni grotescamente deben llegar hoy a la escena aquellas funestas trapisondas, vergüenza de nuestra historia' ('Elections, women's suffrage, members of parliament, republic, etc. Not even in grotesque caricature should those awful, chaotic episodes of shame in our national history be put on stage today'). Francisco Ortiz's report agreed, describing the effect as a kind of 'torpe surrealismo, nada recomendable en el teatro de la nueva generación juvenil y luchadora' ('clumsy surrealism, far from recommendable in theatre intended for the new generation of young warriors') (AGA 1016/40). After more than a month of delay, the work was finally approved with cuts on sixteen pages, with an explicit condition that an inspection of the dress rehearsal was mandatory in each province in which performances were to take place. When an application was submitted in 1971, the revisions had been incorporated into the text. Bautista de la Torre's report declared that it had been toned down enough to be acceptable and could be approved subject to a rigorous inspection of the dress rehearsal (AGA 84/71). None of the three reports written at this time mentions the issue of anachronism: the comic situations based on female emancipation, voting and the dismantling of traditional family structures were now seen not as a threat but as a historical curiosity.

Although musicals written after the war tended to avoid explicitly political topics, censors often found political implications in comic characters, situations and comments. In the case of Muñoz Román's ¡Cinco minutos nada menos! ('Five Minutes, No Less!'), a massively successful show first performed in January 1944, one of the conditions imposed was that the ridiculous, opportunistic character Don Pito was not to be described as a retired colonel. The required cuts included a reference to taking a complaint to the *sindicato* ('trade union'): presumably, the problem here was that the only trade unions allowed by the Franco regime – the *sindicatos verticales* run by the Falange – were not intended to defend workers interests against employers but to bind workers into service to the state. Also marked as inappropriate was a joke about a man due to marry a woman with three children looking forward to collecting the state subsidy for large families the day after wedding. The only explicitly political line was a pun on the word *eje* (referring to the axle of a car but also to the Axis powers), which was cut (AGA 25/44).

However, most of the censors' concerns in relation to ¡Cinco minutos nada menos! were moral matters: actions and gestures, sexual innuendo in the dialogue, and the cut of the costumes. The suppressions recommended by the unidentified censor who submitted a report included a joke about a woman fearing the loss of her *sostén* (the support provided by her husband's wages but also her bra); repeated wordplay on the name of a newspaper, *La Verdad Desnuda* ('the naked truth'); *double entendres* around a woman called Concha (which can be a slang term for female genitals), and various frivolous remarks about marriage. What seemed to trouble the censor most, though, was an apparent lack of decorum in costume design. He insisted that 'no deben permitirse las transparencias ni los semidesnudos' ('see-through garments and partial nudity must not be allowed') and specified that female dancers should wear bras and, under their skirts, 'un pantalón bombacho' ('bloomers') covering their thighs (AGA 25/44).

As always, definitive authorisation was dependent on an inspection of the dress rehearsal, which was carried out by the head of the inspection service for Madrid on 19 January. His report was surprisingly positive: 'Todo el espectáculo es completamente blanco y en él no hay situaciones o gestos inmorales o equívocos' ('The entire show is completely innocent, without any immoral or ambiguous situations or gestures'). He found the costumes to be in much better taste than would normally be expected in a *revista*; indeed, in one musical number, 'las señoritas periodistas salían con unas faldas largas en demasía por lo que se les indicó la conveniencia de recogerlas un poco' ('the young ladies playing the role of journalists came on with skirts that were too long, as a result of which they were advised that the hems could be raised a little'). He found the exaggerated politeness with which a male character kissed the female lead slightly inappropriate. He noted at the end of his report that not all elements of the staging were in place for the rehearsal that he had inspected, and that a full dress rehearsal was due to take place on the evening of 20 January, which raises the suspicion that he was taken in by a classic ruse – disguising the skimpiness of the wardrobe and playing down gestures and intonation just for the inspector, only to dial everything up again on the opening night.

That the gullible inspector had had the wool pulled over his eyes seems to be confirmed by the report submitted on 20 January by another official who attended the final rehearsal (perhaps without notifying the company in advance). His report completely rejected the earlier description of the show and set out a series of conditions that it needed to fulfil: respect for all the cuts imposed; the suppression of all kisses on stage; stricter supervision of poses struck by artistes at various points in the performance; preventing the chorus girls in the 'California' number from lifting up their skirts and showing too much leg; less revealing costumes, and the use of modest underwear; covering-up of the star's *décolletage* in the penultimate scene; and lengthening of the trousers worn by the chorus girls when dressed as cowboys. The report concluded by declaring a general desire to 'arrancar de este género de una manera definitiva lo procaz y a mi juicio lo único que lleva al público' ('rid this genre once and for all of smuttiness, which in my view

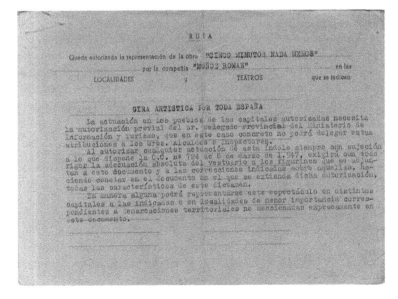

Figure 8: Censorship certificate authorising *Cinco minutos nada menos* (1946)

is the only thing that brings audiences in') (AGA 25/44). A letter signed by the Delegado Nacional de Propaganda was sent to the company on 21 January warning them to respect all the conditions laid down: actors were to stick strictly to the approved script, all costumes were to conform to the approved sketches, and all publicity material needed to be submitted for authorisation.

¡Cinco minutos nada menos! was so successful in Madrid that tours to numerous other places around the country were soon booked. Other documents in the file contain lengthy lists of towns and cities in which performances were authorised between March 1944 and June 1949, specifying that in each place the licence was subject to inspection of the dress rehearsal. Without explanation, some of the places in a list dated 26 March 1945 are crossed out. The locations not approved are generally smaller towns, where the public was thought to be less sophisticated and more impressionable than in the cities, though the list of deleted places included Logroño, a provincial capital – perhaps at the request of the civil governor there.

Female performers' costumes continued to be the most frequent point of contention in the policing of *revistas*. Despite the progressive tightening-up of procedures, constant supervision of performances continued to be needed. *El año pasado sin agua* ('The Old Year Run Dry') by José López de Lerena and Pedro Llabrés, with music by Ernesto Rosillo, was authorised in December 1948 with eight cuts. Reports were submitted by two censors, neither of whom raised significant issues. José Luis García Velasco noted that the humour was coarse but would be adequately mitigated by the cuts that he had marked on the script, which were a mixture of sexual insinuations and references to rationing and shortages of everyday goods. Emilio Morales de Acevedo advised that 'el cuadro 16 tiene un sastre afeminado que no debe remarcarse' ('scene 16 features an effeminate tailor, a role that should not be exaggerated') (AGA 638/48). Camp male roles were a staple ingredient of the humour of the *revista* and other comedy genres; the normal tactic adopted by censors was to tolerate the presence of such figures but insist that the effeminacy should not be played up.

To begin with, *El año pasado sin agua* seems to have been an unremarkable case, but the situation became more interesting just over a month into the show's run. A letter sent on 9 February 1949 by the Director General to the Delegado Provincial for Madrid in-

The Pervasiveness of Censorship during the Dictatorship 185

formed him that complaints had been received about the company not respecting the conditions of the authorisation and instructing him to carry out an unannounced inspection of a performance. He was told to pay particular attention to the musical number entitled 'La zamba', which was apparently arousing ardent enthusiasm among spectators for the sensuality of the dancing and the skimpiness of the costumes. The *zamba* is a traditional Argentinian folk dance, but the dance performed in the show is referred to in an inspector's report as a *samba* (Brazilian and much more sensual), which fits the description above more closely. The spelling *zamba* may have been a deliberate distraction on the part of the authors or the composer, so as not to arouse the suspicions of the censors reading the script. The Delegado Provincial was advised to obtain a seat as close to the stage as possible in order to enable him to check the truth of the allegation that 'por el elemento femenino de la Compañía en cuestión, se ha llegado incluso a la supresión de determinadas prendas femeninas de imprescindible uso por razones éticas y artísticas' ('female members of the company in question have gone so far as to dispense with certain items of ladies' wear that are an essential requirement for reasons both ethical and artistic') (AGA 638/48). There is no report in the file on this inspection, but the official must have confirmed the allegations, as a letter was sent to Mariano Madrid on 14 February 1949 imposing a fine of 5,000 pesetas, banning an entire scene, prohibiting 'La zamba' unless the costumes were changed, and warning that further infractions would result in the permanent withdrawal of the show's licence.[9]

The sanctions imposed in Madrid did not have a lasting effect on the company's respect for regulations. In October 1950, the Delegado Provincial in Badajoz reported that *El año pasado sin agua* was still being performed with a strong emphasis on eroticism, especially in Gracia Imperio's rendering of 'La zamba'. Mariano Madrid was warned that the lascivious moves must be toned down, and an inspector attended a performance. His report confirmed that the company was ignoring his department's admonitions: 'Gracia Imperio repitió el número a que aludo, de la misma forma desvergonzante, por sus insinuaciones y movimientos lúbricos, que se repitieron en las tres veces que se ejecutó la samba antes citada' ('Gracia Imperio performed the number in question in the same shameless way as before, with the same insinuations and lewd movements, which were repeated on the three occasions on which the samba was performed'). The Delegado Provincial reported that not only were his orders being flouted but the company was publicly mocking them. He requested that the Dirección General take action against the artiste and the company, and issued instructions that the samba was to be removed from the show. He must have been disappointed by the reply received more than a week later from the Director General, which merely instructed him to issue a formal warning that any further infringements would be severely punished. The paper trail ends there, without any indication that the authorities succeeded in bringing Madrid and his cast to heel.

Another Lerena and Llabrés show, *Su majestad la mujer* ('Her Majesty, Woman'), with music by Jacinto Guerrero, was approved in April 1950 with numerous cuts and conditions relating to set and costume designs. The Delegado Provincial for Madrid was instructed to carry out a particularly strict inspection, and his report demonstrated commendable zeal in the detailed attention paid to female performers' costumes. He listed four modifications that he had required the company to make. One outfit needed to have an extra piece of fabric inserted so as to connect the top and bottom of what appears to have been a kind of bikini. In another, the straps of bathing suits worn by performers lying down at the front of the stage were to be shortened to limit the amount of cleavage on view. The skirts worn by two dancers in the roles of 'the Psychologist' and 'the Philosopher' were not allowed to feature slits, and the flesh-coloured underwear worn by the chorus line was to be replaced by something in a different colour (AGA 115/50).

In the early 1950s, Matías Colsada was emerging as the leading impresario of the *revista*. He enhanced production values, specialising in opulent staging and lavish publicity, but stuck to the traditional formula of risqué dialogue and songs together with attractive female stars and costumes as skimpy as the censors would allow. The Colsada show *Cirilo, que estás en vilo* ('Cyril, You're as Jumpy as a Squirrel'), by Enrique Paradas, Joaquín Jiménez and Francisco de Torres, with music by Ernesto Rosillo and Juan Mollá, was banned on 4 October 1953. Adolfo Carril's report unhesitatingly recommended prohibition on the grounds that there were unacceptable lines and situations on every page of the script: 'Se trata de un libro de revista, tan burdo y grosero en su argumento y desarrollo que lo estimo totalmente improcedente' ('The text in question is that of a musical comedy that is so crude and distasteful that I consider it totally inadmissible') (AGA 325/53). The extensive cuts marked on the script are all instances of mild sexual *double entendre* – generally less ribald than many earlier examples of the genre, which suggests that some censors were becoming more intolerant of indecency. A revised version of the script was approved on 17 November with a few further cuts. The production did not go ahead in November 1953, but a new application was approved in November 1954.

The standard conditions attached to licences issued for *revistas* and variety shows were now lengthy and meticulous, attempting to make the coordination of central and local censorship decisions as watertight as possible. As well as a list of cuts and amendments to the script, the number of approved set and costume design sketches was specified, with an indication of any changes required, and the responsibility of Delegados Provinciales to carry out inspections and give final approval to all details of staging was emphasised. The conditions for *Cirilo, que estás en vilo* included remarkably detailed specifications for wardrobe modifications. Thirty-two different outfits were required to be worn with petticoats and a type of bloomers known as *truxas*, while eleven others were to be complemented by underwear in a fabric similar to the costume and of the same length. The censors seem to have got their way in this case: an undated report on a performance later in the 1950s recorded that there was no cause for complaint. However, the same report noted that formal warnings had been issued to the Colsada company on several other occasions.

Although the public's enthusiasm for the traditional *revista* was on the wane by the early 1960s, Colsada and a few other impresarios were still making money from the genre – and still fighting skirmishes against the censors. The report on censorship produced for Fraga in 1964 insisted that, despite the general policy of *apertura*, with regard to the *revista* 'la censura ha sido, no más amplia, sino más severa' ('censorship has been more severe, not more lenient') (MIT 1964: 48). This claim seems to be backed up by the case of *Las siete niñas de Écija* ('The Seven Écija Girls') by Pedro Llabrés and Juan de Azaila, with music by José García-Bernalt. An application was made on 12 February 1965 for a production opening on 19 February in Toledo. Arcadio Baquero's report was brief and stringent: 'De acuerdo con la norma 18, y debido a la acumulación de escenas, frases, y situaciones groseras, mi informe es de prohibición' ('With reference to criterion 18, and on account of the accumulation of indecent scenes, phrases and situations, my recommendation is prohibition'). Víctor Aúz Castro agreed, also citing *norma* 18 – the clause in the 1963 regulations which refers to an accumulation of minor issues resulting in an overall impression of unacceptable immorality or violence – and listing ten pages on which cuts would need to be made. José Luis Vázquez Dodero's recommendation was similar: 'Tiene que estar sometida a tantos cortes que o se prohíbe o se reconsidera' ('So many cuts need to be made that the work should either be banned or revised') (AGA 27/65). The suppressions marked by Aúz in the script are almost all to do with a series of inane jokes and *double entendres* about the lack of interest in sex of Chicha I and Chicha II, the kings of an imaginary country.

The decision to ban *Las siete niñas de Écija* was confirmed on 16 February. Two days later Azaila submitted an appeal, accompanied by an extensively revised script, in which the Chichas are no longer kings but businessmen (presumably resulting in changes to costumes), and references to their sexual impotence have been removed or made much more oblique. Azaila's appeal letter provides interesting evidence of the economic impact of censorship decisions. Azaila pointed out that the show was booked to open on 23 February at the Teatro Ruzafa in Valencia (the plan to perform in Toledo must already have been abandoned), for which a cast of forty performers had been taken on, including stars recruited from Argentina, England and France. He added that around half a million pesetas had already been spent, largely on publicity, and spelled out the business problem: 'En el caso de no verificarse el estreno, por falta de programación debido a la premura de tiempo, la empresa de la Compañía habría de indemnizar con una fuerte cantidad a la del Teatro, que habría de permanecer cerrado algunos días con el consiguiente perjuicio económico y moral' ('If the production does not go ahead, the absence of any alternative programming due to the short notice will result in the Company being liable for the payment of substantial compensation to the owners of the Theatre, which will be obliged to remain closed for several days, causing significant financial losses and damage to morale' (AGA 27/65). His collaborator, García-Bernalt, wrote a letter to the prominent radio and television commentator Matías Prats Cañete, pleading with him to use his influence to facilitate the swift approval of the production. He explained that the cast had been rehearsing for twenty-eight days; he had invested everything he owned in the show, and now faced the prospect of having to pay compensation to the Teatro Ruzafa, honour the contracts of the foreign stars, and leave thirty-two Spanish families out on the street (AGA 27/65). The emergency rewriting did the trick: Aúz, Baquero and Vázquez Dodero all recommended authorisation for audiences over eighteen, though they imposed three further cuts.

Luis Escobar, who had taken over the Teatro Eslava in Madrid, developed a successful brand of shows that recycled material from previous hits, beginning with *Te espero en Eslava* ('I'll See You at the Eslava') in December 1957. In 1965, he managed to stage a version of *La corte de Faraón* (*The Court of the Pharaoh*), a racy zarzuela of 1910 banned since 1940, by disguising it as a show about gangsters in 1920s Chicago under the title *La bella de Texas* ('Texas Belle') (Escobar 2000: 210).[10] In September 1971, two complete scenes from his show *Eslava 101* were prohibited. He lodged an appeal, which was rejected by the Junta de Censura. However, Escobar had connections at the highest levels. He spoke to the Director General de Cultura Popular y Espectáculos (Enrique Thomas de Carranza), who promised to see what he could do, and two days later the Subdirector, Mario Antolín Paz, rang him to say that the cuts had been withdrawn and that he himself would attend the inspection of the dress rehearsal – which went without a hitch (Escobar 2000: 269).

The recollections of a member of the chorus line of *Eslava 101*, Teresa del Olmo, cast an interestingly different light on the *revista* and how it was seen by the censors. The second part of the show was played in modern dress, including 'hippy' outfits loosely inspired by Ragni, Rado and MacDermot's rock musical *Hair* (1967, not staged in Spain until 1983). Del Olmo recalls that the inspectors at the dress rehearsal instructed several female members of the cast to change into longer skirts but paid no attention to the costumes worn by the male performers, some of whom appeared in very tight flared trousers, with bare torsos. The male lead asked the costume designer to make him a particularly close-fitting, low-waisted pair of trousers in a stretch fabric. As the show's run got under way, the cast began to notice that the predominantly female audiences that typically attended late-afternoon performances were filling one side of the auditorium much more than the other. The draw was a pose adopted several times by the male lead, who would stand facing across the stage and use a tape sewn into his trousers to pull the front of them taut across his groin, offering a bulging profile to the audience. Inspectors attended several performances but never objected to this piece of business: 'La mente enferma de los censores éramos las mujeres –nosotras, los escotes, las piernas, la tripa, el culo . . . Éramos el pecado. Y sin embargo estaba este señor, con un paquete de padre y muy señor mío, enseñando pectorales . . .' ('The sick minds of the censors were obsessed with us, the women – cleavages, legs, bellies, bums . . . We represented sinfulness. And yet here was this guy showing his pectorals and sporting a packet like a bull's . . .') (Olmo 2019). Despite their repeated complaints over the decades about the tastelessness of the *revista*, the censors had always been complicit in the commercial and sexual exploitativeness of the genre.

The *revista* was an important and immensely popular component of the entertainment industry during the Second Republic and the dictatorship. Looking at it through the lens of the censorship files casts fascinating light on the evolution of the genre, how it was received by audiences and censors, and how it continually challenged not only the moral values of National-Catholicism but also the regime's efforts to regulate, fix and homogenise performance cultures.

The slow re-emergence of Catalan theatre

The censorship decisions discussed so far in this chapter affected individual playwrights, companies, genres, texts and productions, and were motivated by particular political and religious factors. There was another dimension of the Franco regime's regulation of the theatre that constituted a much more wide-ranging and indiscriminate process of censorship: a blanket ban on performances in Catalan, Basque and Galician, which was maintained until 1946. There was no particular piece of legislation prohibiting performances in languages of Spain other than Castilian, as there had been in 1867 (see Chapter 1), but Franco had made clear during the war that language would be a key component of the goal of political unification: national unity was to be 'absoluta, con una sola lengua, el castellano, y una sola personalidad, la española' (Franco 1938). It was Catalan theatre that was most seriously affected by the policy, since Barcelona was the most important centre of theatrical activity outside Madrid. When a new theatrical season got under way in Barcelona in February 1939, productions were exclusively in Castilian, the repertoire heavily dependent on transfers from Madrid and the trends discussed earlier in this chapter.[11]

The AGA contains hardly any evidence of applications for plays in Catalan (or Basque or Galician) being turned down in the early post-war period. It was obvious that it would be pointless, possibly dangerous, even to make the attempt, and for commercial companies this was a risk not worth taking. The only applications between 1939 and 1941 for plays in Catalan were from the Valencian region. Xavier Fàbregas argues that theatre in Catalan-speaking areas outside Catalonia was censored slightly less severely than in Catalonia itself, treated as 'un producte inofensiu' ('an inoffensive product') less likely to be associated with nationalist sentiment (1978: 267). However, *Un revolcó a temps* ('A Tumble in Time') by Francisco Marín Melià must have been submitted too early to benefit from such tolerance, as it was banned in November 1939 (AGA 463/39). *El Negre* ('Blackie'), a Valencian rural drama from 1924 by Fernando Lluch Ferrando, was approved in August 1941. The brief report by José María García Escudero did not comment directly on the fact that the script was mostly in Catalan, though it did complain that the language was 'a veces impropio' ('occasionally improper') (AGA 2428/41). This refers mostly to the slightly irreverent use of religious expressions (several instances of which were cut from the script), but may also have been a way of showing disapproval of the language.

A few dramatists were writing plays in Catalan in the early 1940s with no expectation that they would be staged. Salvador Espriu wrote *Antígona* in 1939 (not performed until 1958); Josep Maria de Sagarra returned from exile in 1940 and devoted much of his time to translating Shakespeare's plays; Joan Brossa began writing experimental 'poetry for the stage' in 1942 which did not begin to be performed regularly until the 1960s. Fàbregas records a small number of unauthorised readings and amateur performances in Catalan in private houses in the early 1940s (1978: 268–9), and Gallén presents evidence of amateur groups staging plays in Catalan in various locations in the early 1940s, below the radar of censorship (2010: 121–2).

The only exceptions to the blanket ban were the traditional Nativity plays (*Pastorets*) and Passion plays, which the Church insisted should continue to be performed in Catalan. In December 1939, the Civil Governor of Barcelona issued a statement confirming that *Pastorets* could be performed in Catalan, with the approval of the office of the Civil Governor, as long as they were of 'un exclusivo carácter religioso familiar' ('an exclusively religious and family character') rather than public spectacles; they could not be performed in venues normally used for theatre, cinema, dances or other entertainment, and tickets were not allowed to be sold (Vanguardia 1939d). Professional productions of Nativity plays in commercial theatres had to be performed in Castilian until 1946, creating a mixed economy of *Pastorcillos* (in Castilian) and *Pastorets* (in Catalan). The genre gradually acquired more and more importance as one of the few channels available for the public use of Catalan, benefiting from a network of well-equipped theatres maintained by parishes. Performances always expanded the core Nativity story to include other scenes centring on the shepherds, creating a safe space for the representation of Catalan folk culture and the celebration of Catalan popular language.[12] The survival of the *Pastorets* tradition helped to nurture community performance groups all over Catalonia and maintain a theatrical infrastructure that later became useful to secular and semi-professional performance groups.

In principle, Nativity and Passion plays were not subject to state censorship, but local authorisation could be refused if there was a suspicion of the purely religious function being compromised. There are a few authorisations for *Pastorets* amongst the notifications in the censorship files held in the Arxiu Nacional de Catalunya. One, for performances in the town of El Vendrell in 1966, even required two cuts to the script and specified that an inspection of the dress rehearsal was required – an unusual condition for performances authorised for audiences of all ages. This production was a new initiative, which may be what attracted the interest of the censors. The offending lines contain what look like innocuous references to Joseph initially suspecting Mary of adultery until he is reassured by an angel that 'el que está engendrat en ella és per obra del Sant Esperit' ('the child has been engendered in her by the Holy Spirit'); the angel is also quoted as referring to Jesus as 'el qui ha de salvar al vostre poble i el qui l'ha d'alliberar dels seus pecats' ('the one who will save your people and free them from their sins'), which may have been judged to hint at political implications (ANC 348/66). Also in the 1966–7 Christmas season, the celebrated *L'Estel de Natzaret* ('The Star of Nazareth') by Ramon Pàmies, performed every year in the Barcelona suburb of Sant Vicenç de Sarrià, was authorised for audiences of all ages, but in this case too an inspection of the dress rehearsal was required (ANC 356/66). It may be that, in the rebellious atmosphere of the mid-1960s, censors were wary of the possibility of *Pastorets* groups introducing subversive elements into their performances.

The lifting of the ban on performances in Catalan in 1946 was part of the shift in power within the regime after the end of the Second World War. Soon after the transfer of responsibility for censorship from the Secretaría General del Movimiento to the Ministerio de Educación Nacional in July 1945, Bartolomé Barba Hernández was appointed as Civil Governor of Barcelona, bringing a more relaxed approach to cultural production in Catalan. In his memoirs (published in 1948), Barba disingenuously claims that the impact of the government's decision to allow performances in Catalan was culturally and politically insignificant:

> La autorización del teatro catalán privó a los elementos catalanistas de la única bandera fácil y popular que les quedaba, fue un paso hacia la normalidad y, por otra parte, no fue acogida con ninguna manifestación extraordinaria de entusiasmo por el público, lo que daba a entender que la masa de población no hace ni pretende hacer bandera de combate de su lengua, como quisieran los cuatro agitadores que aún quedan flotando sin punto posible de apoyo después de estas disposiciones. (Quoted in Gallén 1985: 111)

> The authorisation of theatre in Catalan deprived the Catalanists of the only easy and popular rallying point they had left. It was a step towards normality and was, in any case, not greeted with any great show of enthusiasm by the masses, which indicated that the majority of the population has no desire to use their language as a campaign banner, despite the urgings of the handful of agitators who have been left drifting without support after the introduction of these measures.

Although press censorship ensured that the re-establishment of performances in Catalan was not reported or reviewed, there is evidence that some of the first professional productions were received with considerable enthusiasm. There certainly was popular demand for Catalan theatre, and Barba's confidence that Catalans were uninterested in making a banner of their language was eventually proved to be spectacularly ill-founded. If the impact of the lifting of the ban was limited, this was largely due to continuing restrictions on press coverage and advertising, and limits on the number of venues licensed for productions in Catalan.

The first play authorised for production in Catalan was *Lo ferrer de tall* ('The Knifemaker') by Frederic Soler, a rural drama first staged in 1874. There is no indication in the file that the language of the text was a significant issue, and the censor's report was entirely positive. However, there was a lengthy delay, setting a pattern that remained a feature of theatre in Catalonia long after 1946. The script was inexplicably returned to the applicant on 20 April without a decision, perhaps because the change of policy had not yet been finalised. The application was resubmitted on 30 April and was not approved until 16 June. In the meantime, local authorisation must have been obtained, for the production opened at the Teatro Apolo on 10 May (with a preview at the Fomento Martinense community association on 2 May) and ran until 18 June, advertised as a 'grandioso éxito' ('great hit') (Vanguardia 1946). It ran again at the Apolo from July to September and was taken on tour around Catalonia by the Romea company. There was little about this rather old-fashioned play in itself that would have excited Barcelona audiences in 1946, and no reviews were published in the press: its success must have come primarily from the simple fact of constituting the first opportunity for more than seven years to hear Catalan on a commercial stage.

The success of *Lo ferrer de tall* was not an isolated phenomenon. The season of Catalan theatre offered by the Borràs-Clapera company included revivals of three other classics: Santiago Rusiñol's *La bona gent* ('Good People') from 21 May and *El pintor de miracles* ('The Painter of Miracles') from 26 May, and special tribute performances of Àngel Guimerà's *Terra baixa* (*Marta of the Lowlands*) on 18 June. Other hits in the summer of 1946 were *Lo nuvi* ('The Fiancé') by Feliu i Codina, Rusiñol's *L'auca del senyor Esteve* ('The Ballad of Senyor Esteve') and Sagarra's *L'Hostal de la Glòria* ('Gloria's Guesthouse'). The restriction of the number of theatres licensed for performances in Catalan has sometimes been exaggerated: Ciurans claims that plays in Catalan could be performed in only one Barcelona theatre at a time, with a few venues taking turns (2005: 316). However, listings in the press between 1946 and 1949 frequently show at least three Barcelona theatres simultaneously offering shows with Catalan titles. For example, on 24 July 1946, six productions in Catalan were advertised and seven in Castilian. Long-established companies that had turned themselves into *compañías de teatro español* in 1939 were now re-branding themselves as *compañías de teatro catalán* (Vila-Daví, Borràs-Clapera and Pujol-Fornaguera) and were joined by new companies specialising in theatre in Catalan.

Sagarra is often identified as the first Catalan playwright to have a new play staged: his *El prestigi dels morts* ('The Prestige of the Dead') was authorised in September 1946 and premiered on 17 October at the Teatro Romea. However, the Valencian musical comedy *La cotorra del mercat* ('The Parrot in the Market') by Paco Barchino and Leopoldo Magenti could be regarded as the first new work in Catalan to be staged in Barcelona, at the Teatro Condal from 17 July 1946 following a successful run in Valencia (Soler Carnicer 2007: 161). *El prestigi dels morts* was also preceded by Salvador Bonavia i Panyella's musical *La Pinxeta i el noi maco* ('La Pinxeta and the Likely Lad'), which premiered at the Teatro Victoria on 24 July 1946.

By the early 1950s, performances in Catalan by professional and amateur companies were a normal feature of the Barcelona theatre scene, although not a prominent one. Theatre in Catalan received no official encouragement or investment and little press coverage, and was still overshadowed by theatre in Castilian, largely transfers from Madrid. Advertisements for Catalan plays still had to be in Spanish, and the names of playwrights, directors and actors were still given in their Castilian form. The vernacular repertoire continued to be dominated by classics, and few new plays in Catalan were being produced.[13] Gallén provides figures showing that the number of new plays in Castilian staged in Barcelona between 1947 and 1954 was 630, compared with 116 in Catalan (18 per cent of the total) (1985: Appendices 7 and 11).

The support of the Church in Catalonia for certain non-commercial theatrical initiatives continued to be crucial.[14] FESTA (Foment de l'Espectacle Selecte i Teatre Associació), an organisation established in Barcelona in 1948 to promote amateur theatre in Catalan, was, according to its Honorary President from 1960 to

1972, Tomàs Roig i Llop, frequently protected by the Diocese from censorial interference:

> Aquesta entitat només va poder funcionar emparant-se en la influència de la Diòcesi de Barcelona [. . .] Malgrat això, per part de les autoritats governatives d'aleshores hi va haver les corresponents multes de tant en tant (a mi mateix me'n varen posar per promocionar teatre en català) i jo simplement les portava al Bisbat (al palau del Bisbe) i ells deien: 'No s'hi amoïni, i vostès endavant, que nosaltres en responem.' Efectivament, mai no vàrem pagar-ne cap. (2005: 124)

> The organisation could only function with the protection of the Diocese of Barcelona [. . .] In spite of that, the authorities levied the requisite fines from time to time (I was fined a few times myself for promoting theatre in Catalan), but I just took the papers to the diocesan office (the Bishop's Palace) and they would say: 'Don't worry, you carry on, we'll take care of it.' As it turned out, we never had to pay a single one.

The everyday constraints on Catalan theatre in this period are vividly illustrated by the case of Cecília A. Màntua. She had begun to write in Catalan for theatre and radio before the war, but the plays for which she sought approval in the early 1940s were in Castilian, sometimes with Catalan or Valencian settings. They were usually approved, sometimes with cuts or after revision, but the censorship files repeatedly show unexplained delays and signs of hostility towards a Catalan author. The *zarzuela* written in collaboration with Antonio Losada, *A ti vuela mi canción* ('My Song Flies to You'), was initially prohibited in October 1941 on the grounds that it was 'escrita en pésimo castellano' ('written in appalling Spanish') (AGA 2525/41), though a revised version was judged to be well written and was approved (AGA 2705/41). *La riada* ('The Flood'), a rural drama set in Valencia, featuring some dialogue in Valencian dialect, was approved in August 1944 but on condition that 'la totalidad de la obra se representará en perfecto castellano, sin palabras ni frases algunas en Valenciano' ('the work in its entirety shall be performed in perfect Castilian, without any words or phrases in Valencian') (AGA 497/44). Màntua took several years to reinvent herself as a writer of plays in Catalan after 1946, and her most famous work, *La Pepa maca* ('Our Pepa'), dismissed by the censors as clichéd and sentimental, was held up by the censors for so long in 1950 that the production was abandoned. She made use of performances in small non-commercial venues to pave the way for a commercial premiere in July 1959, and the play became a huge success.[15]

The development of non-commercial and amateur theatre in Barcelona was given a significant boost by the foundation of the Agrupació Dramàtica de Barcelona (ADB) in 1955. Committed to a repertoire exclusively in Catalan and with the aim of creating a model for a national theatre of Catalonia, the group staged forty-one plays by Catalan authors (most of them living) and twenty-four by foreign authors (classics such as Shakespeare, Molière and Chekhov, as well as contemporary playwrights such as Rattigan, Ionesco, Anouilh and Brecht) (Casas 2011: 46–50).[16] In addition to the usual interference from censorship, the ADB's determination to make foreign plays translated into Catalan an important part of their output, and thereby raise the profile of Catalan as a vehicle for international drama, came up against another obstacle erected by the authorities. In 1957, new regulations were introduced governing the performance of plays translated into Catalan. The first clause threatened to make this part of the ADB's mission impossible, as it restricted permission for the performance of plays translated into Catalan to professional theatre, ruling out performances of foreign plays by 'las agrupaciones o cuadros de aficionados que actúan regularmente en locales propios, en la región catalana' ('associations or amateur groups operating regularly in their own venues in the Catalan region') (statement released by the Delegación Provincial del Ministerio de Información y Turismo in December 1957, reproduced in Gallén 2013: 113). However, in a letter of January 1958, the playwright, translator and lawyer Xavier Regàs identified a loophole that could be exploited by the ADB: 'Es evident que vostès no actuen regularment com les companyies a les quals aludeix i que solen fer-ho cada diumenge, ni disposen de local propi. No hi ha dubte, doncs, que han de quedar al marge' ('It's clear that your group doesn't operate regularly in the same way as the companies referred to, which tend to perform every Sunday, and nor do you have a venue of your own. There's no doubt, then, that your case falls outside the scope of that regulation') (CDMAE Fons ADB, E91). The ADB succeeded in continuing to stage foreign drama in Catalan until it was closed down by the authorities in 1963 after a conflict over a production of Brecht's *Threepenny Opera*. This episode was another example of theatremaking in Catalonia being obstructed by the censorship bureaucracy: the correspondence between the ADB, the Delegado Provincial, the Dirección General and other interested parties tells a sorry tale of delays, confusion and obfuscation (CDMAE Fons ADB, E98-08).

A celebration of the Catalan theatrical tradition in 1964 prompted an article in *ABC* lamenting the slow death of Catalan theatre due to 'una ausencia de público, una quiebra de empresa y un desaliento en autores y actores' ('a lack of audiences, the failure of companies, and despondency amongst authors and actors') (Vila-San Juan 1964). Censorship had undoubtedly played a part in hindering the re-emergence of theatre in Catalan after 1946, but it was not the only cause. Its effects were compounded by a range of other factors: a lack of initiative, imagination and investment from impresarios; commercial dependence on the Spanish-language repertoire; insufficient public subsidy and institutional support; a lack of interest from the local bourgeoisie; weaknesses in the training and professional support available to actors and directors. What Vila-San Juan did not acknowledge was that, despite all these impediments, the seeds had already been sown – in the network of community performance groups, the work of the ADB, the unobtrusive emergence of new authors and the establishment of new initiatives such as the Escola d'Art Dramàtic Adrià Gual – for the exciting growth of independent theatre that would become a distinctive feature of Catalan culture in the 1960s and 1970s (which is discussed in Chapter 6).

This chapter has demonstrated that the theatre censorship exercised during the early and middle years of the dictatorship was not a simple matter of a monolithic regime suppressing a specific set of unacceptable ideas and behaviours while promoting its own values. The picture that has emerged is complex, multifactorial and sometimes surprising. None of the examples discussed was a clearly oppositional or subversive work, but the evidence has shown censorship constantly interfering in the everyday work of the theatre industry in a variety of ways, sometimes ineffectually. Censors devoted less time and energy to actively suppressing expressions of dissent than to other mundane forms of control: monitoring obscure ideological issues related to the balance of power within the regime; tidying up inconvenient echoes of Republican social and political circumstances in revived works from the 1930s; paying a prudish degree of attention to irreverence or vulgarity of language and indecency of dress and onstage behaviour. Their efforts were also devoted to policing the boundaries of theatrical genres and attempting to discipline improvisational forms of performance.

Case study

La Infanzona, by Jacinto Benavente
Teatro Calderón (Madrid), 10 January 1947, Compañía Lola Membrives

La Infanzona is darker and more morally problematic than the Benavente plays discussed earlier in this chapter. Its protagonist, Doña Isabel, has concealed from her son José María the identity of his father; José María suspects that his father was murdered by Leoncio, one of his mother's brothers, but when he challenges Leoncio and is wounded, Isabel reveals that Leoncio *is* his father and stabs him to death. This was a risky text to write in 1941. Benavente must have known that the topic of incest and the violent way in which the dramatic crisis was resolved were likely to provoke unease and possibly outrage. The censorship file on this play is interesting not only for the evidence of how the censors weighed up the moral threat of the text, but also for its revelation of a surprising power struggle between different agents of censorship.

The first application for approval of a production of *La Infanzona* was lodged on 11 September 1941 by the López Heredia-Asquerino company. A report submitted by E. Romeu on 13 September recognised that audiences were likely to be attracted to the work but warned that the attraction would be unhealthy and immoral, not only because of the incest and references to violent revenge but also on account of 'el casuismo racionalista y el temor antimisericordiosamente católico en que actúan los personajes' ('the emphasis in the characters' behaviour on rationalistic casuistry and lack of faith in divine mercy') (AGA 2472/41). The problem was not simply the moral unacceptability of building a plot around incest but the ambivalence with which it was treated. Censors were sometimes disapproving of the insouciant intellectual detachment that Benavente tended to display in his comedies; in this case what was dangerous was the refusal to allow the tragic dilemma to be resolved by orthodox Catholic principles. The verdict of 'prohibida' was issued on 15 September.

Benavente did not give up on *La Infanzona*. He was developing his successful partnership with Lola Membrives, who had staged several of his plays before the war. Her company was touring regularly in Spain and South America, and she agreed to include this play in the repertoire. It opened in Buenos Aires on 6 December 1945 and went on to be performed in other cities in Argentina and Chile. On 18 September 1946, Membrives applied for permission to bring her production to Spain. The religious censor Mauricio de Begoña was slightly less condemnatory in his report than Romeu had been in 1941, suggesting that 'los equívocos y conceptos eclécticos y fluctuantes abundan mucho menos que en otras obras del mismo autor' ('the ambiguities and the eclecticism and flexibility of the concepts are much less marked in this work than in others by the same author'). Nevertheless, he insisted that the fact that the plot revolved around incest was enough to warrant prohibition.

Surprisingly, this was not the end of the story. A handwritten note on the report form shows that Begoña's recommendation was overruled, perhaps by García Espina, the Director General: 'Visto el anterior informe y considerando que en la apreciación absoluta de esta obra juegan otros factores muy importantes de índole nacional y política por la condición insigne de su autor, esta Dirección General ha resuelto autorizar la representación en España de "La Infanzona"' ('In view of the above report, and bearing in mind that the overall assessment of this work involves other highly important factors of national politics on account of the prestigious reputation of the author, the Directorate General has decided to authorise performances in Spain of *La Infanzona*') (AGA 2472/41). The case of *Ni al amor ni al mar* showed that Membrives – who in addition to being a leading theatre impresario had a public role as cultural attaché at the Argentinian embassy – was a powerful ally for Benavente, adept at convincing the Francoist authorities that the negative publicity generated by a high-profile ban was more uncomfortable than allowing a controversial production to go ahead. It may be that it was her lobbying that persuaded them to approve *La Infanzona*.

The Membrives production opened at the Teatro Calderón in Madrid on 10 January 1947 and was an immediate hit with audiences and critics. *ABC* published an extended, hyperbolic review praising the staging and the quality of the text – the psychological depth of the characterisation and the consummate skill with which the action was brought to an explosive climax: 'El corazón de los espectadores sube a la garganta y el pulso se detiene y llega a nosotros la auténtica dimensión de la tragedia, de la verdadera, de la única' ('Every spectator feels their heart in their throat and their pulse stopping, and we know that we are in the presence of the authentic dimension of tragedy – true, unique tragedy') (Marqueríe 1947).

Unwilling to lose out altogether, Irene López Heredia re-applied on 12 March for permission to stage *La Infanzona*, which was granted. Both companies set out to tour the play, but further obstacles lay in wait. The Membrives company was booked to open on 5 April at the Teatro Principal in Zaragoza. However, on 22 March the mayor of Zaragoza, José María Sánchez Ventura, decided to ban the production, asserting that the city council, as owner of the venue, had the power to exercise moral censorship over works to be performed in it. He published lengthy justifications of the decision in the local press, citing negative reviews of the play published by Catholic organisations. The ban was supported by Miguel Sancho Izquierdo, Rector of Zaragoza University and an appointed member of the city council, in an open letter published in the local newspaper *El Noticiero* on 25 March. Sancho Izquierdo's lengthy letter went beyond the particulars of the case to offer an interesting general defence of censorship from an intransigent Catholic point of view. He lamented a growing tendency to allow moral absolutes to be blurred in the name of artistic expression:

> Admira el ver cómo católicos [. . .] posponen la Moral y el Bien a un concepto muy discutible de Arte (de esto del Arte habría mucho que hablar) y pretenden justificar lo inmoral y pecaminoso por ir envuelto en las galas del mismo. Y no. Lo malo, lo objetivamente malo, es malo siempre y si va rebozado y como disimulado, doblemente malo por ser más difícil de advertir. (AGA 2472/41)

> It is disconcerting to see Catholics [. . .] subordinating Morality and Goodness to a highly debatable concept of Art (about which much could be said), and attempting to justify immorality and sinfulness on the grounds of it being dressed up as Art. This is wrong. What is objectively branded as evil is always evil, and doubly so if presented in a disguised manner, since that makes it more difficult to identify.

Sancho Izquierdo insisted on the duty of the authorities to protect the public from unpleasant and corrupting material, even if censorship proved to be counterproductive. If the controversy provoked by a ban in Zaragoza resulted in increased attendance elsewhere, at least the city council's conscience was clear and those who insisted on seeing the play could not claim that they did not know it was sinful.

As documented in Chapter 3, the regime had from an early stage been determined to establish a centralised state monopoly over censorship. Certain functions were delegated to provincial representatives of the relevant ministry and civil governors were often consulted, but no competing jurisdictions were allowed. The provincial delegate of the Ministerio de Educación, Félix Ayala, sent a confidential report to the Director General on 26 March, together with copies of the press coverage. Ayala explained that he had been consulted by a representative of the council, who had asked if the authorisation of *La Infanzona* was motivated by political factors and the reputation of Benavente. Ayala had confined himself to pointing out that censorship decisions were made in Madrid and his function was not to question or defend them but simply to ensure that they were implemented. Sánchez Ventura had ignored this warning and proceeded to notify the company of the ban, which was then reported in the local and national press, prompting fierce controversy. Ayala then consulted the Civil Governor, who agreed that the council's action was inconvenient but refused to become involved. Unable to get in touch with José María Ortiz in Madrid, Ayala decided on his own initiative to censor press coverage of the incident and prevent the mayor from disseminating another letter defending his decision, on the grounds that 'el Alcalde no debe usar nuestra Prensa, vinculada a la Subsecretaría de Educación Popular, para crearse un ambiente favorable a una determinación contraria al fallo de otra Dirección General, también vinculada a la misma Subsecretaria' ('the Mayor should not make use of our Press, governed as it is by the Subsecretariat of Popular Education, to create a climate of opinion in favour of a decision that contravenes the ruling of another Directorate General, which is itself part of the same Subsecretariat') (AGA 2472/41).

Ayala reported that public opinion in the city was predominantly opposed to the ban, and offered an eloquent summing-up of the political and public relations problems posed by the situation:

El público en general se pregunta, cuántas censuras hay en España; se indignan contra el precedente que supone este hecho y las consecuencias que acarrearía si cada Alcalde de cada pueblo juzga con su criterio particular y propio la oportunidad y moralidad de una obra. Los comentaristas –casi toda la ciudad–, dejan muy mal parada a la censura, y se preguntan, así mismo, si es que no hay una representación eclesiástica en la Comisión correspondiente, ya que si la hay –arguyen–, debe acatarse su decisión por entender que mayor competencia ha de poseer un eclesiástico en quien delega la Jerarquía de la Iglesia, que un seglar, por acendrado celo apostólico que le adorne. (AGA 2472/41)

The public in general is wondering how many censorship bodies there are in Spain. They are indignant at the precedent set by this incident and what the consequences would be if every mayor in every town and village were to make their own rulings on the suitability and morality of plays. Public opinion – almost the whole city – is criticising the censorship apparatus and people are wondering if there is no ecclesiastical representation on the board, arguing that if there is, their decision should be upheld, since the judgement of a religious representative appointed by the hierarchy of the Church ought to be more authoritative than that of a layman, however pure the apostolic zeal with which he may be invested.

Tantalisingly, the documentation relating to the Zaragoza incident ends there. For the reasons set out by Ayala, the Dirección General would not have been happy to give way to the mayor, and Membrives and Benavente must have been pulling all the strings they had at their disposal. In the end, a compromise was arrived at: the Membrives company performed *La Infanzona* on 15 April, ten days later than originally planned, and in a different theatre, the privately owned Argensola. And as Sancho Izquierdo had foreseen, the controversy stimulated demand for the play. Between June and December 1947, five other companies – including one based in Zaragoza – applied for permission to stage it.

La Infanzona sparked another conflict of jurisdictions in Mallorca in December 1947. The Teatro Principal in Palma was owned by the Diputación de Baleares (the provincial-level local government), which decided at very short notice to prevent *La Infanzona* from being performed there by the López Heredia company. According to the Delegado Provincial's report, the head of the

Diputación recognised that he did not have the power to ban plays, but sent the company a letter requesting them to perform a different work in place of *La Infanzona*, since it was considered to be 'en desacuerdo con la calidad moral que requieren las obras de un teatro propiedad del Organismo que él preside' ('at odds with the moral quality required of works performed in a theatre owned by the body over which he presides') (AGA 2472/41). As in Zaragoza, the Civil Governor was consulted but declined to overrule the Diputación. The management of the theatre demanded that the company fulfil its contract by putting on another work from its repertoire, but López Heredia insisted that they would only perform *La Infanzona*, resulting in the contract being cancelled. She then negotiated with another venue in Palma, the Teatro Lírico, and it was announced that two performances of *La Infanzona* would be given there on 15 December. However, the Delegado Provincial reported that the company cancelled their contract with the Lírico on that same day and departed for Castellón de la Plana, where they had other bookings. He also informed the Director General de Prensa that he had suppressed various comments in the daily newspapers and other publications, 'para evitar polémicas y controversias que hubieran contribuido a enconar el asunto' ('in order to avoid altercations and controversies that would have contributed to aggravating the incident') (AGA 2472/41).

The case of *La Infanzona* illustrates how multifaceted the process of censorship could be. The file provides evidence of the roles of multiple agents – officially appointed *lectores*, their superiors in the Dirección General, Civil Governors, Delegados Provinciales and local authorities – taking part in censorship decisions, and of the regime's continuing struggle to enforce central authority and uniformity of practice. It also provides fascinating glimpses of attempts by various other interested parties – authors, performing companies, theatre managements, religious organisations, academic institutions and the press – to influence the process directly or indirectly, and of overlaps between the censorship of theatre and the press.

Notes
1. Lluch had been an active supporter of the Republic and a member of La Barraca, and had worked with Rivas Cherif and other left-wing

theatremakers. See García Ruiz (2010) for an account of his life and work.
2 See Wahnón (1996) on the failure of the Falangist theatrical project.
3 Although the Falange's Sección Femenina generally reinforced patriarchal values, the social roles in which its activists were engaged could be empowering: Victoria Enders records the testimony of former Sección Femenina members who were perceived as dangerously progressive, their activities considered 'improper for good Catholic women' (2002: 93).
4 Unfortunately, there is no censorship file on this play in the AGA. For a definition of the *sainete*, see Chapter 1.
5 The censors' treatment of this and other plays by Millán-Astray is analysed by Santos Sánchez (2013b).
6 The AGA database does not distinguish reliably between Antonio Paso y Cano and his son Antonio Paso Díaz.
7 Jurado Latorre provides complete lists of cuts for *La Oca* and seven other Muñoz Seca plays, and a sample of the extensive cuts made to ¡Soy un sinvergüenza! (2001: 239–53). Alba Peinado (2009) analyses the files on fourteen plays.
8 Pope Leo XIII had confirmed in an encyclical of 1891 entitled 'Pastoralis officii' that the Catholic Church condemned duelling as sinful and contrary to divine law.
9 At this time, the price of tickets in Madrid ranged from 2 pesetas for the cheapest seats in popular shows up to 15 pesetas in the stalls (figures from ABC 1949). The capacity of the Teatro La Latina is approximately 900 spectators (Teatro La Latina 2018), so the amount of the fine could have been covered from the box-office takings of a single performance.
10 The 1985 film *La corte de Faraón*, directed by José Luis García Sánchez, is a comedy centring on an amateur theatre group in the 1940s arrested by the police for performing the *zarzuela*.
11 See the appendices in Gallén (1985) for lists of works premiered in the post-war period, as well as companies and venues.
12 See the extract from an interview with the playwright Josep Maria Benet i Jornet quoted in Thompson (2018: 42).
13 Censorship files in the AGA on plays by Guimerà, Rusiñol and Sagarra (in Catalan and translated into Spanish) from the 1940s to the 1960s are analysed in Fernández Poza (2011).
14 This phenomenon was part of a wider process beginning in the 1950s. Dowling points to 'a growing tension between the State and Church in Catalonia' by the late 1950s, and 'the growing engagement of the Church with both Catalanism and the social question' (2012: 602–3).
15 The censorship of these and other plays by Màntua is discussed in more detail in Thompson (2018). Censors' and critics' sexist dispar-

aging of popular plays by a female dramatist as over-sentimental has an interesting parallel in the case of Julia Maura, some of whose plays in the 1940s and 1950s trod on dangerous territory in dealing with infidelity and adultery (discussed in Santos Sánchez 2013b).

16 The ADB is also discussed in Chapter 7. For a full account of the group's trajectory, see Coca (1978).

Chapter 5

The Realist Generation: A Spotlight on the Margins of Society

When speech is not free and when a myth becomes the story of national identity, then the impulse to generate a truer portrait of reality is strong. In post-war Spain, the so-called 'realist dramatists' launched a theatrical rebellion that represented a generation's political awakening and angry disillusion, combined with an urgent, if at times naïve, determination to change both theatre and society. Exposing power relationships with a focus on those on the losing side, they enacted their desires and frustrated hopes.

Realist drama emerged as a significant trend in the 1950s. The dictatorship, which had by now established itself at all levels of society, faced a rise in opposition from old and new quarters. The Communist Party had refocused its efforts away from guerrilla warfare and towards other action, some of it cultural. Student protests, particularly in Madrid, highlighted a youthful generation unwilling to accept the status quo, and workers went on strike in Asturias and Catalonia in echoes of earlier politicised acts of dissent.

Drawing on Italian cinematic neo-realism, naturalism, the popular comic form of the *sainete* set amongst the lower classes, and plays by North American authors such as Arthur Miller, Tennessee Williams, Eugene O'Neill and Thornton Wilder, whose works were staged in Spain in the 1950s by some influential directors (see Chapter 7), a generation of Spanish dramatists emerged determined to represent the social reality of Spain under dictatorship. The influence of earlier Spanish writers such as Machado and Unamuno, who wrote of the 'problem of Spain', and Lorca and

Valle-Inclán, who challenged the prevailing theatrical tradition of their time, together with the politicised theatre of the 1930s, can also be discerned. Several of the realists also drew inspiration from foreign political dramatists, such as Bertolt Brecht, Jean Anouilh and Jean-Paul Sartre, as well as the gritty portraits of mid-century British society by playwrights such as Shelagh Delaney and John Osborne. Yet the work of the realists was always grounded in the local and represented a Spanish identity.

While there is some discrepancy among critics regarding who makes up the Realist Generation, the most significant in terms of influence and impact are Antonio Buero Vallejo (1916–2000), the forerunner of the realist dramatists, Alfonso Sastre (1926–2021), perhaps the most radical of the group, José Martín Recuerda (1922–2007), José María Rodríguez Méndez (1925–2009), Carlos Muñiz (1927–94) and Lauro Olmo (1921–94) (Oliva 1979; Monleón 1962; García Pavón 1962). All of them experienced the war as children, except the slightly older Buero Vallejo, who was an active participant in the conflict. While Buero's trajectory was somewhat different and he made a name for himself within the commercial theatre in the late 1940s and early 1950s, most of the realists came up through student or community theatre groups.

Dealing with class, generational differences, poverty, injustice, morality and, albeit indirectly, the dictatorship, they wrote plays that passed judgement on post-war Spanish society and aimed to inspire protest and provoke action. Many of the plays portray a society that is unjust and in need of change and they engage with very contemporary problems, such as unemployment and economic migration, the backdrop to Olmo's *La camisa* (*The Shirt*, written in 1962); poverty-induced death in Rodríguez Méndez's *Los inocentes de la Moncloa* ('The Innocents of La Moncloa', 1961); the miserable existence of the office worker in Muñiz's *El tintero* ('The Inkwell', 1961); moral dilemmas provoked by financial difficulties in Buero Vallejo's *El tragaluz* (*The Basement Window*, 1966); the social and personal impact of the war in Martín Recuerda's *La llanura* ('The Plain', 1947) and social injustice in Sastre's *Muerte en el barrio* ('Death in the Neighbourhood', 1955). Reflecting a collective experience of poverty and inequality, the plays often focus on the crisis or dilemma of a representative individual or group.

The authors of these works wished to discomfort traditional audiences and challenge authority, but also to capture a new generation of theatregoers. This was theatre with a social and political message and a deliberate rejection of the tradition of evasion and entertainment (Ladra 1968; Halsey 1979; Oliva 1979). Many of the plays not only dealt with the everyday concerns of the working class, but also reproduced their language. The sets and props too, reflected a world at odds with the bourgeois interiors of the well-made play. Unsurprisingly, this type of theatre was unpopular with the regime, as it highlighted a reality in conflict with the dictatorship's myth of a successful society, united under its political leaders and benefiting from the legacy of the war. For its authors, the problem was that in order to convey a message of change or revolution to a Spanish public, they had first to get their plays past the censors.

Despite some obvious differences in terms of style and approach and some reluctance to embrace the notion that they formed a coherent group, the realists were united by a determination to create a theatre that engaged with social and human issues and the often uncomfortable reality of life under the dictatorship. Muñiz proposed that what united them was 'una actitud abiertamente crítica ante la realidad sociopolítica española' ('an openly critical attitude towards the sociopolitical reality of Spain') (O'Connor and Pasquariello: 14). Rodríguez Méndez suggested that they were all concerned by 'the problem of Spain' and aimed to reflect and explore the reality of the Spanish people (1997: 77). Martín Recuerda saw them as moving against the prevailing theatrical current, and as dramatists with a mission to reflect Spain as they saw it (Heras 1969: 28–9). Olmo said that they were united in their desire to rescue Spanish theatre from 'un estado de decadencia e inautenticidad' ('a state of decadence and inauthenticity') (Gabriele and Olmo 1991: 385).

As commentators on society and critics of the regime and its values, all suffered significant censorship. This included official censorship of productions and editions of their plays (from relatively minor cuts to extensive deletions and prohibitions, curtailed performance runs and limitations on venues and audiences), negative press, restrictions on travel and other threats to their livelihood. Several also complained of the preferential treatment given to foreign social dramatists and believed themselves to be disadvantaged (Primer Acto 1974c: 13–23; Winecoff 1968: 8).

To avoid clashes with the authorities, the realists adopted certain techniques and strategies. Veiled allusions to politics, historical dramas with implicit criticism of current leaders, social dramas focusing on divided families, as well as the use of dark humour were all part of their armoury. Some, like Buero's *Un soñador para un pueblo* (*A Dreamer for the People*, 1958), Sastre's *La sangre y la ceniza* ('Blood and Ash', 1965) and Muñiz's *Tragicomedia del serenísimo Príncipe don Carlos* ('Tragicomedy of His Serene Highness Prince Carlos', 1971), focus on known historical figures, while plays such as Rodríguez Méndez's *Vagones de madera* ('Wooden Wagons', 1958) and Martín Recuerda's *La llanura* ('The Plain', 1947) centre on an unknown everyman, or on shared or silenced experiences of the past.

While rarely speaking of it directly, the realists also engaged with Spain's civil war and its damaging legacy on society. Conflicts between individuals, generations and family members were often employed to comment on the silenced national one. They represented individuals suffering alienation in a post-war society where community and communication have broken down. One little-studied feature of their work is their engagement with race. Stuart Green points to how Sastre, in *En la red* ('In the Net') and *Mulato* ('Mulatto'), and Muñiz, in *Un solo de saxofón* ('A Saxophone Solo'), employed race to comment on injustices that had parallels with the Spanish dictatorship (2011: 363).

Yet another means of dealing with censorship was to negotiate with the authorities, either directly or via the director of a production. Some, like Buero, were open about their dealings with the censors and claimed that such compromise and concession, which he called *posibilismo* (a term that also incorporated his use of symbolism to make veiled criticisms of society), was a wise choice in difficult circumstances. Others rejected it, deeming it a form of collusion with the authorities, even if they sometimes engaged in it. The fraught discussions around the validity of this stance which played out in the literary press in the late 1950s and 1960s became known as the *posibilismo-imposibilismo* debates and divided authors who had, in the end, much more to unite than to separate them (Schwartz 1968; O'Leary 2005: 112–39).

Realist theatre was particularly popular amongst student and independent theatre groups, but the response of both critics and the public to the representation of a depressed and unjust post-war society was not always favourable (Cañizares Bundorf 2000: 235; Castellano 1955: 291). Of course, the media were controlled by the regime and the most powerful newspapers promoted its values.

The conservative press largely worked in tandem with the regime and, at an everyday level, some influential critics used their columns to silence political messages, stressing costume and performance over content, dismissing works as unworthy or simply not reviewing them. Moreover, some theatre critics were also censors who directly served the state.

The realists' criticism of the mistreatment of the lowly and disenfranchised by those in charge meant that much of the censorship that their theatre attracted was political. Their plays did not often have a religious focus, although their representation of a nihilistic worldview and of a politicised Church more concerned with power than the wellbeing of its flock meant that they also encountered some problems with religious censors. Furthermore, the realists' representation of the 'authentic' language of characters from the margins and of lascivious behaviour at all levels of society led to disapproval from some morally vigilant censors.

For the dramatists themselves, the impact of censorship on their own work and on the cultural landscape of Spain was devastating. Rodríguez Méndez, who wrote in some detail about its negative cultural legacy, deemed censorship the 'aberration of our times' (Primer Acto 1974a: 14). Muñiz observed that their generation was the one to suffer most from state interference (Primer Acto 1968: 24). Martín Recuerda blamed 'una censura feroz' ('fierce censorship') and 'un público mojigato' ('a prudish public') for the relative poverty of Spanish offerings when compared to other European theatres (Isasi Ángulo 1974: 253). Lauro Olmo, for his part, divided Spanish theatre into two groups: the staged and the unstaged (Gómez García 1971: 12).

The 1940s and 1950s

Buero was the only one of the group to interact with the censors in the 1940s and no significant threat was perceived in his work. As a *posibilista*, he negotiated with the censors regarding proposed cuts to *Historia de una escalera* (*Story of a Stairway*), which included politicised references to the unions and to the 'cowards' who had not played their part in the defence of the Republic (AGA 433/49). He found impartial alternatives to these and the only cut that was made in the end was the elimination of a slightly bawdy joke.[1]

The 1950s was the decade in which the realists emerged as a significant force in the Spanish theatre, in influence if not commercial success. Censorship focused on the protection of the regime's institutions, although this overlapped to some extent with protection of the Church and a narrowly moralistic view of what was acceptable in Spanish society.

The system operated in quite a sophisticated way, often making cuts or limiting staging, rather than banning works outright. For example, despite some obvious parallels with the present, Buero's first historical drama, *Un soñador para un pueblo*, set during the reign of Carlos III and focused on the Italian-born minister Esquilache and the popular rising against his reforms that took place in Madrid in Easter Week 1766, was authorised with cuts on 9 December 1958 (AGA 293/58). Sometimes, however, even Buero encountered serious problems and had a play deemed unacceptable. Such was the case of *Aventura en lo gris* ('Adventure in Grey', 1949), which, in its portrait of a post-civil war dictatorship in the imaginary land of Surelia, was considered too suggestive of Spain (AGA 395/53). The censors found it variously 'confusing', 'pessimistic', 'pretentious' and echoing 'new, incoherent' literary trends. The files contain an internal communication suggesting that the regime might tolerate the authorisation of the play for non-commercial theatres but this information does not seem to have been passed on to the author or company. It was not staged in the 1950s and a revised version was finally authorised in 1963, when it was read by the censors as a criticism of war generally, rather than of the now more distant Spanish civil war.

While Buero benefited from his *posibilista* attitude combined with his early success in the commercial sector, collaborating with influential and established directors, other realists who came up through minority theatres found it harder to access the commercial stage. Even those who worked within the independent or student theatre found their work regularly obstructed by censorship. Olmo, for example, was censored much more harshly than Buero from the start of his career in the 1950s and particularly in the 1960s.[2] This is unsurprising, given that he was close to the Communist Party and its politics are echoed in his social and political works. He represented the working-class community he came from in a fresh and unpatronising way and, like the left-wing practitioners of the 1930s, believed in a theatre *del pueblo* – of and for ordinary people. In all his works, he represented the voice of the marginalised and downtrodden, but always with humour and using his – and their – own voice. His *Magdalena*, a play touching on youthful political demonstrations and abuse of power, was submitted to the censors in June 1959 by the Compañía Teatral de Educación y Descanso and was prohibited (AGA 219/59).

Rodríguez Méndez made his mark in the non-commercial sector. His *La tabernera y las tinajas* ('The Landlady and the Wine Jars', 1959) was written for and premiered by La Pipironda. This Barcelona-based theatre collective, which he described as 'a type of guerrilla-theatre group', aimed to learn from the community, rather than to educate it (Isasi Ángulo 1974: 270). The play contains some social commentary in its contrast of the bar owner with the corrupt local elites, but was authorised for over-eighteens and widely staged in the following decades (AGA 95/71).[3] However, this was exceptional in his career under the dictatorship, as he would go on to have many problems with censorship.

Carlos Muñiz also started his theatrical career in the non-commercial sector but he worked as a civil servant as well as a dramatist, and was thus in the difficult position of acting for the state while also wishing to criticise it. In fact, despite his own difficulties with the censors, or perhaps because of them, Muñiz accepted a place on the new Junta de Censura Teatral in 1963, thinking that he could support other writers and 'limar asperezas' ('smooth things over') from the inside, in the words of Jerónimo López Mozo, one of the friends who advised him against the move (2010). As noted in Chapter 3, he was dismissed in the backlash against the signatories of a letter of protest to Fraga on state mistreatment of miners and censorship. In a further twist, an official report from the Ministry of Information and Tourism to the Director General of Radio and Television, dated 28 February 1974, described him as anti-Francoist and anti-Catholic and noted his trajectory from intellectual Falangism (he was part of Dionisio Ridruejo's group) to anarchism and communism (AGA Muñiz).

Muñiz's *El grillo* ('The Cricket', 1955) centres on Mariano, a civil servant, who has economic problems and is ground down by life. Censorship of *El grillo* involved more than simple cuts related to its social commentary. The censors insisted that Mariano's job be recast in the private sector, thus eliminating the commentary on the state's responsibility as an employer. The play was initially approved with cuts but only for a single performance at the Teatro María Guerrero in January 1957, although it would later be approved with the same restrictions on several other occasions (AGA 5/57) (see Santos Sánchez 2013).

In the student theatre sector, one of the most interesting cases from the 1950s relates to Martín Recuerda's *La llanura* (1947), which was approved for *cámara* in November 1953, following an important and detrimental revision. The play focuses on the Madre (mother), who refuses to forget the execution of her husband by Falangists. The censors' reports lay bare the regime's concerns about the portrayal of religion and politics and show the various ways in which they attempted to limit the potential of the play to provide a perspective on the war at odds with the official one. Gumersindo Montes Agudo, while acknowledging the play's literary value, referred in his report to 'alusiones políticas peligrosas' ('dangerous political allusions') and asked for the view of a priest on an act set in a place of worship, a potentially contentious reminder of the Church's role in the war. Brother Mauricio de Begoña, a Capuchin Friar, commented on the play's pessimism but approved it with cuts for the restricted public of the Teatro Español Universitario (TEU). His report notes that the final suicide (a sin and therefore unjustifiable in terms of Catholic dogma) was depicted as evidence of madness, rather than as a premeditated act, and thus considered tolerable. Bartolomé Mostaza, however, suggested prohibition on moral and political grounds, deeming it corrosive, despairing, and open to confused political interpretations (AGA 351/53).[4]

In the end, the play was authorised for *cámara* and a limited number of performances but with a significant cut that would change the tenor of the piece: the play's reference to the civil war and the related killing of a key character were removed (Reyes 2017). Despite some success within the student theatre, Martín Recuerda's experience with the censors left a bitter aftertaste:

> La censura la crucificó. Nos dijeron que no se podía hablar del Albaicín, ni de guerra civil, ni de fusilados. Luego nos dejaron ponerla, hecha por estudiantes, un solo día en el Español en un escenario ocupado por decorados del *Edipo* de Pemán [...] Aquello no era *La llanura*; estaba desvirtuada, pero, así y todo, no veas los 'bravos' que hubo aquella noche. Bueno, pues al día siguiente la crítica me pegaba una patada en el culo sin más [...] Lo cierto

es que *La llanura*, que aborda un tema tan actual como es el de los desaparecidos, no pudo nunca estrenarse tal como era, y sólo se publicó en el año 82. (Vicente Mosquete, quoted in Morón Espinosa 2008: 233)

> It was crucified by censorship. They said that we couldn't mention the Albaicín, or the civil war, or those executed. Later they let us stage it, with students, a single performance in the Español on a stage containing the set of Pemán's *Oedipus* [. . .] That wasn't *La llanura*; it was distorted but, even so, you should have heard the applause that night. Anyway, the next day the critics had a go at me [. . .] The truth is that *La llanura*, which deals with a theme as relevant as that of the Disappeared, could never be staged as intended, and was only published in 1982.

Of all the realist theatre, it was perhaps Alfonso Sastre's that most defined the relationship between drama and censorship in the 1950s. The history of Sastre's interaction with the authorities neatly charts the evolution of dramatist, genre and censorship practice. He was viewed initially as a friend of the regime before eventually being recognised as its political opponent and as a key figure in a new form of theatre that seemed to define itself *against* the regime. Some censors understood from the outset that this was a dramatist whose work undermined the regime's values, while others read it as anti-communist and, therefore, perfectly acceptable.[5]

His earliest plays, *Cargamento de sueños* ('Cargo of Dreams'), written in 1946 (AGA 377/53), and *El cubo de la basura* ('The Rubbish Bin', 1951), despite their revolutionary ideas raised no red flags with the censors.[6] *La mordaza* (*The Gag*, 1953), notwithstanding its focus on a tyrannical patriarch, Isaías Krappo, was another that the censors did not object to: they interpreted it as a rural drama and considered it unproblematic in moral and political terms.[7] In fact, Sastre had written it as a coded protest against the regime and censorship, and was surprised that it did not cause a stir. He later summed up its message: 'Vivimos amordazados. No somos felices. Este silencio nos agobia. Todo esto puede apuntar a un futuro sangriento' ('We are gagged. We are not happy. This silence stifles us. This may all point to a bloody future') (1966: 283).

Sastre's card was marked, however, when a scandal erupted with *Escuadra hacia la muerte* (1953), which was initially approved but later withdrawn by the authorities following military intervention (see case study). In the immediate aftermath of the affair, problems arose with Sastre's next two plays, *Prólogo patético* ('Pathetic Prologue') and *El pan de todos* ('Everyone's Bread'), which although the subject of separate applications and reports, were considered together at the highest levels in discussions both about the wisdom of staging them and about the dramatist himself.

Prólogo patético deals with the moral dilemmas facing revolutionaries plotting to overthrow a dictator. According to Sastre, it was to be the first play in a trilogy about terrorism (1992a: 14). It was initially read by four censors in February and March 1952 and their reports show some unease regarding the play's depiction of the sadistic and cruel police and the honourable 'terrorists' that oppose them. Virgilio Hernández Rivadulla correctly read it as a play about the justification of violent revolution for the betterment of society but suggested that, as no location was specified, it was not identifiably about Spain. Díez Crespo, although noting positively that it was to be staged by university students and not 'the usual delinquents', considered it a dangerous play. Gumersindo Montes Agudo, convinced of Sastre's right-thinking ideas, considered it an anti-Communist play. There is no evidence at this point of a final verdict and *Prólogo patético* was lost in *silencio administrativo*. In late 1953, however, the censors were asked to consider it again, following a new application by Carmen Troitiño and José Luis Alonso. Montes Agudo wrote a second positive report, from which we can deduce that cuts had been made since the previous year. He noted the suppression of two scenes and stated that there was nothing in the play that challenged Falangist orthodoxy. Begoña was more cautious. While he found the play unproblematic from the perspective of Catholic ideology and morals (once some crude language was removed), he suggested that the play's representation of conflicting ideologies could be confusing but recognised that he was not the competent authority to judge the play politically (AGA 438/53).

At around the same time, there was an application from La Máscara theatre company to stage *El pan de todos*, a play about a moral and political dilemma in which the protagonist, David Harko, denounces his mother to the authorities for the sake of an unspecified revolution. She is killed by the authorities and he later commits suicide. Montes Agudo concluded that it was anti-Communist and, therefore, politically tolerable. Bartolomé Mostaza, on the other hand, had some doubts about the author's intentions but recognised the quality and humanism of the play and concluded that it posed no political threat (AGA 401/53).

While the initial censors' reports on the two plays are separate, they were referred together to the military authorities for a verdict that would seal their – and Sastre's – fate. On 4 January 1954, the then Director General de Cinematografía y Teatro, Joaquín Argamasilla, sent both plays to the Ministro Secretario General del Movimiento, Raimundo Fernández Cuesta, for his political judgement.[8] It is clear that the scandal surrounding *Escuadra hacia la muerte* weighed heavily on the decision-makers. Argamasilla, despite assuming that Sastre was well-intentioned, outlined in his letter the danger that might arise from misinterpretation by leftist spectators of both plays. Fernández Cuesta sent *El pan de todos* to another group of censors, all but one of whom considered it a dangerous work with possible references to the regime, and recommended its prohibition.[9] Guided by this, the Minister, in line with Argamasilla's recommendation, gave a verdict of prohibition for both *Prólogo* and *El pan* on 14 January 1954. He seemed almost reluctant, referring to 'the proper intentions of the author' but noting the negative influence of Jean-Paul Sartre on the Spanish dramatist's work and the extreme danger of possible interpretations of the work that would be contrary to the regime's values. Argamasilla, in his final note to Fernández Cuesta, thanked him and vowed to use his political guidance from this case in future decision-making. The censorship of these works was significant, therefore, not just for the author but for the early refinement of the process itself.

This was not the end of the affair, however, and an outraged Sastre wrote to José María Ortiz in February 1954 demanding to know why his plays were banned and his career stunted in this way. Having first ignored him, Ortiz then offered a private meeting and oral explanation, which Sastre rejected, demanding not the practical reasons for the ban, which he supposed might be based on the regime's fears for a repetition of the scandal around *Escuadra hacia la muerte*, but instead 'the objective moral reasons, ones based on the reality of the texts' (AGA 401/53). A handwritten note on Sastre's letter, dated 2 March, states simply 'No hacer caso' ('Ignore'). The conversation was clearly at an end and there was to be no satisfaction for the dramatist. While some doubt about his own motives and politics remained, his work was now clearly identified as open to political abuse by enemies of the regime.

Yet Sastre did not give up and he fought to stage his work when an opportunity again presented itself in 1955. The files contain a letter from Sastre and the actor and director of a new theatre company, José María Rodero, dated 30 April, in which they ask for the verdict of prohibition of *El pan de todos* to be revised.[10] They argue that the play had already been published in its entirety in *Ateneo*, a journal published by the Ministry itself. Sastre's negotiation worked and the play was reviewed.

By now there was a new Director General, Manuel Torres López, and he referred it to the Permanent Reading Commission of the Consejo Superior del Teatro, who unanimously recommended the lifting of the ban, believing the play to be politically and morally sound and 'una tragedia de profundos valores humanos' ('a tragedy of profound human values'), set in a political system which they considered to be recognisably communist and not comparable to the Spanish situation, except in the most skewed of interpretations. They predicted that the play's depiction of communism would cause repulsion and horror in the average spectator and the only negative aspect they found was a certain pessimism around man's ability to maintain his ideological purity and position and the consequent impossibility of revolutionary triumph. Reading it from a Nationalist perspective, this could be seen as undermining their own revolutionary success. Nonetheless, the report stressed their view that the play was not a threat. An additional moral report by Begoña, dated 21 May 1955, indicated a reading of the play as a criticism of the 'inhuman and anti-Catholic' Communist Party and thus its implicit support for the Catholic faith, concluding that it was morally and religiously acceptable.

In light of such a positive review, Fernández Cuesta was consulted again in a letter dated 25 May 1955, which mentioned the commission's views, the publication of the play and its previous dramatised reading at both university and in an educational seminar delivered to the Frente de Juventudes, the youth branch of the Falange. In the letter, Torres López referred to Sastre as an 'already illustrious dramatist' and also noted that much of his work had been censored for a broad variety of reasons. He also consulted the Ministro de Información y Turismo in June. After much lengthy deliberation, *El pan de todos* was authorised in 1956, first with a few cuts and later, on several occasions in the 1960s and 1970s, without. There was a further twist in the tale: Sastre asked the Communist Party for its views on the play and was informed that the party did not approve of it (1992b: 5). In the end, the fact that *El pan de todos*, which Sastre had clearly intended as critical of the regime, could be – and was – read as the opposite, ironically led the dramatist to censor it himself (Sastre 1992b: 7). *Prólogo patético*, on the other hand, remained banned for years.[11]

Religious concerns were to the forefront in the judgement of Sastre's *La sangre de Dios* ('The Blood of God'), which draws on the biblical episode of Abraham's test when asked to sacrifice his son, Isaac. The Teatro de Arte applied to stage the play in March 1955. Br Constancio de Aldeaseca objected to the representation of faith – only the fool is a believer and other characters are at pains to stress their lack of religious belief – but suggested authorisation with cuts, including the phrase, 'O Dios no existe . . . o es un monstruo' ('Either God does not exist . . . or He's a monster'). José María Ortiz thought it should be prohibited for its confusing and dangerous message about faith. The most interesting report, however, is once again from Falangist author, Montes Agudo, who read it much more positively as an example of 'un teatro católico combativo' ('a combative Catholic theatre'), thus in keeping with the most radical right-wing theatre of the 1930s. Indeed, he identified Sastre as the great hope of the Spanish stage, whose pathway should not be closed off. The discrepancy in the interpretations of the play meant that it was subject of a special reading in a sitting of the Permanent Reading Commission. They found that the consoling dénouement allowed for authorisation, albeit with several cuts (AGA 86/55). The file also contains a document in which Sastre's responses to the censors' proposed cuts are indicated. In some cases, he defended his text and in others he appeared willing to change it, a clear example of *posibilismo* at work. The outcome led to *La sangre de Dios* being staged many times by student and amateur groups from the 1950s to the 1970s.

What is without doubt is that Sastre's theatre was now carefully scrutinised by censors alert to potential criticism of the regime. When in 1955 censors could not agree a verdict on Sastre's *Muerte en el barrio* ('Death in the Neighbourhood'), it too, was referred to the Permanent Reading Commission. The play is about the neglect of the poor by a cruel local doctor, whose failure to save a child's life leads to punishment by the people he had earlier so badly treated in what was represented as an episode of natural justice. Despite the Commission's largely positive reading of the play, it was banned in January 1956 due to evident unease at the reputation growing around the author and his works: 'Conviene desvirtuar lo más rápidamente posible, esa aureola de mártir e incomprendido que empieza a forjarse alrededor de él' ('It would be advisable to counteract, as quickly as possible, this image of misunderstood martyr that is beginning to build up around him'). In fact, the regime's own actions in prohibiting his work did much to consolidate his position as a symbol of the cultural opposition.

The relationship between Sastre and the regime worsened and *Tierra roja* ('Red Earth'), a play about the exploitation and mistreatment of miners, was banned in 1958. The preliminary note attached to the text, dated October 1956, cannot have helped. In it, Sastre asserted that while the play was not a direct reference to a Spanish location or a historical event, it dealt with reality and, moreover, he suggested that the incidents depicted happened in Spain 'en uno o en otro momento de su historia reciente' ('at some point in its recent history'). Two of the censors suggested that a performance could turn into a political rally and must not be authorised. The final report assumed that Sastre was being deliberately provocative and aiming to add to his banned works (AGA 98/58).

Following so many prohibitions, it is initially surprising that *Guillermo Tell tiene los ojos tristes* ('Sad Are the Eyes of William Tell') was not banned. The play is a version of the Swiss legend, which tells the story of a heroic folk hero who overthrows a tyrannical leader and is seen as a symbol of political freedom and independence. Sastre's revolutionary take on this was clear and he suggested in his introduction to the published version that it was relevant to situations of oppression elsewhere (1990: 5). The censor's report explains why it was authorised for a single performance in 1959: the tyrannical authorities were read as only applicable to a communist country. Moreover, the unnamed censor suggested that the play would have a brief life (AGA 34/59). He was mistaken. Several other companies applied to stage it over the following years, including Gogo and El Bululú, two of the most political independent theatre groups of the 1960s and beyond. When approved in the

1960s and 1970s, it was stipulated that the uniforms were not to appear Spanish, but rather reflect the place and era in which the play is set (Switzerland in the fourteenth century). Given Sastre's reputation and the politics of those involved in the productions, we can assume that this would have had little effect on the spectators' interpretation of the play. Indeed, it would later be banned twice: in 1961, in a production that referred to the armed forces' machine guns and to the proletariat, and a student production in early 1969 at a time of rising opposition to the regime and clampdowns on university campuses.

The regime's dealings with the realists in the 1950s, and with Alfonso Sastre in particular, show how they identified and sought to control what was, in essence, an enemy within: a generation that had not lived through the war and was not obviously allied to the political opposition, but came to represent it both in their depiction of the misery and injustice of Spain under Franco and in their call for social change.

The 1960s

The 1960s was a period of great transformation in censorship and society and while a certain tolerance of social and political themes and easing of restrictions can be discerned, this was always conditional on the current needs of the regime.

A marked rise in student and popular opposition to the regime led to several clashes with the authorities that were played out to some extent at the level of censorship. Student protests continued and by the mid-1960s the officially approved students' union (the SEU) had effectively been taken over by left-wing forces. One of their goals was to employ the cultural department of the SEU against the regime (Rodríguez Tejada 2014). According to Alberto Castilla, these organisations began to produce 'intense, anti-Francoist activity' (1999: 237). In February 1965, a large demonstration in Madrid supported by academic leaders was brutally repressed. A year later, a new, anti-regime students' union, the Sindicato Democrático de Estudiantes Universitarios, was established in Barcelona and became a focal point for student opposition (Gómez Oliver 2008: 104). Later, a state of exception was declared in Guipúzcoa in August 1968 and across Spain from January 1969. It lasted until March and special university police were brought onto campuses for the duration.

Another factor in the increased problems with the censors in the 1960s was the fact that the realists' plays were increasingly provocative. Several plays represented the brutality of the authorities: Buero's *La doble historia del doctor Valmy* (*Dr Valmy's Double Case History*), Olmo's *El cuerpo* ('The Body') and *Conflicto a la hora de la siesta* ('Conflict at Siesta Time'). Others foregrounded the need for social or revolutionary change: Sastre's *En la red*, Rodríguez Méndez's *El vano ayer* ('Empty Yesterday') Olmo's *La condecoración* ('The Medal', 1964), *Plaza menor* ('Minor Square') and *El cuarto poder* ('The Fourth Estate'). Works such as Rodríguez Méndez's *Los inocentes de Moncloa* and Olmo's *English Spoken* portrayed a damaged and struggling Spanish youth, and others, such as Olmo's *La condecoración*, Rodríguez Méndez's *Vagones de madera* and *La vendimia de Francia* ('Grape-Picking in France'), and Martín Recuerda's *El caraqueño* ('The Man from Caracas', 1968) staged antimilitarism and negative representations of war and its legacy. Establishment figures were negatively portrayed in Buero's *El sueño de la razón*, Olmo's *El cuarto poder* and Martín Recuerda's *Las salvajes en Puente San Gil* ('Wild Women in Puente San Gil', 1961) and plays such as Buero's *El tragaluz*, Olmo's *La camisa* and *English spoken*, Muñiz's *El tintero* and *Las viejas difíciles* ('Difficult Old Ladies', 1962), Rodríguez Méndez's *Bodas que fueron famosas del Pingajo y la Fandanga* ('The Famous Wedding of Pingajo and Fandanga', 1965) show a society not thriving but divided, embittered and often without hope.

The new censorship legislation introduced in the 1960s detailed the prohibitions of criticism of the regime and its supporters. Article 17 specified that attacks on the Roman Catholic Church and its teaching were outlawed. This meant that, even though there was no longer always a priest among the readers of each play, the censors were required to monitor carefully how the Church and religion were represented on stage. Although not prohibited, Buero's *Las Meninas*, Rodríguez Méndez's *El milagro de pan y de los peces* ('The Miracle of the Loaves and Fishes', 1953, first staged in 1960) and Muñiz's *Miserere para medio fraile* ('Miserere for a Half Monk', 1966), all suffered cuts because of their negative portrayals of the clergy (AGA 296/60, AGA 581/71, AGA 14/67). Indeed, Vázquez Dodero denounced Muñiz's play for falsifying history by lauding John of the Cross 'como pretexto para pintar como criminales a los frailes que se oponían a su posición reformadora' ('as a pretext for depicting as criminals the monks who opposed his reforming stance').

In April 1963, Olmo's *El milagro* ('The Miracle', 1955) was prohibited because the three priests who read it objected strongly to its depiction of the futility of faith and its 'groserías' ('vulgarities') (AGA 110/63). The realists often clashed with the censors when it came to expressions considered offensive or in bad taste and to questions of sexual morality, all of which were dealt with in article 13 of the new legislation (BOE 1963a: 3930). Not only did the playwrights employ the earthy language of real Spaniards in their works but they also often pointed to the hypocrisy of a regime that defined itself and society in moral terms, while lacking compassion, forgiveness and basic human decency. While the main issue for the censors was political in the cases of Muñiz's *Un solo de saxofón* and Buero's *La doble historia del doctor Valmy*, they also objected to sexualised language and references to the body in the plays. In the case of the former, censors rejected phrases such as '¡si tienes el sexo negro!' ('but you have a black penis') and '¡El mundo es una mierda!' ('the world is shit') (AGA 14/65). In the latter, Fr González Fierro suggested that the torture scenes were acceptable as they were already commonly featured in cinema and theatre yet expressed a desire to rid the play of references to impotence, which he seemed to consider more distasteful (AGA 147/64).

The realists sometimes ran into trouble for their reproduction of the natural, non-literary speech of ordinary Spanish people. Olmo's earthy language and sometimes bawdy dialogue caused him problems with the censors. One of the most interesting examples is his *La pechuga de la sardina* ('The Breast of the Sardine', 1962), about the situation of single women in Spain, with its portrait of loneliness, sexual desire and frustration and its criticism of exploitation by men and the lack of kindness and understanding on the part of the holier-than-thou *beatas* ('sanctimonious women'). It highlights the impact of an oppressive moral climate and social disadvantage on many Spanish women at a time when much of the western world was celebrating the emergence of sexual and social freedoms. When José Osuna applied in June 1963 to stage it at the Teatro Goya, the censors Marcelo Arroita-Jáuregui, Fr Jorge Blajot and Sebastián Bautista de la Torre sought to eliminate crude language and some references to religion but gave a verdict of authorisation with cuts. Despite this, it was referred to two further censors, Fr Carlos María Staehlin, who suggested prohibition, and Adolfo Prego de Oliver, who thought it could be authorised with cuts. It eventually went to a plenary session of the censorship board where it was authorised for over 18s with many cuts and a clear instruction to monitor the staging.

Cuts based on questions of taste were also made to Olmo's *El cuerpo* (1966), described by one censor as a hedonistic and carnal celebration of the body. The application to stage it on Easter Sunday 1966 in the Teatro Valle-Inclán was surely a provocation, but it was authorised with seven cuts intended to reduce its 'eroticism'.

Muñiz had difficulty with *Las viejas difíciles*, a 'tragedia caótica' ('chaotic tragedy') set in an unspecified country and time. It centres on the miserable existence of a no longer young couple, Antonio and Julita, whose ordinary and innocent dreams have all been frustrated (2007: 358). The society in which they struggle to survive is one of oppressive, moralistic interference in private lives by the so-called 'Damas de Asociación' ('Association Ladies') and the play is at times darkly humorous in its exaggerated depiction of extreme morality and desperate poverty in a cruel society. Following a date in the park, in which they discuss their dreams of happiness and togetherness, Julita and Antonio are imprisoned for offending public morality. They marry in prison but, on their release, they are still rejected by society and are betrayed, or fail, at every turn.

The TEU in San Sebastián applied in February 1966 for permission to stage the play at the Teatro Gran Kursaal. While the censors found fault with the play's morality and depiction of the authorities, they also considered it such a caricature as to be more or less harmless, if certain cuts were introduced and its audience was restricted. Fr Blajot, for example, suggested several cuts on moral and taste grounds, including elimination of the following phrases: p. 226 'me cago en el dinero' ('fuck money!'); p. 245 'ni sentí sobre el vientre la pesadez de un hombre alegre y retozón' ('nor have I felt the weight of a happy and frisky man on my belly'). Permission was granted for a *cámara* performance but the files contain a further document, dated 24 March (several days after it was staged and, presumably, a reaction to the production) in which it is stipulated that all further applications needed to be considered by the Director General, who would monitor the use of expressions and songs in the play (AGA 57/66).

In September 1966, the Teatro Nacional de Cámara y Ensayo applied for permission to stage the play in the Teatro Beatriz for several days in early October. It was allowed for over-eighteens with sixteen cuts, to eliminate bad taste and criticisms of state institutions and it premiered on 7 October. The files also show how the censorship process was, on occasion, subverted. The inspector who viewed it on 19 October noted that not all cuts were respected in the TEU production and that the acting exaggerated certain lewd actions. Nonetheless, there is no indication in the files that punitive action was taken, perhaps because of the public involved. Given what Muñiz revealed about the play, however, it is somewhat surprising that it was ever authorised: 'En el final de mi obra *Las viejas difíciles* las damas de la Asociación aniquilaban a los protagonistas a tiros de metralleta mientras cantaban una canción con música del himno de las SS nazis. Me prohibieron la música y el final quedaba desvirtuado' ('At the end of my play *Las viejas difíciles* the ladies from the Association annihilate the protagonists with machine guns while singing a song set to the music of the Nazi SS anthem. They prohibited the music and the ending was distorted) (O'Connor and Pasquariello 1976: 15). It is likely that its dark humour and exaggeration helped in its approval, even with cuts, as it made it seem less serious and perhaps less political.

Martín Recuerda's work also suffered significant moral and religious censorship. In 1962 an application was made to stage his *Las salvajes en Puente San Gil*, a critique of the world of the *revista*, with its exploitation of young women by ostensibly respectable men. It was authorised with cuts on moral and political grounds, generally to eliminate descriptions of the behaviour of the pillars of society towards the girls (AGA 254/62). His *El Cristo* ('The Christ', 1964), which focuses on the relationship between a parish priest and his wayward flock, was read by several clerical censors in December 1964 and went to a plenary of the censorship board. They objected to the depiction of the lay Catholic group, Acción Católica, and the associated Cursillos de Cristiandad spiritual movement and, once cut, it was authorised for over-eighteens (AGA 232/64). The dramatist was in trouble again in 1965 with ¿*Quién quiere una copla del Arcipreste de Hita?* ('Who Wants a Ditty by the Archpriest of Hita?'), a rather free version of the medieval masterpiece *El libro de buen amor* (*The Book of Good Love*). Several censors expressed unease at the negative portrait of the clergy and some suggested using the programme notes to guide the spectators in their interpretation of the play and the problematic image of a womanising priest. In his initial report, Federico Sainz de Robles's take on the play, and indeed on the role of censorship, seems almost enlightened:

> No admite su representación escénica ni supresiones ni adulteraciones: se toma o se deja; se permite o se prohíbe. Yo me inclino por lo primero porque no debemos ser tan puritanos que nos asustemos en el teatro de lo que nos gloriamos en el libro. La experiencia puede ser interesante. (AGA 139/65)
>
> The staging of this play does not allow for suppressions or adulterations: take it or leave it; allow it or prohibit it. I would opt for the former because we should not be so puritanical that we are shocked by something in the theatre that we celebrate in the book. It could be an interesting experience.

Yet, in his subsequent report for the plenary, Sainz de Robles was more circumspect, arguing that the sections relating directly to *El libro de buen amor* should be left untouched, while those added by Martín Recuerda could be pruned to eliminate pornographic and offensive language. He not only suggested framing the work for the public within the programme but also via the press, demonstrating again how much the press was part of the overall apparatus of cultural control. It was eventually authorised for over-eighteens with several cuts but prohibited for broadcast.

Martín Recuerda's later play, *El caraqueño*, with its theme of economic migration from Spain following the civil war and criticism of religion and post-war Spanish society, was submitted to the censors in May 1968 by Justo Alonso for staging at Madrid's Teatro Cómico in November. It was authorised for over-eighteens with several cuts and an inspection of the dress rehearsal. Unsurprisingly, cuts included a description of the rape of the protagonist Emilio's mother at the hands of Nationalist soldiers during the civil war and criticism of priests (AGA 232/68).

On the political front, the realists' plays tended to depict a people threatened by its rulers. Their portrayal of a miserable and unequal society contradicted the regime's propaganda of peace and prosperity. The solution was often to restrict the public to minimise the impact of such criticism. Carlos Muñiz's use of dark humour only served to exaggerate and highlight the wretched existence of many Spaniards and the injustices that prevailed in society. *El tintero*, a touchstone play of 1960s realist theatre, is an expressionistic, darkly comical play that focuses on the final days in the pitiful life of an office worker, Crock. Its journey through the censorship system reveals how negotiation and adaptation were a normalised part of the control system. The play itself is a Kafkaesque tale of alienation, misfortune, injustice, incomprehension and suicide. Crock's innocent expressions of happiness and freedom – singing, placing flowers on his desk, receiving a visit from his friend – are viewed as an affront to the officially sanctioned way the office should operate. A case against him is cooked up by some sinister bureaucrats and delivered by puppet-like model employees, Pim, Pam and Pum, who insist on 'la vida alegre' ('the happy life') that the office represents.

The files show that the play was originally called *La vida sin ventanas* ('Life without Windows'), and an application was made in 1960 by the Amparo Soler Leal company to stage it as a commercial production (sponsored by Alfonso Sastre's Grupo de Teatro Realista) in the Teatro Recoletos in Madrid, with music by Cristóbal Halffter. It was read by five censors, who were concerned not only by the social element but also by the moral issues raised by the adultery of the protagonist's wife and the suicide of the protagonist himself. The adultery was also deemed problematic because of the man involved: a teacher, and therefore not only a person charged with the (moral) education of the next generation, but also a state employee (AGA 306/60).

In addition to the censors' reports, the file contains correspondence between the censors, the dramatist and the theatre company. It is clear that Muñiz was both well connected and, like Buero, a *posibilista*. In a letter to José María Ortiz, dated 10 January 1961, Muñiz defended his work and set out the moral, aesthetic and social intentions of his expressionistic farce, which he claimed would have no 'efecto pernicioso' ('pernicious effect'). José María de Quinto, from the GTR, also wrote to Ortiz asking for a verdict, stressing both the urgency of the request (actors needed to be hired immediately) and the group's goal of supporting new Spanish authors.

In internal correspondence about the play (now titled *La farsa del tintero* ('The Farce of the Inkwell')), dated 28 January 1961, the censor Avelino Esteban Romero gave his verdict, arguing that the changes made to the title and characters (the protagonist had become Crock and other characters were given non-Hispanic sounding names) had helped, but that some problems remained. He finished, nonetheless, by suggesting that if the teacher character were replaced by another, it could be approved for minority theatres. This letter is interesting, not only because it shows how long the process lasted but also because it reveals Muñiz's *posibilismo* and the changes that he made to the play to render it stageable. The eventual verdict, delivered on 30 January 1961, was authorisation for over-eighteens, without further cuts, and the production limited to Madrid. The following month the name of the play was changed to *El tintero* and it was later authorised more broadly for *cámara*.

Occasionally a work had a greater impact than anticipated, as in the case of Olmo's *La camisa*. Set in the autumn of 1960, it reflects the impact of the regime's economic Stabilisation Plan (BOE 1959b) on the poorest sections of society, here represented by the working-class characters of Lola, Juan and the grandmother. The play undermines the regime's assertions regarding progress and prosperity, making clear that a reasonable standard of living for Spain's working classes is more often the result of emigration than the policies of the government (Berenguer 1997). It also shows the threats (drink, drugs, sexual exploitation) faced by the poorest in society. *La camisa* won the 1961 Valle-Inclán prize (created by Dido Pequeño Teatro), which guaranteed automatic staging in a *teatro de cámara*, but was not premiered until March 1962. It went on to become one of the iconic plays of cultural opposition to the regime in the 1960s but also alerted the censors to Olmo's potential as a voice of dissidence (Primer Acto 1974c: 20–1).

The play's route to success was rather tortured (Muñoz Caliz 2005: 201–4). When Josefina Sánchez Pedreño first applied on behalf of Dido Pequeño Teatro, the play was read by two censors, Adolfo Carril and Fr Andrés Avelino Esteban Romero. The former referred to the play in his report as a social drama, criticised its use of provocative clichés and argued for prohibition. The latter, in his moral report, commented on its bitterness and depiction of social and moral deprivation, but thought it suitable for adult audiences in theatre clubs, only in the more cosmopolitan environments of Madrid and Barcelona. While the summary list of Olmo's works in the AGA indicates that it was authorised at this point, both Patricia O'Connor (1973: 42–3) and Berta Muñoz suggest that it was not (2005: 201). Olmo, in his prologue to the Cátedra edition of the play, throws some light on the contradiction, stating that the prohibition took place during rehearsals: 'Los ensayos de 1961 hubo que suspenderlos. Surgieron dificultades y no se autorizó el estreno' ('The rehearsals in 1961 had to be suspended. Problems arose and the premiere was not authorised') (1997: 130).

Dido applied again in June, this time appealing directly to the Director General, and secured authorisation for a single *cámara* performance, which took place in the Teatro Goya on 8 March 1962 with Alberto González Vergel as director. The same year, it was authorised for commercial productions in Madrid and Barcelona, with cuts to eliminate references to sex and the body but also one, highlighted by Muñoz Cáliz, to a striking scene that juxtaposes financial news on the radio of Spain's 'spectacular' economic recovery with the poverty of those listening (2005:198). Halsey noted its unexpected success: 'Originally scheduled for a single evening, [it] ran for one hundred and six performances at the Goya Theater and another hundred at the Maravillas' (1979: 69). It won prestigious prizes – the Larra and the Premio Nacional de Teatro – and was widely staged at home and abroad. *La camisa* and its welcome by a certain sector of the opposition seems to have encouraged the censors to view Olmo's work as a problem and subsequent works were carefully monitored and many were heavily censored or prohibited (Primer Acto 1973–4: 20–1). Ironically, Monleón notes that Olmo was also the victim of a particular type of censorship of the left: when, following the success of *La camisa*, his subsequent works did not, in the eyes of some, meet the political standards of the opposition, he was deemed a failure (1995: 81–2).

Several other realist works centre on Spain's frustrated young people, who in turn embraced the plays as representative of their experiences. Rodríguez Méndez's *Los inocentes de la Moncloa* (1960), about young people preparing for the *oposiciones*, the state examinations for entry into a world of stable public employment, highlights not only the poverty of some Spaniards, in the character of the young man from Córdoba, but also captured the powerlessness of a whole generation. Interestingly, Rodríguez Méndez presents the eagerness of people to join the system, and thus save themselves, rather than any solidarity or revolt against it. Indeed, the play concludes with the success of the protagonist, José Luis. It was the subject of an application in January 1961 for staging in Barcelona and was authorised for over-eighteens, with eight cuts to eliminate some bad taste and negative references to Spain, including Ana Mari's comment about 'sufriendo como la mayoría de los españoles' ('suffering like the majority of Spaniards') and Paco's suggestion that the students faced 'un destino negro por delante' ('a black destiny ahead'). A similar verdict was delivered for an application to stage the play in Madrid in 1964.

Olmo's *English spoken*, which focused on unemployment and emigration as the legacy of the civil war, portrayed a Spanish society clearly at odds with the regime's presentation of a successful and stable country. Once again, the playwright represented the frustration and lack of opportunity experienced by young, working-class Spaniards. The play is, in some ways, a lament for a lost solidarity. Fr Cea's short report described it as 'lasciva, grosera y morbosa' ('lascivious, crude and sick'), which combined with its problematic and unorthodox political content ensured that it would need to be cut severely (AGA 375/67). Alfredo Mampaso was biting in his criticism but thought the theme alien to the concerns of Spain's youth and so delivered a verdict of authorisation with numerous cuts, including negative allusions to the civil war and elements of poor taste. For example, the cut on page 33 of Act I takes a swipe at politicians, while condemning the state of the economy:

BASILIO.– *¿Y la política, qué?*
MÍSTER.– *A mí, de la política, sólo me interesa un dato. Los que están arriba, son los que se acuestan con las mejores mujeres.* (AGA 375/67)

BASILIO – *And what about politics?*
MÍSTER – I'm only interested in one fact about politics. Those at the top are the ones who sleep with the best women.

The play was finally authorised with thirteen cuts, with monitoring of the dress rehearsal and deemed not suitable for broadcast. Halsey noted that it became a rallying point of opposition to the regime among its youthful audience:

Evidence of the polemical impact of the play is found in an account of the fiftieth performance, which was accompanied by a recital by Paco Ibáñez. While police waited outside uncertain whether to enter, the spectators insulted each other in a carnival atmosphere; and Olmo, himself, was denounced as a 'comunista de mierda' ['a shitty Communist']. When Ibáñez sang Celaya's 'España en marcha', at the refrain 'a la calle que ya es hora de pelear cuerpo a cuerpo' ['to the streets, it's time to fight person to person'] a cry of '¡Eso, a la calle!'

['Yes, to the streets!'] rang out; and at Otero's verse 'aquí no se salva ni Dios' ['no one gets saved here'], anyone who left was accompanied by the ritual shout of '¡Eso, fuera el fascio!' ['Out, Fascists!']. (1979: 85, our translations)

Olmo's *El cuerpo*, which he described as the story of a pair of biceps and a criticism of machismo (2004: 347) seems a less obvious criticism of Spain, yet, as Antonio Fernández Insuela indicates, the play works on two levels: as the story of a middle-aged man, obsessed with bodily strength, who is confronted with his gradual physical decline, and as a symbolic political story of 'poder basado en esa fuerza' ('power based on that strength') (Olmo 2004: 339–45). The censorship files list it as authorised in January 1966 for over-eighteens. In his memoir, José María García Escudero suggested that Olmo had written the play 'para que se le prohíba' ('in order for it to be prohibited') (1978a: 154), thus placing the blame on him and insinuating that the dramatist was playing political games.

Several plays by Rodríguez Méndez centred on the theme of revolution, provoking the ire of the censors. His *El círculo de tiza de Cartagena* ('The Cartagena Chalk Circle', 1963), a darkly comical work (with a significant nod to Brecht's *The Caucasian Chalk Circle*), employs the time of the 1873 Cartagena revolts to represent and comment on the clash between revolution and tradition. When in May 1962 an application to stage the play was made by the Teatro del Candil company, with José Tamayo as director, the response from the censors was mixed. Montes Agudo concluded that nothing could justify the staging of this play, which was 'políticamente peligrosa y teatralmente absurda' ('politically dangerous and theatrically absurd'), but it was eventually authorised in November, too late for the production to go ahead (AGA 106/62). It premiered instead in early 1963 in Barcelona, in the Teatro Guimerá, with cuts to eliminate negative references to religion.

The 1960s also saw an increase in the use of allusion to history or to the family as a way of commenting on contemporary politics. One such play was Buero's *El tragaluz* (1966), a family drama introduced by two researchers from the future whose enlightened viewpoint is supposed to encourage the spectators to view their present from a critical distance. The action focuses on the dysfunctional relationship between two brothers based on the choices they made in the aftermath of the civil war. Vicente has accommodated himself to the new ways and is thriving but continues to make victims of others in his eagerness to succeed in this broken society; Mario judges him and Spanish society negatively but, initially at least, does nothing to change it. When an application was made to stage it in 1967, the censors objected to Mario's sarcastic equation of 'el desarrollo' ('economic development') with the hardship experienced by the millions of people who migrated from the countryside to the cities. Another cut was Mario's damning statement to his brother: 'Nos tocó crecer en un tiempo de asesinos y nos hemos hecho hombres en un tiempo de ladrones' ('It was our lot to grow up in an age of murderers and we have become men in an age of thieves'). This was changed, probably after negotiation between the author and the censorship office, to 'Nos tocó crecer en años difíciles' ('It was our lot to grow up in difficult times'), a much milder comment that did not directly criticise the authorities (ANC 172/67).[12]

In addition to worrying about internal politics, the files show how the regime used censorship to protect its reputation and its relationships with other states. The censors took issue with Muñiz's *Un solo de saxofón*, for example, due to its representation of the United States. The play is based on a racist murder and sordid cover-up that takes place in the Depression-era United States. While it could be argued that the play's criticism of injustice, social inequality and the need for rebellion also applied to Spain under the dictatorship, the censors focused not on these parallels but, instead, on the play's perceived attack on an important ally. In his 1965 report, Bartolomé Mostaza complained of a 'feroz diatriba contra la sociedad norteamericana' ('fierce diatribe against North American society') and as late as 1972 Zubiaurre lamented an attack 'tan manido como pedestre' ('as hackneyed as it is pedestrian') against the United States, while Albizu noted that the dramatist seemed to wish to mock the country (AGA 14/65). In the end, it was restricted to *cámara* and later applications from minority theatres allowed for limited performance runs. Similarly, Rodríguez Méndez's *La Andalucía de los Quintero* ('The Andalusia of the Quintero Brothers'), which was the subject of an application by the Royal School of Dramatic Arts for a tour in 1969, was cut to eliminate a reference to 'puta Alemania' ('bloody Germany') before being authorised for over-eighteens (AGA 200/69).

In the late 1960s, student and worker unrest saw an upsurge in harsh censorship and prohibitions. Plays that might have been allowed in other circumstances now fell foul of censors who were fearful of their impact on a disaffected public. Buero's *El sueño de la razón* (1969), set during the despotic reign of Fernando VII and focusing on the relationship between the authorities and the elderly and deaf painter Goya, evoked certain parallels with contemporary Spain. Buero incorporated the titles of his war etchings and Black Paintings into the disturbing dialogue and portrayed reality as a nightmare. In July 1969, José Osuna applied for permission to stage the play in the Reina Victoria theatre in Madrid in the January 1970 season. All three censors who read it expressed concerns about the scene in which Leocadia is raped by the Royal Volunteers and Bautista de la Torre also accused Buero of going too far with his 'chafarrinón folletinesco y subversivo' ('subversive, melodramatic slander'). Buero's 'tendenciosa intención' ('tendentious intentions') in his condemnation of absolutism and his sympathy for oppressed liberals were noted and the censors objected to the untimeliness of the theme. In late November the play was sent to a further thirteen censors. The definitive verdict was withheld until the censors had seen the rehearsal. In the end, a pragmatic decision was made to authorise it, as the authorities concluded that a further delay in the announcement of a verdict could encourage a political interpretation of the play (AGA 259/69). *El sueño de la razón* was finally staged in Madrid in February 1970.

Muñiz's *Un solo de saxofón* was also considered untimely in January 1969, despite having previously been approved for *cámara*. Records show that the Provincial Delegate received a phone call from Madrid indicating that the play could not be authorised 'en los momentos actuales' ('at the current time'), undoubtedly a reference to the state of emergency introduced the same month in response to widespread organised opposition to the regime from student and workers' groups. Another of Muñiz's plays, the farce *El caballo del caballero: Farsa burguesa para una exposición de pintura* ('The Knight's Steed: Bourgeois Farce for an Exhibition of Paintings'), also ran into difficulties due to political circumstances. The play presents a colourless 'mundo al revés' ('topsy-turvy world'), where nothing is as it should be. Hombre ('Man'), an emblematic character, insists to Hermenegildo and his wife that everyone must lend a hand to achieve 'paz y colores' ('peace and colours') but the tyrannical Señor Don ('Mr Master') offers false happiness in this upside-down world and threatens punishment should things return to the way they were before. He announces that he is 'la mano justiciera que ponga las cosas en su sitio' ('the hand of justice that puts things in their place') and will not tolerate lack of discipline. Hombre argues that said hand must be cut off to set the world to rights, but Señor Don persuades Hermenegildo and his wife to embrace evasion from reality instead. They do and Hermenegildo dies. Señor Don laughs and exits, leaving Hombre to lament both the death and the ongoing loss of peace and colour in the world.

The play was the subject of an application from the university group TEU de Peritos Industriales in March 1965 and was initially approved but subsequent applications, during a period of heightened student unrest, led to a review and when a student group in Palma de Mallorca applied to stage the play in 1969 the censors worried about its political implications. The abstract nature of the play helped, however, and it was authorised for *cámara* with one significant cut, the phrase 'y con los grises' ('and with the greys') (AGA 52/65). This comment, following Hombre's plea for help to 'acabar con el blanco y con el gris, acabar con el negro' ('do away with the white, the grey and the black'), was an obvious reference to the Fuerzas de Policía Armada, commonly known as *los grises* ('the greys') for the colour of their uniform. Inspired by the Nazis, this armed, repressive police force under military command was defined in law as 'instrumento vigilante y represivo de tipo permanente' ('a permanent instrument of vigilance and repression'); it was charged with responding to the political and social needs of the regime and was often involved in clashes with students and repression of protests (BOE 1941b: 1630).[13]

This decade saw not only cuts but also a significant number of prohibitions of realist plays. Some of these were overtly political, dealing with police brutality and torture and revolutionary action against authorities portrayed as tyrannical. The parallels with Spain were patent, particularly when increasing public opposition to the regime was being brutally repressed.

Alfonso Sastre's *En la red*, set in Algeria, is about state torture and the need for revolutionary change. The protagonists, Pablo, Leo and Cecilia are a militant group tasked with helping others to escape. They are suspicious of each other but later realise that Pablo, rather than a traitor, is one of the revolutionary leaders. At the end of the play, while they have succeeded in their mission, they are caught by the authorities and Leo is killed.

An application to stage *En la red* was made in October 1960 but the response was *silencio administrativo*. In December 1960, Sastre wrote to José María Ortiz, demanding to know the status of his play. He referred to the letter about censorship sent to a Minister and signed by 227 writers, including himself, and he restated his opposition to the practice. He received a rather defensive response, explaining that the delays had been due to the detailed and extensive readings necessary, given the play's subject matter. The play was being read, not only by the censorship authorities but also by the Ministry for Foreign Affairs. *En la red* was eventually authorised and premiered by the student theatre group GTR in the Teatro Recoletos on 9 March 1961, with Juan Antonio Bardem as director. Yet when one considers that it centres on a group of freedom fighters struggling to liberate Algeria, with its obvious parallels with the those who would liberate Spain from dictatorship and that the application to stage the play came from the GTR, which had made its political agenda and opposition to the Franco regime clear from the outset, its authorisation is still surprising. A review by Eugenia Serrano in *Pueblo* criticised Western intellectuals for betraying their own blood and homeland to defend the colonised (1961: 3). Alfredo Marquerie's more sophisticated and insidious review in *ABC* reported a positive reception from theatregoers and suggested that, as it was about concrete and current events in another country, it had no symbolic value. In other words, he advised readers that it should not be read as being about Spain. Moreover, he went on to say that some might read it as an echo of the fear experienced by those trapped in 'red' Madrid at the end of the civil war, thus actively framing it for a pro-regime reading (1961: 58).

Yet the censors were taken aback by the public reaction to the play. An internal note reveals that they blamed audience misinterpretation and 'negative political understanding' of the play, rather than recognising Sastre's deliberate criticism. The initial failure of the censors to note Sastre's political agenda is striking, especially as he spelled it out in the programme notes, which suggested that some might find the play intolerable and expressed the hope that it would act as a consciousness-raising piece in the tradition of 'teatro concebido como forma de lucha y de investigación de lo real' ('theatre conceived of as a form of battle and as an investigation of reality') (2001:16). The outcome was a ban on staging in the provinces (Sastre 2001: 18). In a revision of their original verdict, the authorities now assumed that anyone trying to stage it was motivated by their political opposition to the regime. This was an interesting combination of reactive and proactive censorship, as Provincial Delegates were asked to report any attempts, or indeed rumours of attempts, to stage the play (AGA 260/60).

En la red was also prohibited in Oviedo in September 1961, no doubt a result of the heightened unrest in Asturias at the time. Yet it was authorised on several subsequent occasions in the 1960s and 1970s following a review by the censors who referred to the altered political situation that made the play stageable again. This was always subject to change, however, and a Basque version was banned in 1972, even when it was authorised elsewhere in Spain.

After *En la red*, Sastre struggled to have much of his work staged for several years. *Oficio de tinieblas* ('Tenebrae Service', 1962), a play about a politically motivated cover-up of a crime of passion and set during Holy Week, was, according to Martínez-Michel, the subject of an application by José Luis Alonso for staging in the Teatro María Guerrero (2003: 142). The files relating to this application are missing but it was banned, according to the dramatist (Sastre 1966: 945). The AGA file shows, however, that it was later authorised with cuts (relating to religion and morality) in August 1963 for staging at the Teatro de la Comedia, on condition that the dress rehearsal was carefully monitored (AGA 197/63). Yet, according to Martínez-Michel, the production did not go ahead and the play was not staged until 1967 (2003: 144).

Sastre's *La sangre y la ceniza*, based on the life and brutal death of Miguel Servet, which drew fairly obvious parallels between a tyrannical past and contemporary Spain, was prohibited for both stage and print. José María García Escudero wrote to Carlos Robles Piquer, Director General de Información, arguing that works such as this should not be authorised, citing allusions to the regime, blasphemy, vulgarities and religious disrespect (Martínez-Michel 2003: 144). Other works, such as *Crónicas romanas* ('Roman Chronicles', 1968), a free version of Cervantes's *Numancia*, did not even make it to the application stage; its revolutionary theme was too obviously unstageable.

Some of Rodríguez Méndez's plays were also banned. His most contentious works are those set at significant moments in Spain's troubled recent history, highlighting his interest in the people (*pueblo*) as a repository of Spanishness. The fact that establishment figures (and drawing on his own experiences, frequently the military) are often negatively portrayed ensured that these plays often fell foul of the censors. His *Vagones de madera*, although it had been staged in Barcelona in 1959, was prohibited in February 1961, despite the lack of unanimity among censors. The provincial delegate from Guipúzcoa, Miguel Ángel R. Arbeloa, objected to its treatment of religious education and its depiction of King Alfonso XIII and the armed forces. Montes Agudo deemed it 'amarga, tendenciosilla, con un antimilitarismo trasnochado' ('bitter, slightly tendentious, and containing a jaded antimilitarism'), but thought that it could be salvaged by imposing several cuts. José María Cano also thought it suitable for over-eighteens and made the point that the crudeness of the dialogue was an accurate representation of soldiers' language. An application to stage *Vagones* in Madrid in 1962 was also unsuccessful, despite a positive opinion from the military censor Juan Guerra y Romero. Later, however, following an application by Grupo Gestos in Gijón in 1964, it was authorised for over-eighteens and for *cámara*, with cuts to eliminate negative references to General Primo de Rivera and the monarchy, the latter the subject of much debate in Spain in the mid-1960s. Cuts included the call to commit regicide: '¡Que se muera el tío de la corona!' ('Death to the guy with the crown!') (AGA 311/60).

Rodríguez Méndez's *Bodas que fueron famosas del Pingajo y la Fandanga* (1965) is listed several times in the AGA files.[14] It is set among the poor in Madrid in 1898 against the backdrop of Spain's disastrous American wars and reflects a disintegrating society. It traces the escapades of the picaresque Pingajo, from his return from the Cuban wars, to his love affair with Fandanga, his tricking of her lascivious suitor, a lieutenant in the Spanish army, a robbery, his capture and execution. It was decidedly antimilitary in sentiment and mocking of Spain's supposed nobility, features that would lead to problems with the censors. Muñoz Cáliz suggests that *Bodas* was the victim of *silencio administrativo* and its production was halted for eight years (2005: 226). In 1974 the play was finally authorised (AGA 205/74), although it was not premiered until August 1976, after the death of Franco (Thompson 2007a: 126).

Buero's most difficult encounter with censorship was with *La doble historia del doctor Varga* (later changed to the less Spanish-sounding *La doble historia del doctor Valmy*) in 1964. The play, about police torture and public denial of the truth, centres on two separate but related medical case studies from the files of the eponymous doctor. Most of the action focuses on the second of these, the story of Daniel and Mary Barnes, who live with their son and Daniel's mother in the fictional land of Surelia. Daniel is a member of the security police and he tortured and castrated a prisoner called Aníbal Marty, who died as a result. Daniel's own impotence is a reaction to this incident. Mary, like Daniel's mother, lives a life of denial but when Lucila, Marty's widow, tells her the truth, she confronts her husband. Daniel is too weak and fearful of his superiors to change, and Mary kills him. In the end, both Mary and Lucila are arrested by the security police and will, we assume, also be tortured and possibly killed. The first case history is Buero's message to his spectators. In it, a couple dressed like other theatregoers refuse to accept the truth of the Barnes' story and insist that the authorities always act in the best interests of the people. They (and, by extension, the spectators) are diagnosed by the doctor as delusional for their failure to recognise the truth of what is happening around them.

The initial application to stage the play came from the Teatro de la Comedia company in July 1964. It was read by three censors. Mostaza, like Fr González Fierro, deemed the play suitable for over-eighteens, with many cuts. Neither considered it suitable for broadcast. The third censor, Vázquez Dodero, made similar recommendations. The play was authorised with cuts (many of them sexual references) and required the foreignisation of the characters' names. However, the theatre company, not having received a definitive answer in time, did not stage the play.

Later that same year, the Ramón Clemente theatre company sought permission to stage what was now called *La doble historia del doctor Valmy* in Barcelona in October 1964 and in Madrid in early 1965. The renamed and amended play was sent to the same censors once again. All three now suggested that the first case study should be eliminated and Mostaza and Vázquez Dodero proposed cutting references to sex and other examples of 'bad taste'. The play was considered by a plenary of the censorship board. Sebastián Bautista de la Torre thought that the name of the imaginary country, Surelia, was suggestive of a southern European country, such as Spain, and advised changing it for a more neutral term. This, combined with the elimination of the first case history and a long series of other minor cuts, led Buero to refuse the proposed changes and as a result, the play was not authorised. When, in February 1966, the Núria Espert Theatre company applied to stage the play, Manuel Fraga was consulted. Buero's comments in the press about the play and his refusal to accept any cuts were noted. The result was a ministerial prohibition, on 15 March 1966, in accordance with Article 22 of the 1964 regulations. Subsequent applications to stage the play during the dictatorship were refused (AGA 147/64).

Several of Olmo's plays were banned in this period. These included *Plaza menor* and *Junio, siete, stop* ('June, Seven, Stop') in 1967, and *El cuarto poder* in 1968. *Plaza menor* was described by the censor Alfredo Mampaso as typical of the style of the dramatist, focusing on the misery of the oppressed lower classes and the destroyed hopes of the young, and blaming the authorities for their failures. Díez Crespo deemed it subversive and dangerous, and Fr Artola described it as 'el grito de protesta del pueblo aplastado' ('the cry of protest from a downtrodden people'). It was referred to a plenary. The censors took issue with dialogue such as this, from Act I:

> VOZ.– La unión, la unión de los subdesarrollados es la que nos pondrá en marcha hacia una sociedad más justa, más digna, más en consonancia con los sagrados valores humanos que, hoy por hoy, son sacrificados en aras del neocapitalismo . . .
>
> VOICE – The unity, the unity of the disadvantaged is what will set us on the path to a society that is more just, more honourable, more in tune with the sacred human values that are daily being sacrificed on the altar of neocapitalism . . .

The inclusion of the Republican anthem, the 'Himno de Riego', was deemed an intolerable affront to the new regime, and the censors further objected to criticism of the regime's honours system and references to torture in Act II. It was prohibited on the basis of articles 14.3, 15 and 17 of the 1963 legislation, which related to the falsification of historical persons, events or atmosphere; the fostering of hatred between people or classes; and attacks on the Church, the state or Franco (AGA 177/67). Olmo's *Junio, siete, stop* was banned in September 1967 for its morality, rather than its politics. The family drama, with its emphasis on the honour code, was read by some censors as a commentary on Spain under Franco (AGA 222/67).

Another Olmo play, *El cuarto poder*, a montage of six short pieces that attack the manipulation of the press and of censorship, is divided into two parts. The first of these contains *La noticia* ('The News'), *La niña y el pelele* ('The Girl and the Simpleton') and *Conflicto a la hora de la siesta* and explores the political use of the press and the fear of speaking out. The second contains the plays *De cómo el hombre limpión tiró de la manta* ('How the Cleaning Man Let the Cat Out of the Bag'), *Nuevo retablo de las maravillas y olé* ('New Altarpiece of Wonders and Olé') and *Ceros a la izquierda* ('Zeros to the Left').

When an application was made by Justo Alonso in November 1969 to stage the drama, it was read by Fr Cea, Bautista de la Torre and Martínez Ruiz. They delivered a negative verdict and it was prohibited for its attacks on the institutions of the state, its anticlericalism, antimilitarism and its denunciation of censorship and lack of freedom. Articles 14.2, 14.3 and 19 of the 1963 legislation, relating to negative representation of certain ideologies or institutions; the falsification of historical persons, events or atmosphere; and protection of minors and the prohibition of blasphemy, pornography and subversion, were cited in the verdict of prohibition in November 1969 (Muñoz Caliz 2005: 316–17). In December 1969, an appeal was lodged and it went to a plenary. Several censors commented on its quality but prohibited it nonetheless in February 1970. Despite correspondence from the author, asserting its universality, the play was read by the censors as a direct criticism of Spain and of the regime (Muñoz Cáliz 2005: 317). A further application to stage *El cuarto poder* was made by Justo Alonso in October 1970. His argument that changes had been made to the playtext did not convince them. For Pedro Barceló, one of the censors who read it at the time, 'Es más un "mitin protestatario" que una pieza teatral' ('it's more of a protest rally than a theatre piece') (AGA 376/69).

Some of the plays from *El cuarto poder* were also the subject of separate applications. In 1967, *La noticia*, a play about fake news and propaganda, which makes a veiled reference to the notorious Julián Grimau case, was unsurprisingly deemed 'de marcada intención política' ('of marked political intent'), by Ortiz, who consulted the Director General, García Escudero, about an application by the Ateneo de Oviedo for a proposed January tour of the region.[15] Given that his letter is dated mid-February, we can assume that the planned tour did not go ahead. It was authorised on 22 February for *cámara* sessions, without cuts and was premiered in the Ateneo de Oviedo. Despite being banned with the rest of *El cuarto poder* in 1969 and 1970, *La noticia* was authorised again with the same conditions in 1971 (AGA 15/67).

Olmo's family drama, *La condecoración*, caused most consternation, with its hostile depiction of the civil war victors and the conflict's damaging legacy in society. The father, Don José, who fought on the Nationalist side in the civil war, feels betrayed both by his more successful friend, Don Lucas, and by his children Pedro and Luisa, who have benefited from their status as children of the victors, but whose sympathies now lie with the rising youthful opposition to the regime. Even his wife, Doña María, is living a lie, promoting a false family harmony that echoes a false national one. Julia, the family's servant, hails from the defeated side in the war and her presence is a constant reminder of what Republicans lost. In what is a prescient representation, given Spain's later historical memory debates, her initial desire for a quiet life and no return to conflict are gradually replaced by the need to acknowledge painful memories of the past and to apportion blame. The play highlights the disappointing legacy of the civil war, even for some of those on the winning side. While it shows the Francoist old guard glorifying war, their children abhor all that they, their medals, and their uniforms represent and want a better society. In a dialogue with Luisa in Act I, Pedro highlights the damage to broader society done by the war: 'Un día recorrerás conmigo la ciudad. Y te mostraré gente que va hablando sola. Y un excesivo número de borrachos. Y un excesivo número de prostitutas. Y un excesivo número de . . .' ('One day you'll wander the city with me. And I'll show you the people who talk to themselves. And an excessive number of drunks. And an excessive number of prostitutes. And an excessive number of . . .').

He later attacks all that his father – and the regime – stand for: 'La intimidación, el miedo. Eso es lo que habéis creado: el miedo [. . .] Pero la Patria, la Patria auténtica, ¿dónde queda? Te lo diré. (*Firme.*) <u>Abonando los campos</u>' ('Intimidation and fear. That's what you've created: fear [. . .] But the Fatherland, the true Fatherland, where is it now? I'll tell you where. (Firm voice.) <u>Fertilising the fields</u>'). Dialogue such as this laid bare an intolerable truth about the legacy of the war and demanded acknowledgement of a silenced and buried past. The play was banned. The prohibition was upheld on other occasions and the play was not authorised until after Franco's death (AGA 29/65).

The 1970s

Censorship files from the 1970s and the transition period are very revealing of the power shifts and accommodations taking place. Although the aged dictator held on to power, the 1970s saw increased discussion of the future of the regime and a sense that some change was inevitable. The different factions' plans for alternative modes of governance were reflected in sometimes fraught debates about censorship among those charged with its implementation. In this period, we see a continuation of censorship and prohibition of works deemed attacks on the regime or supportive of the opposition. Some of the most interesting cases in the mid-1970s, however, relate to previously banned plays, such as Buero's *La doble historia del doctor Valmy* and Olmo's *La condecoración*.

In terms of morality, religion and taste, it is clear both that the dramatists were bolder in what they attempted to stage and that more was tolerated than before, although the censors were still inclined to prune in order to protect the public from exposed flesh and other supposedly offensive material. For example, some sensitive censors objected to descriptions of women and girls in beachwear in Buero's *Llegada de los dioses* ('Arrival of the Gods') (AGA 323/71), and most of the censors who read his *La Fundación* (*The Foundation*) demanded the elimination of a reference to masturbation and condemned the suggestion of a sexual encounter between Tomás and his girlfriend Berta (AGA 145/73). Martín Recuerda's *El engañao* ('The Deceived'), based on the life of St John of God in Granada, was critical of Church-state relations. Crude language and statements such as 'la Iglesia católica pacta con los reyes para robar' ('the Catholic Church does deals with the monarchs to rob the people') were cut before authorisation in February 1974 (AGA 574/73). The file on Muñiz's *Los condenados* ('The Condemned') contains a copy of the playtext with several censorship marks referring to homosexuality (Juan's relationship with Emilio), the unjust legal system, and the hypocrisy and sexual pecadillos of priests (AGA 618/74). Olmo's *Spot de identidad* ('Identity Ad'), although approved in December 1975 for over-eighteens, was deemed to be in very poor taste by the censors, who were unimpressed by the homosexuality and nudity on display (AGA 703/75).

When it came to political censorship, several works by the realists were authorised with cuts in this period. Buero, again, seems to have got away with more than the others, by trading on his reputation and that of the directors he worked with, and by successfully balancing political commentary with acceptable plotlines. In *La Fundación*, for example, he condemned regimes that imprison, torture and kill the political opposition. Authorisation for staging was sought in February 1973. In his report, Mampaso noted the play's emphasis on the need to fight for a better society and criticised Buero's representation of 'los buenos oprimidos y los malos en el poder' ('the oppressed good guys and the bad guys in power'), which he related directly to the dramatist's own experience as a prisoner of the regime. Despite this, he did not suggest a ban. Several censors noted the universality of the political theme, something that Buero, as a *posibilista*, was eager to emphasise. Of course, the resonance in a country where political opponents were still treated in this way, was not lost on them. It is an indication of changed times and Buero's status that nobody suggested prohibition at the plenary, and a sign of the authorities' nervousness that it was then sent to a special commission for further evaluation. It was finally authorised with cuts in June 1973, more than three months after the application was made. The final verdict demanded that set and costume could in no way be suggestive of Spain (AGA 145/73). It was, of course, interpreted by many as a commentary on the dictatorship.

The regime's concern for its reputation is also evident in the censorship of Olmo's *Historia de un pechicidio* ('Story of a Stab in the Breast'), a version of *Junio, siete, stop*, described in one censor's report as reminiscent of Pedro Muñoz Seca's 1918 farce *La venganza de don Mendo* (*Don Mendo's Revenge*). It was approved for over-eighteens in 1972, although the authorisation was dependent on a green light from the inspection services once they had viewed the dress rehearsal, as there was some concern over the potential for mischief in the costumes (particularly that of the Inquisitor), set and style of performance (AGA 602/72).

Reputation was an issue again in October 1972, when Justo Alonso applied to stage Muñiz's *Tragicomedia del serenísimo Príncipe don Carlos* in the Poliorama in Barcelona under the direction of Alberto González Vergel. The play's take on the country's degenerate leadership sparked unease about the production. García-Cernuda considered it 'irrepresentable bajo cualquier punto de vista' ('unstageable from any perspective'). Florentino Soria objected to the portrait of a sinister Felipe II, surrounded by cruel and fanatical Church figures. Bautista de la Torre acknowledged the importance and quality of the play but found it to be biased in its representation of Felipe II and of the Church and recommended seeking the views of a priest (AGA 576/72).

It was referred to a plenary of the censorship board and was read by twelve censors and the secretary, Ortiz. Both Fr Cea and Fr Artola gave a verdict of prohibition. Fr Cea cited article 14 of the legislation in his verdict and although he praised its quality, construction and dramatic force, he denounced the play's depiction of the close and corrupt relationship between Church and Crown: 'La Iglesia y la Corona son como las cucarachas que hay que desterrar para lograr la libertad' ('The Church and the Crown are like cockroaches that have to be eliminated to achieve liberty'). In addition to the religious and political issues, the censor cited questions of taste, especially the scenes in which the prince's virility is tested (AGA 576/72).

Several of the censors accused Muñiz of propagating the *leyenda negra* of Spain (the anti-Catholic 'Black Legend', propagated by contemporary enemies, which demonised Spain's leadership and played down the country's achievements in the conquest of the Americas) and considered this unacceptable at a time when the regime needed to convince future allies of its stability and integrity. Antonio Zubiaurre, for example, argued that the play constituted an affront to a great king and was in clear breach of article 17 of the legislation in its attack on national dignity.

There were sympathetic readings from some censors, five of whom gave a verdict of authorisation, albeit with extensive cuts. Luis Tejedor was impressed by Muñiz's work and, like the dramatist, argued for the demythification of Spanish history, claiming that this would actually be good for the monarchy. Jesús Vasallo's report also makes for interesting reading. He deemed the play an important work and, while concluding that it could be authorised with cuts for over-eighteens, expressed some concern about parallels with the present day. Like other censors, he objected to the scene representing the testing of the prince's virility, and, in particular, to Don Carlos's sexual relations with his aunt, Juana, in act 1:

> D. Carlos.– Recuerdo que siendo aún muy niño y ella ya viuda, las largas noches de invierno venía a mi lecho a consolarme. Y sentía el vello de su sexo cerca de mi barriga [. . .] Ella solo quiere sentir algo vivo entre las piernas.
>
> D. Carlos – I remember when I was still very young and she was already a widow, she would come to my bed on long winter nights to console me. And I would feel the soft hair of her sex close to my belly [. . .] She only wants to feel something alive between her legs.

There were other references to sex, including with dogs, which caused grave concern among the censors. In addition, the character Barbero's suggestion that 'es grande, muy grande honra la deshonra de una virgen por el Príncipe de España' ('it's a great, great honour to be deflowered by the Prince of Spain') was criticised, as were the mentions of the Prince's 'pajarito' ('little pecker') and whether or not it had been blessed. Of course, this was not just about sex, but rather the negative portrait of a debauched and corrupt leader.

The final verdict, delivered on 31 October 1972, was one of prohibition based on articles 10, 14 and 18, referring to images and scenes that might provoke base passions; falsification of history; and the creation of a lascivious and obscene tone or mood. Justo Alonso tried to negotiate, arguing that the play was not in breach of the legislation and Muñiz wrote a lengthy letter pleading his case. In it, he cited several historical sources that informed his work and reasoned that to ban the work would be to silence Spanish history, but to no avail. It was prohibited again later the same year.

Several of Rodríguez Méndez's plays were prohibited in the 1970s, for what were clearly perceived – both by those who wished to stage them and by the censors – as attacks on the regime's institutions. *Los quinquis de Madriz* ('Down and Out in Madrid', 1967), for example, set in Madrid's shanty towns, highlights both the brutality and the failures of Francoist Spain, which has left a battered group of social outcasts on the edges of the city. Despite the economic revival this fractured community has little hope or opportunity and the play ends with the execution of the protagonist at the hands of the state. Some of the censors who viewed the play objected to its crudeness and its 'anarchist' ideology (Zubiaurre), its exaltation of crooks (Soria) and its glorification of delinquents, but the main criticism related to its political content – the wholly negative depiction of the institutions of the Francoist state, a clear breach of article 14.2 of the legislation. The play was prohibited in 1970 and never staged (AGA 413/70).[16]

In 1972, his *El ghetto, o la irresistible ascención de Manuel Contreras* ('The Ghetto, or The Irresistible Rise of Manuel Contreras', 1964) was prohibited, despite having been staged by La Pipironda in 1966 (Muñoz Caliz 2005: 332). Set in a working-class area, this time in one of the new estates created in the construction boom of the late 1950s and early 1960s, it shows the lives of characters beholden to the demands of a booming economy. Manuel, a likeable character who is doing well, is faced with a dilemma when he is asked to play a role in firing two co-workers, whose politics do not fit with the new Spain. His own success is therefore at the expense of others and the play exposes a corrupt and immoral system behind Spain's much-lauded economic prosperity. Its prohibition in 1972 was due to contemporary political concerns. By now, many of the regime's toothless 'vertical' unions had been infiltrated by communists associated with the outlawed Comisiones Obreras ('Workers' Commissions') union and the play was seen as a subversive attack on the official unions and how they operated in the interests of the state, rather than the workers, and articles 15 and 19 of the 1963 regulations, referring to the fostering of social division and subversion, respectively, were cited in the prohibition (AGA 555/72).

Another of Rodríguez Méndez's plays, *Historia de unos cuantos* ('Anyone's History', 1971), charts the hopes and disappointments of various members of working-class Madrid from the political crisis of 1898 to the early dictatorship, representing the impact on the *pueblo* of corruption and hypocrisy amongst the establishment and the journey of Julián from optimistic socialism towards self-interested capitalism under the new regime (Thompson 2007a: 140). A production by Ricard Salvat was prohibited in 1972 and an application by the Quart 23 company to stage it in Valencia in 1973 led to a plenary meeting of the censorship board. The files show that there was significant disagreement among the many censors who read it. For Mampaso, 'no deja de ser un mitin político de "rojillos" desengañados y derrotados' ('it is a political rally of disillusioned and defeated reds'), while Vázquez Dodero argued that it would need to be cut so severely as to undo the meaning of the play and, therefore, it should be banned. Even though the majority of censors voted to authorise it, the four who advocated prohibition held sway and although no formal verdict was issued, it was not staged. An application for commercial staging made by the Tina Sainz-Manuel Galiana company in December 1974 was not decided until April 1975: in the plenary session of the board, ten censors opted for approval and seven for prohibition. It was eventually authorised for over-eighteens with cuts, including reference to the UGT trade union, to Republican hero Fermín Galán and other leaders of the Jaca uprising, and to praise for the Second Republic, as well as a call for conscripts to rebel against their officers (AGA 251/73). Due to the delay, the play was in fact premiered in April 1975 in a student production in Salamanca, by Martín Recuerda's Juan del Enzina student theatre group, while the commercial production was still under consideration. The first commercial staging of the play did not take place until 28 November 1975, shortly after Franco's death (Thompson 2004).

Finally, although not officially banned, Rodríguez Méndez's *Flor de Otoño: una historia del barrio chino* (*Autumn Flower: A Chinatown Story*, 1972), which explores the sordid, culturally diverse and seductive characters from the margins of Barcelona in 1930 and contrasts them with the staid and judgemental haute bourgeoisie, was hindered by censorship. The protagonist, Lluiset, is a lawyer from a wealthy family but also a gay, risqué nightclub performer and militant anarchist. The play's take on a hypocritical and corrupt elite, complicit with a declining dictatorship, and the rising opposition to it would have had particular resonance at the end of the Franco regime. Its insistence on plurality, linguistic as well as cultural and political (characters speak Castilian and Catalan), was a further insult to the regime's monoculturalism. The play seems to have been authorised for over-eighteens in 1974, but no production took place. The files contain no reports, but the censored text is present and marks suggest that the censors objected to pro-anarchist political statements.

Olmo did not fare much better in the 1970s than he had in the previous decade. His first play of the new decade, *Mare Nostrum*,

S.A. (1970), was banned. Initially read in April, it was eventually prohibited in June for its depiction of an immoral and sordid country prostituting itself for money, in scenes such as the second of the first Act, in which the fisherman says '¡Viva Inglaterra! Luego *me introdujo entre las piernas* cinco libras . . .' ('Long live England! Then she stuffed a fiver between my legs'), and in scene 4, when the character Adriana refers to herself as 'a national prostitute'. The play was doubly problematic, like so many of Olmo's works, being political in intent and immoral in language. Bautista de la Torre condemned its crudeness and the fact that the society criticised was so obviously identifiable as Spanish. He argued for prohibition based on article 14.3, which proscribes the false representation of history (AGA 150/70).

Martín Recuerda's *Las arrecogías del beaterio de Santa María Egipcíaca* (*The Inmates of the Convent of St Mary of Egypt*, 1970), is based on the story of the early nineteenth-century liberal heroine Mariana Pineda. The religious-run house where women judged to be immoral are sent and where the action is set is also a convenient dumping ground for women with suspect political views. Their banishment and confinement is a way of silencing them; Martín Recuerda gives them a voice. The young Rosa, imprisoned for embroidering the opposition flag that Mariana Pineda commissioned, has her hands broken by the cruel governors. The religious authorities are portrayed as the servants of the political class, willing to sacrifice their Christian values in order to keep in with political power. The only solidarity and charity that exists, much like in *Las salvajes*, is found among social outcasts. At one point in the play, the spectators are made to share the experience of being prisoners, as bars descend from the ceiling. It was banned in late 1971, following a plenary of the censorship board that found the political parallels with the present day intolerable. Zubiaurre found much to complain about and cited articles 12, 14.1, 14.3, 17.2 and 18 (referring to representations of cruelty, disrespect for religion, attacks on the state or national dignity and the Head of State and an overall climate of lasciviousness or brutality) in his verdict of prohibition. A report drawn up following the plenary summarised the problems with the play, which included its breathtaking quality (a recognition of its persuasive potential); its representation of absolutist repression; its veiled, subversive messages about the present; its depiction of religious figures, reminiscent of current rebel priests, who reject the links between Church and state, its politicised setting and props and its yearning for freedom (AGA 547/71).

The transition period

Some of the most interesting cases from the period of transition to democracy relate to the fate of previously banned plays and, as Spain moved towards constitutional monarchy with democratic governance structures, the impact of contemporary politics on the theatre was discernible. The 1976–7 theatre season was, according to Frank P. Casa, 'almost a retrospective of Spanish theater of exiles and banned authors' (1988: 171–2).

Sastre's *La sangre y la ceniza* (1965) enjoyed minor success when staged at the Teatro Igualada in 1977. Other previously banned plays to make it to the stage during the transition period included Martín Recuerda's *Las arrecogías del Beaterio Santa María Egipcíaca*, which had successful runs in both 1977 and 1978. Rodríguez Méndez's *Bodas que fueron famosas del Pingajo y la Fandanga* and *Flor de Otoño*, which had been prohibited in 1965 and 1973, respectively, were produced in 1978 and 1982, the former for the inauguration of the new Centro Dramático Nacional. Muñiz's *Tragicomedia del serenísimo Príncipe don Carlos*, banned in 1972, was staged to some critical acclaim in 1980. Olmo's *Plaza menor* was authorised during the transition in July 1976, albeit after much lengthy deliberation and a plenary session of the censorship board. His *El cuarto poder* made it to the stage in March 1976, with a single cut (a mocking reference to the war) and monitoring of the dress rehearsal. Some of the censors expressed concern about the political insensitivity of staging the play's attack on the military in *Conflicto a la hora de siesta* in particular; others felt that it had lost its bite.

Two remarkable cases were the attempts to stage Buero's *La doble historia del doctor Valmy* and Olmo's *La condecoración*. At a time when the power of the old guard was under threat and the more liberal wing of the regime was attempting to accommodate itself to inevitable political change, the censors' reports on these works capture the mounting divisions within the ranks of the authorities, as well as the increased unease around the perceived threat from the theatre in a society undergoing seismic change.

An application was made on 30 October 1975 to stage *La doble historia del doctor Valmy*. The three initial censors did not agree a verdict and it went to a plenary of the censorship board, where members condemned it as dangerous for its immorality, its failure to show due punishment for bad behaviour, its fostering of hatred and social division, its vulgarity and its brutality. Vázquez Dodero suggested that, if not prohibited, it should be set behind the iron curtain or in a Latin American country. Most advised banning it, objecting to its negative representations of political ideologies and institutions. The Secretary and the Subdirector General, however, voted in favour of its authorisation, leading to a deadlock. The decision was referred to the Director General, who returned a verdict of authorisation with three cuts, conditional upon approval of the dress rehearsal (AGA 147/64). The play finally premiered at the Teatro Benavente, Madrid on 29 January 1976 under the direction of Alberto González Vergel. Despite its success at the box office and winning the *El Espectador y la Crítica* Prize, Buero faced an official backlash. On 9 February the Director General of Security issued a report in which the dramatist was condemned for his 'theatrical campaign against the police'. The North American theatre journal, *Estreno*, reported at the time that the dramatist had received threats to his person, and his life, as a response both to the play and for adding his signature to a document calling for an amnesty for political prisoners (1976: 50).

While some in the government embraced it, resistance to political change continued. The files on Olmo's *La condecoración* from February and March 1976 highlight the power politics and pragmatism at play behind the scenes, as well as clear ideological divisions within the authorities.[17] The application came from Justo Alonso, who wished to stage the play in the Teatro Marquina. Some of the censors thought it should be authorised. For example, Juan Emilio Aragonés, rather reasonably, pointed to the fact that public opposition to the regime and the widespread reporting of it in the press made the prohibition of works like this one redundant. He did insist on one cut, however, to eliminate a reference to the execution of political prisoners, as he said that *nowadays* (the stress on the present day is worth noting), execution was reserved for murderers, a debatable assertion. Pedro Barceló demonstrated some concern about public reaction to the

Falangist anthem that features in the play, but in the end recommended authorisation.

Vázquez Dodero, on the other hand, embodied the hardline Francoists' resistance to change, and gave a verdict of prohibition in a report suggesting that the staging of the play could lead to a *deserved* violent reaction. Mampaso described it in his report as 'anti-regime political theatre' and also advocated prohibition. García-Cernuda took issue both with the negative presentation of Spain's heroic nationalists and the positive one of subversive youth. Zubiaurre deplored the play's 'exaltación del inconformismo' ('exaltation of non-conformity') and criticism of the civil war victors. José Moreno Reina found the negative depiction of 'nuestra guerra de Liberación' ('our war of Liberation' – a euphemism often used by Francoists to refer to the civil war) unacceptable in the current political climate. Fr Cea objected to the portrait of the victors as intransigent; the undermining of the justification for war; and the lack of respect for what he, in a throwback to the terminology of the 1930s, termed 'the Crusade'. Vasallo advised retaining prohibition because of the play's attacks on the regime's institutions, principles and symbols and Diez Crespo's short report dismissed the play's literary worth, concluding that it would be very dangerous to stage it. Tejedor, reluctantly, he claimed, considered it 'el momento más inoportuno para autorizar esta obra' ('the most inopportune moment to authorise this work') and so, despite the changing times, it was not approved.

Several months later, in December 1976, Justo Alonso again applied to stage *La condecoración*, this time in the Teatro Arlequín the following January. There had been a shift in mood and personnel in the authorities and internal correspondence dated 15 November 1976 reveals a new policy relating to previously banned works, inspired by the altered political circumstances (the Political Reform bill, which would be passed on 18 November 1976 and would mark a definitive shift away from dictatorship, was being debated in Parliament as the play was being discussed). Works such as *La condecoración* were no longer seen as a threat and, indeed, approving them could help the regime's purpose as it redefined itself in more democratic terms.

The reports reflect the most current political concerns of the authorities, including the internal battles between the *aperturistas* and the uncompromising Francoists. Political circumstances were crucial to the decision-making and Barceló, who thought it suitable for over-eighteens and did not mention cuts, demonstrated his concern that what went on in the theatre could have an impact outside. Mier thought it could be authorised for over-eighteens with two cuts (references to torture and killing) but stressed that the uniform mentioned must not be one currently in use by the armed forces. Guerra's report is interesting for its use of an argument that was also common in the contemporary parliamentary debates about amnesty and later ones about historical memory, that what was represented in the play was a history that was over and done with and without contemporary relevance. But Albizu's report is the most interesting of all as it made clear why the play was suddenly acceptable to the government. He described *La condecoración* as 'una obra antibúnker y en nada perjudicial al Gobierno' ('an anti-bunker work, in no way prejudicial to the government') and went on to say that it could, in fact, work in its favour. Aragonés, on the other hand, believed that times had moved on sufficiently to allow the play to be authorised without cuts and revealed in his report one of the consequences of censorship: the play was a little out of date (AGA 29/65). In the end, it was not staged until after the death of Franco and was premiered in the Teatro Infanta Isabel in Madrid on 10 March 1977, under the direction of Alberto González Vergel.

Aragonés's comment was prescient. The realists, as the dramatists who had most overtly taken on the regime with their politicised works and often politicised productions, were associated with the past at a moment when Spain's leadership and population was determinedly fixed on the future. This was one of the problems facing dramatists when their previously banned works were finally authorised – they were considered old-fashioned or no longer relevant and often struggled to find a company to stage them (See Ruiz Ramón 1989: 574 and Zatlin 1980b: 463).

Furthermore, their association with political opposition to the regime also affected the reception of the realists' newer works. Buero's *Jueces en la noche* (*Judges in the Night*, 1979), which centres on an opportunistic minister from the Franco era who has reinvented himself as a life-long democrat in order to retain power, was apparently too close to the bone. Zatlin observes that the play 'unleashed a violent reaction, mostly political [. . .] Buero was attacked from Right and Left as an opportunist' (1980b: 469).

Yet there were also some successes in terms of new works. Sastre's *Ahola no es de leil* ('No Laughing Matter') enjoyed some success in 1979, but as a minority production. Buero's 1977 play *La detonación* ('*The Shot*'), in which he dealt with censorship and transition politics, was also successful.

In several ways the realists' goals and themes, and the non-commercial venues in which many of their works were performed, echoed the political theatre of the 1930s, although they aimed less to inculcate in the spectators a specific ideology than to use the theatre to bear witness to a damaged post-war society. Their efforts captured a growing mood of dissatisfaction and desire for change, especially among the young. At a time when other avenues were closed off, the theatre offered a relatively anonymous venue in which groups could gather to discuss politics in the guise of art and allowed for a playing out of alternatives to the social order. The importance of this theatre lay in its ability to remind audiences of such alternatives and to keep hope alive, to present on stage a silenced and officially forgotten version of the past, and to explore the ease with which people deceive themselves about their choices and actions.

Yet, this stress on the political was arguably also its weakness. It was naïve in its expectations of action on the part of the spectator and threatened to lose sight of the artistic in favour of the political. Indeed, one might also argue that this theatre also allowed more traditional theatregoers to salve their political consciences by attending performances that called for change, instead of working to achieve it. When political freedom finally arrived, it did not bring recognition and instead the dramatists who had combined artistic, humanistic and social goals in their work were seen as old-fashioned, and their methods obsolete.

Moreover, once censorship of the press was rescinded, people no longer turned to the theatre for political commentary or social testament, but rather for entertainment and – during the *destape* ('post-dictatorship permissiveness') – titillation (see Chapter 8).

Case study

Escuadra hacia la muerte, by Alfonso Sastre
Teatro María Guerrero (Madrid), 18 March 1953, Teatro Popular Universitario, directed by Gustavo Pérez Puig

The 1953 production of Alfonso Sastre's *Escuadra hacia la muerte* at the Teatro María Guerrero was among the most significant in Spain's twentieth-century theatre history. It embodied the clash between culture and the state under the dictatorship and, in many ways, defined the relationship between the realists and the regime thereafter. This was the clash of a new theatrical movement with the repressive powers of Francoism, and Sastre was the most active of the realists in his attempts to redefine and shape the theatre.

In 1945, he and a group of university friends established Arte Nuevo (1945–8), a theatre group with nationalist leanings and ambitious, if somewhat naïve, ideas about revolutionising the stage (Anderson 1997: 13; Doménech 1964: 39). From 1948, he wrote for *La Hora*, which was published by the state-sanctioned Sindicato Español Universitario (SEU – 'Spanish University Students' Union'). Sastre's political awakening came in the late 1940s and early 1950s, when he began his 'enfrentamiento con la censura al compás del descubrimiento paulatino de lo que realmente había sucedido durante la guerra española' ('confrontation with censorship in accord with his gradual discovery of what had really happened during the civil war') (Forest 1997: 23). Along with his fellow student and early collaborator, José María de Quinto, he joined the Spanish Communist Party at the end of the 1950s. Together, they established the ambitious Teatro de Agitación Social (TAS – 'Theatre of Social Agitation') in 1950, which aimed to bring international committed drama to the Spanish stage and bring revolution to society. TAS published a manifesto, which stated that 'lo social, en nuestro tiempo, es una categoría superior a lo artístico' ('in our times, the social is a superior category to the artistic') (Forest 1997: 124; Aznar and Oskam 1992). In 1960, again with de Quinto, he would form the Grupo de Teatro Realista (GTR – 'Realist Theatre Group'), which aimed to 'reclaim popular theatre' and, like the political theatre groups of the 1930s, organised low-priced shows in non-traditional venues to attract a public of students and workers (Sastre 1998: 240). The GTR staged both

Muñiz's *El tintero* and Sastre's own *En la red* but did not survive for long, which is not surprising in view of the outspoken opposition to censorship outlined in its manifesto:

> La existencia de la censura de teatro y especialmente en la forma en que viene ejerciéndose entre nosotros (se trata de una actividad conceptualmente arbitraria, administrativamente irregular, éticamente irresponsible y legalmente amorfa, sin que ni siquiera tenga autoridad para mantener sus propios dictámenes) es una vergüenza pública y privada. Públicamente (objetivamente) lo es porque tiene el carácter de una calamidad cultural. Privadamente (subjetivamente) porque es el signo de nuestro conformismo –el de los autores, directores, actores, empresarios . . .– y de nuestra propia corrupción. Es urgente la absoluta liquidación [. . .] de este mecanismo. (Martínez Michel 2003: 58)

> The existence of theatre censorship and especially the way it has been exercised here (it is a conceptually arbitrary, administratively irregular, ethically irresponsible and legally amorphous activity, that does not even have the authority to uphold its own verdicts) is a public and private disgrace. Publicly (objectively) it is disgraceful because it can be characterised as a cultural calamity. Privately (subjectively) because it is a sign of our conformity – that of authors, directors, actors, theatre managers . . . – and of our own corruption. The total liquidation [. . .] of this mechanism is urgent.

This confrontational stance, which would continue for the duration of the dictatorship was, if not the result of, certainly intensified by, Sastre's relationship with the authorities. The initial confusion about his politics and the sympathetic reading of his plays came to an end with the scandal surrounding the staging of *Escuadra hacia la muerte*.

The plot centres on five soldiers and their Corporal in a situation of almost Gothic confinement in an isolated outpost surrounded by woods. They await orders for an unknown mission. The action takes place in December, not in the present day but during a future Third World War. There is a clear existentialist echo of Sartre in the play's construction and hopeless ending. Yet the characters are drawn with realist strokes, as are the human dilemmas they face.

The men are, in the words of Adolfo, 'una escuadra de castigo' (69) ('a punishment squad'), what Corporal Goban terms 'una escuadra de soldados para la muerte' ('a squad of soldiers for death') (73) and Javier calls, more accurately, 'una escuadra de condenados a muerte' ('a squad of soldiers condemned to death') (78). All of them are there as punishment for crimes committed when serving in the army. Goban is killed in Scene 6 of Part 1, on Christmas Day, by four of the five men. Part 2 shows the various reactions of the men, the breakdown of discipline and order, and their frustration at their continuing purposeless existence.

There are no heroes in the play; all are guilty of something. They are not fighting for a just cause; indeed, they do not seem to understand why they are fighting. Yet their killing of Goban leads to some remorse and humanises the soldiers. The play highlights the senselessness of the conflicts that they, as pawns of their superiors, are engaged in. Sastre described the play as a cry of protest against a new world war, and a negation of the use of language to camouflage the horror of war and the glorification of heroism and death (Blanco Aguinaga *et al.* 1983: 232).

Several critics have highlighted the play's importance, among them Farris Anderson, who considers it reflective of 'the spirit of post-war Europe' and sees Goban as the personification of military tyranny and the men's brutal act as an uprising against it (1987: 22, 29). For London, 'the extreme violence of Sastre's play and the suicide it contains were [...] a torrent in a desert of blandness' (1997: 189). Lauer, noting the play's reflection of concerns about the Cold War and a possible Third World War, nevertheless concludes that it is an optimistic play that suggests that a better world is possible (2008: 439). For this better world to come into being, however, the play seems to suggest that change is necessary. It is easy to see why such a work, with its experimental structure and thematic engagement with war, hopelessness and fatalism, captured the imagination of many young people who were opposed to the regime.

Initially the production of *Escuadra hacia la muerte* was uncontroversial. The application to stage it, dated 16 March 1953, came from the state-supported SEU. The two censors who read the play were not overly concerned by what they saw. Bartolomé Mostaza, although he thought it pessimistic, concluded that there was no moral risk involved and suggested authorisation for over-eighteens. He made no comment on its politics. Gumersindo Montes Agudo, however, whose reports can generally be read as supportive of Sastre, delivered a more astute reading of the play, acknowledging both the play's 'germen de resentimiento' ('seed of resentment') and the possible danger it posed. His proposed solution was to limit the audience, rather than to cut the play: 'No debe darse ante públicos propuestos a dudas y extrañas ideologías' ('It should not be performed in front of a public inclined to doubt or strange ideologies') (AGA 94/53).

It was deemed only suitable for *teatros de cámara y ensayo*, and, interestingly, permission to stage it was only granted to 'organizaciones u organismos de significación política perfectamente definida y encuadrada en la línea doctrinal de nuestro Estado' ('organisations or bodies with a political orientation clearly in keeping with the official doctrine of our State'). The SEU fitted the bill, of course, and *Escuadra* was authorised without cuts. At the time, Sastre was not seen as a dramatist of the opposition.

The unknown student theatre group, the Teatro Popular Universitario, staged it two days later at the Teatro María Guerrero in Madrid. The director was Gustavo Pérez Puig, who remained a champion of the dramatist, and who would become one of the most important directors of both stage and state television. The actors involved were Adolfo Marsillach, Miguel Ángel Gil, Félix Navarro, Juanjo Menéndez, Agustín González and Fernando Guillén. It was an immediate success and was staged also on 22 March and, due to popular demand, on 24 March (Mostacilla 1953).

The initial reviews were positive. Antonio Rodríguez de León in *ABC* waxed lyrical about this manly play, Sastre's theatrical skills and the enthusiastic response of the public 1953: 33). Torrente, in *Arriba*, deemed it the most important work of the season to date and predicted a bright future for Sastre (1953). He noted, however, that this was potentially threatened by Sastre's embrace of certain trendy forms and by his tendency to subordinate his theatre to his ideas. He went on to state that he disagreed with 'sus pretensiones ideológicas' ('its ideological pretensions'), its sociology and metaphysics and its North American structure, but found depth in the human drama and the honouring of values in the character of Pedro (although he suspected that his interpretation did not necessarily chime with the author's intentions). Juan Emilio Aragonés wrote that the play triumphed in Madrid and described it as an example of 'teatro comprometido' ('committed theatre') (1953).

On the third night, however, everything changed. According to Sastre, on the night of 24 March, General José Moscardó, known as the hero of the siege of the Alcázar during the civil war, was in attendance. He was apparently outraged by what he perceived as the play's antimilitarism and lack of patriotism and by the fact that it was staged in a national theatre (Vicente Mosquete 1988: 10).[18] While the files do not contain a direct complaint from him, they do contain a later document, a letter from the Director General to the Jefe del Alto Estado Mayor ('Head of the Armed Forces'), dated 29 November 1955 that refers to 'varias quejas y objeciones de carácter castrense' ('several complaints and objections of a military character') coinciding with the third performance and the decision to prohibit the play.[19]

When the Salvador Soler-Martí company applied in August the same year to stage *Escuadra* in a commercial theatre in October, a new report was drawn up by Montes Agudo, in which he related the play to the Second World War but stressed the play's ambiguity, suggesting that while it could be interpreted as a play about the beauty of a soldier's destiny, or even a Falangist work, it could also be interpreted by others as a Marxist play. He argued, therefore, that it should be limited to *cámara*. The play was banned, presumably due to the earlier military complaints. Subsequent applications to stage the play reiterated the prohibition.

One of the most interesting documents in the file is a letter from Sastre to the Director General, Joaquín Argamasilla, dated November 1954, informing him that the play was being staged regularly, without his permission, by TEUs, experimental groups and *teatros de cámara*. Sastre reminded Argamasilla that in his capacity as a professional dramatist, he had been prohibited from staging it for profit with a commercial company and pointed to the lack of logic and the failure of the censors to do their job properly. He requested a revision of the verdict. Argamasilla wrote back, indicating that he would start a review, although he suggested that Sastre should not get his hopes up. He also stated that Provincial Delegates would be reminded not to authorise what was still a banned play in their regions.

A formal review of the play began in late 1955 following a proposed *posibilista* revision by Sastre (foreignising the names) and was considered by the Permanent Reading Commission. When Mario Antolín Paz, Secretary of the Cultural Department of the SEU, wrote in late January 1956 asking for permission for the SEU in San Sebastián to stage it for a university audience, the response was negative, as the play was still under review. As part of the appraisal process, the Director General wrote to General Carlos Asensio Cabanillas, the Head of the Armed Forces. The letter, dated 29 November 1955, asked for his views on the prohibition and if the play might be deemed allowable if the authority figures were foreignised, thus eliminating any link to the Spanish military.[20] Asensio Cabanillas's detailed response (see Figure 9), dated 15 January 1956, reiterated the need for prohibition, given the portrait of the military leader and the military in general and the likelihood that the Spanish public would see parallels with the División Española de Voluntarios, that is, the Blue Division of Spanish volunteers who fought with the Nazis on the Eastern Front in the Second World War. He thought that the solution of foreignising was insufficient as it still conveyed an impression of antimilitarism to the spectator. The verdict of prohibition was reiterated on 27 January 1956 (see Figure 10).

The situation, therefore, remained much as before. The play was officially banned, but regularly staged by student and other minority groups. As Plaza and González Yuste note, for many years it was the most-performed work by TEUs and theatre clubs (1975: 57). Official files show that while many companies applied for permission to stage the play and were refused it, several illegal productions took place.

Figure 9: Letter from General Asensio recommending the prohibition of *Escuadra hacia la muerte* (1956)

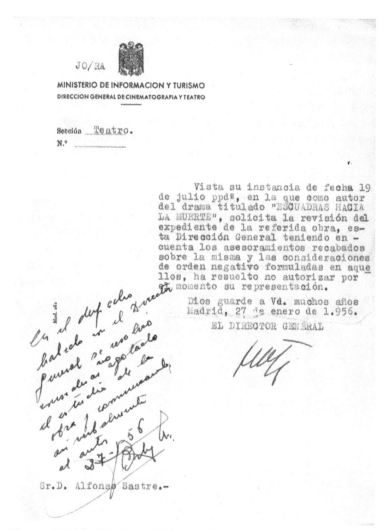

Figure 10: Notification of the prohibition of *Escuadra hacia la muerte* (1956)

The fate of Sastre's play finally changed in 1962, under new leadership at the Ministry and as the regime began to focus less on the triumph of the war and more on the peace and stability it claimed to have delivered. A new report from the Comandante Asesor Técnico del Alto Estado Mayor ('Technical Adviser to

Figure 11: Letter from Commander Guerra y Romero recommending authorisation of *Escuadra hacia la muerte* (1962)

the Chief of Defence Staff') gave a different reading of the play (see Figure 11), suggesting that the characters were not symbolic or identifiable with Spain, nor was the location, and it was not about the armed forces, but rather characters on the margins and was, therefore, allowable. *Escuadra hacia la muerte* was finally authorised, with the stipulation that the names of characters not be Spanish and military uniforms not be identifiable with Spain or another foreign army. Over the next decade there were many successful applications to stage it, before Sastre once again had trouble with the censors as a result of his work, *Askatusuna* ('*Freedom*', 1971), a version of *En la red*, provocatively set in the Basque country. This version, written for Swedish television, led to Sastre being blackballed until 1974 (Martínez-Michel 2003: 81).

The case of *Escuadra hacia la muerte* marked Sastre out as an important cultural voice of the opposition to the regime. With this play, the censors realised that the revolution he yearned for was not theirs. Indeed, as we have seen in this chapter, the scandal surrounding this play had a damaging impact on attempts to stage Sastre's subsequent works for much of the 1950s and beyond and hindered the dramatist's goal of making a living in the commercial theatre. By the end of the decade, he could claim to be the most censored Spanish dramatist: 'No existo. He sido borrado de todas las listas ... Salvo de las listas negras, por supuesto: por lo que se refiere a éstas, estoy en todas' ('I don't exist. I've been deleted from all the lists ... Except for the blacklists, of course: I'm on all of those') (Primer Acto 1974b: 5; see also Avril (1982) and Cramsie (1984)).

The play itself took on iconic status as a work of opposition, highlighting how the politics of a play can have as much to do with how it is read, interpreted and used as with its content. Alfonso Sastre, in many ways, captured the significance of the realists to a young generation of Spaniards, many of whom, like him, became politicised at university and challenged the regime's – and often their families' – values. In the aftermath of the scandal, Sastre too moved ever more to the left and became more vocal in his opposition to the regime and its lack of freedoms.

Notes

1 For a complete analysis of the censorship of Buero's theatre, see O'Leary 2005.
2 Despite significant problems with the censors, Olmo managed to have a theatrical career that included some commercial productions, as well as co-authoring successful children's theatre with his wife, Pilar Enciso. These, too, were often censored (see Muñoz Cáliz 2005).
3 See Muñoz Cáliz (2005: 225–7) for more details.
4 See Muñoz Cáliz (2005: 113–17) for more details.
5 For more information on the social and political context of the 1950s, see Cazorla Sánchez (2010), Ellwood (1987), Graham (2016) and Preston (1993).
6 *El cubo de la basura* was not presented for theatre censorship but was authorised for publication.

7 See Muñoz Cáliz (2006b) and Martínez-Michel (2003) for more on this case.
8 This correspondence and report are contained in the file on *Prólogo patético*. They are also mentioned in a letter from the Minister to Manuel Torres López, Argamasilla's successor as Director General (dated 8 June 1955), which is contained in the *El pan de todos* file (AGA 401/53).
9 In a letter to Argamasilla's successor in 1956, Fernández Cuesta revealed that the dissenting reader of *El pan de todos* was the Falangist author Gonzalo Torrente Ballester, who had instead suggested some modifications to the work. These included emphasising the interior torment and awareness of sin of the protagonist; the expansion of the dialogue between Aunt Paula and Jocobo Fessler to show the heartlessness of the latter (a representative of the revolution); further emphasis on Jacobo's lack of humanity; and the elimination of some of Marta's words at the end, including 'pase lo que pase estás salvado' ('whatever happens, you're saved').
10 Rodero's acting career spanned from the 1940s until his death in 1991. He acted in many significant productions, including Lluch's *España, Una, Grande y Libre* (1940), Buero Vallejo's *En la ardiente oscuridad* (1950), Albert Camus's *Calígula* (1963) and Alberti's *El hombre deshabitado* (1988).
11 The ban on *Prólogo patético* was confirmed in July 1971, unsurprisingly, given Sastre's notoriety by this stage. The play was to have been performed at the Sitges Festival in the summer, but the censors considered that its justification of violence and terrorism and its denial of an afterlife could lead to public disturbances. Yet it had been authorised for publication in 1963, which once again highlights the inconsistency in the implementation of censorship and the regime's fear of live performance.
12 The AGA file on *El tragaluz* contains only a copy of the script with a provisional set of cuts marked. The definitive cuts and revisions, including the replacement of 'el desarrollo' by 'como tantos otros' ('like so many others'), are listed in a notification sent to Barcelona in September 1967, three months after the original decision.
13 The *grises* were also the subject of Olmo's hard-hitting family drama, *Conflicto a la hora de la siesta* ('Conflict at Siesta Time'), part of *El cuarto poder*.
14 There is no verdict listed in 1967 or 1970 and files on these applications are incomplete (Muñoz Caliz 2005: 232 and Thompson 2007a: 126). Expediente O-003/70, although linked to a proposed production in Barcelona in 1970, does not contain any censors' reports.
15 Ángel Berenguer states that Olmo confirmed the Grimau reference to him (1997: 91). The Communist leader, Julián Grimau, was arrest-

ed in November 1962 and tortured by the regime before being tried at a military tribunal, found guilty of 'continued military rebellion' and executed on 20 April 1963. His political killing for crimes that dated back to the civil war led to an international outcry and condemnation of the regime (Novais 2015).

16 For a study of the censorship of this play in relation to the politics of the time, see García del Río (2020).
17 See Muñoz Cáliz (2005: 253–6) for more detail.
18 Ironically, Sastre's humble 'Autocrítica' was published on 18 March 1953 in the right-wing paper, *El Alcázar*.
19 Although the theatre production was banned, a different branch of the censorship authorities allowed publication of the play by Escélicer the same year.
20 Asensio Cabanillas, a personal friend of Franco's, was a much-decorated military leader, notoriously implicated in the massacre of Badajoz of August 1936.

Chapter 6
Experimental, Avant-Garde and Independent Theatre: Pushing the Boundaries

The wave of theatrical innovation in Spain in the 1920s and 1930s could not be continued after the civil war. By April 1939, the most prominent avant-garde playwrights and directors had disappeared from the scene. Ramón María del Valle-Inclán and Miguel de Unamuno had died in 1936; Federico García Lorca had been killed at the beginning of the war; Rafael Alberti, Max Aub, María Teresa León, Cipriano Rivas Cherif, Margarita Xirgu and many others went into exile. The Franco regime was hostile to modernism, especially the work of writers associated with the Republic, and the theatrical establishment had little interest in reviving their legacy in the 1940s and 1950s. By the late 1950s, some of the more adventurous directors and fringe groups would find theatrical and political inspiration in the pre-war avant-garde and begin to seek opportunities to stage plays that were being performed to acclaim outside Spain. The work of Valle-Inclán and Lorca in particular made an important contribution to the reimagining of theatrical forms and search for new audiences by the postmodernist avant-garde that emerged in the 1960s.

This chapter traces the slow thawing of the regime's antipathy to Valle-Inclán, Lorca and Alberti. The distinctive case of Fernando Arrabal will then be examined, followed by examples of the censorship of a range of experimental, absurdist, symbolist and independent theatre of the 1960s and 1970s, including developments in Catalonia.

The pre-war avant-garde

The famously eccentric Valle-Inclán had not been an unconditional supporter of the Second Republic. His political stance veered between nostalgia for Carlist monarchism, calls for socialist revolution and sympathy for Mussolini's fascism.[1] Nevertheless, his association with prominent figures of the Republic, together with his tendency to satirise the Borbón monarchy, the Catholic Church and the armed forces, led Francoists to view his work with suspicion and sometimes hostility.

The censorship of Valle Inclán's work during the dictatorship is surveyed by Muñoz Cáliz (2011), who identifies two phases.[2] In the 1940s and 1950s the only applications for productions of his work were submitted by amateur and student groups. Most were approved, often with cuts. Despite the usual *cámara* conditions (small venues, tickets not on sale to the general public, permission normally for a single performance), some of these stagings were influential in raising awareness of the theatrical potential of Valle-Inclán's texts. In the second phase, from 1960, student and independent groups were increasingly interested in his work as an expression of dissidence (Cardona 1992: 167). The censors of the *apertura* period were reasonably relaxed about this trend, as long as scripts were trimmed and they could be confident that the productions were not reaching large audiences. At the same time, the first attempts were made to gain approval for commercial productions, most of which were blocked.

Divinas palabras (*Divine Words*) was internationally celebrated long before the first application was made for staging in Spain. Marcel Herrand directed a version in Paris in 1946, and Ingmar Bergman's Swedish production was a controversial success in Göteborg in 1950. An application by the group Dido Pequeño Teatro for a performance at the Teatro Bellas Artes in Madrid was rejected in 1958. One censor found the work crude but magnificent, and articulated a position that would be taken up repeatedly over the next decade: 'Lástima que no pueda el censor admitir en su integridad la hermosa tragicomedia, ni se atreva a colaborar con imperdonables correcciones ni supresiones que harían perder su valor literario y su enorme fuerza y realismo' ('Regrettably, I am unable to approve this fine tragicomedy intact, nor would I dare to go along with unforgivable corrections or suppressions that would deprive it of its literary value and its enormous power and realism') (AGA 2/58). The second censor argued that the play was so shameless and dangerous that it should not be authorised even for *cámara* performances.

José Tamayo's application to stage *Divinas palabras* at the Teatro Español in 1960 was the first attempt to mount a major professional production of a Valle-Inclán play. Despite the fact that the script had already been adapted to remove some of the most irreverent and erotic elements, the censors found it unacceptably crude, immoral and irreligious (AGA 2/58). Tamayo eventually obtained approval for performances by his own commercial company rather than at the state-sponsored Teatro Español. The premiere, inaugurating the Teatro Bellas Artes (Madrid) in November 1961, was hailed as a historic event, finally giving Valle-Inclán the public recognition he deserved (Pombo Ángulo 1961).

Luces de Bohemia (*Bohemian Lights*) had a longer and more difficult journey to a commercial premiere. A *cámara* application by Escena in 1957 was initially refused. After revision of the script by the director, including the removal of scenes six (Max Estrella's dialogue with the anarchist) and ten (Max and Don Latino's encounter with the prostitutes), it was approved for a single performance at the Teatro de la Comedia in Madrid, which does not seem to have taken place (AGA 214/57). Approval was given in 1962 for a commercial production at the Teatro Goya in Madrid by the José Osuna company, subject to extensive cuts. However, the author's son Carlos refused to give permission for performance with cuts. The centenary of the playwright's birth in 1966 prompted two more non-commercial productions of *Luces de Bohemia*, and major productions were staged in Paris, Buenos Aires and Edinburgh.

Tamayo took up the cause in 1967, applying for permission for the Lope de Vega company to stage *Luces de Bohemia* as part of the officially sponsored Festivales de España. The Junta de Censura was not prepared to license performances under that banner, which would have attracted large audiences in multiple locations, but authorisation was eventually given in October 1967 for normal commercial performances by the Lope de Vega company in Madrid and Barcelona, with eighteen cuts including the whole of scene six (ANC 214/57a). Carlos Valle-Inclán still insisted that the play could only be performed intact, which left the case in limbo. An appeal in 1968 was met with silence. Finally, a second appeal was successful and Tamayo's production was approved without cuts in July 1970. The censors were now in general agreement about the author's classic status, and most agreed that this meant that the integrity of the text should be respected. One of them remarked: 'Personalmente, me parece algo así como una herejía suprimir una sola palabra del por excelencia esperpento de Valle-Inclán, en 1970' ('Personally, I would see it as a kind of heresy to suppress, in 1970, even a single word of Valle-Inclán's *esperpento* par excellence' (AGA 214/57). The Junta attached the following condition, hoping to discourage audiences from drawing current parallels with the play's political and religious satire: 'Montaje y puesta en escena realista. Con absoluto rigor histórico situando la acción en los años del Madrid descrito por Valle-Inclán' ('A realist style of production. With absolute historical accuracy, situating the action in Madrid at the time depicted by Valle-Inclán') (ANC 214/57b).

The first commercial performance of *Luces de Bohemia* took place in Valencia in October 1970, and the Madrid premiere at the Bellas Artes in October 1971 was another major success for Tamayo. The work had not lost its power to shock faithful Francoists, however: Cardona (1992: 171) notes that performances in Bilbao, San Sebastián, Vitoria y Pamplona scheduled for December 1970 were suspended, presumably as a result of the respective civil governors judging it to be unsuitable for local audiences.

Los cuernos de don Friolera (*The Horns of Don Friolera*) had also been performed several times overseas before it was accepted in Spain: in Buenos Aires in 1940, Naples in 1950, and Bordeaux, Paris, Grenoble and Brussels in 1955 (Lima 2003: 210). A single *cámara* performance by a *teatro de cámara* group at the Teatro Goya in Madrid, directed by Víctor Andrés Catena, was approved with cuts in September 1958 but did not take place. Montes Agudo and Mostaza praised the play in their reports, but recommended that authorisation should be restricted to *cámara* productions (AGA 223/58).[3]

An application by Juan José Alonso Millán in November 1958 was for a performance by a student group at the Teatro María Guerrero. Authorisation was given, but it seems to have been decided that a national theatre was not a suitable venue, since the performance took place at the Teatro de la Comedia. The script had already been subjected to some self-censorship, anticipating censors' objections to elements such as the word 'cabrón' ('cuckold'), sardonic comments on Spain and religion, Don Friolera's references to his regiment, Curro's cynical remarks about corruption in high places, and the conversation between Friolera's fellow officers revealing their decadent behaviour in the colonies. Further cuts were imposed by the censors, including the removal of the horns from the title, a self-defeating intervention in the case of such a well-known work, merely serving to draw attention to the act of censorship.

Reports from 1969 on a proposed commercial production of *Los cuernos de don Friolera* were in favour of authorisation with cuts or restrictions, though one warned that there was still a danger of provoking 'protestas en algunos sectores militares demasiado susceptibles' ('protests in certain over-sensitive military circles') (AGA 223/58). There is no record of a decision: the outcome seems to have been *silencio administrativo*. It was not until February 1976 that a commercial production was authorised, without cuts but restricted to audiences over the age of eighteen. Although the application was for a production by the Barcelona-based Adrià Gual company, it was the Lope de Vega company under the direction of Tamayo that ended up performing the play at the Teatro Bellas Artes in Madrid. Valle-Inclán's prestige was now a decisive factor and the risk of a military backlash was dismissed: 'Ante *Los cuernos de don Friolera* el militar que se enfadase –de cabo o sargento a general– no tendría razón' ('Any military man – from a corporal or sergeant up to a general – who was aggrieved by *The Horns of Don Friolera* would simply be wrong') (AGA 223/58).

All Valle-Inclán's plays posed a dilemma for the censors, who showed increasing respect for his international reputation and were prepared to recognise literary quality and powerful theatricality in the texts. However, the crudeness, the violence and the anarchic satire of religion, nationalism and authority continued to be regarded as a threat requiring careful handling. The strategy of confining Valle-Inclán to the *cámara* circuit worked for a while, limiting the impact of his work while allowing the authorities to show that they were not banning it altogether. Eventually, the persistence of Tamayo and others, meeting diminishing resistance during the period of *apertura* in the 1960s, succeeded in claiming Valle-Inclán's central place in the modern theatrical canon.

While the censors' objections in the case of Valle-Inclán were mostly to the content and tone of his plays, the problem with Federico García Lorca was primarily the man himself, as seen in the *La casa de Bernarda Alba* case study at the end of Chapter 3. He was simply blacklisted by the Dirección General de Seguridad throughout the 1940s. The growth of his iconic status as a martyr and cultural figurehead of the Republic was not impeded by the banning of productions of his work. On the contrary, as pointed out repeatedly by Montes Agudo in his censorship reports, the suppression of Lorca's work played into the hands of those who aimed to use him as a 'banner' – a focus for opposition to the social and cultural values of the regime. Although the blanket ban was relaxed in the 1950s, Lorca's association with the Republic continued to be an obstacle to the definitive approval of his plays and a stimulus for those who wished to stage them.[4]

Even a work as innocuous as *Doña Rosita la soltera* (*Doña Rosita the Spinster*) did not receive a professional staging until after the end of the dictatorship. The first censorship application was made by the Falangist Tomás Borrás on 16 October 1943 for a commercial production at the Teatro Lara. Montes Agudo's report on the script was favourable and recommended approval with cuts, though he acknowledged that the author's name might be politically problematic (AGA 284/43). The authorisation was confirmed on 10 November, subject to various cuts and amendments. However, the final censorship certificate issued on 17 November, presumably following intervention by *la Superioridad*, recorded the decision as 'prohibida' (AGA 284/43). Two other commercial productions – by María Victoria Durá's and Eugenia Zuffoli's companies – appear to have been authorised in 1945 and 1947 but did not go ahead.

An amateur production of *Doña Rosita la soltera* was staged without authorisation in a small town near Alicante in 1948 (Salvat and Coll 2001: 276). The director, Alberto González Vergel, commented in an interview that the play had not been banned by the government but by Lorca's estate, 'porque la familia no quería que se representara bajo el mismo régimen que lo asesinó' ('because the family didn't want it to be performed under the same regime that killed him') (Información 2010). His general assertion in the same interview that Lorca was never censored by Franco but by the author's own family is disproved by the records of prohibition decisions in the censorship files, but refusal of permission by the author's sisters may well account for the failure of productions of

Doña Rosita to reach the stage despite official authorisation having been given.

The authorities continued to display anxiety about Lorca in the 1950s. A letter of 28 November 1953 from the Director General de Cinematografía y Teatro to the Delegado Provincial in Valladolid confirmed that the Department had no objection to a proposed student production of *Doña Rosita*, but instructed that the authorisation should be subject to confirmation by the Civil Governor, in view of 'las circunstancias políticas que concurren alrededor del referido autor' ('the political circumstances surrounding the author of this play') (AGA 284/43).

Professional companies continued to seek to perform *Doña Rosita* in the 1960s, and in 1969 Núria Espert was in discussions with the García Lorca family seeking permission to stage the play (ABC 1969). However, it took another eleven years for this project to come to fruition. As director of the Centro Dramático Nacional, Espert presided over a hugely successful production in 1980 directed by Jorge Lavelli. The forty-five-year gap between the original premiere and this triumphant revival may have been largely the result of the family's recalcitrance, but the censorship file confirms that there was a period during which this play was banned by the regime.

Luis Escobar was invited to direct *Yerma* as part of the Spoleto Festival in 1960 and won the support of the author's brother Francisco for the production to be performed at the Eslava as well as in Italy (2000: 206). Escobar claims that the censors approved the text in its entirety, but the file in the AGA shows that one cut was imposed for religious reasons: the line in which the old woman says to Yerma 'A mí no me ha gustado nunca Dios. ¿Cuándo os vais a dar cuenta de que no existe?' ('I've never liked God. When are you people going to realise that God doesn't exist?') (AGA 300/58). Several censors had expressed reservations about the text. Morales de Acevedo's report, written in December 1958, recognised the work's literary quality but declared that 'su realismo expresivo solo la hace tolerable para teatro de cámara' ('its expressive realism makes it suitable only for theatre clubs'). In 1960 Fr Villares recommended authorisation, arguing that the fame of the playwright and the text, as well as the political circumstances surrounding the author, justified a lenient response to the irreligious elements. Montes Agudo put the political argument in favour of authorisation more bluntly, repeating his assertion that 'hay que arrebatar ya al contrario la bandera lorquiana' ('it's high time we seized the Lorca banner from the hands of the opposition') (AGA 300/58).

Escobar's production of *Yerma* was licensed, but with several restrictions: the line specified above was cut, the minimum age of spectators was set at eighteen, and the authorisation was limited to Madrid and Barcelona. According to Ricardo Doménech, the authorities also instructed newspapers to give the premiere – the first commercial production of a Lorca play since the war – minimal publicity (2008: 79). The performances in Madrid were closely monitored. Escobar remembers the presence at every performance in the first week of plainclothes policemen watching out for expressions of anti-government feeling (2000: 209). Trouble was also expected in Barcelona in January 1961, but the Delegado Provincial reported that there was little threat to public order:

> En los anfiteatros se pudo observar efectivamente la asistencia 'en grupo' de universitarios y estudiantes de arte dramático y bellas artes y otros no identificados, que sólo oscurecerse la Sala ovacionaron a telón corrido insistentemente [. . .] Al terminar la representación partieron de éstos los gritos ¡Lorca! ¡Lorca! [. . .] no siendo secundados por el resto del público. (AGA 300/58)

> Up in the galleries, it was noticeable that there were groups of drama and art students, together with other unidentified students, who as soon as the house lights went down applauded continuously [. . .] At the end of the performance, their shouts of 'Lorca! Lorca!' [. . .] were not shared by the rest of the audience.

Such incidents did not worry the authorities unduly. An internal memo of 24 November 1971 summarising *Yerma*'s censorship history since 1960 reported: 'Se carece de antecedentes sobre alteraciones o problemas creados con las representaciones de esta pieza en Madrid, Barcelona y otras plazas' ('There is no record of disturbances or problems caused by performances of this play in Madrid, Barcelona or other locations') (AGA 300/58). Nevertheless, there was some concern about the potential for performances of Escobar's *Yerma* to cause difficulties in particular places. There were repeated applications by the Eslava company in 1960–1 for performances in various cities beyond Madrid and Barcelona, several of which were turned down. The fact that it was ecclesiastical censors who were asked for their views on these requests suggests that the problem with certain locations was the likelihood of local opposition from the Church or Catholic organisations.

Núria Espert's company submitted an application on 23 March 1971 for authorisation of the daringly innovative version of *Yerma* that she was developing with the director Víctor García and the designer Fabià Puigserver, to be performed in Granada. No further reports were required, and the licence was issued in only two days. A second application made on 8 July for performances at the Teatro Griego in Barcelona was approved. However, the performances in Granada and Barcelona did not go ahead. Although the Junta de Censura Teatral no longer had any objections to the play or its author, it was now the production and its creators that were problematic. Espert and García had collaborated two years earlier on a production of Fernando Arrabal's *Los dos verdugos* (*The Two Executioners*), which had been banned at the last minute following the inspection of the dress rehearsal. Espert had then had several more conflicts with the censors over plans to stage works by Genet, Alberti and Buero Vallejo (Espert and Ordóñez 2002: 104–38).

It was the García Lorca family who refused permission for performances in Granada. According to Espert, 'no querían, bajo ningún concepto, que *Yerma* se hiciera en Granada, donde le habían fusilado' ('under no circumstances were they willing to allow *Yerma* to be put on in Granada, where he [Federico] had been murdered') (Espert and Ordóñez 2002: 139). They gave the go-ahead for performances in Barcelona, but two weeks before the planned opening, official authorisation to perform at the Teatro Griego was withdrawn. Espert attributes the ban to 'una orden gubernativa' ('a government order') (Espert and Ordóñez 2002: 143), and a report in the *New York Times* claimed that the Barcelona performances were 'forbidden by the police' (Eder 1971). However, it was reported in the press that the decision was taken by Barcelona City Council, which did not explain the cancellation but claimed that it had discovered that urgent repairs to the theatre were needed (Vila San Juan 1971).

The next attempt was a production at the Teatro de la Comedia in Madrid, which was prepared but banned twice, in October and November 1971, causing significant financial losses for the company (Espert and Ordóñez 2002: 145). Only after numerous protests did the approval finally come through. For the opening on 30 November, the theatre was surrounded by a massive contingent of police. There was no disturbance of public order, and the production was a huge success. The short run at the Comedia was followed by an acclaimed national and international tour that lasted four years and ran to more than 2,000 performances.

By the early 1970s, Lorca had indisputably gained iconic status at home and abroad. The last of his plays to be approved during the dictatorship was *Mariana Pineda*, a poetic drama about the Granadan heroine executed for supporting liberal opponents of Fernando VII in 1831. The file on this case provides striking evidence of official attitudes towards Lorca in the final phase of the regime. There is no record of any attempt to stage the play until 1966. It was unlikely to be approved in the early years of the dictatorship, largely because it was closely associated with the Second Republic. It had been performed in homage to Lorca as part of the programme of the Second International Writers' Congress in Defence of Culture in July 1937, making a decisive contribution to the consecration of Lorca as a martyr of the Republic.[5]

The 1966 application was submitted on 1 December by Lorca's nephew, Manuel Fernández-Montesinos, for a production of *Mariana Pineda* directed by Alfredo Mañas at the Teatro Bellas Artes in Madrid, to open in late January 1967.[6] All three censors' reports made light of the political content of the text. Martínez Ruiz remarked that the emphasis was poetic and the setting lacked historical or political substance. Bautista de la Torre added: 'Su tono de romance y el distanciamiento del ambiente aleja cualquier identificación con problemas actuales' ('The lyrical, romantic tone and the distancing of the setting make any identification with present-day issues unlikely'). Mostaza agreed that the sentimental approach removed any political threat and opined that, in any case, the play was unlikely to have a strong impact on audiences (AGA 334/66).

The Junta de Censura Teatral approved the production on 20 December, for audiences of any age and without cuts. However, the Director General (García Escudero) decided to consult the Minister. He wrote to Fraga informing him of the Junta's decision and noting that the play had in its time been regarded as an 'exaltación de la heroína de la República, circunstancia comentada recientemente por algunos periódicos extranjeros que dieron al mismo tiempo la noticia de su autorización por la censura española' ('celebration of the heroine of the Republic, a circumstance that has been commented upon recently by foreign newspapers, which have at the same time reported that the play has already been authorised by the Spanish censorship' (AGA 334/66). Fraga, apparently displeased by the anticipation of the censorship decision, decided on 21 January 1967 to overrule the Junta and ban the production. Fernández-Montesinos lodged an appeal on 26 January, insisting that neither the company nor the theatre management had been responsible for briefing the press. The French newspaper *Le Monde* had reported the ban on 25 January, claiming that it was motivated by the director's intention to have Mariana (anachronistically) embroidering a republican flag.[7] Fernández-Montesinos, realising that this story could jeopardise the appeal, wrote to *Le Monde* asking them to publish a correction pointing out that an appeal was in progress and clarifying that the claim about the flag had been a misunderstanding (AGA 334/66).

The consideration of the appeal prompted a remarkable series of communications. Carlos Robles Piquer (Director General de Información) wrote to Fraga on 14 February 1967 advising him to allow the production to go ahead. With startling candour, he referred to the murder of Lorca and that of his brother-in-law, Fernández-Montesinos's father: 'De todas maneras, no hay que olvidar que el crimen fue cometido, que nunca se ha investigado sobre él y que hubo otros análogos' ('In any case, it should not be forgotten that the crime was committed, that it has never been investigated, and that there were other similar ones').[8] Robles Piquer's summing-up of the situation provides striking confirmation that the regime was still uncomfortably aware that it had not yet succeeded in 'wresting the Lorca banner' from the hands of the opposition:

> En mi opinión, no tiene justificación suficiente el mantenimiento de la prohibición [. . .] porque en este caso se dan inevitables factores políticos en un tema que ha dado ya muchos disgustos y que no me parece razonable mantener vivo sin necesidad, sobre todo cuando ello contrasta con la línea general de tu política que trata de normalizar el tema Lorca o el tema Machado. (AGA 334/66)

> In my opinion, there is insufficient justification for maintaining the ban [. . .] because there are unavoidable political factors in an affair that has already caused a great deal of trouble. I do not think it is advisable to keep drawing attention to the issue unnecessarily, especially when that goes against your general policy aim of normalising the Lorca business – and the Machado business.

García Escudero offered similar advice on 15 February. He reassured the Minister that his overruling of the Junta's authorisation had been perfectly in order, but concluded that the banning of the play, 'con lo que representa el nombre de García Lorca en España y sobre todo en el extranjero, tendría una repercusión política inconveniente que me parece oportuno evitar máxime cuando la obra en sí no ofrece reparos de importancia' ('in the light of what García Lorca's name represents in Spain and above all outside Spain, would have unwelcome political repercussions, which I believe we should strive to avoid, especially when the play itself poses no significant problems'). He recommended authorisation but suggested that the company should be warned that permission could be withdrawn at any point if performances became the focus of 'un clima inconveniente' ('an undesirable atmosphere') (AGA 334/66).

Fraga accepted the advice of his subordinates and authorisation was issued on 21 February 1967. The play opened at the Teatro Marquina without incident. Perhaps as a result of a warning given by García Escudero, Mañas's production did little to bring out the political dimension of the protagonist's heroism or to make parallels with the present explicit. Most of the reviews published at the time were complicit with the regime's desire to depoliticise the play: 'No hay en *Mariana Pineda* ideas políticas. No hay, en rigor, ideas. Hay sensibilidad y sentimentalismo' ('There are no political ideas in *Mariana Pineda*. In fact, there are no ideas at all. There is only sensibility and sentimentality') (López Sancho 1967: 119). In 1927, the inspector's report on the opening night had noted that the audience's enthusiastic reception of the play appeared to be due primarily to the ideas it advocated (see Chapter 1). Forty years later, Mañas's production was also a great success, thanks in large part to the now irresistible allure of Lorca himself, which was unavoidably tied to his political significance, habitually acknowledged by the custom of applauding the empty stage after the final curtain.

The other great poet-dramatist of the 'Generation of 1927', Rafael Alberti, had been more politically active than Lorca during the Republic and continued to oppose the Franco regime from exile throughout the dictatorship. Muñoz Cáliz (2010) cites various sources that provide evidence of the regime's view of Alberti. An article of 6 July 1939 in the Falange newspaper *Arriba* refers vindictively to 'uno de los seres más abyectos que nacieron, por error, en nuestro suelo: el poeta Alberti, uno de los agentes de Rusia en España, que figuró y agitó cuanto pudo, sin coger las armas para defender lo que propugnaba con su pluma' ('one of the most abject beings that have ever been born, by mishap, on our soil: the poet Alberti, one of Russia's agents in Spain, who stirred up trouble and drew attention to himself as much as he could, without actually taking up arms to defend what he advocated with his pen' (quoted in Muñoz Cáliz 2010: 150). Charges had been laid against him under the Ley de Responsabilidades Políticas but were dropped in June 1946 (BOE 1946: 1642): the authorities must have abandoned any hope of arresting him or confiscating his assets.

The classification of Alberti as an enemy of the regime made it unthinkable that any of his plays – either pre-war works such as *El hombre deshabitado* (*Uninhabited Man*) and *Fermín Galán*, or postwar ones such as *El adefesio* (*The Freak*) and *Noche de guerra en el Museo del Prado* (*A Wartime Night in the Prado Museum*) – would be approved for staging in Spain in the 1940s or 1950s.[9] This situation was exacerbated by the scarcity of published editions. The earliest application stored in the AGA, submitted on 5 January 1968, was for a production of *El adefesio* in Barcelona by the Independent Theatre group Teatro Gogo. The play was written in Argentina in 1943 and premiered by Margarita Xirgu in Buenos Aires a year later. Ricard Salvat, director of the EADAG drama school (Escola d'Art Dramàtic Adrià Gual) in Barcelona, developed a production that was performed in Reggio Emilia (Italy) and Paris in 1966. He did not apply for authorisation in Spain, but a few performances were given in the school's own studio theatre without notifying the authorities (Salvat 1975: 12).

For Salvat, the political significance of the work was powerfully clear: 'Era una denuncia de la realidad española, denuncia que quedaba muy vigente aún en el momento en que la estrenamos' ('It was a denunciation of Spanish reality, a denunciation that felt very relevant to the time in which we performed it') (1975: 12). However, the three censors who evaluated the script in 1968 produced bland reports praising its lyricism and recommending authorisation for audiences over eighteen, without cuts. The religious censor, Jesús Cea, was the only one to bring up the issue of the identity of the author: 'Queda a juicio de la Junta el nombre de su autor por su significación política' ('It is up to the Junta to come to a decision with regard to the name of the author on account of his political reputation') (AGA 12/68). The Junta evidently decided that a few *cámara* performances in a small, obscure venue could be tolerated. The production, directed by Mario Gas, was performed in February 1968 at the Instituto de Estudios Norteamericanos in Barcelona, as well as in Mataró and Olesa de Montserrat in March.

The following year, Gas secured a commercial booking for *El adefesio* at the Teatro CAPSA in Barcelona, opening on 21 November 1969. It is likely that permission was given locally on the grounds that approval had already been given on three occasions and the CAPSA was a relatively small venue. Productions by seven different companies in various other places were also approved in 1972 and 1973, but those that were proposed by commercial companies with well-known directors (María Paz Ballesteros and José Luis Alonso) did not take place. The play finally received a high-profile premiere at the Teatro Reina Victoria in Madrid in September 1976, directed by José Luis Alonso, starring the exiled actor María Casares and featuring a scene in which Victoria Vera appeared almost nude, becoming one of the emblematic liberating moments of the transition to democracy.

The identity and political affiliation of the author became a decisive factor in the case of *Égloga para tres voces y un toro ante la muerte lenta de un poeta* ('Eclogue for Three Voices and a Bull on the Slow Death of a Poet'), which provides an illuminating example of interaction between the work of the Junta in Madrid – focusing on the script – and action at local level investigating the performers and potential circumstances of performance. The script was based on Alberti's poem 'Égloga fúnebre a tres voces y un toro para la muerte lenta de un poeta' ('Funereal Eclogue for Three Voices and a Bull for the Slow Death of a Poet'), the third section of *Pleamar* (*High Tide*), published in Buenos Aires in 1944. The poetic dialogue is a lament for the destruction of the Second Republic and the deaths of three poets closely associated with it: Antonio Machado, Federico García Lorca and Miguel Hernández. The wounded bull is usually interpreted as a symbol of Spain, as represented by the Republic and the common people (Casado 2017: 198–200).

The application, submitted on 27 December 1968 for performances in Morón de la Frontera in early January 1969 by the amateur group Talía, seems to have been designed to play down the political and historical significance of the piece. The title is given on the application form as *Égloga para tres voces y un toro*, omitting the reference to death; when not qualified as 'funereal', the term *égloga* might suggest a pastoral composition about love amongst Arcadian shepherds. The synopsis written by the applicant is calculatedly vague: 'Es un poema en el cual Alberti nos da su visión de las interioridades de un hombre (El toro) representante de un pueblo. Las voces, voces de 3 poetas, lo que piensan de este toro-pueblo' ('It is a poem in which Alberti gives us his vision of the internal world of a man (The Bull) who represents a people. The Voices, voices of three poets, tell us what they think of the bull-people figure'). The synopsis insists that the work is surrealist and abstract. Furthermore, the applicant attached a note stating that the work would be performed without a set, giving no indication of time or place (AGA 1/69).

Nevertheless, the censors' reports suggest that they were suspicious. Martínez Ruiz warned that although the poetic quality of the piece would justify a degree of leniency, 'no cabe engañarse de la intención "anti" del texto y de la actitud de su autor' ('there is no mistaking the dissident intention of the text and the attitude of the author'). Bautista de la Torre claimed to be happy to authorise works by Alberti if they were purely poetic and apolitical, but 'en aquéllas en que aparece como escritor comprometido, y en temas como el presente de tan marcada orientación, no creo que sea lo más prudente darle entrada' ('when it comes to works that show him to be a politically committed writer, and topics as obviously tendentious as the present one, I do not think it is wise to give him a platform'). Father Artola made the absurd suggestion that a single performance might be allowable if the audience could be guaranteed to 'escuchar la pieza en un nivel poético, y no político' ('listen to the piece on a poetic level, not a political one') (AGA 1/69).

The Delegado Provincial in Sevilla reported that of the eighteen members of the group, only two were resident in the town, the others being students at the University of Sevilla, and that the group had been newly established and did not have a registered address. This information intensified the censors' suspicions and provided a convenient administrative reason for not authorising the production. They may also have found out more about the person who had submitted the application: José Julio Vélez Noguera was a budding poet and a literature student at Sevilla becoming involved in dissident political activity, which led to his expulsion from the university in 1970 and several spells in prison thereafter (Cabrera 2012). It was decided on 21 January 1969 that a licence should not be issued until the group regularised its legal position (AGA 1/69). The general political climate may have contributed to this outcome: strikes and student protests had been growing in late 1968, Fraga and García Escudero were no longer in charge of censorship, and a nationwide state of exception was imposed on 24 January. The production did not take place, and there is no record of further applications to perform the *Égloga*.

The challenge posed by *La Lozana andaluza* ('Lozana, the Andalusian Beauty'), an adaptation of Francisco Delicado's picaresque novel of 1528 about a Spanish woman building a career in the bordellos of Rome, was moral rather than political. The text was written around 1960 and published in Buenos Aires in 1964. An application for a commercial production at the Teatro Fígaro in Madrid was submitted on 14 July 1970 by Núria Espert's company, which was by this time viewed with considerable mistrust by the authorities. Reports were submitted by sixteen censors, most of whom felt that Alberti had gone too far in focusing on the most immoral aspects of the story, producing a script that was unacceptably indecent, even pornographic.[10] Although the first three reports recommended prohibition on the grounds that the extent of the cuts required for authorisation would be excessive, it was decided that the author should be invited to revise the script. Guided by Armando Moreno, the company manager, Alberti made a number of changes, mostly involving finding euphemisms for references to prostitution and body parts (a list is included in the file). The revised version was read in September by the same three censors, none of whom felt that Alberti had done enough to make it acceptable. The remaining members of the Junta all issued reports on the text between September and November. Most of them agreed that extensive cuts and amendments were still required, but there was an interesting degree of disparity in their assessments of the quality of the work. Mampaso judged it to be full of theatricality and a magnificent evocation of the period, while García-Cernuda felt that the author should have had the self-respect to keep the work 'dentro de unos límites de decoro que han sido gigantescamente desbordados. La obra es absolutamente intolerable, sobre carecer de valores literarios' ('within the limits of decorum, which have been outrageously exceeded. The work is utterly intolerable, as well as being devoid of literary value') (AGA 280/70).[11]

On 10 November 1970, Moreno was informed that further revision of the script was required. The fact that 'NO' was written across the top of a copy of a letter sent to him suggests that the censors' patience had run out, but no formal decision to refuse authorisation was recorded. The application remained in the limbo of *silencio administrativo* for three years, until Moreno wrote to the Director General in November 1973 to complain about the delay. The reply from Mario Antolín Paz claimed that the authorities were waiting for the company to submit the further revisions, and the impasse continued. When Moreno wrote again in September 1975 requesting a decision, no response was sent. In the meantime, another application for a commercial production of *La Lozana andaluza* (to be directed by Ángel Facio at the Teatro Beatriz in Madrid) was submitted by the Collado company in June 1974. Eight censors voted for prohibition and seven for authorisation with cuts, and still no definitive verdict was issued. Alberti's text was finally staged in September 1980, by María José Goyanes's company at the Teatro Maravillas in Madrid (directed by Carlos Giménez).

La Gallarda, a mythological poetic tragedy composed in 1945, offered no overt political or moral challenges, and an application to stage it in late 1971 was approved by the Junta without delay. However, the licence issued on 5 October was overridden on the same day by an internal memo advising that 'el dictamen definitivo de esta pieza plantea un problema de carácter político determinado por la personalidad de su autor, que la Superioridad debe considerar ante la posibilidad de reacciones o incidencias ajenas a la obra teatral objeto de esta nota' ('the definitive verdict on this piece raises a problem of a political nature due to the personality of the author, which should be considered by a higher authority in view of the possibility of reactions or incidents unrelated to the play itself') (AGA 516/71). The very name of the author was still judged to be potentially inflammatory. There is no record of a final decision and the production did not go ahead: another case of *silencio administrativo*. The play was not premiered until 1992, when it was directed by Miguel Narros as part of the Universal Exposition in Sevilla.

Valle-Inclán, Lorca and Alberti all posed the same fundamental dilemma for the authorities. The political inconvenience of their personal profiles could be outweighed by a perception of literary value, which the censors preferred to see as an essentially poetic quality suitable for relatively highbrow or specialised audiences, though this was too often compromised by regrettable elements of dissidence or immorality. The censors' desire to acknowledge these dramatists' plays as classics while trying to restrict their dissemination and neutralise their political potential conflicted with the works' growing international reputation and with theatremakers' determination to make the most of their theatricality and subversiveness.

The post-war avant-garde

The emergence of a new theatrical avant-garde in post-war Spain was an extremely slow process, but there is little evidence that it was held up by the direct effect of censorship. The allegorical existentialist experiments produced by Alfonso Sastre and the Arte Nuevo group in the mid-1940s were approved without reservations by the censors, though José María Conde-Salazar's report on *Ha sonado la muerte* ('Death Has Sounded') judged the purely literary value of the work to be negligible (AGA 33/46) and Bartolomé Mostaza described *Cargamento de sueños* ('Cargo of Dreams') as nebulous and lacking metaphysical depth (AGA 309/46). The brevity of the life of this initiative was due to a lack of resources rather than repressive action by the state (Paco 1993). There is no doubt, however, that the stifling, conservative cultural environment fostered by censorship in the 1940s and 1950s, conditioned by hostility to the work of Valle-Inclán and Lorca, helped to make it difficult to win professional, commercial or official support for theatrical experimentation. Other pioneers such as Fernando Arrabal, Francisco Nieva and José Ruibal began writing plays in the 1950s but did not at first have access to opportunities to have them staged. It was not until the mid-1960s – as Valle-Inclán, Lorca and foreign influences such as Brecht, Artaud and the Absurdists were becoming accepted presences on the Spanish theatrical scene and a wave of new fringe groups and festivals was gathering pace – that the new avant-garde became prominent and came regularly to the attention of the censors.

Arrabal tended to be automatically associated by critics and censors with the Theatre of the Absurd, though the influence on him of the Spanish neo-surrealist Postismo movement predated that of Beckett, Ionesco or Adamov (Berenguer 1987: 45–56), and Arrabal himself has declared that the author who interests him most is Valle-Inclán (1958). This uncritical assumption worked in his favour to some extent: being able to assign a text to an established aesthetic category with a degree of international prestige often seemed to have a reassuring effect on censors. On the other hand, it contributed to the view that theatre of this kind was a minority taste, not suitable for commercial productions in mainstream theatres.[12]

It was the Dido group that gave Arrabal his first premiere. *Los hombres del triciclo* ('The Tricycle Men', usually known as *The Tricycle*) was approved in January 1957 for a single *cámara* performance without cuts. The censors were puzzled by the script but did not see it as a political or moral threat. Morales de Acevedo described the play as 'obra de un bromista o de un perturbado. Como broma, puede pasar y aceptarse' ('the work of a prankster or a crackpot. As a prank, it can be allowed to go ahead') (AGA 359/56). There was a delay of a whole year before the performance took place (in January 1958), but there is no evidence that this was caused by censorship. The premiere was a more high-profile event than the censors had expected, filling the Teatro Bellas Artes and receiving substantial reviews. The reception by both audience and critics was mixed. Alfredo Marqueríe made the usual accusation that Arrabal was imitating Ionesco and Adamov, and reported that while the cast and director received unanimous applause, the audience showed some hostility to the author when he took his curtain call (1958: 51).

The unenthusiastic reception of *Los hombres del triciclo* in 1958 contributed to Arrabal's decision to remain in France, maintaining little contact with the theatre world in Spain while he built up an international reputation. His early plays were regularly authorised between 1964 and 1968, but only for *cámara* productions, which led him to publish a disgruntled public letter in the theatre journal *Primer Acto*. He complained that the confinement of his work to under-resourced amateur and student productions did his reputation more harm than good: 'Estas representaciones pueden parecer coartadas para paliar ciertas carencias; no hay que olvidar que estos grupos representan obras mías prohibidas y tan sólo autorizadas en teatros de cámara' ('Such performances seem to be allowed as a way of covering up certain deficiencies; it should not be forgotten that these groups are performing plays of mine that are banned and only authorised for theatre clubs') (Arrabal 1967). The accusation that the regime was cynically using authorisation for *cámara* to whitewash an oppressive cultural policy was valid, yet Arrabal's disparaging attitude to the efforts of non-commercial companies won him few friends in the Spanish theatre industry.

The absence of fully professional or commercial productions of Arrabal's plays in Spain was in most cases not the direct result of bans imposed by the Junta de Censura. The files for *El triciclo*, *Ceremonia por un negro asesinado* ('Ceremony for a Murdered Black'), *Guernica*, *La juventud ilustrada* ('Illustrated [or Enlightened] Youth') and *Y pusieron esposas a las flores* (*And They Put Handcuffs on the Flowers*) do not contain any applications by commercial companies. Only the most adventurous directors were willing to challenge mainstream audiences by putting these radical, disconcerting spectacles on commercial stages. Antonio Guirau's application to stage *Fando y Lis* (*Fando and Lis*) and *Los dos verdugos* (*The Two Executioners*) at the Teatro Marquina was approved in 1967 but there is no record of the production taking place. Teatro ARA, a semi-professional company based in Málaga, was given approval in May 1966 for a *cámara* production of *El cementerio de automóviles* (*Automobile Graveyard*) at the Teatro Infanta Beatriz in Madrid, as part of an officially sponsored Teatro Nacional de Cámara programme, but this performance also seems not to have gone ahead. At the end of June 1966, ARA applied for permission for a commercial production of *El cementerio de automóviles*, but the Junta confirmed that the authorisation was valid only for *cámara* (AGA 127/66).

It was Núria Espert who made the most determined efforts to mount professional productions of Arrabal's plays, submitting applications for *El cementerio de automóviles*, *Los dos verdugos* and *El gran ceremonial* (*The Grand Ceremonial*) in 1968. By now, however, the regime had become considerably more hostile towards the playwright. On a visit to Madrid in 1967, he had been asked to write a dedication in one of his books. Unwisely, he had written: 'Me cago en dios, en la patra y en todo lo demás' ('I shit on god, *la patra* and all the rest') (Cela Trulock 2002). He was arrested and charged with blasphemy and insulting the nation. His defence argued unconvincingly that the dedication referred to the god Pan and to Arrabal's cat [Cleo]patra (not *la Patria*, the Fatherland), and that he was suffering from the side-effects of combining a glass of Marie Brizard with amphetamine tablets. Various public figures in Spain and abroad expressed their support, and he was acquitted after spending three weeks in custody.

Although none of the sixteen censors who wrote reports on *El cementerio de automóviles* in 1968 referred to the author's notoriety, all but one of them condemned the work's combination of blasphemy and eroticism, recommending restriction to *cámara* or outright prohibition. Father Cea described it as the product of a diabolical mind, and Manuel Díez Crespo heavily underlined his recommendation: 'De ninguna manera en teatro comercial' ('Absolutely not for a commercial production'). An undated note attached to the Junta's decision to confirm the limiting of the approval to *cámara* shows that a decision had already been taken in principle to blacklist Arrabal (probably in December 1968): 'Se consulta con el Dtor. Gral. si este autor se considera como vetado y decide demorar la decisión. –Vetado' ('Director General consulted over whether this author is to be considered banned and the decision delayed. – Banned') (AGA 127/66). *El gran ceremonial* was also prohibited in December 1968 for its accumulation of sadomasochism, necrophilia, fetishism and blasphemy (AGA 391/68). Arrabal was still not being rejected out of hand: the report by Florentino Soria praised his undeniable talent and originality. However, what had been tolerable as childlike whimsy in the author's earliest works was in the censors' view now being replaced by 'pura provocación' ('pure provocation') (AGA 391/68).

What became the most controversial of Espert's attempts to stage Arrabal was *Los dos verdugos*. Since approval for both *cámara* and commercial theatres had already been given, there was initially no objection to the production opening at the Teatro Reina Victoria on 8 February 1969, though an internal memo of 6 February noted that there was to be a strict inspection of the dress rehearsal in order to prevent any 'exceso o inconveniencia' ('excess or inappropriateness'), and that the company had been warned that the licence for the production would be cancelled at the slightest sign of trouble (AGA 1/64). There is interesting variation between different accounts of the banning of *Los dos verdugos*. Patricia O'Connor attributes the decision to the notes written by Arrabal for the programme, in which he spelled out the political significance of the work, resulting in all copies of it being confiscated from the printers (1973: 37). Espert's own account also mentions the destruction of programmes and posters, but focuses primarily on Víctor García's set design, which featured a tank with its gun pointing out at the audience:

> Los censores se presentaron en el Reina Victoria en pleno ensayo general, vieron el tanque y pusieron una cara que no presagiaba nada bueno [. . .] A la mañana siguiente, Robles Piquer convocó a Armando en el Ministerio de Cultura y le recibió a gritos. Le dijo que ya nos habían tolerado demasiadas cosas y que lo del tanque era la gota que desbordaba el vaso. (Espert & Ordóñez 2002: 104–5)

> The censors turned up at the Reina Victoria in the middle of the dress rehearsal, and when they saw the tank the look on their faces was not a good sign [. . .] The next morning, Robles Piquer summoned Armando [Moreno] to see him in the Ministry and started shouting at him. He told him they had already let us get away with too much and the business with the tank was the last straw.

Presumably, the tank was thought to make the link between Arrabal's anonymous torturers and the military-led regime excessively obvious, especially in the circumstances of heightened political tension marked by the national state of exception decreed on 24 January. This was such a high-profile case that the authorities took the unusual step of issuing a statement to the press explaining their reasons for the ban and attempting to discredit Arrabal. The elements of the set not specified in the text were allegedly designed to provoke 'efectos políticos directamente relacionados con dolorosas circunstancias pasadas de la vida española' ('political effects directly related to painful circumstances of Spain's past'), and the author's published interpretation of the work was assumed to have the same intent (Agencia Cifra 1969). The statement also referred to Arrabal's trial for blasphemy and insulting the nation, alleging that on his return to Paris he declared that he had lied to the judges and had indeed intended to insult the *patria* (Agencia Cifra 1969).

Arrabal and his work were now completely unacceptable to the Spanish authorities. His public pronouncements against the regime were becoming more pugnacious and his new plays were increasingly explicit in their subversion of authoritarianism and Catholicism and their protests against torture and oppression. All applications for productions of new plays and previously authorised ones were now routinely rejected: 'The authorities feared that productions of Arrabal's plays were becoming rallying points for rising protest and dissidence' (O'Leary 2008: 42).

Guernica was banned in December 1968 on the grounds that it contravened article 14.2 of the 1963 *Normas*, which referred to attacks on national institutions or ceremonies (AGA 393/68). *La juventud ilustrada* was initially approved in March 1969, but two of the three reports recommended that the case should be referred to *la Superioridad* on account of the risk posed by the author (AGA 82/69). After three weeks of silence, senior officials decided to ban the production, using the power granted to the Minister by article 22 of the *Normas*. *Fando y Lis*, approved since 1966, was now prohibited. A handwritten note attached to the application stated simply: 'Prohibido el autor 15/IX/1969' ('Author prohibited 15/09/1969') (AGA 168/66). Three applications for *cámara* performances of *El triciclo* in 1972 were turned down, the notification for one of them stipulating that 'las obras del autor Fernando Arrabal están prohibidas en todo el territorio nacional' ('the works of the author Fernando Arrabal are prohibited in all parts of the country') (AGA 359/56).

The file on *El arquitecto y el emperador de Asiria* (*The Architect and the Emperor of Assyria*) shows the whole trajectory from wary tolerance of Arrabal in the *apertura* period to outraged rejection towards the end of the dictatorship, and finally cautious rehabilitation in the transition to democracy. In November 1966, Bautista de la Torre, Artola and Baquero were inclined to authorise an officially sponsored production for the Teatro Nacional de Cámara y Ensayo with extensive cuts, though the production did not go ahead. In June 1973, an adaptation to be performed at the Peruvian Embassy was banned after ferociously hostile reports by three censors. Mampaso referred to 'la significación política de Fernando Arrabal, su línea de teatro obsceno, irreverente y antisocial, irrepresentable en España' ('the political significance of Fernando Arrabal, his obscene, irreverent and antisocial brand of theatre, unperformable in Spain'). Zubiaurre pointed to subversive political symbolism, obscene language and actions, blasphemy and irreverence; and

García-Cernuda tersely concluded: 'Es irrepresentable. Incide en la totalidad de las normas prohibitivas' ('It is unperformable. It infringes every single one of the criteria for prohibition') (AGA 307/66).

Provisional approval was given in March 1976 for a commercial production of *El arquitecto* directed by Adolfo Marsillach, but was not confirmed until 6 July, three days after Adolfo Suárez's appointment as Prime Minister. The minutes of the meeting of the censorship board noted that 'por la Jerarquía competente para ello ha sido levantado el veto que pesaba sobre su autor' ('the veto that applied to this author has been lifted by the relevant senior authority'), and that from now on Arrabal's works were to be judged 'atendiendo exclusivamente a su contexto literario, tema, condicionamientos de su puesta en escena, etc., prescindiendo de cualquier otra consideración ajena al juicio que los elementos básicos de apreciación precedentemente citados merezca' ('exclusively with reference to the literary context, the subject matter, the details of staging, etc., without any consideration of other factors not pertinent to the evaluation of the work itself') (AGA 307/66).

Arrabal was therefore one of the first beneficiaries of the change of government of July 1976 which marked the real beginning of the transition to democracy. However, this did not mean an unconditional green light for his work, which still had the capacity to shock the establishment. *En la cuerda floja* (*On the Tightrope*) was banned on 13 August 1976. Antonio Albizu's report described the work as 'un alegato contra todo lo que fue el Régimen' ('a diatribe against everything the Regime stood for'), and Antonio de Zubiaurre argued that it could jeopardise current efforts to promote political reconciliation: 'Es más bien una injusta y disparatada queja, con aguijones de revanchismo' ('It is an unfounded and preposterous protest, driven by a desire for revenge') (AGA 1116/76). The last of Arrabal's plays to be censored was *Y pusieron esposas a las flores* (*And They Put Handcuffs on the Flowers*), which had been inspired by the author's spell in prison in 1967. Although four censors proposed that it could be tolerated with cuts, the majority were outraged and the production was banned on 15 October 1976. Jesús Vasallo complained of its 'nauseabunda indecencia en todos los aspectos' ('nauseating indecency in every aspect'), and Fr Cea declared: 'Nada queda por ensuciar en esta alucinación teatral: Dios, la patria, las instituciones estatales y religiosas, todo ello dentro de un cúmulo de groserías del peor gusto' ('Nothing remains unsullied in this theatrical delirium: God, the fatherland, national and religious institutions, all wrapped up in a conglomeration of crudity in the worst possible taste'). Less than nine months later, while the veteran Manuel Díez Crespo described the work as blasphemous and designed to shock, his new colleague José Luis Guerra Sánchez commented dispassionately that it was 'una crítica de la España de Franco' (AGA 1180/76). The production was approved (for audiences over eighteen, with two cuts) in early July 1977, as the first democratically elected government since 1936 was taking power and setting up the new Ministerio de Cultura y Bienestar.

Arrabal's response to the Franco regime's determination to restrict performances of his work was consistently and radically *imposibilista*.[13] He was not willing to be docile or negotiate over cuts and rewrites. He summed up his approach to censorship in 1974: '¡La censura es una barbaridad! Pero en realidad yo *ignoro* la censura: jamás he escrito una línea preocupado por ella. Soy optimista: lo que hoy se nos prohíbe mañana verá la luz' ('Censorship is barbaric! But the fact is that I pay no attention to it. I've never written a single line worrying about how it was likely to be affected by censorship. I'm an optimist: what's banned today will see the light tomorrow') (Primer Acto 1974b: 6–7). This uncompromising stance, maintained by a writer with a high international profile, had a valuable effect in drawing attention to censorship and prompting unfavourable comparisons with other, more liberal countries. On the other hand, if there was anything likely to reassure censors that they were still – even in 1976 – performing a useful function in protecting the theatregoing public from seditious and unsavoury spectacles, it was the innovative output of Fernando Arrabal.

Like Arrabal, Francisco Nieva began to develop his carnivalesque aesthetic in the Postismo movement in Madrid in the 1940s before moving to Paris in 1952, where he absorbed avant-garde influences, especially from Artaud.[14] However, the plays he wrote while he was building up an international reputation as a painter and stage designer remained virtually unknown until several years after his return to Spain in 1964. They were not picked up by student or *cámara y ensayo* groups, and Nieva did not at first make much effort to persuade directors or producers to attempt to stage them. He recalls that friends had commented: '"Eso está muy bien, es muy sorprendente, pero no vas a poder estrenarlo nunca." Llevaban toda la razón, pero yo no podía dejar de expresarme, ni desarrollar mi dramaturgia autocensurándome' ('"It's great stuff, very original, but you'll never get any of it staged." They were absolutely right, but I had to go on expressing myself and I wasn't going to try to advance my theatre by self-censoring') (Nieva 2010).

Nieva's first clash with the censors came with *Es bueno no tener cabeza* ('It's Good to Have No Head').[15] On 5 May 1969, the Teatro Moratín company applied for approval for a commercial triple bill of this play alongside *El corazón acelerado* ('The Accelerated Heart') and *El maravilloso catarro de Lord Bashaville* ('Lord Bashaville's Marvellous Catarrh'). The latter was approved, no decision was made with regard to the former, and *Es bueno no tener cabeza* was prohibited on 19 August after three rounds of readings. The censors were almost unanimous in finding it completely unacceptable, principally for its sexual (and transsexual) content. Soria complained of perversion and amoral cynicism, and Cea described it as pornographic and unperformable (AGA 171/69).

It is important to note that despite the censors' indignation at the content and language of these plays, many of them made a point of praising their literary and theatrical quality. Bautista de la Torre referred to the 'muy moderno tratamiento y muy destacada ambición' ('very modern treatment and extraordinary ambition'). Soria saw 'indiscutible altura literaria' ('undeniable literary distinction') in all three, and Muelas, Mampaso, Barceló and Martínez Ruiz all stressed their literary and theatrical value (AGA 171/69). There is little sign of the censors misunderstanding or being hostile to Nieva's innovative approach in itself. They took his work seriously, but were not prepared to tolerate what they saw as unacceptable levels of profanity and indecency.

Not long after this episode, Nieva obtained a post at the Real Escuela de Arte Dramático ('Royal School of Dramatic Art') in Madrid, teaching stage design. Taking advantage of an informal understanding that private performances in the college by staff and students could take place without official authorisation, he directed a production of *Es bueno no tener cabeza* in June 1971. Far from attempting to stay under the radar of the authorities, he invited all his numerous contacts in the Madrid theatre industry and set out to cause a sensation:

Nadie faltó, y la dirección del centro fue sorprendida en el curso de la representación. No pudo hacer nada. Y la función resultó un éxito rotundo [. . .] Teníamos previstas tres actuaciones, pero a la segunda, con las escaleras llenas de público, entró la policía desalojando a todo el mundo. Bueno, yo había conseguido mi objetivo. Ya no era decorativamente maldito, sino un autor a tener en cuenta. (Nieva 2010)

Absolutely everyone came, and the college management knew nothing about it until the performance was under way. There was nothing they could do. And it was a great success [. . .] We were going to do three performances, but on the second night, with the stairs full of people coming in, the police charged in and threw everyone out. Anyway, I had achieved my objective. Now I wasn't just a decoratively accursed author; I was a force to be reckoned with.

This act of defiance may have resulted in an unofficial blacklisting for Nieva. A commercial production of *Malditas sean Coronada y sus hijas* ('Coronada and Her Daughters Be Damned') by the Justo Alonso company was approved with cuts in July 1971 but did not go ahead. The censors expressed concerns about how the excesses of the text might be realised on stage and insisted on rigorous inspection of the dress rehearsal. Indeed, the conditions stipulated in the authorisation recommended that several inspections might be needed (AGA 250/71). There is no indication in the file of a decision to withdraw the authorisation; perhaps an inspection led to a last-minute ban, or perhaps *la Superioridad* decided to overrule the Junta.

With *Pelo de tormenta* ('Storm Hair'), Nieva once again transgressed the limit of what the censors were willing to tolerate. Justo Alonso applied in August 1973 for authorisation of commercial performances at the Teatro Marquina. Although Martínez Ruiz proposed that it could be approved for *cámara*, the view of the religious censor Fr Cea was decisive: the work was 'inaceptable por su burla de las instituciones religiosas y virtudes cristianas y morales' ('unacceptable on account of its mockery of religious institutions and of Christian and moral virtues') (AGA 436/73). The author lodged an appeal against the ban in September 1973. His letter to the Junta de Censura was defiant and erudite, arguing that the carnivalesque representation of religious rites was not a denunciation of Catholicism as currently practised in Spain, since the Church itself had left behind archaic 'exterioridades rituales y folklóricas' ('ritual, folkloric displays') and inquisitorial practices, and had embraced the modernising spirit of the Second

Vatican Council. He insisted that the emphasis on sexuality was stylised, much less indecent than many of the popular mainstream shows now being allowed to proliferate in the country's theatres, and that far from attacking the regime or the nation, his play was a sincere celebration of Spanish popular culture (AGA 436/73). His tongue-in-cheek ingenuity made little impact on the members of the Junta, however: the verdict of prohibition was confirmed in October 1973 and again in 1974 following another application by Alonso.

The application for *Pelo de tormenta* was revived in July 1975 and Alonso's production was approved for audiences of over-eighteens. The reports written at this time show signs of an awareness among censors that they were on the verge of moving into a new era. Juan Emilio Aragonés declared: 'Si hay obras que salvar, pese a sus desmanes −compensados por su excelente texto−, estamos ante una de ellas' ('If there are plays worth saving, this is one of them, despite its excesses, which are compensated for by the high quality of the script'). Pedro Barceló argued that the play's grotesque, fantastic qualities removed any risk of parallels being drawn with current circumstances and institutions: 'Hay expresiones chocantes y algunas que pueden parecer críticas globales de estratos o instituciones, pero entiendo que ese desgarramiento sitúa perfectamente al espectador en un plano inconcreto' ('There are shocking expressions and lines that could be taken as general critiques of power structures or institutions, but in my view the exorbitance of the whole thing takes the spectator onto an abstract level') (AGA 436/73). Despite the shift in attitudes signalled by these remarks, there were still obstacles of some kind in the way of getting *Pelo de tormenta* onto the stage. It was not performed until 1983, at the Teatro Lope de Vega in Sevilla, finally reaching Madrid in a triumphant production at the Teatro María Guerrero in 1997.

Nieva's work began to be published in Spain from the early 1970s, but his first professional premieres did not come until 1976, when *Sombra y quimera de Larra* ('Shadow and Mirage of Larra') was staged in March at the Teatro María Guerrero, followed in April by a double bill of *La carroza de plomo candente* ('The Carriage of White-Hot Lead') and *El combate de Ópalos y Tasia* ('The Battle between Opalos and Tasia') at the Teatro Fígaro in Madrid, directed by José Luis Alonso. An application for *La carroza de plomo candente* had been submitted in June 1975 but appears to have been held up. It is unfortunate that there are no reports or records of a decision in the censorship file: it would have been interesting to see how the authorities assessed the risk posed by this play in the tense period between June 1975 and April 1976. In an interview published on the day of the premiere, Nieva suggested that a broad historical idea lay at the centre of his theatre: 'El absolutismo político y religioso produce un pueblo agobiado, desganado, fatalista; un pueblo niño, dolorido, rencoroso, ingobernable según sus tiránicos gobernantes' ('Political and religious absolutism leaves the people enervated, jaded and fatalistic – a population that is infantile, distressed, resentful, and ungovernable according to its tyrannical rulers'). He added: 'El error de la censura, al haberla prohibido por tanto tiempo, consiste en la idea de que yo atacaba ciertas instituciones cuando, en realidad, yo atacaba un modo de ser español desde su fase más negativa' ('The error committed by the censors in banning it for so long lies in their assumption that I was attacking specific institutions when, in reality, I was attacking a whole conception of Spanishness in its most negative form') (Laborda 1976).

Careful reading of the censors' reports on other plays indicates that some of them did understand this distinction and were able to look beyond the immediate task of suppressing images, words and actions that posed an obvious risk of offending the hierarchy of Church and regime. Martínez Ruiz, for example, argued that while *Pelo de tormenta* 'lastima algunas tradicionales formas sociales, rituales, de nuestra historia y religión' ('damages certain traditional social and ritual constituents of our history and religion'), it did so in the form of an irrational, fantastical experiment, which could be tolerated under *cámara* conditions (AGA 436/73).

In 1976, with the climate of *destape* (uncovering) gathering pace in the theatre, cinema and magazines, the shock value of Nieva's work could be used as a marketing tactic. Shortly after the opening of *La carroza* and *El combate*, the theatre management published an announcement in the press warning the public that 'debido a las crudas situaciones y diálogos jamás vistas ni oídos aquí en un escenario, pero nunca gratuitas, se advierte a los espectadores de estrecha mentalidad que se abstengan de asistir a este espectáculo' ('owing to the crude situations and dialogue, never before seen or heard on stage in this country, but never gratuitous, narrow-minded spectators are advised to refrain from attending this spectacle')

(ABC 1976a). The fact that the Church issued a 'moral classification' of 4 ('extremely dangerous') (ABC 1976b) was now likely to attract more customers than it repelled. Some conservative theatregoers whose sensibilities censorship was supposed to protect were certainly still susceptible to shock. A critic later recalled witnessing the scandalised departure of a respectable middle-aged couple: '"Vámonos, Mariano, que pequen ellos", decía la señora mientras libraba a su marido del desnudo rubio y venial de Rosa Valenty en cueros de Venus Calipigia' ('"Let's go, Mariano, they can sin if they want", the lady was saying as she dragged her husband away from the blonde and venial nakedness of Rosa Valenty in all her glory as Venus Callipyge') (Cuevas 1980: 65).

According to Nieva, the company simply ignored cuts ordered by censors and inspectors: 'Aún existía la censura, pero no se hizo el menor caso de ella. En el ensayo para la censura, por el que era necesario pasar, ésta se manifestó haciendo indignadas tachaduras por todas partes, bajo nuestra mirada compasiva. Un acto de venganza' ('There was still censorship, but no one took any notice of it. In the rehearsal for the censors, which was still a requirement, they tried indignantly to impose cuts all over the place, while we just looked on pityingly. An act of revenge') (Nieva 2010).

Nieva condemns censorship unequivocally: 'El efecto de la censura fue desastroso a nivel general' ('In general, the effect of censorship was disastrous' (2010). In his own case, however, he maintains that he never made concessions or practised self-censorship:

> Nunca he dejado caer la toalla. Cuanto escribiera entonces y ahora no ha tenido más vigilancia que mi propio sentido estético. El periodo de silencio forzoso me sirvió de acicate y no pocas de aquellas obras las escribí en el extranjero, en Dublín, en Berlín, en Roma. Es la demostración más palpable de que las prohibiciones invitan a la más completa rebeldía. (Nieva 2010)

> I've never thrown in the towel. Everything I wrote then and everything I write now has been subject to no control other than my own aesthetic judgement. The period of enforced silence I went through acted as a stimulus, and many of those early works were written outside Spain, in Dublin, Berlin, Rome. It's the most tangible proof of the fact that prohibitions just provoke the most radical rebellion.

Nieva came to be associated with the generation of avant-garde playwrights often referred to as the *Nuevo Teatro Español* ('New

Spanish Theatre'). This movement first made its presence felt between 1965 and 1966, though some of its members had been writing plays since the 1950s and were contemporaries of the Realist Generation discussed in Chapter 5. Their work, however, marked a decisive break from that of the realists and from mainstream commercial theatre, experimenting in diverse ways with symbolism, ritual, carnival, abstraction and improvisation, and drawing inspiration from Valle-Inclán, Grotowski, Artaud, Jarry, Brecht, the Living Theatre and popular culture.[16] The New Spanish Theatre was a loosely defined movement encompassing at least twenty authors, the most prominent of whom were José Ruibal, Jerónimo López Mozo, Alberto Miralles, Luis Riaza, Ángel García Pintado and Manuel Martínez Mediero. Thanks to new prizes and festivals, editions, and influential academic studies, especially by the US critic George Wellwarth (1972), by the early 1970s their work was well known but still infrequently performed, largely confined to *cámara* productions.

Varied as their methods were, these playwrights shared a conviction that aesthetic experimentation went hand in hand with political dissidence – specifically against the dictatorship and more generally against consumerist capitalism, conservative values and social injustice. They specialised in satirical allegories of political and economic power, which unsurprisingly caught the attention of the censors. López Mozo characterises the New Spanish Theatre as 'una generación castigada por la censura' ('a generation castigated by censorship') (1986: 30). Some of these playwrights tended to assume that the censors were instinctively hostile to innovation and incapable of grasping the point of their symbolism, the significance of which was not always tied to the immediate political situation: 'Los censores tachan lo que entienden, pero sobre todo lo que no entienden' ('The censors delete what they can understand, but above all what they don't understand') (García Pintado 1979: 65). As demonstrated earlier in this chapter, some censorship decisions were indeed the product of obtuse conservatism or moral panic. However, many of the censors showed themselves to be capable of more nuanced assessments and willing to give the benefit of the doubt to works by the historical avant-garde or the New Spanish Theatre which they found artistically challenging or puzzling, as long as they did not find them gratuitously provocative.

The experimental forms favoured by the new wave – symbolism, allegory, abstraction, ritual, 'Aesopian' fables – could be a double-edged sword in the struggle against censorship. For theatremakers seeking ways of smuggling subversive material past the censors, such techniques often seemed an attractive option. A leading member of the New Spanish Theatre has acknowledged that camouflaging political dissidence behind symbolism became a defining – and not always subtle – feature of the genre:

> Ante esa situación, nuestro autor, o bien suaviza su obra, perdiendo acaso su validez, o no renuncia, sino que cambia la táctica del cuerpo a cuerpo y se enmascara. Y en ese sentido doy como característica principal y peligrosa [. . .] el virtuosismo de muchos escritores, demostrado en el momento de disimular personajes incómodos, geografías próximas y actualidades innombrables para conseguir, contando con la complicidad del público que habrá de aceptar el juego, el permiso de la Junta de Censura para la representación. (Miralles 1979: 47)

> Faced with this situation, our author has two choices: either water down his work, at the risk of it becoming pointless, or refuse to give ground, instead changing the tactics of engagement by using masks. Consequently, I would say that the most characteristic and most dangerous feature [of this kind of theatre] is the virtuosity of many playwrights, manifested in their tendency to disguise inopportune personages, proximate geographies and unmentionable actualities, assuming the complicity of audiences primed to go along with the game, all with the aim of gaining the approval of the Censorship Board for performances.

Josep Maria Benet i Jornet, when asked if he wrote in a coded way in order to ensure that his plays were staged (and published), replies: 'Sí, claro que sí, con segundas lecturas, que por otra parte el público captaba inmediatamente [. . .] Los censores eran bastante tontos' ('Yes, of course, with double meanings, which, mind you, the audience would get straight away [. . .] The censors were pretty stupid') (2010). He emphasises that the hidden meanings or links to current realities were not always encoded in the words of the script but were to be brought out by gestures, intonation and details of staging. The game could be subversive fun – for authors, performers, often in fringe theatre groups, and spectators of the kind targeted by such groups (predominantly younger and more left wing than the consumers of mainstream commercial theatre), who could all enjoy a frisson of subversive complicity and feel superior to the dim-witted functionaries who had apparently failed to crack the code.

Reports in the AGA files show, however, that members of the Junta de Censura were often perfectly capable of spotting disguised allusions to dictators, ecclesiastical hierarchies complicit with tyrants, oppressively patriarchal families, fratricidal wars, or underdeveloped countries kowtowing to the United States. Censors recommending authorisation would frequently emphasise in their reports that they were aware of implicit *intenciones* (a term normally used in the sense of 'political intentions') but judged them not to pose a serious threat. Or else they would indicate that they assumed that spectators would not capture the intended meanings, or that they could be neutralised by selective cuts. The censors were also playing a game, anxious to prove – if only to one another – that they knew what the theatremakers were up to and that they remained in control by allowing the opposition to think that they were scoring a few points here and there.

The other edge of the sword of *enmascaramiento* was that its use could be counterproductive. If authors assumed that censors were on the lookout for coded dissent and that it was therefore necessary to make the coding more cryptic, the result could be 'un juego adivinatorio para cómplices' ('a guessing game for the complicit') leaving all but the most thoroughly initiated spectators in the dark (Miralles 1979: 143). And if censors assumed that authors were always building in hidden meanings and audiences were always expecting to find them, they were likely to become hyper-sensitive, over-interpreting symbols and possible parallels with current realities. José Ruibal comments wryly that if his technique of using animals as symbolic characters was supposed to be a way of evading censorship, it was not very successful. Instead, 'constantemente veían en todos y cada uno de los muchos animales que pueblan mis obras, la imagen de la irrepetible personalidad que durante tan luengos años nos ha gobernado' ('they constantly saw in every single one of the many animals that populate my plays the image of the unrepeatable personage who has governed us for so many years') (1977a: 14). Looking through transcriptions of censors' reports on his plays, Benet i Jornet remarked: 'Era imposible entender cómo es que a veces no veían lo que había, y otras veces veían cosas que no estaban. Era una situación exasperante y terrible en realidad' ('It was impossible to understand how they could sometimes not see what was there, and at other times see things that weren't there. It really was an exasperating and awful situation' (2010).

While the authors of the New Spanish Theatre considered themselves particularly harshly affected by censorship, their tendency towards abstraction and symbolism, together with their enthusiasm for foreign avant-garde influences, was regarded by some members of the Realist Generation as a distraction from engagement with historical and political reality, and therefore complicit with censorship. Rodríguez Méndez argued that their productions were 'estéticamente avanzados en su maquinaria técnica, pero muy desviados de la crítica social y sobre todo de la crítica concreta de la sociedad española' ('aesthetically advanced in their technical apparatus but very detached from social critique, and particularly from specific critique of Spanish society') (1974: 162). Ruibal insisted that the main point was not to avoid representing social reality but to deconstruct it through poetic theatre that created its own verisimilitude (1984: 24). Symbolism was never merely a ruse to evade censorship but a way of freeing political theatre from anecdotal, localised detail and achieving 'dimensión poética y trascendencia mítica, a la vez que intemporalidad' ('poetic substance and mythical transcendence, as well as intemporality') (Ruibal 1984: 40). While censors sometimes showed that they understood this ambition, they nevertheless felt compelled to intervene whenever they felt that the poetic became too obviously and topically political (or morally objectionable).

Although Ruibal began writing plays in the mid-1950s while working as a journalist in Latin America, the first censorship application for one of his works was made in 1969. He had gained some recognition in the United States, with translations of *Los mendigos* (*The Beggars*), *El asno* (*The Jackass*) and *El rabo* (*Tails*) published in academic theatre journals and a student production of *The Beggars* at Penn State University in 1968. His breakthrough in Spain came in 1969: between April and October, five applications for permission to perform short pieces by Ruibal were made by Daniel Bohr's company Nuevo Teatro Experimental, and one by the *cámara* group La Cabala. The applications were for productions in small fringe theatres, including three at a new venue in Madrid, the Café-Teatro Lady Pepa, which was pioneering a model of independent commercial theatre that would thrive in the early 1970s. The Lady Pepa provided a low-cost, flexible space that could harbour small-scale experimental productions with short runs, appealing to young and liberal-minded audiences but without the restrictions normally applied to *cámara y ensayo* groups.

These first productions were almost all authorised with little fuss. The censors saw no reason to fear that Ruibal's satires of capitalism, consumerism and US economic imperialism would be taken as attacks on Francoism. A triple bill at the Lady Pepa, entitled *Café-teatro*, was to consist of *La secretaria* ('The Secretary'), *Los mutantes* ('The Mutants') and *El rabo* (*Tails*), The first piece, about a secretary whose successive 'promotions' all involve serving increasingly junior members of the patriarchal corporate hierarchy, was considered innocuous. The second, about a married couple crushed under a growing mountain of consumer goods, was judged to be authorisable despite Soria identifying an ambiguous critical intention. *El rabo*, with its references to dogs sniffing each other's rear ends and protesting against humans' insistence on misinterpreting this habit, was more problematic. García Carrión complained that 'se trata de una verdadera indecencia en su contenido' ('its content is truly indecent') and recommended prohibition, while Mampaso suggested that there were politically loaded phrases and identified a problem that would arise frequently in relation to this kind of theatre: 'Habría que estar a un visado especial del ensayo general para poder pronunciarse por una autorización de Censura' ('It would be necessary to attend a special inspection of the dress rehearsal to be able to come to a decision on whether to authorise this piece') (AGA 152/69). Authorisation for audiences of over-eighteens was issued on 29 April 1969 for all three pieces (with six cuts from one page of *El rabo*), though *El rabo* was omitted from some of the performances (López Mozo 2018), perhaps as a result of a last-minute ban imposed after a dress rehearsal inspection.

Daniel Bohr, keen to capitalise on the surge of interest in Ruibal's work, submitted an application on 17 July 1969 for a more ambitious project: a commercial production of *El hombre y la mosca* (*The Man and the Fly*), a full-length play written in 1968, to be staged in Barcelona and Madrid. Objections from the censors were to be expected, since this text is a ferocious satire of autocracy and its tendency to strive to perpetuate itself.[17] The ageing Hombre, a military dictator whose regime – symbolised by a glass dome – is founded on the skulls of enemies killed in a civil war long ago, trains a younger Doble to be an exact double of himself so that the regime can continue apparently unchanged after his death. Despite the grotesque symbolic approach, the censors identified references to current political circumstances that were unacceptably obvious. Two of the first three reports submitted on 29 July recommended prohibition. Vázquez Dodero commented that 'parece una alegoría del Jefe del Estado y el Príncipe D. J. Carlos' ('it looks like an allegory of the Head of State and Prince Juan Carlos'), while Sunyer, listing eighteen pages containing unacceptable material, concluded that 'la intención de la obra es tan clara y los lugares pueden ser tan comunes que no considero oportuno autorizarla' ('the intention of the work is so clear and the references so obvious that I do not consider authorisation appropriate'). Bautista de la Torre agreed, but was more cautious than his colleagues and recommended that the decision be referred to higher authority, as a result of which two further readings were commissioned (AGA 273/69).

Both of the additional reports recommended prohibition. Suevos drew attention to the topicality of the central theme, which was partly accidental. When the play was written in 1968, Prince Juan Carlos had not yet been confirmed as Franco's successor. His official nomination as king-in-waiting, swearing loyalty to the principles of the *Movimiento Nacional*, was made in a law of 22 July 1969, five days after Bohr submitted his application to the censorship office (BOE 1969b). Suddenly, the Hombre's project of reproducing himself and his regime by means of a ruthlessly groomed double looked startlingly close to what the *Caudillo* was planning. The parallel seemed to be cemented by one of the lines marked as problematic in the script, where the Doble attempts to assert his inherited power: 'Haré lo que me dé la real gana. Y mi gana, mi real gana, será la ley y el orden que todos acatarán sin rechistar' ('I'll do as I royally please. And my will, my sovereign will, shall be the law and the order that all must obey without question') (Ruibal 1977b: 97–8).

The decision to ban *El hombre y la mosca* was confirmed on 5 August 1969. On 3 October, Bohr submitted an appeal in which he undertook to ensure that no connection with Spain or current political circumstances would be suggested by the staging, argued that there was no satirical intention, and promised that he and Ruibal would make any amendments that were required (AGA 273/69). Not only were these protestations of innocence disingenuous but the timing was – once again – unfortunate. As the process of obtaining reports from all the remaining members of the Junta dragged on through November and December, Manuel Fraga was replaced by Alfredo Sánchez Bella, which made it even more unlikely that a more lenient attitude might be adopted.

When the Junta finally met on 13 January 1970, the prohibition was ratified by fourteen votes to three. Several censors made a point of praising the quality of the writing and lamenting the fact that the blatant political references obliged them to ban the production. Barceló summed up the problem concisely: 'La situación personal y política que se refleja en la obra es una continua alusión a hechos, personas, actos de la más inmediata realidad circundante, que, pese a la indudable calidad del texto examinado, parece insalvable la norma diecisiete en sus apartados segundo y tercero' ('The personal and political situation reflected in the work refers continuously to facts, persons and actions from the most immediate surrounding reality, as a result of which, despite the text's undoubted quality, article 17, clauses 2 and 3 of the regulations must be brought to bear') (AGA 273/69).[18] As always, what the censors were attempting to gauge was the likely response of audiences. Muelas considered the political intention clumsy, but was convinced that 'el público aun irá más allá y los actores procurarán echar leña al fuego' ('the audience will go even further and the actors will do what they can to add fuel to the fire') (AGA 273/69).

Another attempt to stage *El hombre y la mosca* in Spain was made at an even more politically tense moment six years later.[19] Justo Alonso Osorio submitted an application on 21 June 1976 for a commercial production at the Teatro Marquina in Madrid. On this occasion, history turned in Ruibal's favour: Arias Navarro, the prime minister appointed by the late dictator, was replaced on 3 July by Adolfo Suárez, who appointed Andrés Reguera Guajardo as Ministro de Información y Turismo. The new government quickly began to loosen censorship. The three censors appointed to write new reports on *El hombre y la mosca* were doing so while these momentous changes were taking place. Martínez Ruiz, Mier and Barceló all recommended approval for audiences over eighteen, judging that any threat the play might have posed had become insignificant. Ironically, Barceló now argued that potential links to present political circumstances would be avoided because of the play's distorted representation of reality and 'porque el final no tendría correlación con la historia' ('because the ending would not correspond to historical fact'). Juan Carlos's moves towards democratisation were indeed pointing towards a real-world dénouement very different from the Doble's abortive attempt to exercise the absolute power inherited from his mentor, but the outcome of Spain's transition to democracy was far from settled in early July 1976. Barceló's comment betrays a desire to depoliticise Ruibal's text, consigning it to the past and denying the continuing relevance of what Mier's report described as an 'ataque durísimo a los dictadores' ('extremely hard-hitting attack on dictators') (AGA 273/69).

The censorship board authorised *El hombre y la mosca* on 9 July 1976, without cuts and for audiences over eighteen. Moreover, the Dirección General de Teatro y Espectáculos awarded a subsidy to support Justo Alonso's production. Rehearsals began in March 1977, but the production was abandoned (El País 1977b). Ruibal, disillusioned, returned to the United States. The play was not performed in Spain until 1983, when a bilingual production by the Puerto Rican Traveling Theater transferred from New York.

Ruibal had also experienced official encouragement followed by frustration in the case of *La máquina de pedir* ('The Begging Machine'), a text that envisages an extravagant spectacle parodying global capitalism and Christian ideals of charity. Enrique de la Hoz, Subdirector General de Cultura Popular and head of the government agency Teatros Nacionales y Festivales de España, invited Ruibal in 1968 to submit a play to be performed at a national theatre, with an official subsidy. The text of *La máquina de pedir* was submitted for censorship on 21 October 1969, while the appeal against the banning of *El hombre y la mosca* was being considered. At the same time, De la Hoz instructed Ortiz to consult members of the Comisión Asesora de Teatros Nacionales (Advisory Board for National Theatres, part of the Consejo Superior del Teatro) on the play's suitability for performance at the María Guerrero. Censorship approval was issued on 28 October for audiences over eighteen, without cuts, but on condition that the inspection of the dress rehearsal paid special attention to 'la realización de aquellas escenas que por motivaciones de caracter religioso y erótico pueden ofrecer especiales reparos' ('the staging of those scenes in which religious or erotic elements may be of particular concern') (AGA 358/69). The members of the Comisión Asesora voted four to one in favour of the production, although several of them were unenthusiastic and had concerns about the practicability of the work's complicated staging (AGA Serie O-31/69). However, just as with the earlier play, the consideration of *La máquina de pedir* was overtaken by the end of *apertura* in late October to early November 1969, and the case sank into indefinite *silencio administrativo*. The censorship file contains an interesting exchange of letters from December 1975 and January 1976, in which Ruibal, hoping that the death of the dictator might change the situation, complained about the ministry reneging on the contract to stage his play. The recently appointed Ministro de Información y Turismo, Adolfo Martín-Gamero, promised to investigate: he consulted his subordinates and was advised that the main reason for the failure to go ahead with *La máquina de pedir* had been the extravagance of the proposed staging, which was judged to be too expensive. No further action was taken.

Ruibal's inventive theatre had appeared to be on the verge of a breakthrough in 1968 and 1969, only to be blocked by adverse political circumstances. Another vocal spokesperson for the New Spanish Theatre, Alberto Miralles, also found the development of his work obstructed by the state of exception in early 1969 and the reversal of *apertura* later that year. Having worked with university student groups in the early 1960s, he began teaching in 1966 at the Escuela Superior de Arte Dramático in Barcelona, part of the Instituto del Teatro, and in 1967 formed the Cátaro company with former students.[20] The group was one of the pioneers of the *Teatro Independiente* ('Independent Theatre') movement, which flourished between the late 1960s and mid-1970s. These groups developed new ways of working based on collective creation, improvisation, Brechtian techniques, mime, physical theatre and choral elements, all of which tended to inconvenience the censors, who preferred to deal with fixed scripts by named authors, and staging that adhered predictably to the directions in the text, so that control could be exercised over the end-product. The works written and directed by Miralles with Cátaro were dynamic and variable, sometimes comprising short pieces that could be performed in different combinations and under different titles, usually licensed under *cámara* conditions. As a result, there is a confusing collection of files associated with Miralles in the censorship archive; in some cases, multiple *expedientes* refer to what is essentially the same work.

The group's debut show, first performed at the Instituto del Teatro on 18–20 May 1967, was known as *Espectáculo Cátaro*, or by the titles of its component parts, *La guerra* ('War') and *El hombre* ('Man'), and was later turned into *El hombre es lo que importa* ('Man is What Matters'), *Espectáculo Collage* ('Collage Show') and *El espectáculo no ha terminado* ('The Show's Not Over'). To begin with, authorisation in March 1967 for *sesiones de cámara* was unproblematic. The premiere in Barcelona was followed by performances in Madrid, Valladolid and Palafrugell (Centro de Documentación Teatral 2015). However, authorisation of a performance in Alcoy in February 1968 was denied. All three readers recommended approval but no decision was made at the meeting of the Junta on 5 March. A handwritten note, dated 12 March, tersely recorded: 'No se hace la autorización por orden Superior' ('The licence is not being issued, on superior orders') (AGA 54/67). As the company had given the performance in Alcoy on 27 February without waiting for permission, this retrospective suspension must have been intended to be taken into account in the consideration of future applications. It did not prevent further performances in March–June 1968 but demonstrates the unpredictability with which Independent Theatre groups had to contend.

The growing reputation of Cátaros was boosted by their participation in Adolfo Marsillach's controversial production of *Marat-Sade* in October 1968 (discussed in Chapter 7). A *cámara* performance of *La guerra* in Elche was approved in December, but an application submitted in January 1969 for a performance in Ripollet (Barcelona) was rejected. A national state of exception had been imposed on 25 January to combat what were claimed to be foreign-inspired attempts to disrupt public order (BOE 1969a). Several articles of the *Fuero de los españoles* ('Spanish Bill of Rights') were suspended, including article 12, which ostensibly guaranteed citizens' right to free expression of ideas as long as they did not threaten the fundamental principles of the State (BOE 1945b: 358). The papers for this application are contained in a folder on which it is specified that 'esta autorización no se tramitó, por orden de la Superioridad, debido al Estado de Escepción [*sic*]' ('this permit was not issued, on orders from higher authority, due to the State of Exception'). Five other companies applied for permission to perform one or both pieces in February and March 1969 and

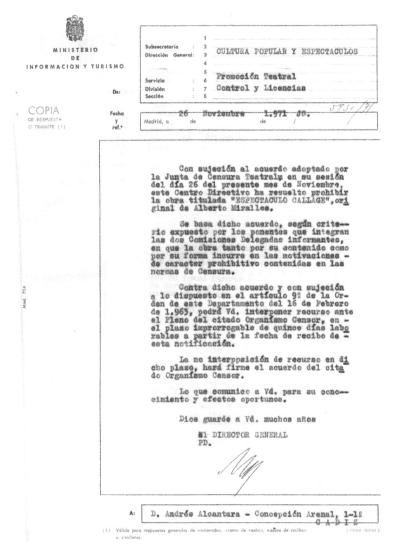

Figure 12: Notification of the prohibition of *Espectáculo collage* (1971)

all were turned down. A note on one of them confirmed that the pieces 'no se autorizan en las actuales circunstancias' ('are not being authorised under current circumstances') (AGA 54/67). Two of these applications were subsequently approved after the end of the state of exception on 25 March.

Taking advantage of the speeding-up of the transition to democracy in July 1976, Miralles submitted an application on 26 July for the Cátaro group to perform an updated version of the work, with the title *El espectáculo no ha terminado*, in a nationwide tour. Some of the censors were still concerned about the possibility of the impassioned protests against global war, tyranny, dehumanisation and exploitation being interpreted as relevant to current national politics, especially as the planned commercial tour would reach a wider audience than earlier *cámara* performances. Six reports were written and the process dragged on into September. In the end, the majority considered that the work no longer presented a significant political risk. Martínez Ruiz commented: 'En realidad, se trata de una acusación totalizante, pero por eso mismo muy universalizada y menos directa, que puede inscribirse en una intelectualización de gran espectáculo' ('In reality, the protest expressed is totalising, which makes it very universal and indirect and amounts to a very intellectualised entertainment') (AGA 1114/76). The licence was issued on 10 September 1976, for audiences over eighteen, without cuts.

The group's best-known production was *Catarocolón*, a satirical demythologisation of Columbus's 'discovery' of the New World.[21] An application in January 1968 for a performance at the Instituto del Teatro in March prompted fierce condemnation from a majority of the members of the Junta de Censura. The targets of Miralles's critique in this case – the history of empire, Isabel the Catholic, the political role of the Church – were more easily identifiable as specifically Spanish and relevant to the regime's construction of a partisan version of national history, as evidenced by the numerous cuts marked in copies of the script in the file. Soria complained that the work was 'una manipulación torpe, entre la parodia y la falsedad, de un gran momento histórico de España [. . .] La representación de esta obra, incluso en sectores minoritarios, creo que constituiría un verdadero escándalo' ('a clumsy manipulation, somewhere between parody and outright falsification, of one of Spain's great historical moments [. . .] The performance of this work, even for a minority audience, would in my view constitute a veritable outrage'). Mampaso conceded that the work had undeniable literary and theatrical value, but described it as an unacceptable attack on 'páginas gloriosas de nuestra Historia' ('glorious pages of our History') (AGA 36/68). The Junta voted on 26 March to ban the work, citing *norma* 14.3 (which prohibits the tendentious falsification of historical facts, personages and settings). The same file contains records of three banned productions of the play by other companies in 1972 and 1973.

The prohibition issued in March 1968 was not the end of the story, however. Later that year, Miralles entered the play – under its alternative title, *Versos de arte menor por un varón ilustre* ('Popular Verses for an Illustrious Gentleman') – for the Sitges Theatre Festival, an officially sponsored event that was rapidly becoming an important showcase for new work and for the regime's display of cultural *apertura*. The fact that the application was specifically for the festival prompted the censors to be less hostile in their assessments. Both reports expressed mild concern about the satirical representation of history but recommended approval solely for Sitges. Martínez Ruiz emphasised that the representation of Queen Isabel must be 'en todo momento digna y no se preste a la hilaridad' ('dignified at all times and not encouraging hilarity') (AGA 209/68). The licence was issued on 16 July 1968, cutting two of Columbus's lines. In one, he complains of the difficulty of winning royal support for his voyage and asks irreverently: '¿Será que el mundo se ha vuelto loco y para conseguir el triunfo hay que leer el "Kempis" en vez de "El Kamasutra" y "Camino" en vez de "Mein Kampff" y "Las moradas" de Santa Teresa, en vez de "Cómo ganar amigos", de Dale Carnegie?' ('Can it be that the world has gone crazy and in order to succeed you have to read Kempis [*The Imitation of Christ*] instead of the *Kama Sutra*, *The Way* [by Josemaría Escrivá, founder of Opus Dei] instead of [Hitler's] *Mein Kampf*, and Saint Teresa's *The Interior Castle* instead of Dale Carnegie's *How to Win Friends and Influence People*?'). In the other, he disparagingly describes Isabel as 'una pobre mujer inepta y orgullosa que refugia su escasa valía en el reducto de un confesionario' ('a poor, proud, inept woman who conceals her limited merits behind the barricade of the confessional').[22]

The group gave two performances in Sitges and won the main festival prize. This success led to further performances in Valladolid, Sabadell and Madrid in November and December. The group continued to perform *Versos de arte menor* in various locations during 1969, 1970 and 1971. The show's popularity on the *cámara* circuit prompted Miralles to attempt a production by Cátaros at the Poliorama in Barcelona in April 1972. The application was accompanied by a note in which Miralles explained that he had carried out self-censorship in order to enable approval for a fully professional commercial production (AGA 209/68). The author's deletions and adaptations marked on one of the typescripts focus mostly on moments in which Columbus claims divine inspiration for his quest, or where the sacred mission is juxtaposed with more worldly motives: the hero gazing heavenwards with a gesture of studied mysticism; the chorus chanting 'Es misión primordial / conseguir nuevos mercados / para evangelizar' ('The primordial mission is to find new markets to evangelise'); the jokey reference to Kempis, *Camino* and *Las moradas*; disrespectful references to Isabel such as 'Virtuosa, mucho corazón y poca cabeza' ('virtuous, a lot of heart but not much head'), and the line about the 'barricade of the confessional' (Miralles 2004: 119, 128, 140, 148). Also removed were a sailor's fanciful remark about the Earth taking the form of a woman's breast and a pun about the need to keep everyone moving, the political significance of which could have been made obvious by gesture or intonation: 'A los españoles siempre les gustó el movimiento' ('Spaniards have always liked [the] movement' (2004: 112, 117). The usual censorial concerns – religion, sex, institutions of the regime, and icons of Catholicism and imperialism – were therefore covered.

Despite the author's careful self-censorship, the work was still judged to be unsuitable for a commercial theatre. Soria considered this version to be a more serious threat than the earlier one and recommended prohibition, and Zubiaurre argued that it flouted *norma* 14.3 (tendentious falsification of history) and should be confined to *cámara*. Bautista de la Torre found the irreverence and the lampooning of Spain's evangelising mission in the Americas unacceptable. He insisted on maintaining the restriction to *cámara*, 'jamás para representaciones normales dada la índole corrosiva del panfleto' ('in no circumstances for normal performances, given the corrosive nature of the invective') (AGA 209/68). At the end of May 1972, the company submitted a lengthy appeal challenging the validity of the application of *norma* 14 and suggesting that other regulations had not been properly followed. It pointed to the number of performances already carried out, the various prizes won and forms of support received from official bodies, and cited favourable opinions published by several theatre critics, including the censor Juan Emilio Aragonés and Gabriel García Espina (the former Director General de Cinematografía y Teatro). Their ingenuity was to no avail, however. Twelve more reports were submitted and the final vote at a meeting of the Junta on 20 June was four for outright prohibition, seven for restriction to *cámara*, and only six for authorisation. The appeal was rejected (AGA 209/68). A revised version of the work finally received its commercial premiere in Madrid in 1981, performed by the Teatro 80 group (Pérez 1996: 261–2).

Looking back on his work with Cátaro, Miralles emphasises their theatrical innovation, the democratic experiment of the group's working methods, and the radicalness of their political protest against both Francoism and broader global processes:

> En los años sesenta los 'cátaros' hacíamos un teatro esencialmente antifranquista. Sin embargo, no se podía criticar abiertamente a la dictadura y dábamos rodeos. Éramos antiamericanos, porque en aquel tiempo se desarrollaba la guerra en Vietnam, y entonces le pegábamos a Franco en el culo del presidente americano. (Miralles 2003: 56)
>
> In the 60s, the theatre the 'Cátaros' were making was essentially anti-Francoist. However, we couldn't criticise the dictatorship openly, so we found indirect ways of doing it. We were anti-American, since the Vietnam War was going on at the time, which was a way of having a go at Franco by laying into the US president.

In some respects, Cátaro and other Independent Theatre groups were successful. They managed to make theatre that protested – sometimes incisively, sometimes naïvely, sometimes openly, sometimes surreptitiously – about a range of issues of national and international scope. They often responded creatively to censorship and generated productive complicity with spectators. They frequently got away with improvising, sometimes with reintroducing prohibited lines or bits of stage business, and occasionally with performing without official approval.[23] They experimented playfully with avant-garde and popular theatrical forms. They attracted new, enthusiastic audiences and used novel spaces, extending the scope and ambition of the *cámara y ensayo* sector. They won prizes and shone at festivals, and were sometimes given official encouragement. Many of the leading figures of the Independent Theatre went on to enjoy successful professional careers in commercial and publicly subsidised theatre after the end of the dictatorship. And yet this exciting little world of radical creativity was tightly constrained. Shows that could have appealed to wider audiences were excluded from the mainstream commercial circuit, while groups were forced to keep reapplying for permission for performances in different locations, to undergo repeated inspections, and to put up with unexpected withdrawals of authorisation.

Independent groups played a particularly influential role in the development of theatre in Catalan from the late 1960s. The importance of amateur and student groups, fringe venues and Church support in Catalonia in the 1940s and 1950s, against a backdrop of mediocre commercial theatre dominated by transfers from Madrid, was noted in Chapter 4. In the 1960s, these factors were intensified and gave rise to a lively and innovative performance culture (in Castilian and Catalan) led by *Teatre Independent* groups and centred in Barcelona on the Institut del Teatre, the Escola d'Art Dramàtic Adrià Gual (EADAG), the commercial CAPSA and Romea theatres, the nightclub La Cova del Drac, and other studio theatres and cultural centres.[24]

Just as the emergence of the New Spanish Theatre was nourished by the rediscovery of Valle-Inclán and Lorca, the growth of independent Catalan theatre in the 1960s and 1970s drew partly on a Catalan avant-garde that originated in the Republican, civil war and post-war periods, especially Joan Oliver, Salvador Espriu, Manuel Pedrolo and Joan Brossa. The Agrupació Dramàtica de Barcelona had played a groundbreaking role in promoting the dramatic output of these writers, staging Espriu's *Antígona* (*Antigone*) and *Primera història d'Esther* (*The Story of Esther*) in 1957; Pedrolo's absurdist *Homes i No* ('Men and No') in 1958; several plays by Oliver in 1958 and 1959; and Brossa's poetic *Or i sal* ('Gold and Salt') in 1961.

The EADAG under the direction of Ricard Salvat continued this process in the 1960s with productions of *Primera història d'Esther* in 1962 and *Antígona* in 1963, and attempts to stage Oliver's *Lloguem-hi cadires* ('Let's Rent Chairs') in 1966 and *La fam* ('Hunger') in 1970, which were both blocked by censorship, due partly to the author's Republican past and partly to the political content of the texts.²⁵ The other promoter of Oliver's work in the 1970s was Ventura Pons, who staged the less politically contestatory works *Allò que tal vegada s'esdevingué* ('What Might Have Happened') and *Bestiari* ('Bestiary') in 1970, and *Vivalda i l'Àfrica tenebrosa* ('Vivalda and Darkest Africa') in 1971, all at the CAPSA.²⁶

The first of these – a satirical version of the story of Adam and Eve – was initially authorised, but Pons and the theatre manager were forced to close down the production after protests published in Falangist and Catholic magazines (Feldman and Foguet 2016: 113–15). As the approval was not formally withdrawn, Pons was able to stage *Allò que tal vegada* with great success in Barcelona in April 1974 (Pons 2011: 103–4). The right-wing campaign against the play was revived, however, when Pons was invited to take his production to Madrid: the police took him in for questioning on the day of the performance and surrounded the theatre, preventing spectators from entering, and beating some of them in the street (Pons 2011: 104–5). *Bestiari* was approved after Pons agreed to the replacement of a monologue described by one censor as 'la escena del mitin catalanista' ('the scene with the Catalanist political meeting') (AGA 508/70). *Vivalda* had earlier been approved for *cámara* only, but this was relaxed in 1971 to allow performances at the CAPSA alongside *Bestiari* (ANC 234/71).

Productions of work by Brossa and Pedrolo were not seriously affected by censorship, but cuts and restrictions on staging were occasionally imposed. Brossa's *El rellotger* ('The Clockmaker') was approved in July 1967 with two cuts that may have been the result of censors over-interpreting the surrealist text. The first must have been taken to be a coded reference to the *Movimiento Nacional*: 'I la roda del moviment, que no engranava bé' ('And the wheel of the movement, which wasn't engaging properly'). The second also read a political message into a discussion of watch components: 'L'agulla esquerra està aixecada enlaire com una arma' ('The hand on the left is sticking up in the air like a weapon') (ANC 199/67). In Pedrolo's *Homes i No*, caged characters struggle for freedom against their mysterious and implacable jailer No, who turns out also to be imprisoned within a larger cage. It was approved in May 1967 for performance by the Teatre Experimental Català group, but subject to a condition intended to discourage links with the political situation in Spain: 'El vestuario no permitirá identificación con la actualidad, ni con fuerzas del orden o ejército concreto' ('The costumes must not suggest any identification with the present time, nor with any specific army or law enforcement agency') (ANC 164/67).

The censors were frequently puzzled by Pedrolo's work, which in most cases led them to consider it of minority interest and politically innocuous (Feldman and Foguet 2016: 171–2). However, *Xit!* ('Shhh!'), a short symbolic piece about the suppression of freedom of expression, was banned in October 1975, a period of heightened tension, as hinted at in Aragonés's report: 'Farsa que en nada se corresponde con la realidad española de ayer mismo, pero quizá inoportuna en las circunstancias de hoy' ('A farce that bears no resemblance to the reality of Spain in the recent past, but which is perhaps inappropriate in current circumstances'). The company's lengthy appeal, submitted on 4 November, made a carefully argued legal case for the invalidity of the decision, on the grounds that the notification of the prohibition did not specify which of the 1963 *normas* had been infringed. The appeal argued that the work was merely a harmless 'chiste escenificado' ('theatrical joke') and suggested that the censors had been carried away by an excess of professional zeal (AGA 539/75). The play was authorised, apparently with little argument, on 2 December, which may be a reflection of the heightened unpredictability of censorship decisions around the time of Franco's death. It was performed by Grup A-71 at the Teatre CAPSA in January 1976.

By the 1960s, the Catalan language itself was rarely an issue for the censors as long as it was not associated with any expression of Catalan nationalism. The ANC file containing censorship notifications for Barcelona from late 1966 and the whole of 1967 shows that of 245 works authorised, sixty-nine (28.2 per cent) were in Catalan. Relatively few were works translated into Catalan: twelve out of the seventy-six plays by foreign authors (15.8 per cent). The file for 1970 contains notifications for 264 works, sixty-four of which (24.2 per cent) were in Catalan. Of sixty-four works by foreign authors, eleven (17.2 per cent) were translated into Catalan. In 1971, the number of plays in Catalan fell to forty-five out of 320 (only 14.1 per cent); only four out of sixty-four works by foreign authors were translated into Catalan (6.2 per cent). The decline in the proportion of productions in Catalan was not directly attributable to censorship: while seven of the ten plays prohibited in

1970 were in Catalan, only four out of eleven banned in 1971 were Catalan scripts.

Although the delays involved in paperwork having to be sent back and forth between Delegaciones Provinciales and Madrid often hampered theatrical activity in Catalonia, there is evidence that officials in Barcelona in the late 1960s and 1970s were sometimes prepared to help theatre companies circumvent censorship restrictions. According to Ventura Pons, permission to perform *Allò que tal vegada s'esdevingué* in Barcelona in 1974 was given by Marita Julbe, the administrator in charge of theatre censorship in the Delegación Provincial, who accepted the original licence from 1970 and remarked that 'no estava pas obligada a remenar calaixos buscant vells expedients' ('she wasn't obliged to rummage around in all the drawers looking for old files') (2011: 103). Pons's production of a Catalan version of Christopher Hampton's *When Did You Last See My Mother?* in 1974 also benefited from the complicity of Julbe, who arranged for the application to be sent to Madrid when Manuel Fraga de Lis, the strict head of the Negociado de Licencias (the department that issued licences once authorisation was confirmed by the Junta de Censura), was away from the office (Pons 2011: 111).

The director Josep Anton Codina, who worked in the EADAG between 1963 and 1967, also remembers Julbe and several other local MIT officials being surprisingly helpful. He had the impression that both dress rehearsal inspections and the monitoring of performances tended to be less rigorous in Barcelona than in Madrid, which meant that companies more frequently got away with restoring lines cut from the script by the censors in Madrid. Having left the EADAG following a disagreement with Salvat over whether to risk keeping an important line that had been cut by the inspectors of the dress rehearsal of *Balades del clam i la fam* ('Ballads of Hunger and Protest') by Maria Aurèlia Capmany and Xavier Fàbregas in 1967, Codina staged musical shows at the cabaret La Cova del Drac. These were billed as *varietats* ('musical variety shows'), as responsibility for the censorship of this genre was largely left to the Delegación Provincial: 'Marita Julbe hacía la vista gorda a veces, dejando pasar como "variedades" espectáculos teatrales que sí tenían diálogo' ('Marita Julbe used to turn a blind eye, letting productions go through as "variety" when they did in fact contain dialogue') (Codina 2012).

La Cova del Drac was a key centre of Catalan counterculture, also hosting concerts by leading singer-songwriters of the *Nova Cançó* (New Song), plays by Capmany, and performances by the theatre collective Els Joglars. Making innovative use of mime, Els Joglars took advantage of the freedom afforded to the venue and were rarely troubled by censorship. Their leader, Albert Boadella, suggests that the censors did not take their work seriously: 'Que la censura fuera relativamente tolerante con sus contenidos, quizá era porque les parecía teatro infantil' ('The fact that censorship was relatively tolerant towards its content may have been because they saw it as children's theatre') (2001: 153). However, the enthusiasm with which La Cova del Drac promoted cultural expression in Catalan occasionally provoked repressive action by the authorities: 'Un día nos comunicaron que nos cerraban el local. Fui a ver al comisario del barrio. Me dijo: "Mire, por nosotros pueden hacer strip-tease y cosas atrevidas que no tendrán problemas, pero si siguen con eso del catalán . . ."' ('One day they announced that they were closing the venue down. I went to see the police inspector. He said to me: "Look, as far as we're concerned you can put on stripteases and other racy stuff and there'll be no trouble, but if you insist on doing things in Catalan . . ."') (Josep Maria Espinàs quoted in Vila-Sanjuán 2011).

The links between Catalan language, cultural identity and nationalism are thoughtfully interrogated in several of Josep Maria Benet i Jornet's plays.[27] His imaginary territory of Drudània, impossibly situated somewhere between Greece and Albania and enclosed within a well-known state (Benet i Jornet 1970: 117), its language and cultural traditions almost erased by assimilation into *la Integració* ('the Integration'), first features in *Cançons perdudes* ('Lost Songs') written in 1968. When Salvat applied on 15 June 1968 for permission for the EADAG to perform this play, the censors had little difficulty in identifying Drudània as Catalonia. Aragonés described the play as clearly separatist, and Pardo saw the intention as transparent: 'Drudania quiere representar a Cataluña, sin lugar a duda. La comedia tiene un marcado carácter de protesta contra la integración de Cataluña en España' ('Drudania is meant to represent Catalonia, without a doubt. The play is a clear expression of protest against the integration of Catalonia into Spain'). Barceló acknowledged those links but made a more critically astute reading of the political implications, arguing that 'la solución no es en modo alguno de índole "separatista", sino todo lo contrario' ('the outcome is not at all separatist in nature but exactly the opposite'), since the leading representatives of Drudanian identity end up dead and the people resign themselves to subjugation (AGA 195/68). None of the censors proposed outright prohibition, judging that the message could be sufficiently neutralised by cutting lines such as 'Hem perdut finalment la llengua i s'han atenuat els nostres sentiments de poble: si, aquesta es la part negativa' ('We've ended up losing our language and our sense of identity as a people has been ground down: yes, that's the negative part') (Benet i Jornet 1970: 133). Authorisation was given on 23 July for audiences over eighteen, with the deletion of five short phrases and an extended passage of almost a page.

The EADAG production of *Cançons perdudes* did not go ahead. When the independent theatre group La Tartana applied for permission for a production in Reus in 1970, it was approved without cuts, the debate about Catalan identity appearing to provoke much less concern than in 1968. Barceló suggested that the work could be seen as 'un lamento por lo catalán perdido pero, en todo caso, está hecho con dignidad y respeto, sin politizaciones' ('a lament for lost Catalanness, but in any case, it is done with dignity and respect, without being over-politicised'). Aragonés agreed, and disingenuously argued that there was no need for cuts because declarations such as 'we've lost our language' disproved themselves simply by being uttered in Catalan (AGA 195/68). La Tartana performed *Cançons perdudes* at the Teatre Estudi de Reus in January 1971.

The only play by Benet i Jornet to be banned was *L'ocell Fènix a Catalunya, o Alguns papers de l'auca* ('The Phoenix in Catalonia, or Characters from a Comic-Strip'), a short absurdist play written in 1970, inspired by Santiago Rusiñol's classic novel *L'auca del senyor Esteve* (*The Epic Life of Mr Esteve*), as well as by the tradition of using the phoenix as an emblem of the nineteenth-century *Renaixença* (the Catalan cultural and political renaissance). Although the text appears to be less direct than the earlier work in its expression of Catalanism, an application for a performance in June 1971 by an amateur company in Cornellà de Llobregat was refused. Three of the four censors who reported on the text were initially inclined to authorise it for *cámara* only, but there were concerns about its 'marcado tufillo separatista' ('strong whiff of separatism'). Zubiaurre expressed concern about the work's 'oportunidad' ('opportuneness') – a term normally used to refer to political sensitivity in particular circumstances. An intensification of Catalanist opposition to Francoism had been triggered by the well-publicised protest at the monastery of Montserrat in December 1970. Benet i Jornet was one of almost 300 writers, artists and intellectuals who locked themselves in the chapel for three days and issued a manifesto demanding civil rights and self-determination for the Basques and Catalans. It may have been this climate of increased tension that aroused Zubiaurre's concern about the play's 'natural efecto en el público de hoy' ('natural effect on an audience at the moment') and led to the decision to prohibit it (AGA 297/71). The censors appeared to be unaware that the company had already performed the work without repercussions under a different title, *Mort i resurrecció del senyor Esteve* ('Death and Resurrection of Mr Esteve') (Feldman and Foguet 2016: 219).

In general, avant-garde and independent theatre may not have suffered more severely from censorship than other genres, but its public impact was certainly limited by the regime's strategy of confining it to the *cámara y ensayo* circuit and other small venues. For some authors, directors and companies, outside the mainstream commercial market was exactly where they wanted to be, developing new relationships with audiences that were younger, more liberal and more socially diverse. With the complicity of those audiences, the kinds of theatre discussed in this chapter were the most creative in resisting and discrediting censorship, and in the process, exploring ways of redefining the relationship between theatre and politics. Our case study for this chapter is an iconic example of the *Teatro Independiente* posing an inventive and impudent challenge to the dead hand of Francoist cultural control.

Case study

Castañuela 70, by Tábano and Las Madres del Cordero
Teatro Marquina (Madrid), 21 June 1970, and Teatro de la Comedia (Madrid), 28 August 1970

The collective Tábano was formed in 1967 by Juan Margallo, Enriqueta Carballeira, Alberto Alonso, and the playwright and director José Luis Alonso de Santos. The group's name, meaning 'gadfly', evoked Socrates's defiant characterisation of his role as a public goad in ancient Athens, as recounted in Plato's *Apology*. Their first clash with the authorities was provoked by the unauthorised performance of *El juego de los dominantes* ('The Domination Game'), a collective creation inspired by Artaud, in which characters were arbitrarily punished for committing inexplicably prohibited acts, and a brutal interrogation consisted of the absurd recitation by torturers and victim of a biography of José María Pemán. The group managed to give three performances at a university residence in Madrid before the production was closed down and a fine imposed (Margallo 2006: 139–42 and Longoni 2015: 315–16).

Moving away from the Theatre of Cruelty aesthetic of the earlier piece, *Castañuela 70* was devised with the band Las Madres del Cordero in the style of a traditional *revista*. In a deceptively frivolous and populist manner calculated to 'buscar la complicidad del público para burlar la censura' ('seek the complicity of the audience in order to evade censorship') (Margallo 2006: 149), the songs and sketches satirised bourgeois and Catholic values, consumerism, folk culture stereotypes, the alienating effect of mass media and the country's subservience to US imperialism. The feature of a conventional *revista* that would normally provoke censorial intervention – the display of female flesh – was carefully avoided, however.

The show was initially authorised on 2 June 1970 under the title *Tic... tac... un, dos, tres* ('Tick-Tock, One, Two, Three') for a single *cámara* performance as part of a Teatro Nacional de Cámara y Ensayo series at the Teatro Marquina in Madrid. The censors were not fooled by the *revista* form. Soria perceived 'una intención crítica y paródica' ('a critical, parodic intention'), and Bautista de la Torre and Muelas recommended an especially strict inspection of the dress rehearsal (AGA 206/70). All three, together with José María Ortiz, insisted on the suppression of the whole of the final scene, which satirised Catholic education and ended with an ironic song, performed in flamenco costumes, parodying the regime's nationalistic rhetoric of 'Spain is different':

Dónde vas a ir que mejor estés.
Piénsalo un momento, luego quédate.
No sé por qué gritan tanto,
hablando de democracias,

esos inventos modernos
siempre acaban en desgracia.
(Tábano and Las Madres del Cordero 2006: 440)

Where can you go where you'll be better off than here? Think about it for a moment, then stick around. I don't know why they rant on so much about democracy, those modern inventions always end in tears.

When the company replaced the deleted material with a less localised sketch about mindless consumerism, the licence was reissued on 16 June without requiring cuts. The single performance at the Marquina, in a double bill following *Oraciones laicas del siglo XX* ('Secular Prayers of the 20th Century') by the student company Taller 1, went ahead in a feverish atmosphere of subversive excitement. The theatre was packed with mostly young spectators. Taller 1 caused a stir by prefacing their performance with a reading of their censorship notification, including details of cuts made to the script. The self-consciously Artaudian style of their piece tested the patience of the audience and they were booed off the stage (Margallo 2006: 148). The more playful satire of *Castañuela 70* came as a welcome contrast and was received with enthusiasm:

> El grupo 'Tábano' alegró a los espectadores, les hizo reír mucho y aplaudir calurosamente con su parodia de revista musical 'Castañuela 70', compuesta de números llenos de ironía, desenfado, buen humor y aguda crítica, a la que no escapan ni acontecimientos actuales ni criterios políticos o propagandas. (López Sancho 1970a)

> Tábano delighted the spectators, making them a laugh a lot and applaud warmly, with their parody of a musical comedy, *Castanets 70*. The show is made up of a series of numbers full of irony, levity, good humour and sharp criticism, focusing on current affairs, political issues and propaganda.

Twelve further *cámara* performances followed in Madrid and various locations in Catalonia in July 1970, including a successful night at the Teatro Romea in Barcelona. Approval for these performances and for the change of title to *Castañuela 70* was given without any fuss. However, an attempt by the company to obtain permission for the reintroduction of the 'Dónde vas a ir que mejor estés' song was rebuffed by the censors on 28 July, after most of these performances had taken place. Soria remarked that the subversive intention was obvious, and Muelas declared: 'Debe prohibirse esta torpe visión de España' ('This crass vision of Spain should be banned') (AGA 206/70).

The success of these performances led to an application on 30 July for a commercial production at the Teatro de la Comedia in Madrid. Although Vasallo recommended authorisation with cuts, Martínez Ruiz proposed that it should be restricted to *cámara* performances. Zubiaurre argued that the impact of references to political issues such as the exploitation of agricultural workers and corruption, or the cynical view of treaties with the United States and the role of the media, would be made more dangerous by the appeal to a larger lowbrow public: 'La absoluta falta de calidad artística de la pieza, su crítica facilona, plebeya y burda atraerían a públicos de bajo nivel, lo que empeoraría el efecto' ('The piece's total lack of artistic quality and its facile, crude and plebeian criticism would attract low-level audiences, which would exacerbate the effect') (AGA 206/70).

Two more reports were commissioned, which offered more relaxed assessments of the risk. Tejedor recommended approval with one cut, while Aragonés was happy to authorise the production without any cuts. The production was approved on 18 August for audiences over eighteen, with substantial cuts on seven pages and, unusually for a commercial authorisation, a limit on the length of the run – it was specified that the licence was valid only until 3 October. The cuts included the opening song (urging spectators to open their eyes and see Spain as it really is); most of the song 'La caída del imperio romano' ('The fall of the Roman Empire'), in which the emperor Meconio is persuaded to sign a deal with the CIA offering protection from barbaric Siberians in exchange for territory and weapons; a parody of the temptation in the Garden of Eden; and most of a sketch satirising the traditional patriarchal family – and implicitly Franco's role as father and captain of the nation. In this sketch, as the son observes that the ship of the family is going down in a storm, the father declares 'Mientras yo lleve el timón, en esta casa no hay peligro' ('As long as I'm at the helm, there's no danger in this house') (AGA 206/70, Tábano and Las Madres del Cordero 2006: 434).

The approval of the closing song ('Dónde vas a ir que mejor estés'), was now left to the judgement of the Delegado Provincial. Margallo gives a vivid account of the negotiation with the inspectors after the dress rehearsal. They objected not to the song itself but to the plywood panel painted with the figures of a footballer, a bullfighter, a flamenco dancer, a businessman, a priest and a nun, behind which the cast stood with their heads showing. The company immediately agreed to remove the priest and the nun from the line-up, but did so in a way that made the suppression obvious: 'Los tachamos al estilo con que los servicios de limpieza borraban las consignas políticas que aparecían en las paredes. ¿Y qué pasó? ¡Que fue peor! Cuando el panel bajaba para la canción final, el público se daba cuenta de que estaban censuradas las dos figuras y gritaba contra la censura' ('We roughly painted over them in the way that official cleaning services used to blot out political graffiti that appeared on walls. And what happened? It was even worse! When the panel came down for the final song, the audience saw that those two figures had been censored and shouted protests against censorship') (2006: 151). The company must have attempted to keep the 'Fall of the Roman Empire' song in the show, since this was also rejected by the inspectors. Again, the company agreed to remove it, but did so in a way that drew attention to the censorship, singing 'La, la, la, la. . .' in place of the lyrics.

The show opened on 21 August 1970 to acclaim and controversy. It played to rowdy full houses, with officials monitoring virtually every performance, a pair of policemen stationed in the gallery, and hecklers trying to disrupt proceedings:

> Tábano y las Madres del Cordero divirtieron mucho, entusiasmaron al público y derrotaron estrepitosamente a los grupos de reventadores que desde el primer cuadro intentaron aguar la representación. Las ovaciones, los bravos y los aplausos demostraron que el público apreciaba su juvenil humor y su sátira bien intencionada. (López Sancho 1970b)
>
> Tábano and Las Madres del Cordero were tremendously entertaining. They delighted the public and completely routed the troublemakers who tried to disrupt the performance right from the first scene. The cheers and the applause demonstrated that the audience appreciated the groups' youthful humour and well-meaning satire.

Margallo recalls that repeated warnings were received from the censorship office, imposing new conditions and threatening to withdraw the licence (2006: 151). The censorship file contains an inspection report written on 17 September, which noted 'las extralimitaciones que en el texto e interpretación del mismo hacían los

Figure 13: Photograph by Martín Santos Yubero of a performance of *Castañuela 70* (1970)

actores' ('the liberties that the actors were taking with the script and their performances'). The inspectors had observed some irregularities but decided not to take formal action; they merely advised the company that if the show was not toned down, permission would not be given for future bookings (AGA 206/70).

Events took an alarming turn during the late-night performance on 27 September, after seventy-four performances. The company was expecting trouble, as it was known that members of the extreme right-wing Catholic group Guerrilleros de Cristo Rey (Warriors of Christ the King) had been showing an interest in the production, and the usual police presence was suspiciously missing (Margallo 2006: 152). The press reported the incident as a clash between left and right-wing agitators:

> Desde el último piso del teatro –que estaba abarrotado de público, en su mayoría jóvenes– se lanzaron miles de octavillas de tipo comunista. Antes de caer al patio de butacas, un grupo de jóvenes –que ya se habían hecho notar al 'patear' la obra– comenzó a proferir gritos de '¡Arriba España!', y otros, y casi simultáneamente se produjeron agresiones a algunos de los espectadores que leían los panfletos. (Europa Press 1970)

Thousands of leaflets of a communist nature were thrown from the top gallery of the theatre, which was crammed with spectators, most of them young. Before the leaflets had reached the stalls, another group of young people, who had already been booing the performance, began to shout 'Long live Spain!' and similar slogans. At more or less the same time, some of the spectators who were reading the leaflets were attacked.

Trancón's analysis of *Castañuela 70* includes a reproduction of the typewritten leaflet (2006: 124), which purported to be a statement by a non-existent Marxist-Leninist-Maoist Revolutionary Front. It condemned the show for the feebleness of its critique of dictatorship and capitalism, and called for violent revolution. The following day, the company received an order from the Dirección General de Seguridad to close down the production 'por alteración del orden público' ('for disturbance of public order') (Margallo 2006: 153). They were convinced that the whole episode was set up by the authorities. Margallo reports that when the theatre management's lawyer went to the Dirección General de Seguridad to appeal against the closure, he was told not to bother, since 'el panfleto lo hemos editado aquí' ('we printed the leaflet ourselves here') (2006: 153). The original authorisation for *cámara* was in principle still valid, but when Tábano applied for permission to perform the show at the Lido in Madrid in October 1970, the application was turned down on the grounds that the venue was not licensed for *cámara y ensayo* productions.

Tábano's next production, *Piensa mal y acertarás* ('Think the Worst and You'll Be Right'), another musical satire in a similar style to be performed at the Teatro Beatriz in Madrid, was judged to be a more serious threat and banned in April 1971. In his report Aragonés seems to confirm the suspicion that the incident at the Teatro de la Comedia was a set-up by the Dirección General de Seguridad: 'Está indicada la prohibición, no nos vaya a enmendar la plana otro Ministerio, como en *Castañuela 70*' ('Prohibition seems to be the way to go, so that we don't find ourselves outflanked by another Ministry, as happened with *Castañuela 70*') (AGA 155/71). The application for their version of *El retablo del flautista* (*The Legend of the Piper*) by Jordi Teixidor was approved in June 1971, but the day after the opening at the Teatro Reina Victoria in Madrid on 4 August, the production was banned on the grounds of 'graves extralimitaciones de interpretación, acción, montaje y dirección escénica' ('serious excesses in the performances, action, staging and direction') (AGA 293/71).

While their work was repeatedly being blocked in Spain, Tábano and Las Madres del Cordero took *Castañuela 70* on tours around Europe and Latin America in 1971 and 1973, performing in thirty-eight different locations and reaching a total of over 86,000 spectators (Tábano and Las Madres del Cordero 2006: 154–209). Many of those spectators were Spanish emigrants, including political exiles, and the tours cemented an international reputation for Tábano as heroes of the anti-Francoist counterculture. This did not help back home, however. A final attempt to obtain approval for a commercial production of *Castañuela 70* in November 1974 was unsuccessful. The application was in the name of Ángel Frías Cayuela, mentioning Tábano only as the author of the text, which prompted Ortiz to check the identity of the company. Mampaso's report argued that caution was required on account of 'los antecedentes del espectáculo y las pocas garantías que ofrece el grupo Tábano para una responsable aceptación de los condicionamientos que la autorización le imponga' ('the track record of the show and the lack of any guarantee that Tábano would respect the conditions attached to authorisation'). The censors agreed that a strict inspection should be enough to limit the danger and approval was given on 13 December, but *la Superioridad* must have intervened, since a memo records that the application and the copies of the script were to be archived, consigning the production to *silencio administrativo* (AGA 206/70).

Castañuela 70 may not have been the most hard-hitting or thought-provoking critique of the ideological, social and cultural values of late Francoism. However, its subversive popularity and the impudence with which Tábano and Las Madres del Cordero continuously challenged the constraints imposed on them probably did more than any other theatrical production of the time to discredit the creaking edifice of authoritarian censorship.

Notes
1 For an account of Valle-Inclán's political and cultural activities during the Republic, see Dougherty (1986).
2 See also Paz Gago (2012), who places the battles with censors within a broader context of the conception and reception of productions of Valle-Inclán's plays.

3   The reports are quoted in full in Pérez-Rasilla and Soria Tomás (2011: 5).
4   See Huerta Calvo (2019: 41–9) on critical views and performances of Lorca's work in Spain in the 1940s; and Vilches de Frutos (2008) and Delgado (2008) for discussions of the 'afterlives' of the author and his work.
5   See Aznar Soler (2010: 577–8) for further details of this performance.
6   Santos Sánchez (2011a) discusses this case in detail.
7   The flag embroidered by Mariana is usually understood to be purple, with a green triangle in the middle surrounded by the words 'Ley, Libertad, Igualdad' ('Law, Liberty, Equality'). To replace this with the red, yellow and purple tricolour of the Second Republic certainly would have been provocative.
8   Robles Piquer's claim that the crime had never been investigated seems disingenuous: he must have been aware of the police report of July 1965 which confirmed that Lorca had been shot by Nationalist troops on the orders of the Civil Governor (quoted in Gibson 2018).
9   Muñoz Cáliz (2010) discusses the censorship of all Alberti's plays in detail, and of the work of other exiled playwrights. See also Isabel-Estrada (2002).
10 This case is discussed in detail by Muñoz Cáliz (2010: 169–76) and Santos Sánchez (2016).
11 A similar challenge was posed by theatrical adaptations of Fernando de Rojas's bawdy classic *La Celestina*, which repeatedly suffered self-censorship by adaptors (including Luis Escobar) and censorship by the authorities between 1940 and 1965. See Bastianes (2018).
12 The censorship of Arrabal's theatre is discussed in detail by Muñoz Cáliz (2005: 118–19 and 233–52) and O'Leary (2008).
13 For discussion of this term, see Chapter 5.
14 See Aggor (2006) for a penetrating analysis of Nieva's theatre and its roots in Valle-Inclán and Postismo.
15 The censorship of Nieva's theatre is discussed in detail by Muñoz Cáliz (2005: 345–65).
16 For surveys of the New Spanish Theatre, see Miralles (1979), Pörtl (1986), Ruiz Ramón (1989: 527–71) and Cornago Bernal (1999).
17 The case is discussed in Thompson (2007b).
18 These clauses forbade anything that constituted an attack on the fundamental principles of the State, the dignity of the nation and the internal or external security of the country, or on the person of the Head of State (BOE 1963a: 3930).
19 The play had been premiered in English at the State University of New York Binghamton in 1971 (see Gillespie 1972).

Experimental, Avant-Garde and Independent Theatre 325

20 The Institute is now usually referred to in Catalan (Institut del Teatre), but the official name during the dictatorship was the Castilian form.
21 This play is discussed by Thompson (1993), and its censorship history by Santos Sánchez (2011b).
22 *Teatro escogido* edition (Miralles 2004: 140, 148).
23 In an interview for our project, López Mozo mentions his own *Collage occidental* ('Western Collage') and productions by Tábano and Teatro Lebrijano as instances of bypassing censorship altogether (2010). Feuillastre (2019) gives further examples.
24 A lively first-hand account of the development of this cultural phenomenon from the 1950s to the 1980s is provided by Muñoz Pujol (2009).
25 The censorship of these and other works by Oliver is examined in Feldman and Foguet (2016: 97–138).
26 Pons has worked in film since 1977.
27 For discussion of the censorship of productions and editions of Benet i Jornet's works, see Feldman and Foguet (2016: 203–36).

Chapter 7

The Censorship of Foreign Theatre: From Taming the Text to Disruptive Drama

Foreign versus domestic theatre

Spanish playwrights during the dictatorship often complained that they were more harshly treated by the censors than their foreign counterparts, a perception that the documents held in the censorship archives seem to confirm. This disparity of treatment had complex and contradictory roots. Members and supporters of the regime expressed a curious mixture of hostility towards the foreign and a dependence on it; a nationalistic and at times xenophobic rhetoric of Spanish superiority, coupled with a sense of cultural isolation; and, as revealed by the censors' reports, a certain feeling of inferiority. Playwright José María Rodríguez Méndez, writing about the long-term legacy of the regime's cultural policies, complained of the negative impact on homegrown Spanish theatre of this leniency towards the foreign (1974: 83). Spanish authors learned to play safe and avoid controversial themes and practices, while these were tolerated in foreign-authored drama. This chapter shows that, although European classics and evasionist or 'safe' dramas were staged throughout the dictatorship, an interesting pattern can be traced in terms of a general movement over time from adaptation to Spanish norms and values, through the emergence of a challenge to the status quo limited by what it was possible to stage, to a more intentionally disruptive phase, involving translations of newer foreign works.

Foreign drama was attractive to practitioners and spectators for several reasons. Many of those involved in running the state theatres were interested in reform and development, and they staged foreign drama in order to showcase certain trends absent in Spain. Sometimes it reflected a business decision by producers, assuming that a hit from Broadway or the West End (especially if already adapted for cinema) would be a success in Madrid and Barcelona. There was also a certain demand for canonical foreign works to satisfy the public's image of itself as cosmopolitan and sophisticated. Moreover, foreign drama was often considered less problematic than domestic fare, as it could be argued that it did not reflect badly on Spanish national identity, even when representing values or ideas that were anathema to the regime. This trend fits with translation theorist Maria Tymoczko's general observation that 'translation is often less controlled than cultural production from within a culture itself' (2009: 26). Yet, under a regime that was so concerned with a unified national identity and with stability, Michelle Woods's notion that translations are targeted by censors 'because they tend to challenge the "natural" or normative order of things' (2012: 3), must also be considered, as must the ideas of Lawrence Venuti (1995 and 2008), Mona Baker (2007), Tymoczko (2010) and others on the politics of translation. In short, the picture is a complicated one and, as this chapter shows, foreign drama was used politically, both to support and to attack the regime, which worked in a variety of ways.

While foreign drama was not a new phenomenon in Francoist Spain and there was an established tradition of translations, rewritings and adaptations in the decades preceding the dictatorship, most of this was neither experimental nor political. Nevertheless, we can discern a precedent of the use of foreign theatre to influence and attempt to change the Spanish stage. As we saw in Chapter 2, avant-garde theatre groups in the early twentieth century experimented with forms and ideas imported from abroad. Then, with the declaration of the Second Republic came an increase in productions of foreign theatre allied to socialist politics. In fact, it was even used as a tool to inculcate radical political ideas into Spain by agitprop collectives such as the Nosotros Group.[1] Although the status of foreign drama underwent significant transformation during the Franco period, by tracing developments in its staging and censorship, we can analyse how it was used strategically. We can therefore come to some conclusions regarding its importance in the public representation of alternative ideas about political, social and moral values.

The role of translation (as neutral, censoring or politically activist) in shaping and presenting a public narrative (sometimes at odds with the official one) and influencing how certain social groups were publicly perceived was important, as was its function in linking a foreign narrative to contemporary issues in Spain.[2] Before considering this, however, it is worth contemplating the other factors at play, namely the directors at the helm of the National Theatres; the Teatro Español Universitario and the creation of the Teatro Nacional de Cámara y Ensayo; the special relationship with the United States; the easing of censorship during the *apertura* period of the 1960s and the growth in independent and experimental theatre groups; and the regime's concern for reputation, both its own and that of the foreign dramatists.

The Teatro Español and the Teatro María Guerrero were designated national theatres in March 1940 and played a significant role in the staging of foreign drama in Spain (Vilches de Frutos 1998 and Pérez-Rasilla 2000). The men running the theatres were appointed by the regime and were tolerated – if not favoured – by it, which gave them a certain influence when negotiating with the censors. Moreover, as people who were ardent champions of theatre, they often went beyond their conservative remit and supported thought-provoking foreign drama.

Another important factor was the establishment in 1954 of the Teatro Nacional de Cámara y Ensayo, initially directed by Modesto Higueras, which drew on the expertise and personnel of many pre-existing independent theatre groups but – crucially – had the imprimatur of the state.[3] Higueras's experience of student and independent theatre allowed him to form a bridge between more experimental drama and the state-sanctioned theatre and to gradually introduce more radical works onto the national stage (Castro Jiménez 2018). In fact, much of what might be termed politically, socially or morally challenging to the values of the regime was brought in via the *teatros de cámara* and many of the directors who helped to advance new ideas – both theatrical and political – in the Spanish stage throughout the dictatorship came up from the ranks of university, club, and other independent theatre groups.

Also worth considering is the special relationship that Spain enjoyed with the United States following the signing of the Pact of Madrid in 1953. This led to a greater tolerance of American ideas and values, including in the arts.[4] Loyalty to the regime became compatible with a more outward-looking view and north-American influence was increasingly accepted. Some in the theatre took advantage of this new state of affairs. American dramas reflecting ideas and morals alien to the regime's traditional values were domesticated to the degree considered necessary to stage them in Spain; this stressed the foreignness of problematic issues, while still bringing alternative ideas into the public sphere. It was in this altered atmosphere of a new-found political alliance between Spain and the United States that dramas by such international figures as Arthur Miller, Tennessee Williams, Eugene O'Neill and Thornton Wilder made it to the national and commercial stages, albeit in bowdlerised form.

The later growth in more overtly political translations in Spain coincided with the liberal phase of so-called *apertura* (1962–9), described by one of its authors, Director General José María García Escudero, as 'censura inteligente' ('intelligent censorship') (1978a: 46). At the same time, Spain saw the continued growth of independent and experimental theatre groups, an increase in theatre festivals and a rise in opposition to the regime. Clamp-downs on home-grown criticism of the regime led some politicised Spanish writers to seek alternative ways of communicating their message to an audience. In this context, translations and versions of foreign plays were created by some as an indirect way to comment on the contemporary political moment.

But they had to contend with the censors, whose decision to expurgate a foreign play was at times based on the reputation or notoriety of the original author, or of the translator or adaptor, rather than the quality of the work. Reputation worked in two ways, however, and it was also linked to the regime's self-image and concern about how it might be perceived abroad. This was sometimes exploited in negotiations between translators or directors and the censors, and the archives show evidence of how the prestige of foreign plays and dramatists outside Spain was used as an argument in favour of authorisation. This worked particularly when the regime's political interests lay in further alliances with Europe, as international press stories about the censorship of globally feted dramatists did the regime's reputation no good.[5]

Despite the neutralising and sanitising efforts of the censors and some translators, other translators, directors and theatre practitioners were able to use foreign texts, with their distance from the domestic political circumstance, to bring into the public sphere a series of taboo subjects. These included criticism of the regime and its supporters; denunciation of repression and its consequences; discussion of rebellion and political violence; and explorations of alternative visions of society and sexual morality. Of course, it can also be argued that the introduction of challenging foreign theatre, often through the *teatros de cámara*, was simply the regime's canny way of managing the opposition to its rule. Although they functioned as a liberal theatre space where new and challenging ideas could be represented, the *teatros de cámara* were also used strategically by the regime to curb the growing voice of opposition and to claim a degree of liberalism that was in reality very contained (Zatlin 1999: 228).

The role of translation and adaptation

Susan Bassnett argues that 'just as the norms and constraints of the source culture play their part in the creation of the source text, so the norms and conventions of the target culture play their inevitable role in the creation of the translation' (1998: 93). When 'the norms and conventions of the target culture' are set by a dictatorial regime, such as in Spain under Franco, then translation becomes a political act – either of complicity or of resistance. Translation is rarely neutral (Baker 2005: 12 and Venuti 1995: 18). As Rundle and Sturge suggest, 'by importing ideas, genres and fragments of different cultural worlds, translations will affirm or attack domestic realities' (2010: 4). Any analysis of foreign theatre in Spain must therefore reflect on the role and agency of the translator.

In Spain, translators and adaptors worked within the constraints imposed by the regime, the theatre directors and managers, and themselves. As Tymoczko argues, 'a translator's sensitivity to norms, especially when intuitive or subconscious, can easily slide into being (often unconsciously) submissive to and collusive with dominant cultural norms (especially those of the target culture)'

(2009: 37). Hence, through a combination of coercive pressure and conscious or unconscious self-regulation, much of the foreign drama presented to the censorship offices reflected, or did not contest, the official values of the regime. Yet this was not the only way in which translation was used: at times adaptations of foreign plays embodied an act of subversion, or a means to evade restrictions applied to domestic works. They became an attempt to create or reinforce countercultural identities, by introducing alternative ideas into the target culture. While temporal and geographical contexts can distance a play from the domestic situation, the *ideas* about social justice, class and revolt that are presented within the source texts are not culturally bound. They can evoke other time periods and struggles, and activate what Mona Baker has termed 'public narratives' that are already familiar to the target audience (2007: 165).

Translators and adaptors working under the dictatorship ranged from pro-regime, to *posibilista* (staging what was possible within the restrictions of censorship), to actively anti-regime. Not all translators or adaptors fit neatly into a single category, however, and some balanced evasive, amusing fare with more challenging pieces.[6] As with theatre directors involved in the staging of foreign drama, the relationships of translators or adaptors with the regime had some bearing on their success. It is also worth remembering that even those who sanitised and neutralised foreign drama for domestic consumption were generally motivated by their desire to improve the Spanish theatre, regardless of their politics.

In some cases the translator was invisible, sometimes because of low status, although at times also for political expediency. In such cases, the AGA represents an invaluable source of data, as applications for staging had to include the name of the translator or adaptor of any foreign play. Interestingly, however, the documents show that these sections were not always completed by the applicant (Merino Álvarez 2016: 38). Some translators were complicit in their invisibility, as to draw attention to themselves might also place a spotlight on their left-wing politics and put their livelihood at risk. Arturo del Hoyo revealed in an interview in 1997 that several supposed enemies of the state continued to work as translators, albeit unnamed, for Spanish publishing houses during the dictatorship (Rodríguez Espinosa 1997; see also Pérez López de Heredia 2004: 121). Moreover, Merino Álvarez tells us that José Méndez

Herrera, a professional translator before the war, continued his work from exile and was among the most prolific translators of theatre during the dictatorship (2016: 39). Yet not all were invisible: in the case of adaptors in particular, especially when they were well-known authors or directors, their names were often used as part of a process of 'framing' the play, presenting it in a particular way with an eye either to appeasing the censors or to challenging the regime.

To add to the complexity of analysing the reception of foreign theatre in Spain, some productions were based on texts that had been translated elsewhere (often Latin America), or had been translated before the dictatorship and, therefore, in different political circumstances not subject to the normative pressures imposed by the regime.[7] Such translations could be considered neutral in the context of the regime, due to their temporal or geographical distance from the dictatorship. They were, however, censored again when used for a contemporary production, and were sometimes used as source material for new versions of plays.[8]

This echoed another common practice, as Merino Álvarez has shown, which was the contracting of a translator, usually unnamed, to produce a 'fair copy' translation of the original text, which was then the material used by a better-known adaptor to produce a version for the stage. She mentions, for example, that in the cases of dramatists José María Pemán, Vicente Balart and José López Rubio, a large proportion of the works listed under their names in the AGA are in fact adaptations, which may have been based on other people's initial translations (2007: 245, footnote 9).

In the early years, some of the translators and adaptors, like some of the censors, were intellectuals allied to the Falange who recognised the importance of culture in the consolidation of a National-Catholic state. Among those who tamed the text for a Spanish audience, the journalist (with the Catholic newspaper *Ya*), literary critic, and sometime censor, Nicolás González Ruiz is a key figure. In his book *La literatura española* he made clear his views on the theatre: 'Creemos que todo gran teatro es, en verdad, teatro religioso' ('We believe that all great theatre is, in truth, religious theatre') (1943: 171). He was an advocate of censorship, which he considered a tool for the betterment of the stage, a significant attitude in a man responsible for many translations of Shakespeare's works staged in the early years of the dictatorship. In an essay titled 'Una gran tarea de dignificación del teatro' ('A great task of dignifying the theatre'), he wrote of the need to 'coordinar una función moral y política con una función literaria' ('harmonise a moral and political function with a literary one'), a creative task, as he saw it, to protect the moral as well as political values of the new Spain (1944). Pemán, politician, poet, essayist and dramatist, was another enthusiastic supporter of the regime, and was possibly the most active of those acculturating canonical texts to fit with its values.[9] Alfredo Marqueríe, a Falangist, sometime censor, and influential theatre critic, also adapted foreign classics for the stage.

So while there were some who worked to support the regime's ideology, there were very few translators who actively worked against the regime. This was understandable, given the risk-averse business model of commercial theatres and the fear of punishment for breaching the norms. More typical were those who either sought to avoid trouble, or who accommodated their translations to the values of the day. There are some notable names among those who translated for the stage, and many of them fall into this *posibilista* category. They range from journalists and writers such as José Monleón (*Primer Acto* and *Triunfo*), Enrique Llovet (*ABC, Informaciones*), Federico Carlos Sainz de Robles and Gonzalo Torrente Ballester, to dramatists and directors such as José López Rubio and José Luis Alonso. Even Trino Martínez Trives, a director with the influential and experimental Dido Pequeño Teatro group, who translated and staged radical works by Beckett, Ionesco and Osborne among others, was not beyond making pervasive changes to the original text (see Fernández Quesada 2011). In many cases and for much of the life of the regime, this was the only way to bring foreign drama and alternative political ideas into the public sphere.

It is, therefore, only a small group of Spanish translators and a small number of plays that could be described as activist in the sense of deliberately disruptive. Indeed, politically engaged translators who took on the regime were often themselves politically engaged writers, such as Alfonso Sastre, Antonio Buero Vallejo and Jaime Salom. As always within the collaborative world of the theatre, they worked with others; figures such as Núria Espert and Adolfo Marsillach, while cognisant of what was possible, were at times part of this concerted activism. Alfonso Sastre seems to have been the most prolific translator working against the regime. He was drawn to the works of Weiss, Strindberg, Langston Hughes, O'Casey and Sartre, particularly when much of his own work was banned in the 1960s and 1970s.[10] Buero Vallejo, although he had less trouble with the censors than some of his contemporaries, also turned on occasion to adaptation, producing versions of Shakespeare's *Hamlet* and Brecht's *Mother Courage* (*Madre Coraje y sus hijos*) in the 1960s, and Ibsen's *The Wild Duck* (*El pato silvestre*) in 1982. Jaime Salom, another member of the Realist Generation, was responsible for a 1970 version of Mart Crowley's taboo-shattering *The Boys in the Band* (*Los chicos de la banda*).

Although a detailed analysis is beyond the scope of this book, it is worth mentioning those who translated challenging foreign theatre into Catalan, dealing as they were with the double bind of the notoriety of the foreign dramatist and the suspicions surrounding the use of the Catalan language itself. As we have documented in Chapters 3 and 4, public performances of plays in Catalan were not allowed on the professional stage in Barcelona until 1946. Enric Gallén argues that the damage this did to the previously thriving Catalan theatre scene was compounded by the fact that there was also a 'specific prohibition of translations of foreign plays (which lasted until the late 1950s)', resulting in a theatrical environment that 'tended to be inward-looking and provincial until 1954' (1996: 19, 20). Pilar Godayol notes that this affected other regional languages also: 'During the first two decades of the dictatorship, translations into Catalan, Galician and Basque were banned' (2016: 60). Even later, as John London indicates, Catalan translations were subject to a two-year delay (1997: 162 and 2001: 428).

The Agrupació Dramàtica de Barcelona (ADB), formed in 1955 with the intention of fostering a Catalan theatre, was pioneering in terms of staging foreign drama, including works by Shakespeare, Ionesco and Brecht. As Gallén writes, 'the main aim of the ADB was to revive artistic and social interest so as to enable Catalan theatre to relate once more to the dominant currents of contemporary foreign theatre' (1996: 23). It was closed by government decree in 1963, following a controversial production of Brecht's *Threepenny Opera* (*L'òpera de tres rals*) (London 1997: 103, 166; Duprey 2014: 26). Despite its premature dissolution, its influence was lasting, and various members went on to influence the Catalan theatre scene, including Ricard Salvat and Maria Aurèlia Capmany, founders of the Escola d'Art Dramàtic Adrià Gual, a significant motor both in strengthening the theatrical culture in Catalonia and in staging foreign drama. Salvat, who had trained with Piscator in Germany, was instrumental in promoting Brecht's theatre in Spain.

As already mentioned, the selection and timing of works for translation are the first choices made by the 'activist' translator, but there are several other strategies employed at textual and paratextual levels in order to mobilise translation for political purposes. It should not be assumed, however, that the regime's censors were unaware of this; rather, they sought to balance the protection of its reputation with the need to regulate cultural expression.

The strategies employed by translators and adaptors of foreign texts included, most obviously, omissions and additions. This can be seen, for example, in Federico Sainz de Robles's 1968 version of Camus's *The State of Siege* (*El estado de sitio*), which excised all mention of Spain (AGA 494/72), and in Enrique Llovet's 1969 *Tartuffe* (*El Tartufo*), which inserted references to Opus Dei ministers (AGA 280/68).[11]

While there are some examples of foreign words retained in the Spanish translations in order to avoid a problematic choice, there is little evidence in the theatre translations of the period of what Lawrence Venuti termed 'foreignisation'– a form of resistance that highlights the differences between the source culture and the target culture and 'enables a disruption of target-language cultural codes' (2008: 34). In some sense, however, the very act of producing a play translated from a foreign language, particularly when it was by an avant-garde or political author, was considered provocative and destabilising. Moreover, there is evidence that Spain's shortcomings were often highlighted in the framing of works.

While retaining 'otherness' in the setting and character names, plays were usually domesticated to the values of conservative bourgeois sensibilities. Just as acculturation includes accommodating the drama to local performance norms, linguistic norms and paradigms of humour, it can also draw parallels between the society portrayed in a foreign work and the domestic circumstance.

The Aesopian strategy of disguising or veiling criticisms through the use of parable and allusion in order to convey a social or political message to an audience was common. Representations of corrupt leadership, social injustice and revolutionary struggles set in different times and foreign places were used to suggest parallels with the situation in Spain. The censors' reports on several foreign plays reveal a real concern about costume and set design, as they were aware that these could be used to reduce the impact of the geographical and temporal distance of the works. The revival of canonical texts by both pro-regime and anti-regime translators was also part of this tactic. The high status of such plays tended to lead to their acceptance by the audience, and the temporal and cultural distance of the events portrayed allowed for substantial explanation, within programme notes for example, which presented an opportunity for the activist translator to suggest certain readings or imply certain parallels with the contemporary situation. Gregor points to several examples of Shakespearean dramas used in this way (2010: 102–7), and Ragué Arias analyses the use of Greek tragedy by dramatists who opposed the regime, as well as those who supported it. She lists Alfonso Jiménez Romero, José Martín Elizondo, Carlos de la Rica, J. J. Vega González, Agustín García Calvo and Luis Riaza as playwrights who used Antigone, for example, 'como símbolo de una ideología progresista' ('as a symbol of a progressive ideology') (1992: 140). Jean Anouilh's version of *Antigone* was also staged several times in Spain in the 1950s and 1960s.

The framing of a play – within the programme or other publicity material, or within correspondence with the censors – could influence how it was interpreted. This strategy was generally employed in one of two ways by the translator or adaptor: either to reduce the threat of censorship by presenting a work as neutral, moralistic or even pro-regime; or alternatively to highlight negative parallels with Spain. A good example of this technique in an attempt to anticipate and see off criticism is producer Andrés de Kramer's framing of Mart Crowley's *The Boys in the Band* in correspondence with the censors, to suggest that homosexuality is a universal issue to be dealt with in a serious, objective and moralising way (Merino Álvarez 2007: 286).

Fine examples of the second type of framing can be seen in productions of works by Brecht and Sartre, which became popular among independent and university theatre groups from the mid-1960s. The political ideology of the original dramatist was used as an implied frame within which the work was to be received by the spectators in search of a political message: reminding them that similar repressive regimes have been successfully challenged in other places; associating the national authorities with demonised groups elsewhere; drawing on the internationally recognised reputation of the original author; and reinforcing or reactivating a discourse of resistance. Similarly, in the case of Irish drama, the Irishness of the dramatist was often used as a frame. When works by Brendan Behan and Sean O'Casey were staged, for example, references to Ireland were used as shorthand for a revolutionary (and often romanticised) armed struggle.[12]

Multiple framings were also possible, as we see in the case of Arthur Miller's *The Crucible* (*Las brujas de Salem*), staged at the Teatro Español in December 1956 by José Tamayo's Lope de Vega Company. This was the year in which Miller appeared before the House Committee on Un-American Activities. Following his refusal to name others, he was convicted of contempt of Congress (Miller 2000). The translator, Diego Hurtado, denied the political parallels and the politics of the dramatist, stressing instead the moral correctness of the work. Some critics, in contrast, highlighted the political aspect. Each hoped to influence how the spectator would receive the work. Hurtado wrote a revealing article about the play and his translation, which was published in *Primer Acto*. In it he stated that his interventions in terms of censorship were both harmless and necessary domestication:

> Mi labor, arte de verterla al castellano, se limitó a reducir las tremendas dimensiones de la obra original, pero guardando en todo su esencia. Y si alguna modificación se introdujo en ella fue solo y exclusivamente pensando en la diferencia de psicología que existe entre los dos países. (1957: 16)

> My work, the art of transferring it into Spanish, was limited to reducing the enormous size of the original work, while retaining its essence throughout. And if any modifications were introduced, it was simply and exclusively the result of thinking of the psychological differences between the two countries.

Domingo Pérez Minik, on the other hand, while not mentioning parallels with Spain, did argue that the work was a political one 'de la cabeza a los pies' ('from head to toe'), in which the past is used to comment on MacCarthyism (1957: 8–9). For Espejo Romero, the focus in the translation on the inappropriate relationship between John Proctor and Abigail distracted from the political and social commentary, but for those willing to receive it, the political message was there (2005: 502–4).

From taming the text to activist translation

We can trace the development in the use of foreign drama over time, from a tamed theatre, focused on entertainment, distraction and popular classics during the early years as the dictatorship established itself, to the limited introduction of new ideas via a process of adaptation to local norms and *posibilismo* in the late 1940s and 1950s, to the emergence of a more disruptive use of translation during the *apertura* and transition periods and beyond.

In the initial years of the dictatorship, successful, evasionist foreign drama was the mainstay in terms of popular productions, complemented by a regular repertoire of foreign classics. John London, in his study of foreign theatre in Spain, notes that in the early years, foreign dramas by Noel Coward, Peter Ustinov, Somerset Maugham and Eduardo de Filippo, while they 'challenged the indigenous culture with differing aesthetic and moral values', were distorted and toned down in the process of adaptation to the Spanish stage and essentially 'became escapist' (1997: 56, 54). The critics too, in their responses to such works, focused on the comedy, rather than on any social commentary.

The success of escapist foreign drama can also be linked to theatre managers tailoring their offerings to the conservative tastes of the Spanish theatregoing public as well as avoiding clashes with the new authorities. In this context, foreign dramas were clearly chosen for their temporal and geographic distance from the Spanish reality, either as entertainment or as high-status canonical works to showcase the prestige of the national theatres (see Monleón 1971: 48; Zatlin 1999: 223, and Zatlin 1994: 103). Apolitical, entertaining foreign dramas were the norm in the commercial theatres, from French boulevard drama, to American detective plays, to Italian farces, and even adulcinated versions of French, British and Irish classics; works that had been popular before the war and were seen as apolitical were also acceptable.

In the 1940s the national theatres were run by Falangist intellectuals who, although sharing some of the values of the regime, were also passionate about the theatre, often had experience of innovations abroad, and saw the potential of foreign drama to influence and reform the Spanish stage. Luis Escobar was an aristocrat and a nationalist. Named 'jefe nacional de Teatro' ('National Director of Theatre') in 1938, he had worked with Dionisio Ridruejo and, as Director of the Teatro Nacional de la Falange, involved himself in propaganda theatre of the right during the civil war. Having presided briefly over theatre censorship, he became the first post-war director of the Teatro María Guerrero in Madrid. His political values and social connections placed him above suspicion and allowed him to introduce foreign drama to the Spanish commercial stage without it being perceived as a threat to the status quo. He was responsible for the staging of works by Eliot, Priestley, Coward and Wilder, albeit in sanitised form. Yet even men as powerful as Escobar were not protected from political interference, and in 1953, according to Adolfo Marsillach, he was forced out by Minister Gabriel Arias-Salgado for what seems to have been a moral judgement of his behaviour at a party. His co-director on many of these productions and subdirector of the theatre, Huberto Pérez de la Ossa, himself a translator and adaptor of plays, was sacked by Arias-Salgado at the same time (1998: 110).[13]

Felipe Lluch was the first director of the Teatro Español before his early death in 1941.[14] An interesting character who had been involved in Rivas Cherif's Teatro Escuela de Arte, he was both a Falangist and a committed Catholic. In the post-war period, he proposed a national theatre along fascist lines and while this did not come to pass as he envisaged it, his influence should not be overlooked. Cayetano Luca de Tena took over from him at the Teatro Español in 1941, and for the next decade he oversaw a repertoire of Spanish classics, Molière and Shakespeare.[15] Like his fellow directors at the María Guerrero, he was the victim of a purge by Arias-Salgado (1998: 110).

While activist translators and dramatists had employed canonical and classical texts to great political effect during the civil war, in the initial years of the dictatorship such plays tended to be used to reinforce ideas about the regime's imperial pretensions rather than to challenge them. This fitted with the cultural ambitions of the Falangist intellectuals who held sway during the early years of the dictatorship and such texts were also generally accepted by the conservative Catholic forces that came to dominate when the Falange was sidelined post-World War II. So while Shakespeare's works were easily accepted by the censors because of their status, it is worth remembering that the versions of his plays staged in early post-war Spain were generally purified and emptied of any potential political significance. Keith Gregor and Elena Bandín note that in the 1940s the Teatro Español favoured Shakespeare's tragedies over his comedies:

> The potentially subversive nature of some of these tragedies (particularly *Macbeth* and *Richard III*, plays which appear to demonise the 'illegitimate' seizure of power and its tyrannical maintenance) was neutralised by having them doctored by self-censoring authors and, perhaps more decisively, by staging them in such a way that the texts' political content could be viewed as distant, both temporally and spatially, from the 'time-space' of mid 20th-century Spain. (2011: 145)

Other classics, such as Euripides' *Medea* and Aristophanes' *The Clouds* (*Las Nubes*) were staged in 1955 in versions prepared by Alfredo Marqueríe. Unsurprisingly, given his political allegiances, the potential of these works to criticise society was not drawn upon and they were instead presented as prestigious classics to show off the greatness of the Spanish theatrical establishment. José María Pemán too, adapted classics, and his *Antígona* (*Antigone*, 1946); *Electra* (1955); *Tiestes* (*Thyestes*, 1956); and *La Orestíada* (*Oresteia*, 1959) were examples of canonical works used to support rather than to challenge the regime. As María José Ragué Arias argues, Pemán's use of Greek myths 'es paradigmática en cuanto a las posibilidades de instigación de falsos triunfalismos populares' ('is paradigmatic in terms of the possibilities for the encouragement of false, popular triumphalism') (1992: 55).

Gregor, commenting on the Teatro Español's limited resources and conservative tendencies, refers to both González Ruiz and Pemán as 'politically docile' authors employed to create versions of Shakespeare's works. He observes that these influential translators 'were careful to erase all smut and, if necessary, the character(s) who produced it, in favour of more maneagable, morally sanitized and "poetic" renderings of familiar plays for predominantly middle-class audiences hungry for such quality "aesthetic" events' (Gregor 2010: 90, 92). In fact they, and especially Pemán, were not merely docile, but rather politically active in favour of the regime.

When Arias-Salgado was at the helm of the Ministerio de Información y Turismo (MIT) from 1951 until 1962, censorship boards were dominated by those whose concerns were moral, rather than political, as the Falange censors lost ground. Despite the influence of ecclesiastical censors during this period, however, other factors increasingly came into play, and there was a certain inevitability to the change that would occur in the late 1940s and 1950s. Foreign plays that were tolerated or even promoted had heretofore either been apolitical (including canonical works considered above politics), or in keeping with the values of the regime. Yet the reception of foreign works was subject to change in line not only with cultural developments, such as the creation of the Teatro Nacional de Cámara y Ensayo, but also with ideological shifts or political expediency.

While translators and adaptors may have internalised the dominant cultural norms of the day, and prepared the text by self-censoring in advance of submission to the censors, there were also attempts to stage daring works. The situation in Spain in this period was one of 'strategic self-censorship', as Tymoczko describes the practice whereby 'translators accept and acquiesce in some norms but oppose and challenge others, setting priorities and undertaking some cultural self-censorship for what they see as a greater good' (2007: 258). This was a period of *posibilismo*, adapting the text in anticipation of censorship, or negotiating with the censors to stage what was tolerable or possible to stage within the restrictive environment of the dictatorship, or as García Escudero defined it, 'el respeto a las circunstancias' ('respect for the circumstances') (1978a: 41).

Many of the influential directors who emerged at this point had learned their craft in independent theatre groups, but – crucially – had the support of some of the older, more established figures who preceded them in the commercial and national theatres. As Marsillach acknowledged, 'todos los que hoy hacemos – o hicimos – teatro en España somos, en parte, consecuencia de aquel trabajo' ('all of us who work, or have worked in theatre in Spain are, in part, a consequence of that work') (1998: 109). Luis Escobar was succeeded at the María Guerrero by Claudio de la Torre, a playwright as well as director, who was in charge from 1954 to 1960, and who brought further innovative and challenging foreign drama to Spain. After a brief period with Modesto Higueras at the helm (1952–4), José Tamayo, founder of the influential and successful Lope de Vega theatre company, became the Director of the Teatro Español in 1954, remaining there until 1962, where he was at the forefront of the internationalisation of the Spanish stage (Hera 2000, Bravo 2003). One of his earliest successes there, in December the same year, was Jean Anouilh's *The Lark* ('*La alondra*'), in a version by José Luis Alonso. For Monleón, who noted in particular his productions of *The Crucible* and *Mother Courage*, Tamayo was a link between critical ideas in the theatre and a conservative public, which unfortunately was more interested in the spectacle than in the revelatory power of the plays (1971: 117–18).

Meanwhile, Higueras, installed as Director of the newly established Teatro Nacional de Cámara y Ensayo in 1954, staged works including 'many of the most important plays of the North American naturalist dramatists, epic theatre, the Theatre of Cruelty, existentialist theatre, German expressionism, the Theatre of the Absurd and the Living Theatre' (Vilches de Frutos 1998: 12). While both public and production runs were severely limited for studio theatres, they nonetheless allowed a series of subjects considered taboo to enter by the back door.

The *posibilismo* of this period, which saw a combination of moderating strategies and the introduction of new ideas and values, can best be seen in the changed status of North American drama. Authors such as Thornton Wilder, Tennessee Williams, Eugene O'Neill and Arthur Miller were brought in from the cold in the 1950s, tolerated following the political reconciliation of Spain with the United States, although as London claims, 'American drama became a tame beast in Spanish hands, just as Spain itself had developed into America's pet ally' (1997: 108). Pérez López de Heredia dates this shift in the treatment of US drama to the end of the 1940s, and she too stresses the alteration of the plays by both adaptors and censors (2004: 151).

Reputation was clearly a factor here and, in the changed political circumstances, the regime was conscious of the need to be seen to tolerate internationally renowned authors from the United States, even if their values were at odds with its own (See Merino Álvarez 2007: 244). Therefore, by the late 1940s and increasingly over the decade that followed, the political climate presented certain opportunities for measured resistance to the National Catholicism of the regime.

A good example of this shift from prohibition to respectability is the case of Thornton Wilder. The official change in attitude towards this dramatist was gradual, but clear. In the early years of the dictatorship, foreign drama or dramatists representing alternative values were taboo. In October 1941, Wilder's *Our Town* ('*Una ciudad pequeñita*') was the subject of an application from the López Heredia-Asquerino company, and was rejected: 'Prohibida por razón del autor' ('Prohibited because of the author') (AGA 2571/41). Another application from the same company in March 1942 was rejected for the same reason. By the mid-1940s, the situation was beginning to change. The play was staged at the María Guerrero in 1944 (and again in 1945), and in 1945 and 1946 in Barcelona (at the Romea and Calderón theatres respectively), directed by Luis Escobar and Huberto Pérez de la Ossa, but in a production with Catholic symbolism in set design, an adaptation which, according to London, 'mocks the austerity of the original' (1997: 89; 91). Thereafter all versions were approved for *cámara*, though in some cases with a cut to a section of dialogue that questions the idea that marriage is a sacrament. Wilder's *The Long Christmas Dinner* (*Navidades en la casa Bayard*) had a similar trajectory from prohibition to authorisation with cuts or the imposition of other limitations.[16] We can see, therefore, that Wilder's status altered as the regime's perspectives on the United States and its values loosened. The plays were staged, but either adapted to the conservative tastes of the public in the state theatres, or restricted to minority audiences in *teatros de cámara*.

Several of Arthur Miller's works were staged in Spain in the 1950s, but once again in versions prepared in accordance with the prevailing values of the day. Ramón Espejo Romero is very critical of the adaptor, José López Rubio:

> His Spanish *Muerte de un viajante* is a seriously mutilated and distorted version of Miller's original. López Rubio actually offered the Spanish audience a mere summary of the play, from which nearly all of the stage directions, some of the most relevant speeches of the play and even a few characters had been wiped out. (2005: 496, 506)

López Rubio also translated Miller's *A View from the Bridge* (*Panorama desde el puente*), which was premiered at the Teatro Lara in Madrid in 1958, and once again, as Espejo Romero shows, he lessened its impact it by changing it drastically.[17] Yet this was understandable given the context. However bowdlerised, it should not obscure the fact that his translation and adaptation work also broadened the theatrical offerings in Spain.

Much more contentious, but again demonstrating the workings of *posibilismo*, is the case of Tennessee Williams.[18] His *A Streetcar*

Named Desire (*Un tranvía llamado Deseo*), translated by José Méndez Herrera, was the subject of an application by the Ana María Noé company in May 1950, for staging in October in Barcelona. The three initial censors variously described the play as 'muy peligrosa' ('very dangerous'), 'inmoral, de una crudeza extraordinaria' ('immoral, of extraordinary crudeness'), or suitable for over-eighteens. It was sent to two further censors, and one of them, Fr Constancio de Aldeaseca, damned the atmosphere of the play as 'moralmente hediondo' ('morally repulsive'), commenting further that 'en toda la obra se halla ni la más mínima insinuación de que pueda existir algún freno de los instintos bestiales del hombre' ('in the entirety of the work there is not even the slightest suggestion that there exists a possible constraint on the animal instincts of man'). The final, unsigned report, dated 5 July, refers to the crudeness of the play and, naturally, it was prohibited.

What happened next reveals how the censorship system and taming process worked. The original ending was removed by Méndez Herrera, and 'un cierto tono de denuncia moral' ('a certain tone of moral denunciation') introduced. In this further self-censored form it was resubmitted to the censors and was rewarded with authorisation for a single staging in a studio theatre. It was not until 1956, and in a new and heavily modified version adapted by Juan Guerrero Zamora from Méndez Herrera's one, that it was finally approved for the commercial stage (Pérez López de Heredia 2004: 63–4; 168). This, of course, came after the important foreign policy developments of 1953. Moreover, it demonstrates how the studio theatres could function as the first stage in the introduction of alternative values into Spain.

O'Neill's *Desire under the Elms* (*Deseo bajo los olmos*) was also censored at various levels, including by translators. Pérez López de Heredia, for example, outlines how it moved from an initial highly restricted *teatro de cámara* performance at the Teatro María Guerrero in 1953, based on a translation by Antonio de Cabo that incorporated the many cuts stipulated by the censors, to commercial productions in Barcelona and Madrid by Armando Moreno and Núria Espert in 1962 (2004: 175–9). Their 1961 application was based on León Mirlas's translation, which had been published in Argentina. Mirlas's text had been banned in Spain in 1959, however, so Moreno's success lay in his ability to convince the censors of the status of O'Neill and to frame his own *adaptation* as a more refined version of an important dramatic work. The censors balanced their apprehension regarding the crudeness of certain scenes against the moral outcome, apparently viewing the work as a link between modern theatre and classical tragedy, and it was authorised (Pérez López de Heredia 2004: 177).

All these cases are characterised by a process of – often drastic – reworking of the foreign playtext to fit with what was possible within the still conservative Spanish context. Nonetheless, this was a period that brought to the Spanish stage ideas and values that were at odds with those put forward by the regime and would not have been tolerated in domestic works. The ground was being laid for a more radical theatrical challenge to come.

The period of *apertura* under Manuel Fraga between 1962 and 1969 brought a degree of liberalisation, which was nonetheless balanced against the political needs of the moment. He was succeeded in 1969 by the Catholic conservative Alfredo Sánchez Bella, who tried to reimpose the moral certitude of previous decades. Although a return to the cultural conservatism of earlier times was not possible, cases such as the crusade against *El Tartufo*, as we shall see, demonstrate the continuing power of Catholic moralists during the late dictatorship. As society changed and censorship adapted to it, so too did the situation of foreign drama evolve. By the 1960s and in particular once *apertura* began, a new pattern can be traced in the use of translated drama to convey a political message of change to the Spanish audience. Yet the impact of disruptive practices should not be overstated, as unchallenging foreign drama continued to dominate.

The state theatres in this period were increasingly influenced by the international focus and experience of those in charge, many of whom had cut their teeth in independent theatre groups and had ties abroad. José Luis Alonso, who took over the directorship of the Teatro María Guerrero in 1961, had previously worked with Carmen Troitiño at the Teatro de Cámara de Madrid, among other independent groups (Vilches de Frutos 1998: 11–12). He had also worked as a theatre critic and travelled abroad in this capacity, covering work for *Primer Acto* from the Royal Court in London for example. His time at the María Guerrero, coinciding with *apertura* and a change in censorship legislation, was marked by an increase in challenging foreign works, most notably Ionesco's *Rhinoceros* (*El rinoceronte*) in January 1961 and Brecht's *The Caucasian Chalk Circle*

(*El círculo de tiza caucasiano*) in 1971, as well as many French plays.[19] Zatlin notes that he had close links with Anouilh and was responsible for several productions of his plays in Spain (1994: 113–14). For Quirós Alpera, 'Alonso can be positioned as a key propeller of interdisciplinary and international formation. He brought international currents and ideas into Spain and promoted them at a time when it was not officially fashionable to do so' (2013: 282–3). Not only did he translate and adapt many important foreign plays, including classics and experimental works but, as José María Pou notes, he used his influence and reputation, whenever possible, to stage them (2000: 301).

At the Español, Tamayo was succeeded in 1962 by Luca de Tena, who returned to the helm following a period in commercial theatres. His second spell lasted from 1962 until 1964, and he was succeeded initially by José Luis Alonso and then by the provisional triumvirate of José López Rubio, Federico Carlos Sainz de Robles and Francisco García Pavón. They, in turn, were succeeded by Adolfo Marsillach, who struggled with the role from 1965 until his resignation in 1966 (García Escudero 1978a).[20] Once freed from the restrictions of the role, Marsillach went on to stage some of the most important and risqué productions of foreign drama of the dictatorship, including Peter Weiss's *Marat/Sade* in 1968 and Llovet's provocative adaptation of Molière's *Tartuffe* in 1969.

Those who followed were also international in their outlook, and the democratic period brought many more foreign productions to Spain (Vilches de Frutos 1998: 17–18). Miguel Narros, whose appointment was described by García Escudero as 'un experimento' ('an experiment'), took over until 1970, and would return to the role from 1984 until 1989 (1978a: 212). A product of the RESAD and the Teatro Español Universitario (TEU), Narros made his mark in the experimental and influential Teatro Estudio de Madrid (TEM, 1961–8), and later in the Teatro Español Independiente (TEI, 1968–78). He had worked in French theatre in the early 1950s before returning to Spain and his theatrical career had an international focus from the outset.[21] Alberto González Vergel was in charge during the early transition, from 1970 until 1976, and the ever-present José Luis Alonso, who had earlier been at the María Guerrero, took over from 1979 until 1983, succeeded by José Luis Gómez, who had trained in Germany (1983–4). The greatest structural change came with the creation of the Instituto de las Artes Escénicas y de la Música in 1985. No longer needed as a political tool, foreign drama was nonetheless part of the ongoing effort to modernise the Spanish theatre. For the period of the dictatorship, however, foreign drama played a hugely important, and sometimes overlooked, political role.

The 1960s and 1970s saw the growth of what can be termed translation (or adaptation) as political activism. A notable number of plays chosen in this period were selected for their partisan message and for the known political stance of their authors. Of course, the notoriety of a foreign author was also a consideration for the censors, whose reports on their works show that they were extremely conscious of both the global status and acceptance of these writers, and of Spain's reputation abroad. The censors, like those forced to negotiate with them, recognised the political game-playing in the attempts to stage these dramatists, and they were cognisant of their task of damage limitation.

Some dramatists, such as Jean-Paul Sartre and Bertolt Brecht, known for their associations with particular ideologies, and therefore useful for conveying a message to the target culture, were the subject of regular applications for staging, particularly by university groups.[22] Also popular was Albert Camus, who was judged to be less hostile towards the Spanish regime than the others by various censors who were seemingly unaware of his negative comments on Spain in *Combat* and elsewhere (Golsan 1991). Those who translated and staged these plays tended to highlight the reputation or notoriety of the original author, drawing on his authority and foregrounding his alternative social and political philosophy. Tymoczko refers to this as 'engaged translation', following Sartre's 'littérature engagée'. These, she argues, are translations that 'incite to rebellion' (2007: 213).

One of the most controversial productions of foreign theatre under the dictatorship was Adolfo Marsillach's 1968 staging of Peter Weiss's *Marat-Sade* (AGA 149/66). The play had been translated by Alfonso Sastre using the pseudonym Salvador Moreno Zarza, as his own notoriety might work against him.[23] The censorship process lasted two years, from 1966. Two scenes were cut by the censors but, according to Marsillach, he – and Weiss – were willing to accept this in order to stage this revolutionary work in Spain (1998: 305).[24] Even when viewing the revised version, the censors expressed some concerns and José María Artola, Florencio Martínez

Ruiz and Arcadio Baquero all referred in their reports to the mention of censorship in scene 4, which they suspected was a deliberately provocative insertion, rather than an element of the original playtext. Stage design was by Francisco Nieva and two of the best independent theatre groups operating at the time participated: the Cátaro group took on the role of the asylum inmates, and Antonio Malonda (of Bululú fame) and some of his students from the Escuela de Arte Dramática formed the chorus. It was staged at the Teatro Español, under the auspices of the Teatro Nacional de Cámara y Ensayo for a three-night run, from 2 to 4 October 1968 and was seen as a game-changing production in terms of staging, but also in terms of political theatre.[25] Marsillach recalls that the first night had the usual audience of critics, civil servants and those who made it their business to be seen at premieres; the second night was when it really got political. He described the audience: 'Se les notaba excitados, nerviosos, palpitantes y, sobre todo, "politizados". La frialdad inicial de la noche anterior fue sustituida por una ansiedad expectante. Advertí enseguida que aquella función iba a transformarse en un acto de oposición al regimen. Y así fue' ('One could see that they were excited, nervous, palpitating and above all, politicised. The initial coldness of the previous night had been replaced by an expectant anxiety. I realised immediately that that show was going to turn into an act of opposition to the regime. And so it was') (1998: 308).

The showering of the spectators with French revolutionary pamphlets at the end, which was part of the performance, was complemented on the second night by a second shower of pamphlets, this time anti-Franco ones, that some of the politicised audience members had brought with them. On the third night, according to Marsillach, the security forces gathered outside the theatre to deal with the crowds. Following its brief but ground-breaking public and critical success in Madrid, it went on to similar triumph the same month at Barcelona's Poliorama (though not without threats of closure), and eventually proceeded to a longer run there in the 1968–9 season. The play was staged for a few days in January 1969 before Weiss withdrew his permission in protest at the regime's introduction of state of emergency legislation in January 1969. Marsillach comments that those involved wished to continue to perform the play, as they considered it politically timely. However, Weiss's decision, coupled with the government's desire for the production to continue in order to give the appearance of normality and to protect its reputation, led him to pull the production (Marsillach 1998: 311–12). The government responded by imposing a ban on productions or film adaptations of any of Weiss's works.

Politics and religion also merged in Marsillach's staging of Molière's *Tartuffe* in October 1969, which took potshots at Opus Dei ministers. The play became a weapon in the ongoing power struggle between the Opus Dei technocrats and the more culturally and socially liberal Falangists. Manuel Fraga, who was allied to the latter faction, commented in his diary on the negative allusions to the political leadership, and presumably enjoyed them following his own fall from grace (1980: 260).[26] Marsillach claims that Fraga told him directly that not only would such a play not bother him, but that he would enjoy it, and the director later suspected that the translator, Enrique Llovet, and Fraga had conspired to have it staged (1998: 316, 319).[27] The play became a focal point of opposition to the regime and the run at the Teatro de la Comedia in Madrid was a huge success. The ministers had their revenge, however, and the proposed tour of the provinces did not go ahead.

The censorship files reveal the behind-the-scenes battle (AGA 280/68). The play was authorised under Fraga, without cuts, despite some very obvious swipes at contemporary – technocrat – politicians. It had permission for staging between 3 October 1969 and 29 June 1970, and was to move from Madrid to the provinces. In October, the Head of the Theatre Section wrote to the Director General expressing his concerns about the play and asking if the references to Opus Dei could be cut. In March, shortly before the play was to begin its tour, the Director General consulted the Attorney General about the legality of banning the provincial tour. The Attorney General's detailed response goes through and rejects various options: (a) using Marsillach's error in the application against him (he incorrectly put down el Grupo de Teatro 70 as the company applying to stage the play), as this had been rectified; (b) invoking article 22 of the 1964 legislation, which allowed the minister to impose a prohibition directly, due to political circumstances, as this would have had to be done at the time of the plenary meeting of the censorship board; (c) the revision of the verdict of authorisation given on 16 August 1969. It was clear that none of these would suffice to overthrow legally the earlier authorisation, so a more imaginative solution was suggested: 'De aquí la precisión de analizar si la representación del "Tartufo" en provincias, por su naturaleza, puede o no ser considerada lesiva para el interés público' ('Hence the necessity of analysing whether the representation of *Tartuffe* in the provinces could be considered dangerous to the public interest by its very nature').

The Attorney General cited Article 110-1 of the *Ley de Procedimiento Administrativo* and article 56 of the *Ley de la Jurisdicción Contencioso-Administrativa*. Provincial delegates were subsequently sent a telegram advising them that the play could not be advertised. Therefore Marsillach's claim in his memoir that the tour was not banned, but rather blocked by more insidious means is correct: all of the provincial theatre managers and owners were informed that the play should be stopped, and it did not go ahead (1998: 320–1). The response from the ministry's spokesperson to the halting of the tour was to deny any official knowledge of a tour, or its prevention by the provincial delegates. The files also contain many cuttings from the provincial press, detailing Marsillach's statement that he had received no notification of a ban. The regional press also took it personally, and seem to have interpreted events as an elitist attack on the provinces, rather than a targeted attack on Marsillach (Gallego 1970).

It is clear that the censors were generally less sure-footed when it came to judging avant-garde drama, much of which was less overtly political than *Marat-Sade*. The texts themselves were often minimalist and the politics in them absent or unclear, but their very structure challenged the status quo and suggested a break with accepted conventions. The politics of some of the dramatists concerned was also highlighted to defy the conservative regime. The files show that the censors did not always understand the works, but they suspected – often correctly – bad intentions on the part of those wishing to stage them.

Beckett's *Endgame* (*Final de partida*), translated by Luce Moreau, wife of Fernando Arrabal, was staged on 11 June 1957 at the Teatro Bellas Artes in Madrid, although the application had been for staging in April. Morales de Acevedo in his report of 26 March suggested that the play is for 'perturbados o curiosos de novedad' ('the mentally unbalanced or those curious for novelty') and said: 'No es posible entender semejante teatro. Solo puede tolerarse para teatro experimental ultra-futurista' ('It is not possible to understand such theatre. It can only be tolerated for experimental ultra-futurist theatre'). In his moral report on the play, Fr Avelino Esteban Romero wrote: 'Este informe tiene el valor que puede tener un juicio sobre una obra que no se ha entendido del todo, y hasta casi nada' ('This report has the limited value that a judgement can have of a play that I have not completely, indeed almost not at all, understood') (AGA 69/58).

Another Beckett play, *Act without Words* (*Acto sin palabras*), was first authorised in 1959 for staging at the Teatro Maravillas by the Los Independientes group (run by José Sedó Torrent), in a translation prepared by the director, Javier Lafleur. Morales de Acevedo's report, dated 21 January 1959, is interesting for its complete dismissal of Beckett's theatre as 'una extravagancia sin interés alguno' ('an extravagance without any interest'), 'solo tolerable, por su inocuidad, para teatro de ensayo' ('only tolerable because of its innocuousness for club theatres'). In response to the question '¿Se juzga la obra tolerable o recomendable para menores?' ('is it judged tolerable or recommended for minors?'), he wrote 'para perturbados' ('for the mentally unbalanced') (AGA 19/59). Yet it was authorised without cuts. In fact, as late as 1967, censors' reports demonstrate that they were still not sure what to do with Beckett. On foot of an application from Los Goliardos to stage *Espectáculo de mimo y pantomima* (a combination of mime by Julio Castronuovo and Beckett's *Act without Words*) in university halls of residence in Valladolid and Madrid, Bautista de la Torre wrote, 'de todos modos conviene el visado del ensayo general para una mejor comprensión del alcance argumental' ('in any case it is advisable to view the dress rehearsal in order to better understand the significance of the plot') (AGA 320/67).[28]

The censors' lack of understanding of the plays offered some opportunities to stage such theatre in experimental and sometimes politically radical ways. Their failure to comprehend the works was compounded by their suspicions about those wishing to stage them and their assumption that the conservative Spanish public would not have great interest in seeing them, all of which meant that these works, hailed elsewhere as important examples of world theatre, were relegated in Spain to minority theatres.

Disruptive practices became increasingly visible during the *destape* (a period of rule-testing cultural experimentation) and the transition to democracy. Taboos were challenged and new freedoms were verified. Foreign works were staged, although not with the same political urgency as before. From a conservative, Catholic perspective, on the other hand, things were clearly getting worse. In October 1975, in a survey carried out by the agency Prensa y Radio Española, S. A. (Pyresa), a representative of the association of Catholic priests (HSE – Hermandad Sacerdotal Española), complained of pornography on the stage and castigated practising Catholics who attended the theatre to see immoral works. He reserved particular disparagement for the influence of European works: 'Si en Europa se hacen esas cosas, aquí no queremos ni debemos imitar a esas democracias europeas cuyas estructuras están llenas de suciedad y porquería' ('Even if in Europe such things are done, here we have no desire nor obligation to imitate those European democracies whose structures are full of filth and indecency') (AGA MIT/00.584).[29] In this period when Spanish identity was again being redefined, the foreign, it seems, was once more considered a threat.

By the back door: saying the unsayable through foreign theatre

There is sufficient evidence, therefore, to conclude that foreign drama was generally more leniently treated by the censors than Spanish-authored works. This circumstance was used as an opportunity by some translators, adaptors and theatre practitioners to bring into Spain surreptitiously subjects that were considered problematic, in terms of religion, sexual morality and politics. Files in the AGA reveal that the censors were aware of this, but struggled to balance a variety of mutable considerations: potential reputational damage, *apertura*, the various possible interpretations of the legislation, and the political circumstances. They did this, not simply by cutting or banning works, but also by restricting production runs, limiting staging to *teatros de cámara*, and by paying particular attention to costume and set design.

Over time, as the influence of the Roman Catholic Church waned and Spain opened up to more foreign influence, the representation of religion, sexual morality and homosexuality also changed. The fact that such representations were less problematic if the plays were foreign, and therefore not taken to represent Spanish morals, was an opportunity for those wishing to harness the power of the theatre for social change. While early translators and adaptators such as González Ruiz and Pemán had promoted and protected Catholic moral values, these were later challenged by subsequent generations of translators and theatre practitioners.

Overall, the power and influence of the Church on theatre censorship is difficult to overstate, however, and its role on state boards was complemented by its own ecclesiastical censorship and by Catholic lobby groups.[30] For example, when Albee's *Who's Afraid of Virgina Woolf?* (*¿Quién teme a Virginia Woolf?*) was staged at the Teatro Goya in 1966, the Asociación de Padres de Familia decried it to the hierarchy. In the same year, a report purported to have been commissioned by the Archbishop of Madrid-Alcalá denouncing 'la ola de pornografía' ('the wave of pornography') in the theatre and naming in particular two foreign works – Brecht's *Mother Courage* and O'Casey's *Bedtime Story* (*Cuento para la hora de acostarse*) – was sent to the Director General, García Escudero (1978a: 194–6; 230).

Religion, morality, sexual mores and questions of taste often merged in censors' judgements. In fact, the line between moral and political censorship was also often blurred – unsurprising under a regime that defined itself as Catholic and nationalist. The representation of sinful and immoral behaviour and of religion and clergy in foreign drama was a cause for much concern on the part of the ecclesiastical censors. As always, temporal and geographical distance could assuage some of their nervousness, and the source of the translations was also an important consideration when delivering a verdict.

Suicide, for example, which was considered a sin, was generally deemed intolerable by religious censors on state boards. One solution was to excise the offence: London mentions, for example, that a 1943 version of Ibsen's *Hedda Gabler*, staged in Barcelona, simply eliminated the suicide of the protagonist (2012: 345). Espejo Romero, writing about a 1952 application to stage Miller's *Death of a Salesman* (*Muerte de un viajante*), notes that, despite initial authorisation, an attempt was made to persuade Tamayo 'to eliminate Willy's final suicide, in accordance with the precepts of the Catholic Church', on this occasion without success (2005: 496, 506; 2002). Yet when John Millington Synge's *Deirdre of the Sorrows* (*Deirdre de los pesares*), in a translation by Alfredo Marquerie, was the subject of an application from the ARA company in Málaga in

May 1964, the play was approved for over-fourteens, without cuts or further restrictions, despite the suicide of the protagonist (AGA 125/64). By now *apertura* had begun and the Church's influence on state boards had diminished. Of interest is the note on the report by Marcelo Arroita-Jáuregui Alonso, which states that 'el distanciamiento que supone la época de la acción y el tono poético de la obra, resta toda peligrosidad al suicidio de la protagonista' ('the distancing effect created by the time period of the action and the poetic tone of the play removes all danger from the protagonist's suicide'). Even the religious censor, Fr Artola, commented on the temporal distance and the morality of the times represented, but thought it suitable only for over-eighteens. Reputation, in this case of both dramatist and translator, also played a part in its authorisation. Not only was Synge considered apolitical, a respected dramatist whose work had been staged in Spain prior to the civil war, but the translator in this case – Alfredo Marqueríe – was also unproblematic.

Aside from particular representations of morality at odds with the Church's teaching, certain foreign authors were considered problematic from a religious point of view. Albert Camus's atheism was sometimes a concern for the censors, as was the existentialism and nihilism that they identified in his works. Yet, on other occasions, Camus's rejection of conventional bourgeois morality was overlooked by the censors, who alluded to the ethical nature of his work. His *Caligula* (*Calígula*), a play about the Emperor, is an interesting case. Eight applications were made to stage it between 1957 and 1971 (AGA 17/57, AGA 142/60, AGA 294/62, AGA 347/71, AGA 639/71). Despite the play's potential for political readings, censorship of the work focused more on the references to adultery and incest and the cruelty and stupidity of the Gods. The religious censor, Manuel Villares, for example, wrote in his January 1957 report: 'El autor se complace en acumular todos los sentimientos más bajos y más perversos de la naturaleza humana en la personalidad de Calígula, loco y degenerado' ('The author takes pleasure in amassing all of the most base and perverse feelings of human nature in the character of Caligula, who is mad and degenerate') and concluded that it ought to be banned (AGA 17/57). Although the other two censors who read the play considered it suitable for *cámara*, the priest's report led to the prohibition of the play. Later, as the influence of the Church weakened, it was authorised for *cámara*.

More problematic was Jean-Paul Sartre and his 'immoral', 'negative', 'false and atheist' works (O'Leary 2021). *Huis clos* was prohibited four times between 1964 and 1966, despite *apertura* and the lessening of the Church's influence. Fr Blajot seems to have been responsible for this verdict. In his December 1964 report, he recommended prohibition for a variety of reasons, including the author's ideology, the portrayal of homosexuality and, crucially, the fact that the play featured in the Catholic Church's *Index of Forbidden Books* (AGA 250/64).[31] A subsequent version by Alfonso Sastre, originally translated as *El infierno* ('Hell') and later changed to *A puerta cerrada* ('In Camera'), went to a plenary of the censorship board in 1967. Fr Cea's report was damning: 'En toda la obra se advierte una concepción liberal y naturalista del infierno en clara contradicción con la doctrina Cristiana' ('In the whole of the play one can see a liberal and naturalist conception of Hell that is in clear contradiction of Christian doctrine'). He concluded that the play would create doctrinal confusion and was in breach of article 17.1 of the legislation, for its attacks on Catholic dogma (AGA 125/67).

There was no agreement among the censors on the value, aesthetic or moral, of the work and the files reveal the different factors that the censors weighed against their religious concerns. Federico Muelas considered it a brilliant creation, and went so far as to suggest that it contained a theological lesson. Manuel Díez Crespo, while very critical of the play from a religious point of view, was cognisant of the importance of the dramatist's work. Florencio Martínez Ruiz, on the other hand, thought that it was of minority interest and therefore not much of a threat. In the end it was authorised for over-eighteens for staging at the mainstream Teatro de Comedia with José María de Quinto as director. The dress rehearsal was to be viewed, the title changed and one cut made, a reference to bad language: 'Es un cabrón, eso es todo [. . .] Un verdadero cabrón' ('He's a bastard, that's all [. . .] A real bastard') (AGA 125/67). The same version was approved for staging by Marsillach and Espert in Barcelona in 1967–8, along with *La Putain respectueuse* (*La respetuosa*). It was again approved, but when they wished to incorporate some readings of work by Simone de Beauvoir after the season had begun, permission was refused. Feminism, it seems, was a step too far.

Avant-garde writers such as Samuel Beckett caused great confusion among the religious censors. His works were the subject of several reports by priests, which were commissioned to give moral guidance on the interpretation of the plays. The problem was that many of the censors simply did not understand the works and dismissed them as worthless. Fr Mauricio de Begoña suggested in 1955 that *Waiting for Godot* (*Esperando a Godot*) 'pudiera originar alguna confusión en espíritus no formados' ('could cause some confusion in those uneducated spiritually'). Apart from cuts to eliminate some crude language, however, he judged that it would be 'ininteligible e inofensiva en el orden moral' ('unintelligible and inoffensive from the moral point of view') (AGA 107/55).

Fr Andrés Avelino Esteban Romero was the author of a report on Beckett's *Krapp's Last Tape* (*La última cinta de Krapp*) in 1959 (see Figure 14), which asked: '¿Qué puede interesar a un público sano y normal, no digo ni siquiera católico, estas anomalías y extravagancias de autores extraños, que tal vez en sus climas sociales encuentran un motivo para estos subproductos...?' ('What interest can a sane and normal – I'm not even saying Catholic – public have in these anomalies and extravagances of strange authors, who perhaps in their own social climes can find a motive for these subproducts?') (AGA 374/59). The play, translated by Daniel de Linos, was the subject of an application in December 1959 from Javier Lafleur for the Los Independientes theatre group, and Adolfo Marsillach was to play Krapp. It was to be staged at the Teatro Lara, Madrid, but was instead banned as a result of the report, which questioned whether it even constituted a play, described it as 'absurdo y tremendista' ('absurd and grotesque'), and claimed 'que parece saboear [*sic*] lo morboso y extravagante' ('that it seems to savour the sordid and outlandish'). By 1962, in more outward-looking times, it was authorised for *cámara* (albeit for one night only) with no cuts.

Brecht was considered even more tricky from both a moral and political perspective. Given the regime's official response to the German playwright (see the case study at the end of this chapter), the 1962 moral report on *Mother Courage* authored by Fr Esteban is surprising for its focus on 'el posible sentido pacifista que encierra su trama, al presentar la inutilidad de las guerras' ('the possible pacifist meaning contained in the argument, in its presentation of the futility of war'). For the sake of the common good, rather than the protection of the Church's reputation, the author of the report advocated the suppression of the chaplain's attempts

"LA ÚLTIMA CINTA DE KRAPP"/

Monologo en magnetofon, original de SAMUEL BECKETT, en versión española de Daniel de Linos————

Informe moral:

Ya hacia tiempo que no llegaba a mi informe este tipo - de teatro(?) absurdo y tremendista, que parece saborear lo morboso y extravagante!

La trama es un monologo del protagonista oyendose en - la cinta de un magnetofon, en la va recordando su vida pasada, llena de morbosidades sexuales, a las que él pone el acompañamiento directo y oral de unos "juramentos que suponemos, aunque el autor con habilidad se limita a señalar que "jura", que no será exclamaciones gramaticales ni jaculatorias...

Me pregunto:¿qué puede interesar a un publico sano y - normal, no digo ni siquiera católico, estas anomalías y extravagancias de autores extraños, que tal vez en sus climas sociales encuentren un motivo para estos subproductos...?

No tiene finalidad alguna sino el propio placer del protagonista en recordar su pasado, sin más. Me parece propio de ciertas salas de fiestas, pero no de escenarios - teatrales...
En la versión hay además un anacronismo curioso y es - que protagonista, que se describe como un"viejo cascarrabias", cuando era de pantalón corto, iba a misas vespertinas-pga.5.-¡qué pronto a envejecido este pobre hombre ya que las misas vespertinas son de hace cuatro o cinco años!O tambien se ocurre pensar los muchos años que este tipo extravagante ha estado de "pantalon corto"!
Tal vez esto ha sido una "concesion" del traductor a la censura, ya que supongo que el autor debe saber poco de misas vespertinas!

Madrid, 13 de diciembre 1959

A.-Avelino Esteban y Romero.-

Figure 14: Esteban Romero's report on *La última cinta de Krapp* (1959) to seduce the protagonist, 'teniendo en cuenta la sensibilidad del público español ante escenas de esta *índole,* en referencia a los sacerdotes' ('taking into consideration the sensitivity of the Spanish public faced with scenes of this type, when referring to priests') (AGA 227/64).

As time went on, the rift between the Church and the state censors became more pronounced and the censorship files reflect this. Theatre, and foreign theatre in particular, increasingly challenged established taboos around questions of taste and traditional Catholic morality. In some cases, plays considered trouble-free by the state were heavily censored by the Church, disturbed by the easy virtue on display. In 1963, for example, two works by Félicien Marceau, *The Egg* (*El huevo*) and *The Good Soup* (*La buena sopa*), which were staged at the Goya and the Reina Victoria respectively, caused a public scandal. The Church argued that 'nuestra inconsciente e inexperta juventud' ('our unaware and inexpert youth') were not ready for this 'europeanisation' of theatre and the plays, which had been authorised by the state censors, were given a 4 rating by the Church's own censors (García Escudero 1978a: 58–61, 63–71). George Wellwarth noted also, that by the end of the 1960s, while official attitudes towards foreign drama had softened, not much had changed overall:

> Brecht and Sartre have been shown in Spain for the first time, but for the most part the imports have been of the bedroom farce variety, a genre that the government – probably correctly – thinks has a pacifying effect on the populace. On this point the Church is now officially against the government. (1969: 156)

Notwithstanding the increasing division between Church and State regarding matters of morality, the censors' reactions to representations of sex, homosexuality and the body – especially the female body – reveal a prudery at the heart of the regime's cultural regulation. Yet, as always, the response to individual works was not predictable. Some potentially problematic works had an easy passage through the censorship process, while others, as we shall see, did not. Responses ranged from light pruning to radical cuts or prohibition. At stake was not simply the reputation of the regime, but the impressionable minds and corruptible souls of the spectators. With foreign drama, the pretence that such transgressive behaviour and immorality was alien to the Spanish national character could be upheld. One constant, however, was an emphasis on set and costume design and performance, in order to control – where possible – representations of both body and behaviour.

Sexual morality was the concern of the censors tasked with judging Seán O'Casey's rather bawdy one-act piece, *Bedtime Story*, which was the subject of applications in 1966, 1968 and 1971. The 1966 version by Renzo Casali led to a mixed response from the censors, with both Vázquez Dodero and Fr Fierro advocating prohibition because of the sexual content and Barceló proposing authorisation for over-eighteens with cuts (AGA 274/66). The problematic combination of eroticism and mockery of religion led to ardent objections on the part of some censors. The files show that it was authorised for the Teatro Nacional de Cámara y Ensayo without cuts, once the costumes (the characters' revealing nightwear) were fixed to reduce the 'excesivo contenido erótico' ('excessive erotic content'). Further documents in the file show that Casali made changes to make it more acceptable, including toning down the religious aspect.

Balancing the various considerations was always key. In 1971, Natividad Zaro's translation of George Bernard Shaw's *Mrs Warren's Profession* (*La profesión de la Señora Warren*), a play about prostitution, was approved without cuts for staging by the Mary Carrillo company, albeit with a stipulation that the dress rehearsal be viewed. Both the dramatist and the translator were considered unproblematic, and Bautista de la Torre's report is revealing of the balancing act within the censors' judgement regarding the moral content: 'Obra excelente, de irónico sarcasmo, en la que se palían las posiciones de extremada inmoralidad de la protagonista con el contrapunto del personaje antagonista. Puede autorizarse' ('An excellent work of sarcastic irony in which the extreme immorality of the protagonist is mitigated by the counterpoint of the antagonist') (AGA 626/71).[32]

Interestingly, the link in some plays between transgressive behaviour and social or political injustice was often simply ignored by the censors, who tended to react to questions of taste and morality more often than social commentary. When Shelagh Delaney's taboo-shattering 1958 play, *A Taste of Honey*, was staged in Spain in 1961, the censors focused their criticism almost entirely on the representation of a homosexual character, despite the play's broad criticism of racism, class snobbery, misogyny, poverty and social injustice.[33] According to files held at the Centro Dramático Nacional, it was first staged in the Teatro María Guerrero in January 1961, by the Dido Pequeño Teatro company, in a version by José María de Quinto (working from a translation by Antonio Gobernado). Miguel Narros directed. An application from Milagros Leal-Amparo Soler Leal company on 6 March 1969 for staging at the Club de Madrid was authorised for over-eighteens but not for broadcast. A note on the verdict expressed the censors' concern and insistence on monitoring the representation of the homosexual character. The single cut, on page 13 of Act 1, was a reference to Helen not wearing a bra and how her breasts move, a concern about the body echoed in later transition-period reports that expressed disquiet not about the exposure of flesh in art *per se*, but curiously about the dangers posed by 'nudity in motion' (AGA MIT/00.584). Subsequent applications for staging in Madrid in 1971 and the provinces in 1972 and 1973 led to authorisation, with the same stipulation regarding the careful monitoring of the representation of homosexuality.

There was a similar response to versions of Brendan Behan's *The Hostage* (*El rehén*), translated by Genoveva Dieterich, which were the subject of applications in 1967 and 1968. The files show that the censors were aware of the political content – presumably why the plays were selected at this time of heightened opposition to the regime – but considered the political and temporal distance from Spain sufficiently great so as not to pose a threat. Instead, the censors were more concerned with bawdiness, nudity and representations of homosexuality (AGA 62/67). While authorised for *cámara* with cuts for staging in the provinces in 1967, when it was proposed to stage *El rehén* in the Teatro Beatriz in Madrid in 1968, under the direction of José María Loperena, more problems ensued and it was referred to a plenary of the Junta de Censura. The reports on the play reveal that it was authorised for *teatros de cámara* only (though not for the Nacional de Cámara at the Teatro Beatriz), and show that the censors required 'especial atención a las escenas de ambientación de bajos fondos sociales y morales' ('special attention to the scenes set in the social and moral underworld'). They objected to the name Gilchrist, translated as Gilycristo, which, they argued, sounded irreverent. In addition, the humorous but lewd song 'La Grecia antigua' was cut. The fact that Brendan Behan himself was known as an anti-establishment figure and political revolutionary (and IRA member) was ignored by the censors, who perhaps correctly decided that to draw attention to it would favour the opposition.

Yet, at times, foreignness was not enough to mollify the censors when the content was deemed too offensive. John Arden's provocative *Live Like Pigs* (*Vivir como cerdos*) was the subject of an application in 1968. The translation was by Álvaro del Amo. The play, deemed 'deliberadamente sucio' ('deliberately filthy') by one of the censors who read it, was banned in accordance with article 18 of the 1964 legislation, which prohibited works due to an accumulation of scenes leading to a whole that was brutal, lascivious, vulgar or gruesome (AGA 365/69).[34]

Almost a decade later, at the start of the *destape* period, Peter Schaffer's *Equus*, directed by Collado, was staged in the Teatro de la Comedia in Madrid in October 1975. Described by Torres Nebrera as 'el estreno más polémico de todo el teatro extranjero visto en 1975' ('the most controversial premiere of any foreign play in 1975'), it brought full frontal male and female nudity to the Spanish stage for the first time, to the delight of some and the consternation of others (2005: 32). It caused quite a scandal and a group calling itself the Comité de Moralidad Pública ('Public Morality Committee') sent threats to the theatre management, as well as to the actors, whom they termed pornographic delinquents. This vigilante group attempted to arrest the decline in Spain's virtue, as they saw it, by vowing to burn down the theatre and to disfigure the actress, María José Goyanes, if the production was not halted (AGA MIT/00.710). It was not, and the threats were not carried out. While such violent antagonism was not common, it did occasionally erupt during the transition period, showing how the theatre was perceived by some as an ideological battleground during this era of profound political change.

Besides sex and the body, open discussion of homosexuality was taboo. The work done by Raquel Merino Álvarez and the TRACE project has shown that it was through translation of foreign drama that the theme of homosexuality was first represented positively on the Spanish stage, despite the existence not only of prudish censorship legislation, but also laws such as the *Ley de Vagos y Maleantes* or the *Ley de Peligrosidad Social*.[35] Merino Álvarez claims that Tennessee Williams' *A Streetcar named Desire* was the turning point and was followed by 'a trend of translations of plays by foreign playwrights

(E. Albee, R. Anderson, M. Crowley and P. Shaffer) that helped introduce topics barred for native playwrights' (2007; 2010: 154 and 2016: 38).

One of the most interesting cases, which would surely have been banned for longer had the author been Spanish, was Robert Anderson's *Tea and Sympathy* (*Tě y simpatía*). It was translated by María Luz Regás and initially prohibited in 1955, but it was further adapted and authorised for *cámara* in 1956. A new translation was completed by Juan Ignacio Luca de Tena in 1956, and it was eventually authorised with cuts for the commercial stage. In those *posibilista* times, the domestication was drastic. One of the cuts, according to Pérez López de Heredia, was the complete elimination of the final scene in which the teacher's wife seduces the protagonist in an effort to 'cure' him (2004: 179–82). The combination of female sexuality, adultery and homosexuality contained in the scene was obviously too much for the censors to bear.

The treatment of the theme of homosexuality eventually changed, however. Merino Álvarez highlights the case of Mart Crowley's 1968 play, *The Boys in the Band*, and the history of its censorship in Spain (2007). She traces the play's trajectory from the first application on 22 June 1970 made by producer, Andrés de Kramer, for staging in the Teatro Beatriz, leading to prohibition by censors on 30 June, to its eventual authorisation five years later. In their verdicts on the initial application to stage it, the three censors denounced *The Boys in the Band* for its obscenity and perversion. Both Soria and Martínez Ruiz termed it scandalous, but Fr Cea's report was particularly damning: 'Desde que se levanta el telón hasta el final la escena está absorbida totalmente por homosexuales, con sus gestos, sus gritos, sus celos, etc. La mezcla con todo este ambiente de algún sentimiento religioso hace a la obra todavía más inaceptable' ('From the raising of the curtain to the ending, the stage is totally taken up with homosexuals, with their gestures, their cries, their jealousies, etc. The mixing of some religious sentiment in all of this atmosphere makes the work even more unacceptable').

Kramer's appeal against the verdict is dated 24 July and is interesting for what it reveals about the game-playing and negotiation that went on behind the scenes. In it he referred to the play's 'auténtico manifiesto en contra de la aberración expresada' ('genuine protest against the expressed aberration'), and he even went so far as to argue that the play was moralistic. He seemed to be trying to take the moral high ground and to employ the legislation in favour of the play, which he also claimed 'en ningún momento [la obra] es soez' ('at no time is the work crude'). Indeed, he also hoped to play on the prejudices of the censors by highlighting the location of this 'problem' in American, rather than Spanish, society. It didn't work, however, and when the play was considered by the plenary of the censorship board on 27 October, the prohibition was upheld. The language used in the reports is pejorative and evidence of the generally hostile attitude to homosexuality of the time, with characters described as: 'maricas', 'anormales', 'tarados', 'invertidos' ('sissies', 'abnormal', 'defectives', 'inverted') and even the most sympathetic report, by Bautista de la Torre, sees the characters as 'personajes atormentados y enfermos, no viciosos y degenerados' ('tormented and sick rather than depraved and degenerate characters'). The verdict was not unanimous, however, and attitudes towards the portrayal of gay characters were softening. The documents that Merino Álvarez reproduces in her article show that several of the censors who read the work considered it suitable for limited authorisation and a couple even accepted the argument put forward by Kramer that it was a moral work. Others did not, and García-Cernuda in particular took umbrage at Kramer's argument, suggesting that he was taking the members of the censorship board for 'deficientes mentales' ('people who are mentally deficient') (2007: 265; 279–84). A further application to stage it in 1972 was refused for the same reason and, although Merino Álvarez did not find the reports (but did see the text), it is clear that the play was eventually authorised three years later. *Los chicos de la banda* finally made it to the Spanish stage on 3 September 1975, five years after the first application was made to stage it in Spain. The play, translated by dramatist Jaime Salom, and adapted for the stage by Ignacio Artime and director Jaime Azpilicueta, was staged in the mainstream Teatro Barceló in Madrid, an indication of just how much things had changed.

While religious, moral and sexual concerns seemed to have dominated some of the censors' discussions, the political use of foreign theatre had the potential to cause serious alarm. Some foreign plays, particularly from the 1960s on, were used to attack Francoism or to suggest political alternatives to it. When considering these works, the censors read them not only for their political content and parallels with Spain, but also bearing political circumstances in mind. Therefore, during a period of civil unrest or heightened protest against the regime, a play that had previously been authorised might be banned or limited to *teatros de cámara*.

In terms of political content, translators, adaptors and directors sometimes foregrounded positive depictions of political revolt, as we can see in Alfonso Sastre's versions of the works of Jean-Paul Sartre or Seán O'Casey. His version of the latter's *Red Roses for Me* (*Rosas rojas para mí*), staged in the Teatro Beatriz in 1969 presented the theme of socialist revolution and armed struggle at a time when the Franco regime was weak and opposition to it was growing (O'Leary 2017b). It is a clear example of the production of a foreign play that reveals as much about the social and political struggles in Spain in the late 1960s as it does about the socialist struggle in Ireland in 1913 (AGA 258/69). Yet reviews focused not on parallels with Spain but with Northern Ireland, despite the obvious equivalences (López Sancho 1969b: 85–6).

Political violence and its justification is the touchy subject of several other works that made it to the Spanish stage in translation, including Camus's *The State of Siege* (*El estado de sitio*) and *The Just Assassins* (*Los justos*). While the latter, which deals with the political assassination of a Russian noble and focuses on the ethical dilemma posed by violent action for a political end, was staged more frequently and with more success in Spain, Camus's most significant play in terms of political censorship was *The State of Siege*. The Plague, which arrives in Cadiz, is represented on stage as a military dictator, and his successful rise to power is aided by the collusion of the bourgeoisie and the Church. A reign of fear and terror ensues for the ordinary citizens, stripped of their most basic rights. One can see why staging this play might have appealed to opponents of the regime. A total of six applications were made to stage the play under Franco and two further applications during the transition period. The first of the applications, by the TEU de Oviedo in January 1960, shows the censors' unease about political parallels with the dictatorship and it was banned. Some other versions of the play eliminated references to Spain, making it more palatable to the censors. However, restrictions and cuts were applied to all subsequent applications, and authorisations were for *teatros de cámara*, even when the application was for a commercial venue. In short, the criticism of the regime was neutralised and managed. The potential for scandal was reduced, the opposition silenced and the show went on.

Many examples show that geographical and temporal distance from Spain were important considerations when the play was a foreign one, and often allowed for the staging of politically challenging works that might otherwise have been prohibited. The moral report drawn up in 1962 on Buero's version of Brecht's *Mother Courage* is interesting for its conclusion that the historical distance employed would preclude parallels being drawn between the Thirty Years War and recent events in Spanish history: 'Al fin, estamos en Alemania y en el siglo XVII y en *épocas* revueltas en todos los *órdenes*' ('After all, we are in Germany and in the seventeenth century and in revolutionary times') (AGA 227/62).[36] This can be seen again in reports on *The Good Person of Szechwan* in 1966, for a production in Barcelona in a Catalan version by Carme Serrallonga (*La bona persona de Sezuan*) (AGA 270/66), and in 1967 for a production in Madrid, adapted by Armando Moreno and José Monleón (*La persona buena de Sezuán*) (AGA 11/67), in both cases with Ricard Salvat as director and Núria Espert in the main role. Sebastián Bautista de la Torre wrote in his report: 'Mantenida en el montaje con ese aire de lejanía no encuentro reparos para su autorización' ('I have no objection to authorisation provided the air of distance is maintained in the staging'). Yet another example of censors requiring that distance be maintained is contained in the file on Brecht's *Fear and Misery of the Third Reich* (*Terror y miseria del Tercer Reich*) (AGA 201/71). The report by Florentino Soria, dated 27 April, states:

> Yo no pongo reparos esenciales a esta representación pero siempre que se ajuste en su puesta en escena a las circunstancias de lugar y tiempo, suprimiendo todo lo que convierta a los marxistas en 'los buenos' y los llamamientos a la lucha de clases y otros detalles que encuentro inconvenientes.
>
> I have no essential objections to this production, as long as the setting is adjusted to the circumstances of place and time, suppressing everything that turns the Marxists into 'the good guys' and the calls for a class struggle, and other details I find inconvenient.

As with the works of Spanish playwrights, the political circumstances at the time an application was made had an impact on the verdict of the censors. While *apertura* and changes to censorship allowed for more challenging foreign drama to be staged, the rise in opposition to the regime meant that the timing of productions mattered, as it was recognised that they could be used as rallying points for protest.

The censors, despite the apparent nonsense of some of their rulings, were not stupid, and their reports show that they generally, and usually correctly, suspected the political motivation behind applications to stage the works of particular dramatists in Spain at particular moments in time. An application in 1967 to stage Alfonso Sastre's version of Sartre's *The Victors* ('*Muertos sin sepultura*'), highlights this. In his report, the censor Soria noted the parallels between the suicide in the play and the recent 'defenestration' of a political opponent of the regime in Spain, and those drawn between the heroic members of the resistance and members of the Communist Party. Moreover, he noted the political allegiances of both author and translator, all of which combined to make the work politically inconvenient (AGA 363/67). The application from the Justo Alonso company was for a commercial production, but it was only authorised for studio theatres, in a clear example of managed opposition.

An application from the university theatre company of the Escuela de Bellas Artes to stage the play earlier that same year was authorised without cuts for *cámara*. The interesting thing about Bautista de la Torre's report is its explicit reference to similar works by Spanish authors and the justification for different treatment of them. The report demonstrates many of the regime's concerns, as well as its sense of inferiority. Temporal, spatial and political distance from the Spanish circumstance is cited as the reason for allowing works by a foreign author. For this censor, the French text is superior to Spanish equivalents. Moreover, he points to the fact that it is set in France during the Resistance, and that its existentialism also distances it from political specificity:

> Conocida obra de Sartre. En ella se nos presentan las distintas reacciones físicas y morales, de unos detenidos políticos frente a la tortura a que los someten sus aprehensores. *Con la misma intención se han escrito dos obras de autores españoles, Buero Vallejo y Alfonso Sastre; pero la del francés tiene una superior categoría ya que la preocupación por la hondura del concepto dentro de sus posiciones existencialistas aleja manifiestas parcialidades políticas. La acción se sitúa en Francia en la época de la resistencia.* Por mi parte –salvo que existan especiales prevenciones

contra el autor que a estas alturas no creo después de autorizarse casi toda la producción de Brecht– puede darse para teatros de cámara siempre que se conserve su auténtica localización y previo el visado de la puesta en escena. (AGA 150/67)

> Well-known play by Sartre. In it we are presented with the different physical and moral reactions of some political prisoners to the torture their captors subject them to. Spanish authors, Buero Vallejo and Alfonso Sastre have written two works with the same intention, but the French work is in a superior category, as the concern for the profundity of the concept within his existential position distances it from manifest political bias. The action takes place in France at the time of the Resistance. For my part – unless there are special measures against the author, which I doubt these days since almost all of Brecht's work has been authorised – it can be authorised for studio theatres, as long as its authentic localisation is retained and the dress rehearsal is viewed.

Brecht's *Antigone*, which had been banned in 1961, was the subject of several subsequent applications, including one by the widely respected Núria Espert Theatre Company to stage a version by José Monleón and Armando Moreno in March 1969. The censors expressed serious reservations about the timing of the production. A state of emergency had been declared in January and the potential for provocative parallels between the theme of the play and the situation in Spain led the censor Fr Cea to conclude that 'se supone mala intención el ponerla ahora en escena' ('one can assume bad intentions in staging it now'). Bautista de la Torre also referred to the 'marcada intención política' ('marked political intention') of the work and the risk of staging what he termed a 'tendentious' version in the current political climate (AGA 89/69). Despite the company's efforts to frame the play in a way that emphasised its theatricality rather than its politics, another censor, Soria, was to conclude: 'Hay una evidente intención de acercar la obra a las coordenadas políticas de hoy' ('There is a clear intention to draw parallels with the politics of today'). In the end, however, and despite the censors' reservations regarding the timing of the application, the play was authorised in mid-April, with a stipulation that the dress rehearsal be closely monitored. The fact that it was eventually permitted, despite many censors' serious reservations, suggests that the potential for scandal and reputational damage for the regime outweighed the possible damage to audiences from exposure to such contentious material.

Under a dictatorship that prohibited political meetings and outlawed political parties, the regime was conscious of the theatre's potential to act as a space for collective expression of dissent. The very fact that the censors, or other officials, intervened to control these translated political works, or attempted to curtail or manage their staging, suggest that they perceived a threat from works that foregrounded opposing values or an alternative social order, or that suggested change was both necessary and achievable.

Conclusion

Over the course of the dictatorship, foreign drama played an important and ever-adapting role in challenging the values established by the regime, and in influencing the development of Spanish theatre. It was frequently staged with political intent, either to distract from reality, to support the dictatorship, or to highlight absent freedoms. It is evident from the archival material in the AGA that while most translation of foreign drama texts conformed to the normative pressures at play, certain translators and adaptors (mostly authors and directors themselves) considered foreign drama to be another weapon in their battle with the regime, and were prepared to manipulate the original works in the process of preparing them for the stage.

During the transition to democracy, as political circumstances changed again, so too did the framing of foreign drama. Following the *destape*, when nudity and sexual content provided the censors with plenty to occupy them, foreign drama came to form part of a renewed attempt at improvement and modernisation, rather than a political battle, and it had few problems with the censors or classification boards. Some directors, such as Marsillach and Salvat, who had been influential in bringing foreign drama to Spain under the dictatorship, were in positions of authority in the post-Franco cultural scene, and continued to use their influence to stage foreign works.

We might ask how successful the strategies of adaptation and activist translation really were, as, according to Venuti, 'the social impact of a politically engaged translation depends on the ways in which diverse cultural constituencies receive it' (2008: 18). Considering the reception of these works by censors, audience and critics, we can get some idea of their impact. Foreignness mattered: both activist translator and censor stressed the otherness of the work – the former to highlight freedoms that were absent in Spain; the latter to distance the criticisms from the Spanish situation. It is clear that censors were generally aware of what was going on, but tried to control the damage by placing restrictions on audiences and venues (often authorised for one performance only, and in studio theatres). While there was often a political message to be decoded in the works, the regime recognised, or determined, that the audience for these works was a minority one.

This ability to adapt to the times and circumstances in matters cultural as well as political, is part of the history of the survival of the regime. By managing the opposition in this way, the regime could make a case for its liberal credentials and dismiss arguments about dictatorship by citing its authorisation of these works. The Director General, García Escudero, writing in 1966, suggested that 'con un punto de vista estrictamente político, lo aconsejable sería quitar hierro a la subversión, convertirla de oposición salvaje en oposición civilizada, metiéndola en los Teatros Nacionales' (1978a: 191) ('from a strictly political point of view, it would be advisable to weaken the subversion, turning it from savage opposition to civilised opposition, by putting it in the National Theatres').

In addition to managed opposition, which allowed the regime to protect its reputation by favouring the limited staging of foreign political works, there is a question still to be resolved about the long-term damage done to the reputations of foreign authors in Spain. Practices of taming the text and activist translation had immeasurable impact on the name and status of certain foreign dramatists in Spain, and many of their works are still known only in their censored form. There is work to be done on the recovery of the creations and reputations of some who were censored and disparaged by the regime, or whose work was radically transformed in order to convey a political message to the target culture.

To conclude, both *posibilista* translation with its compromises, and activist translation with its disruptive intentions, were significant aspects of the cultural resistance to the Franco regime. While it cannot be claimed that they ignited a revolution, these adaptations of imported works did allow foreign influence and unorthodox viewpoints into Spain. Politicised Spanish authors and directors used them to communicate messages to their own audiences despite censorship, and to keep political ideas in the public domain. In sum, foreign drama transposed onto the Spanish situation not only highlighted in form and theme the freedoms absent in Spain, but also in their harnessing of narratives of liberation and revolt served as encouragement to the politically active in society in their efforts to achieve change.

Case study

El círculo de tiza caucasiano, by Bertolt Brecht
Teatro Nacional Universitario at the Teatro María Guerrero (Madrid), 29 March 1965

By 1965, previously banned authors such as Bertolt Brecht, while still treated with much suspicion, were finally being authorised, albeit generally with cuts and for *cámara*, with the restrictions in terms of audience and production run that this implied. The staging of Brecht's *El círculo de tiza caucasiano* (*The Caucasian Chalk Circle*) by the Teatro Nacional Universitario (TNU) at the Teatro María Guerrero was important, as it came at a significant moment in the regime's relationship with the student body. The regime's unease with the growth of student opposition had come to a head in late February, when a peaceful demonstration organised by students and some staff of the University of Madrid was brutally put down by the police. The tension within Spain was heightened by the regime's concerns about its reputation abroad, as it was attempting (unsuccessfully as it turned out) to negotiate entry into the European Common Market at the time (Rodríguez Tejada 2014: 535).

The archives show that there were many applications made to stage Brecht's work in Spain from the late 1950s, although many of these were prohibited. In total, twenty-one plays suffered cuts at the hands of the Spanish censors, and sixteen plays (or versions of plays) were prohibited, from the earliest applications in 1957 to as late as 1975.[37] The MIT internal report on Brecht sent from the Secretario General Técnico to the Secretario General de Cinematografía y Teatro in 1958 reflected the regime's fears about his negative influence in Spain: 'Su teatro es absolutamente racionalista, frío, despiadado. Intenta mostrar la bajeza y ruindad de la sociedad actual, muy especialmente del capitalismo burgués y la posibilidad de librarse de él por el materialismo técnico marxista y la actuación colectiva sobre estas bases' ('His theatre is absolutely rational, cold, merciless. It aims to represent the baseness and meanness of contemporary society, most especially bourgeois capitalism, and the possibility of liberating oneself from it through technical Marxist materialism and collective action based on it').[38] In addition to his politics, concerns were expressed about his morals, and it is therefore logical that Brecht's theatre was both carefully monitored by the censors and attractive to those interested in politically activist translation.

The application in 1965 from the TNU to stage Brecht's *El círculo de tiza caucasiano* at a university theatre competition in Salamanca (later moved to Madrid) was momentous in the history of Spanish theatre because it was the first time that Brecht was staged in a major Madrid theatre, and opened the door to further bold productions. Anticipating possible problems with the censors, the adaptor and representative of the TNU, Alberto Castilla, had framed the work in a neutral fashion in his correspondence with them. He claimed, as the files reveal, that this was a version already adulcinated to suit Spanish tastes:

NOTAS DEL ADAPTADOR:

1. En la presente adaptación ha sido eliminada (por motivos de dificultad escenográfica) la última escena de la parte II, cuando el personaje Grusa intenta cruzar por un puente en las montañas.
2. La primera escena, o prólogo, que recoge varios párrafos o diálogos de carácter 'propagandístico', ha sido suprimida y sustituída por un breve resumen de dicha escena, incluído al principio de la presente adaptación. (AGA 13/65)

ADAPTOR'S NOTES:

1. The last scene in part II, when the character Grusa tries to cross a bridge in the mountains, has been eliminated from this adaptation (because of staging difficulties).
2. The first scene, or prologue, which contains various propagandistic pararaphs or dialogues, has been suppressed and replaced by a summary of said scene, included at the start of this adaptation.

What his notes did not state was the fact that the play still offered a political message, not only within the plot, but in its very staging; this, after all, was by a dramatist associated in the public mind with left-wing revolutionary politics. Castilla, who had adapted the play from an Argentinian translation by Oswald Bayer, was at pains to stress that the play had been denounced by Eastern Bloc countries and, therefore, could be considered acceptable in Spain. This framing of the play seems to have worked, to some extent at least, and the play was authorised with cuts for staging by students of the University of Madrid in the María Guerrero for one night. While the AGA files clearly demonstrate that the censors held negative views of Brecht and his work, they weighed this against distance from Spain, and the impact of a prohibition in sensitive political times. Three censors read the play and all suggested cuts. Fr Artola considered it stageable for *cámara* without cuts and Vázquez Dodero suggested that certain of his recommended cuts applied to both commercial and minority venues. Bautista de la Torre's report, written in rather elegant prose, is the most interesting, and highlights the censor's cognisance of the need to monitor the political circumstances in Spain when delivering a verdict:

> La obra nos ofrece la marca típica del autor: exaltación del pueblo contra los poderes opresores, burla religiosa, antimilitarismo, venalidad de la justicia, despotismo del mando, crueldad de sus agentes. Pero a lo largo de la pieza estas intenciones se diluyen y pierden dejando solo a flote la noble y ejemplar acción de la protagonista. La distancia en el tiempo le resta peligrosidad al destacar sus valores morales por encima de cualquier otro propósito. Por eso y salvo otras razones de orden extrateatral yo me inclino por autorizarla con algunas modificaciones de diálogo o situación que estimo inconvenientes para comercial. (AGA 13/65)

> The play offers us the typical hallmarks of the author: exaltation of the masses against oppressive powers, religious mockery, antimilitarism, corruption of justice, despotism of rulers and cruelty of their agents. Over the course of the piece, however, these intentions are diluted and lost, leaving only the noble and exemplary action of the protagonist. The temporal distance removes the danger given its highlighting of her moral values above any other purpose. Therefore, and unless there are other reasons beyond the theatre, I'm inclined to authorise it with some modifications to the dialogue and location that I consider inappropriate for the commercial stage.

It was authorised with four cuts, three of them relating to the avarice of the clergy and the fourth, a pejorative reference to the army:

p. 34
LAURENTI.– Ya me ocuparé de eso. Pero ¿por qué llamó a un fraile, en lugar de a un cura?
SUEGRA.– ¡Qué más dá! Mi fallo fué pagarle por adelantado. <u>Seguro que se me fué a la taberna</u>. En seguida vuelvo. (SALE CORRIENDO).
LAURENTI.– <u>Desgraciada, por ahorrarse el cura, llamó a un fraile, que es más barato.</u>

LAVRENTI: I'll take care he doesn't. But why only a monk? Why not a priest?
THE MOTHER-IN-LAW: Oh, he's just as good. I only made one mistake: I paid half his fee in advance. Enough to send him to the tavern. I only hope . . . [*She runs off.*]
LAVRENTI: She saved on the priest, the wretch! Hired a cheap monk.
(Brecht 1966: 159)

p. 35
GRUSA.– Claro que lo está. ¿No escuchaste el "sí"?
<u>FRAILE.– Muy bien. Entonces, declaro formalizado el matrimonio. ¿Y la extremaunción?</u>
SUEGRA.– <u>Ni hablar. Ya fué bastante cara la boda. Ahora tengo que preocuparme de los que han venido a darme el pésame.</u> (A LAURENTI). Ya sabes, setecientos, como quedamos.

THE MOTHER-IN-LAW: Of course he is! Didn't you hear him say yes?
THE MONK: All right. We declare the marriage contracted! How about the extreme unction?
THE MOTHER-IN-LAW: Nothing doing! The wedding cost quite enough. Now I must take care of the mourners. [*To* LAVRENTI] Did we say seven hundred?) (Brecht 1966: 160)

p. 36
SUEGRA.– Se está vengando. <u>No debí tomar un fraile tan barato. Este bien vale lo que cuesta. Uno más caro se habría comportado mejor. En Sura tienen uno en estado de santidad, pero, claro, pide una fortuna. Un fraile de cincuenta piastras como éste no tiene dignidad. Cincuenta piastras de dignidad. Y nada más . . .</u>

THE MOTHER-IN-LAW: He's getting his own back. I shouldn't have hired such a cheap one. It's what you'd expect. A more expensive monk would behave himself. In Sura there's one with a real air of sanctity about him, but of course he charges a fortune. A fifty-piastre monk like that has no dignity, and as for piety, just fifty piastres' worth and no more!) (Brecht 1966: 161)

p. 53

AZAK.– 8.240.000 piastras para manutención de soldados. Soldados comer mierda.

ADZAK: 8,240,000 piastres for food supplies not produced. (Brecht 1966: 182) ['Soldiers eat shit' – an addition to the Spanish version.]

The poem included in the production was also read by two censors. Neither Bautista de la Torre nor Arroita Jáuregui had any objections. The show went ahead. An air of anticipation surrounded the production. After all, this was the first time that a play by Bertolt Brecht was to be staged in a national theatre, albeit in a student production and for one night only. The fear was that it would become a rallying cry for further protest; the benefit was that at a time when Spain needed to enhance its standing abroad, this was a perfect opportunity for managed opposition.

The audience was made up largely of students, although there were also some serious theatre critics in the house. When the curtain came down, a shift had occurred. This performance, taking place when it had, was to become a symbol of student opposition to the regime, and a milestone in the employment of the theatre as part of such opposition. Unlike many other student performances, this was recognised as a significant production and reviewed – generally positively – in the mainstream press, although as was to be expected, several of the reviewers avoided mentioning the political content (Castilla 1999: 249–50). Even Nicolás González Ruiz penned a review for *Ya*, in which he referred to the importance of Brecht as a theatrical innovator, although he did not refer to the politics of the piece. Victoriano Fernández Asís, in his review for *El Español*, stressed the poetry of the play over its politics. Pérez Gallego in the *Heraldo de Aragón*, deemed the production 'apoteósico' ('triumphant') and praised the work of Castilla and the TNU in bringing Brecht to the national theatre at last.[39] Joaquín Puig's review in *Primer Acto*, while praising the bravery of those who had brought Brecht to the stage, also stressed the corresponding responsibility to stage it well. He complimented Castilla on beginning the performance with the recitation of Brecht's poem 'To Those Born After' ('Oda a las generaciones venideras'), but his verdict on the production was not so positive: 'Fue una representación arriesgada que, desgraciadamente, no salvó el riesgo' ('It was a risky production that, unfortunately, did not succeed') (1965: 53).

An official inspector, Rafael Salazar Ruiz, was also present, and his report is surprisingly neutral (see Figure 15). He wrote that the youthful audience responded well to the piece and that the atmosphere in the theatre was agreeable. The response outside the theatre, however, was more mixed. Castilla recalls that there

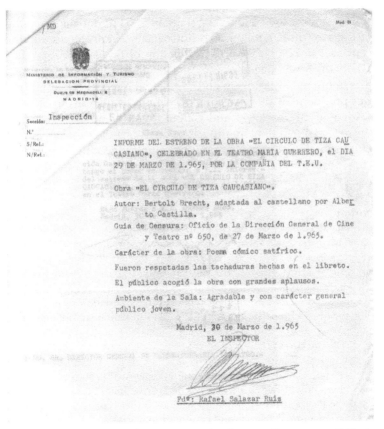

Figure 15: Salazar Ruiz's report on the first performance of *El círculo de tiza caucasiano* (1965)

were criticisms and threats of violence from the hard left and the extreme right also, 'unos acusando a los miembros del TNU de "comunistas" por presentar a Brecht, y otros acusándolos de "fascistas", de hacer el juego al SEU' ('some accusing the members of the TNU of being communists for staging Brecht, and others accusing them of being fascists, for playing the SEU's game') (1999: 250).[40]

This 1965 student performance was followed by many more productions of Brecht's most political theatre, and while some were severely cut or banned, many made it to the stage, including the commercial stage, something unthinkable a decade before. These included Buero Vallejo's version of *Madre Coraje*, which had a successful run on the commercial stage in 1966 under the direction of Tamayo (though following serious delays and problems with the censors), and Núria Espert's production of *El círculo de tiza caucasiano*, which was staged at the María Guerrero in 1968 at a time of heightened civil unrest, and was halted after a few days by the vice-president of the government, Admiral Luis Carrero Blanco (Monleón 1977a: 253–4 and García Escudero 1978a: 263). The theatre, as it had done in the 1930s, once again became an important forum for expressing mounting opposition to the regime. Brecht's work, and foreign drama more generally, was an influential part of this expression.

Notes
1. See McGaha (1979) and O'Leary (2003; 2017a).
2. The material available in the AGA is therefore the key to our understanding not only of the censorship of foreign drama in Spain, but also of its history. Merino Álvarez's work (1994: 24–7; 2016), and that of the TRACE project generally, has been crucial in bringing into the public domain information about theatre translation from the censorship archives, although its focus is a translation studies one, comparing source and target-language texts (TRAnslations CEnsored, www.ehu.es/trace).
3. The organisation was created by a law of 10 August 1954 (BOE 1954a). Vilches de Frutos lists the independent groups active at the time (1998: 10). See also Vilches de Frutos (1995).
4. The Pact was the culmination of years of negotiation and led to an agreement on defence and economic aid that saw the establishment of US military bases in Spain in exchange for economic aid and the end of Spain's political isolation (US Department of State 1957).

5   For further information about Spain's attempts to form a closer alliance with other European states, see Rudnick (1976: 134–41) and Ortuño Anaya (2001: 26–39).
6   For example, Adolfo Lozano Borroy, a minor dramatist himself, was the translator of Aldo de Benedetti's popular escapist theatre. Such entertaining works, though not the focus of this chapter, were the mainstay of commercially staged foreign theatre throughout the dictatorship. Yet Lozano Borroy also produced a version of the controversial British play *A Taste of Honey* (*Sabor a miel*), by Shelagh Delaney (see Martín Clavijo 2011 and 2012).
7   In the aftermath of the civil war, paper restrictions in Spain led to the growth of imports of books from Latin America, and Argentina in particular (see Abellán 1980: 172).
8   Pérez López de Heredia notes that some of those credited with translations in an earlier period may not have been their authors either, as figures such as María de la O Lejárraga and Zenobia Camprubí were sidelined at the time for their gender, and their labours were credited to their husbands, Gregorio Martínez Sierra and Juan Ramón Jiménez. She points out that the exception to this rule was Pilar Millán-Astray, whose original dramas and translations appeared under her own name (2004: 40–1).
9   See García Ruiz (2004) and Santiago Muñoz (2006).
10 According to the censorship files on *Huis clos*, Sastre acted as Sartre's representative in Spain (AGA 250/64 and AGA 125/67). For more on Sastre's translations of Sartre and of O'Casey, see O'Leary (2017b and 2021).
11 For a review of the latter, see López Sancho (1969: 71–2).
12 In the hands of non-activist translators and directors, and in an earlier period, Irishness tended to be associated with conservatism and Catholicism, rather than armed revolution.
13 Marsillach makes the point elsewhere that Escobar did not allow his politics to colour his choice of work or actor (2000: 292–3). See also García Lorenzo (2014a) and Hidalgo (2001). Escobar was later owner and manager of the Teatro Eslava from 1956 until 1963, a period in which he embraced the *posibilismo* mode.
14 See García Ruiz (2000) and Aguilera Sastre (1993).
15 See García Lorenzo (2014b).
16 The document is signed off by the Head of Censorship (el Jefe de censura): 'Por Dios, por España y su Revolución Nacionalsindicalista' ('For God, for Spain and for the National-Syndicalist Revolution'), and dated Madrid, 21 March 1941 (AGA 2027/41).
17 See Espejo Romero (2002) and Merino Álvarez (1994).
18 The censorship documents are reproduced in Pérez López de Heredia (2004: 84–101).

19 Prior to taking over at the María Guerrero, Alonso had already demonstrated an interest in foreign drama and his earliest experience in his home-based theatre, La Independencia, staged works by Sartre and O'Neill. He later worked for the María Jesús Valdés company, and with her staged works by Shakespeare and Arthur Miller, among others. For more detail about him and the other directors mentioned, see Vilches de Frutos (1998), London (1997: 120–30) and García Lorenzo (2014c).

20 See also García Lorenzo (2014e) and Rodríguez (2000).

21 See García Lorenzo (2014d). Narros's time at the Teatro Español saw the staging of works by Cervantes and Valle-Inclán, as well as many foreign dramas. When he left the Español, he continued to stage foreign drama, first with the Teatro Estable Castellano and later the Teatro del Arte.

22 For a detailed analysis of the censorship of Brecht, Sartre and Camus in Spain, see O'Leary (2007, 2017b, 2019 and 2021).

23 By July 1968, however, when the play was to be staged in the Poliorama theatre in Barcelona, Sastre wished to be acknowledged as the translator, and Marsillach wrote to José María Ortiz asking to change the name on the censorship form and explaining that Sastre had not wanted to diminish his own reputation as an author by appearing in 1966 as the author of too many translations.

24 These were scenes 13 ('La liturgia de Marat') and 14 ('Lamentable intermedio'), and corrections were made following initial cuts to scene 30. See AGA 149/66.

25 See Marsillach (1998: 303–12), Monleón (1968: 11), Zatlin (1999: 228) and Cornago (2000: 78–81). See also Ordóñez's reconstruction of José María Pou's memories of the production (2007).

26 See the entry dated Thursday 4th. See also Llovet's obituary in *El País*, where from 1976 until 1979 he was also theatre critic (Ordóñez 2010).

27 Llovet, son-in-law of the translator, diplomat and writer Ricardo Baeza, was both a regime diplomat and an influential theatre critic himself, which proved useful when he employed his adaptations of foreign dramas to engage in social criticism. In the official reports on his adaptation of O'Casey's *Juno and the Paycock* (*Juno y el pavo real*), for example, the subject of a 1955 application from Carmen Troitiño as representative of the Teatro Nacional de Cámara y Ensayo, reference is made to the fact that he is the Spanish Consul in Paris, thus framing the play as acceptable to the censors (AGA 109/55).

28 See also Rodríguez-Gago (2010: 405), and Andaluz Pinedo and Merino Álvarez (2020) for a list of *expedientes* on Beckett plays.

29 At the height of its popularity, the HSE had more than 8,000 members (Jaubert 2016).

30 See Chapter 3 for further information about the Catholic Church's own censorship procedures. While influential, these did not carry the legal weight of the state's censorship legislation.
31 The *Index* was formally abolished by the Vatican in 1966. Despite this, Sartre's earlier inclusion was cited by Fr Cea in a 1967 report on *A puerta cerrada*.
32 Although she had been associated with Rivas Cherif and his experimental theatre in the 1930s, Zaro was the wife of writer and Falangist Eugenio Montes and, we can therefore assume, would not have been perceived as hostile to the regime.
33 '*A Taste of Honey* showed working-class women from a working-class woman's point of view, had a gay man as a central and sympathetic figure, and a black character who was neither idealised nor a racial stereotype' (Barker 2011). For details of how the play was described to the Spanish theatregoing public, see José María de Quinto (1960: 20–2), who praises the work for its social commentary but gives no detail of its content.
34 Del Amo was a playwright as well as theatre and film director and came to prominence as one of the directors of the Centro Dramático Nacional in the later 1970s.
35 See Gaceta de Madrid (1933: 874–7); BOE (1954c: 4862); BOE (1970: 12551–7).
36 *Madre Coraje* was not staged until 1966.
37 For further information about the reception and censorship of Brecht's theatre in Spain, see O'Leary (2007: 73–86).
38 Two-page report, sent from the Secretario General Técnico to the Secretario General de Cinematografía y Teatro (MIT), a copy of which appears in the file on *Madre Coraje y sus hijos* (AGA 227/62).
39 'El círculo de tiza caucasiano en el María Guerrero', *Ya*, 30 March 1965; 'María Guerrero: El círculo de tiza caucasiano de Bertolt Brecht', *El Español*, 5 April, 1965; 'Brecht', *Heraldo de Aragón*, 31 March 1965. All reviews are quoted in Castilla (1999: 250).
40 The Sindicato Español Universitario (or SEU), the students' union established by the Falange in 1933, was the only officially recognised one during the dictatorship. It was disbanded in 1965. See Ruiz Carnicer (1996).

Chapter 8
Dénouement: Dismantling the Apparatus during the Transition to Democracy

The transition gets under way

The preceding chapters have examined the effect of official censorship on theatre in Spain up to the middle of 1976. This was the point at which the hesitant transition to democracy began to accelerate. Adolfo Suárez was appointed head of government by the King on 3 July and brought in Andrés Reguera Guajardo as Ministro de Información y Turismo. Francisco José Mayans Jofre, who had been Director General de Teatro y Espectáculos since February, remained in post. Clear evidence of the new team's intention to liberalise censorship can be seen in a letter sent by Mayans on 15 November 1976 to the secretary of the Junta de Ordenación de Obras Teatrales, copies of which can be found in the *expedientes* of a number of plays that had been banned and were now being reassessed:[1]

> Motivaciones de carácter circunstancial pueden justificar, y de hecho así ha sucedido, la adopción de dictámenes censores de signo prohibitivo, cuya permanente vigencia, una vez modificadas sustancialmente las situaciones de hecho o causas que la aconsejaron, no sería lícito mantener sin grave detrimento de una objetividad a ultranza en el ejercicio de una función que tan directamente afecta a valores culturales, sociales, éticos y políticos. Estimando que en tal situación se hallan obras de calificados autores y considerando así mismo que la propia norma vigente reconoce la capacidad de revisión de dictámenes de que dispone la Administración, esta Dirección General ha resuelto proceder en tal sentido en aquellos casos en los que

aparezcan datos suficientes para entender que la dinámica social y política del país aconseja la revisión de calificaciones claramente superadas. (AGA 29/65)

Proscriptive decisions by censorship bodies may be justified by motives of a circumstantial nature, and at times this has indeed been the case. However, it would not be legitimate to allow such prohibitions to remain in force indefinitely when the material circumstances or causes that prompted them have changed significantly, as this would result in serious damage to the absolute objectivity with which a function that has such a direct effect on cultural, social, ethical and political values must be exercised. Having found that there are works by eminent authors in such a situation, and in view of the fact that current regulations empower the Department to review earlier decisions, the Directorate General has resolved to carry out such reviews in cases that provide sufficient evidence to indicate that the social and political dynamic of the country demands reconsideration of judgements that have clearly been superseded.

This cautiously worded statement did not quite amount to a repudiation of censorship, but it recognised that the political, social and cultural climate was changing rapidly and that the criteria by which the censors had been operating were increasingly indefensible. Ruibal's *El hombre y la mosca* (*The Man and the Fly*) was one of the first works to benefit from the new liberalisation. Banned since 1969, it was authorised on 9 July 1976. Olmo's *Plaza Menor* ('Minor Square'), banned since 1967, was approved on 13 July. Rodríguez Méndez's *Bodas que fueron famosas del Pingajo y la Fandanga* ('The Famous Wedding of Pingajo and Fandanga'), banned since 1966, was authorised for performance at the Festival Grec in Barcelona in August 1976. Olmo's *La condecoración* ('The Medal'), which had been prohibited in 1965 and again in March 1976, was approved in December 1976 and staged in Madrid the following March. Alfonso Sastre's *La sangre y la ceniza* ('Blood and Ashes'), prohibited since 1971, was authorised in September and performed in Barcelona in February 1977 in a production by El Búho, a group led by former members of Tábano. This production became the target of a new, unofficial form of censorship carried out by extremists opposed to the transition to democracy. A bomb was thrown into the foyer of the theatre during a performance, causing damage but no injuries. Responsibility was claimed by the Alianza Apostólica Anticomunista (Apostolic Anti-communist Alliance), one of several right-wing Catholic groups that had been threatening companies and performers since late 1975 (Vanguardia 1977).

The censors at this time were also becoming more tolerant of sexual references, swearing, nudity and irreligiousness, but there were still limits. Fernando Arrabal's *En la cuerda floja* (*On the Tightrope*) and *Y pusieron esposas en las flores* (*And They Put Handcuffs on the Flowers*) were banned in August and October 1976 respectively, on the grounds of obscenity and profanity combined with political subversiveness. At the more popular end of the market, Antonio Fos Fernando's suggestively titled *El moño de la Bernarda* ('French Twist')[2] was strongly disapproved of by the religious censor, Antonio Albizu: 'Estimo que hay excesiva grosería y, sobre todo, que da ocasión para toda clase de acciones y que ni las supresiones ni el visado tendrían eficacia' ('In my view the indecency is excessive and, most importantly, it is likely to give rise to all kinds of actions, which neither cuts nor an inspection would be effective in curbing') (AGA 1134/76). Albizu was outvoted by the other censors and authorisation was given in September 1976 for *café-teatro* performances. Two cuts were imposed, however, both involving ribald references by a prostitute to her profession. The *café-teatro* sector was enjoying a brisk trade in bawdy comedies, riding the growing wave of the erotic *destape* led by magazines and films. A typical example of the genre appears in the same box in the archive: *Amor, amor... destápame* ('My Love, My Love... Strip Me'), authorised in September 1976 without cuts (AGA 1130/76).

The diminution of the Catholic Church's power to intervene directly in cultural control is visible in episodes such as Albizu's failure to persuade his colleagues to prohibit *El moño de la Bernarda*, and in the fact that he and Father Jesús Cea were now the only ecclesiastical censors among the fourteen members of the Junta. Episcopal statements issued in this period showed a recognition of the limits of ecclesiastical power and a post-conciliar emphasis on urging public authorities – in the words of Pope Paul VI's *Octogesima Adveniens* – to encourage constructive forms of expression, while at the same time acting 'de manera que eviten oportunamente la difusión de cuanto menoscabe el patrimonio común de valores, sobre el cual se funda el ordenado progreso civil' ('in such a way as to prevent the spread of what would harm the common heritage of values on which orderly civil progress is based' (Iribarren 1974: 479).

The Church, together with Catholic lay associations, continued to exercise considerable social and cultural influence, and was still publishing its own guides warning of the moral dangers of certain books, films and plays. The list of moral classifications published in *ABC* in October 1976, for example, gives seven theatrical productions the highest rating of 'gravemente peligrosas' ('gravely dangerous'): two popular *revistas*, *Lo tengo rubio* ('I've Got Virginia') and *El desnudo de Venus* ('Nude Venus'); Peter Shaffer's *Equus*; Francisco Nieva's *La carroza de plomo candente* ('The Carriage of White-Hot Lead') and *El combate de Ópalos y Tasia* ('The Battle between Opalos and Tasia'); Ray Cooney and John Chapman's hit farce *Sé infiel y no mires con quién* (*Not Now, Darling*), which had been playing since 1972; Jaime Salom's thoughtful drama about the newly controversial topic of divorce, *La piel del limón* (*Bitter Lemon*); and Manuel Martínez Mediero's anticlerical comedy *Mientras la gallina duerme* ('While the Chicken Sleeps') (ABC 1976b).

By early 1977, it was becoming clear that Catholic moral values were losing the battle against the *destape*, as nudity and eroticism became increasingly prominent on stage and screen, and increasingly profitable at the box office.[3] The actor Teresa del Olmo refused to work in Spain during the late 1970s because so many of the roles on offer in plays and films required female performers to take part in nude scenes (Olmo 2019). While sexual liberation had earlier tended to be associated with progressive, anti-Franco politics, some of those cashing in on the new permissiveness were pursuing reactionary agendas, satirising the country's movement towards democracy, Europeanisation and modernisation in a way that was reminiscent of comedies that lampooned Republican reforms between 1931 and 1936. Pablo de Villamar's *¡Jo, qué corte. . . estamos en Europa!* ('A Right Royal Mess. . . We're in Europe Now!') premiered in April 1977 in Madrid, directed by the author. Billed as a 'farsa porno-política' ('pornopolitical farce'), it derided progressive political activism, sneered at European cultural stereotypes and disingenuously denounced the commercialisation of sex. One review commented: 'Todo el irreflexivo, sombrío y torpe odio del franquismo a Europa está aquí presente, en montón, sin que Villamar se preocupe ni poco ni mucho de hacerlo inteligible' ('All the dreary, boorish, knee-jerk hatred of Francoism towards Europe is on show here, in abundance, without Villamar making much of an effort to render it intelligible') (Álvarez 1977).

Villamar's show was received with enthusiasm at first by rightwing militants, but before long the production faced public hostility and fell apart amidst sexual and financial scandal. The theatre manager, Francisco Banegas, accused the author of embezzling box-office takings, and declared to the press that the play contained little more than gratuitous slander, which he had attempted to persuade Villamar to tone down: 'En muchas ocasiones me he visto obligado a cursarle telegramas, prohibiéndole toda alusión injuriosa a personas e instituciones públicas, sin que hiciera el menor caso' ('Many times I've had to send him telegrams telling him not to include slanderous references to individuals and public institutions, without him taking the slightest notice') (Gracia 1977). This is the kind of material that Republican censors in the 1930s would have been inclined to suppress, on the grounds that it threatened to undermine public confidence in fragile, embryonic democratic institutions at a time of political tension. Banegas presumably attempted to take on the role of unofficial censor for fear of being sued for libel.

The official censors were now subject to conflicting political imperatives. On the one hand, the Suárez government was under public pressure to forge ahead with the dismantling of the structure of the dictatorship and was keen to legitimise the idea of parliamentary democracy. On the other hand, the authorities were painfully aware of the risk of a reactionary backlash led by the armed forces, which might be provoked by a perception that social unrest was out of control and that the reputation and interests of the institutions that had been at the heart of the dictatorship were under threat. An early sign of this nervousness about discrediting components of the former regime had been seen in the official reaction to the success of Buero Vallejo's previously banned *La doble historia del doctor Valmy* (*The Double Case History of Dr Valmy*) in early 1976. As discussed in Chapter 5, the censors had been worried about the potential impact of the play's denunciation of police brutality, and the personal file on Buero held by the Dirección General de Seguridad contains a report from February 1976 in which the play is described as part of an orchestrated 'theatrical campaign against the police' (AGA Buero Vallejo).

Censors were still liable to be alarmed by plays that made critical or satirical references to the late dictator and components of his regime. In September 1976, García-Cernuda argued that Juan

Antonio Castro's satire of authoritarianism and Catholic values, *De la buena crianza del gusano* ('On the Correct Breeding of Worms'), should be prohibited on the grounds that it contained 'claras alusiones a Franco y a su sucesor, presentándoles como indeseables' ('obvious references to Franco and his successor, presenting them as undesirable'). An earlier version of the play had been performed in August 1975, and the revised script was more explicit in its politics. In the end the production was approved for *cámara* on 10 September, with the deletion of a line that included Franco's own confident boast of 1969: Víctor, the jackbooted fascist plotting a comeback from retirement, declares '¡Y todas las posibilidades han sido previstas! Todo está atado y bien atado' ('And all the possibilities have been foreseen! Everything is well and truly tied up') (AGA 1144/76).

It was not only the reputation of the *Caudillo* himself that was at stake. *No hablaré en clase* ('I Must Not Talk in Class') by Joan Ollé and Josep Parramon, the show with which the Catalan independent theatre group Dagoll Dagom made its name, was banned in September 1976 for its satirical recreation of Catholic and Falangist indoctrination (alongside the suppression of the Catalan language) in post-war primary schools.[4] Zubiaurre's report described the content as very delicate, and Barceló expressed concern about the risk of performances provoking 'fuertes reacciones extrateatrales' ('strong reactions outside the theatre'). Albizu, apparently naively, seemed to be unsure about whether the scenes recreating lessons about the Falange were to be taken ironically, and was particularly worried about the evocation of the heroism of Colonel Moscardó at the siege of the Alcázar in 1936, one of the foundational legends of Francoism (AGA 1138/76) (see Figure 16). The decision to ban the work was taken on 21 September, citing *norma* 14, clauses 1 and 2 of the 1963 regulations, which forbade the disrespectful presentation of religion and attacks on national institutions and ceremonies.

Dagoll Dagom responded by sending a spoof announcement of the premature death of *No hablaré en clase* to Barcelona newspapers, which published it without charge, a stunt that would have been unthinkable only a few months earlier (Ollé 2014). The group submitted a revised version of the text on 10 November 1976, though the changes made to the script left in place the elements to which censors had had the strongest objections. Some of the changes

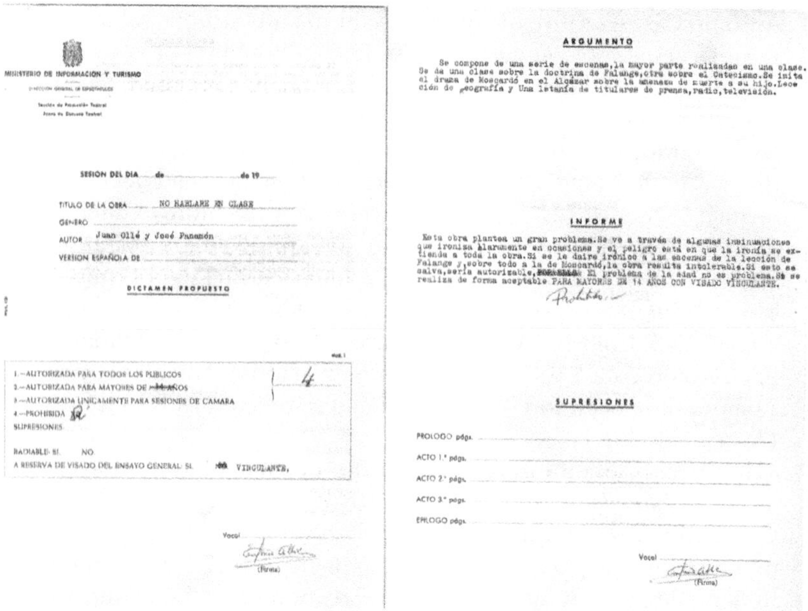

Figure 16: Antonio Albizu's report on *No hablaré en clase* (1976)

of detail in the final 'litany' – in which the cast were to intone an apparently random list of names, cultural phenomena and political institutions over a coffin – were significant, however.[5] Ollé and Parramon omitted 'La Benemérita' ('the Civil Guard'), assuming that the censors feared the displeasure of the still powerful armed police force. They also deleted 'Mártir de la Cruzada' ('Martyr of the Crusade') and 'Arriba España' ('Long live Spain'), which were presumably judged to be too dear to the hearts of supporters of the dictatorship. An account of the episode written by a member of Dagoll Dagom claims that the script was resubmitted under a different title in order to fool the censors (Bozzo 2015: 16), but the censorship file shows that this was not the case. The revised version bore the same title as the original, with the addition of *Pa amb oli i sucre i altres lletanies* ('Bread with Oil and Sugar and Other Litanies') as a subtitle.

All three censors who read the revised script of *No hablaré en clase* recommended authorisation without cuts, which was agreed on 23 November. Barceló was still worried about the risk of 'extra-theatrical reactions', but found that in general the text had been sufficiently toned down. Aragonés now dismissed the play's evocation of the historical memory of a whole generation of Spaniards – particularly traumatic for many Catalans – as 'situaciones y lugares comunes sin vigencia hoy' ('situations and clichés without any relevance to the present') and suggested that its critique of the Falange was pointless, since the Movement's influence was now so diminished. Tejedor considered the work innocuous, but was more worried than Aragonés about the relevance of the recreation of Francoist political indoctrination at a time when the Falange was splitting into four competing parties: '¿No pueden ser, en las actuales circunstancias de división del Partido, altamente peligrosos los puntos de la página 10, referentes a Falange?' ('In the current circumstances of division of the Party, mightn't the points on page 10 referring to the Falange be highly dangerous?'). The scene referred to uses an authentic extract from a textbook published by the Falange, based on rote learning of questions (spoken by a voice offstage) and approved answers (recited by an actor in school uniform). The passage condemns universal suffrage and the liberal state, and advocates its replacement with a totalitarian state devoted to the service of eternal truths. Ollé and Parramon's revision of this part of the script included some canny self-censorship, removing the term 'totalitario' and omitting the last two questions, which focused on the difference between totalitarianism and tyranny. They also added a note identifying the source, in order to underline its historical authenticity (AGA 1138/76).

No hablaré en clase opened at the Aliança del Poblenou in Barcelona on 25 February 1977. It made such an impact that it transferred to the larger Saló Diana in April and was revived at the commercial Sala Villarroel in September, and again in June 1978. Events demonstrated that the censors' fears of a right-wing reaction against the show and the company were not misplaced. Bozzo recalls: 'Les trucades amb amenaça de bomba eren habituals i gairebé rutinàries' ('Phone calls with bomb threats were frequent, almost routine') (2015: 20). The theatre would be evacuated, the police would be called and would make a suspiciously cursory check of the premises before declaring the all-clear. During the play's successful run at the Sala Cadarso in Madrid, a Molotov cocktail was thrown through a window of the theatre on 20 November, the second anniversary of Franco's death. On tour with the show in the spring of 1978, members of the group were assaulted in Jaén by right-wing militants shouting '¡Arriba España!' (Bozzo 2015: 21–2).

The transfer to Madrid brought Dagoll Dagom into conflict with a manifestation of censorship that seemed to be oblivious to the environment of political and social change. Despite the staging having been approved in Barcelona, an official insisted on carrying out an inspection of the dress rehearsal and demanded so many cuts that 'la funció quedava gairebé impossible de representar' ('it would have been almost impossible to go ahead with the show') (Bozzo 2015: 17). The theatre management pulled all the strings at their disposal and succeeded in persuading the new Director General de Teatro y Espectáculos, Rafael Pérez Sierra, to intervene and overrule the inspector.

Another Catalan play held up for political reasons in 1977 was Manuel de Pedrolo's *Aquesta nit tanquem* ('We're Closing Tonight'), written in 1973.[6] The Assemblea de Treballadors de l'Espectacle (an anarchist-affiliated association) applied on 5 March for permission to perform it in the space they managed in Barcelona, the Saló Diana. Although the play's condemnation of torture and censorship in an imaginary dictatorship is symbolic and highly metatheatrical, the censors found obvious parallels with Francoism. Guerra Sánchez's report noted: 'En un país llamado Istmo, unos actores representan la opresión y represión que sufren los ciudadanos (represión policial, social, etcétera). El paralelo es claro y se refiere a España' ('In a country called Isthmus, some performers act out the oppression and repression suffered by the citizens – police brutality, social repression, etc. The parallel is clear: it refers to Spain'). Albizu's report made it clear why such a critique still mattered: 'Estimo que todo ello es contraproducente y viene a despertar resentimientos que no se avienen con el espíritu de convivencia que se ha de desarrollar' ('In my view, this is all counterproductive and likely to provoke feelings of resentment unhelpful to the spirit of harmony that needs to be developed'). This desire to suppress revelations about the oppressive nature of the dictatorship in the interests of reconciliation would become a dominant theme of the transition to democracy. The fiercest rejection of Pedrolo's text came from Zubiaurre, who claimed that it was inaccurate and reminded his colleagues that the 1963 regulations (revised in 1975) were still legally in force:

El conjunto es una calumnia de grandes proporciones por cuanto acumula todos los defectos, arbitrariedades y crímenes sobre una etapa *que no fue así* [. . .] Creo que un espectáculo así, aparte de ser un acto político, es también un propósito indigno: incluye tendenciosidad, falsedad y un fondo de odio y revancha especialmente indeseable en la hora actual. (AGA 176/77)

> This adds up to a monstrous calumny, since it attributes a mountain of defects, abuses of power and crimes to a period that *was not like that* [. . .] I believe that a work of this nature, apart from being a political act, is also ignominious in its intentions, driven by tendentiousness, dishonesty and an undertone of hatred and vindictiveness that is especially unwelcome at the present moment.

Two censors, Mier and Tejedor, were in favour of authorisation, as long as the more incendiary elements – a scene of police brutality and a revolutionary call to arms – were deleted. The Delegado Provincial in Barcelona suggested that the audience was likely to be small, and advised that allowing the production to go ahead would cause less trouble than banning it. Authorisation was issued on 26 April, with substantial cuts on six pages. The company, however, was not prepared to accept the outcome. In the past, applicants had tended to lodge formal appeals only against outright prohibitions, but in this case the aim was to have the cuts withdrawn. The appeal submitted by Roman Heras on 22 September was detailed and forceful, alleging procedural defects and challenging the legal basis of the Junta's judgement. The dispute dragged on until January 1978, when the production was finally authorised without cuts – not on the grounds that the original decision had been unjustified but because circumstances were now different.

While the case of *Aquesta nit tanquem* was under consideration, major political change had been taking place. A law of 1 April 1977 established freedom of expression in the press and broadcasting, though there were still limitations: the authorities retained the right to seize pornography and material that threatened the unity of Spain, showed disrespect for the monarchy or attacked the reputation of the armed forces (BOE 1977a: 7928). Following the *Ley para la Reforma Política* ('Political Reform Act') of September 1976, the first democratic general election since 1936 took place on 15 June 1977. The election was peaceful with a high turnout and returned Adolfo Suárez to power at the head of a centre-right coalition, constituting a clear mandate for reform. The Socialist Party (the PSOE) did unexpectedly well, while none of the far-right parties advocating a return to authoritarianism, including the scattered remnants of the Falange, won a single seat. On the day before the election, Francisco José Mayans, Director General de Teatro y Espectáculos, gave an interview to *El País* in which he outlined the priorities for his department under a democratically elected government. They included 'libertad de expresión para el teatro, suprimiendo la censura previa administrativa, sin abandonar la protección del menor y la mera orientación del adulto' ('freedom of expression for the theatre, abolishing official prior censorship while continuing to provide protection for the young and impartial guidance for adult spectators'), and he explained that 'mi opinión es que la sociedad ha evolucionado con espléndida salud y que la creación artística debe desarrollarse sin cortapisa de ningún género' ('my opinion is that our society has evolved in splendid health and artistic creativity should be allowed to develop without restraint of any kind') (El País 1977a).

On 4 July 1977, Suárez's new government created a Ministerio de Cultura y Bienestar ('Ministry of Culture and Welfare'), headed by Pío Cabanillas Gallas, who had been a member of Manuel Fraga's team during the *apertura* of the 1960s.[7] He was Subsecretario de Información y Turismo between 1962 and 1969, and Minister between January and October 1974. The Dirección General de Teatro y Espectáculos was transferred to the new ministry, with Mayans remaining in post until replaced on 2 November by Rafael Pérez Sierra, Director of the Real Escuela Superior de Arte Dramático y de Danza in Madrid. The structure and functions of the ministry were confirmed in a law of 27 August, which defined the remit of the Dirección General as follows: 'A la Dirección General de Teatro y Espectáculos le competen las funciones de protección, fomento y difusión de la creación y de la actividad teatral' ('The Directorate General of Theatre and Public Spectacles shall be responsible for the protection, promotion and dissemination of theatrical creation and activities') (BOE 1977b: 19583). An earlier definition of the functions of the Dirección General de Cultura Popular y Espectáculos had included, alongside the supportive terms 'protección' and 'fomento', the more normative terms 'ordenación' ('ordering') and 'regulación' ('regulation'), and the article defining the role of the Sección de Teatro had added 'vigilancia' ('invigilation, supervision') (BOE 1968: 828). That piece of legislation and one that modified it in 1970 had both included the Junta de Censura de Obras Teatrales in the list of sections within the Dirección General, but there was no mention in the 1977 act of its successor, the Junta de Ordenación de Obras Teatrales.

Although the Junta continued to operate during the rest of 1977 with most of its membership intact (and Ortiz still in post as its secretary), their political masters had sent a clear signal that leniency was expected. Cuts were still being imposed for moral and political reasons, but there are no records of plays being banned by the Junta in the second half of 1977. Many of the files from this year do not contain reports or records of decisions, which suggests that much of the business was being carried out in a perfunctory way. When reports were written, they tended to be briefer than in the past. In some cases, censors were asked to review cuts made on earlier occasions. In November 1977, for example, an independent theatre group requested cancellation of the cuts imposed in 1974 on Luis Riaza's *El desván de los machos y el sótano de las hembras* ('Males in the Attic, Females in the Basement'), which was swiftly granted with little debate (AGA 380/73).

The government was now committed – with clear public support – to the removal of official censorship, yet the old authoritarian habit of suppression was still deeply engrained in the establishment. It reasserted itself in late 1977, with the controversial banning of *La torna* ('The Rounding-Up') by Els Joglars, which brought the tension between democratisation and the bunker into alarming focus (discussed in the case study at the end of this chapter).

(Almost) complete abolition

Following the abolition of film censorship in November 1977, the *Real Decreto 262/1978 sobre libertad de representación de espectáculos teatrales* ('Royal Decree on the Freedom to Perform Theatre Productions') was passed on 27 January 1978. The primary guiding principle set out in the preamble is respect for fundamental human rights:

La libre expresión del pensamiento a través del teatro y demás espectáculos artísticos, como manifestación de un derecho fundamental de la persona, no puede tener otros límites que los que resulten del ordenamiento penal vigente, así como del respeto debido a los derechos e intereses generales. Se hace por ello necesaria una norma por la que quede suprimida toda censura administrativa de los espectáculos teatrales y artísticos. (BOE 1978a: 5153)

The free expression of thought by means of the theatre and other artistic spectacles, as a manifestation of a fundamental right of the individual, must not be subject to any limits other than those determined by the penal code or the respect due to general rights and interests. Legislation is therefore required to abolish all administrative censorship of theatre and other forms of performance.

The phrase referring to the penal code was an important proviso. In the still turbulent circumstances of the transition, it was judged necessary to make clear that freedom of expression did not give artists immunity from prosecution if their work was found to be in breach of specific laws. This might be considered a sensible precaution consistent with liberal principles, but the wide range of actions that could constitute criminal offences meant that theatrical activities were potentially still vulnerable to official repression. Spain's *Código Penal* ('Penal Code') had last been revised in 1973 and many of its definitions of offences dated from the 1940s or earlier. A minor change in 1976 had deleted clauses referring to expressions of hostility to national pride and unity, and support for separatist activities (BOE 1976: 14136), while another adjustment in March 1978 had removed references to offences against the *Movimiento Nacional*, its principles and its national council (BOE 1978b: 6502). Still in place were a number of offences – punishable by fines or imprisonment – that might be considered to be committed (or advocated) in the course of theatrical performances: insulting the Spanish nation; undermining the authority of the state; insulting the head of state or the government; making public calls for changes in the form of government; offending religious sentiments or mocking the Catholic religion; blasphemy; insulting ministers or public officials; causing a disturbance in a public place or during a performance; inciting rebellion or sedition; offending against public decency or advocating immoral doctrines; adultery committed by a woman; slander or libel (BOE 1973). Giving public performances without the required licence or contravening the terms of the licence also continued to be an offence. Articles 239 and 567, referring to blasphemy, were not revoked until 1988, and a reference to the Catholic religion in article 209 remained in force until 1983. One of the primary purposes of establishing a prior censorship apparatus in the first place had been to provide a means of taking preventative action without having to resort to formal legal proceedings to punish transgressions. The law of January 1978 removed that option, bringing the legal framework for regulating the theatre and entertainment industry back to more or less the same scope it had had before 1935, allowing intervention only on a legal basis, by judicial authorities and not by a censorship office.

Another safeguard built into the act – unsurprising in the context of the *destape* and the moral panic it provoked in some social sectors – was the retention of classification according to the age of spectators, in parallel with the system applied to the cinema, justified as a 'defensa de la infancia y de la adolescencia, así como del derecho de todo el público a una correcta información sobre el contenido de los espectáculos' ('defence of childhood and adolescence, as well as of the public's right to accurate information regarding the content of performances') (BOE 1978a: 5153). A special category was created for cases in which 'el espectáculo puede herir de modo especial la sensibilidad del espectador medio' ('the production may be particularly offensive to the sensibilities of the average spectator') (1978a: 5153–4). The understanding of what the levels of tolerance of the 'average spectator' might be had shifted significantly in recent years, and in practice, this special 'S' category was reserved for shows that were blatantly erotic.[8]

In some respects, the new arrangements for *calificación* ('classification') looked similar to the old censorship system. Theatre companies were required to apply for a licence at least thirty days in advance of the opening, proposing a classification and submitting three copies of the script, on which three members of the Comisión de Calificación de Teatro y Espectáculos would write reports. The classification would be decided by a majority vote at a meeting of the commission. An important change from previous practice was that failure to issue a decision within fifteen days (*silencio administrativo*) would automatically result in the confirmation of the classification proposed by the applicant, rather than leaving the project in limbo as used to be the case. The theatre was required to display the classification in publicity material and at the box office. La Dirección General had the power to change the classification and to order the suspension of the show if the conditions of the licence were not fulfilled.

The new body was based on the existing Junta de Ordenación, with a nationwide remit, still administered by José María Ortiz and with some of the same members. The minutes of a meeting of the commission in July 1978 name four *vocales* who had served as theatre censors (Fr Jesús Cea Buján, José Luis Guerra Sánchez, Carmelo Romero Andrés and Antonio Zubiaurre Martínez) and three who were newly appointed: Francisco Martínez García (a literary scholar), Ramón Regidor Arribas (a professor of vocal performance) and Juan Wesolowski Fernández de Heredia (a musician who had served as a film censor in the early 1970s) (AGA 193/43). They were later joined by Julia Arroyo Herrera (a journalist and theatre critic), Carlos Hernández Morán (a civil servant in the Tourism department and Director of Teatros Nacionales y Festivales de España in 1978), Paloma Notario Bodelón (also a civil servant in the Tourism department), and Pilar Mateos Martín (a writer of children's books and scriptwriter for radio and television).

Article 6 of the January 1978 act confirmed that the commission did not have censorship powers: 'La calificación a que se refiere el presente Real Decreto no producirá otros efectos que los meramente administrativos' ('The classification to which the present Royal Decree refers shall have a purely administrative effect') (BOE 1978a: 5154). The classification did not in itself provide any protection from legal sanctions against performances, which could only be imposed by a judicial authority. The commission could, however, have a role in initiating or heading off that process: 'Si con ocasión de la calificación de un espectáculo la Administración advirtiera que su representación pudiera ser constitutiva de delito, lo pondrá en conocimiento del Ministerio Fiscal, lo que comunicará previamente al interesado' ('If in the course of the classification of a production the Administration should come to the view that the performance of the work might constitute a criminal offence, this should be reported to the State Prosecution Service, after notifying the interested party') (1978a: 5154).

A second law passed on 7 April 1978 defined the classification categories: 'todos los públicos' ('all audiences'), audiences over fourteen years, audiences over eighteen, and the special category 'S' (BOE 1978c: 8611). It also established a Subcomisión de Valoración ('Quality Assessment Subcommission'), its membership selected from the Comisión de Calificación, responsible for advising on the award of financial and other support for productions judged to be of particularly high quality, from which S-rated works were excluded. This detail is uncomfortably reminiscent of the old system's overlap between censorship and the evaluation for prizes and subsidies through the Consejo Superior del Teatro.

The provision indicating that potential breaches of the Penal Code could be reported to the Ministerio Fiscal was now made more specific: the responsibility was assigned to the Dirección General rather than to the 'Administración', a vague term denoting the government as a whole. This aspect of the new system could potentially be used as an indirect form of prior censorship, or consultative censorship – advising applicants that their work might be liable to prosecution unless changes were made. A search in the database of court judgements maintained by the official Centro de Documentación Judicial ('Judicial Documentation Centre') does not turn up any cases between 1978 and 1985 of prosecutions under the Penal Code brought against theatrical productions.[9] Further investigation of theatrical *calificación* files would be needed to assess how frequently the commission reported productions to the judicial authorities or warned companies that this was likely to happen. There was one controversial case in 1978 which certainly came about in this way:

> A little later in August, the use – or abuse – of sex in theater reached its apotheosis in *Ven a disfrutar*, the Spanish version of Earl Wilson's *Let My People Come*. Through song and dance, this erotic collage urged the abandonment of all taboos and restraints as it ran the gamut of sexual activities. (O'Connor 1984: 67)

Although Earl Wilson Jr's ebullient 'Sexual Musical' (first staged in New York in 1974) did not break new ground in terms of what was shown on stage, its uninhibited celebration of sexual language was designed to smash taboos – one of the songs is entitled 'Dirty Words'. O'Connor reports that it was the language of the show that led to the government closing it down twenty-eight days after its opening (1984: 67). A report in the magazine *Blanco y Negro* dismisses any suggestion that the Madrid public was offended: 'Pero no crean que el público se escandalizó, ¡qué va! Se reían a más y mejor. Y es que nos estamos colocando a nivel europeo, aunque sólo sea en esto' ('But don't imagine that the audience was scandalised. Far from it! They were roaring with laughter. After all, we're putting ourselves on the same level as the rest of Europe, even if it's only in this') (Blanco y Negro 1978: 43).

Further press reports reveal how the ban came about. The Teatro del Príncipe was closed down on 15 September, half an hour before that evening's performance of *Ven a disfrutar*, by order of the government. The producer, Jaime Azpilicueta, was notified that the work 'incurre en delito contra la moral pública conforme al artículo 451 del Código Penal' ('represents a criminal offence against public morality according to article 451 of the Penal Code') (ABC 1978). In fact, the relevant article of the 1973 *Código Penal* is 431: 'El que de cualquier modo ofendiere el pudor o las buenas costumbres con hechos de grave escándalo o trascendencia incurrirá en las penas de arresto mayor, multa de 5.000 a 25.000 pesetas e inhabilitación especial' ('Whosoever should offend in any way against decency or propriety by committing acts of grave outrage or notoriety shall be liable to imprisonment for a term of between one and six months, a fine of between 5,000 and 25,000 pesetas, and professional disqualification') (BOE 1973: 24210–11).[10] Azpilicueta confirmed to the press that the script had been revised after a warning from the Comisión de Calificación that it risked prosecution:

> Tenemos todos los permisos en regla y el acta de la Junta de Clasificación no señala en ninguna parte que la obra, en esta versión, pueda incurrir en delito penal. Con anterioridad presentamos otra versión que, aunque autorizada, advertía de este riesgo. Entonces hicimos una segunda, la que estaba en cartel, a la que la Junta no hizo indicación de ningún tipo. (ABC 1978a)

> We've got all the permits in order and the notification from the Classification Board doesn't say anything about this version of the show committing a criminal offence. We had submitted an earlier version, which, although it was authorised, did lead them to warn us that there was a risk of that. So we produced a second version, the one that was being performed, and the Board didn't have anything to say about it.

In a sense, Azpilicueta's predicament was worse than it would have been if prior censorship had still been in place, since authorisation by the Junta de Censura used to confer protection from intervention by mayors, civil governors, Church authorities or the armed forces. He coordinated a vigorous protest campaign, writing to Adolfo Suárez and several government ministers, and the show reopened on 11 October (El País 1978). In a press conference in late October, the Fiscal del Reino (head of the Prosecution Service), Juan Manuel Fanjul, confirmed that the report of a potential breach of the penal code had come from the Ministerio de Cultura in June, that his department had asked the Civil Governor to investigate, and that the producers had agreed to make changes to the script and title of the show. He claimed that the problem was that the company was found to be performing the original version: 'Un buen día el Gobierno Civil de Madrid descubrió, contrastando los libretos, que se estaba ofreciendo lo que en un principio se consideró que constituía delito de escándalo público' ('One fine day the office of the Civil Governor of Madrid discovered, by comparing the scripts, that what was on offer was what had originally been considered likely to constitute an offence of public immorality') (ABC 1978b). A news report about the reopening of the theatre gives a different story, suggesting that there was confusion about the two versions and the one being performed was the revised script (ABC 1978c). Strictly speaking, then, the act of censorship was carried out not on the grounds of an offence under article 431 but of breaching the conditions of the Comisión de Calificación's certification, though this was probably an error. In any case, the episode demonstrated that freedom of expression in the theatre was still vulnerable to repressive action by the state.

The vast majority of applications dealt with by the Comisión de Calificación appear to have been unproblematic. Many plays that had previously been authorised only for audiences over the age of eighteen were now routinely classified as suitable for spectators over fourteen, including Lorca's *La casa de Bernarda Alba*, which had prompted expressions of outrage by ecclesiastical censors before being licensed for over-eighteens in 1963. Romero, who had been a censor since 1970, commented in July 1978: 'Considero que actualmente se han levantado numerosos tabúes sexuales que pesaban sobre nuestra sociedad y que los mayores de 14 años pueden asumir perfectamente este canto de libertad, a la vez que feroz crítica de la represión sexual, que entraña la obra' ('My view is that many sexual taboos that used to weigh on our society have now been lifted, and that spectators over the age of fourteen are perfectly capable of engaging with this song of liberty, this fierce critique of sexual repression embodied in the play'). Regidor's report echoed earlier censors' complaints about 'crudeza' ('crudity, rawness'), but only to argue that this, together with 'la violencia interior que desprende' ('the interior violence with which the work is suffused'), made it unsuitable for children under fourteen (AGA 193/43). Lorca's *Así que pasen cinco años* (*When Five Years Have Passed*) had been authorised in 1970 for audiences over eighteen, but in September 1978 was judged suitable for spectators of any age (AGA 87/70). The revision of age limits was significant in the case of classic texts, opening them up to school-age audiences.

Miralles's previously troublesome *Catarocolón*, restricted to over-eighteens in 1968, was considered politically innocuous enough in June 1978 to be classified as suitable for over-fourteens. Fr Cea commented: 'Es una crítica a la historia tradicional, pero sin motivos para poder considerarla como un atentado a los valores nacionales y mucho menos, una página de la Leyenda Negra' ('It's critical of the traditional view of history, but there is no reason to see it as an attack on national values, and even less as a contribution to the Black Legend') (AGA 36/68). The ideological links in Alberti's *Noche de guerra en el Museo del Prado* ('A Night of War in the Prado Museum') between the civil war and paintings by Goya and Velázquez were brought up in Guerra Sánchez's report of October 1978, but only to argue that the cultural and historical knowledge required to understand them was likely to be beyond spectators under the age of fourteen. In contrast, Zubiaurre mentioned partial nudity and a few elements of coarse language as reasons for a classification of over-fourteen (AGA 690/78). Rodríguez Méndez's *Historia de unos cuantos* ('Anyone's History'), which had divided opinion among the censors in 1973 because of its bitter vision of Spanish history between 1898 and the 1940s, was classified as suitable for all audiences in January 1980 (AGA 7/80). None of the three readers offered any comment, which suggests that at this stage the system was no longer being run with great diligence.

Other motives for recommending restriction to audiences over fourteen included a plot revolving around adultery in the case of Ana Diosdado's *Olvida los tambores* ('Forget the Drums') in April 1978 (AGA 216/70), and crudity of language in Manuel Martínez Mediero's *El último gallinero* ('The Last Henhouse') in September 1978 (AGA 663/78). Reports by Arroyo and Cea on the latter play noted its allegory of political and sexual repression but did not suggest that this posed a problem. Incidentally, this file provides confirmation that the Comisión de Calificación was still operating – with the same membership and still managed by Ortiz – in December 1981, when Alberto Miralles submitted an application for a production of a revised version of *El último gallinero* by the Cátaro group. The classification of over-fourteen was confirmed. As in the case of *Historia de unos cuantos*, none of the readers bothered to write comments.

Another revival of a political satire from the New Spanish Theatre had caused some concern in September 1978, however: José Ruibal's *Los mendigos* (*The Beggars*), which had been banned in 1970.[11] Romero's classification report noted that the political symbolism 'tiene claras concomitancias con la España del régimen de Franco' ('shows clear parallels with the Spain of Franco's regime'), but the reason for classifying it as suitable for over-fourteens was the representation – albeit highly stylised – of violence. Zubiaurre, on the other hand, was worried about scenes featuring starving beggars being eliminated and swept away by the forces of order, in which 'el blanco de la crítica son las fuerzas armadas y las del orden público' ('the targets of the critique are the armed forces and the police'), and which threatened to be 'realmente conflictivos en el momento presente' ('seriously conflictual at the present moment'). He suggested that the case warranted special attention (AGA 184/70). These remarks seem to indicate a desire to return to suppressive censorship as a way of avoiding a backlash by reactionary forces. His colleagues must have convinced him that this was no longer possible, since the outcome was the routine classification of the work for over-fourteens.

The principle of freedom of expression was formally enshrined in the Spanish legal system by the Constitution of 1978, which was ratified by referendum on 6 December and came into force on 29 December. Article 20 guaranteed the right to 'expresar y difundir libremente los pensamientos, ideas y opiniones mediante la palabra, el escrito o cualquier otro medio de reproducción' ('the right to freely express and disseminate thoughts, ideas and opinions through words, in writing or through any other medium') and to 'la producción y creación literaria, artística, científica y técnica' ('literary, artistic, scientific and technical production and creation'); it also declared that 'el ejercicio de estos derechos no puede restringirse mediante ningún tipo de censura previa' ('the exercise of these rights may not be restricted by any form of prior censorship') (BOE 1978d: 6). The process of bringing the Penal Code into line with the principles of the Constitution dragged on for more than a decade. Article 578 (defining the offence of staging a performance or screening a film without a licence, or breaching the terms of the licence) was not revoked until 1989. The process culminated in a comprehensive reform of the Code in 1995, in which, as the preamble states, 'se otorga a la libertad de expresión toda la relevancia que puede y debe reconocerle un régimen democrático' ('freedom of expression is given the highest degree of importance that a democratic system of government can and should accord it') (BOE 1995: 8).

While the institutions of the state had now renounced official censorship, some of the right-wing extremists still resisting democratisation continued to interfere with freedom of theatrical expression through intimidation. The actor Teresa del Olmo took part in a production of Juan Antonio de Castro's historical drama ¡Viva la Pepa! ('Long Live the Constitution!'), which opened at the Teatro Fígaro in Madrid on 16 January 1980.[12] She recalls that for the entire month of the show's run, bomb threats by the Guerrilleros de Cristo Rey were received every evening, forcing the evacuation of the theatre and the abandonment of the late performance (the afternoon performances were able to go ahead). The production made a loss, which the members of the company, a small cooperative, were obliged to make up from their own pockets (Olmo 2019).

The Comisión de Calificación remained in existence until 1985, under a succession of ministers: Manuel Clavero Arévalo (1979–80), Ricardo de la Cierva (1980), Íñigo Cavero Lataillade (1980–1), Soledad Becerril Bustamante (1981–2), and following the electoral victory of the Socialist Party in October 1982, Javier Solana Madariaga (1982–8). The Dirección General de Teatro y Espectáculos became la Dirección General de Música y Teatro in 1980, and minor adjustments to the legal and administrative framework were made during the early 1980s. In June 1981, a category of over-sixteen was added to the classification system, bringing theatre into line with cinema (BOE 1981). The *Reglamento de Policía de Espectáculos* of 1935 was reformed in August 1982. This was mostly a matter of updating technical, safety and employment standards, but the regulations retained a provision that gave civil governors and mayors the power to close down performances 'que sean inconvenientes o peligrosas para la juventud y la infancia, que puedan ser constitutivos de delito o atenten gravemente contra el orden público o las buenas costumbres' ('which are inappropriate or dangerous for young people and children, which may constitute a criminal offence, or which pose a grave threat to public order or decency'), or which included material inconsistent with the age classification (BOE 1982).[13] There is, however, no evidence that this power has been used since 1982. Finally, the 'S' rating for theatre and other kinds of live performance was abolished in June 1983 by the Socialist administration of Felipe González, 'ya que su mantenimiento resulta anacrónico y no es en modo alguno determinante para un público mayor de edad' ('since the category is now anachronistic and is not in any way a deciding factor for an adult public') (BOE 1983). Cultural policy finally recognised that grown-ups could be trusted to make their own judgements about what they might find offensive in live performance.

The Comisión de Calificación, the last remaining component of the censorship apparatus, was scrapped as part of the restructuring of the Ministerio de Cultura in 1985, following the creation of the Instituto Nacional de las Artes Escénicas y de la Música ('National Institute for Performing Arts and Music') in December 1984. The INAEM was established as a department with the status of a Dirección General, which meant the abolition in April 1985 of the Dirección General de Teatro y Música, together with its component sections. The act specified that films would continue to be classified by the Comisión de Calificación de Películas Cinematográficas, but no such function was mentioned for theatre. The main mission of the INAEM was defined as 'la promoción, protección y difusión de las artes escénicas y de la música en cualquiera de sus manifestaciones' ('the promotion, protection and dissemination of performance arts and music in any form') (BOE 1985: 11988), without any mention of control, ordering, regulation or supervision. The dismantling of the censorship apparatus was completed by the repeal of Royal Decree 262/1978, which had created the classification system (BOE 1985: 11993).

Case study

La torna, by Els Joglars/Albert Boadella
Teatro Argensola (Barbastro), 7 September 1977

La torna ('The Rounding-Up'), a dark, *commedia dell'arte*-style farce by Els Joglars, is based on the trial and execution by the Spanish state in 1974 of the mysterious drifter known as Heinz Chez for the killing of a police officer. The play implies that the garrotting of Chez on the same day as the controversial execution of the Catalan anarchist Salvador Puig Antich was a manoeuvre designed to delegitimise Puig Antich's political motivation by associating his offences with the apparently motiveless criminality of Chez. It includes a scene in which the protagonist is condemned by a military tribunal whose members are under the influence of copious quantities of Rioja. The production was approved by the censorship board on 6 September 1977, though there is no record of the censors' views, as the file contains only a copy of the script (AGA 427/77). A member of the cast recalls that the inspector viewing the dress rehearsal complained mildly about the language and some of the female performers' costumes but said nothing about the depiction of the military tribunal (Crehuet *et al.* 2008: 76). The premiere went ahead on 7 September in Barbastro (Aragón) without interference from the authorities, followed by forty performances in various locations around Catalonia, Navarra, Alicante and Mallorca. The tour was to culminate in Barcelona in January 1978.

The leader of Els Joglars, Albert Boadella, comments in his memoirs that 'aun cuando la muerte del dictador elevaba implícitamente las cotas de libertad de expresión, continuaba estando claro que la estructura franquista seguía casi inmune, y que, en el caso del ejército, más bien existía un ánimo muy beligerante' ('even though the death of the dictator was implicitly raising the level of freedom of expression, it was still clear that the structure of Francoism remained largely untouched, and that in the case of the army, their attitude was downright belligerent') (2001: 258). On 30 November 1977, Boadella received a telephone call from a legal officer in the army ordering *La torna* to be closed down. Boadella refused to accept the validity of such an order given by telephone, but it was confirmed a few days later by the Civil Governor's office and the show closed definitively. He and other members of the group were arrested on multiple charges of insulting and defaming the armed forces, offences which still came under military jurisdiction. The arrests sparked a national and international campaign of protests, including a general strike in the theatre industry, and the affair became a dangerous focus of tension between a government trying to consolidate democratic principles and a military establishment determined to hold onto its privileges. A feigned illness allowed Boadella to be transferred to a hospital, from which he escaped and fled to France. Four other members of Els Joglars were tried by a military tribunal and sentenced in March 1978 to two years of imprisonment, which provoked further demonstrations and protests.

The military case against Els Joglars rested partly on an interpretation of the licence issued by the Junta de Ordenación de Obras Teatrales for *La torna*. Two of the accused argued that their actions constituted the legitimate exercise of a civil right, recognised in the military code of justice as a valid defence, since the production had been authorised by the competent authority. However, the prosecution asserted that the authorisation – and therefore the right to perform the play – had been invalidated by the distribution of a printed programme in which the unspecific action of the play (centred on a fictional protagonist named Sánchez) was explicitly linked to the real-life circumstances of the executions of Chez and Puig Antich, thereby breaching one of the conditions of the permit, which is quoted in the court's judgement: 'Cualquier alteración del texto aprobado que no cuente con la aprobación expresa de la Dirección General del Espectáculo será considerada como causa de caducidad de esta guía de censura' ('Any alteration of the approved text without the express approval of the Directorate General for Theatre shall be considered grounds for the annulment of the present censorship permit') (cited in López Rodríguez 2008: 51). The script itself had not been changed but the military authorities took the view that the programme notes – making explicit a political meaning not spotted by the censors – constituted part of the performance and should have been submitted for authorisation.[14] A press release issued by the army also argued that the costumes used in performances had broken the terms of the licence issued by the censorship office, since they were identifiable as Spanish army and civil guard uniforms (Els Joglars 2016).

The Franco regime's censorship apparatus had been designed to ensure that its use would be strictly controlled by central government. The Church was given an influential role within the system, civil governors were frequently asked for advice on local factors affecting central decisions, and the army was occasionally consulted when its interests or reputation were at stake, but none of these bodies was allowed to intervene directly to ban plays on their own authority. The army now broke with that tradition, using military law to perpetrate a more draconian act of censorship than any carried out during the dictatorship, while disingenuously claiming to be upholding the civil authority's ruling. The irony was deepened by the fact that the body that had issued that ruling had been abolished in the period between the performances in September–November 1977 and the trial in January–March 1978.

The convictions were overturned in January 1979, but Boadella was re-arrested on his return to Spain. The military continued to be intent on court-martialling him, reinflaming the conflict with the government, until some deft political manoeuvring secured his conditional release in July 1979 (Boadella 2001: 332). The case was not definitively closed until it was passed from military to civil jurisdiction in 1981, following the crisis in which the armed forces' resistance to democratisation came to a head and was finally overcome: the attempted *coup d'état* of 23 February. The banning of *La torna* had been one of the most controversial episodes of the transition to democracy, transforming what Boadella describes as 'una obra de teatre incompleta i esvalotada' ('an incomplete and impetuous piece of theatre') into 'un símbol indiscutible de llibertat') ('an indisputable symbol of liberty') (2001: 267). As Wheeler shows, the episode brought into the open the army's determination to 'reinforce their role as privileged auditors of the new regime, ensuring democracy was constantly in the dock between 1975 and 1981' (2020: 116–18). Its continuing resonance beyond the transition was marked by *La torna de la torna* ('The Return of *La torna*'), a show in which Boadella revived the group's most provocative piece and commented on the events of 1977.[15]

Notes

1 The euphemistic new name of the censorship board had been introduced in 1975, but some of the paperwork dating from 1976 and 1977 still featured the name Junta de Censura Teatral.

2   This colloquial expression is a euphemistic variant of *el coño de la Bernarda* ('Bernarda's fanny'), which usually means something like a shambles – a frenetic and chaotic situation.
3   See O'Connor 1984 for a survey of nudity in Spanish theatre between 1975 and 1980, by which time 'the sexual revolution in Spanish theater, brief and intense, had flamed out' (70).
4   See Rodriguéz Solás (2017) for a detailed study of the censorship of this play.
5   A recording of this scene from a performance in 1997 can be viewed on YouTube, *www.youtube.com/watch?v=vUEAXbZ1v0c*.
6   This case is discussed in detail in Feldman and Foguet (2016: 166–70).
7   'Bienestar' was dropped from the name of the ministry in August 1977.
8   A few examples of works rated 'S' are described in O'Connor (1984: 66–8).
9   Prosecutions for immorality in the late 1970s and early 1980s tended to be for pornographic content in magazines, or in films shown at venues not licensed for S-rated material. Some of the judgements in such cases argued that prosecution was warranted more often for printed publications than for theatrical performances, as audiences were forewarned about offensive material by the theatre classification system. The CENDOJ database can be consulted online at *www.poderjudicial.es/search/indexAN.jsp*.
10 Article 451 referred to adultery, allowing a husband to pardon his wife. The wording of article 431 remained in force until it was replaced in 1989 with a definition concerning indecent exposure in front of children.
11 The AGA file on *Los mendigos*, though initiated in 1970, contains no documentation from that year (AGA 184/70). Information from other sources (for example Arjona 1970) confirms that this play was banned in May when it was due to be performed at the Festival Cero in San Sebastián. Its publication had also been blocked in 1969.
12 The liberal Constitution of 1812 is popularly known as *la Pepa* because it was promulgated in Cádiz on 19 March, St Joseph's Day (the familiar form of José is Pepe).
13 Article 71.1 of the 1982 law combined articles 8 and 26 of the 1935 *Reglamento*, which allowed for suspensions and bans on public order grounds, together with article 32, which required the authorities to report breaches of the Penal Code.
14 The full text of the programme note is reproduced on the group's website (Els Joglars 2016).
15 *La torna de la torna* is analysed by Breden (2006).

Conclusion

Theatre censorship during the Franco regime was more severe than at any time since the starting point of this study, the tyrannical reign of Fernando VII in the early nineteenth century. The historical parallel is powerfully dramatised in Antonio Buero Vallejo's *El sueño de la razón*, in which Fernando, like Saturn devouring his children, ruthlessly crushes dissent and silences his liberal opponents, while the ageing, deaf, isolated Francisco de Goya daubs his fury and despair onto the walls of his house. Father Duaso, the king's chaplain and censor who attempts to protect Goya, argues for the necessity of censorship and claims to be working for the public good: 'El hombre siempre será pecador, y en nuestra mano sólo está evitarle algunas ocasiones de pecado . . . Soy censor de publicaciones por eso' ('Man will always be a sinner, and all we can do is to help him avoid some of the opportunities for sin . . . That is why I'm a censor of publications') (Buero Vallejo 1995: 153). He is soon made aware of the brutality of the political regime that he serves and realises that he has been used as a pawn in the king's plot to break the painter's resistance. His well-meaning work ends up not saving souls but propping up the corrupt power of a tyrant.

Censorship always purports to work on behalf of a social consensus, defending shared moral and cultural values, preventing threats to public order, ensuring respect for institutions, and protecting humanity from its own base instincts. There is always a degree of truth in such claims: some individuals and organisations will support or even demand the suppression of certain forms of expression.[1] However, the more authoritarian a state is and the more draconian its practice of censorship, the more the supposed consensus is revealed as constructed and illusory, employed to defend particular interests rather than the general good.

Each of the historical periods examined in this book gave rise to a distinctive approach to cultural control and a different way of constructing the ostensible consensus underlying it. The liberal bourgeois system that developed in Spain over the course of the nineteenth century varied in the degree to which it constrained cultural production, but it did make a general commitment to the principle of freedom of expression (allied to the protection of intellectual property) and to the premise that constraints on this freedom should be applied through judicial proceedings rather than direct, anticipatory state intervention. The Primo de Rivera dictatorship in the 1920s brought a temporary abandonment of those constitutionalist principles. Its turn to arbitrary repressive action was defended on the grounds that the Restoration establishment had allowed moral values, public order and national dignity to collapse, yet in practice that action was largely directed at protecting specific institutional interests, primarily those of the armed forces and the Church.

The Second Republic restored constitutionalism in 1931 and reinforced the principle of freedom of expression, taking a more permissive approach to the management of cultural production than any previous regime. However, it struggled to maintain public order and became increasingly anxious to defend its institutional legitimacy against threats from both ends of the political spectrum, which led to a tightening of censorial control in 1935. The civil war, unsurprisingly, meant that both individual freedom of expression and commercial freedom were subordinated to ideological and military priorities in both zones, as cultural production was dispersed and censorship in various forms was practised by multiple agencies. In the Republican zone, a new consensus was rapidly constructed around the idealisation of the proletariat, the rejection of bourgeois social values, the defence of the Republic and resistance to Fascism. While official censorship by the state remained relatively tolerant for most of the war, other interventions affecting what could be performed were difficult to distinguish from programming decisions made by workers' committees. In the Nationalist zone, the Falange led the process of subordinating cultural production to a propaganda apparatus seeking unquestioning obedience to a totalitarian state that combined militarism with an element of theocracy.

The Franco dictatorship was unconstrained by any commitment to constitutionalism or human rights. One of its foundational acts was to turn legality upside down by declaring itself the authentic national government and the embodiment of the Spanish people, and condemning the defenders of the democratically elected Republic as rebels and traitors. This audacious claim to total legitimacy was asserted through extreme violence and a far-reaching campaign of propaganda and indoctrination, with the collaboration of the Catholic Church. National-Catholicism was founded on a set of ideals and values that did not constitute a consistent or well theorised ideology but were pragmatically bound together by the balance of forces within the regime and by the need to justify its very existence: national unity and order guaranteed by an authoritarian state; a heroic, messianic vision of history culminating in the nationalist victory of 1939; and the centrality of Catholicism to cultural identity, education and morality.[2] Although there were significant shifts in the political make-up of the dictatorship and the rhetoric it employed, these underlying values were remarkably durable.

Censorship of all media was therefore an essential tool for the maintenance of an ideological orthodoxy which was intended to be all-embracing and permanent, disseminated through Ideological State Apparatuses such as the education system, the Church and associated organisations, cultural institutions, the press and the Falange's propaganda machine.[3] At first, censorship was seen as part of an active attempt to foster a theatrical culture that would embody National-Catholic values. Like similar ambitions in the Republican zone during the war, the attempt was hindered by a shortage of suitable scripts and the dependence of the theatre industry on the established repertoire of conventional commercial fare. Once those illusions had faded, it became increasingly clear that the main business of theatre censorship was merely reactive policing. Rather than providing moral education and aesthetic guidance, its main function was to limit the dissemination of ideas, stories, language or images that might challenge or undermine the official orthodoxy, expose its hollowness, or discredit any of the specific institutions that constituted the regime. The erratic evolution of Francoist cultural control is neatly summarised by Duncan Wheeler: 'A fluctuating combination of patronage, permissiveness and prohibition characterised the regime until its very end, different aspects coming in and out of focus' (2020: 103).

In the absence of explicit dissent in the early 1940s, one of the central preoccupations of Francoist censorship was the management of the internal politics of the regime. An important part of the legitimisation of Francoism was the balancing of the roles of the different 'families' of the regime in order to construct a unity of purpose out of a disparate coalition of forces (as demonstrated by the examples in Chapter 4 of the prohibition and cutting of pro-Nationalist plays). That need for unity also led to the suppression of performance in Catalan, Basque and Galician, an indiscriminate, far-reaching act of censorship that was cynically treated as if it were completely uncontroversial and inconsequential.

The period of Catholic hegemony from the decline in Falange influence in the mid-1940s up to the early 1960s revolved around the merging of political and religious priorities. If censorship for Arias-Salgado was about saving souls, that salvation depended on the imposition of a single National-Catholic 'truth', alongside a pragmatic defence of the Church's social and political influence. The Church was a crucial pillar of the structure and discourse of the regime not only because religion provided a tool for social control but also because the ideal of national unity was founded on the proposition that Catholicism was an essential defining feature of Spanishness. Loyalty to the Church was still – alongside a desire for social and political stability – the most powerful factor driving the production of an ostensible consensus in support of strict cultural control. The two apparently distinct dimensions of the censorship criteria applied throughout the dictatorship – political on the one hand, religious and moral on the other – were therefore always intertwined. The suppression of material judged to be indecent, irreverent or disrespectful to the Church was not a purely moral or doctrinal matter but inherently political.

The cautious *apertura* that began in the early 1960s revealed a growing scepticism within the system about the state's ability to maintain the illusion that censorship was being practised with the consent of a majority of the public, and that it reflected the values and tastes of 'normal' spectators. The strategy pursued by Fraga and García Escudero, based on an implicit recognition that censorship was driven largely by the defence of factional interests that were increasingly unrepresentative of public opinion, was more pragmatic than the absolutist approach of their predecessors. The main aim was damage limitation and management of the pace of a process of social and cultural change that was accepted as inevitable.[4] More specifically, the aim was to hinder or obscure the politicisation of cultural innovation – to limit the extent to which the theatre could contribute to and be conditioned by the spread of a dissident counterculture in which political opposition, secularism, social liberalism and artistic experimentation intersected. The device of confining certain kinds of performance to the *cámara y ensayo* circuit was a key component of that strategy.

Even the Church hierarchy itself came to acknowledge that the moral and religious crusade waged since 1939 had had little success in forcing the Spanish people into a National-Catholic mould. An episcopal statement issued in 1950 had called for a united front of clergy, critics, writers, educators and civil authorities in condemning pernicious texts, films and plays, in order to 'purificar moralmente el ambiente que respiramos' ('morally purify the atmosphere that we breathe') and restore 'la dignidad y prestigio de España y de todo lo auténticamente español' ('the dignity and prestige of Spain and all that is authentically Spanish') (Iribarren 1974: 257). A similar document issued in 1971 cautiously welcomed an increase in the public's concern for social justice and solidarity, but lamented 'una alarmante y progresiva decadencia moral en muchos sectores de nuestra comunidad eclesial y civil' ('an alarming and progressive moral decay in many sectors of our ecclesiastical and civil community'), caused in part by 'corrientes de cultura que, con pretextos humanistas, erosionan inhumanamente el campo de las ideas morales' ('cultural trends that, under humanist pretexts, viciously erode the field of moral ideas') (Iribarren 1974: 474). While the statement condemned consumerism, secularism, materialism and a lack of respect for traditional authority, it acknowledged at the same time that they were increasingly accepted as normal features of social life. As in previous periods, it was proposed that the state could play a part in remedying the decay, but the Church was losing faith in the efficacy of coercion: no mention was made in the 1971 document of repressive measures such as censorship.

As social change – intensified by increasing contact with other cultures – accelerated around them in the 1970s, the censors' business was more and more to do with attempting to manage that change. The principal challenge was to balance progressive and reactionary forces, both within the regime and outside it. As dissidence became more overt, the argument that allowing performances to go ahead would be less damaging than banning them was made more frequently. The proposition that a play might introduce dangerous ideas and behaviours to an innocent, defenceless public was being replaced by the assumption that such ideas and behaviours were already in circulation and the most that could be done was to ensure that they were not manifested too blatantly, so as not to stimulate unhelpful debate or provoke apoplexy in the political or religious bunker. Censors continued to be subject to conflicting pressures during the transition. There was irresistible public demand for social and political liberalisation but surviving elements or supporters of the old regime were liable to react viciously – threatening a kind of privatisation of censorship – if they felt that immorality or hostile reassessments of Francoism and National-Catholicism were being pushed too far.

In an important sense, then, forty years of laborious, bureaucratic, pervasive theatre censorship failed. The very fact that the regime felt the need to continue practising it for so long demonstrated that any ambition to effect a lasting purification – or at least subjugation – of cultural production was a delusion. The kind of perfect, 'invisible' censorship postulated by Bourdieu (1992: 138), was clearly not achieved. Theatremakers, some more deliberately than others, continued to challenge the norms, to use unauthorised discourses and to oblige coercive censorship to draw attention to itself, thereby showing that implicit, structural censorship was not working. Some other censorship systems in the twentieth century, particularly those of communist regimes in eastern Europe, attempted to get round this problem by pretending that censorship was not taking place. As the Franco regime did not resort to such subterfuge, its use of censorship became more and more counterproductive, falling into the 'performative contradiction' trap outlined by Judith Butler: 'Explicit forms of censorship are exposed to a certain vulnerability precisely through being more readily legible. The regulation that *states what it does not want stated* thwarts its own desire' (1997: 130). Moreover, theatrical culture in Spain was not a closed system. The banning and restriction of plays that were being performed in other countries made Spanish censorship increasingly visible internally and internationally, which became more and more of a concern to the regime from the mid-1950s onwards. Arrabal, whose success did not depend on having his plays performed in Spain, sees censorship as entirely counter-productive, welcoming it as a tribute: 'I was receiving the gift that only regimes of that kind can give. The gift of censorship' (2016: 40). Nieva too has noted that as a result of his friendships with prominent cultural figures associated with opposition to the regime, 'se me fue conociendo como "autor maldito", y esto confiere cierto prestigio' ('I became known as a "cursed author" and that brings with it a certain prestige') (2010).

Nevertheless, the evidence that we have presented clearly shows that serious damage was done to theatre and theatremakers, and that the impact was not confined to explicitly dissident work. The most severe acts of censorship – blanket prohibitions of whole categories of output – were few and relatively short-lived, such as the ban on theatre in Catalan from 1939 to 1946, the blacklisting of García Lorca between 1939 and the early 1950s, and of Arrabal between 1968 and 1976. Much more frequent was the refusal to allow particular plays to be performed. Estimating how many individual plays were prohibited between 1939 and January 1978 is not straightforward, partly because only a fraction of the more than 22,600 *expedientes de censura teatral* stored in the AGA have been examined, and partly because a decision by the censorship board to reject a particular application was often not the end of the story. In some cases, a revised script was submitted shortly after the initial decision and approved; in others, an application by a different company in new circumstances received a different verdict. Certain bans were tactical and temporary, linked to particular events or political circumstances, such as the state of exception in early 1969. Some plays were authorised for *cámara* productions but not for commercial ones, and some were authorised during the transition, after many years of prohibition.

In total, we have firm data for 1,086 plays, drawn from our own examination of AGA and ANC files, from Muñoz Cáliz's *Expedientes de la censura teatral franquista* (2006a), and from other published sources (Jurado Latorre 2001, Muñoz Cáliz 2011, Feldman and Foguet 2016, and Payá Beltrán 2018). Of those, 120 (11 per cent) were refused a licence for performance, and forty-five (4.1 per cent) remained prohibited until the abolition of censorship, in many cases because no further applications for approval were submitted. Some of those banned plays have never been staged. In Muñoz Cáliz's sample (2006), explicitly selected as representative of *teatro crítico* (critical theatre), the rate of prohibition was, unsurprisingly, higher (23 per cent). Across the other 878 cases, including the work of numerous clearly non-dissident authors, the prohibition rate was 8.3 per cent, with eighteen (2.1 per cent) remaining banned up to January 1978. Some years – particularly 1943 and 1975 – stand out as periods with markedly higher rates of prohibition. Since the 21,500 unexamined files in the archive cover thousands of innocuous commercial works unlikely to have been banned, the total rate of prohibition over the whole period cannot have been higher than 8 per cent and may have been significantly lower. If a global rate of 6 per cent were assumed, the total number of works prevented either temporarily or permanently from being staged would amount to approximately 1,350, an average of roughly thirty-four per year.

It is not possible to say with certainty that the banned plays would have been the thirty or forty most important in each year, but in many cases the textual or theatrical qualities that prompted prohibition were features that would have offered valuable contributions to the theatrical environment of the time. Each prohibition meant an author being denied the chance to see his or her work staged, to learn from that experience in order to develop their craft, to earn royalties, and gain professional and critical recognition in Spain and abroad. Efforts to revive banned plays during the transition offered important but limited compensation for the lost years. The prohibition of foreign plays – and restrictions on visits by foreign companies – resulted in Spanish theatre being deprived of aesthetic and professional models, as well as business opportunities. Each banned production also meant a director being prevented from choosing what to stage; a company losing work and wages; a theatre losing revenue; audiences being deprived of the right to choose what to see; an experiment nipped in the bud; and Spanish culture suffering one more dose of impoverishment. As José Monleón has stated, censorship 'no nos ha dejado crecer; no nos ha dejado pensar; no nos ha dejado dialogar' ('did not allow us to grow; to think; to engage in dialogue') (2011). Disruption and financial loss were particularly severe when prohibitions were imposed at the last minute, sometimes as a result of the dress rehearsal inspection, or even during a production's run.

Censorship was therefore a serious risk factor in programming decisions, making mainstream directors and impresarios reluctant to take on challenging projects and producing a general dampening effect on theatrical activity – especially any work offering serious social critique. What cannot be quantified is the extent to which the threat of prohibition acted successfully as a deterrent, producing total self-censorship – the decision not to write, or not to submit scripts for performance. The playwrights we have interviewed have tended to say that they managed to write more or less what they aimed to write despite the constraints, some showing greater pliability than others in order to get their work staged. Rodríguez Méndez claimed never to have taken censorship into account, neither deliberately challenging it nor attempting to evade it, and never quite understanding the reasons for decisions to ban his plays (private conversation, 2006). José Monleón, however, suggests that 'una autocensura profunda' ('a profound self-censorship') was normalised under the dictatorship (2011), while Alfonso Guerra speaks of 'una castración cultural espantosa' ('a shocking cultural castration') (2010). Ricardo Rodríguez Buded, a playwright whose work began to be noticed in the early 1960s and was linked to the emerging Realist Generation, found the environment so hostile that he gave up the struggle:

> En aquellos años, decir la verdad en nuestro país constituía un grave problema. La censura institucionalizada no lo permitía; la censura espontánea y gratuita de empresarios y gentes bien instaladas en el mundo teatral lo consideraba peligroso para sus intereses. Lo cierto es que nos encontramos frente a una carencia absoluta de estímulos y una amplia diversificación de dificultades. Resultaba, pues, prácticamente imposible llevar adelante una tarea que fuera medianamente compensadora. (Quoted in O'Connor and Pasquariello 1976: 22)

> At that time, speaking the truth in our country was a serious problem. Institutional censorship didn't allow it, and it was considered a threat to the interests of the unofficial, arbitrary censorship practised by impresarios and people in positions of influence in the world of the theatre. The fact is that we were up against an absolute lack of encouragement and wide range of impediments. As a result, it was practically impossible to produce work that would be even moderately worthwhile.

Ángel Facio also points to the impact of self-censorship on the selection of works for staging, making the point that 'hasta que no estrenó Brecht Tamayo, pues Brecht era imposible' ('until Tamayo staged Brecht, Brecht was impossible'); once that influential director had introduced Brecht to the mainstream, other directors took it as an indication that the dramatist was no longer banned (2011).

Although explicit censorship criteria were not made public until 1963, it was obvious to theatremakers throughout the dictatorship that there were certain kinds of subject matter that would render a play unperformable: a positive view of the Republic, or an account of the civil war from the Republican point of view; experiences of the deprivation, violent persecution and mass incarceration of the post-war period; the impossibility of identifying or recovering the thousands of bodies in mass graves all over Spain, or of holding to account the perpetrators of human rights abuses; the cultural memory and political aspirations of suppressed nationalisms; the complicity of the Church in oppression, indoctrination and social injustice; the unevenness of development and the prevalence of corruption in the economic boom of the 1960s; the violence of patriarchy, the oppressiveness of Catholic family values, and the repression of homosexuality. The regime thus succeeded in preventing vast areas of the collective memory and daily experience of Spaniards from being represented on stage. With newspapers, radio and television tightly controlled and non-fiction publishing constrained even after the 1966 Press Law, there was an acute need for dramatic and cinematic explorations of all these issues – a need that could not be fulfilled until the end of the dictatorship.

If the number of plays banned was small in relation to the sector's total output, the incidence of other constraints on theatrical production was much higher. We estimate that around one-third of plays were authorised with textual cuts, the extent of which ranged from single phrases to entire scenes or complete musical numbers. All genres were affected, as the range of material that could be judged unacceptable was extremely broad. In many cases, especially at the more commercial end of the market, cuts were relatively trivial, focusing on indecorous or irreverent language. Bowdlerisation of this kind was not often textually or dramatically significant, but it could have a deadening effect on the atmosphere of a production and its appeal to audiences. As *revistas* were particularly reliant upon sexual innuendo and vivacious colloquial banter, their commercial success could be threatened by prudish trimming of the dialogue and banning of songs. The majority of the plays staged by Alfonso Paso, the most prolific and successful dramatist of the 1960s, were subject to cuts, in some cases so extensive that the censors' initial decision was prohibition. A significant component of his appeal to mainstream audiences was an urbane, mildly cynical, slightly flippant treatment of sex, marriage and Catholicism, often designed to expose the narrow-mindedness and hypocrisy of conventional middle-class morality, an approach that frequently incurred the disapproval of the censors. However, he became so adept at rapidly rewriting his scripts and using his commercial pre-eminence to negotiate with the censorship office that the impact on the success of his work was minimal.[5] For Paso and the producers of *revistas*, the skirmishes with censorship were a game in which they constantly pushed at the boundaries to test what they could get away with.

For many authors, however, the stakes were higher. The point of suppressions was often to render a social or political critique – or parallel with current real-life circumstances – less explicit, which could have a significant impact on the communication of ideas to the audience. Buero Vallejo, one of the few other playwrights whose prestige afforded significant leverage in negotiations with the censorship office over cuts, could be tenacious in his insistence on retaining lines that he regarded as dramatically and thematically crucial, while giving way on less significant elements. Most authors, however, had little choice: cuts were usually non-negotiable and were often carried over into published editions of their plays. The obsessive attention to the printed text and the insistence on fixing and policing a single authorised version of each script also had the stifling effect of discouraging improvisation and adaptation, threatening to suck the essential energy out of *revistas*, avant-garde experiments and the collective creations of independent theatre groups.

The imposition of other conditions on theatrical productions, driven largely by the desire to depoliticise cultural activity, was also frequent and invasive, limiting the creative options of everyone involved in them. Plays set in unspecified or foreign locations, or in periods remote from the present, were often approved on condition that the staging did not suggest links to current circumstances in Spain. This constrained directors' visions of how to connect with audiences, as well as the creativity of set and costume designers, inhibiting innovation and immediacy by favouring a literal or highly conventional approach to indications of time and place in scripts. Professionals working on *revistas* were kept busy moving hemlines down and necklines up. The work of performers was also controlled at times through stipulations on censorship certificates. They were instructed, for example, to play religious characters with reverence and figures of authority with dignity; to avoid making a character's homosexuality obvious, showing bare flesh or suggesting sexual activity; to tone down a rebellious character's passion or to ensure that immoral behaviour was not made attractive.

While the imposition of minimum ages for audiences may not in itself have created severe difficulties for playwrights or companies, it contributed to the overall message that access to culture was not a right available to all but a concession, conditional and strictly regulated by the state. Only works clearly designed for young children, or with purely religious content, were classified as suitable for spectators of all ages. In a sample of 509 censorship notifications sent to the Delegado Provincial in Barcelona in 1966–7 and 1970, sixty-nine works (13.6 per cent) were approved for all ages, thirty-eight (7.5 per cent) for over-fourteens, and 402 (79 per cent) for over-eighteens. The normal conditions for authorisation for *cámara* included restriction to audiences over eighteen. Approval for children did not necessarily exempt a production from other controls: a passage of four lines was cut from Lauro Olmo's *Asamblea general* ('General Assembly') and an inspection was required, which was to be 'especialmente cuidado por ser obra destinada a público infantil' ('particularly attentive as this is a work for children') (ANC 328/66). In the case of Jorge Audifredd's *La imaginación de Pepito* ('Pepito's Imagination'), the authorisation specified that the inspection should ensure that the staging 'se mantenga dentro de las directrices y características de espectáculos infantiles, a tenor de la clasificación otorgada a la obra, ya que a ello queda condicionado tal dictamen' ('conforms to the approved criteria and normal characteristics of children's entertainment, in line with the classification issued for the work, since this authorisation is conditional upon such conformity') (ANC 295/67). The author's name would not have aroused the same suspicions as Olmo's, but the tradition of jokes in which Pepito mischievously misinterprets instructions from his teacher may have put the censors on their guard.

The exclusion of young people under the age of eighteen from 70 to 80 per cent of theatrical productions did not have a significant direct impact on education, since contemporary dramatic texts barely featured in a secondary school literature curriculum dominated by the study of the classics. Productions of plays from Spain's Golden Age were not often affected by censorship, though experimentation involving updating classics or bringing out political implications was strongly discouraged. Specialised drama studies did not become widespread in schools until the late 1970s, as part of the gradual diversification of the curriculum initiated by the Education Law of 1970 (Vieites 2014: 343–5). Any extra-curricular interest in theatre attendance that teenagers might have developed, especially in the 1960s and 1970s with the emergence of new styles, groups, venues and festivals, was frustrated by the censors' highly conservative application of the criteria for age classifications (which were drastically loosened under the 1978 *calificación* system). It was evident that the regime was anxious to prevent young people from being drawn into the ambit of theatrical counterculture.

The requirement for an inspection of the dress rehearsal (*visado del ensayo general*) was the norm, usually waived only for plays clearly targeted at children or with purely religious content. Although inspections rarely resulted in outright bans, the threat of the last-minute withdrawal of permission tended to create considerable anxiety and uncertainty. Much more frequent was the imposition of new textual cuts or restrictions on elements of staging that were not envisaged by the readers of the script. It was here that the sharp end of censorship was experienced by theatremakers in the form of humourless bureaucrats insisting on adherence to the approved script, nit-picking over details of intonation, movement or costume, stifling innovation and improvisation. Although companies' attempts to negotiate with inspectors (or pull the wool over their eyes) were sometimes successful, the frequent need to fight these small battles was a tiresome burden on the profession and a constant reminder of the vulnerability and conditionality of their creative freedom.

Decisions to allow performances of a play in some locations but not in others may have exacerbated the impression of arbitrariness and inconsistency in the system, yet they tended to be motivated by factors that made sense to the regime: either the patronising assumption that audiences outside Madrid and Barcelona were more susceptible to moral or political outrage than sophisticated city-dwellers, or the political need to appease particular civil governors, generals or bishops and maintain support for the regime among conservative social groups. Access to culture was therefore unequal and some sectors of the population were deemed to be incapable of making choices that were available to other citizens. Although Fraga's reforms in the 1960s made the censorship apparatus slightly more consistent and subject to explicit rules, the maintenance of a degree of arbitrariness was deliberate – a reminder that there was no real legal or political accountability. Such restrictions could also have a damaging impact on the financial viability of productions, adding to the difficulty of planning tours.

The power to authorise productions only for *cámara* conditions was an important part of the apparatus of control, especially between the late 1950s and early 1970s. It constituted a genuine concession on the part of the regime, allowing the performance of work that many censors and officials would have preferred to suppress altogether. To some extent the *cámara y ensayo* system also represented a commitment to the support of innovation and experimentation, backed up – albeit not very generously – with prizes, festivals and subsidies. However, its main purpose was not enabling but restrictive. The regime was determined to maintain a clear separation between the commercial and *cámara* sectors, labelling certain kinds of experimental or politically problematic performance as unsuitable for large mainstream audiences in order to confine them to a restricted market in which their influence would be limited, while ensuring that the fare offered to commercial theatre audiences was as politically anodyne and aesthetically conventional as possible. Restricting authorisation to *cámara* was therefore also a way of policing genre boundaries and audience expectations, as well as a propaganda weapon, allowing the regime to deny that the work of challenging authors and groups was being banned while limiting its dissemination and impact.

The policy of confinement to the *cámara* circuit was largely effective and caused significant damage. There were many shows that could have been successful in larger venues with longer runs, higher production values and more extended tours (though they would have been subject to more severe textual cuts). The commercial sector could have been usefully opened up by such crossovers, diversifying its audiences and increasing its social relevance. Even when this was not the case, the system simply made life difficult for amateur, semi-professional and independent companies.

By obliging them to continually reapply for permission for repeat performances, it effectively kept them under surveillance and in a state of provisionality.

It should also be recognised, however, that the system suited some theatremakers who were not seeking to appeal to the commercial market. Their experiments with theatrical form were bound up with the development of new collective ways of working and an ambition to reach out to new, mostly younger audiences. Confinement to a *cámara* 'bubble' could in some ways encourage the creation of a loyal customer base with shared expectations and a tendency towards complicity with coded meanings, dissident ideas and countercultural values. This was particularly the case in Catalonia, where the commercial sector was an unappealing environment, short of both public support and private investment, its repertoire dominated by transfers from Madrid, its workforce lacking modern professional training. The *teatre independent*, in contrast, took advantage of its marginalisation to create its own dynamic, which had a lasting impact on Catalan theatre, as Josep Maria Benet i Jornet argues:

> Teníamos que llegar con mucha frecuencia a escenarios paralelos, a los cuales iba solamente un tipo de público determinado, y las obras se hacían solamente siete u ocho veces. Pero bueno, era tu público y entonces había una libertad, tanto política como de nuevas formas de entender el teatro. Si escribías con esta influencia, se hacían obras mucho más modernas, que se estrenaban o se publicaban poco pero que eran mucho más modernas. (2010)

> We often had to make do with alternative venues, which attracted only a certain type of audience, and we would do no more than seven or eight performances. But then it was *your* public and as a result you'd have a kind of freedom, both in terms of politics and of new ways of understanding theatre. If you wrote with that kind of influence, you tended to produce work that was much more modern, plays that didn't get staged or published a lot but were much more up to date.

The overall impact of censorship on theatremaking in Spain was therefore heterogeneous, variable and pervasive. The multiple controls and restrictions affected all kinds of performance, professional and amateur, commercial and 'fringe', politically engaged and escapist. It was an ever-present, banal irritant which, even when it did not result in high-profile bans, imposed on the profession a daily burden of uncertainty, tedious bureaucratic procedures, delays (especially outside Madrid), financial losses, occasional fines, and a general drag on creativity. It was less a matter of absolute suppression or silencing than an ongoing process of policing: delimiting, channelling, labelling and distributing cultural production as part of an effort to fix and maintain an oppressive social and discursive order. Productions were defined as suitable only for certain audiences, certain companies, certain times, certain locations, certain types of space, and certain ways of performing. The main aim was to make theatrical performance docile and unproblematic, to obscure its destabilising political potential. This goal of depoliticisation is best understood in terms of Jacques Rancière's distinction between 'politics' and 'police':

> Politics is generally seen as the set of procedures whereby the aggregation and consent of collectivities is achieved, the organization of powers, the distribution of places and roles, and the systems for legitimizing this distribution. I propose to give this system of distribution and legitimization another name. I propose to call it *the police* [. . .] The police is thus first an order of bodies that defines the allocation of ways of doing, ways of being, and ways of saying, and sees that those bodies are assigned by name to a particular place and task; it is an order of the visible and the sayable that sees that a particular activity is visible and another is not, that this speech is understood as discourse and another as noise.' (1999: 28–9)

Theatre censorship literally orders bodies (of performers and spectators), allocates ways of doing, being and saying, and distributes places and roles. It aims to make theatrical expression understandable as merely inconsequential noise rather than meaningful discourse, that is, to neutralise its power to act as a form of political activity, which Rancière defines as 'whatever shifts a body from the place assigned to it or changes a place's destination. It makes visible what had no business being seen and makes heard a discourse where once there was only place for noise' (1999: 30). In this sense, it is not only explicitly dissident or nonconformist theatre that can act as *politics* and call into question a particular consensus or 'order of the visible and the sayable', especially when that order is as inflexible and artificial as that constructed by Francoism. Rancière rejects the notion of 'committed art', arguing that 'the politics of works of art plays itself out to a larger extent – in a global and diffuse manner – in the reconfiguration of worlds of experience based on which police consensus or political dissensus are defined' (2004: 65). Thus, even the gestures of deleting a few words of sexual innuendo, specifying how the role of a priest was to be played or ordering a costume adjustment in a *revista* were police actions designed to limit or efface a manifestation of politics that threatened the stability and legitimacy of the discursive order.

As the examples analysed in this book have shown, the policing carried out by the censorship apparatus in Spain had limited success in depoliticising theatrical expression. Indeed, in many ways it achieved the opposite. José Monleón, discussing the evolution of the Independent Theatre, argues that this was inevitable:

> El caso es que la oposición entre el poder y la cultura acaba siempre radicalizando a esta última, en tanto que perturba sus deseables niveles de independencia o –lo que es lo mismo– el libre compromiso con una opción política y el debate público de las restantes. Así que el franquismo acabó consiguiendo exactamente lo contrario de lo que se proponía: la politización de la cultura, la evidencia de que toda expresión de la realidad que no se correspondiera con el ideario oficial –y ahí estaban los censores para recordárnoslo– era un acto de subversión política. (1988: 7)

> The fact is that the opposition between power and culture always ends up radicalising culture, since it obstructs its desire for independence, which is to say, its freedom to commit to a particular political option and engage in public debate about the remaining options. Consequently, Francoism ended up achieving exactly the opposite of what it intended: the politicisation of culture, making it obvious that any representation of reality that did not match the official worldview – and the censors were always there to let us know when that was the case – was an act of political subversion.

Since theatrical performance is by its nature collective and public, theatre as a staging of political dissensus always involves collectivities – teams of theatremakers together with the spectators who choose to participate in the events they create. Francoist theatre censorship was energetically and imaginatively resisted by both the makers and the spectators. Authors defied the constraints and challenged the system at the cost of the suppression of their work, or else found inventive ways of working within the system and testing its boundaries. In some cases, pushing against the constraints acted as a stimulus, as Martínez Mediero asserts: 'Con la imaginación calenturienta de la que Dios me ha dotado, para mí fue un acicate. Gracias a la censura escribí mis obras más creativas' ('With the overheated imagination that God has blessed me with, censorship was a stimulus. It was thanks to censorship that I wrote my most creative plays') (interviewed in Grada 2020). Symbolic structures and abstract or historical settings were seldom chosen purely as a device to circumvent censorship, but the friction and ambiguity generated by the political possibilities of such techniques were often powerfully suggestive. Absences and silences in dramatic texts were often filled with significance by the surrounding context of concealment, suppression and unmentionable losses.

Companies found ways of distracting censors' attention while injecting immediacy, emotional impact and significance into staging and performance. They resisted the authorities' tendency to hinder theatrical experimentation. Moves by some companies in the 1960s away from texts towards physical theatre and improvisation were prompted to some extent by the constraints of censorship and its obsession with fixing texts but were also an integral part of the companies' own aesthetic evolution. Spectators' responses were also politicised. One of the more positive aspects, according to Ángel Facio of the independent theatre group Los Goliardos, was the creation of a special relationship of 'claves compartidas' ('shared codes') between practitioner and public (2011). Jesús Campos suggests that censorship 'hizo muy activo el espectador' ('made the spectator very active') (2010). They became adept at reading between the lines, interpreting silences, metaphors and visual signals, and through their complicity became active participants in the acts of dissensus. In a sense, the censors were afraid of the public: beneath their confidence in their power, there was always an undertone of uncertainty about the accuracy of their efforts to predict audiences' responses, and anxiety about the risks of unforeseen controversy and being judged by their political masters to have shown excessive leniency. In settings such as the second night of *Marat/Sade* in 1968 or the Festival Cero in San Sebastián in 1970, the audience became a central, defining component of the theatrical and political event.

The response to strict censorship could be dynamic and energising, described by the director and playwright Fermín Cabal as 'muy efímero, muy del momento – muy vivo' ('very ephemeral, very of the moment, very alive') (2010). For those who succeeded in making theatre despite censorship, there was a sense of excitement and engagement with the current social and political moment. However, this can also be viewed as a distortion of normal theatrical practices and an effacing of the powerful ambiguity that normally lies at the centre of a dramatic conflict. The theatre was no longer judged by artistic values alone but rather by the ideological values associated with its author, performers, public and critics.

The mixed picture built up in this book of the erosion of the efficacy of a draconian system of cultural control by multiple, distributed acts of resistance which generated artistic and political energy is pithily summed up by Monleón, who played a hugely important role as director, critic, producer and publisher in supporting theatrical initiatives in Spain from the late 1950s onwards:

> Fue una lucha donde la censura quería llegar a cien y la oposición consiguió que llegara a sesenta. Gracias a nuestras alegorías, a porque íbamos al extranjero y veíamos cómo se hacía lo que no podíamos ver, y entonces lo traíamos aquí y lo integrábamos como podíamos. Todo eso hacía que la acción de la censura estuviera un poco frenada por la respuesta social [. . .] El teatro ofrecía la posibilidad de representar realidades conflictivas que en el orden cotidiano no se podían comentar. Cuando no podía haber discurso político más que el discurso partidario del régimen, yo creo que uno de los espacios fundamentales para articular la crítica del régimen fue el teatro. (2011)

> It was a struggle in which the censorship system aimed to reach one hundred and the opposition prevented it from getting further than sixty. Thanks to our allegories, and to the fact that we would go abroad to see how people there were doing what we weren't allowed to see, and then we'd bring it back here and integrate it into our work as best we could. All of that meant that the action of censorship was curbed to some extent by the response of society [. . .] Theatre offered the possibility of representing conflictive realities that couldn't be discussed in the sphere of everyday life. At a time when there could be no political discourse other than the partisan discourse of the regime, I believe that one of the crucial spaces in which a critique of the regime could be articulated was the theatre.

The maintenance of this resistance did not depend on heroic headline instances of explicitly political action. Theatremakers and their audiences were playing their part simply by continuing to do their work in their own way, and sometimes by connecting directly with political activism outside the theatre. In the process they showed that the regime did not have total control over the discursive order – that other languages, identities, versions of history, forms of cultural capital and visions of society were possible. Alberto Miralles appears to mock the proposition that political and cultural opposition to Francoism had any real effect: 'Los que estudiáis historia sabéis que las izquierdas fuimos de victoria en victoria hasta la derrota final porque Franco murió en la cama cuando Dios quiso y no cuando los hombres lo decidieron' ('Those of you who study history know that the left went from victory to victory until final defeat because Franco died in his bed when God willed it and not when human beings decided it') (2003: 58). But he then pivots and suggests: 'Pero nunca se sabrá en qué medida la lucha antidictatorial debilitó el régimen permitiendo que la Transición fuera posible' ('But we'll never know to what extent the struggle against the dictatorship weakened the regime and made the Transition possible') (2003: 58).

Recent historical explanations of the transition to democracy have argued for a shift away from a top-down model – emphasising change driven by high-level negotiation between remnants of the Franco regime and leaders of the labour movement and left-wing parties – towards a bottom-up model focusing on much more widely distributed forms of social, civic and cultural action, with their roots in earlier movements that accelerated during the 1960s and 1970s:

> The growing tension between the rigid political structure and a dynamic consumer society became more obvious, as social mobilisation expanded from the traditional foci of conflict – the factories and the universities – and reached neighbourhoods, women's and consumers' associations, professional sectors, artists and other groups of the middle classes. (Groves, Townson, Ofer and Herrero 2017: 9)

Theatrical activity, explicitly in some cases and implicitly in others, was enmeshed in that network of resistance. Franco retained sufficient control to enable him to die in his bed, yet by then the discursive order that he and his agents of cultural control had gone to so much trouble to construct and maintain was thoroughly discredited. By pushing back against censorship and asserting its independence, theatre – like other cultural forms – played an important role in that process.

Notes

1 The general applicability of this idea is argued in Thompson (2016: 262), with reference to theatre censorship in a number of countries and periods (2016: 262).
2 The debate about whether Francoism possessed a clearly defined ideology is summarised by Giménez Martínez (2015).
3 On Ideological State Apparatuses, see Althusser (1984).
4 See the Introduction for a statement by Fraga to this effect.
5 The censorship file on *Víspera de domingo* ('The Night before Sunday') contains correspondence between Paso and José María Ortiz which shows the head of the censorship office going out of his way to help the playwright make the script acceptable (AGA 92/65). See Payá Beltrán (2018) for discussion of other examples.

Bibliography

Archival sources are listed first. The archives are: Archivo General de la Administración in Alcalá de Henares, Madrid (AGA); Arxiu Nacional de Catalunya in Sant Cugat del Vallès, Barcelona (ANC); Centro Documental de la Memoria Histórica in Salamanca (CDMH); and Centre de Documentació i Museu de les Arts Escèniques in Barcelona (CDMAE). AGA files for plays between 1939 and 1978 are identified by their *Expediente* code, which consists of a number followed by the year in which the file was set up (e.g., AGA 205/39 is application number 205 from 1939). The *Expedientes* ('files') are envelopes of documents stored in cardboard boxes; each box is identified by a *Caja* number (e.g., 73/08163). The *Instrumento de Descripción* (IDD) code identifies the section of the archive and the shelf location in which the box is stored; the prefix 03 refers to the 'culture section' of the archive. Theatre censorship files from 1939 to 1978 are in IDD (03)46.000. *Expedientes* initiated during the Republic (1931–9) were given a four-digit number not coded by year; we have added the prefix R to make the labelling of these items clear (e.g., AGA R6565). When a specific *Expediente* number is unavailable, the item is identified by the *Caja* code (e.g., 21/0646).

In the ANC, *Fons* ('collection') 318 contains the censorship notifications sent from Madrid to the Provincial Delegation in Barcelona, in some cases accompanied by inspection reports or correspondence. These documents are referenced by their *Expediente* number preceded by ANC (e.g., ANC 356/66) to distinguish them from the complete files held in the AGA.

Documents in the CDMAE are referenced by the name of the *Fons* followed by the *Caixa* ('box') number (e.g., CDMAE Fons ADB, E91). Some CDMAE materials can be consulted online at *http://colleccions.cdmae.cat*.

The documents consulted in the CDMH are mostly from the *Fondos Político-Sociales* ('Politico-Social Collections'): documents collected after the civil war to be used by the Francoist authorities as evidence of 'political' activity during the Republican period. They are referenced by *Fondo*, *Caja* and *Expediente* (e.g., CDMH PS-Madrid 1120, 29).

Spanish legislation is listed in the second section, referenced by the title of the official gazette in which each measure was published. Republican legislation was published in the *Gaceta de Madrid* (up to 8 November 1936) and the *Gaceta de la República* (10 November 1936 to 28 March 1939). The Nationalists' provisional government from 25 July to 2 October 1936 issued its decrees in the *Boletín Oficial de la Junta de Defensa Nacional*. Legislation passed by the Franco regime from 2 October 1936 appeared in the *Boletín Oficial del Estado* (BOE). All legislation is accessible online at *www.boe.es/legislacion*.

All other sources, including newspaper articles, are listed in the third section.

Archival sources

AGA 1/64. Censorship file: Fernando Arrabal, *Los dos verdugos* (1964–77). Archivo General de la Administración: IDD (03)046.000, Caja 71/00776, Expediente 1/64.

AGA 1/69. Censorship file: Rafael Alberti, *Égloga para tres voces y un toro ante la muerte lenta de un poeta* (1968–9). Archivo General de la Administración: IDD (03)046.000, Caja 73/09692, Expediente 1/69.

AGA 2/58. Censorship file: Ramón María del Valle-Inclán, *Divinas palabras* (1958–60). Archivo General de la Administración: IDD (03)046.000, Caja 73/09247, Expediente 2/58.

AGA 5/57. Censorship file: Carlos Muñiz, *El grillo* (1956–68). Archivo General de la Administración: IDD (03)046.000, Caja 73/9212, Expediente 5/57.

AGA 6/39. Censorship file: Ramón Cué, *Y el Imperio volvía...* (1939). Archivo General de la Administración: IDD (03)046.000, Caja 73/08147, Expediente 6/39.

AGA 7/68. Censorship file: Bertolt Brecht, *El círculo de tiza caucasiano* (*Der kaukasische Kreidekreis*) (1968). Archivo General de la Administración: IDD (03)046.000, Caja 73/10282, Expediente 7/68.

AGA 7/80. Classification file: José María Rodríguez Méndez, *Historia de unos cuantos* (1980). Archivo General de la Administración: IDD (03)046.000, Caja 73/10285, Expediente 7/80.

AGA 9/39. Censorship file: Gabriel Orizana, *El Alcázar de Toledo* (1939). Archivo General de la Administración: IDD (03)046.000, Caja 73/08147, Expediente 9/39.

AGA 11/67. Censorship file: Bertolt Brecht, *El alma buena de Sezuan (Der gute Mensch von Sezuan)*, adap. Armando Moreno and José Monleón (1967). Archivo General de la Administración: IDD (03)460.000, Caja 73/09577, Expediente 11/67.

AGA 12/68. Censorship file: Rafael Alberti, *El adefesio* (1968–73). Archivo General de la Administración: IDD (03)046.000, Caja 73/09633, Expediente 12/68.

AGA 13/65. Censorship file: Bertolt Brecht, *El círculo de tiza caucasiano (Der kaukasische Kreidekreis)* (1965). Archivo General de la Administración: IDD (03)046.000, Caja 73/09492, Expediente 13/65.

AGA 14/65. Censorship file: Carlos Muñiz, *Un solo de saxofón* (1965–73). Archivo General de la Administración: IDD (03)046.000, Caja 73/9492, Expediente 14/65.

AGA 14/67. Censorship file: Carlos Muñiz, *Miserere para medio fraile* (1967). Archivo General de la Administración: IDD (03)046.000, Caja 73/09577, Expediente 14/67.

AGA 15/67. Censorship file: Lauro Olmo, *La noticia* (1967–71). Archivo General de la Administración: IDD (03)046.000, Caja 73/09577, Expediente 15/67.

AGA 17/57. Censorship file: Albert Camus, *Caligula* (1957–60). Archivo General de la Administración: IDD (03)046.000, Caja 73/09213, Expediente 17/57.

AGA 19/59. Censorship file: Samuel Beckett, *Acto sin palabras (Act without Words)*, trans. Javier Lafleur (1959). Archivo General de la Administración: IDD (03)046.000, Caja 73/09282, Expediente 19/59.

AGA 19/66. Censorship file: Lauro Olmo, *El cuerpo* (1966). Archivo General de la Administración: IDD (03)046.000, Caja73/09526, Expediente 19/66.

AGA 20/61. Censorship file: José María Rodríguez Méndez, *Los inocentes de la Moncloa* (1961–4). Archivo General de la Administración: IDD (03)046.000, Caja 73/09353, Expediente 20/61.

AGA 21/0046. Letter from the Jefe de la Sección de Cinematografía y Teatro (Vicesecretaría de Educación Popular) to the Sección de Asuntos Generales (6 October 1942). Archivo General de la Administración: IDD (03)049.000, Caja 21/0046.

AGA 21/0064. Collection of applications for approval of visual material by Vicesecretaría de Educación Popular, Delegación Nacional de Propaganda, Sección de O.A.P. y Plástica (February–August 1943). Archivo General de la Administración: IDD (03)049.000, Caja 21/0064.

AGA 21/0646. Collection of correspondence and associated documents relating to the Vicesecretaría de Educación Popular, Delegación

Nacional de Propaganda, Sección de Cinematografía y Teatro (January–December 1943). Archivo General de la Administración: IDD (03)049.000, Caja 21/0646.

AGA 21/1477. Circular ('Normas de Funcionamiento e Informe') sent to censors by the head of the Sección de Censura, Dirección General de Propaganda (23 January 1940). Archivo General de la Administración: IDD (03)049.000, Caja 21/1477.

AGA 21/5797. Censorship file: Eduardo Marquina, *En el nombre del padre* (1935). Archivo General de la Administración: IDD (03)036.000, Caja 21/5797.

AGA 21/5804. Censorship file: Ramón Sender, Rafael Dieste and Rafael Alberti, *La llave, Al amanecer* and *Los salvadores de España* (1936). Archivo General de la Administración: IDD (03)036.000, Caja 21/5804.

AGA 21/5814a. Censorship file: José María Acebo, *Bandera de amor* (1937). Archivo General de la Administración: IDD (03)036.000, Caja 21/5814.

AGA 21/5814b. Censorship file: Luis Pérez de León, *Noches de bombardeo* (1937). Archivo General de la Administración: IDD (03)036.000, Caja 21/5814.

AGA 21/5822a. Censorship file: Federico García Lorca, *Mariana Pineda* (1927). Archivo General de la Administración: IDD (03)036.000, Caja 21/5822.

AGA 21/5822b. Censorship file: Federico García Lorca, *La zapatera prodigiosa* (1937). Archivo General de la Administración: IDD (03)036.000, Caja 21/5822.

AGA 21/5849. Censorship file: Honorio Maura, *Un negociante excelente* (1935). Archivo General de la Administración: IDD (03)036.000, Caja 21/5849.

AGA 25/44. Censorship file: José Muñoz Román and Jacinto Guerrero, *¡5 minutos nada menos!* (1944–56). Archivo General de la Administración: IDD (03)046.000, Caja 73/08552, Expediente 25/44.

AGA 27/65. Censorship file: Pedro Llabrés, Juan de Azaila and José García-Bernalt, *Las siete niñas de Écija* (1965–8). Archivo General de la Administración: IDD (03)046.000, Caja 73/09493, Expediente 27/65.

AGA 29/65. Censorship file: Lauro Olmo, *La condecoración* (1965–76). Archivo General de la Administración: IDD (03)046.000, Caja 73/09493, Expediente 29/65.

AGA 31/75. Censorship file: Tim Rice and Andrew Lloyd Webber, *Jesus Christ Superstar* ('*Jesucristo Superstar*'), adap. Nacho Artime and Jaime Azpilicueta (1975). Archivo General de la Administración: IDD (03)046.000, Caja 73/10106, Expediente 31/75. Other applications contained in Caja 73/9984, Expediente 605/72 and Caja 73/10153, Expediente 266/76.

AGA 33/46. Censorship file: Alfonso Sastre and Medardo Fraile, *Ha sonado la muerte* (1946). Archivo General de la Administración: IDD (03)046.000, Caja 78/00272, Expediente 33/46.

AGA 34/59. Censorship file: Alfonso Sastre, *Guillermo Tell tiene los ojos tristes* (1959–69). Archivo General de la Administración: IDD (03)046.000, Caja 73/09284, Expediente 34/59.

AGA 36/68. Censorship file: Alberto Miralles, *Catarocolón* (also known as *Versos de arte menor por un varón ilustre*) (1968–78). Archivo General de la Administración: IDD (03)046.000, Caja 73/09636, Expediente 36/68.

AGA 52/65. Censorship file: Carlos Muñiz, *El caballo del caballero* (1965–71). Archivo General de la Administración: IDD (03)046.000, Caja 73/09495, Expediente 52/65.

AGA 54/67. Censorship file: Alberto Miralles, *Espectáculo Cátaro* (*La guerra y El hombre*) (1967–70). Archivo General de la Administración: IDD (03)046.000, Caja 73/09583, Expediente 54/67.

AGA 57/66. Censorship file: Carlos Muñiz, *Las viejas difíciles* (1966). Archivo General de la Administración: IDD (03)046.000, Caja 73/09531, Expediente 57/66.

AGA 62/67. Censorship file: Brendan Behan, *El rehén* ('*The Hostage*'), trans. Genoveva Dieterich (1967–8). Archivo General de la Administración: IDD (03)046.000, Caja 73/09639, Expediente 62/67.

AGA 69/58. Censorship file: Samuel Beckett, *Final de partida* (*Fin de partie*), trans. Luce Moreau de Arrabal (1958). Archivo General de la Administración: IDD (03)046.000, Caja 73/09253, Expediente 69/58.

AGA 82/69. Censorship file: Fernando Arrabal, *La juventud ilustrada* (1969). Archivo General de la Administración: IDD (03)046.000, Caja 73/09702, Expediente 82/69.

AGA 84/71. Censorship file: Emilio González del Castillo, José Muñoz Román and Francisco Alonso, *Las de Villadiego* (1971). Archivo General de la Administración: IDD (03)046.000, Caja 73/08230, Expediente 84/71.

AGA 86/55. Censorship file: Alfonso Sastre, *La sangre de Dios* (1955). Archivo General de la Administración: IDD (03)046.000, Caja 73/09146, Expediente 86/55.

AGA 87/70. Censorship file: Federico García Lorca, *Así que pasen cinco años* (1970–8). Archivo General de la Administración: IDD (03)046.000, Caja 73/09762, Expediente 87/70.

AGA 89/69. Censorship file: Bertolt Brecht, *Antígona* ('*Antigone*') (1969). Archivo General de la Administración: IDD (03)046.000, Caja 73/09937, Expediente 89/69.

AGA 92/65. Censorship file: Alfonso Paso, *Víspera de domingo* (originally submitted under the title *El sábado por la noche*) (1965–7). Archivo

General de la Administración: IDD (03)046.000, Caja 73/09501, Expediente 92/65.

AGA 94/53. Censorship file: Alfonso Sastre, *Escuadra hacia la muerte* (1953–62). Archivo General de la Administración: IDD (03)046.000, Caja 73/09057, Expediente 94/53.

AGA 95/71. Censorship file: José María Rodríguez Méndez, *La tabernera y las tinajas* (1971). Archivo General de la Administración: IDD (03)046.000, Caja 73/09833, Expediente 95/71.

AGA 98/58. Censorship file: Alfonso Sastre, *Tierra roja* (1958). Archivo General de la Administración: IDD (03)046.000, Caja 73/09255, Expediente 98/58.

AGA 106/62. Censorship file: José María Rodríguez Méndez, *El círculo de tiza de Cartagena* (1962–3). Archivo General de la Administración: IDD (03)046.000, Caja 73/09398, Expediente 106/62.

AGA 107/55. Censorship file: Samuel Beckett, *Esperando a Godot* (*En attendant Godot*) (1955). Archivo General de la Administración: IDD (03)046.000, Caja 73/09149, Expediente 107/55.

AGA 109/55. Censorship file: Seán O'Casey, *Juno y el pavo real* ('*Juno and the Paycock*'), adap. Enrique Llovet (1955). Archivo General de la Administración: IDD (03)046.000, Caja 73/09149, Expediente 109/55.

AGA 110/63. Censorship file: Lauro Olmo, *El milagro* (1963). Archivo General de la Administración: IDD (03)046.000, Caja 73/09439, Expediente 110/63.

AGA 111/39. Censorship file: Pepe Romeu (pseudonym of José Rizo Navarro), *Yo quiero divorciarme* (1939). Archivo General de la Administración: IDD (03)046.000, Caja 73/08156, Expediente 111/39.

AGA 115/50. Censorship file: José López de Lerena, Pedro Llabrés and Jacinto Guerrero, *Su majestad la mujer* (1950–1). Archivo General de la Administración: IDD (03)046.000, Caja 73/08916, Expediente 115/50.

AGA 115/74. Censorship file: José María Rodríguez Méndez, *Flor de Otoño* (1974). Archivo General de la Administración: IDD (03)046.000, Caja 73/10075, Expediente 115/74.

AGA 121/63. Censorship file: Lauro Olmo, *La pechuga de la sardina* (1963). Archivo General de la Administración: IDD (03)046.000, Caja 73/09440, Expediente 121/63.

AGA 124/39. Censorship file: Jacinto Benavente, *La malquerida* (1939–67). Archivo General de la Administración: IDD (03)046.000, Caja 73/08157, Expediente 124/39.

AGA 125/64. Censorship file: John Millington Synge, *Deirdre de los Dolores* ('*Deirdre of the Sorrows*') (1964). Archivo General de la Administración: IDD (03)460.000, Caja 73/09474, Expediente 125/64.

AGA 125/67. Censorship file: Jean-Paul Sartre, *El infierno* (*Huis clos*), trans. Alfonso Sastre (1967–73). Title later changed to *A puerta cerrada*. Archivo General de la Administración: IDD (03)046.000, Caja 73/09593, Expediente 125/67.

AGA 127/39. Censorship file: José María Cabeza and Luis Felipe Solano, *Por el Imperio hacia Dios* (1939). Archivo General de la Administración: IDD (03)046.000, Caja 73/08157, Expediente 127/39.

AGA 127/66. Censorship file: Fernando Arrabal, *El cementerio de automóviles* (1966–77). Archivo General de la Administración: IDD (03)046.000, Caja 73/09541, Expediente 127/66.

AGA 139/65. Censorship file: José Martín Recuerda, *¿Quién quiere una copla del Arcipreste de Hita?* (1965). Archivo General de la Administración: IDD (03)046.000, Caja 73/10276, Expediente 139/65.

AGA 142/60. Censorship file: Albert Camus, *Calígula* (1961). Archivo General de la Administración: IDD (03)046.000, Caja 73/10269, Expediente 142/60.

AGA 144/61. Censorship file: Lauro Olmo, *La camisa* (1961–2). Archivo General de la Administración: IDD (03)046.000, Caja 73/09365, Expediente 144/61.

AGA 145/73. Censorship file: Antonio Buero Vallejo, *La Fundación* (1973). Archivo General de la Administración: IDD (03)046.000, Caja 73/10017, Expediente 145/73.

AGA 147/64. Censorship file: Antonio Buero Vallejo, *La doble historia del doctor Valmy* (1964–76). Archivo General de la Administración: IDD (03)046.000, Caja 73/09477, Expediente 147/64.

AGA 149/66. Censorship file: Peter Weiss, *Persecución y asesinato de Jean-Paul Marat (Marat-Sade)*, trans. Salvador Moreno Zarza [Alfonso Sastre] (1966–8). Archivo General de la Administración: IDD (03)046.000, Caja 73/09544, Expediente 149/66.

AGA 150/67. Censorship file: Jean-Paul Sartre, *Muertos sin sepultura* (*Morts sans sépulture*), trans. Alfonso Sastre (1967–73). Archivo General de la Administración: IDD (03)046.000, Caja 73/09596, Expediente 150/67.

AGA 150/70. Censorship file: Lauro Olmo, *Mare Nostrum, S.A.* (April–June 1970). Archivo General de la Administración: IDD (03)046.000, Caja 73/09770, Expediente 150/70.

AGA 152/69. Censorship file: José Ruibal, *Café-teatro* (*La secretaria, Los mutantes, El rabo*) (1969–72). Archivo General de la Administración: IDD (03)046.000, Caja 73/09710, Expediente 152/69.

AGA 155/71. Censorship file: Emilio Martínez Suárez [Grupo Tábano], *Piensa mal y acertarás* (1971). Archivo General de la Administración: IDD (03)046.000, Caja 73/09839, Expediente 155/71.

AGA 156/69. Censorship file: José Ruibal, *Los ojos* (1969–72). Archivo General de la Administración: IDD (03)046.000, Caja 73/09710, Expediente 156/69.

AGA 158/51. Censorship file: Federico García Lorca, *La zapatera prodigiosa* (1951–78). Archivo General de la Administración: IDD (03)046.000, Caja 73/08971, Expediente 158/51.

AGA 168/66. Censorship file: Fernando Arrabal, *Fando y Lis* (1966–9). Archivo General de la Administración: IDD (03)046.000, Caja 73/09547, Expediente 168/66.

AGA 170/69. Censorship file: Francisco Nieva, *Tórtolas, crepúsculo y. . . telón* (1969). Archivo General de la Administración: IDD (03)046.000, Caja 73/09712, Expediente 170/69.

AGA 171/69. Censorship file: Francisco Nieva, *Es bueno no tener cabeza* (1969–72). Archivo General de la Administración: IDD (03)046.000, Caja 73/10187, Expediente 171/69.

AGA 176/77. Censorship file: Manuel de Pedrolo, *Aquesta nit tanquem* (1977–8). Archivo General de la Administración: IDD (03)046.000, Caja 73/10201, Expediente 176/77.

AGA 177/67. Censorship file: Lauro Olmo, *Plaza Menor* (1967–76). Archivo General de la Administración: IDD (03)046.000, Caja 73/09600, Expediente 177/67.

AGA 192/39. Censorship file: Mariano Tomás, *Santa Isabel de España* (1939–47). Archivo General de la Administración: IDD (03)046.000, Caja 73/08162, Expediente 192/39.

AGA 193/43. Censorship file: Federico García Lorca, *La casa de Bernarda Alba* (1943–78). Archivo General de la Administración: IDD (03)046.000, Caja 73/08489, Expediente 193/43.

AGA 195/68. Censorship file: Josep Maria Benet i Jornet, *Cançons perdudes* (1968–70). Archivo General de la Administración: IDD (03)046.000, Caja 73/09657, Expediente 195/68.

AGA 197/63. Censorship file: Alfonso Sastre, *Oficio de tinieblas* (1963). Archivo General de la Administración: IDD (03)046.000, Caja 73/09449, Expediente 197/63.

AGA 200/69. Censorship file: José María Rodríguez Méndez, *La Andalucía de los Quintero* (1969). Archivo General de la Administración: IDD (03)046.000, Caja 73/09716, Expediente 200/69.

AGA 201/56. Censorship file: Pedro Peña y Giménez, *¡Ay qué loca!* (1956–9). Archivo General de la Administración: IDD (03)046.000, Caja 73/09197, Expediente 201/56.

AGA 201/71. Censorship file: Bertolt Brecht, *Terror y miseria del Tercer Reich* (*Furcht und Elend des Dritten Reiches*) (1971). Archivo General de la Administración: IDD (03)046.000, Caja 73/09845, Expediente 201/71.

AGA 205/39. Censorship file: José Echegaray, *El gran Galeoto* (1939–63). Archivo General de la Administración: IDD (03)046.000, Caja 73/08163, Expediente 205/39.

AGA 205/74. Censorship file: José María Rodríguez Méndez, *Bodas que fueron famosas del Pingajo y la Fandanga* (1974). Archivo General de la Administración: IDD (03)046.000, Caja 73/10079, Expediente 205/74.

AGA 206/70. Censorship file: Alberto Alonso and Juan Margallo [Grupo Tábano], *Castañuela 70* [*Tic... tac... un, dos, tres*] (1970–5). Archivo General de la Administración: IDD (03)046.000, Caja 73/09777, Expediente 206/70.

AGA 209/68. Censorship file: Alberto Miralles, *Versos de arte menor por un varón ilustre* (also known as *Catarocolón*) (1968–74). Archivo General de la Administración: IDD (03)046.000, Caja 73/09660, Expediente 209/68.

AGA 214/57. Censorship file: Ramón María del Valle-Inclán, *Luces de Bohemia* (1957–71). Archivo General de la Administración: IDD (03)046.000, Caja 73/09233, Expediente 214/57.

AGA 216/70. Censorship file: Ana Diosdado, *Olvida los tambores* (1970–8). Archivo General de la Administración: IDD (03)046.000, Caja 73/09779, Expediente 216/70.

AGA 219/59. Censorship file: Lauro Olmo, *Magdalena* (1959). Archivo General de la Administración: IDD (03)046.000, Caja 73/09299, Expediente 219/59.

AGA 222/67. Censorship file: Lauro Olmo, *Junio, siete, stop* (later staged with the titles *Cronicón del medioevo* and *Historia de un pechicidio*) (1967–74). Archivo General de la Administración: IDD (03)046.000, Caja 73/09606, Expediente 222/67.

AGA 223/58. Censorship file: Ramón María del Valle-Inclán, *Los cuernos de don Friolera* (1958–76). Archivo General de la Administración: IDD (03)046.000, Caja 73/09269, Expediente 223/58.

AGA 227/62. Censorship file: Bertolt Brecht, *Madre Coraje y sus hijos* (*Mutter Courage und ihre Kinder*) (1962–6). Archivo General de la Administración: IDD (03)046.000, Caja 73/09412, Expediente 227/62.

AGA 232/64. Censorship file: José Martín Recuerda, *El Cristo* (1964). Archivo General de la Administración: IDD (03)046.000, Caja 73/09487, Expediente 232/64.

AGA 232/68. Censorship file: José Martín Recuerda, *El caraqueño* (1968). Archivo General de la Administración: IDD (03)046.000, Caja 73/09663, Expediente 232/68.

AGA 242/54. Censorship file: Alfonso Sastre, *La mordaza* (1954). Archivo General de la Administración: IDD (03)046.000, Caja 73/09119, Expediente 242/54.

AGA 250/64. Censorship file: Jean-Paul Sartre, *A puerta cerrada* (*Huis clos*) (1964–73). Archivo General de la Administración: IDD (03)046.000, Caja 73/09489, Expediente 250/64.

AGA 250/71. Censorship file: Francisco Nieva, *Malditas sean Coronada y sus hijas* (1971). Archivo General de la Administración: IDD (03)046.000, Caja 73/09851, Expediente 250/71.

AGA 251/73. Censorship file: José María Rodríguez Méndez, *Historia de unos cuantos* (1973–5). Archivo General de la Administración: IDD (03)046.000, Caja 73/10027, Expediente 251/73.

AGA 254/62. Censorship file: José Martín Recuerda, *Las salvajes en Puente San Gil* (1962). Archivo General de la Administración: IDD (03)046.000, Caja 73/09415, Expediente 254/62.

AGA 258/69. Censorship file: Seán O'Casey, *Rosas rojas para mí* ('*Red Roses for Me*'), trans. Alfonso Sastre (1969). Archivo General de la Administración: IDD (03)046.000, Caja 73/09714, Expediente 258/69.

AGA 259/69. Censorship file: Antonio Buero Vallejo, *El sueño de la razón* (1969). Archivo General de la Administración: IDD (03)046.000, Caja 73/09724, Expediente 259/69.

AGA 260/60. Censorship file: Alfonso Sastre, *En la red* (1960–3). Archivo General de la Administración: IDD (03)046.000, Caja 73/09343, Expediente 260/60.

AGA 270/66. Censorship file: Bertolt Brecht, *La bona persona de Sezuan* (*Der gute Mensch von Sezuan*), trans. Carme Serrallonga (1966). Archivo General de la Administración: IDD (03)460.000, Caja 73/09563, Expediente 270/66.

AGA 271/56. Censorship file: Ramón María del Valle-Inclán, *Melodrama para marionetas* [*La cabeza del Bautista*] (1956–63). Archivo General de la Administración: IDD (03)046.000, Caja 73/09204, Expediente 271/56.

AGA 273/69. Censorship file: José Ruibal, *El hombre y la mosca* (1969–76). Archivo General de la Administración: IDD (03)046.000, Caja 73/09726, Expediente 273/69.

AGA 274/66. Censorship file: Seán O'Casey, *Cuento para la hora de acostarse* ('*Bedtime Story*'), trans. Renzo Casali (1966–71). Archivo General de la Administración: IDD (03)460.000, Caja 73/09563, Expediente 274/66.

AGA 280/68. Censorship file: Molière, *El Tartufo* (*Tartuffe*), trans. Enrique Llovet (1968–74). Archivo General de la Administración: IDD (03)046.000, Caja 73/09671, Expediente 280/68.

AGA 280/70. Censorship file: Rafael Alberti, *La Lozana andaluza* (1970–4). Archivo General de la Administración: IDD (03)046.000, Caja 73/09786, Expediente 280/70.

AGA 284/43. Censorship file: Federico García Lorca, *Doña Rosita la soltera* (1943–73). Archivo General de la Administración: IDD (03)046.000, Caja 73/08497, Expediente 284/43.

AGA 293/58. Censorship file: Antonio Buero Vallejo, *Un soñador para un pueblo* (1958). Archivo General de la Administración: IDD (03)046.000, Caja 73/09278, Expediente 293/58.

AGA 293/71. Censorship file: Jordi Teixidor, *El retablo del flautista* (1971–6). Archivo General de la Administración: IDD (03)046.000, Caja 73/09857, Expediente 293/71.

AGA 294/62. Censorship file: Albert Camus, *Caligula* (1962–7). Archivo General de la Administración: IDD (03)046.000, Caja 73/09420, Expediente 294/62.

AGA 296/60. Censorship file: Antonio Buero Vallejo, *Las Meninas* (1960). Archivo General de la Administración: IDD (03)046.000, Caja 73/09347, Expediente 296/60.

AGA 297/71. Censorship file: Josep Maria Benet i Jornet, *L'ocell Fènix a Catalunya, o Alguns papers de l'auca* (first performed with the title *Mort i resurrecció del senyor Esteve*) (1971–7). Archivo General de la Administración: IDD (03)046.000, Caja 73/09857, Expediente 297/71.

AGA 300/58. Censorship file: Federico García Lorca, *Yerma* (1958–73). Archivo General de la Administración: IDD (03)046.000, Caja 73/09279, Expediente 300/58.

AGA 306/60. Censorship file: Carlos Muñiz, *El tintero* (1960–8). Archivo General de la Administración: IDD (03)046.000, Caja 73/09348, Expediente 306/60.

AGA 307/66. Censorship file: Fernando Arrabal, *El arquitecto y el emperador de Asiria* (1966–76). Archivo General de la Administración: IDD (03)046.000, Caja 73/09568, Expediente 307/66.

AGA 309/46. Censorship file: Alfonso Sastre, *Cargamento de sueños* (1946). Archivo General de la Administración: IDD (03)046.000, Caja 78/00294, Expediente 309/46.

AGA 311/60. Censorship file: José María Rodríguez Méndez, *Vagones de madera* (1960–8). Archivo General de la Administración: IDD (03)046.000, Caja 73/09349, Expediente 311/60.

AGA 320/67. Censorship file: Los Goliardos, *Espectáculo de mimo y pantomima* (adapted from Samuel Beckett, *Acte sans paroles*) (1967). Archivo General de la Administración: IDD (03)046.000, Caja 73/09621, Expediente 320/67.

AGA 323/71. Censorship file: Antonio Buero Vallejo, *Llegada de los dioses* (1971). Archivo General de la Administración: IDD (03)046.000, Caja 73/10250, Expediente 323/71.

AGA 325/53. Censorship file: Enrique Paradas, Joaquín Jiménez, Francisco de Torres, Ernesto Rosillo and Juan Mollá, *Cirilo, que estás en vilo* (1953–8). Archivo General de la Administración: IDD (03)046.000, Caja 73/09082, Expediente 325/53.

AGA 334/66. Censorship file: Federico García Lorca, *Mariana Pineda* (1966–73). Archivo General de la Administración: IDD (03)046.000, Caja 73/09572. Expediente 334/66.

AGA 347/71. Censorship file: Albert Camus, *Caligula* (1971). Archivo General de la Administración: IDD (03)046.000, Caja 73/09863, Expediente 347/71.

AGA 351/53. Censorship file: José Martín Recuerda, *La llanura* (1953–4). Archivo General de la Administración: IDD (03)046.000, Caja 73/09085, Expediente 351/53.

AGA 352/39. Censorship file: Pedro Muñoz Seca, *Anacleto se divorcia* (1939). Archivo General de la Administración: IDD (03)046.000, Caja 8168, Expediente 352/39.

AGA 358/69. Censorship file: José Ruibal, *La máquina de pedir* (1969–76). Archivo General de la Administración: IDD (03)046.000, Caja 73/09737, Expediente 358/69.

AGA 359/56. Censorship file: Fernando Arrabal, *Los hombres del triciclo* (1956–72). Archivo General de la Administración: IDD (03)046.000, Caja 73/09211, Expediente 359/56.

AGA 363/67. Censorship file: Jean-Paul Sartre, *Muertos sin sepultura* (*Morts sans sépulture*), translated by Alfonso Sastre (1967). Archivo General de la Administración: IDD (03)046.000, Caja 73/09627, Expediente 363/67.

AGA 365/69. Censorship file: John Arden, *Vivir como cerdos* ('*Live Like Pigs*'), trans. Álvaro del Amo (1969). Archivo General de la Administración: IDD (03)046.000, Caja 73/09738, Expediente 365/69.

AGA 374/59. Censorship file: Samuel Beckett, *La última cinta de Krapp* (1959–62). Archivo General de la Administración: IDD (03)046.000, Caja 73/09314, Expediente 374/59.

AGA 375/39. Censorship file: Manuel Linares Rivas and Alejandro Pérez Lugín, *Currito de la Cruz* (1939–65). Archivo General de la Administración: IDD (03)046.000, Caja 73/08171, Expediente 375/39.

AGA 375/67. Censorship file: Lauro Olmo, *English spoken* (1967–8). Archivo General de la Administración: IDD (03)046.000, Caja 73/09628, Expediente 375/67.

AGA 376/69. Censorship file: Lauro Olmo, *El cuarto poder* (1969–70). Archivo General de la Administración: IDD (03)046.000, Caja 73/09739, Expediente 376/69.

AGA 377/53. Censorship file: Alfonso Sastre, *Cargamento de sueños* (1953). Archivo General de la Administración: IDD (03)046.000, Caja 73/08706, Expediente 377/53.

AGA 380/73. Censorship file: Luis Riaza, *El desván de los machos y el sótano de las hembras* (1973–7). Archivo General de la Administración: IDD (03)046.000, Caja 73/10040, Expediente 380/73.

AGA 391/68. Censorship file: Fernando Arrabal, *El gran ceremonial* (1968). Archivo General de la Administración: IDD (03)046.000, Caja 73/09687, Expediente 391/68.

AGA 393/39. Censorship file: Antonio Quintero, *El delirio* (1939–44). Archivo General de la Administración: IDD (03)046.000, Caja 73/08173, Expediente 393/39.

AGA 393/68. Censorship file: Fernando Arrabal, *Ciugrena* [*Guernica*] (1968). Archivo General de la Administración: IDD (03)046.000, Caja 73/09687, Expediente 393/68.

AGA 395/53. Censorship file: Antonio Buero Vallejo, *Aventura en lo gris* (1953–63). Archivo General de la Administración: IDD (03)046.000, Caja 73/09089, Expediente 395/53.

AGA 397/39. Censorship file: Jacinto Benavente, *El nido ajeno* (1939–78). Archivo General de la Administración: IDD (03)046.000, Caja 73/08173, Expediente 397/39.

AGA 401/53. Censorship file: Alfonso Sastre, *El pan de todos* (1953). Archivo General de la Administración: IDD (03)046.000, Caja 73/09090, Expediente 401/53.

AGA 413/70. Censorship file: José María Rodríguez Méndez, *Los quinquis de Madriz* (1970). Archivo General de la Administración: IDD (03)046.000, Caja 73/09803, Expediente 413/70.

AGA 427/77. Censorship file: Els Joglars/Albert Boadella, *La torna* (1977). Archivo General de la Administración: IDD (03)046.000, Caja 73/10213, Expediente 427/77.

AGA 433/49. Censorship file: Antonio Buero Vallejo, *Historia de una escalera* (1949). Archivo General de la Administración: IDD (03)046.000, Caja 73/08892, Expediente 433/49.

AGA 436/73. Censorship file: Francisco Nieva, *Pelo de tormenta* (1973–6). Archivo General de la Administración: IDD (03)046.000, Caja 73/10045, Expediente 436/73.

AGA 438/53. Censorship file: Alfonso Sastre, *Prólogo patético* (1953–71). Archivo General de la Administración: IDD (03)046.000, Caja 73/09093, Expediente 438/53.

AGA 450/48. Censorship file: Federico García Lorca, *Bodas de sangre* (1948–72). Archivo General de la Administración: IDD (03)046.000, Caja 73/08839, Expediente 450/48.

AGA 463/39. Censorship file: Francisco Marín Melià, *Un revolcó a temps* (1939). Archivo General de la Administración: IDD (03)046.000, Caja 73/08179, Expediente 463/39.

AGA 476/39. Censorship file: Jesús Morante Borrás, *Arriba España* (1939–47). Archivo General de la Administración: IDD (03)046.000, Caja 73/08180, Expediente 476/39.

AGA 494/72. Censorship file: Albert Camus, *L'Etat de siège* (*El estado de sitio*), trans. Federico Sainz de Robles (1972). Archivo General de la Administración: IDD (03)046.000, Caja 73/09969, Expediente 494/72.

AGA 497/44. Censorship file: Cecília A. Màntua, *La riada* (1944). Archivo General de la Administración: IDD (03)046.000, Caja 73/08595, Expediente 497/44.

AGA 508/70. Censorship file: Joan Oliver, *Bestiari* (1970–4). Archivo General de la Administración: IDD (03)046.000, Caja 73/09817, Expediente 508/70.

AGA 516/71. Censorship file: Rafael Alberti, *La Gallarda* (1971). Archivo General de la Administración: IDD (03)046.000, Caja 73/09884, Expediente 516/71.

AGA 539/75. Censorship file: Manuel de Pedrolo, *Xit!* (1975–6). Archivo General de la Administración: IDD (03)046.000, Caja 73/10134, Expediente 539/75.

AGA 546/71. Censorship file: José Martín Recuerda, *Las arrecogías del beaterio de Santa María Egipcíaca* (1971). Archivo General de la Administración: IDD (03)046.000, Caja 73/09888, Expediente 546/71.

AGA 555/72. Censorship file: José María Rodríguez Méndez, *El ghetto, o la irresistible ascención de Manuel Contreras* (1972). Archivo General de la Administración: IDD (03)046.000, Caja 73/09977, Expediente 555/72.

AGA 574/73. Censorship file: José Martín Recuerda, *El engañao* (1973–4). Archivo General de la Administración: IDD (03)046.000, Caja 73/09998, Expediente 574/73.

AGA 576/72. Censorship file: Carlos Muñiz, *Tragicomedia del serenísimo Príncipe don Carlos* (1972–3). Archivo General de la Administración: IDD (03)046.000, Caja 73/09979, Expediente 576/72.

AGA 581/71. Censorship file: José María Rodríguez Méndez, *El milagro del pan y de los peces* (1971). Archivo General de la Administración: IDD (03)046.000, Caja 73/09893, Expediente 581/71.

AGA 602/72. Censorship file: Lauro Olmo, *Historia de un pechicidio (Cronicón del medioevo)* (1972). Archivo General de la Administración: IDD (03)046.000, Caja 73/09984, Expediente 602/72.

AGA 618/74. Censorship file: Carlos Muñiz, *Los condenados* (1974). Archivo General de la Administración: IDD (03)046.000, Caja 73/10102, Expediente 618/74.

AGA 626/71. Censorship file: George Bernard Shaw, *La profesión de la señora Warren* (*Mrs Warren's Profession*), trans. Natividad Zaro (1971). Archivo General de la Administración: IDD (03)046.000, Caja 73/09898, Expediente 626/71.

AGA 638/48. Censorship file: José López de Lerena, Pedro Llabrés and Ernesto Rosillo, *El año pasado sin agua* (1948–50). Archivo General de la Administración: IDD (03)046.000, Caja 73/08853, Expediente 638/48.

AGA 639/71. Censorship file: Albert Camus, *Calígula* (1971). Archivo General de la Administración: IDD (03)046.000, Caja 73/09900, Expediente 693/71.

AGA 663/78. Censorship file: Manuel Martínez Mediero, *El último gallinero* (1978–81). Archivo General de la Administración: IDD (03)046.000, Caja 73/10249, Expediente 663/78.

AGA 690/78. Classification file on Rafael Alberti, *Noche de guerra en el Museo del Prado* (1978). Archivo General de la Administración: IDD (03)046.000, Caja 73/10250, Expediente 690/78.

AGA 703/75. Censorship file: Lauro Olmo, *Spot de identidad* (1975). Archivo General de la Administración: IDD (03)046.000, Caja 73/10143, Expediente 703/75.

AGA 782/40. Censorship file: Carlos Arniches, Antonio Estremera and Jacinto Guerrero, *Peccata Mundi* (1940). Archivo General de la Administración: IDD (03)046.000, Caja 73/08207, Expediente 782/40.

AGA 828/40. Censorship file: Jacinto Benavente, *Alfilerazos* (1940–9). Archivo General de la Administración: IDD (03)046.000, Caja 73/08211, Expediente 828/40.

AGA 852/40. Censorship file: Felipe Lluch Garín, *Espectáculo de la España Una, Grande y Libre* (1940). Archivo General de la Administración: IDD (03)046.000, Caja 73/08213, Expediente 852/40.

AGA 932/40. Censorship file: Jacinto Benavente, *Aves y pájaros* (1940–5). Archivo General de la Administración: IDD (03)046.000, Caja 73/08222, Expediente 932/40.

AGA 1016/40. Censorship file: Emilio González del Castillo, José Muñoz Román and Francisco Alonso, *Las de Villadiego* (1940–1942). Archivo General de la Administración: IDD (03)046.000, Caja 73/08230, Expediente 1016/40.

AGA 1114/76. Censorship file: Alberto Miralles, *El espectáculo no ha terminado* (version of *Espectáculo Cátaro*) (1976). Archivo General de la Administración: IDD (03)046.000, Caja 73/10173, Expediente 1114/76.

AGA 1116/76. Censorship file: Fernando Arrabal, *En la cuerda floja, o Balada del tren fantasma* (1976). Archivo General de la Administración: IDD (03)046.000, Caja 73/10173, Expediente 1116/76.

AGA 1130/76. Censorship file: *Amor, amor. . . destápame* (1976). Archivo General de la Administración: IDD (03)046.000, Caja 73/10175, Expediente 1130/76.

AGA 1134/76. Censorship file: Antonio Fos Fernando, *El moño de la Bernarda* (1976). Archivo General de la Administración: IDD (03)046.000, Caja 73/10175, Expediente 1134/76.

AGA 1138/76. Censorship file: Joan Ollé and Josep Parramon, *No hablaré en clase* (1976). Archivo General de la Administración: IDD (03)046.000, Caja 73/10175, Expediente 1138/76.

AGA 1144/76. Censorship file: Juan Antonio Castro, *De la buena crianza del gusano* (1976). Archivo General de la Administración: IDD (03)046.000, Caja 73/10175, Expediente 1144/76.

AGA 1180/76. Censorship file: Fernando Arrabal, *Y pusieron esposas a las flores* (1976–7). Archivo General de la Administración: IDD (03)046.000, Caja 73/10178, Expediente 1180/76.

AGA 1279/40. Censorship file: Pedro Muñoz Seca, *Marcelino fue por vino* (1940–53). Archivo General de la Administración: IDD (03)046.000, Caja 73/08246, Expediente 1279/40.

AGA 1330/40. Censorship file: Pedro Muñoz Seca and Pedro Pérez Fernández, *La Oca* (1940–71). Archivo General de la Administración: IDD (03)046.000, Caja73/08251, Expediente 1330/40.

AGA 1371/40. Censorship file: Jacinto Benavente, *Lo increíble* (1940–63). Archivo General de la Administración: IDD (03)046.000, Caja73/08254, Expediente 1371/40.

AGA 1431/40. Censorship file: Jacinto Benavente, *Señora ama* (1940–65). Archivo General de la Administración: IDD (03)046.000, Caja 73/08260, Expediente 1371/40.

AGA 1489/40. Censorship file: Pilar Millán-Astray, *Regina la bien plantá* (1940–4). Archivo General de la Administración: IDD (03)046.000, Caja 73/08265, Expediente 1489/40.

AGA 1579/40. Censorship file: Jacinto Benavente, *Lo cursi* (1940–54). Archivo General de la Administración: IDD (03)046.000, Caja 73/08273, Expediente 1579/40.

AGA 1687/40. Censorship file: José Echegaray, *Mancha que limpia* (1940–61). Archivo General de la Administración: IDD (03)046.000, Caja 73/8281, Expediente 1687/40.

AGA 2027/41. Censorship file: Thornton Wilder, *Navidades en la casa Bayard* ('*The Long Christmas Dinner*') (1941). Archivo General de la Administración: IDD (03)046.000, Caja 73/08312, Expediente 2027/41.

AGA 2428/41. Censorship file: Fernando Lluch Ferrando, *El Negre* (1941). Archivo General de la Administración: IDD (03)046.000, Expediente 2428/41.

AGA 2472/41. Censorship file: Jacinto Benavente, *La Infanzona* (1941–51). Archivo General de la Administración: IDD (03)046.000, Caja 73/08354, Expediente 2472/41.

AGA 2525/41. Censorship file: Cecília A. Mántua and Antonio Losada, *A ti vuela mi canción* (1941–2). Archivo General de la Administración: IDD (03)046.000, Caja 73/08359, Expediente 2525/41.

AGA 2571/41. Censorship file: Thornton Wilder, *Una ciudad pequeñita* ('*Our Town*') (1941). Archivo General de la Administración: IDD (03)046.000, Caja 73/08362, Expediente 2571/41.

AGA 2705/41. Censorship file: Cecília A. Mántua and Antonio Losada, *Serenata de Schubert, o A ti vuelan mis canciones* (revised version of *A ti vuela mi canción*, 1941). Archivo General de la Administración: IDD (03)046.000, Caja 73/08374, Expediente 2705/41.

AGA 2993/42. Censorship file: Jacinto Benavente, *Ni al amor ni al mar* (1940–65). Archivo General de la Administración: IDD (03)046.000, Caja 73/08401, Expediente 2993/42.
AGA Buero Vallejo. Security dossier on Antonio Buero Vallejo (1963–77). Gabinete de Enlace, Ministerio de Información y Turismo. Archivo General de la Administración: IDD (03)107.001, Caja 42/08804, Expediente 03.
AGA MIT/00.584. 'Encuesta sobre la pornografía y el desnudo' (18 October 1975). Report for Ministerio de Información y Turismo by Agencia Pyresa (Prensa y Radio Española, SA). Archivo General de la Administración: IDD 104.04, Caja 581.
AGA MIT/00.710. 'Notas sobre obras en general' (1976). Internal report, Ministerio de Información y Turismo. Archivo General de la Administración: IDD 104.04, Caja 576.
AGA Muñiz. Security dossier on Carlos Muñiz (1974). Gabinete de Enlace, Ministerio de Información y Turismo. Archivo General de la Administración: IDD (03)107.001, Caja 42/08885, Expediente 11.
AGA R5907. Censorship file: Lope de Vega, *Fuente Ovejuna* (1932). Archivo General de la Administración: IDD (03)036.000, Caja 21/5802, Expediente 5907.
AGA R5971. Censorship file: Francisco Ramos de Castro, *Las del Beni* (1932). Archivo General de la Administración: IDD (03)036.000, Caja 21/5820, Expediente 5971.
AGA R5993. Censorship file: Pilar Millán-Astray, *Las andanzas de Ginesillo* (1932). Archivo General de la Administración: IDD (03)036.000, Caja 21/5849 Expediente 5993.
AGA R6005. Censorship file: Antonio Paso Díaz and Federico López de Saá, *Chungonia* (1932). Archivo General de la Administración: IDD (03)036.000, Caja 21/5792, Expediente 6005.
AGA R6033. Censorship file: Jacinto Benavente, *La duquesa gitana* (1932). Archivo General de la Administración: IDD (03)036.000, Caja 21/5792, Expediente 6033.
AGA R6061. Censorship file: Miguel de Unamuno, *El otro* (1932). Archivo General de la Administración: IDD (03)036.000, Caja 21/5793, Expediente 6061.
AGA R6077. Censorship file: Manuel de Jesús Moreno, *De muy buen barro* (1932). Archivo General de la Administración: IDD (03)036.000, Caja 21/5797, Expediente 6077.
AGA R6078. Censorship file: José Martín Villapecellín, *República Inmoral* (1933). Archivo General de la Administración: (03)036.000, Caja 21/47, Expediente 6078.
AGA R6117. Censorship file: Federico García Lorca, *Bodas de sangre* (1933). Archivo General de la Administración: IDD (03)036.000, Caja 21/5800. Expediente 6117

AGA R6125. Censorship file: Ramón del Valle-Inclán, *Divinas palabras* (1933). Archivo General de la Administración: IDD (03)036.000, Caja 21/5795, Expediente 6125.

AGA R6158. Censorship file: Emilio Gómez de Miguel and Eduardo Borrás, *No hay novedad en el frente* (1933). Archivo General de la Administración: IDD (03)036.000, Caja 21/5820, Expediente 6158.

AGA R6177. Censorship file: Alejandro Casona, *La sirena varada* (1934). Archivo General de la Administración: IDD (03)036.000, Caja 21/5835, Expediente 6177.

AGA R6192. Censorship file: Vicente Mena Pérez, *Santa Teresita del Niño Jesús* (1933). Archivo General de la Administración: IDD (03)036.000, Caja 21/5835, Expediente 6192.

AGA R6208. Censorship file: Enrique Jardiel Poncela, *Usted tiene ojos de mujer fatal* (1933). Archivo General de la Administración: IDD (03)036.000, Caja 21/5804, Expediente 6208.

AGA R6211. Censorship file: José María Pemán, *El divino impaciente* (1933). Archivo General de la Administración: IDD (03)036.000, Caja 21/5546, Expediente 6211.

AGA R6214. Censorship file: Carlos Arniches, Antonio Estremera and Jacinto Guerrero, *Peccata Mundi* (1934). Archivo General de la Administración: IDD (03)036.000, Caja 21/5837, Expediente 6214.

AGA R6222. Censorship file: Julio G. Miranda, *Pinitos fascistas* (1933). Archivo General de la Administración: (03)036.000, Caja 21/5810, Expediente 6222.

AGA R6243. Censorship file: José María Pemán, *Cuando las Cortes de Cádiz* (1934). Archivo General de la Administración: IDD (03)036.000, Caja 21/5846, Expediente 6243.

AGA R6279. Censorship file: José María Pemán, *Cisneros* (1934). Archivo General de la Administración: IDD (03)036.000, Caja 21/5843, Expediente 6279.

AGA R6293. Censorship file: Federico García Lorca, *Yerma* (1934). Archivo General de la Administración: IDD (03)036.000, Caja 21/5822, Expediente 6293.

AGA R6306. Censorship file: Eduardo Marquina, *La Dorotea* (1935). Archivo General de la Administración: IDD (03)036.000, Caja 21/5820, Expediente 6306.

AGA R6333. Censorship file: Pedro Muñoz Seca, *Ciudadano de honor* (1935). Archivo General de la Administración: IDD (03)036.000, Caja 21/5827, Expediente 6333.

AGA R6364. Censorship file: Enrique Jardiel Poncela, *Un adulterio decente* (1935). Archivo General de la Administración: IDD (03)036.000, Caja 21/5823, Expediente 6364.

AGA R6439. Censorship file: Hilario Torres, *Por triunfar* (1935). Archivo General de la Administración: IDD (03)036.000, Caja 21/5848, Expediente 6439.

AGA R6444. Censorship file: Vicente Castro Les, *¡La bolsa o la vida!* (1935). Archivo General de la Administración: IDD (03)036.000, Caja 21/5823, Expediente 6444.

AGA R6446. Censorship file: Manuel Soler Chamizo, *Los dientes de un lobo* (1935). Archivo General de la Administración: IDD (03)036.000, Caja 21/5823, Expediente 6446.

AGA R6465. Censorship file: Francisco Ramos de Castro and José Luis Mayral, *La Colasa de Pavón* (1935). Archivo General de la Administración: IDD (03)036.000, Caja 21/5802, Expediente 6465.

AGA R6467. Censorship file: Manuel García, *Guerra a la guerra* (1935). Archivo General de la Administración: IDD (03)036.000, Caja 21/47, Expediente 6467.

AGA R6497. Censorship file: Nonato Ovejuna Inia [Antonio Juan Onieva], *Hambre atrasada* (1935). Archivo General de la Administración: IDD (03)036.000, Caja 21/5848, Expediente 6497.

AGA R6530. Censorship file: Azorín, *La guerrilla* (1936). Archivo General de la Administración: IDD (03)036.000, Caja 21/5814, Expediente 6530.

AGA R6546. Censorship file: Martin Flavin, *Los hombres grises* ('*The Criminal Code*') (1936). Archivo General de la Administración: IDD (03)036.000, Caja 21/5839, Expediente 6546.

AGA R6554. Censorship file: Alejandro Casona, *Nuestra Natacha* (1936). (03)046.000, Archivo General de la Administración: IDD (03)036.000, Caja 21/5843. Expediente 6554.

AGA R6562. Censorship file: Julio Sánchez Godínez and Florencio Domínguez, *La obrera del tejar* (1936). Archivo General de la Administración: (03)036.000, Caja 21/5839, Expediente 6562.

AGA R6565. Censorship file: Manuel García Adanero, *El confidente* (1934–6). Archivo General de la Administración: IDD (03)049.001, Caja 21/5839, Expediente 6565.

AGA R6613. Censorship file: Aurelio González Rendón, *Ya están de pie los esclavos sin pan* (1936). Archivo General de la Administración: IDD (03)036.000, Caja 21/5805, Expediente 6613.

AGA R6633. Censorship file: Arturo González Verdú, *¡Comunista!* (1936). Archivo General de la Administración: IDD (03)036.000, Caja 21/5831, Expediente 6633.

AGA R6669. Censorship file: Pedro Muñoz Seca, *Bronca en el ocho* (1936). Archivo General de la Administración: IDD (03)036.000, Caja 21/5778, Expediente 6669.

AGA R6678. Censorship file: Luis Mussot, *¡No pasarán!* (1936). Archivo General de la Administración: IDD (03)036.000, Caja 21/5805, Expediente 6678.

AGA R6681. Censorship file: Rafael Alberti, *Los salvadores de España* (1936). Archivo General de la Administración: IDD (03)036.000, Caja 21/5804, Expediente 6681.

AGA R6862. Censorship file: José Ricardo Navas, *Ropa limpia* (1937). Archivo General de la Administración: IDD (03)036.000, Caja 21/5839, Expediente 6862.

AGA Serie O-31/69. Reports commissioned by the Sección de Teatro for the Comisión Asesora de Teatros Nacionales, relating to José Ruibal, *La máquina de pedir* (October-November 1969). Archivo General de la Administración: IDD (03)046.000, Caja 73/10285, Expediente Serie O no. 31 año 69.

ANC 164/67. Censorship notification: Manuel de Pedrolo, *Homes i No* (May 1967). Arxiu Nacional de Catalunya: Fons 318, Registre 429, Caixa 1, Expediente 164/67.

ANC 172/67. Censorship notification: Antonio Buero Vallejo, *El tragaluz* (September 1967). Arxiu Nacional de Catalunya: Fons 318, Registre 429, Caixa 1, Expediente 172/67.

ANC 199/67. Censorship notification: Joan Brossa, *El rellotger* (July 1967). Arxiu Nacional de Catalunya: Fons 318, Registre 429, Caixa 1, Expediente 199/67.

ANC 214/57a. Censorship notification: Ramón María del Valle-Inclán, *Luces de Bohemia* (October 1967). Arxiu Nacional de Catalunya: Fons 318, Registre 429, Caixa 1, Expediente 214/57.

ANC 214/57b. Censorship notification: Ramón María del Valle-Inclán, *Luces de Bohemia* (July 1970). Arxiu Nacional de Catalunya: Fons 318, Registre 429, Caixa 2, Expediente 214/57.

ANC 234/71. Censorship notification: Joan Oliver, *Vivalda i l'Àfrica tenebrosa* (August 1971). Arxiu Nacional de Catalunya: Fons 318, Registre 429, Caixa 2, Expediente 234/71.

ANC 295/67. Censorship notification: Jorge Audifredd, *La imaginación de Pepito* (October 1967). Arxiu Nacional de Catalunya: Fons 318, Registre 429, Caixa 2, Expediente 295/67.

ANC 297/71. Censorship notification: Josep Maria Benet i Jornet, *L'ocell Fènix a Catalunya* (June 1971). Arxiu Nacional de Catalunya: Fons 318, Registre 429, Caixa 2, Expediente 297/71.

ANC 328/66. Censorship notification: Lauro Olmo, *El raterillo* and *Asamblea general* (December 1966). Arxiu Nacional de Catalunya: Fons 318, Registre 429, Caixa 1, Expediente 328/66.

ANC 348/66. Censorship notification: Rosendo Fortunet, *Los pastorets musicals del Vendrell* (December 1966). Arxiu Nacional de Catalunya: Fons 318, Registre 429, Caixa 1, Expediente 348/66.

ANC 356/66. Censorship notification: Ramon Pàmies, *L'Estel de Natzaret* (January 1967). Arxiu Nacional de Catalunya: Fons 318, Registre 429, Caixa 1, Expediente 356/66.

CDMAE Fons ADB, E91. Letter from Xavier Regàs to Frederic Roda Pérez on the subject of official restrictions on the translation of foreign plays translated into Catalan (29 January 1958). Centre de Docu-

mentació i Museu de les Arts Escèniques (Barcelona). Fons Agrupació Dramàtica de Barcelona, *Caixa* E91, document 02.
CDMAE Fons ADB, E98-08. Correspondence relating to a production of *Òpera de tres rals* ('*The Threepenny Opera*') by Bertolt Brecht (1963). Centre de Documentació i Museu de les Arts Escèniques (Barcelona). Fons Agrupació Dramàtica de Barcelona, *Caixa* E98-08, files 01 to 04. Scans accessible online (Escena Digital): *http://colleccions.cdmae.cat/catalog?locale=ca*.
CDMH PS-Barcelona 584, 28. Documents relating to the Comité Central de Espectáculos Públicos de Barcelona (1936). Centro Documental de la Memoria Histórica. Fondo: Político-Social, Barcelona. Caja 584, Expediente 28.
CDMH PS-Barcelona 821, 1. Documents relating to theatre business conducted by the Dirección General de la Seguridad (1938–9). Centro Documental de la Memoria Histórica. Fondo: Político-Social, Barcelona. Caja 821, Expediente 1.
CDMH PS-Barcelona 1067, 7. Documents relating to the Comité Económico del Teatro de Barcelona (1937). Centro Documental de la Memoria Histórica. Fondo: Político-Social, Barcelona. Caja 1067, Expediente 7. Digitised: CDMH_PS_BAR_C1067_Exp007.pdf.
CDMH PS-Barcelona 1421, 9. Documents relating to the Comité Económico del Teatro de Barcelona (1936–7). Centro Documental de la Memoria Histórica. Fondo: Político-Social, Barcelona. Caja 1421, Expediente 9. Digitised: CDMH_PS_BAR_C1421_Exp009.pdf.
CDMH PS-Madrid 1120, 27. Carbon copy of a handwritten document reporting an incident in a theatre in Málaga during a performance of a Muñoz Seca play (8 January 1932). Centro Documental de la Memoria Histórica. Fondo: Político-Social, Madrid. Caja 1120, Número 27.
CDMH PS-Madrid 1120, 29. Document relating to collectivisation of the theatre industry (4 October 1936). Centro Documental de la Memoria Histórica. Fondo: Político-Social, Madrid. Caja 1120, Número 29.
CDMH Ridruejo 5, 1. Letter to Dionisio Ridruejo from the Marqués de Lozoya, Director General de Bellas Artes, Ministerio de Educación Nacional (5 March 1940). Centro Documental de la Memoria Histórica. Fondo: Ridruejo (Director General de Propaganda: Correspondencia). Caja 5, Número 1.
CDMH Santander-HA, 5, 10. Official letter relating to regulation of the theatre industry (9 December 1936). Centro Documental de la Memoria Histórica. Fondo: Santander-Hacienda. Caja 5, Número 10.

Legislation

BOE (1936). 'Relación [de 1° de noviembre] de Gobernadores Civiles de las provincias ocupadas', *Boletín Oficial del Estado* 20 (3 November 1936), p. 95. *www.boe.es/datos/pdfs/BOE//1936/020/A00095-00095.pdf.*

BOE (1937a). 'Decreto núm. 180 [de 14 de enero]. Creando la Delegación para Prensa y Propaganda', *Boletín Oficial del Estado* 89 (17 January 1937), pp. 134–5. *www.boe.es/datos/pdfs/BOE//1937/089/A00134-00135.pdf.*

BOE (1937b). 'Asimilaciones. Orden [de 11 de febrero]. Concede la asimilación a Alférez para los efectos de haberes a los sacerdotes civiles y soldados presbíteros comprendidos en la relación que empieza con D. Aniceto Vecilla Turiño y termina en D. Leoncio Malmierca Calvo', *Boletín Oficial del Estado* 116 (13 February 1937), pp. 398–9. *www.boe.es/datos/pdfs/BOE//1937/116/A00398-00399.pdf.*

BOE (1938a). 'Ley de Prensa [de 22 de abril]', *Boletín Oficial del Estado* 549 (23 April 1938), pp. 6915–17. Corrected version *Boletín Oficial del Estado* 550 (24 April 1938), pp. 6938–40. *www.boe.es/datos/pdfs/BOE//1938/550/A06938-06940.pdf.*

BOE (1938b). 'Decreto [de 26 de abril] creando la Delegación del Estado para Recuperación de Documentos', *Boletín Oficial del Estado* 553 (27 April 1938), pp. 6986–7. *www.boe.es/datos/pdfs/BOE//1938/553/A06985-06986.pdf.*

BOE (1938c). 'Orden [de 29 de abril] sobre edición y venta de publicaciones no periódicas', *Boletín Oficial del Estado* 556 (30 April 1938), pp. 7035–6. *www.boe.es/datos/pdfs/BOE//1938/556/A07035-07036.pdf.*

BOE (1938d). 'Orden circular [de 11 de julio] encareciendo a los Gobernadores Civiles pongan especial cuidado y atención en la represión de la blasfemia y la difamación', *Boletín Oficial del Estado* 11 (11 July 1938), p. 160. *www.boe.es/datos/pdfs/BOE//1938/011/A00160-00160.pdf.*

BOE (1939a). 'Ley de 9 de febrero de 1939 de Responsabilidades Políticas', *Boletín Oficial del Estado* 44 (13 February 1939), pp. 824–47. *www.boe.es/datos/pdfs/BOE//1939/044/A00824-00847.pdf.*

BOE (1939b). 'Orden [de 15 de julio] creando una Sección de Censura dependiente de la Jefatura del Servicio Nacional de Propaganda y afecta a la Secretaría General', *Boletín Oficial del Estado* 211 (30 July 1939), pp. 4119–20. *www.boe.es/datos/pdfs/BOE//1939/211/A04119-04120.pdf.*

BOE (1939c). 'Ley [de 8 de agosto] por la que se modifica la organización de la Administración Central del Estado establecida por las de 30 de enero y 29 de diciembre de 1938', *Boletín Oficial del Estado* 221 (9 August 1939), pp. 4326–7. *www.boe.es/datos/pdfs/BOE//1939/221/A04326-04327.pdf.*

BOE (1939d). 'Decreto de 7 de octubre de 1939 suprimiendo el Consejo de Trabajo y resolviendo sobre la situación de los funcionarios adscritos al mencionado Organismo', *Boletín Oficial del Estado* 300 (27 October 1939), pp. 6019–20. *www.boe.es/datos/pdfs/BOE//1939/300/A06019-06020.pdf.*

BOE (1940). 'Anuncios de incoación de expedientes de Responsabilidades Políticas', *Boletín Oficial del Estado* 59, Anexo único (28 February 1940), pp. 1034–54. *www.boe.es/datos/pdfs/BOE//1940/059/C01034-01054.pdf.*

BOE (1941a). 'Decreto de 10 de octubre de 1941 por el que se organizan los servicios de la Vicesecretaría de Educación Popular de F.E.T. y de las J.O.N.S.', *Boletín Oficial del Estado* 288 (15 October 1941), pp. 7987–8. *www.boe.es/datos/pdfs/BOE//1941/288/A07987-07988.pdf.*

BOE (1941b). 'Decreto de 31 de diciembre de 1941 por el que se dispone la ejecución de la Ley reorganizadora de la Policía, de 8 de marzo de 1941', *Boletín Oficial del Estado* 65 (6 March 1942), pp. 1627–32. *www.boe.es/datos/pdfs/BOE//1942/065/A01627-01632.pdf.*

BOE (1944). 'Decreto por el que se aprueba y promulga el "Código Penal, texto refundido de 1944", según la autorización otorgada por la Ley de 19 de julio de 1944', *Boletín Oficial del Estado* 13 (13 January 1945), pp. 427–72. *www.boe.es/datos/pdfs/BOE//1945/013/A00427-00472.pdf.*

BOE (1945a). 'Decreto-Ley de 27 de julio por el que se organiza la Subsecretaría de Educación Popular en el Ministerio de Educación Nacional', *Boletín Oficial del Estado* 209 (28 July 1945), p. 686. *www.boe.es/datos/pdfs/BOE//1945/209/A00686-00686.pdf.*

BOE (1945b). 'Fuero de los españoles, texto fundamental definidor de los derechos y deberes de los mismos y amparador de sus garantías', *Boletín Oficial del Estado* 199 (18 July 1945), pp. 358–60. *www.boe.es/datos/pdfs/BOE//1945/199/A00358-00360.pdf.*

BOE (1946). 'Administración de Justicia: Comisión Liquidadora de Responsabilidades Políticas, Sala Instancia número 2, Edictos de sobreseimientos', *Boletín Oficial del Estado* 168 (17 June 1946), pp. 1642–4. *www.boe.es/datos/pdfs/BOE//1946/168/C01642-01644.pdf.*

BOE (1947a). 'Orden de 31 de diciembre de 1946 por la que se crea el Consejo Superior del Teatro, dependiente de la Dirección General de Cinematografía y Teatro', *Boletín Oficial del Estado* 25 (25 January 1947), p. 572. *www.boe.es/datos/pdfs/BOE//1947/025/A00572-00572.pdf.*

BOE (1947b). 'Orden de 31 de diciembre de 1946 por la que se nombran los componentes del Consejo Superior del Teatro', *Boletín Oficial del Estado* 25 (25 January 1947), p. 572. *www.boe.es/datos/pdfs/BOE//1947/025/A00572-00572.pdf.*

BOE (1948). 'Orden del 26 de enero de 1948 sobre inspección de los espectáculos públicos', *Boletín Oficial del Estado* 30 (30 January 1948), pp. 441–2. *www.boe.es/datos/pdfs/BOE//1948/030/A00441-00442.pdf.*

BOE (1951a). 'Decreto-Ley de 19 de julio de 1951 por el que se reorganiza la Administración central del Estado', *Boletín Oficial del Estado*

201 (20 July 1951), p. 3446. *www.boe.es/datos/pdfs/BOE//1951/201/ A03446-03446.pdf.*

BOE (1951b). 'Orden de 29 de noviembre de 1951 por la que se modifica la constitución del Consejo Superior del Teatro', *Boletín Oficial del Estado* 351 (17 December 1951), p. 5675. *www.boe.es/datos/pdfs/ BOE//1951/351/A05675-05675.pdf.*

BOE (1954a). 'Orden de 10 de agosto de 1954 por la que se crea el Teatro Nacional de Cámara y Ensayo bajo una dirección artística oficialmente designada por este Departamento', *Boletín Oficial del Estado* 263 (20 September 1954), p. 6326. *www.boe.es/datos/pdfs/ BOE//1954/263/A06326-06326.pdf.*

BOE (1954b). 'Orden de 30 de noviembre de 1954 por la que se dictan normas sobre la asistencia de menores a los espectáculos públicos no deportivos', *Boletín Oficial del Estado* 348 (14 December 1954), pp. 8228–89. *www.boe.es/datos/pdfs/BOE//1954/348/A08228-08229. pdf.*

BOE (1954c). 'Ley de 15 de julio de 1954 por la que se modifican los artículos·2° y 6° de la Ley de Vagos y Maleantes del 4 de agosto de 1933', *Boletín Oficial del Estado* 198 (17 July 1954), pp. 4862–3. *www. boe.es/datos/pdfs/BOE//1954/198/A04862-04862.pdf.*

BOE (1955a). 'Orden de 16 de febrero de 1955 por la que se regulan las autorizaciones y licencias para la representación de revistas y espectáculos arrevistados', *Boletín Oficial del Estado* 67 (8 March 1955), p. 1562. *www.boe.es/datos/pdfs/BOE//1955/067/A01562-01562.pdf.*

BOE (1955b). 'Orden de 25 de mayo de 1955 por la que se reglamentan y protegen las actividades de los Teatros de Cámara o Ensayo y Agrupaciones escénicas de carácter no profesional', *Boletín Oficial del Estado* 196 (15 July 1955), pp. 4291-2. *www.boe.es/datos/pdfs/ BOE//1955/196/A04291-04292.pdf.*

BOE (1956a). 'Orden de 5 de noviembre de 1956 por la que se rectifica el apartado segundo de la de 29 de noviembre de 1951, relativa a composición del Consejo Superior del Teatro', *Boletín Oficial del Estado* 357 (22 December 1956), p. 8042. *www.boe.es/datos/pdfs/ BOE//1956/357/A08042-08042.pdf.*

BOE (1956b). 'Ley de 27 de diciembre de 1956 reguladora de la Jurisdicción contencioso-administrativa', *Boletín Oficial del Estado* 363 (28 December 1956), pp. 8138–58. *www.boe.es/datos/pdfs/BOE//1956/363/ A08138-08158.pdf.*

BOE (1959a). 'Orden de 28 de abril de 1959 por la que se designa el Tribunal que ha de fallar el Concurso Nacional de Autores Noveles de Teatro', *Boletín Oficial del Estado* 108 (6 May 1959), p. 6659. *www.boe. es/datos/pdfs/BOE//1959/108/A06659-06659.pdf.*

BOE (1959b). 'Decreto-Ley de 21 de julio de 1959, de nueva ordenación económica'. Jefatura del Estado. *Boletín Oficial del Estado* 174 (22 July

1959), pp. 10005–7. *www.boe.es/datos/pdfs/BOE//1959/174/A10005-10007.pdf*.

BOE (1962). 'Orden de 26 de noviembre de 1962 por la que se crea en el Ministerio de Información y Turismo una Oficina de Enlace', *Boletín Oficial del Estado* 292 (26 November 1962), pp. 17333–4. *www.boe.es/boe/dias/1962/12/06/pdfs/A17333-17334.pdf*.

BOE (1963a). 'Orden de 9 de febrero de 1963 por la que se aprueban las "Normas de censura cinematográfica"', *Boletín Oficial del Estado* 58 (8 March 1963), pp. 3929–30. *www.boe.es/boe/dias/1963/03/08/pdfs/A03929-03930.pdf*.

BOE (1963b). 'Orden de 16 de febrero de 1963 por la que se constituye una Junta de Censura de Obras Teatrales', *Boletín Oficial del Estado* 58 (8/ March 1963), p. 3931. *www.boe.es/boe/dias/1963/03/08/pdfs/A03931-03931.pdf*.

BOE (1963c). 'Orden de 26 de febrero de 1963 por la que se designan los miembros integrantes de la Junta de Censura Teatral', *Boletín Oficial del Estado* 65 (16 March 1963), p. 4426. *www.boe.es/boe/dias/1963/03/16/pdfs/A04426-04426.pdf*.

BOE (1964). 'Orden de 6 de febrero de 1964 por la que se aprueba el Reglamento de Régimen Interior de la Junta de Censura de Obras Teatrales y las normas de censura', *Boletín Oficial del Estado* 48 (25 February 1964), pp. 2504–6. *www.boe.es/boe/dias/1964/02/25/pdfs/A02504-02506.pdf*.

BOE (1966). 'Ley 14/1966, de 18 de marzo, de Prensa e Imprenta', *Boletín Oficial del Estado* 67 (19 March 1966), pp. 3310–15. *www.boe.es/boe/dias/1966/03/19/pdfs/A03310-03315.pdf*.

BOE (1967). 'Decreto 2764/1967, de 27 de noviembre, sobre reorganización de la Administración Civil del Estado para reducir el gasto público', *Boletín Oficial del Estado* 284 (28 November 1967), pp. 16429–31. *www.boe.es/boe/dias/1967/11/28/pdfs/A16420-16424.pdf*.

BOE (1968). 'Decreto 64/1968, de 18 de enero, de reorganización del Ministerio de Información y Turismo', *Boletín Oficial del Estado* 18 (20 January 1968), pp. 825–31. *www.boe.es/boe/dias/1968/01/20/pdfs/A00825-00831.pdf*.

BOE (1969a). 'Decreto-ley 1/1969, de 24 de enero, por el que se declara el estado de excepción en todo el territorio nacional', *Boletín Oficial del Estado* 22 (25 January 1969), p. 1175. www.boe.es/boe/dias/1969/01/25/pdfs/A01175-01175.pdf.

BOE (1969b). 'Ley 62/1969, de 22 de julio, por la que se provee lo concerniente a la sucesión en la Jefatura del Estado', *Boletín Oficial del Estado* 175 (23 July 1969), pp. 11607–8. *www.boe.es/boe/dias/1969/07/23/pdfs/A11607-11608.pdf*.

BOE (1970). 'Orden de 27 de octubre de 1970 por la que se reorganiza la Junta de Censura de Obras Teatrales', *Boletín Oficial del Estado* 275

(17 November 1970), pp. 18612–13. *www.boe.es/boe/dias/1970/11/17/ pdfs/A18612-18613.pdf.*

BOE (1973). 'Decreto 3096/1973, de 14 de septiembre, por el que se publica el Código Penal, texto refundido conforme a la Ley 44/1971, de 15 de noviembre', *Boletín Oficial del Estado* 297 (12 December 1973), pp. 24004–291. *www.boe.es/datos/pdfs/BOE/1973/297/R24004-24291. pdf.*

BOE (1976). 'Ley 23/1976, de 19 de julio, sobre modificación de determinados artículos del Código Penal relativos a los derechos de reunión, asociación, expresión de las ideas y libertad de trabajo', *Boletín Oficial del Estado* 174 (21 July 1976), pp. 14135–6. *www.boe.es/boe/ dias/1976/07/21/pdfs/A14135-14136.pdf.*

BOE (1977a). 'Real Decreto-ley 24/1977, de 1 de abril, sobre libertad de expresión', *Boletín Oficial del Estado* 87 (12 April 1977), pp. 7928–9. *www.boe.es/boe/dias/1977/04/12/pdfs/A07928-07929.pdf.*

BOE (1977b). 'Real Decreto 2258/1977, de 27 de agosto, sobre estructura orgánica y funciones del Ministerio de Cultura', *Boletín Oficial del Estado* 209 (1 September 1977), pp. 19581–4. *www.boe.es/boe/ dias/1977/12/01/pdfs/A26420-26423.pdf.*

BOE (1978a). 'Real Decreto 262/1978, de 27 de enero, sobre libertad de representación de espectáculos teatrales', *Boletín Oficial del Estado* 53 (3 March 1978), pp. 5153–4. *www.boe.es/boe/dias/1978/03/03/pdfs/ A05153-05154.pdf.*

BOE (1978b). 'Ley 17/1978, de 15 de marzo, sobre modificación del artículo 161 y derogación de los artículos 164 bis, a), b) y c) del Código Penal', *Boletín Oficial del Estado* 66 (18 March 1978), p. 6502. *www.boe. es/boe/dias/1978/03/18/pdfs/A06502-06502.pdf.*

BOE (1978c). 'Orden de 7 de abril de 1978 por la que se dictan normas sobre calificación de espectáculos teatrales', *Boletín Oficial del Estado* 89 (14 April 1978), pp. 8611–13. *www.boe.es/boe/dias/1978/04/14/ pdfs/A08611-08613.pdf.*

BOE (1978d). 'Constitución Española', *Boletín Oficial del Estado* 311 (29 December 1978). Referencia: BOE-A-1978-31229. *www.boe.es/buscar/ pdf/1978/BOE-A-1978-31229-consolidado.pdf.*

BOE (1981). 'Orden de 3 de junio de 1981 por la que se modifica el artículo 2 de la Orden de 7 de junio de 1978, que dicta normas sobre calificación de espectáculos teatrales', *Boletín Oficial del Estado* 138 (10 June 1981), p. 13122. *www.boe.es/boe/dias/1981/06/10/pdfs/ A13122-13122.pdf.*

BOE (1982). 'Real Decreto 2816/1982, de 27 de agosto, por el que se aprueba el Reglamento General de Policía de Espectáculos Públicos y Actividades Recreativas', *Boletín Oficial del Estado* 267 (6 November 1982), pp. 30570–82. *www.boe.es/boe/dias/1982/11/06/pdfs/A30570- 30582.pdf.*

Bibliography 453

BOE (1983). 'Orden de 30 de junio de 1983 sobre calificación de los espectáculos teatrales y artísticos', *Boletín Oficial del Estado* 171 (19 July 1983), p. 20095. *www.boe.es/boe/dias/1983/07/19/pdfs/A20095-20095. pdf.*

BOE (1985). 'Real Decreto 565/1985, de 24 de abril, por el que se establece la estructura orgánica básica del Ministerio de Cultura y de sus Organismos autónomos', *Boletín Oficial del Estado* 103 (30 April 1985), pp. 11986–94. *www.boe.es/boe/dias/1985/04/30/pdfs/A11986-11994.pdf.*

BOE (1995). 'Ley Orgánica 10/1995, de 23 de noviembre, del Código Penal', *Boletín Oficial del Estado* 281 (24 November 1978). Referencia: BOE-A-1995-25444. *www.boe.es/buscar/pdf/1995/ BOE-A-1995-25444-consolidado.pdf.*

Boletín Oficial de la JDN (1936a). 'Decreto núm. 13 [de 27 de julio]. Disponiendo la destitución de los Gobernadores civiles a partir del día 19 del actual', *Boletín Oficial de la Junta de Defensa Nacional de España* 3 (30 July 1936), p. 11. *www.boe.es/datos/pdfs/BOE//1936/003/J00011-00011.pdf.*

Boletín Oficial de la JDN (1936b). 'Bando [de 28 de julio] haciendo extensivo a todo el territorio nacional el Estado de Guerra declarado ya en determinadas provincias', *Boletín Oficial de la Junta de Defensa Nacional de España* 3 (30 July 1936), pp. 9–10. *www.boe.es/datos/pdfs/ BOE//1936/003/J00009-00010.pdf.*

Boletín Oficial de la Provincia de Barcelona (1867). 'Real orden [de 15 de enero] disponiendo que en adelante no se admitan a la censura obras dramáticas que estén exclusivamente escritas en cualquiera de los dialectos de las provincias de España', *Boletín Oficial de la Provincia de Barcelona*, 26 January 1867.

Butlletí Oficial de la Generalitat de Catalunya (1936). 'Decret [de 26 de juliol] creant la Comissaria d'Espectacles de Catalunya', *Butlletí Oficial de la Generalitat de Catalunya* 211 (29 July 1936), p. 785. *http://dogc. gencat.cat/web/.content/continguts/serveis/republica/1936/19360211.pdf.*

Diari Oficial de la Generalitat de Catalunya (1938). 'Ordre [de 19 de gener] per la qual és disposada la intervenció tècnica i administrativa de totes les empreses d'espectacles públics de Catalunya', *Diari Oficial de la Generalitat de Catalunya* 21 (21 January 1938), p. 274. *http://dogc. gencat.cat/web/.content/continguts/serveis/republica/1938/19380021.pdf.*

Diario Oficial del País Vasco (1936). 'Decreto [de 14 de diciembre] sobre incautaciones de cines y teatros en el territorio de Euzkadi', *Diario Oficial del País Vasco* 81 (18 December 1936), pp. 577–80. *www.euskadi.eus/y22-bopv/es/bopv2/datos/1936/12/3600634a.pdf.*

Gaceta de la República (1937a). 'Decreto [de 30 de enero] facultando al Ministro para organizar bajo el título de "Milicias de la Cultura" un cuerpo de Maestros e Instructores escolares para enseñanza de los combatientes', *Gaceta de la República* 33 (2 February 1937), p. 600. *www.boe.es/datos/pdfs/BOE//1937/033/B00600-00600.pdf.*

Gaceta de la República (1937b). 'Decreto [de 22 de agosto] creando el Consejo Central de Teatro, dependiente de la Dirección general de Bellas Artes de este departamento, con las facultades y cometido comprendido en el articulado y apartado que se insertan', *Gaceta de la República* 236 (24 August 1937), p. 769. *www.boe.es/datos/pdfs/ BOE//1937/236/B00769-00769.pdf.*

Gaceta de la República (1937c). 'Orden [de 13 de octubre] nombrando a los señores que han de integrar el Consejo Central del Teatro en la forma que se expresa', *Gaceta de la República* 287 (14 October 1937), p. 162. *www.boe.es/datos/pdfs/BOE//1937/287/B00162-00162. pdf.*

Gaceta de la República (1937d). 'Decreto [de 28 de octubre] reorganizando la Junta de Espectáculos de Madrid, la que estaba integrada en la forma que se establece', *Gaceta de la República* 304 (31 October 1937), p. 393. *www.boe.es/datos/pdfs/BOE//1937/304/B00393-00393. pdf.*

Gaceta de la República (1937e). 'Orden [de 27 de diciembre] resolviendo se proceda a la intervención provisional de las Empresas de espectáculos públicos de la ciudad de Alicante, ajustándose a las normas vigentes establecidas', *Gaceta de la República* 364 (30 December 1937), p. 1502. *www.boe.es/datos/pdfs/BOE//1937/364/B01502-01502. pdf.*

Gaceta de la República (1938a). 'Orden [de 14 de enero] interviniendo provisionalmente por el Estado, todas las Empresas de espectáculos públicos de Madrid y disponiendo se nombre un Delegado Interventor general de las mismas', *Gaceta de la República* 17 (17 January 1938), p. 244. *www.boe.es/datos/pdfs/BOE//1938/017/B00244-00244. pdf.*

Gaceta de la República (1938b). 'Orden [de 12 de febrero] disponiendo que un funcionario del Departamento ejerza, cerca del Consejo Central del Teatro, y como Secretario administrativo e interventor de fondos, las funciones especificadas en el articulado que se inserta', *Gaceta de la República* 48 (17 February 1938), p. 893. *www.boe.es/datos/ pdfs/BOE//1938/048/B00893-00893.pdf.*

Gaceta de la República (1938c). 'Orden [de 2 de marzo] dictando normas para el funcionamiento de las distintas actividades pendientes del Consejo Central del Teatro, en tanto se tramita la petición de los créditos extraordinarios precisos para su pleno funcionamiento', *Gaceta de la República* 78 (19 March 1938), p. 1379. *www.boe.es/datos/ pdfs/BOE//1938/078/B01379-01379.pdf.*

Gaceta de Madrid (1834a). 'Real orden [de 13 de enero] permitiendo que en Carmona y demás pueblos del reino haya representaciones

teatrales', *Gaceta de Madrid* 22 (18 February 1834), p. 100. *www.boe.es/ datos/pdfs/BOE//1834/022/A00100-00100.pdf.*
Gaceta de Madrid (1834b). 'Real decreto [de 27 de marzo] suprimiendo el destino de juez protector de los teatros del reino, y mandando que los subdelegados de Fomento desempeñen por ahora las atribuciones que correspondían a dicho destino', *Gaceta de Madrid* 39 (29 March 1834), p. 181. *www.boe.es/datos/pdfs/BOE//1834/039/A00181-00181.pdf.*
Gaceta de Madrid (1834c). 'S.M. se ha dignado disponer [el 28 de octubre] que el sueldo asignado al censor político de los teatros de esta corte, se entregue a la comisión nombrada para formar el plan de enseñanza primaria del reino', *Gaceta de Madrid* 257 (29 October 1834), p. 1075. *www.boe.es/datos/pdfs/BOE//1834/257/A01075-01075. pdf.*
Gaceta de Madrid (1837). 'Constitución de la Monarquía Española', *Gaceta de Madrid* 935 (24 June 1837), pp. 1–2. *www.boe.es/datos/pdfs/ BOE//1837/935/A00001-00002.pdf.*
Gaceta de Madrid (1847). 'Real decreto [de 30 de agosto] organizando el teatro nacional', *Gaceta de Madrid* 4743 (9 September 1847), pp. 1–2. *www.boe.es/datos/pdfs/BOE//1847/4743/A00001-00002.pdf.*
Gaceta de Madrid (1849). 'Real decreto orgánico [de 7 de febrero] de los teatros del reino', *Gaceta de Madrid* 5262 (8 February 1849), pp. 1–3. *www.boe.es/datos/pdfs/BOE//1849/5262/A00001-00003.pdf.*
Gaceta de Madrid (1852). 'Real decreto [de 28 de julio] resolviendo que los teatros del reino se rijan en lo sucesivo con arreglo al decreto orgánico sobre el régimen de los teatros del reino que se expresa', *Gaceta de Madrid* 6613 (31 July 1852), pp. 1–2. *www.boe.es/datos/pdfs/ BOE//1852/6613/A00001-00002.pdf.*
Gaceta de Madrid (1857). 'Real orden [de 24 de febrero] disponiendo que para la aplicación de la censura de teatros se observen las disposiciones que se citan', *Gaceta de Madrid* 1515 (26 February 1857), p. 1. *www.boe.es/datos/pdfs/BOE//1857/1515/A00001-00001.pdf.*
Gaceta de Madrid (1868). 'Decreto [de 16 de enero] estableciendo la libertad de teatros', *Gaceta de Madrid* 16 (16 January 1868), p. 1. *www. boe.es/datos/pdfs/BOE//1869/016/A00001-00001.pdf.*
Gaceta de Madrid (1869). 'Constitución del Estado', *Gaceta de Madrid* 158 (7 June 1869), p. 1. *www.boe.es/datos/pdfs/BOE//1869/158/A00001- 00002.pdf.*
Gaceta de Madrid (1876). 'Constitución de la Monarquía Española', *Gaceta de Madrid* 184 (2 July 1876), pp. 9–12. *www.boe.es/datos/pdfs/ BOE//1876/184/A00009-00012.pdf.*
Gaceta de Madrid (1881). 'Real Orden Circular [de 26 de febrero] derogando la Real orden de 27 de Febrero de 1879, que impulsa a los Gobernadores la obligación de remitir al Ministerio de la Gobernación los ejemplares de cada obra dramática diez días antes de ser

puesta en escena', *Gaceta de Madrid* 58 (27 February 1881), p. 565. *www.boe.es/datos/pdfs/BOE//1881/058/A00565-00565.pdf.*

Gaceta de Madrid (1886). 'Real Decreto [de 2 de agosto] aprobando el Reglamento de Policía de Espectáculos', *Gaceta de Madrid* 217 (5 August 1886), pp. 368–9. *www.boe.es/datos/pdfs/BOE//1886/217/A00368-00369.pdf.*

Gaceta de Madrid (1913). 'Real orden [de 19 de octubre] aprobando el Reglamento de Policía de Espectáculos, de construcción, reforma y condiciones de los edificios destinados a los mismos', *Gaceta de Madrid* 304 (31 October 1913), pp. 347–55. *www.boe.es/datos/pdfs/BOE//1913/304/A00347-00355.pdf.*

Gaceta de Madrid (1924). 'Real orden [de 28 de mayo] disponiendo que compete a los Gobernadores civiles conocer de la imposición de multas por embriaguez y escándalo, faltas a la moral y a los Reglamentos de espectáculos públicos', *Gaceta de Madrid* 150 (29 May 1924), p. 1013. *www.boe.es/datos/pdfs/BOE//1924/150/A01013-01013.pdf.*

Gaceta de Madrid (1931a). 'Decreto [de 29 de mayo] creando un "Patronato de Misiones Pedagógicas" encargado de difundir la cultura general, la moderna orientación docente y la educación ciudadana, en aldeas, villas y lugares, con especial atención a los intereses espirituales de la población rural', *Gaceta de Madrid* 150 (30 May 1931), pp. 1033–4. *www.boe.es/datos/pdfs/BOE//1931/150/A01033-01034.pdf.*

Gaceta de Madrid (1931b). 'Ley [de 21 de octubre] declarando actos de agresión a la República los que se mencionan', *Gaceta de Madrid* 295 (22 October 1931), pp. 420–1. *www.boe.es/datos/pdfs/BOE//1931/295/A00420-00421.pdf.*

Gaceta de Madrid (1931c). 'Constitución de la República Española', *Gaceta de Madrid* 344 (10 December 1931), pp. 1578–88. *www.boe.es/datos/pdfs/BOE//1931/344/A01578-01588.pdf.*

Gaceta de Madrid (1932). 'Ley de 27 de octubre de 1932 autorizando al Ministro de este Departamento para publicar como Ley el Código penal reformado, con arreglo a las bases establecidas en la Ley de 8 de septiembre del corriente año', *Gaceta de Madrid* 310 (5 November 1932), pp. 818–56. *www.boe.es/datos/pdfs/BOE//1932/310/A00818-00856.pdf.*

Gaceta de Madrid (1933). 'Ley de Vagos y Maleantes [de 4 de agosto]', *Gaceta de Madrid* 217 (5 August 1933): pp. 874–7. *www.boe.es/datos/pdfs/BOE//1933/217/A00874-00877.pdf.*

Gaceta de Madrid (1935). 'Orden [de 3 de mayo] aprobando el Reglamento de Policía de Espectáculos públicos y de construcción y reparación de los edificios destinados a los mismos', *Gaceta de Madrid* 125 (5 May 1935), pp. 1055–70. *www.boe.es/datos/pdfs/BOE//1935/125/A01055-01070.pdf.*

Other sources

AAT (1995). *Lauro Olmo. Fe de vida.* Madrid: Asociación de Autores de Teatro.
ABC (1929). 'Informaciones y noticias teatrales', *ABC,* 7 February 1929, p. 39.
ABC (1930). 'Las audiencias del presidente', *ABC,* 23 April 1930, p. 17.
ABC (1932). 'Comedia Chungonia', *ABC,* 6 August 1932, p. 35.
ABC (1933). 'Informaciones y noticias teatrales. Del Beatriz a la Comedia', *ABC,* 9 July 1933, p. 57.
ABC (1934a). 'Guía del espectador', *ABC,* 27 May 1934, p. 58.
ABC (1934b). 'Guía del espectador', *ABC,* 8 June 1934, p. 48.
ABC (1936a). 'Van a desaparecer la obscenidad y la grosería de los escenarios', *ABC,* 15 August 1936, p. 13.
ABC (1936b). 'Se confirma el asesinato de Federico García Lorca', *ABC,* 8 September 1936, p. 7.
ABC (1937a). 'Espectáculos: La disposición sobre teatros y cinematógrafos', *ABC,* 24 January 1937, pp. 9–10.
ABC (1937b). 'José Carreño España autocritica su actuación al frente de la Delegación de Propaganda y Prensa', *ABC,* 26 April 1937, pp. 11–12.
ABC (1937c). 'Otra prórroga al Grupo García Lorca', *ABC,* 16 May 1937, p. 18.
ABC (1939a). 'Informaciones teatrales: El teatro en la España Nacional', *ABC,* 29 March 1939, p. 14.
ABC (1939b). 'Informaciones y noticias teatrales: Don Jacinto Benavente, rescatado', *ABC,* 1 April 1939, p. 22.
ABC (1939c). 'Informaciones y noticias teatrales', *ABC,* 4 April 1939, p. 28.
ABC (1939d). 'Informaciones y noticias teatrales: Normas para los empresarios de espectáculos públicos', *ABC,* 8 April 1939, p. 28.
ABC (1939e). 'Informaciones y noticias teatrales: En honor de Serafín Álvarez Quintero', *ABC,* 11 April 1939, p. 26.
ABC (1939f). 'Informaciones y noticias teatrales: Inauguración de la Zarzuela', *ABC,* 25 April 1939, p. 24.
ABC (1939g). 'Guía del espectador: *Currito de la Cruz*', *ABC,* 12 July 1939, p. 17.
ABC (1939h). 'Guía del espectador: Silva Aramburu', *ABC,* 13 July 1939, p. 24.
ABC (1939i). 'Informaciones y noticias de Madrid: La censura de obras nuevas teatrales y la revisión de repertorios', *ABC,* 7 October 1939, p. 19.
ABC (1940). 'Reposición en el Colisevm de *Peccata mundi*', *ABC,* 28 May 1940, p. 14.
ABC (1943a). 'Guía del espectador: *El pan comido en la mano,* en Calderón', *ABC,* 13 March 1943, p. 11.

ABC (1943b). 'Notas teatrales: Reposición de *La otra honra* en Fontalba', *ABC*, 17 September 1943, p. 13.

ABC (1946a). 'El Consejo de Ministros de ayer: Se adoptaron severas medidas contra la confabulación de los carniceros, que han dejado sin carne los mercados al ser tasado el producto, y se designaron altos cargos de Educación Popular y Asuntos Exteriores', *ABC*, 12 January 1946, pp. 7–8.

ABC (1946b). 'El Ministro de Educación Nacional da posesión de sus cargos a los señores Ortiz Muñoz, Cerro Corrochano, Rocamora, Guijarro, García Espina y Alcázar', *ABC*, 15 January 1946, p. 19.

ABC (1949). 'Informaciones y noticias teatrales, de música y cinematográficas: Cartelera madrileña', *ABC*, 30 April 1949, p. 22.

ABC (1964). 'Teatro Goya: Compañía Maritza Caballero, *La casa de Bernarda Alba* de Federico García Lorca confirma su éxito universal con el triunfo clamoroso obtenido en Madrid', *ABC*, 23 January 1964, p. 21.

ABC (1969). 'Informaciones teatrales y cinematográficas: La escena, al día', *ABC*, 12 August 1969, p. 57.

ABC (1970). 'Junta de Censura de Obras Teatrales', *ABC*, 20 August 1970, p. 51.

ABC (1976a). 'Espectáculos: Aviso', *ABC*, 15 May 1976, p. 89.

ABC (1976b). 'Clasificación moral: teatro, variedades y revista', *ABC*, 15 October 1976, p. 57.

ABC (1978a). 'Suspendida, por orden gubernativa, *Ven a disfrutar*, en el Principe', *ABC*, 16 September 1978, p. 42.

ABC (1978b). 'Fanjul Sedeño, en Cuenca: "El aumento de la delincuencia no tiene nada que ver con la democracia"', *ABC*, 1 October 1978, p. 80.

Abellán, Manuel L. (1978). 'Censura y práctica censoria', *Sistema*, 22, 29–52.

Abellán, Manuel L. (1980). *Censura y creación literaria en España (1939–1976)*. Barcelona: Península.

Abellán, Manuel L. (1984). 'Literatura, censura y moral en el primer franquismo', *Papers: Revista de Sociología*, 21, 153–72.

Abellán, Manuel L. (ed.) (1987). *Censura y literaturas peninsulares* (Diálogos hispánicos de Amsterdam, 5). Amsterdam: Rodopi.

Abellán, Manuel L. (1988). 'Apuntes sobre la censura teatral durante la II República', *Ojáncano. Revista de Literatura Española*, 1, 14–22. Reproduced in *Represura*, 7 (2011). *www.represura.es/represura_7_febrero_2011_articulo12.html*.

Abellán, Manuel L. (1989a). 'La censura teatral durante el franquismo', *Estreno*, 15(2), 20–3.

Abellán, Manuel L. (1989b). 'Problemas historiográficos en el estudio de la censura literaria del último medio siglo', *Revista Canadiense de Estudios Hispánicos*, 13(3), 319–29.

A.C. (1933). 'Informaciones y noticias teatrales. Beatriz: *Santa Teresita del Niño Jesús*', *ABC*, 30 June 1933, pp. 49–50.
A.C. (1939). 'Fontalba: *El divino impaciente*', *ABC*, 9 April 1939, p. 27.
Agencia Cifra (1969). 'El estreno de *Los dos verdugos*, de Arrabal, suspendido en Madrid', *ABC* (Sevilla), 7 February 1965, p. 65.
Aggor, Komla (2006). *Francisco Nieva and Postmodernist Theatre*. Cardiff: University of Wales Press.
Aguilera Sastre, Juan (1992). 'El debate sobre el teatro nacional durante la dictadura y la república' in Dru Dougherty and María Francisca Vilches de Frutos (eds), *El teatro en España: Entre la tradición y la vanguardia. 1918–1939*. Madrid: CSIC/Fundación Federico García Lorca/Tabacalera, pp.175–87.
Aguilera Sastre, Juan (1993). 'Felipe Lluch Garín, artifice e iniciador del Teatro Español Nacional' in Andrés Peláez Martín (ed.), *Historia de los teatros nacionales (1939–1962)*. Madrid: Centro de Documentación Teatral, pp. 41–67.
Aguilera Sastre, Juan (2013). 'Entre dos exilios: Rivas Cherif y García Lorca', *Archivum*, 63, 7–58.
AHMD (2016). Informe per a l'Ajuntament de València (Regidoria de Patrimoni Cultural i Recursos Culturals) sobre els noms de carrer de la ciutat que remeten a figures de la dictadura franquista. València: Aula d'Història i Memòria de la Universitat de València. *www.valencia.es/ayuntamiento/publicaciones.nsf/vDocumentosTituloAux/Tu%20calle%20cambia%20de%20nombre*.
Alba Peinado, Carlos (2009). 'La censura del teatro republicano de Pedro Muñoz Seca y Pedro Pérez Fernández', *Teatr@: Revista de Estudios Escénicos*, 2, 144–82.
Alberti, Rafael (1937). 'Numancia, Tragedia de Miguel de Cervantes', *El Mono Azul*, 43 (2 December 1937). Reproduced in José Monleón (1979). *El mono azul: Teatro de urgencia y romancero de la guerra civil*. Madrid: Ayuso, pp. 254–7.
Alberti, Rafael (1938). 'Teatro de urgencia', *Boletín de Orientación Teatral*, 1 (15 February 1938). Reproduced in Francisco Mundi Pedret (1987). *El teatro de la guerra civil*. Barcelona: PPU, p. 21.
Alcocer, Santos (1944). 'Labor del Departamento de Teatro de la Delegación Nacional de Propaganda en 1943', *Ya*, 13 January 1944. Reproduced in *DHTE* (*Documentos para la historia del teatro español*), *http://teatro.es/contenidos/documentosParaLaHistoria/Docs1944/index.html*.
Alonso, José Luis (1960). 'Un sabor a miel, ante el público', *Primer Acto*, 17, 23.
Althusser, Louis (1971). 'Ideology and Ideological State Apparatuses: Notes towards an Investigation' in *Lenin and Philosophy and Other Essays*, trans. Ben Brewster, London: NLB, pp. 121–73.
Althusser, Louis (1984). *Essays on Ideology*. London/New York: Verso.

Altolaguirre, Manuel (2010). *El caballo griego. Reflexiones y recuerdos (1927–1958)*. Madrid: Diario Público.

Alvar, Manuel *et al.* (1975). *El teatro y su crítica. Reunión de Málaga de 1973*. Málaga: Instituto de Cultura de la Diputación Provincial de Málaga.

Álvarez, Carlos Luis (1977). 'No es el camino: *¡Jo, qué corte. . . estamos en Europa!*, de Pablo Villamar, en el Benavente', *Blanco y Negro (ABC)*, 11 May 1977, pp. 59.

Amorós, Andrés (2016). 'Muñoz Seca: ingenio y tragedia de un gran humorista', *ABC*, 28 November 2016, pp. 80, 85.

A. M. T. (1970). 'Un curioso espectáculo: *Castañuela 70*', *La Vanguardia Española*, 31 July 1970, p. 32.

Andaluz Pinedo, Olaia, and Raquel Merino Álvarez (2020). 'La censura del teatro de Samuel Beckett en España (1955–1978)' in José Francisco Fernández (ed.), *Samuel Beckett en España*. Valladolid: Universidad de Valladolid, pp. 91–115.

Anderson, Farris (1971). *Alfonso Sastre*. New York: Twayne.

Anderson, Farris (1978). 'The Madrid Theatre Season, 1976–77: Problems of Transition', *Estreno*, 4(1), 8–11.

Anthropos (1993). 'Guerra Civil y producción cultural', *Anthropos* 148.

Anuario teatral (El Público), 1985 (1986). Madrid: Centro de Documentación Teatral.

Aragonés, Juan Emilio (1971). *Teatro español de posguerra*. Madrid. Publicaciones Españolas.

Araquistáin, Luis (1930). *La batalla teatral*. Madrid: Mundo Latino.

Araujo-Costa, Luis (1933). 'Veladas teatrales BEATRIZ.– Presentación de compañía. Estreno de la comedia en tres actos, divididos en dos viñetas cada uno, de don Vicente Mena, *Santa Teresita del Niño Jesús*'. *La Época* (Madrid), 30 June 1933, p. 4.

Araujo-Costa, Luis (1939a). 'Informaciones y noticias teatrales. Fontalba: *El divino impaciente*', *ABC*, 9 April 1939, p. 27.

Araujo-Costa, Luis (1939b). 'Comedia: Inauguración de la temporada y homenaje a Muñoz Seca', *ABC*, 16 April 1939, pp. 24–5.

Araujo-Costa, Luis (1940). 'Función de gala en el Español', *ABC*, 9 April 1940, p. 15.

Arias-Salgado, Gabriel (1960). *Textos de Doctrina y Política española de la Información*, vol. 1: *Discursos y declaraciones*. Madrid: Ministerio de Información y Turismo.

Arozamena, José María de (1939). 'Comedia: Estreno de *Los rojillos*', *ABC*, 17 June 1939, pp. 21–2.

Arrabal, Fernando (1958). 'Antecrítica de *Los hombres del triciclo*', *ABC*, 29 January 1958, p. 51.

Arrabal, Fernando (1967). 'Con todo cariño', *Primer Acto*, 82, 4.

Arrabal, Fernando (1969). 'Autocrítica de *Los dos verdugos*, que se estrena hoy', *ABC*, 7 February 1969, p. 65.

Arrabal, Fernando (2016). 'The Dictator's Gift of Censorship', trans. Michael Thompson, in Catherine O'Leary, Diego Santos Sánchez and Michael Thompson (eds), *Global Insights on Theatre Censorship*. New York/Abingdon: Routledge, pp. 35–42.

Arriba (1939). 'Los espectáculos de Madrid', *Arriba*, 30 March. 1939. Reproduced in *DHTE (Documentos para la historia del teatro español)*, *www. teatro.es/contenidos/documentosParaLaHistoria/Docs1939/documentos. php?tema=1&sec=1*.

Artime, Ignacio (2013). 'Tras el infarto, un productor de *Evita* me invitó al Hospital Monte Sinaí de Nueva York (Memorias)', *La Nueva España* (Asturias), 6 August 2013. *www.lne.es/asturias/2013/08/06/infarto-productor-evita-invito-hospital/1451889.html*.

Audiencia Nacional (2008). 'Auto del 18 de noviembre de 2008, por Baltasar Garzón', Juzgado Central de Instrucción N°5 de la Audiencia Nacional. *https://e00-elmundo.uecdn.es/documentos/2008/11/18/auto_memoria_historica.pdf*.

Augustine, Saint (2003). *The Works of Saint Augustine: A Translation for the 21st Century. Exposition of the Psalms (Enarrationes in Psalmos) 99–120*, trans. Maria Boulding. New York: New City Press.

Aznar Soler, M. (1987). *Literatura española y antifascismo (1927–1939)*. Valencia: Conselleria de Cultura, Educació i Ciència.

Aznar Soler, M. (1992). '"El Buho": Teatro de la F.U.E. de la Universidad de Valencia' in Dru Dougherty and María Francisca Vilches de Frutos (eds), *El teatro en España entre la tradición y la vanguardia, 1918–1939*. Madrid: CSIC/Fundación Federico García Lorca/Tabacalera, pp. 415–27.

Aznar Soler, Manuel. (1993). 'María Teresa León y el teatro español durante la Guerra Civil', *Anthropos*, 148, 25–34.

Aznar Soler, Manuel (1997). 'El teatro español durante la II República (1931–1939)', *Monteagudo*, 2, 45–58.

Aznar Soler, Manuel (2010). *República literaria y revolución (1920–1939)*. Sevilla: Renacimiento.

Aznar Soler, Manuel, and Jeroen Oskam (1992). 'Entrevista con José María de Quinto', *Ojáncano*, 6 (1992), 44–52.

Azorín (José Martínez Ruiz) (1943). 'El siglo XIX', *ABC*, 30 March 1943, p. 3.

Baker, Mona (2005). 'Narratives in and of Translation', *Journal of Translation and Interpretation*, 1(1), 4–13.

Baker, Mona (2007). 'Reframing Conflict in Translation', *Social Semiotics*, 17(2), 151–69.

Balbontín, José Antonio (2007). *La España de mi experiencia. Reminiscencias y esperanzas de un español en el exilio*. Sevilla: Junta de Andalucía.

Banegas, Francisco J. (2015). *La televisión que yo viví y otras historias paralelas*. Madrid: Liber Factory.

Barker, Dennis (2011). 'Shelagh Delaney Obituary', *The Guardian*, 21 November 2011. *www.theguardian.com/stage/2011/nov/21/shelagh-delaney*.
Bassnett, Susan (1998). 'Still Trapped in the Labyrinth: Further Reflections on Translation and Theatre' in Susan Bassnett and André Lefevere (eds), *Constructing Cultures: Essays on Literary Translation*. Clevedon: Multilingual Matters, pp. 90–108.
Bastianes, María (2018). 'Un clásico difícil. Censura y adaptación escénica de *La Celestina* bajo el franquismo', *Hispanic Research Journal*, 19(2), 117–34.
Benet i Jornet, Josep Maria (1970). *Fantasia per a un auxiliar administratiu; Cançons perdudes*. Palma de Mallorca: Moll.
Benet i Jornet, Josep Maria (2010). Unpublished interview with Michael Thompson for the *Theatre Censorship in Spain* project (12 December 2010).
Beneyto, Antonio (1979). *Censura y política en los escritores españoles*. Barcelona: Plaza y Janes.
Beneyto Pérez, Juan (1987). 'La censura literaria en los primeros años del franquismo: las normas y los hombres' in Manuel L. Abellán (ed.), *Censura y literaturas peninsulares*. Amsterdam: Rodopi, pp. 27–40.
Berenguer, Ángel (1987). 'Introducción' in Fernando Arrabal, *Pic-Nic, El triciclo, El laberinto*. Madrid: Cátedra, pp. 11–126.
Berenguer, Ángel (1988). *El teatro en el siglo XX (hasta 1939)*. Madrid: Taurus.
Berenguer, Ángel (1997). 'Introducción' in Lauro Olmo, *La camisa; El cuarto poder*. Madrid: Cátedra.
Berenguer, Ángel (2004). 'Introducción al teatro de Lauro Olmo' in Lauro Olmo, *Teatro Completo*, 1. Madrid: Asociación de Autores de Teatro, pp. 11–38.
Berenguer, Ángel (2005). 'El teatro español durante la Segunda República' in Fidel López Criado (ed.), *La República de las letras y las letras de la República*. A Coruña: Universidade da Coruña/Xunta de Galicia, pp. 179–95.
Berenguer, Ángel, and Manuel Pérez (1998). *Tendencias del teatro español durante la transición política (1975–1982)*. Madrid: Biblioteca Nueva.
Bilbatúa, Miguel (1976). *Teatro de agitación política (1933–1939)*. Madrid: Cuadernos para el Diálogo/Edicusa.
Blanco Aguinaga, Carlos, Julio Rodríguez Puértolas and Iris M. Zavala (1983). *Historia social de la literatura española*, III. Madrid: Castalia.
Blanco y Negro (1932). 'La actualidad escénica: La OCA', *Blanco y Negro* (*ABC*), 3 January 1932, pp. 131–3.
Blanco y Negro (1978). 'Gente', *Blanco y Negro* (*ABC*), 23 August 1978, pp. 42–3.
Blinkhorn, Martin (1988). *Democracy and Civil War in Spain, 1931–1939*. London/New York: Routledge.

BNE (2016a). 'Honorio Maura' in *Escritores en la BNE*. Madrid: Biblioteca Nacional de España, *http://escritores.bne.es/web/authors/honorio-maura-1886-1936*.
BNE (2016b). 'Pedro Muñoz Seca' in *Escritores en la BNE*. Madrid: Biblioteca Nacional de España, *https://escritores.bne.es/web/authors/pedro-munoz-seca-1879-1936/*.
Boadella, Albert (2001). *Memòries d'un bufó*. Madrid: Espasa.
Bonsaver, Guido (2007). *Censorship and Literature in Fascist Italy*. Toronto: University of Toronto Press.
Borrás, Tomás (1942). 'Movimiento teatral', *Cuadernos de Literatura Contemporánea*, 3–4, 167–73.
Bourdieu, Pierre (1992). *Language and Symbolic Power*, trans. Gino Raymond and Matthew Adamson. Cambridge: Polity Press.
Bozzo, Joan Lluís (2015). *Memòries trobades en una furgoneta: Els primers èxits de Dagoll Dagom*. Barcelona: Empúries.
Bravo, Julio (2003). 'Muere José Tamayo, el director que abrió la puerta de la modernidad al teatro español', *ABC*, 27 March 2003, p. 64.
Brecht, Bertolt (1966). *Parables for the Theatre: Two Plays by Bertolt Brecht*, trans. Eric Bentley. London: Penguin.
Breden, Simon (2006). '*La torna de la torna* by Els Joglars: history and production. Teatre Romea, Barcelona, October 2005', *Gestos*, 42, 149–57.
Brenan, Gerald (2012 [1943]). *The Spanish Labyrinth, An Account of the Social and Political Background of the Spanish Civil War*. Cambridge: Cambridge University Press.
Bryan, T. Avril (1982). *Censorship and Social Conflict in the Spanish Theatre: The Case of Alfonso Sastre*. Lanham: University Press of America.
Buero Vallejo, Antonio (1994). *Obra completa*, ed. Luis Iglesias Feijoo and Mariano de Paco, 2 vols. Madrid: Espasa-Calpe.
Buero Vallejo, Antonio (1995). *El sueño de la razón*. Madrid: Espasa Calpe.
Burguera y Serrano, Amado de Cristo (1915). *Suplemento a la obra Representaciones escénicas malas, peligrosas y honestas: calificación moral de cerca de 2.750 comedias, tragedias, dramas, óperas, zarzuelas, sainetes y juguetes cómicos, sobre todo castellanos, antiguos y, muy en especial, modernos y contemporáneos, con datos biográficos de autores dramáticos*. Valencia: Antonio López y Compañía.
Burt, Richard. 1998. '(Un)censoring in Detail: The Fetish of Censorship in the Early Modern Past and the Postmodern Present' in Robert C. Post (ed.), *Censorship and Silencing: Practices of Cultural Regulation*. Los Angeles: The Getty Research Institute for the History of Art and the Humanities, pp. 17–41.
Butler, Judith (1997). *Excitable Speech: A Politics of the Performative*. Abingdon/New York: Routledge.
Butler, Judith (1998). 'Ruled Out: Vocabularies of the Censor' in Robert C. Post (ed.), *Censorship and Silencing: Practices of Cultural Regulation*.

Los Angeles: The Getty Research Institute for the History of Art and the Humanities, pp. 247–59.

Cabal, Fermín (2010). Unpublished interview with Diego Santos Sánchez for the *Theatre Censorship in Spain* project (9 March 2010).

Cabañas Bravo, Miguel (2011). 'Miguel Prieto y la escenografía en la España de los años treinta', *Archivo Español de Arte*, 84(336), 355–78.

Campos, Jesús (2010). Unpublished interview with Diego Santos Sánchez for the *Theatre Censorship in Spain* project (8 March 2010).

Cañizares Bundorf, Nathalie (2000). *Memoria de un escenario. Teatro María Guerrero 1885–2000*. Madrid: Instituto Nacional de las Artes Escénicas y de la Música.

Cardona, Rodolfo (1992). 'El teatro de Valle-Inclán dentro y fuera de España (1899–1975)', *Anales de la Literatura Española Contemporánea*, 17(1–3), 163–78.

Carmona, Alfredo (1935). 'Pavón: *La Colasa del Pavón*', *ABC*, 1 December 1935, p. 61.

Carr, Raymond (2001 [1980]). *Modern Spain, 1875–1980*. Oxford: Oxford University Press.

Carreras, Albert, and Xavier Tafunell (eds) (2005). *Estadísticas históricas de España: Siglos XIX–XX*, vol. 1, 2nd ed. Bilbao: Fundación BBVA.

Casa, Frank P. (1988). 'The Assimilation of Ramón del Valle-Inclán's Dramas into Contemporary Spanish Theater' in Martha T. Halsey and Phyllis Zatlin (eds), *The Contemporary Spanish Theater: A Collection of Critical Essays*. Lanham: University of America Press, pp. 163–82.

Casa, Frank P. (1979).'Theatre after Franco: The First Reaction', *Hispanófila*, 22(66), 109–22.

Casado, Marina (2017). *La nostalgia inseparable de Rafael Alberti: oscuridad y exilio íntimo en su obra*. Madrid: Ediciones de la Torre.

Casas, Joan (2011). 'Notes sobre el repertori de l'ADB i el seu espai d'influència' in Francesc Foguet, Núria Santamaria and Mercè Saumell (eds), *L'Agrupació Dramàtica de Barcelona: entre el mite i la realitat?* Barcelona: Punctum/GRAE, pp. 45–60.

Casona, Alejandro (1936). 'Autocrítica. *Nuestra Natacha*. Comedia de Alejandro Casona, que se estrena esta noche en el Teatro Victoria', *ABC*, 6 February 1936, p. 14.

Castellano, Juan R. (1955). 'Los premios nacionales de teatro en España', *Hispania*, 38(3), 291–3.

Castellet, José María (ed.) (1976). *Literatura, ideología y política*. Barcelona: Anagrama.

Castellet, José María (ed.) (1977). *La cultura bajo el franquismo*. Barcelona: Anagrama.

Castellón, Antonio (1976). 'Proyectos de reforma del teatro español, 1920–1939', *Primer Acto*, 76, 4–13.

Castro, Cristóbal de (1939). 'La dignificación escénica. Teatro Nacional de Falange. Orígenes, propósitos, realización', *Arriba*, 22 May 1939, p. 8. Centro de Documentación de las Artes Escénicas y de la Música, *www.teatro.es/catalogo-integrado/teatro-1423699-3*.
Castro Jiménez, Antonio (2018). 'Modesto Higueras Cátedra' in *Biografías*. Madrid: Real Academia de la Historia, *http://dbe.rah.es/biografias/46247/modesto-higueras-catedra*.
Cataslán García, Pedro (2008). '*Ak y la humanidad*: Una obra bajo sospecha', *Teatro: Revista de Estudios Culturales/A Journal of Cultural Studies*, 22, 167–95.
Cazorla, Hazel (1965). 'Simbolismo en el teatro de Carlos Muñiz', *Hispania*, 48(2), 230–3.
Cazorla Sánchez, Antonio (2010). *Fear and Progress: Ordinary Lives in Franco's Spain, 1939–1975*. Oxford: Wiley Blackwell.
Cela Trulock, Jorge (2002). 'El testigo de Arrabal', *El Cultural*, 17 January 2002, *https://elcultural.com/El-testigo-de-Arrabal*.
Centro de Documentación Teatral (n.d.). 'Efemérides: Ionesco en España', *Teatro.es*. Madrid: Centro de Documentación Teatral, *http://teatro.es/efemerides/ionesco-en-espana*.
Centro de Documentación Teatral (2015). 'Actuaciones del grupo Cátaro, 1967–1970' in *El Teatro Independiente en España, 1962–1980*, *http://cdaem.mcu.es/teatro-independiente/espacios/giras-de-cataro.php*.
Chabás, Juan (1933). 'El teatro religioso', *Luz. Diario de la República*, 03 July 1933, p. 5.
Checa Puerta, Julio E. (2013). 'Claves 1941: Escena y política', *DHTE (Documentos para la historia del teatro español)*. Madrid: Centro de Documentación Teatral, *http://teatro.es/contenidos/documentosParaLaHistoria/Docs1941*.
Ciurans, Enric (2005). 'El teatro catalán: una dramaturgia de la imagen' in Osvaldo Pelletieri (ed.), *Teatro, memoria y ficción*. Buenos Aires: Galerna, pp. 315–22.
Clemente, Josep Carlos (ed.) (1973). *Una cultura en crisis*. Barcelona: Plaza y Janés.
Cobb, Christopher (1985). *El teatro de agitación y propaganda en España: El Grupo 'Nosotros' (1932–1934): César Falcón, intérprete de la Inglaterra de los años veinte en la prensa Española*. Intro. J. Falcón. Lima: Hora del hombre.
Cobb, Christopher H. (1992–3). 'El agit-prop cultural en la Guerra Civil', *Studia Histórica-Historia Contemporánea*, 10–11, 237–49.
Cobb, Christopher H. (1995). *Los milicianos de la cultura*. Bilbao: Universidad del País Vasco.
Cobo Rivas, A. (1998). *José Martín Recuerda: vida y obra dramática*. Granada: Caja General de Ahorros de Granada.
Coca, Jordi (1978). *L'Agrupació Dramàtica de Barcelona: intent de teatre nacional (1955–1963)*. Barcelona: Institut del Teatre/Edicions, p. 62.

Coca, Jordi (2008). 'Les polítiques teatrals' in Francesc Foguet i Boreu (ed.), *Teatre en temps de guerra i revolució (1936–1939)*. Barcelona: Punctum/Generalitat de Catalunya, pp. 37–53.

Codina, Josep Anton (2012). Unpublished interview with Michael Thompson for the *Theatre Censorship in Spain* project (7 July 2012).

Comisión Episcopal de Ortodoxia y Moralidad (1950). *Instrucciones y Normas para la censura moral de espectáculos: Aprobadas por la Comisión Episcopal de Ortodoxia y Moralidad, de acuerdo con la dirección central de Acción Católica*. Madrid: Acción Católica Española.

Conferencia Episcopal Española (1977). *Los valores morales y religiosos ante la Constitución Española*. Madrid: XXVII Asamblea Plenaria de la Conferencia Episcopal Española, https://archivodelatransicion.es/fondo-documental/fondo-documental-poderes-publicos/la-iglesia-catolica.

Cornago Bernal, Óscar (1999). *La vanguardia teatral en España, 1965–1975: del ritual al juego*. Madrid: Visor.

Cornago Bernal, Óscar (2000). *Discurso teórico y puesta en escena en los años sesenta: la encrucijada de los 'realismos'*. Madrid: Consejo Superior de Investigaciones Científicas.

Cornejo Ibares, María Paz (2007). 'El polémico montaje de *La casa de Bernarda Alba* en 1950' in Fidel López Criado (ed.), *La literatura, la iglesia y el reino de este mundo: estudios de literatura española contemporánea*. A Coruña: Deputación da Coruña, pp. 209–18.

Cotarelo y Mori, Emilio (1904). *Bibliografía de las controversias sobre la licitud del teatro en España*. Madrid: Biblioteca Nacional, https://archive.org/details/bibliografadela00morigoog.

Crehuet, Elisa et al. (2008). *Joglars 77, del escenario al trullo: libertad de expresión y creación colectiva, 1968/1978*. Barcelona: Icaria.

Cuevas, David (1980). 'Estreno en Vitoria de *El rayo colgado*, de Francisco Nieva: Una historia mágica de España', *ABC*, 1 August 1980, pp. 65–6.

Cramsie, Hilde F. (1984). *Teatro y censura en la España franquista: Sastre, Muñiz y Ruibal*. New York: Peter Lang.

Cueto Asín, Elena (2005). '*Sombras de héroes* de Germán Bleiberg o el primer 'Guernica' sobre el escenario', *Revista Hispánica Moderna*, 58(1–2), 93–106.

Cueto Asín, Elena (2008). *Reconciliaciones en escena. El teatro de la Guerra Civil*. Madrid: Orto.

Cueva, Jorge de la (1939). '*El delirio*. Comedia de don Antonio Quintero', *Ya*, 24 September 1939. Centro de Documentación de las Artes Escénicas y de la Música, www.teatro.es/catalogo-integrado/teatros-1425147-3.

Delgado, Maria M. (2008). *Federico García Lorca*. Abingdon: Routledge.

Delgado, Maria, and David Thatcher Gies (eds) (2012). *A History of Theatre in Spain*. Cambridge: Cambridge University Press.

Dennis, Nigel, and Emilio Peral Vega (2009). *Teatro de la Guerra Civil. El bando republicano*. Madrid: Fundamentos.

Dennis, Nigel, and Emilio Peral Vega (2010). *Teatro de la guerra civil: el bando nacional.* Madrid: Fundamentos.
DHTE (2015). *Documentos para la historia del teatro español* (database). Madrid: Centro de Documentación Teatral, http://teatro.es/contenidos/documentosParaLaHistoria/Docs1943/estrenos.php.
Díaz, Carlos (1983). 'Los españoles y Sartre: crónica de un retraso', *Arbor*, 114 (April 1983), 452–62.
Díaz Fernández, José (1930). *El nuevo romanticismo, polémica de arte, política y literatura.* Madrid: Zeus. Reprinted with intro. by Nigel Dennis. Madrid: Fundación Santander Central Hispano, 2006.
Díez, Emeterio (2007). 'La censura teatral en Madrid durante la Segunda República (1931–1936)', *Anales de la Literatura Española Contemporánea*, 32(2), 423–46.
Díez, Emeterio (2008). 'La censura teatral bajo el franquismo: la Vicesecretaría de Educación Popular (1941–1945)', *Teatro: Revista de Estudios Culturales*, 22, 316–33, https://digitalcommons.conncoll.edu/teatro/vol22/iss22/.
Díez, Emeterio (2009). 'La institución de la censura teatral franquista (1938–1941)', *Cuadernos para investigación de la literatura hispánica*, 34, 371–86.
Diez, Xavier (2008). 'La socialtzació dels espectacles públics' in Francesc Foguet i Boreu (ed.), *Teatre en temps de guerra i revolució (1936–1939).* Barcelona: Punctum/Generalitat de Catalunya, pp. 15–35.
Díez-Canedo, Enrique (1968). *Artículos de crítica teatral. El teatro español de 1914 a 1936, vol. 4: Elementos de renovación.* México: Joaquín Mortiz.
Doménech, Ricardo (2008). *García Lorca y la tragedia española.* Madrid: Fundamentos.
Donahue, Francis (1973). 'Carlos Muñiz and the Expressionist Imagination', *Romance Notes*, 15(2), 230–3.
Dosa, J. (1934a). 'Martín: *Peccata Mundi*', *ABC*, 30 May 1934, pp. 47–8.
Dosa, J. (1934b). 'Martín: Inauguración de la temporada con la reposición de *Peccata Mundi*', *ABC*, 1 September 1934, p. 41.
Dougherty, Dru (1986). *Valle-Inclán y la Segunda República.* Valencia: Pre-textos.
Dougherty, Dru (1999). 'Theater and Culture, 1868–1936' in David T. Gies (ed.), *Cambridge Companion to Modern Spanish Culture.* Cambridge: Cambridge University Press, pp. 211–21.
Dougherty, Dru (2013). '*Fuente Ovejuna* en clave republicana: la refundición de Enrique López Alarcón (1932)', *Anales de la Literatura Española Contemporánea*, 38(1–2), 127–47.
Dougherty, Dru, and Andrew A. Anderson (2012). 'Continuity and Innovation in Spanish Theatre, 1900–1936' in Maria Delgado and David T. Gies (eds), *A History of Theatre in Spain.* Cambridge: Cambridge University Press, pp. 282–309.

Dougherty, Dru, and María Francisca Vilches de Frutos (eds) (1992). *El teatro en España: Entre la tradición y la vanguardia, 1918–1939*. Madrid: CSIC/Fundación Federico García Lorca/Tabacalera.
Dowling, Andrew (2012). 'For Christ and Catalonia: Catholic Catalanism and Nationalist Revival in Late Francoism', *Journal of Contemporary History*, 47(3), 594–610.
Duprey, Jennifer (2014). *The Aesthetics of the Ephemeral: Memory Theaters in Contemporary Barcelona*. Albany NY: SUNY Press.
Eder, Richard (1971). 'Madrid: Triumph of Lorca's *Yerma*', *The New York Times*, 27 December 1971, p. 36.
Edwards, Gwynne (1985). *Dramatists in Perspective: Spanish Theatre in the Twentieth Century*. Cardiff: University of Wales Press.
Edwards, Gwynne (1999). '*Yerma* on Stage', *Anales de la Literatura Española Contemporánea*, 24(3), 433–51.
Edwards, Gwynne (2000). 'Productions of *La casa de Bernarda Alba*', *Anales de la Literatura Española Contemporánea*, 25(3), 699–728.
El Español (2017). 'El primer 18 de julio de Franco como caudillo: "No puedo ser un poder interino"', *El Español*, 16 July 2017, www.elespanol.com/reportajes/20170716/231726948_0.html.
El País (1977a). '"El teatro debe plantearse como servicio público": Entrevista con Francisco José Mayans, director general de Teatro y Espectáculos', *El País*, 15 June 1977, https://elpais.com/diario/1977/06/15/cultura/235173601_850215.html.
El País (1977b). 'Ruibal renuncia a la subvencion para su obra *El hombre y la mosca*', *El País*, 1 August 1977, https://elpais.com/diario/1977/08/02/cultura/239320806_850215.html.
El País (1978). 'Los actores de *Ven a disfrutar* esperan que vuelva a autorizarse la obra', *El País*, 18 September 1978, https://elpais.com/diario/1978/09/19/sociedad/275004012_850215.html.
El Perpetuo Socorro (1945). *Películas y obras de teatro censuradas mensualmente en la Revista 'El Perpetuo Socorro' durante los años 1939–1944*. Madrid: El Perpetuo Socorro.
El Sol (1933). 'Una carta: El incidente derivado de unas protestas en el teatro Beatriz', *El Sol* (Madrid), 2 July 1933, p. 12.
El Sol (1937). 'Las normas en que ha de inspirarse la actuación del Consejo Central de Teatro', *El Sol* (Madrid), 5 December 1937, p. 2.
Els Joglars (2016). *Joglars*, https://elsjoglars.com/.
Ellwood, Sheelagh M. (1987). *Spanish Fascism in the Franco Era: Falange Española de las JONS, 1936–76*. New York: St Martin's Press.
Enders, Victoria L. (2002). '"And We Ate Up the World": Memories of the *Sección Femenina*' in Paolo Bacchetta and Margaret Power (eds), *Right-Wing Women: From Conservatives to Extremists Around the World*. New York/London: Routledge, pp. 85–100.

Escobar, Luis (2000). *En cuerpo y alma: Memorias de Luis Escobar, 1908–1991*. Madrid: Temas de Hoy.

Escolar, Hipólito (1987). *La cultura durante la guerra civil*. Madrid: Alhambra.

Espejo Romero, Ramón (2002). '*Death of a Salesman*, de Arthur Miller, en España durante los años 50', *Atlantis*, 24, 85–107.

Espejo Romero, Ramón (2005). 'Some Notes about Arthur Miller's Drama in Francoist Spain: Towards a European History of Miller', *Journal of American Studies*, 39(3), 485–509.

Espejo Trenas, Antonio (2009). 'Álvaro de Orriols, pionero del teatro de masas: los estrenos de *Rosas de sangre* y *Los enemigos de la República*', *Stichomythia*, 10, 20–32.

Estreno (1976). 'Cartelera', *Estreno*, 2, 50.

Espert, Nuria, and Marcos Ordóñez (2002). *De aire y fuego: Memorias*. Madrid: Aguilar.

Estévez, Mayca (2018). Unpublished interview with Michael Thompson for the *Theatre Censorship in Spain* project (7 December 2018).

Europa Press (1970). 'Incidentes en el Teatro de la Comedia de Madrid', *ABC* (Sevilla), 29 September 1970, p. 58.

Fàbregas, Xavier (1978). *Història del teatre català*. Barcelona: Millà.

Facio, Ángel (2011). Unpublished interview with Diego Santos Sánchez for the *Theatre Censorship in Spain* project (18 January 2011).

Falcón, César (1934). 'El teatro proletario en Asturias', *La Lucha* (Madrid), 30 January 1934, p. 19. Reproduced in José Esteban and Gonzalo Santonja (eds) (1988), *Los novelistas sociales españoles (1928–1936). Antología*. Barcelona. Anthropos, pp. 104–7.

Feldman, Sharon, and Francesc Foguet (2016). *Els límits del silenci: La censura del teatre català durant el franquisme*. Barcelona: Abadia de Montserrat.

Fernández, José Francisco (2009). 'A Long Time Coming: The Critical Response to Samuel Beckett in Spain and Portugal' in Mark Nixon and Matthew Feldman (eds), *The International Reception of Samuel Beckett*. London/New York: Continuum, pp. 272–90.

Fernández Insuela, Antonio (2004). 'Introducción (a *El cuerpo*)' in Lauro Olmo, *Obra Completa*, tomo I. Madrid: AAT, pp. 339–45.

Fernández Poza, Óscar (2011). 'Un primer acercamiento a la censura en el repertorio teatral catalán en el Archivo General de la Administración', *Revista de Lenguas y Literaturas Catalana, Gallega y Vasca*, 16, 41–56.

Fernández Quesada, Nuria (2011). 'Under the Aegis of the Lord Chamberlain and the Franco Regime: the Bowdlerisation of *Waiting For Godot* and *Endgame*' in Catherine O'Leary and Alberto Lázaro (eds), *Censorship across Borders: The Reception of English Literature in Twentieth-Century Europe*. Newcastle upon Tyne: Cambridge Scholars Publishing, pp. 193–209.

Fernández Torres, Alberto (1974). 'El autor en su entorno social. Madrid. Mesa Redonda', *Pipirijaina*, 6–7, 48–53. Reproduced in Teatro. es (CDAEM), *www.teatro.es/catalogo-integrado/el-autor-en-su-entorno-social-madrid-mesa-redonda-31310-2*.

Feuillastre, Anne-Laure (2019). 'La calle como escenario de protesta política en la España de los setenta', *Crisol*, 5 (*Callejeando/La Rue dans tous ses états/A rua em todas as vias*), 377–88, *http://crisol.parisnanterre.fr/index.php/crisol/article/view/114/107*.

Foguet i Boreu, Francesc (1998). 'Cultura y teatro en las trincheras: La 31ª División del Ejército Republicano', *Teatro: Revista de Estudios Culturales/A Journal of Cultural Studies*, 13–14, 137–72.

Foguet i Boreu, Francesc (2000). 'El teatro universitario en la Cataluña de la Segunda República (1933/5–7)', *Anales de la Literatura Española Contemporánea*, 25(3), 821–88.

Foguet i Boreu, Francesc (2002). *Las Juventudes Libertarias y el teatro libertario: Cataluña (1936–1939)*. Madrid: Fundación de Estudios Libertarios Anselmo Lorenzo.

Forest, Eva (ed.) (1997). *Alfonso Sastre o la ilusión trágica: Cincuenta años de teatro*. Hondarribia: Hiru.

Foucault, Michel (1978). *The History of Sexuality*. New York: Pantheon.

Foucault, Michel (1979). *Discipline and Punish: The Birth of the Prison*, trans. Alan Sheridan. New York: Vintage.

Foucault, Michel (1980). *Power/Knowledge: Selected Interviews and Other Writings 1972–77*, ed. Colin Gordon. Harlow: Pearson.

Foxá, Agustín de (1938). 'Ambo ato', *ABC* (Sevilla), 1 January 1938, pp. 3–4.

Fraga Iribarne, Manuel (1980). *Memoria breve de una vida pública*. Barcelona: Planeta.

Fraga Iribarne, Manuel (2010). Unpublished interview with Diego Santos Sánchez for the *Theatre Censorship in Spain* project (19 February 2010).

Franco, Francisco (1938). 'Declaraciones al enviado especial del periódico brasileño *Jornal do Brasil*' (January 1938), reproduced in *Generalísimo Francisco Franco* (2003–6), *www.generalisimofranco.com/Discursos/prensa/00018.htm*.

Franco, Francisco (1939). *Palabras del Caudillo: 19 abril 1937–31 diciembre 1938*. Barcelona: Ediciones Fe.

Freshwater, Helen (2004). 'Towards a Redefinition of Censorship' in Beate Müller (ed.), *Censorship and Cultural Regulation in the Modern Age*. Amsterdam and New York: Rodopi, pp. 225–45.

Freshwater, Helen (2009). *Theatre Censorship in Britain. Silencing, Censure and Suppression*. Houndsmills: Palgrave Macmillan.

Fuentes, Víctor (2006). *La marcha al pueblo en las letras españolas, 1917–1936*. Madrid: Ediciones de la Torre.

Gaborik, Patricia (2021). *Mussolini's Theatre: Fascist Experiments in Art and Politics*. Cambridge: Cambridge University Press.
Gabriele, John Philip, and Candyce Leonard (1990). 'Perspectivas sobre el teatro español a los quince años de la democracia', *Anales de la Literatura Española Contemporánea*, 15(1–3), 253–73.
Gabriele, John P. (1991). 'Conversación con Lauro Olmo', *Anales de la Literatura Española Contemporánea*, 16(3), 383–7.
Gabriele, John P. (1997). 'Diálogo con José María Rodríguez Méndez, Cronista Teatral', *Iberoamericana*, 21(2)(66), 75–83.
Gagen, Derek (2008). 'Collective Suicide: Rafael Alberti's Updating of Cervantes's *La destrucción de Numancia*', *The Modern Language Review*, 103(1), 93–112.
Gallego, Juan María (1970). 'Reloj sin horas: *El Tartufo* y su gato encerrado' *El Progreso* (Lugo), 1906/1970. Contained in the AGA file on *El Tartufo* (AGA 280/68, Caja 73/09671).
Gallén, Enric (1985). *El teatre a la ciutat de Barcelona durant el règim franquista (1939–1954)*. Barcelona: Institut del Teatre.
Gallén, Enric (1996). 'Catalan Theatrical Life: 1939–1993' in David George and John London (eds), *Contemporary Catalan Theatre: An Introduction*. Sheffield: The Anglo-Catalan Society, pp. 19–42.
Gallén, Enric (2000). 'Censura i moral en el teatre representat a Barcelona durant el primer franquisme' in Ferran Carbó et al (eds), *Les literatures catalana i francesa: Postguerra i 'engagement'*. Barcelona: Abadia de Montserrat, pp. 163–86.
Gallén, Enric (2010). 'Sobre el teatre professional, amateur i independent a Catalunya durant el règim franquista' in Josep Massot i Muntaner (ed.), *Miscel·lània Joaquim Molas, 6*. Barcelona: Abadia de Montserrat (Estudis de Llengua i Literatura Catalanes, 61), pp. 109–46.
Gallén, Enric (2013). 'Traducció i censura teatral sota la fèrula franquista dels anys cinquanta', *Quaderns: Revista de Traducció*, 20, 95–116, www.raco.cat/index.php/QuadernsTraduccio/issue/view/19955/showToc.
García Álvarez, Cristina. (1990). 'El teatro de la Guerra civil en la zona nacional' in Roy Boland R. and Alun Kenwood (eds), *War and Revolution in Hispanic Literature*. Melbourne/Madrid: Voz Hispánica, pp. 197–209.
García del Río, Antonio (2020). 'De vagos y maleantes, bandidos y censores. La contraimagen del quinqui durante el franquismo en obras de Rodríguez Méndez', *Kamchatka*, 16, 129–54.
García Escudero, José María (1952). 'Censura y Libertad', *Arbor*, 23(83), 177–97.
García Escudero, José María (1978a). *La primera apertura: diario de un director general*. Barcelona: Planeta.
García Escudero, José María (1978b). 'Los doce Ministros de Hacienda de la República'. *Revista de economía política*, 79, 7–51.

García Escudero, José María (1995). *Mis siete vidas. De las brigadas anarquistas a juez del 23-F*. Barcelona: Planeta.
García Iniesta, César (1937). 'El Teatro en Madrid durante la guerra', *Crónica*, 10 October 1937, p. 5.
García Lorca, Federico (2007). *Amor de Don Perlimplín con Belisa en su jardín*, ed. Margarita Ucelay. Madrid: Cátedra.
García Lorenzo, Luciano (2014a). 'La dirección de escena en España (3). Luis Escobar', *Rinconete*, http://cvc.cervantes.es/el_rinconete/anteriores/mayo_14/13052014_01.htm.
García Lorenzo, Luciano (2014b). 'La dirección de escena en España (4). Cayetano Luca de Tena', *Rinconete*, http://cvc.cervantes.es/el_rinconete/anteriores/mayo_14/29052014_01.htm.
García Lorenzo, Luciano (2014c). 'La dirección de escena en España (5). José Luis Alonso Mañés', *Rinconete*, http://cvc.cervantes.es/el_rinconete/anteriores/junio_14/09062014_01.htm.
García Lorenzo, Luciano (2014d). 'La dirección de escena en España (6). Miguel Narros', *Rinconete*, http://cvc.cervantes.es/el_rinconete/anteriores/julio_14/03072014_01.htm.
García Lorenzo, Luciano (2014e). 'La dirección de escena en España (7). Adolfo Marsillach', *Rinconete*, http://cvc.cervantes.es/el_rinconete/anteriores/julio_14/24072014_01.htm.
García Pascual, Raquel (2006). 'La mirada del bufón de corte: *Tragicomedia del serenísimo príncipe don Carlos*, de Carlos Muñiz', *Dicenda: Estudios de Lengua y Literatura españolas*, 24, 95–116, https://revistas.ucm.es/index.php/DICE/article/view/DICE0606110095A.
García Pavón, Francisco (1962): *El teatro social en España (1895–1962)*. Madrid. Taurus.
García Pintado, Ángel (1979). 'La vanguardia en los nuevos autores españoles (Sólo una introducción)', *Primer Acto*, 182, 65–6.
García Ruiz, Víctor. (1996). 'Los mecanismos de censura teatral en el primer franquismo y *Los pájaros ciegos* de V. Ruiz Iriarte (1948)', *Gestos*, 22, 59–85.
García Ruiz, Víctor (1997). 'Sociedad, prensa y autocensura en el franquismo: la frustrada recepción de *Los pájaros ciegos* de V. Ruiz Iriarte (1948)', *Gestos*, 24, 119–33.
García Ruiz, Víctor (2000). 'Un teatro fascista para España: los proyectos de Felipe Lluch', *RILCE: Revista de Filología Hispánica*, 16(1), 93–134.
García Ruiz, Víctor (2003a). 'El teatro español entre 1939 y 1945' in Víctor García Ruiz (ed.), *Historia y antología del teatro español de posguerra (1940–1975), Vol. 2: 1945–1950*. Madrid: Fundamentos, pp. 11–134. Biblioteca Virtual Miguel de Cervantes, *www.cervantesvirtual.com/obra/el-teatro-espanol-entre-1939-y-1945*.
García Ruiz, Víctor (2003b). 'El teatro español entre 1945 y 1950' in Víctor García Ruiz (ed.), *Historia y antología del teatro español de posguerra*

(1940–1975), Vol. 1: *1945–1945*. Madrid: Fundamentos, pp. 11–140. Biblioteca Virtual Miguel de Cervantes, *www.cervantesvirtual.com/obra/el-teatro-espanol-entre-1945-y-1950*.

García Ruiz, Víctor (2004). 'Alta comedia y comedia de evasión: Pemán, Calvo Sotelo, Ruiz Iriarte y otros autores' in Javier Huerta Calvo (ed.), *Historia del teatro español*, vol. 2: *Del siglo XVIII a la época actual*. Madrid: Gredos, pp. 2731–56. Biblioteca Virtual Miguel de Cervantes, 2013), *www.cervantesvirtual.com/nd/ark:/59851/bmc1c3p7*.

García Ruiz, Víctor (2010). *Teatro y fascismo en España. El itinerario de Felipe Lluch*. Madrid/Frankfurt: Iberoamericana/Vervuert.

García Ruiz, Víctor, and Gregorio Torres Nebrera (2005). *Historia y antología del teatro español de posguerra (1940–1975)*, vol. VII: *1971–1975*. Madrid: Fundamentos.

García Tortosa, F., *et al.* (1986). *Literatura popular y proletaria*. Sevilla: Universidad de Sevilla.

George, David (2002). *Theatre in Madrid and Barcelona 1892–1936: Rivals or collaborators?* Cardiff: University of Wales Press.

Gibson, Ian (1985). *Federico García Lorca*, vol. 1: *De Fuente Vaqueros a Nueva York (1898–1929)*. Barcelona: Grijalbo.

Gibson, Ian (2018). *El asesinato de García Lorca*, 2nd ed. Madrid: Penguin Random House.

Gies, David Thatcher (1994). *The Theatre in Nineteenth-Century Spain*. Cambridge: Cambridge University Press.

Gies, David Thatcher (ed.) (1999). *The Cambridge Companion to Modern Spanish Culture*. Cambridge: Cambridge University Press.

Gil Fombellida, María Carmen (2003). *Rivas Cherif, Margarita Xirgu y el teatro de la II República*. Madrid. Fundamentos.

Gillespie, Gerald (1972). 'Estreno mundial de *El hombre y la mosca*', *Primer Acto*, 142, 74. Reproduced in Ruibal, José (1977). *El hombre y la mosca*. Madrid: Fundamentos, pp. 137–9.

Giménez Martínez, Miguel Ángel (2015). 'El corpus ideológico del franquismo: principios originarios y elementos de renovación', *Estudios Internacionales*, 180, 11–45. *https://scielo.conicyt.cl/scielo.php?script=sci_abstract&pid=S0719-37692015000100002*.

Godayol, Pilar (2016). 'The Francoist censorship and the Catalan Translations of Jean-Paul Sartre', *Perspectives*, 24(1), 59–75.

Golsan, Richard J. (1991). 'Spain and the Lessons of History: Albert Camus and the Spanish Civil War', *Romance Quarterly*, 38(4), 407–17.

Gómez Díaz, Luis Miguel (1993). 'Luis Mussot Flores: su labor teatral durante la Guerra Civil', *Anales de la Literatura Española Contemporánea*, 18(3), 519–37.

Gómez Díaz, Luis Miguel (2006). *Teatro para una guerra (1936–1939). Textos y documentos*. Madrid: Centro de Documentacion Teatral/Ministerio de Cultura.

Gómez García, Manuel (1971). '1971: así piensan 40 profesionales de la escena española sobre la censura, teatro social y teatro político', *Primer Acto*, 131, 8–24.

Gómez García, Manuel (1997): *Diccionario Akal de teatro*, Madrid: Akal.

Gómez Oliver, Miguel (2008). 'El movimiento estudiantil español durante el Franquismo (1965–1975)', *Revista crítica de ciencias sociais*, 81, 93–110.

Gómez Pérez, Rafael (1986). *El franquismo y la Iglesia*. Madrid: Rialp.

Gómez-Reino y Carnota, Enrique (1981–2). 'La libertad de expresión en la II República', *Revista de Derecho Político*, 12, 159–87.

González, Luis Mariano (1996). 'La escena madrileña durante la II República (1931–1939)', *Teatro: Revista de Estudios Culturales/A Journal of Cultural Studies*, 9–10, 7–624.

González, Luis Mariano (2007). *El teatro español durante la II República y la crítica de su tiempo (1931–1936)*. Madrid: Fundación Universitaria Española.

González Olmedilla, Juan (1936). 'Una noche feliz para autor, intérpretes y público. Con extraordinario éxito, legítimamente alcanzado, se estrena en el Victoria *Nuestra Natacha*, de Alejandro Casona', *Heraldo de Madrid*, 7 February 1936, p. 14.

González Ruiz, Nicolás (1943). *La literatura española*. Madrid: Pegaso.

González Ruiz, Nicolás (1944). 'Una gran tarea de dignificación del teatro', *Ya*, 18 July 1944. Reprinted in Abellán, Manuel L. (ed.) (1987). *Censura y literaturas peninsulares*. Amsterdam: Rodopi, pp. 173–5. Reproduced in *DHTE* (*Documentos para la historia del teatro español*): http://teatro.es/contenidos/documentosParaLaHistoria/Docs1944/index.html.

González Tuñón, Raúl (2006). 'La Tarumba (los títeres al servicio de la Guerra)' in Eugenio Otero Urtaza (ed.), *Las Misiones Pedagógicas 1931–1936*. Madrid: Sociedad Estatal de Conmemoraciones Culturales/Residencia de Estudiantes, pp. 499–501. Originally published in *Ahora* (Madrid), 12 May 1937, pp. 7–8.

Gracia, Fernando (1977). 'Teatro Benavente: "No fuimos violadas." Coaccionadas por su director, acusaron al empresario', *Diario 16*, 3 June 1977, p. 28.

Gracia y Justicia (1936). 'El aplaudido Casona', *Gracia y Justicia*, 15 February 1936, p. 14.

Grada (2020). 'Perfil: Manuel Martínez-Mediero', *Grada* 148, 15 September 2020, www.grada.es/manuel-martinez-mediero-historia-del-teatro-contemporaneo-en-extremadura-grada-148-perfil/revista-grada/perfil.

Graham, Helen (2002). *The Spanish Republic at War 1936-1939*. Cambridge: Cambridge University Press.

Graham, Helen (ed.) (2016). *Interrogating Fascism: History and Dictatorship in Twentieth-Century Spain*. London: Bloomsbury.

Grau Gatell, Jordi (2015). 'Testimonio que el soldado Eduardo Sánchez Lázaro, soldado activo en la Base de Hidros del Atalayón, dio a su esposa Angelina Gatell sobre el asesinato del capitán Virgilio Leret Ruiz', *Memòria Repressió Franquista* (blog). Reproduces a letter sent by Angelina Gatell to Carlota Leret O'Neill, *http://memoriarepressiofranquista.blogspot.com/2015/07/testimonio-que-el-soldado-eduardo.html*.

Green, Stuart (2011). 'El conflicto racial como táctica de camuflaje en el teatro durante el segundo franquismo', *Anales de la Literatura Española Contemporánea*, 36(2), 351–67.

Gregor, Keith (2010). *Shakespeare in the Spanish Theatre: 1772 to the Present*. London: Continuum.

Gregor, Keith, and Elena Bandín (2011). 'The Role of the Censor in the Reception of Shakespearean Drama in Francoist Spain: The Strange Case of *The Taming of the Shrew*' in Catherine O'Leary and Alberto Lázaro (eds), *Censorship across Borders: The Reception of English Literature in Twentieth-Century Europe*. Newcastle upon Tyne: Cambridge Scholars Publishing, pp. 143–60.

Groves, Tamar, Nigel Townson, Inbal Ofer and Antonio Herrera (2017). *Social Movements and the Spanish Transition: Building Citizenship in Parishes, Neighbourhoods, Schools and the Countryside*. Cham: Palgrave Macmillan.

G.T. (1933). 'Un Suceso: *Santa Teresita del Niño Jesús* en el Beatriz', *Luz. Diario de la República*, 1 July 1933, p. 6.

Guerra, Alfonso (2010). Unpublished interview with Diego Santos Sánchez for the *Theatre Censorship in Spain* project (7 April 2010).

Halsey, Martha T. (1980). 'The Violent Dramas of Martín Recuerda', *Hispanófila*, 70, 71–93.

Halsey, Martha T. (2007). 'José Martín Recuerda (1925–2007)', *Estreno: Cuadernos del Teatro Español Contemporáneo*, 33(1), 5–6.

Halsey, Martha T., and Phyllis Zatlin (eds) (1988). *The Contemporary Spanish Theatre: A Collection of Critical Essays*. Lanham: University of America Press.

Haro Tecglen, Eduardo (1958). 'Introducción a Alfonso Sastre', *Primer Acto*, 6, 16–18.

Hera, Alberto de la (2000). 'Tamayo', *ADE Teatro*, 82, 294–6.

Heraldo de Madrid (1936). '*Nuestra Natacha*, de Alejandro Casona, es la comedia de los estudiantes de hoy, que tienen un sentido social, ciudadano, humano, de su misión generosa', *Heraldo de Madrid*, 5 February 1936, p. 8.

Heras, Santiago de las (1969). 'Un autor recuperado. Entrevista con José Martín Recuerda', *Primer Acto*, 107, 28–31.

Hidalgo, Susana (2001). 'La otra vida del "marqués de Leguineche"', *El País*, 30 October 2001, *http://elpais.com/diario/2001/10/30/madrid/1004444678_850215.html*.

Higuera Estremera, Luis Felipe (1999). 'El primer estreno comercial de García Lorca en la posguerra española (*Yerma*, Teatro Eslava, 1960)', *Anales de la Literatura Española Contemporánea*, 24(3), 571–92.
Holquist, Michael (1994). 'Corrupt Originals: The Paradox of Censorship', *PMLA*, 109(1), 14–25.
Huerta Calvo, Javier (2019). 'Introducción' in Federico García Lorca, *Teatro completo*. Madrid: Verbum, pp. 9–52.
Hurtado, Diego (1957). 'Las brujas de la política', *Primer Acto*, 2, 16.
Iglesias Santos, Montserrat (1999). 'La II República y el teatro renovador: la búsqueda de un nuevo público para una nueva dramaturgia', *ADE Teatro*, 77, 51–61.
Información (2010). 'Alberto González Vergel: Decano de los directores de teatro de España', *Diario Información*, 18 April 2010, *www.diarioinformacion.com/dominical/2010/05/17/lorca-censuro-franco-familia-prohibio-representarlo-regimen/1000138.html*.
Informaciones (1939). 'Un funeral por el alma de varios escritores y artistas, víctimas de la barbarie roja', *Informaciones* (Madrid), 1 May 1939. Reproduced in *DHTE* (*Documentos para la historia del teatro español*), *http://teatro.es/contenidos/documentosParaLaHistoria/Docs1939/documentos.php*.
Iribarren, Jesús (ed.) (1974). *Documentos colectivos del Episcopado español, 1870–1974*. Madrid: Editorial Católica.
Isabel-Estrada, María Antonia de (2002). *De lo vivo y cercano: censura y representación del teatro de Rafael Alberti en España durante el franquismo*. Madrid: Sociedad Estatal de Conmemoraciones Culturales.
Isasi Ángulo, Amando C. (1974). *Diálogos del teatro español de la postguerra*. Madrid: Ayuso.
Izcaray, Jesús (1934). '*Peccata Mundi*, en Martín', *Luz*, 30 May 1934, p. 6.
Jackson, Gabriel (1970). 'The Spanish Popular Front, 1934–7', *Journal of Contemporary History*, 5(3), 21–35.
Jansen, Sue Curry (1988). *Censorship: The Knot that Binds Power and Knowledge*. Oxford: Oxford University Press.
Jaubert, Luis Joaquín (2016). 'Hermandad Sacerdotal Española', *Ya*, 30 January 2016, *www.diarioya.es/content/hermandad-sacerdotal-española*.
J.G.O. (1933). 'Anoche en el Beatriz', *El Heraldo de Madrid*, 30 June 1933, p. 5.
J.L.S. (1936). 'Tres estrenos en el Español', *La Voz*, 21 October 1936, p. 3.
J.M.A. (1939). 'El teatro y la horda. Honorio Maura cayó también asesinado por los rojos', *Madrid*, 15 April 1939. Reproduced in *DHTE* (*Documentos para la historia del teatro español*, *www.teatro.es/profesionales/honorio-maura-17899/documentos-on-line/prensa*.
Jover, Francisco (1965). 'Entrevista con Lauro Olmo', *Yorick*, 2, 8–9.
Jurado Latorre, María Rosario (2011). 'La censura franquista y el teatro conservador: el caso de Muñoz Seca', *Teatro: Revista de Estudios Teatrales*, 13–14, 237–55.

Kany, C. E. (1930). 'Un homenaje a Benavente', *Bulletin of Spanish Studies*, 7(26), 69–74.
Kronik, John W. (1997). 'Antonio Sánchez Barbudo', *Hispania*, 80(2) 277–9.
La Prensa (1932). 'Comedia suspendida por burlarse de la República', *La Prensa*, 8 August 1932, p. 2.
La Voz (1933). 'Un alboroto en el Teatro Beatriz', *La Voz*, 30 June 1933, p. 3.
La Voz (1936). 'Manifiesto de la Alianza de Escritores Antifascistas para la Defensa de la Cultura', *La Voz*, 30 July 1936, p. 3.
Laborda, Ángel (1976). 'El estreno de esta noche: *La carroza de plomo candente*, de Nieva', *ABC*, 23 April 1976, p. 64.
Ladra, David (1964). 'Reflexión, aquí y ahora, sobre el teatro español comprometido', *Primer Acto*, 51, 18–24.
Laertes (1937). 'También hay ranas en la charca teatral', *La Voz*, 9 December 1937, p. 3.
Lauer, A. Robert (2008). 'Alfonso Sastre's *Escuadra hacia la muerte*: A Liminal Approach', *Revista Canadiense de Estudios Hispánicos*, 32(3), 439–52.
Lénárt, András (2009). 'Un hombre de la apertura franquista: García Escudero', *Acta Scientiarum Socialium*, 30, 37–48.
León, María Teresa (1977). *Memoria de la melancolía*. Barcelona: Laia/Picazo.
León, María Teresa (1979 [1937]). 'Gato por liebre', *El Mono Azul*, 14 October 1937. Reproduced in José Monleón, *'El mono azul': Teatro de urgencia y romancero de la guerra civil*. Madrid: Ayuso, pp. 228–9.
Libertad (2011). 'Certificado de defunción de Federico García Lorca', *Aquella Granada del 1936* (blog). Copy of document held in the *Registro Civil*, Granada, http://aquellagranadadel1936.blogspot.com/2011/08/certificado-de-defuncion-de-federico.html.
Lima, Robert (2003). *The Dramatic World of Valle-Inclán*. Woodbridge: Tamesis.
Linares, Francisco (1996). 'Theatre and Falangism at the Beginning of the Franco Régime' in Günter Berghaus (ed.), *Fascism and Theatre: Comparative Studies on the Aesthetics and Politics of Performance in Europe, 1925–1945*. Providence, RI/Oxford: Berghahn, pp. 210–28.
London, John (1997). *Reception and Renewal in Modern Spanish Theatre: 1939–1963*. London: Modern Humanities Research Association.
London, John (2001). 'Catalan Language and Culture: since 1939' in Derek Jones (ed.), *Censorship: A World Encyclopedia*. London/Chicago: Fitzroy Dearborn, pp. 427–9.
London, John (2012). 'Theatre under Franco (1939–1975): Censorship, Playwriting and Performance' in Maria M. Delgado and David T. Gies (eds), *A History of Theatre in Spain*. Cambridge: Cambridge University Press, pp. 341–71.

Longoni, Ana (2015). 'Tras la pista de Uviedo: experimentos (socio)teatrales de un paria', *Badebec*, 5(9), 310–29, *https://rephip.unr.edu.ar/handle/2133/15376*.
López Criado, Fidel (ed.) (2005). *La República de las letras y las letras de la República*. A Coruña: Universidade da Coruña/Xunta de Galicia.
López Mozo, Jerónimo (1986). 'El Nuevo Teatro Español, hoy', in Klaus Pörtl (ed.), *Reflexiones sobre el Nuevo Teatro Español*. Tübingen: Max Niemeyer, pp. 30–8.
López Mozo, Jerónimo (2010). Unpublished interview with Diego Santos Sánchez for the *Theatre Censorship in Spain* project (19 May 2010).
López Mozo, Jerónimo (2018). 'Datos sueltos para una biografía de José Ruibal', *Las puertas del drama*, 51, *www.aat.es/elkioscoteatral/las-puertas-del-drama/drama-51/testimonio-datos-sueltos-para-una-biografia-de-jose-ruibal*.
López Rodríguez, Fernando (2008). 'Vivencia y creatividad del actor teatral: un derecho de autoría', PhD thesis, Universidad de Alcalá, *https://ebuah.uah.es/dspace/handle/10017/8961*.
López Sancho, Lorenzo (1967). 'Espectáculos: *Mariana Pineda*, de García Lorca, en el Marquina', *ABC*, 12 March 1967, pp. 119–20.
López Sancho, Lorenzo (1969a). 'Un Gran *Tartufo* actualizado en el Teatro de la Comedia', *ABC*, 5 October 1969, pp. 71–2.
López Sancho, Lorenzo (1969b). '*Rosas rojas para mí* de O'Casey en el Beatriz', *ABC*, 8 October 1969, pp. 85–6.
López Sancho, Lorenzo (1970a). 'Doble sesión de cámara en el Teatro Marquina', *ABC*, 23 June 1970, p. 75.
López Sancho, Lorenzo (1970b). '*Castañuela 70*, un feliz ensayo juvenil en la Comedia', *ABC*, 23 August 1970, p. 53.
Luz (1933). 'Una carta: El incidente del teatro Beatriz', *Luz: Diario de la República*, 3 July 1933, p. 11.
Machado, Manuel (1938). 'Intenciones. Teatro Español', *ABC* (Sevilla), 4 August 1938, p. 3.
Madrid (1939). 'Recepción en la Academia de la lengua de D. Eduardo Marquina y jura de académicos', *Madrid*, 4 August 1939. Reproduced in *DHTE* (*Documentos para la historia del teatro español*), *http://teatro.es/contenidos/documentosParaLaHistoria/Docs1939/documentos.php*.
Mainer, José Carlos (1981). *La edad de plata (1902–1939): Ensayo de interpretación de un proceso cultural*. Madrid: Cátedra.
Mainer, José Carlos (2006). *Años de vísperas: La vida de la cultura en España (1931–1939)*. Madrid: Espasa-Calpe.
Mainer, José Carlos (2010). *Historia de la literatura española*, vol. 6, *Modernidad y nacionalismo 1900–1939*. Madrid: Crítica.
Mally, Lynn (2003). 'Exporting Soviet Culture: The Case of Agitprop Theater', *Slavic Review*, 62(2), 324–2.

Margallo, Juan (2006). 'Andanzas y malandanzas de *Castañuela 70*' in *Tábano y Las Madres del Cordero, Castañuela 70: esto era España, señores*. Madrid: Rama Lama Music, pp. 137–61.
Marqueríe, Alfredo (1947). 'Informaciones y noticias teatrales y cinematográficas: En el Calderón se estrenó con éxito resonante *La Infanzona* de Benavente', *ABC*, 11 January 1947, p. 16.
Marqueríe, Alfredo (1950). 'Una representación del Teatro de Ensayo La Carátula: Estreno de *La casa de Bernarda Alba*, de García Lorca', *ABC*, 22 March 1950, p. 21.
Marqueríe, Alfredo (1958). '"Dido" estrenó *Los hombres del triciclo*, de Fernando Arrabal', *ABC*, 30 January 1958, pp. 51–2.
Marquina, Eduardo (1938). 'El gran teatro de España', *ABC (Sevilla)*, 8 November 1938, pp. 3–4.
Marrast, Robert (1955). 'Essai de bibliographie de Rafael Alberti', *Bulletin Hispanique*, 57(1–2), 147–77.
Marrast, Robert (1978). *El teatre durant la guerra vivil española: Assaig d'història i documents*. Barcelona: Institut del Teatre.
Marrast, Robert (1986). 'El teatro durante la guerra civil española': *Cuadernos El Público*, 15, 19–31.
Marsillach, Adolfo (1998). *Tan lejos, tan cerca: Mi vida*. Barcelona: Tusquets.
Marsillach, Adolfo (2000). 'Luis Escobar', *ADE Teatro*, 82, 292–3.
Martín, Sabas (1985). 'José Martín Recuerda: El drama ibérico': *Cuadernos Hispanoamericanos*, 418, 120–7.
Martín Clavijo, Milagro (2011). 'La recepción del teatro de Aldo de Benedetti en la España franquista', *Transfer*, 6(1), 27–42.
Martín Clavijo, Milagro (2012). 'El teatro italiano en la España de los años sesenta', *Transfer*, 7(1–2), 73–88.
Martín Gijón, Mario (2011). 'El teatro durante la Guerra Civil española en el frente y la retaguardia de la zona republicana', *Lectura y Signo*, 6, 263–74.
Martínez Cachero, José María (1986). 'Talía en la Guerra Civil: sobre el Teatro de la zona nacional', *Studium Ovetense*, 14, 83–99. Alicante: Biblioteca Virtual Miguel de Cervantes (2001), *www.cervantesvirtual. com/obra/tala-en-la-guerra-civil–sobre-el-teatro-de-la-zona-nacional-0*.
Martínez Gallego, Francesc A., and Antonio Laguna Platero (2014). 'Agit-Prop comunista en la Guerra Civil: entre el Frente Popular y el Partido Único Obrero', *Historia Contemporánea*, 49, 675–706.
Martínez-Michel, Paula (2003). *Censura y represión intelectual en la España franquista: El caso de Alfonso Sastre*. Hondarribia: Hiru.
Martínez Riaza, Ascención (2004). *¡Por la República! La apuesta política y cultural del peruano César Falcón en España, 1919–1939*. Lima: Instituto de Estudios Peruanos.
Mata Induráin, Carlos (1995). 'Notas sobre el teatro proletario español de la preguerra: *Guerra a la Guerra* y *Miserias*', *RILCE*, 11(1) 68–87.

Mata Induráin, Carlos (2007). 'Risas contra la II República: *La Oca* (Pedro Muñoz Seca y Pedro Pérez Fernández, 1931)', *Revista Stichomythia*, 5, 72–81, *http://parnaseo.uv.es/Ars/ESTICOMITIA/Numero5/maquetacion/gonzalez.pdf.*

Maura, Honorio (1933). 'Lo ocurrido anoche en el teatro Beatriz', *La Época* (Madrid), 30 June 1933, p. 4.

McCarthy, Jim (1999). *Political Theatre during the Spanish Civil War.* Cardiff: University of Wales Press.

McCarthy, Jim (2003a). 'Luis Mussot: observaciones sobre su teatro de urgencia', *ADE Teatro*, 97, 86–88.

McCarthy, Jim (2003b). 'Soldados como espectadores. Teatro de agitación y propaganda y estética de la representación en la Guerra Civil española (1936–1939)', *ADE Teatro*, 97, 139–47.

McCarthy, Jim (2012). 'Theatrical Activities during the Spanish Civil War, 1936–1939' in Maria M. Delgado and David T. Gies (eds), *A History of Theatre in Spain*. Cambridge: Cambridge University Press, pp. 310–22.

McGaha, Michael D. (1979). *The Theatre in Madrid during the Second Republic*. London: Grant & Cutler.

Membrez, Nancy J. (1992). 'The Bureaucratization of the Madrid Theater: Government Censorship, Curfews and Taxation (1868–1925)', *Anales de la Literatura Española Contemporánea*, 17(1–3), 99–123.

Merino Álvarez, Raquel (1994). *Traducción, tradición y manipulación. Teatro inglés en España, 1950–1990*. Leon: Universidad de León/Universidad del País Vasco.

Merino Álvarez, Raquel (ed.) (2007a). *Traducción y censura en España (1939–1985). Estudios sobre corpus TRACE: Cine Narrativa, Teatro*. Bilbao: Universidad del País Vasco/Universidad de León.

Merino Álvarez, Raquel (2007b). 'La homosexualidad censurada: estudio sobre corpus de teatro TRACEti inglés-español (desde 1960)' in Raquel Merino Álvarez (ed.), *Traducción y censura en España (1939–1985). Estudios sobre corpus TRACE: Cine Narrativa, Teatro*. Bilbao: Universidad del País Vasco/Universidad de León, pp. 243–86.

Merino Álvarez, Raquel (2015). 'Musicales traducidos y censurados en los escenarios españoles (1955–1985)', *Quaderns de Filologia: Estudis Literaris*, 20, 219–35, *https://ojs.uv.es/index.php/qdfed/article/view/7538*.

Merino Álvarez, Raquel (2016). 'The censorship of theatre translations under Franco: the 1960s', *Perspectives*, 24(1), 36–47.

Miller, Arthur (2000). 'Are You Now Or Were You Ever. . .?', *The Guardian*, 17 June 2000, *www.theguardian.com/books/2000/jun/17/history.politics*.

Miralles, Alberto (1966). 'Hombres de teatro: Alfonso Sastre', *Yorick*, 11, 1966, p. 11. Reproduced in Julio Huélamo (ed.) (1984). *Yorick 1965–1974: Historia, antología e índices*). Madrid: Centro de Documentación Teatral, pp. 53–54.

Miralles, Alberto (1979). *Nuevo teatro español: una alternativa cultural social*. Madrid: Villalar.
Miralles, Alberto (2003). 'El grupo Cátaro y el teatro independiente', *Assaig de teatre: revista de l'Associació d'Investigació i Experimentació Teatral*, 37, 55–64.
Miralles, Alberto (2004). *Teatro escogido*, vol. 1. Madrid: Asociación de Autores de Teatro. Biblioteca Virtual Miguel de Cervantes, www.cervantesvirtual.com/obra/teatro-escogido-de-alberto-miralles-tomo-1–1.
MIT (1964). *Informe sobre la censura cinematográfica y teatral*. Dirección General de Cinematografía y Teatro. Madrid: Ministerio de Información y Turismo. (Unpublished report held at the Biblioteca General, Ministerio de Cultura, Madrid.)
Molero Manglano, Luis (1974). *Teatro español contemporáneo*. Madrid: Editora Nacional.
Monleón, José (1962). 'Nuestra generación realista', *Primer Acto*, 32, 1–3.
Monleón, José (1968). 'Notas a un estreno muy importante', *Primer Acto*, 102, 11.
Monleón, José (1971). *Treinta años de teatro de la derecha*. Barcelona: Tusquets.
Monleón, José (1977a). 'El teatro. Presente y future del teatro español' in J. M. Castellet (ed.), *La cultura bajo el franquismo*. Barcelona. Ediciones del bolsillo, pp. 241–62.
Monleón, José (1977b). '*La condecoración*, de Lauro Olmo', *Triunfo*, 738 (19 March 1977), 56–7.
Monleón, José (1979). '*El mono azul': Teatro de urgencia y romancero de la guerra civil*. Madrid: Ayuso.
Monleón, José (1988). 'La llegada de La Cuadra a la escena española', *Cuadernos El Público*, 35, 7–15. Reproduced in *Biblioteca Virtual de Prensa Histórica*, http://prensahistorica.mcu.es/es/publicaciones/numeros_por_mes.do?idPublicacion=1002549&anyo=1988.
Monleón, José. (1995). 'Lauro Olmo o la denuncia cordial', *Teatro: Revista de Estudios Culturales/A Journal of Cultural Studies*, 8, 73–82.
Monleón, José (2011). Unpublished interview with Diego Santos Sánchez for the *Theatre Censorship in Spain* project (2 February 2011).
Montijano Ruiz, Juan José (2009). *Historia del teatro olvidado: La revista (1864–2009)*. Granada: Universidad de Granada (PhD thesis).
Montijano Ruiz, Juan José (2010). *Historia del teatro frívolo (1864–2010)*. Madrid: RESAD/Fundamentos.
Moradiellos, Enrique (2000). *La España de Franco, 1939–1975: política y sociedad*. Madrid: Síntesis.
Morón Espinosa, Antonio César (2008). 'El teatro universitario durante los años 50: La presencia de José Martín recuerda dentro del TEU de Granada', *Teatro: Revista de Estudios Culturales/A Journal of Cultural Studies*, 22, 217–41.

Müller, Beate (2004). 'Censorship and Cultural Regulation: Mapping the Territory' in Beate Müller (ed.), *Censorship and Cultural Regulation in the Modern Age*. Amsterdam/New York: Rodopi, pp. 1–31.

Mundi Pedret, Francisco (1987). *El teatro de la guerra civil*. Barcelona: PPU.

Muñiz, Alfredo (1934). '*Yerma*, el poema trágico de Federico García Lorca, admirablemente interpretado por Margarita Xirgu y su compañía, alcanzó en el Español un triunfo clamoroso', *El Heraldo de Madrid*, 31 December 1934, p. 4.

Muñiz, Carlos (1962). 'Antonio Buero Vallejo: ese hombre comprometido', *Primer Acto*, 38, 8–10.

Muñiz, Carlos (1965). 'En mi décimo aniversario como autor dramático, reflexion impúdica', *Primer Acto*, 63, 12.

Muñiz, Carlos (2007). *Teatro escogido*. Alicante: Biblioteca Virtual Miguel de Cervantes, www.cervantesvirtual.com/obra/teatro-escogido-1.

Muñoz Cáliz, Berta (2005). *El teatro crítico español durante el franquismo, visto por sus censores*. Madrid: Fundación Universitaria Española, www.bertamuñoz.es/censura/indice.html.

Muñoz Cáliz, Berta (2006a). *Expedientes de la censura teatral franquista*, 2 vols. Madrid: Fundación Universitaria Española, www.bertamuñoz.es/exedientes/indice.html.

Muñoz Cáliz, Berta (2006b). 'La mordaza que asfixiaba a los españoles' in Alfonso Sastre, *Teatro escogido, Tomo 1*. Madrid: Asociación de Autores de Teatro, pp. 163–70. Reproduced in the *Biblioteca Virtual Miguel de Cervantes* (2008), www.cervantesvirtual.com/obra/la-mordaza-que-asfixiaba-a-los-espaoles-0/.

Muñoz Cáliz, Berta (2010). *Censura y teatro del exilio: Incidencia de la censura en la obra de siete dramaturgos exiliados*. Murcia: Editum.

Muñoz Cáliz, Berta (2011). 'Valle-Inclán y la censura de representaciones durante el franquismo', *Don Galán: Revista de Investigación Teatral*, 1, 1(2), http://teatro.es/contenidos/donGalan/pagina.php?vol=1&doc=1_2.

Muñoz Pujol, Josep Maria (2009). *El cant de les sirenes: Petita crònica del teatre independent a Catalunya (1955–1990)*. Barcelona: Edicions 62.

Mussot, Luis et al. (1936). 'El Comité del Grupo del Teatro Popular se incauta del Fontalba', *ABC*, 26 July 1936, p. 32.

Mussot, Luis (1937). '*El actor y la guerra*', *Espectáculos*, 3, 2–3. Reproduced in L. M. Gómez Díaz, *Teatro para una guerra (1936–1939). Textos y documentos*. Madrid: Centro de Documentación Teatral, 2006. [Digital appendix].

Ní Chuilleanáin, Eiléan, Cormac Ó Cuilleanáin and David Parris (eds) (2009). *Translation and Censorship: Patterns of Communication and Interference*. Dublin: Four Courts Press.

Nieva, Francisco (2010). Unpublished response to survey issued by the Theatre Censorship in Spain project (January 2010).

Nieva de la Paz, Pilar (1993). *Autoras dramáticas españolas entre 1918 y 1936*. Madrid: CSIC.
Nieva de la Paz, Pilar (1994). 'Las autoras teatrales españolas frente al público y la crítica (1918–1936)' in Juan Villegas (ed.), *Actas de XI Congreso de la Asociación Internacional de Hispanistas*, vol. 2. Irvine CA: University of California Press, pp. 129–39.
Nieva de la Paz, Pilar (2013). 'Concha Méndez y Manuel Altolaguirre: La memoria de una vocación teatral', *Anales de la Literatura Española Contemporánea*, 38(3), 757–83.
Novais, José Antonio (2015). 'Julián Grimau, el último muerto de la guerra civil', *El País*, 20 April 2015, *https://elpais.com/elpais/2015/04/20/ eps/1429519997_868869.html*.
Obregón, Antonio de (1939a). 'Crónica del teatro: Reposición de la obra del señor Pemán, *Cuando las Cortes de Cádiz*, en el Reina Victoria', *Arriba*, 22 April 1939. Centro de Documentación de las Artes Escénicas y de la Música, *www.teatro.es/catalogo-integrado/cronica-de-teatro-1423254-3*.
Obregón, Antonio de (1939b). 'Comediógrafos caídos por España', *Arriba*, 17 October 1939. Centro de Documentación de las Artes Escénicas y de la Música, *www.teatro.es/catalogo-integrado/comediografos-caidos-por-espa%C3%B1a-1424737-3*.
O'Connor, Patricia W. (1966). 'Government Censorship in the Contemporary Spanish Theatre', *Educational Theatre Journal*, 18(4), 443–9.
O'Connor, Patricia W. (1969). 'Censorship in the Contemporary Spanish Theater and Antonio Buero Vallejo', *Hispania*, 52(2), 282–8. Reprinted in Mariano de Paco (ed.), *Estudios sobre Buero Vallejo*. Murcia: Universidad de Murcia, pp. 81–92, *www.lluisvives.com/servlet/SirveObras/scclit/12818302026708273321435*.
O'Connor, Patricia W. (1973). 'Torquemada in the Theatre: A Glance at Government Censorship', *Theatre Survey: The American Journal of Theatre History*, 14(2), 33–45.
O'Connor, Patricia W. (1984). 'Post-Franco Theater: From Limitation to Liberty to License', *Hispanic Journal*, 5(2), 55–73.
O'Connor Patricia W., and Anthony M. Pasquariello (1976). 'Conversaciones con la Generación Realista', *Estreno*, 2(2), 8–28.
O'Leary, Catherine (2003). 'From "República Inmoral" to "La Peste Fascista": Agit-prop Theatre of the Second Republic', *Teatro: Revista de Estudios Teatrales*, 19, 177–96.
O'Leary, Catherine (2005). *The Theatre of Antonio Buero Vallejo: Ideology, Politics and Censorship*. Woodbridge: Tamesis.
O'Leary, Catherine (2007). 'The Theatre of Bertolt Brecht in Francoist Spain' in Hector Brioso and José V. Saval (eds), *Nuevas aportaciones a los estudios teatrales (del siglo de Oro a nuestros días)*. Alcalá de Henares: Universidad de Alcalá de Henares, pp. 73–86.

O'Leary, Catherine (2008) '"Irrepresentable en España": Fernando Arrabal and the Spanish Censors', *Journal of Iberian and Latin American Research*, 14(2), 29–52.
O'Leary, Catherine, Diego Santos Sánchez and Michael Thompson (eds) (2015). *Global Insights on Theatre Censorship*. New York/London: Routledge.
O'Leary, Catherine (2017a). 'Staging the Revolution: The Nosotros Theatre Group and the *teatro proletario* of the Second Republic', *Modern Language Review*, 112, 611–44.
O'Leary, Catherine (2017b). 'Translating the Armed Struggle: Alfonso Sastre and Sean O'Casey in Spain', *Translation Studies*, 11(1), 47–65.
O'Leary, Catherine (2019). 'Censoring the Outsider: The Theatre of Albert Camus in Franco's Spain', *Modern Drama*, 62(3), 292–319.
O'Leary, Catherine (2020). *La censura del teatro durante la guerra civil española*. Madrid: Guillermo Escolar.
O'Leary, Catherine (2021). 'From *littérature engagée* to engaged translation: Staging Jean-Paul Sartre's theatre as a challenge to Franco's rule in Spain', *Perspectives*, 29(1), 124–40.
Oliva, César (1989). *El teatro desde 1936*. Madrid: Alhambra.
Oliva, César (2013). 'La escena universitaria española', *Anales de la Literatura Española Contemporánea*, 38(1–2), 239–54.
Ollé, Joan (2014). 'Todo empezó en la parroquia', *El Periódico*, 19 September 2014, *www.elperiodico.com/es/cuaderno/20140919/todo-empezo-en-la-parroquia-3535500*.
Olmo, Lauro (1997). *La camisa; El cuarto poder*. Madrid: Cátedra.
Olmo, Lauro (2004). *Teatro*, vol. 1. Madrid: AAT.
Olmo, Teresa del (2019). Unpublished interview with Michael Thompson for the *Theatre Censorship in Spain* project (23 May 2019).
Ordóñez, Marcos (2010). 'Las muchas vidas del crítico y escritor Enrique Llovet', *El País*, 26 August 2010, *http://elpais.com/diario/2010/08/26/necrologicas/1282773602_850215.html*.
Ordóñez, Marcos (2016). 'Aquel *Marat-Sade* del 68', *El País*, 3 May 2016, *http://elpais.com/diario/2007/05/03/cultura/1178143209_850215.html*.
Orriols, Álvaro de (2000). 'Curriculum vitae', *Renacimiento*, 27–30, 151–3.
Ortuño Anaya, Pilar (2001). 'The EEC, the Franco regime, and the Socialist group in the European Parliament, 1962–1977', *International Journal of Iberian Studies*, 14(1), 26–39.
Otero Urtaza, Eugenio, and María García Alonso (2006). 'Cronología' in Eugenio Otero Urtaza (ed.), *Las Misiones Pedagógicas 1931–1936*. Madrid: Sociedad Estatal de Conmemoraciones Culturales/Residencia de Estudiantes, pp. 33–59.
Paco, Mariano de (ed.) (1984). *Estudios sobre Buero Vallejo*. Murcia: Universidad de Murcia.

Paco, Mariano de (1993). 'Alfonso Sastre y *Arte Nuevo*' in Mariano de Paco (ed.), *Alfonso Sastre*. Murcia: Universidad de Murcia, pp. 129–39.
Paco, Mariano de (2010). *El teatro de los hermanos Álvarez Quintero*. Murcia: Universidad de Murcia/Editum.
Paco, Mariano de (2019). 'Cronología de Alfonso Sastre', *Biblioteca Virtual Miguel de Cervantes, www.cervantesvirtual.com/portales/alfonso_sastre/*.
Panse, Barbara, and Meg Mumford (1996). 'Censorship in Nazi Germany: The Influence of the Reich's Ministry of Propaganda on German Theatre and Drama, 1933–1945' in Berghaus, Günter (ed.), *Fascism and Theatre: Comparative Studies on the Aesthetics and Politics of Performance in Europe, 1925–1945*. Providence RI: Berghahn, pp. 140–56.
Parker, Jason T. (2010). 'Recruiting the Literary Tradition: Lope de Vega's *Fuenteovejuna* as Cultural Weapon during the Spanish Civil War', *Bulletin of the Comediantes*, 62(1), 123–43.
Pasquariello, Anthony (1983). 'Government Promotion, Honours and Awards: A Corollary to Franco Era Censorship in Theater', *Cuadernos de ALDEEU*, 1 (Monograph on Twentieth Century Spanish Theatre, no. 1), 67–81.
Pavlović, Tatiana (2011). *The Mobile Nation: España cambia de piel (1954–1964)*. Bristol/Chicago: Intellect.
Payá Beltrán, José (2018). *Alfonso Paso, autor*. Sant Vicent del Raspeig: Universitat d'Alacant.
Payne, Stanley G. (2012). *The Spanish Civil War*. Cambridge: Cambridge University Press.
Paz Gago, José María (2012). *La revolución espectacular: El teatro de Valle-Inclán en la escena mundial*. Madrid: Castalia.
Pemán, José María (1937). '*Almoneda*: Autocrítica', *ABC* (Sevilla), 8 April 1937, p. 11.
Pemán, José María et al. (1960). 'El problema de la censura', *Boletín Informativo, Centro de Documentación y de Estudios* (Paris), 4, 15–17. *Filosofía en Español* (2012), *www.filosofia.org/hem/dep/clc/bicde04j.htm*.
Peral Vega, Emilio (2012). '*Altavoz del frente*: una experiencia multidisciplinar durante la Guerra Civil española', *Hispanic Research Journal*, 13(3), 234–49.
Pérez, Janet (1989). 'Fascist Models and Literary Subversion: Two Fictional Modes in Postwar Spain', *South Central Review*, 6(2), 73–87.
Pérez, Janet (2010). 'El teatro de GTB' in Carmen Becerra (ed.), *Los mundos de Gonzalo Torrente Ballester*, vol. 2: *Aproximaciones a la obra de Gonzalo Torrente Ballester*. Madrid: Ministerio de Cultura/Sociedad Estatal de Conmemoraciones Culturales, pp. 47–65.
Pérez, Manuel (1998). *El teatro de la transición política (1975–1982)*. Kassel: Reichenberger.
Pérez-Bowie, José Antonio (2010). 'Torrente Ballester, teórico y crítico del teatro' in Carmen Becerra (ed.), *Los mundos de Gonzalo Torrente*

Ballester, vol. 2: *Aproximaciones a la obra de Gonzalo Torrente Ballester*. Madrid: Ministerio de Cultura/Sociedad Estatal de Conmemoraciones Culturales, pp. 67–85.

Pérez-Domenech, José (1933). 'Hablan los jovenes autores: Rafael Alberti dice que la burguesía tiene el teatro que se merece', *El Imparcial*, 23 April 1933, p. 6.

Pérez Ferrero, Miguel (1934). 'Yerma, en el público', *El Heraldo de Madrid*, 31 December 1934, p. 4.

Pérez López de Heredia, María (2004). *Traducciones censuradas de teatro norteamericano en la España de Franco (1939–1963)*. Bilbao: Universidad del País Vasco.

Pérez Minik, Domingo (1957). 'Libertad y compromiso en el drama moderno', *Primer Acto*, 2, 8–9.

Pérez-Montaner, Jaume (1977). 'Una aproximación al teatro de la guerra civil española', *Cuadernos Americanos*, 5, 169–76.

Pérez-Rasilla, Eduardo, and Guadalupe Soria Tomás (2011). 'El primer estreno de *Los cuernos de don Friolera* en la España franquista, por el TEU de Madrid, bajo la dirección de Juan José Alonso Millán, en 1958', *Don Galán: Revista de Investigación Teatral* 1, http://teatro.es/contenidos/donGalan/pagina.php?vol=1&doc=1_3.

Pérez Zalduondo, Gemma (2011). 'Música, censura y Falange: el control de la actividad musical desde la Vicesecretaría de Educación Popular (1941–1945)', *Arbor*, 751, 876–86, http://arbor.revistas.csic.es/index.php/arbor/article/view/1357/1366.

Pine, Lisa (2017). *Hitler's 'National Community': Society and Culture in Nazi Germany*, 2nd ed. London: Bloomsbury.

Piscator, Erwin (1930). *El teatro político*. Madrid: Cenit.

Plaza Plaza, Antonio (2010). 'El teatro y compromiso en la obra de Luisa Carnés', *Acotaciones*, 25, 95–122.

Pombo Ángulo, Manuel (1961). 'Inauguración del Teatro Bellas Artes con *Divinas palabras*, de don Ramón María del Valle-Inclán: Nota crítica de la representación', *La Vanguardia Española*, 19 November 1961, p. 9.

Pons, Ventura (2011). *Els meus (i els altres)*. Barcelona: Proa.

Popkin, Louise B. (1975). *The Theatre of Rafael Alberti*. London: Tamesis.

Pörtl, Klaus (ed.) (1986). *Reflexiones sobre el Nuevo Teatro Español*. Tübingen: Max Niemeyer.

Post, Robert C. (ed.) (1998). *Censorship and Silencing: Practices of Cultural Regulation*. Los Angeles: The Getty Research Institute for the History of Art and the Humanities.

Pou, José María (2000). 'Una vision personal: José Luis Alonso', *ADE Teatro*, 82, 297–302.

Pou, Josep Maria (2010). Unpublished interview with Michael Thompson for the *Theatre Censorship in Spain* project (10 December 2010).

Preston, Paul (1986). *The Triumph of Democracy in Spain*. London: Routledge.
Preston, Paul (1993). *Franco: A Biography*. New York: Harper Collins.
Preston, Paul (1994). *The Coming of the Spanish Civil War: Reform, Reaction and Revolution in the Second Republic*. London: Routledge.
Preston, Paul (2012). *The Spanish Holocaust: Inquisition and Extermination in Twentieth-Century Spain*. London: Harper Press.
Primer Acto (1961–2). 'Encuesta (sobre el teatro)', *Primer Acto*, 29–30, 5–15.
Primer Acto (1968). 'Coloquio sobre el naturalismo, el costumbrismo, el sainete y el futuro de nuestro teatro', *Primer Acto*, 102, 20–9.
Primer Acto (1971). '1971: así piensan 40 profesionales de la escena española sobre censura, teatro social y teatro político en España', *Primer Acto*, 131, 8–24.
Primer Acto (1974a). 'Encuesta sobre la censura: 25 autores cuentan sus experiencias con la censura', *Primer Acto*, 165, 4–14.
Primer Acto (1974b). 'Encuesta sobre la censura: otros 14 autores cuentan sus experiencias', *Primer Acto*, 166, 4–11.
Primer Acto (1974c). 'Cinco preguntas a autores que estrenaron', *Primer Acto*, 170–1, 13–23.
Primer Acto (1974d). 'Teatro último de Rodríguez Méndez', *Primer Acto*, 173, 10–11.
Primo de Rivera, José Antonio (1976). *Discursos y escritos: Obras completas (1922–1936)*, ed. Agustín del Río Cisneros. Madrid: Instituto de Estudios Políticos. Reproduced in *Obras completas de José Antonio, www.rumbos.net/ocja/jaoc0075.html*.
Puig, Joaquín (1965). '*El círculo de tiza caucasiano* por el Teatro Nacional Universitario', *Primer Acto*, 64, 53.
Pulpillo Leiva, Carlos (2014). 'La configuración de la propaganda en la España nacional (1936–1941)', *La Albolafia: Revista de Humanidades y Cultura*, 1, 115–36.
Quinto, José María de (1960). '5 notas al margen de *Un sabor a miel*', *Primer Acto*, 17, 20–2.
Quinto, José María de (1986). 'Sobre el verdadero estreno en España de *La casa de Bernarda Alba*', *Insula: Revista de letras y ciencias humanas*, 476–7, 8.
Quiroga, Alejandro (2012). 'Miguel Primo de Rivera: Overture to Franco' in Alejandro Quiroga and Miguel Ángel del Arco (eds), *Right-Wing Spain in the Civil War Era: Soldiers of God and Apostles of the Fatherland, 1914–45*. London/New York: Continuum, pp. 27–59.
Quirós Alpera, Gabriel (2013). *José Luis Alonso. Historia de la dirección escénica en España*. Madrid: Fundamentos.
RAE/CGPJ (2016). *Diccionario del español jurídico*. Madrid: Real Academia Española/Consejo General del Poder Judicial, *https://dej.rae.es/*.

Ragué Arias, María José (1992). *Lo que fue Troya. Los mitos griegos en el teatro español actual*. Madrid: Asociación de Autores de Teatro.
Ragué Arias, María José (1996). *El teatro fin de milenio en España (De 1975 hasta hoy)*. Barcelona: Ariel.
Ramiro de la Mata, Javier (2018). 'Fermín Galán Rodríguez' in Real Academia de la Historia, *Diccionario Biográfico electrónico*, http://dbe.rah.es/biografias/10038/fermin-galan-rodriguez.
Rancière, Jacques (1999). *Disagreement: Politics and Philosophy*, trans. Julie Rose. Minneapolis/London: University of Minnesota Press.
Rancière, Jacques (2004). *The Politics of Aesthetics*, trans. Gabriel Rockhill. London: Continuum.
Rey Faraldos, Gloria (1992). 'El teatro de las Misiones Pedagógicas', in Dougherty and Vilches de Frutos (eds), *El teatro en España: Entre la tradición y la vanguardia. 1918–1939*. Madrid: CSIC/Fundacion Federico Garcia Lorca/Tabacalera, pp. 153–64.
Reyes, Gabriel de los (1984). 'Comentarios de Buero Vallejo sobre su teatro', *Estreno*, 10(1), 21–4.
Reyes, José Manuel (2017). 'Teología de la información y doctrina de la censura: *La llanura* (1947, 1954), de José Martín Recuerda, y *Diálogos de la herejía* (1961, 1964), de Agustín Gómez-Arcos', *Anales de la Literatura Española Contemporánea*, 42(2), 405–26.
Richards, Michael (1998). *A Time of Silence: Civil War and the Culture of Repression in Franco's Spain, 1936–1945*. Cambridge: Cambridge University Press.
Rico, Francisco, and Domingo Ynduráin (1981). *Historia crítica de la literatura española, VIII: Época contemporánea, 1939–1980*. Barcelona: Crítica.
Ridruejo, Dionisio (1976). *Casi unas memorias*. Barcelona: Planeta.
Ródenas, Miguel (1940). 'Notas teatrales: El estreno de *Aves y pájaros* constituyó otro gran éxito de Benavente en Lara', *ABC*, 31 October 1940, p. 7.
Rodrigo, Antonina (1974). *Margarita Xirgu y su teatro*. Barcelona: Planeta.
Rodríguez, Juan Carlos (2009). 'Notas sobre el teatro en la Segunda República' in José Luis Casas Sánchez and Francisco Durán Alcalá (eds), *1931–1936. De la República democrática a la sublevación militar: Actas del IV Congreso sobre Republicanismo*. Córdoba: Diputación de Córdoba/Universidad de Córdoba, pp. 193–216.
Rodríguez, Carlos (2000). 'Adolfo Marsillach, o la pasión teatral', *ADE Teatro*, 82, 303–6.
Rodríguez Espinosa, Marcos (1997). 'Editores y traductores difusores de la historia literaria: El caso de Arturo de Hoyo en la editorial Aguilar', *TRANS*, 2, 153–64.
Rodríguez-Gago, Antonia (2010). 'Staging Beckett in Spain: Theater and Politics' in S. E. Gontarski (ed.), *A Companion to Samuel Beckett*. London: Wiley-Blackwell, pp. 403–15.

Rodríguez Méndez, José María (1974a). *La incultura teatral en España*. Barcelona: Laia.
Rodríguez Méndez, José María (1974b). 'Conmigo mismo', *Primer Acto*, 173, 14–16.
Rodríguez Puértolas, Julio (1986). *Literatura fascista española*. Madrid: Akal.
Rodríguez Puértolas, Julio (2003). 'El teatro fascista durante la Guerra civil', *ADE Teatro*, 97, 150–8.
Rodríguez Puértolas, Julio (2008). *Historia de la literatura fascista española*, 2nd ed., vol. 1. Madrid: Akal.
Rodríguez Puértolas, Julio (2009). 'Guerra civil, fascismo y teatro (1936–1939)', *Teatro: Revista de Estudios Culturales*, 23, 93–103, *https://digitalcommons.conncoll.edu/teatro/vol23/iss23/14*.
Rodríguez Solás, David (2013). 'The New Angulo el Malo's Company: Misiones Pedagógicas and the Teatro del Pueblo', *Anales de la Literatura Española Contemporánea*, 38(3), 785–812.
Rodríguez Solás, David (2014). *Teatros Nacionales Republicanos. La Segunda República y el teatro clásico español*. Madrid/Frankfurt: Iberoamericana/Vervuert.
Rodríguez Solás, David (2017). 'Dagoll Dagom's *No hablaré en clase*, a Postdramatic Response to Francoism' in Diego Santos Sánchez (ed.), *Theatre and Dictatorship in the Luso-Hispanic World*. New York: Routledge, pp. 140–54.
Rodríguez Tejada, Sergio (2014). 'Surveillance and student dissent: The case of the Franco dictatorship', *Surveillance and Society*, 12(4), 528–46, *www.surveillance-and-society.org*.
Roig i Llop, Tomàs (2005). *El meu viatge per la vida 1939–1975*. Barcelona: Abadia de Montserrat.
Romero Cabrera, Alejandro (2012). 'Breve biografía de Julio Vélez'. Blog: *Julio Vélez (. . .y alrededores)*, 19 October 2012, *http://juliovelez1946.blogspot.com/2012/10/breve-biografia-de-julio-velez.html*.
Romero Salvadó, Francisco J. (2013). *Historical Dictionary of the Spanish Civil War*. Lanham/Toronto/Plymouth: Scarecrow.
Rudnick, David (1976). 'Spain's Long Road to Europe', *The World Today*, 32(4), 134–41.
Ruibal, José (1969). 'Sobre el estreno de mis obras en café-teatro', *Primer Acto*, 112, 60.
Ruibal, José (1977a). 'Crónica descocada o no sé si teoría de la venganza' in José Ruibal, *El hombre y la mosca*. Madrid: Fundamentos, pp. 5–21.
Ruibal, José (1977b). *El hombre y la mosca*. Madrid: Fundamentos.
Ruibal, José (1984). 'Introducción' in José Ruibal, *Teatro sobre teatro*. Madrid: Cátedra, pp. 11–46.
Ruiz Carnicer, Miguel Ángel (1996). *El Sindicato Español Universitario (SEU), 1939–1965: La socialización política de la juventud universitaria en el franquismo*. Madrid: Siglo Veintiuno.

Ruiz Ramón, Francisco (1989). *Historia del teatro español: Siglo XX*, 8th ed. Madrid: Cátedra.
Rundle, Christopher, and Kate Sturge (2010). 'Translation and the History of Fascism' in Christopher Rundle and Kate Sturge (eds), *Translation under Fascism*. London: Palgrave, pp. 3–12.
S. (1936). 'Escena y bastidores. Teatro Español: Presentación de Nueva Escena, compañía de la Alianza de Intelectuales Antifascistas', *El Sol*, 21 October 1936, p. 3.
Sala Valldaura, Josep Maria (2012). 'Popular theatre and the Spanish stage, 1737–1798' in Maria M. Delgado and David T. Gies (eds), *A History of Theatre in Spain*. Cambridge: Cambridge University Press, pp. 134–56.
Salazar López, José María (1966). *Diccionario legislativo de cinematografía y teatro*. Madrid: Editora Nacional.
Salguero Rodríguez, José María (1996). 'El primer Sender (1916–1939) y sus textos teatrales', *Anales de la Literatura Española Contemporánea*, 21(3), 351–64.
Salvat, Ricard (1975). 'De *El adefesio* a *Noche de guerra en el Museo del Prado*', *Primer Acto*, 178, 11–17.
Salvat, Ricard, and August Coll (2001). 'Entrevista a Alberto González Vergel (Madrid, 22 de mayo de 2001)', *Assaig de teatre: revista de l'Associació d'Investigació i Experimentació Teatral*, 26–7, 275–86, www.raco.cat/index.php/AssaigTeatre/issue/view/11680.
SAM (1937a). 'Espectáculos: Los teatros y la revolución', *ABC*, 8 April 1937, p. 14.
SAM (1937b). 'Espectáculos: Los teatros y la revolución. Habla el presidente de la Junta de Espectáculos', *ABC*, 11 April 1937, pp. 13–14.
SAM (1937c). 'Acuerdos de la Junta de Espectáculos', *ABC*, 9 May 1937, pp. 13–14.
SAM (1937d). 'Maravillas: *Tatí, Tatí*', *ABC*, 15 October 1937, p. 6.
SAM (1937e). 'Suspensión del Comité de Lectura', *ABC*, 16 October 1937, p. 6.
Samaniego, Fernando (1977). 'José Ruibal estrenará su obra *El hombre y la mosca*. Estaba retenida por la censura desde 1968', *El País*, 10 February 1977, https://elpais.com/diario/1977/02/11/cultura/224463602_850215.html.
Sánchez Sánchez, Juan Pedro (2006). '*La señorita de Trevélez*: tragedia grotesca de Carlos Arniches', *Revista de Filología*, 24, 225–36.
Santiago Muñoz, Fernando (2006). 'El Pemán franquista', *El País*, 31 July, http://elpais.com/diario/2006/07/31/andalucia/1154298128_850215.html.
Santolaria, Cristina (2004). 'Bibliografía' in Lauro Olmo, *Teatro*, vol. 1. Madrid: AAT, pp. 53–77.

Santos Sánchez, Diego (2009). 'El teatro de Lorca y la censura franquista: *La casa de Bernarda Alba*' in Jesús G. Maestro (ed.), *Federico García Lorca y el teatro (Theatralia* 11). Vigo: Editorial Academia del Hispanismo, pp. 113–25.
Santos Sánchez, Diego (2011a). '*Mariana Pineda*'s Struggle against Censorship', *Bulletin of Hispanic Studies*, 88(8), 931–44.
Santos Sánchez, Diego (2011b). 'La historia silenciada: el descubrimiento de América y la censura teatral franquista', *Neophilologus*, 95, 79–93.
Santos Sánchez, Diego (2013a). 'El fracaso del proyecto teatral falangista' in Miguel Ángel Ruiz Carnicer (ed.), *Falange, las culturas políticas del fascismo en la España de Franco (1936–1975)*, vol. 2, pp. 564–77.
Santos Sánchez, Diego (2013b). 'Dramaturgas y censura en el primer franquismo: Pilar Millán Astray y Julia Maura', *Revista Canadiense de Estudios Hispánicos*, 37(2), 319–38.
Santos Sánchez, Diego (2013c). 'Staging *la España eterna*: Rise and Fall of the National-Catholic Theatrical Canon in the Civil War Aftermath', *Modern Language Review*, 108(4), 1156–76.
Santos Sánchez, Diego (2016). 'Exilio, reescritura y censura: *La lozana andaluza* de Rafael Alberti', *Estreno*, 42(1), 64–94.
Saporiti, Piero T. (1950). 'Spain: A Window Closes', *Time*, 3 April 1950, p. 26.
Sartre, Jean-Paul (1973). *Un Théâtre de situations*, ed. Michel Contat and Michel Rybalka. Paris: Gallimard.
Sastre, Alfonso (1953). 'Autocrítica de *Escuadra hacia la muerte*', *El Alcázar*, 18 March 1953. Centro de Documentación de las Artes Escénicas y de la Música, www.teatro.es/estrenos-teatro/escuadra-hacia-la-muerte-7451/documentos-on-line/prensa.
Sastre, Alfonso (1960). 'Teatro imposible y pacto social', *Primer Acto*, 14, 1–2.
Sastre, Alfonso (1961–2). 'Teatro para el año nuevo', *Primer Acto*, 29–30, 26–7.
Sastre, Alfonso (1966). *Obras completas*. Madrid: Aguilar.
Sastre, Alfonso (1967). 'Autocrítica', *ABC*, 19 October 1967, p. 3.
Sastre, Alfonso (1974). *Anatomía del realismo*, 2nd ed. Barcelona: Seix Barral (Biblioteca Breve).
Sastre, Alfonso (1987). 'Teoría del teatro: el estado de la cuestión', *Gestos*, 4, 37–46.
Sastre, Alfonso (2001). *En la red*, 2nd ed. Hondarribia: Hiru.
Sastre, Alfonso (1990). 'Una nota actual: No sólo es Guillermo Tell' in Alfonso Sastre, *Guillermo Tell tiene los ojos tristes*. Hondarribia: Hiru, pp. 4–5.
Sastre, Alfonso (1992a). *Teatro de Vanguardia*. Hondarribia: Hiru.
Sastre, Alfonso (1992b). *El pan de todos*. Hondarribia: Hiru.

Schwartz, Kessel (1965). 'Culture and the Spanish Civil War – A Fascist View: 1936–1939', *Journal of Inter-American Studies*, 7(4), 557–77.
Schwartz, Kessel (1968). '*Posibilismo* and *Imposibilismo*. The Buero Vallejo-Sastre Polemic', *Revista Hispánica Moderna*, 34(1–2), 436–45.
Sender, Ramón J. (1931). *Teatro de masas*. Valencia: Orto.
Serrano, Eugenia (1961). 'Actualidad de la tortura', *Pueblo*, p. 3. Contained in AGA file on Alfonso Sastre, *En la red* (AGA 260/60).
Serrano Anguita, F. (1939). 'Ante los autores que cayeron. "Y somos hoy, porque ellos fueron antes!"', *Informaciones* (Madrid), 23 May 1939. Centro de Documentación de las Artes Escénicas y de la Música: *Documentos para la historia del teatro*, http://teatro.es/contenidos/documentosParaLaHistoria/Docs1939/documentos.php?tema=1&sec=1.
Sirera, Josep Lluís (2008). 'El teatre al País Valencià' in Francesc Foguet i Boreu (ed.), *Teatre en temps de guerra i revolució (1936–1939)*. Barcelona: Punctum/Generalitat de Catalunya, pp. 153–67.
Soler Carnicer, José (2007). *Valencia pintoresca y tradicional, 2*. Valencia: Carena.
Sotomayor Sáez, María Victoria (1998). *Teatro, público y poder: la obra dramática del último Arniches*. Madrid: Ediciones de la Torre.
Sotomayor Sáez, María Victoria (2001). 'Incidencia de la censura en el teatro de Carlos Arniches' in Marieta Santos Casenave and Alberto Romero Ferrer (eds), *El teatro de humor en la guerra y la posguerra española (1936–1948)*. Cádiz: Fundación Pedro Muñoz Seca/Universidad de Cádiz, pp. 183–91.
Surwillo, Lisa (2007). *The Stages of Property: Copyrighting Theatre in Spain*. Toronto: University of Toronto Press.
Surwillo, Lisa (2012). 'Copyright, buildings, spaces and the nineteenth-century stage' in Maria M. Delgado and David T. Gies (eds), *A History of Theatre in Spain*. Cambridge: Cambridge University Press, pp. 244–63.
Tábano and Las Madres del Cordero (2006). *Castañuela 70: esto era España, señores*, ed. Santiago Trancón. Madrid: Rama Lama Music.
Teatro La Latina (2018). 'Ficha técnica', *Teatro La Latina: El teatro*, www.teatrolalatina.es/el-teatro.
Thomas, Hugh (2013). *The Spanish Civil War*, revised ed. London: Penguin.
Thompson, Michael (1993). 'El mito del Descubrimiento y el descubrimiento del mito en el teatro español contemporáneo' in Alan Deyermond and Ralph Penny (eds), *Actas del Primer Congreso Anglo-Hispano*, vol. 2: *Literatura*. Madrid: Castalia, pp. 261–71.
Thompson, Michael (2004). 'Rodríguez Méndez en el laberinto de la censura: el confuso expediente sobre *Historia de unos cuantos*', *Estreno*, 30(1), 19–27.

Thompson, Michael (2007a). *Performing Spanishness: History, Cultural Identity and Censorship in the Theatre of José María Rodríguez Méndez*. Bristol: Intellect.
Thompson, Michael (2007b). '"Una cosa ofensiva": la vanguardia teatral española frente a la censura (el caso de *El hombre y la mosca*)' in Héctor Brioso and José Saval (eds), *Nuevas aportaciones a los estudios teatrales (del Siglo de Oro a nuestros días)* (Alcalá de Henares: Universidad de Alcalá), pp. 87–98.
Thompson, Michael (2016). 'Conclusion: The Power of Theatre' in Catherine O'Leary, Diego Santos Sánchez and Michael Thompson (eds), *Global Insights on Theatre Censorship*. New York/Abingdon: Routledge, pp. 259–67.
Thompson, Michael (2018). '"La totalidad de la obra se representará en perfecto castellano": Censorship of theatre in Catalonia after the civil war' in Lloyd Hughes Davies, John B. Hall and David Gareth Walters (eds), *Catalan Culture: Experimentation, Creative Imagination and the Relationship with Spain*. Cardiff: University of Wales Press, pp. 35–59.
Torreblanca López, Agustín (1995). 'Fuentes documentales para la historia del control administrativo de la representación de obras teatrales (1939–1985)', *Signo: Revista de Historia de la Cultura Escrita*, 2, 77–98.
Torrente Ballester, Gonzalo (1937). 'Razón y ser de la dramática futura', *Jerarquía*, 2, 61–80. Reproduced in Luis Miguel Gómez Díaz, *Teatro para una guerra (1936–1939): Textos y documentos*. Madrid: Centro de Documentación Teatral, 2006 (CD-ROM).
Torrente Ballester, Gonzalo (1953). 'Teatro. María Guerrero. Estreno de *Escuadra hacia la muerte*', *Arriba*, 19 March 1953. Centro de Documentación de las Artes Escénicas y de la Música, *www.teatro.es/estrenos-teatro/escuadra-hacia-la-muerte-7451/documentos-on-line/prensa*.
Torrente Ballester, Gonzalo (1957). *Panorama de la literatura española contemporánea*. Madrid: Guadarrama.
Torres Nebrera, Gregorio (1986). 'Construcción y sentido del teatro de Carlos Muñiz', *Anuario de Estudios Filológicos*, 9, 295–316, *http://hdl.handle.net/10662/3322*.
Torres Nebrera, Gregorio (1991–2). 'María Teresa León: Los espacios de la memoria', *DRACO: Revista de literatura española*, 3–4, 349–78.
Torres Nebrera, Gregorio (2003). 'María Teresa León y la Guerra Civil española (De teatro y otros textos)', *ADE Teatro*, 97, 16–24.
Torres Nebrera, Gregorio (2005). 'El teatro español en el ultimo quinquenio del Franquismo (1971–1975)' in Víctor García Ruiz and Gregorio Torres Nebrera (eds), *Historia y Antología del teatro español de posguerra (1940–1975)*, vol. VII: *1971–1975*. Madrid: Fundamentos, pp. 11–158.

Torres Nebrera, Gregorio (2013). 'Las memorias teatrales de José Gordón: "Arte Nuevo" y "La Carátula", *Don Galán*, 3, 2(1), http://teatro.es/contenidos/donGalan/donGalanNum3/pagina.php?vol=3&doc=2_1.
Toulet, Paul-Jean (1929). *Les Contrerimes: Poèmes*. Paris: Émile-Paul Frères.
Townson, Nigel (2000a). *The Crisis of Democracy in Spain: Centrist Politics under the Second Republic, 1931–1936*. Brighton/Portland OR: Sussex Academic Press.
Townson, Nigel (2000b). 'La ruptura de un consenso: los escándalos "Straperlo" y "Tayá"', *Historia y política*, 4, 31–42.
Townson, Nigel (2007). 'Introduction' in Nigel Townson (ed.), *Spain Transformed: The Franco Dictatorship, 1959–1975*. Houndmills/New York: Palgrave Macmillan, pp. 1–29.
Trancón, Santiago (2006). 'Primer acto: De un tiempo y un país' in Tábano and Las Madres del Cordero, *Castañuela 70: esto era España, señores*. Madrid: Rama Lama Music, pp. 15–131.
Trapiello, Andrés (2010). *Las armas y las letras. Literatura y Guerra Civil (1936–1939)*, Barcelona: Destino.
Tymoczko, Maria (2007). *Enlarging Translation, Empowering Translators*. Manchester: St Jerome.
Tymoczko, Maria (2009). 'Censorship and Self-Censorship in Translation: Ethics and Ideology, Resistance and Collusion' in Eiléan Ní Chuilleanáin, Cormac Ó Cuilleanáin and David Parris (eds), *Translation and Censorship: Patterns of Communication and Interference*. Dublin: Four Courts Press, pp. 24–45.
Tymoczko, Maria (2010). 'Translation, Resistance, Activism: An Overview' in Maria Tymoczko (ed.), *Translation, Resistance, Activism*. Amherst/Boston MA: University of Massachusetts Press, pp. 1–22.
Ucelay, Margarita (2007). 'Introducción' in Federico García Lorca, *Amor de Don Perlimplín con Belisa en su jardín*. Madrid: Cátedra, pp. 9–248.
US Department of State (1957). 'Military Facilities in Spain: Agreement Between the United States and Spain, September 26, 1953' in *American Foreign Policy 1950–1955*. Washington DC: US Government Printing Office. Reproduced in *The Avalon Project* (Lillian Goldman Law Library, Yale University, 2008), http://avalon.law.yale.edu/20th_century/sp1953.asp.
Valbuena Prat, Ángel (1956). *Historia del teatro español*. Barcelona: Noguer.
Valdés, Roberto (1938). 'Los comediógrafos y la República', *Mi Revista* (Barcelona), 1 December 1938, p. 15
Vandaele, Jeroen (2010). 'It Was What it Wasn't: Translation and Francoism' in Christopher Rundle and Kate Sturge (eds), *Translation under Fascism*. London: Palgrave, pp. 84–116.
Vanguardia (1938). 'Notas teatrales: Inauguración de la temporada en el Parthenon', *La Vanguardia*, 17 September 1938, p. 5.

Bibliography 495

Vanguardia (1939a). 'Servicio Nacional de Propaganda: Actividades del Teatro, Música, Espectáculos', *La Vanguardia Española*, 9 February 1939, p. 5.
Vanguardia (1939b). 'Los teatros: Nota del Departamento Nacional de Teatro', *La Vanguardia Española*, 8 March 1939, p. 3.
Vanguardia (1939c). 'En el Barcelona: *María Magdalena*, comedia gitana en tres actos y prólogo, original de Rafael de León, con ilustraciones musicales del maestro Quiroga', *La Vanguardia*, 14 May 1939, p. 6.
Vanguardia (1939d). 'Gobierno Civil: Sobre la representación de obras navideñas religioso-teatrales', *La Vanguardia Española*, 31 December 1939, p. 3.
Vanguardia (1940). 'TIVOLI – *Y el Imperio volvía*...', *La Vanguardia Española*, 13 April 1940, p. 6.
Vanguardia (1943). 'Cartelera: Teatros', *La Vanguardia Española*, 22 May 1943, p. 5.
Vanguardia (1946). 'Cartelera: Teatros', *La Vanguardia Española*, 14 May 1946, p. 11.
Vanguardia (1977). 'Reivindicada por la Triple A: Bomba, sin heridos y con daños, en la Sala Villarroel', *La Vanguardia Española*, 8 February 1977, p. 19.
Venuti, Lawrence (1995). *The Translator's Invisibility*. New York: Routledge.
Venuti, Lawrence (2008). 'Translation, simulacra, resistance', *Translation Studies*, 1(1), 18–33.
Vicente Hernando, César de (1999). 'Concepto y tendencias del teatro revolucionario y de agitación social entre 1900 y 1939', *ADE Teatro*, 77, 133–43.
Vicente Hernando, César de (ed.) (2013). *Una generación perdida. El tiempo de la literatura de avanzada (1925–1935)*. Doral FL: Stockcero.
Vicente Mosquete, José Luis (1988). 'Alfonso Sastre: un largo viaje desde Madrid a Euskadi', *Cuadernos El Público*, 38, 5–27.
Vieites, Manuel F. (2014). 'La educación teatral: nuevos caminos en historia de la educación', *Historia de la Educación: Revista Interuniversitaria*, 33, 325–50.
Vila-San Juan, Pablo (1964). 'Barcelona al día', *ABC*, 14 January 1964, p. 42.
Vila-San Juan, Pablo (1971). 'La semana teatral en Barcelona', *ABC*, 4 August 1971, pp. 51–2.
Vila-Sanjuán, Sergio (2011). 'Cuando Tuset era una "street"', *La Vanguardia*, 13 February 2011, p. 51.
Vilches de Frutos, María Francisca (1995). 'El Teatro Nacional de Cámara y Ensayo. Auge de los grupos de teatro independiente (1960–1975)' in Andrés Peláez (ed.), *Historia de los Teatros Nacionales (1960–1985)*. Madrid: Centro de Documentación Teatral, pp. 127–50.

Vilches de Frutos, María Francisca (1998). 'Directors of the Twentieth-century Spanish Stage' in Maria Delgado (ed.), *Spanish Theatre 1920–1995*, vol. 2, *Strategies of Protest and Imagination. Contemporary Theatre Review*, 7(3), 1–24.

Vilches de Frutos, María Francisca (1999a). 'La representación en España del teatro de Federico García Lorca durante la década de los sesenta', *Boletín de la Fundación Federico García Lorca*, 25, 80–106.

Vilches de Frutos, María Francisca (1999b). 'La otra vanguardia histórica: cambios sociopolíticos en la narrativa y el teatro español de preguerra (1926–1936)', *Anales de la Literatura Española Contemporánea*, 24(1–2), 243–68.

Vilches de Frutos, Francisca (2008). 'El teatro de Federico García Lorca en la construcción de la identidad colectiva española (1936–1986)', *Anales de la Literatura Española Contemporánea*, 33(2), 283–326.

Vilches de Frutos, María Francisca, and Dru Dougherty, (eds) (1992). *El teatro en España entre la tradición y la vanguardia, 1918–1939*. Madrid: CSIC/Fundacion Federico García Lorca/Tabacalera.

Vilches de Frutos, María Francisca, and Dru Dougherty (1997). *La escena madrileña entre 1926 y 1931: un lustro de transición*. Madrid: Fundamentos.

Villamil-Acera, Rakhel (2014). '¡Qué divertido es divorciarse!: La desentimentalización del divorcio en el teatro madrileño antes y después de la Segunda República', *Hispania*, 97(2), 233–43.

Vincent, Mary (2011 [1996]). *Catholicism in the Second Spanish Republic: Religion and Politics in Salamanca 1930–1936*. Oxford: Oxford University Press.

Vogeley, Nancy (1981). 'Alfonso Sastre on Alfonso Sastre: Interview', *Hispania*, 64(3), 459–65.

V.T. (1933). 'Los estrenos celebrados ayer en los escenarios de Madrid. En el Beatriz *Santa Teresita del Niño Jesús*', *La Voz*, 30 June 1933, p. 3.

Wahnón, Sultana (1996). 'The Theatre Aesthetics of the Falange' in Günter Berghaus (ed.), *Fascism and Theatre: Comparative Studies on the Aesthetics and Politics of Performance in Europe, 1925–1945*. Providence RI/Oxford: Berghahn, pp. 191–209.

Wellwarth, George (1965). *The Theatre of Protest and Paradox: Developments in the Avant-Garde Drama*. London: MacGibbon & Kee.

Wellwarth, George (1969). 'In Spain...', *The Drama Review*, 13(4), 156–7.

Wheeler, Duncan (2020). *Following Franco: Spanish Culture and Politics in Transition, 1962–92*. Manchester: Manchester University Press.

Woods, Michelle (2012). *Censoring Translation: Censorship, Theatre and the Politics of Translation*. London: Continuum.

Ya (1939). 'En breve abrirán sus puertas quince teatros madrileños', *Ya*, 12 April 1939. Reproduced in *DHTE* (*Documentos para la historia del teatro*

español), *www.teatro.es/contenidos/documentosParaLaHistoria/Docs1939/ documentos.php?tema=1&sec=2#*.
Ya (1944). 'Todos los elementos de las revistas teatrales serán sometidos a previa censura', *Ya*, 12 January 1944. Reproduced in *DHTE* (*Documentos para la historia del teatro español*), *http://teatro.es/contenidos/documentosParaLaHistoria/Docs1944/index.html*.
Yorick (1971). 'Con Mario Antolín, nuevo Subdirector General de Teatro', *Yorick*, 49–50, 63–5.
Zatlin Boring, Phyllis (1980a). 'Encuesta sobre el teatro madrileño de los años 70', *Estreno*, 6(1), 11–22.
Zatlin Boring, Phyllis (1980b). 'Theatre in Madrid: The Difficult Transition to Democracy', *Theatre Journal*, 32(4), 459–74.
Zatlin, Phyllis (1994). *Cross-cultural Approaches to Theater: The Spanish-French Connection*. New Jersey/London: Scarecrow Press.
Zatlin, Phyllis (1999). 'Theater and Culture, 1936–1996' in David T. Gies (ed.), *Cambridge Companion to Modern Spanish Culture*. Cambridge: Cambridge University Press, pp. 222–36.
Zozaya, Antonio (1939). 'Bajo el hierro y el fuego: "La censura teatral"', *Nuestra Lucha*, 9 January 1939. Reproduced in Maribel Martínez López (2003), *El Romea y otros teatros de Murcia durante la Guerra Civil*. Murcia: Universidad de Murcia, pp. 174–6.

Index

A

Absurd, Theatre of the 265, 282, 283, 310, 315, 342
Acción Católica (Catholic organisation) 116, 225
Acebo, José María (playwright) 70–1, 430
Adamov, Arthur (playwright) 283
adaptation of foreign plays 34, 327, 330–4, 343–4, 346–9, 368–9, 371
aesthetic criteria for censorship 4, 5, 102–5, 109, 114, 118, 137, 143–4, 162–3, 172, 355, 408, 419
age, classification of productions by 116, 119, 132, 136, 141, 149, 150–1, 189, 192, 193, 213, 225–6, 228, 229, 231, 232, 237, 238, 243, 245, 247, 252, 256, 269, 272, 277, 289, 292, 299, 301, 302, 306, 315, 319, 344, 354, 355, 359, 360, 393–5, 397–9, 401, 417–18
agitprop theatre xxxi, 28, 55–7, 60, 62, 66–9, 327
Agrupació Dramàtica de Barcelona (theatre group) 197–8, 310, 334, 446, 447
Albee, Edward (playwright) 353, 362

Alberti, Rafael (playwright) 16, 18, 29, 39, 52, 55, 60–2, 66–9, 84, 123, 265, 273, 277–82, 398, 428, 429, 430, 436, 440, 441, 445, 459
Albizu Salegui, Antonio (censor) 138, 232, 252, 288, 382, 385–6, 388
Alcocer Bárdena, Francisco (censor) 112
Aldeaseca, Constancio de (censor) 108, 175, 178, 219, 344
Alfonso XIII (King of Spain) 13, 43, 160, 237
Alianza Apostólica Anticomunista (right-wing militant organisation) 381
Alianza de Intelectuales Antifascistas (cultural organisation) 29, 60–1, 67, 69, 83
allegory xxxiii, 173, 296, 300, 399
Alonso, Alberto (actor) xxxiv, 316, 435
Alonso, Francisco (composer) 441
Alonso, José Luis (director) 123, 216, 236, 278, 292, 333, 342, 345–6
Alonso, Justo (director, producer) 226, 240, 244–5, 250, 251, 291–2, 301–2, 366
Alonso de Santos, José Luis (playwright) 316

Alonso Millán, Juan José (playwright, director) 268
Altavoz del Frente (theatre group) 61–2
Altolaguirre, Manuel (director, playwright, poet) 61, 69
Álvarez, José Antonio (director) 63
Álvarez de Cienfuegos, Alberto (playwright) 73
Álvarez Quintero, Joaquín and Serafín (playwrights) 89, 165
Amadeo (King of Spain) 1
amateur theatre 95, 101, 118, 124, 191, 195, 197, 219, 266, 270, 278, 283, 310, 315, 419, 420
Amo, Álvaro del (playwright, translator) 361, 438
Amo y Gilí, Fermín del (censor) 112
Anderson, Maxwell (playwright) 12
Anderson, Robert (playwright) 362
Angélico, Halma (playwright) 74
Anouilh, Jean (playwright) 197, 208, 336, 342, 346
Antolín Paz, Mario (Director General de Espectáculos, theatre director) 124, 139, 189, 258, 281
apertura (opening-up) 114, 122–36, 139, 146, 150, 151, 187, 266, 269, 287, 303, 307, 328, 329, 338, 345, 352, 354, 355, 365, 390, 409
appeals against censorship decisions 28, 101, 113–14, 122, 131–4, 177, 188–9, 229, 240, 267–8, 275, 291–2, 300–2, 308–9, 312, 322, 362–3, 389
Aragonés Daroca, Juan Emilio (censor, critic) 122, 127, 250, 252, 257, 292, 309, 312, 314–15, 319, 322, 387

Arbeloa, Miguel Ángel (censor, Delegado Provincial) 237
Arden, John (playwright) 361, 438
Argamasilla de la Cerda y Elío, Joaquín (Jefe del Departamento de Teatro, Director General de Cinematografía y Teatro) 100, 115, 146–7, 217, 258
Arias Navarro, Carlos (Presidente del Gobierno) 141, 301
Arias-Salgado, Gabriel (Ministro de Información y Turismo) xxv, xxvi, 99, 100, 102, 111, 115, 119, 123, 125, 339, 340, 409
armed forces, involvement in censorship 8–9, 16, 17, 18, 123, 124, 130, 140, 159, 164, 166, 221, 234, 237, 252, 258, 259, 261, 266, 312, 373–4, 384, 386, 389, 397, 399, 402–4, 407
Arniches, Carlos (playwright) 44, 45, 165, 168–9, 441, 444, 490
Arquelladas, Manuel (playwright) 73
Arrabal, Fernando (playwright) 135, 265, 273, 282–9, 350, 382, 411–12, 428, 431, 433, 434, 437, 438, 439, 441, 442
Arrese, José Luis (Secretario General del Movimiento) 111
Arroita-Jáuregui Alonso, Marcelo (censor) 127, 151, 223, 354
Arroyo Herrera, Julia (censor) 394, 398
Artaud, Antonin (playwright, director) 282, 289, 295, 317, 318
Arte Nuevo (theatre group) 254, 282
Artime, Nacho (producer) 141, 363, 430
Artola Barrenechea, José María (censor) 127, 138, 150, 239, 244, 279, 287, 347, 354, 372

Asensio Cabanillas, Carlos (general) 259
Asociación Católica Nacional de Propagandistas (lay Catholic organisation) 88, 100, 111, 115
Asociación de Padres de Familia (Catholic association) 353
Assemblea de Treballadors de l'Espectacle (theatre association) 388
Aub, Max (playwright) 265
audience reactions or participation xxviii–ix, 7, 10, 15, 19, 26, 28, 44–5, 46, 48, 50, 56, 79–83, 129, 130, 133, 134, 140, 145, 148, 151, 156, 159, 174, 178, 180, 185, 189-90, 194, 201, 217, 218, 221, 226, 230, 235, 252, 253, 268, 272, 274, 276, 279, 283, 293–4, 296–7, 301, 309, 316, 317–23, 336, 348, 369, 374–5, 393, 395–6, 397–8, 419–20, 422–4
Audifredd, Jorge (playwright) 417, 446
Aúz Castro, Víctor (censor, theatre director) 127, 188–9
avant-garde theatre xxii, xxxiii–iv, 13, 52–4, 76, 121, 265–6, 282–3, 289, 294, 295, 298, 309, 316, 327, 335, 350, 355, 416
Ayala, Félix (Delegado Provincial) 202–3
Azaila, Juan de (playwright) 187–8, 430
Azaña, Manuel (Presidente de la República Española) 14, 17, 21, 49, 78
Azorín (pseudonym of José Martínez Ruiz) (playwright, novelist) 20, 172, 445
Azpilicueta, Jaime (director, producer) 141, 363, 396, 430

B
Balart, Vicente (playwright, adaptor/translator) 332
Ballesteros, María Paz (actor, director) 278
Banegas, Francisco (theatre manager) 384
Baquero Goyanes, Arcadio (censor) 127, 187, 189, 287, 348
Barba Hernández, Bartolomé (Gobernador Civil de Barcelona) 112, 193–4
Barceló Roselló, Pedro (censor) 127, 138, 240, 250, 252, 290, 292, 301–2, 314–15, 359, 385, 386
Barchino, Paco (playwright) 195
Bardem, Juan Antonio (film and theatre director) 142, 150–1, 235
Basque theatre 6, 23–5, 112, 190–1, 236, 262, 334, 409
Bautista de la Torre, Sebastián (censor) 127, 138, 181, 223, 233, 238, 240, 244, 248, 274, 279, 287, 290, 300, 308, 317, 351, 359, 363, 365, 366, 367, 372, 374
Bayer, Oswald (translator, writer) 372
Beauvoir, Simone de (writer) 355
Becerril Bustamante, Soledad (Ministro de Cultura) 400
Beckett, Samuel (playwright) xxxv, 134, 283, 333, 350–1, 355–6, 429, 431, 432, 437, 438
Begoña, Mauricio de (censor) 108, 113, 145, 200, 214, 216, 218, 356
Behan, Brendan (playwright) 337, 360–1, 431
Benavente, Jacinto (playwright) xxxiii, 11, 40, 52, 157, 165,

172–9, 199–204, 432, 439, 441, 442, 443
Benet i Jornet, Josep Maria (playwright) 296, 297, 314–16, 420, 434, 437, 446
Beneyto Pérez, Juan (censor) 93
Berenguer, Dámaso (Presidente del Consejo de Ministros) 1, 12–13
Bergamín, José (poet, playwright) 60–1
Bergman, Ingmar (film and theatre director) 266
Blajot Pena, Jorge (censor) 127, 223, 224, 355
blasphemy 90, 97, 108, 131, 140, 236, 240, 267, 285, 286, 287, 289, 392, 409
Bleiberg, Germán (playwright) 62
Boadella, Albert (playwright, director) 314, 402–4, 439
Bohr, Daniel (director) 298–301
Bonavia i Panyella, Salvador (playwright) 195
books (censorship of) xxvii–viii, 6, 8, 14, 91, 95, 96, 117, 135–6, 355, 383
Borrás, Eduardo (playwright) 56, 444
Borrás, Enrique (actor, director) 53, 169, 177, 178, 194, 195
Borrás Bermejo, Tomás (director, playwright, Jefe del Sindicato Nacional del Espectáculo) 143, 270
Bourdieu, Pierre (theorist) xxiv, 411
Brecht, Bertolt (playwright, director) xxxv, 126, 134, 136, 141, 197, 208, 231, 282, 295, 303, 334, 335, 336, 345, 347, 353, 356, 358, 365, 367, 370–6
Brossa, Joan (playwright) 191, 310, 311, 446

Buero Vallejo, Antonio (playwright) xxviii, xxxiii, 123, 124, 208, 210–12, 222, 223, 227, 231, 233, 237–9, 242–3, 249–50, 252–3, 273, 333–4, 365, 366–7, 376, 384, 406, 416, 433, 436, 437, 439, 443, 446, 463, 482
Búho, El (theatre group) 381
Bululú, El (theatre group) 220, 348
Buñuel, Luis (film director) 61
Burguet i Ardiaca, Francesc (playwright) 140
Butler, Judith (theorist) xxiv, 411

C
Cabal, Fermín (playwright) 423
Cabala, La (theatre group) 298
Cabanillas Gallas, Pío (Ministro de Información y Turismo, Ministro de Cultura) 139, 390
Cabeza, José María (playwright) 158–9, 433
Calderón de la Barca, Pedro (playwright) 52, 76, 158
Calvo Sotelo, Joaquín (playwright) 62, 89
cámara y ensayo, teatro de (fringe/non-commercial theatre) xxxiv, 102, 118–19, 122, 131, 132, 134–5, 146, 147, 214, 224, 228, 229, 232, 233, 234, 237, 241, 257, 258, 266–9, 271, 278, 283–5, 287, 289, 291, 293, 295, 299, 304, 306, 308–9, 310, 311, 315, 316, 317–19, 322, 328, 330, 343, 344, 352, 354, 356, 360, 362, 364, 366–7, 370, 372, 385, 410, 412, 417, 419–20
Caminals Girbent, Pere Lluís (playwright) 139

Camus, Albert (playwright, novelist) 335, 347, 354, 364, 429, 433, 437, 438, 439, 440
Cano Lechuga, José María (censor) 115, 237
Capmany Maria, Aurèlia (director, playwright) 123, 140, 313, 314, 334
CAPSA (theatre) 278, 310, 311, 312
Caracol, El (theatre group) 11
Carátula, La (theatre group) 142, 145–6
Carballeira, Enriqueta (actor) 316
Carreño España, José (Presidente de la Junta de Espectáculos de Madrid) 29–30
Carrero Blanco, Luis (admiral, Presidente del Gobierno) 124, 125, 137, 376
Carril Gómez, Adolfo (censor) 112, 162, 186, 228
Casali, Renzo (actor, director, adaptor) 359, 436
Casares, María (actor) 278
Casona, Alejandro (playwright) 40, 53, 54–5, 66, 444, 445
Castilla, Alberto (adaptor) 371–2, 374–5,
Castro, Juan Antonio (playwright) 384–5, 400, 441
Castro, Horacio de (playwright, translator) 12
Castro Les, Vicente (playwright) 42, 445
Castronuovo, Julio (actor, director) 351
Catalan theatre xxxi, xxxiii, xxxiv, 5–6, 112, 135, 137, 190–8, 247, 310–16, 334, 365, 385–9, 402–4, 409, 412, 420
Cátaro (theatre group) 303–9, 348, 398, 399, 431, 435, 441

Catena, Víctor Andrés (director) 268
Catholic Church, censorship by xxvii, xxix, xxxi, 2–3, 4, 51, 75, 88, 93, 97, 106, 108, 113–14, 115–17, 123, 126, 127, 145, 147, 150, 151, 171–2, 203, 211, 273, 294, 340, 347, 353–5, 358, 382–3, 396, 404, 408–10
Catholic values xxxii, 13, 18, 32, 35, 40, 49, 62, 63, 74, 78, 87, 88, 89, 93, 97, 98, 108, 115, 117, 121, 124, 128–30, 147, 158, 159–60, 163, 165, 170, 171, 178, 190, 200, 201, 212, 214, 216, 219, 222, 287, 291, 317, 343, 345, 352–63, 382–4, 385, 392, 408–11, 415
see also National-Catholicism
Cavero Lataillade, Íñigo (Ministro de Cultura) 400
Cea Buján, Jesús (censor) 127, 138, 230, 240, 244, 251, 277, 285, 288, 290, 291, 355, 362, 367, 382, 394, 398
censorship in other countries xxvii, 90, 411
censura plástica (censorship of printed or manufactured visual materials) 163–4, 429
Centro Dramático Nacional (national theatre) 249, 271, 360
Cernuda, Luis (poet) 61
Chacel, Rosa (writer) 61
Chaparrieta Torregrosa, Joaquín (politician) 43
Chapman, John (playwright) 383
Chekhov, Anton (playwright) 52, 197
Clemente, Ramón (producer) 238
Cierva, Ricardo de la (Ministro de Cultura) 400
civil war xxi, xxiii, xxvi, xxvii, xxx, xxxi, 1, 20, 21–35, 38, 48,

59–76, 85, 87, 89, 112, 123, 124, 136, 168, 176, 210, 212, 214–15, 226, 230, 231, 235, 241, 251, 254, 257, 265, 300, 310, 339, 354, 398, 407, 415
Clavero Arévalo, Manuel (Ministro de Cultura) 400
Codina, Josep Anton (director) 137, 140, 313
Colsada, Matías (producer) 186–7
Comisión de Calificación de Obras Teatrales 393–7, 399, 400–1
Comisión Permanente de Lectura (section of the Consejo Superior del Teatro) 114, 218, 219, 258
Comissaria d'Espectacles de la Generalitat de Catalunya 22
Comité de Control de Espectáculos Públicos (Madrid) 23, 26
Comité de Moralidad Pública (right-wing organisation) 361
Comité Económico del Teatro/ Comité Econòmic del Teatre (Barcelona) 22, 27, 34, 447
Conde-Salazar y Manzano, José María (censor) 112, 178–9, 282
Confederación Española de Derechas Autónomas (CEDA, political coalition) 17, 41, 47, 50, 78, 85
Confederación Nacional del Trabajo (CNT, anarchist trade union) 22–3, 25–7, 29, 31, 33–4, 72, 74, 85
Consejo Central del Teatro 31–4, 62, 64, 70–1, 73–4, 172
Consejo Superior del Teatro 113, 218, 302, 395
constitutions 3, 6, 8, 14, 41, 399–400
Cooney, Ray (playwright) 383
copyright 1, 2, 4,

costumes xxviii, 12, 50, 68, 102, 116, 119–20, 132, 169, 181–2, 184–90, 221, 243, 252, 261, 311, 317, 336, 352, 259, 402, 403, 416–17, 418, 422
Cova del Drac, La (entertainment venue) 310, 313–14
Coward, Noel (playwright) 338, 339
criteria for censorship xxi, xxxii, 4, 5, 94, 96, 97–8, 102–3, 105–9, 116–17, 128–34, 150, 155, 158, 163–4, 288, 381, 409, 415, 418
Crowley, Mart (playwright) 141, 334, 336, 362–3
Cué, Ramón (playwright) 76, 158, 428

D

Dagoll Dagom (theatre group) 385–8
Delaney, Shelagh (playwright) 208, 359
destape (stripping-off) xxxv, 253, 293–4, 351–2, 361, 368, 382–4, 393
Díaz de Mendoza, Fernando (actor, director) 156, 169
Díaz de la Espina, Jesús (censor) 112
Dido Pequeño Teatro (theatre group) 228–9, 266, 283, 333, 360
Dieste, Rafael (playwright) 29, 40, 60–1, 67–8, 84, 430
Dieterich, Genoveva (translator) 360, 431
Díez Crespo, Manuel (censor) 112, 127, 138, 216, 239, 251, 285, 289, 355
Diosdado, Ana (playwright, actor) 398, 435
Domingo, Marcelino (politician) 49

Domínguez, Florencio (playwright) 57, 445
Durá, María Victoria (actor) 270

E
Echegaray y Eizaguirre, José (playwright) 169–72, 434, 442
Eliot, Thomas Stearns (poet, playwright) 339
Elorriaga Fernández, Gabriel (censor) 124
Escena (theatre group) 267
Escobar, Luis (director, actor, producer, Jefe del Departamento de Teatro) 63, 90, 91–2, 95, 113, 124, 147, 157, 159, 189, 271–2, 338–9, 341, 343
Escola d'Art Dramàtic Adrià Gual (EADAG, theatre school) 198, 277, 310, 313, 314, 315, 335
Espert, Núria (actor, director) 123, 239, 271, 273, 280, 284–6, 333, 344, 355, 365, 367, 376
Esplandiú Peña, Juan (censor) 112
Espriu, Salvador (playwright, poet) 191, 310
Esteban Romero, Andrés Avelino (censor) 112, 114, 147, 149–50, 227, 228, 351, 356–8
Estévez, Mayca (actor) 124
Estremera, Antonio (playwright) 44, 441, 444
Euzkadi *see* Basque theatre
evasion of censorship xxxiii, xxxiv, 140–1, 180, 182, 189, 296–8, 314, 317, 323, 331, 335
exile xxxiv, 30, 76, 85, 95, 168, 191, 249, 265, 276, 278, 323, 332

F
Fàbregas, Xavier (playwright, critic) 313
Facio, Ángel (director) 281, 414, 423

Falange (FET y de las JONS, political organisation) xxiii, xxxii, xxxiii, 21, 62, 75, 88–93, 95–6, 98–9, 101, 111, 126, 130, 143, 144, 151, 156–60, 162, 164, 172, 174, 175, 179, 181, 214, 216, 218, 251, 258, 276, 311, 332, 338–9, 340, 349, 385, 387, 390, 407–9
Falcón, César (director, playwright) 55, 61–2
Falcón, Irene (director, playwright) 55, 62
Fanjul, Juan Manuel (Fiscal del Reino) 397
Fascism (Italian) 88, 90, 115, 160, 266
Feliu i Codina, Josep (playwright) 194
Fernández, Juan (censor) 148, 150
Fernández Cuesta, Raimundo Ministro (Secretario General del Movimiento) 217–18
Fernández-Montesinos García-Lorca, Manuel (producer, lawyer) 274–5
Fernández Palomero, Manuel (playwright) 12
Fernández-Shaw e Iturralde, Rafael (censor, playwright) 112
Fernández y González, Francisco (censor) 112
Fernando VII (King of Spain) 2, 233, 274, 406
festivals, theatre xxvii, xxxiv, 114, 118, 135, 140, 141, 179, 267, 271, 282, 295, 307, 310, 329, 381, 418, 419, 423
Filippo, Eduardo de (playwright, actor, director) 338
film censorship xxv–vi, 8, 23–4, 30, 34, 90, 92–3, 96, 100, 106, 111, 114, 113, 116–17, 119, 124–5, 128–31, 133, 134, 136, 139,

164, 349, 382, 383, 391, 393, 400, 401, 410, 415
Flavin, Martin (playwright) 57, 445
Foment de l'Espectacle Selecte i Teatre Associació (amateur theatre association) 195
Fortunet, Rosendo (playwright) 192, 446
Fos Fernando, Antonio (playwright) 382, 441
Foxá, Agustín de (playwright) 89
Fraga de Lis, Manuel (censor) 313
Fraga Iribarne, Manuel (Ministro de Información y Turismo) xxv, 123–6, 131–6, 139, 146, 150, 187, 213, 239, 274–6, 280, 301, 345, 349, 390, 409, 419
Fraguas Saavedra, Antonio (Jefe del Departamento de Teatro) 100, 171
Fraile, Medardo (playwright) 431
Fraile Clivilles, Manuel María (Director General de Espectáculos) 139
Franco Bahamonde, Francisco (general, Presidente del Gobierno) xxi, xxv, 1, 20, 35, 41, 58, 75–6, 88, 91, 93, 95, 98–9, 111, 122, 124, 137, 139, 141, 142, 144, 156–7, 158, 160, 173, 190, 237, 239, 242, 247, 252, 300, 303, 309, 312, 319, 384, 387, 402, 425
Frente Popular (political coalition) 21, 32, 47, 54, 57–9, 60, 66, 71
fringe theatre *see cámara y ensayo*

G
Gabinete de Enlace (MIT surveillance office) 123–4, 443
Galarza, Valentín (general, Ministro de Gobernación) 99
Galiana, Manuel (actor, director) 247

Galician theatre 6, 112, 190–1, 334, 409
Garau, Antonio (censor) 148
García, Manuel (playwright) 56
García, Víctor (director) 273, 286
García Adanero, Manuel (playwright) 17, 58, 445
García-Bernalt, José (composer) 187–9, 430
García Calvo, Agustín (playwright) 336
García Carrión, Marcelo (censor) 299
García-Cernuda Calleja, José María (censor) 138, 244, 251, 280, 288, 363, 384
García Escudero, José María (Director General de Cinematografía y Teatro) xxv, xxvi, 115, 124–6, 131, 133–4, 136, 146, 150, 151–2, 191, 231, 236, 240, 274, 276, 280, 329, 341, 346, 353, 369, 409
García Escudero y Fernández de Urrutia, Pío (censor) 115
García Espina, Gabriel (Director General de Cinematografía y Teatro) 111, 145–6, 200, 309
García Lorca, Federico (playwright, director, poet) xxxii, 9, 10–11, 16, 40, 48, 52, 53, 60, 62, 64, 66, 123, 125, 134, 142–52, 172, 207, 265, 270–6, 278, 282, 310, 397–8, 412, 430, 431, 434, 436, 437, 439, 443, 444
García Lorca family 270–3
García Pavón, Francisco (critic, writer) 151, 346
García Pintado, Ángel (playwright) 295
García Velasco, José Luis (censor) 112, 184
Gas, Mario (director) 278

Gil-Robles y Quiñones, José María (politician) 50, 78
Giménez, Carlos (director) 281
Giménez Arnau, José Antonio (Director General de Prensa, writer) 91
Gobernado, Antonio (translator) 360
Goebbels, Paul Joseph (German politician) 90
Gogo (theatre company) 220, 277
Goliardos, Los (theatre group) 351, 423, 437
Gómez, José Luis (director) 346
Gómez de Miguel, Emilio (playwright) 56, 444
González de Canales, Patricio (Secretario Nacional de Propaganda) 100, 102, 105
González del Castillo, Emilio (playwright) 16, 180, 431, 441
González Fierro, Luis (censor) 127, 223, 238, 359
González Márquez, Felipe (Presidente del Gobierno) 401
González Rendón, Aurelio (playwright) 65, 445
González Ruiz, Nicolás (translator, theatre critic) 104, 114, 122, 332, 340, 358, 374
González Verdú, Arturo (playwright) 57, 445
González Vergel, Alberto (director) 229, 244, 250, 252, 270, 346
Gordon Paso, José (director) 142, 145
Gorky, Maxim (playwright) 52
Grotowski, Jerzy (director) 295
Grup A-71 (theatre group) 312
Grupo de Teatro Realista (theatre group) 227, 235, 254
Grupo García Lorca (theatre group) 61, 64

Guerra González, Alfonso (politician, theatre director) xxiv, xxxv, 414
Guerra Gutiérrez, José (censor) 138
Guerra Sánchez, José Luis (censor) 138, 252, 289, 388, 394, 398
Guerra y Romero, Juan (military censor) 237, 261
Guerrero, Jacinto (composer) 44, 186, 430, 432, 444
Guerrero, María (actor, director) 156, 169,
Guerrero Zamora, Juan (director, adaptor) 344
Guerrillas de Teatro (theatre group) 34, 62, 69
Guerrilleros de Cristo Rey (right-wing militant group) 321, 400
Guillén, Pascual (playwright) 30
Guimerà, Àngel (playwright) 194
Guirau, Antonio (director) 284

H

Halffter, Cristóbal (composer) 227
Hampton, Christopher (playwright) 313
Heras, Roman (producer) 389
Hermandad Sacerdotal Española (Catholic association) 352
Hernández, Miguel (poet) 278
Hernández Morán, Carlos (censor) 394
Hernández Rivadulla, Virgilio (censor) 110, 161–2, 216
Hernández Tomás, Jesús (Ministro de Instrucción Pública) 65
Herrand, Marcel (director) 266
Herrera Esteban, León (Ministro de Información y Turismo) 139
Hickerson, Harold (playwright) 12
Higueras, Modesto (Director del Teatro Nacional de Cámara y Ensayo) 328, 341–2

historical theatre xxxiii, 18, 40, 41–2, 78, 89, 138, 140, 159–60, 165, 167, 170, 180, 209–10, 212, 222, 231–2, 237, 243–7, 248–9, 306–9, 365, 385–7, 398, 423

Hitler, Adolf (German politician) 60, 307

homosexuality, censorship of representations of 128, 140, 141, 242, 243, 336, 352, 355, 358–63, 415, 417

Hoz, Enrique de la (Subdirector General de Cultura Popular) 302

Hughes, Langston (playwright, poet) 334

Hurtado, Diego (translator) 337

I

Ibáñez Martín, José (Ministro de Educación Nacional) 111

Ibsen, Henrik (playwright) 334, 353

Iglesia, Celedonio de la (press censor) 9

immorality, censorship of 18, 49–50, 55, 56, 73, 116–17, 124, 126, 148, 172, 180, 199, 201, 250, 267, 280–1, 282, 344, 352–5, 358–61, 397, 411, 417

Imperio, Gracia (stage name of Emilia Argüelles Catalina) (actor, singer) 185

implicit censorship xxiv–v, 411

Independent Theatre (*Teatro independiente/Teatre independent*) 121, 135, 137, 140–1, 198, 210, 220, 265, 266, 277, 303–10, 315, 316–23, 328–9, 336, 341, 345, 348, 385, 391, 416, 419, 420, 422, 423

Independientes, Los (theatre group) 348, 356

inspections of dress rehearsals or performances xxviii, 88, 113, 119, 131–2, 137, 141, 180–1, 182, 184–7, 189, 192–3, 243, 273, 285, 291, 299, 302, 310, 313, 317, 320, 323, 388, 413, 417, 418

Institut del Teatre (theatre school) 303–4, 306, 310

Instituto de las Artes Escénicas y de la Música (INAEM, government department) xxx, 346–7, 401

Ionesco, Eugène (playwright) 125, 197, 283, 333, 334, 345

Isabel I (Queen of Spain) 159–60, 164, 306–8

Isabel II (Queen of Spain) 1–2, 6, 16

J

Jaquotot, Carlos (playwright) 12

Jardiel Poncela, Enrique (playwright) 44, 444

Jarry, Alfred (playwright) 141, 295

Jato Miranda, David (Delegado Nacional de Propaganda) 99, 113

Jiménez, Joaquín (playwright) 16, 186, 437

Jiménez Romero, Alfonso (playwright) 336

Joglars, Els (theatre group) xxxv, 314, 391, 402–4, 439

Juan Carlos (King of Spain) 141, 300, 302

Juan de Borbón (Conde de Barcelona) 160

Juan del Enzina (theatre group) 247

Julbe, Marita (Ministerio de Información y Turismo official) 313

Junquera Fernández-Carvajal, Juan (Gobernador Civil de Zaragoza) 147

Junta de Censura (nineteenth century) 4–5
Junta de Censura Teatral/Censura de Obras Teatrales 123–4, 126–8, 131–9, 150–1, 189, 213, 224–5, 238, 244, 246–50, 268, 273–6, 277–8, 280–1, 284–5, 288, 291–2, 296–7, 301–2, 304, 306–7, 309, 313, 340, 349, 353–4, 355, 363, 391, 396, 412
Junta de Defensa de Madrid/Junta Delegada de la Defensa de Madrid 29
Junta de Defensa Nacional 89
Junta de Espectáculos (Madrid) 29–34, 64–5, 73–4, 167
Junta de Ordenación de Obras Teatrales 139, 141, 380, 382, 389, 391, 394, 402, 403
Junta Superior de Censura 92–3

K
Kramer, Andrés de (writer, translator) 336, 362

L
Lady Pepa (*café-teatro* venue) 298–9
Lavelli, Jorge (director) 271
Lafleur, Javier (director, translator) 351, 356, 429
legislation relating to censorship xxi–ii, xxv–xxxii, xxxvi, 2, 3–9, 13–15, 17–19, 22, 26, 31–4, 44, 45, 46, 48, 50, 51, 54, 56–7, 64, 78, 91–2, 96, 97, 100, 112–14, 118–20, 128–38, 141, 160, 190, 222, 223, 234, 239–40, 244–6, 300, 345, 348, 349, 352, 355, 361, 363, 389–95, 415, 418, 428, 448–56
  Ley de Defensa de la República (1931) 13–14
  Ley de Orden Público (1933) 14, 17, 90
  Ley de Prensa (1938) xxv, 91
  Ley de Prensa e Imprenta (1966) 135–6
  Ley de Responsabilidades Políticas (1939) 94–5, 277
  Ley para la Reforma Política (1976) 389
  Reglamento de Policía de Espectáculos (1886) 7–8
  Reglamento de Policía de Espectáculos (1913) 8, 15–16
  Reglamento de Policía de Espectáculos (1935) 17–19, 25, 29, 400–1
Lenormand, Henri-René (playwright) 52
Leo XIII (Pope) 79
León, María Teresa (director, writer) 32, 55, 61–2, 69, 265
Lerroux, Alejandro (politician) 42, 49,
Linares Rivas, Manuel (playwright) 438
Linos, Daniel de (translator) 356
Liñán y Zofio, Fernando de (Ministro de Información y Turismo) 139
Living Theatre (theatre group) 295, 342
Llabrés, Pedro (playwright, songwriter) 184, 186, 187, 430, 432, 440
Llovet, Enrique (playwright, director, translator, critic) 333, 335, 336, 349, 432, 436
Lloyd Webber, Andrew (composer, producer) 141, 430
Lluch Ferrando, Fernando (playwright) 191, 442

Lluch Garín, Felipe (director) 62, 157–8, 339, 441
locations, banning of performances in specific xxv, 102, 132, 149, 184, 272–3, 310, 418–19, 421
Lope de Vega, Compañía (theatre company) 267, 269, 337, 341
Loperena, José María (director) 360
López de Lerena, José (playwright) 184, 432, 440
López de Saá, Federico (playwright) 49, 443
López Heredia, Irene (actor) 174–5, 199, 201, 203–4, 343
López Mozo, Jerónimo (playwright) 213, 295
López Rubio, José (playwright) 66, 332–3, 343, 346
Losada, Antonio (composer) 196, 442
Luca de Tena, Cayetano (director, producer) 339, 346
Luca de Tena, Juan Ignacio (playwright) 89, 362

M
MacDermot, Galt (composer) 189
Machado, Antonio (poet) 207, 275, 278
Machado, Manuel (poet, playwright) 62
Madres del Cordero, Las (musical group) 316–17, 320, 323, 479
Magariños Torres, Santiago (censor) 96
Magenti, Leopoldo (composer) 195
Malonda, Antonio (actor, director) 348
Mampaso Bueno, Alfredo (censor) 138, 239, 243, 247, 251, 280, 287, 290, 299, 307, 323

Màntua, Cecília A. (pseudonym of Cecília Alonso i Bozzo) (playwright) 196–7, 440, 442
Mañas, Alfredo (director) 274, 276
Marceau, Félicien (playwright) 358
Margallo, Juan (actor, director, playwright) xxxiv, 316–23, 435
María Cristina de Habsburgo-Lorena (Queen of Spain, wife of Alfonso XII) 11
María Cristina de Borbón-Dos Sicilias (Queen Regent of Spain) 2
Marín Melià, Francisco (playwright) 191, 439
Marqueríe, Alfredo (critic, translator) 235, 283, 333, 340, 353–4
Marquina, Eduardo (playwright) 35, 40, 52, 157, 159, 430, 444
Marsillach, Adolfo (actor, director, translator) 257, 288, 304, 333, 339, 341, 346–50, 355–6, 368
Martín Elizondo, José (playwright) 336
Martín-Gamero, Adolfo (Ministro de Información y Turismo) 139, 303
Martín Recuerda, José (playwright) xxxiii, 208–11, 214–15, 222, 225–6, 242, 247–9, 433, 435, 436, 438, 440
Martínez García, Francisco (censor) 394
Martínez Mediero, Manuel (playwright) 295, 383, 398, 423, 441
Martínez Ruiz, Florencio (censor) 127, 138, 240, 274, 279, 290, 291, 293, 301, 306, 307, 319, 347, 355, 362
Martínez Suárez, Emilio (producer) 433

Martínez Trives, Trino (director, translator) 333
Masferrer i Cantó, Santiago (director) 60
Mateos Martín, Pilar (censor) 394
Maugham, William Somerset (playwright, novelist) 338
Maura, Honorio (playwright) 43–4, 76, 81–5
Mayans Jofre, Francisco José (Director General de Teatro y Espectáculos) 430
Mayral, José Luis (playwright) 49, 445
Membrives, Lola (actor, producer) 177, 199–203
Mena Pérez, Vicente (playwright) xxxii, 51, 78–80, 85, 444
Méndez Herrera, José (translator) 344
Miaja, José (general, Presidente de la Junta de Defensa de Madrid) 73
Mier, Fernando (censor) 138, 252, 301–2, 389
military censorship xxxiii, xxxv, 8–9, 88, 215, 217, 237, 257–61, 269, 402–4
Millán-Astray, Pilar (playwright) 40, 52, 81–2, 85, 161, 442, 443
Miller, Arthur (playwright) xxxv, 207, 329, 337, 342–3, 353
Miralles, Alberto (playwright, director) 295, 303–9, 398–9, 425, 431, 435, 441
Miranda, Julio G. (playwright) 56, 444
Mirlas, León (translator) 344
Misiones Pedagógicas (Republican cultural initiative) 39–40, 67, 83
Molière (stage name of Jean-Baptiste Poquelin) (playwright) 197, 339, 346, 349, 436

Mollá, Juan (playwright, composer) 186, 437
monarchy, representation of 14, 39, 47, 160, 166, 168, 237, 244–5, 266, 300, 389
Monleón, José (director, critic, translator) xxiii, xxviii, 135, 229, 333, 342, 365, 367, 413–14, 422, 424, 429
Montes Agudo, Gumersindo (censor) 100, 143, 144, 146, 167, 170–2, 176, 178–9, 214, 216, 219, 231, 237, 256, 258, 268, 270, 271
Morales, María Luz (censor) 127
Morales de Acevedo, Emilio (censor) 112, 113, 160, 184, 271, 283, 350, 351
Morante Borrás, Jesús (playwright) 162, 439
Moreno, Armando (actor, producer) 280–1, 365, 367, 429
Moreno, Manuel de Jesús (playwright) 51, 443
Moreno Reina, José (censor) 138, 251
Mostaza Rodríguez, Bartolomé (censor) 100, 114, 127, 146, 151, 214, 216, 232, 238, 256, 268, 274, 282
Moscardó, José (general) 76, 257, 385
Movimiento Nacional (political movement) 88, 94, 97–9, 111, 130, 143, 160–3, 174, 193, 217, 300, 308, 311, 392
Muelas Pérez de Santa Coloma, Federico (censor) 124, 128, 138, 290, 301, 317, 318, 355
Muñiz, Carlos (playwright, censor) xxxiii, 123, 127, 208–11, 213–14, 222–8, 232–4, 242, 244–5,

249, 255, 428, 429, 431, 437, 440, 443
Muñoz Fontán, José (Director General de Cinematografía y Teatro) 115
Muñoz Román, José (playwright) 16, 180–4, 430, 431, 441
Muñoz Seca, Pedro (playwright) 18, 35, 45–8, 76, 81–5, 165–7, 243, 438, 442, 444, 445, 447
music censorship 72, 93–4, 95–6, 119–20, 185, 225, 313, 415
Mussolini, Benito (Italian politician) 60, 90, 266
Mussot, Luis (playwright) 60, 66–7, 445

N

Narbona González, Francisco (censor) 112, 179
Narros, Miguel (director) 281, 346, 360
National-Catholicism 32, 89, 117, 129, 157–8, 163–4, 190, 332, 408–11
Navas, José Ricardo (playwright) 72, 446
Nazism 78, 90–1, 158, 168, 225, 234, 259
negotiation with censors xxviii, xxx, xxxiii, xxxiv, 47, 69, 132, 210, 211, 218, 227, 232, 245, 289, 319, 328–9, 341, 347, 362, 416, 418
New Spanish Theatre (*Nuevo teatro español*) xxxiv, 294–8, 303, 310, 399
Nieva, Francisco (playwright) 282, 289–94, 348, 383, 412, 434, 435, 439, 445
normas de censura (1963–4) 128–32, 137, 139, 150, 188, 287–8, 301, 307, 308, 312, 385

Nosotros (theatre group) 55, 60–1, 327
Notario Bodelón, Paloma (censor) 394
nudity, censorship of 48, 181, 243, 278, 294, 360–1, 368, 382–3, 398, 443
Nueva Escena (theatre group) 29, 61, 67, 69
Nuevo Teatro Experimental (theatre group) 298

O

obscenity, censorship of 25–6, 129, 131, 138, 245, 287, 362, 382
O'Casey, Seán (playwright) 334, 337, 353, 359, 364, 432, 436
Oficina Nacional Permanente de Vigilancia de Espectáculos 116
Oliver, Federico (playwright) 52,
Oliver, Joan (playwright) 310–11, 440, 446
Ollé, Joan (playwright, director) 385–7, 441
Olmo, Lauro (playwright) xxxiii, 123, 135, 208–9, 211–12, 222–5, 228–31, 239–43, 247–52, 381, 417, 429, 430, 432, 433, 434, 435, 438, 441, 446
Olmo, Teresa del (actor) 189–90, 383, 400
O'Neill, Eugene (playwright) 207, 329, 342, 344
Opus Dei (Catholic organisation) 120, 138, 307, 335, 349
Orizana, Gabriel de (pseudonym of Nazario González Ramos, playwright) 75, 158, 429
Orriols, Álvaro (playwright) 16, 39
Ortiz Muñoz, Francisco (censor) 100, 110, 180
Ortiz Martínez, José María (Jefe de la Sección de Teatro) 105,

110–11, 115, 126, 143, 146, 168, 202, 217, 219, 227, 235, 240, 244, 302, 317, 323, 391, 394, 399
Ortiz Muñoz, Luis (censor) 110–11
Osborne, John (playwright) 208, 333
Osuna, José (director) 223, 233, 267
Ovejuna Inia, Nonato (pseudonym of Antonio Juan Onieva, playwright) 52, 443, 445

P
Palazón, J. (censor) 99, 178
Pàmies, Ramon (playwright) 193, 446
Paradas, Enrique (playwright) 16, 186, 437
Paraíso, El (theatre group) 146–7
Pardo, Antonio (censor) 128, 314
Parramon, Josep (playwright) 385–8, 441
Partido Comunista de España (PCE, communist party) 21, 31, 33, 61–2, 65, 74, 124, 207, 212, 218–19, 246, 254, 366
Partido Socialista Obrero Español (PSOE, socialist party) 17, 21, 22, 26, 33, 47, 49, 56–7, 390, 400–1
Paso Díaz, Antonio (playwright) 12, 49, 160, 165, 443
Paso Gil, Alfonso (playwright) 123, 145, 415–16, 431
Paso y Cano, Antonio (playwright) 35, 165
Pastor Bela, Antonio (censor) 100
pastorets (Catalan Nativity plays) 192–3, 446
Paul VI (Pope) 382
Pedrolo, Manuel de (playwright) 123, 310–12, 388–9, 434, 440, 446

Pemán, José María (playwright, poet, adaptor, politician) 35, 41–2, 44, 62–3, 75, 89, 122, 123, 131, 156–7, 159, 214, 317, 332–3, 340, 353, 444
penal code 7, 15, 97, 392–3, 395–7, 400
Peña y Giménez, Pedro (playwright) 434
Pérez de Echenique, Francisco (playwright) 140
Pérez de la Ossa, Huberto (director, translator) 339, 343
Pérez de León, Luis (playwright) 72, 430
Pérez Fernández, Pedro (playwright) 45, 442
Pérez Galdós, Benito (novelist, playwright) 64
Pérez Lugín, Alejandro (novelist) 32, 438
Pérez Puig, Gustavo (director) 254, 257
Pérez Sierra, Rafael (Director General de Teatro y Espectáculos) 388, 390
Peris Celda, Josep (playwright) 71
Perpiñán, Rafael (playwright) 58
Pipironda, La (theatre group) 213, 246
Piscator, Erwin (director) 335
political theatre xxii–iii, 55–72, 75–6, 157–65, 207–11, 214–22, 226–31, 234–42, 243–9, 251, 253, 254, 298, 348, 376
Pons, Ventura (film and theatre director) 311, 313
posibilismo/imposibilismo (strategy for dealing with censorship) 125, 210–12, 219, 227–8, 243, 258, 289, 331, 333, 338, 341–3, 362, 369
Pou, Josep Maria/José María (actor, director) 132, 346

Prego de Oliver, Adolfo (censor) 127, 224
press censorship xxxv–vi, 9, 89, 91, 99–100, 114, 135, 145–6, 193–4, 202, 204, 226, 253, 389, 408, 415
Priestley, John Boynton (playwright, novelist) 339
Prieto, Indalecio (politician) 49
Prieto, Miguel (director, stage designer) 55, 60–1, 68, 84
Primo de Rivera, José Antonio (politician) 175
Primo de Rivera, Miguel (general, Presidente del Consejo de Ministros) 1, 8–13, 16, 87, 237, 407
prizes, links with censorship xxvii, 113–14, 118, 112, 295, 309, 395, 419
propaganda and censorship xxxii, 1, 31, 71, 87–111, 115, 407–8, 419
provincial censorship offices xxix, 1, 2, 8, 24, 91, 96, 99–102, 106, 112–13, 119, 131, 137, 184–7, 197–8, 202–4, 233, 236, 237, 258, 271–2, 279, 313, 319, 350, 389, 417
Puerto Rican Traveling Theater (theatre group) 302
Puigserver, Fabià (theatre designer) 273

Q

Quart 23 (theatre group) 246
Queipo de Llano, Gonzalo (general) 60, 68
Quintero Ramírez, Antonio (playwright, composer, songwriter) 30, 75, 89, 165, 167, 439
Quinto, José María de (director) 135, 142, 145–6, 227, 254, 355, 360
Quiroga, Manuel (composer) 75

R

Rado, James (actor, playwright, director, composer) 189
Ragni, Gerome (actor, singer, playwright) 189
Ramos de Castro, Francisco (playwright) 48–9, 443, 445
Rancière, Jacques (theorist) xxv, 421–2
Rattigan, Terence (playwright) 197
Real Escuela Superior de Arte Dramático (RESAD, theatre school) 290, 346, 390
Realist Generation (*Generación Realista*) xxvi, xxxiii–iv, 207–54, 262, 295, 298, 334, 414
Regás, María Luz (translator, playwright) 362
Regàs, Xavier (playwright, director, translator) 197, 446
Regidor Arribas, Ramón (censor) 394, 398
Reguera Guajardo, Andrés (Ministro de Información y Turismo) 141, 301, 380
regulations for theatre (*see* legislation)
Republic (First) 1, 6
Republic (Second) xxi–iii, xxvi, xxx–iv, 1, 9, 11, 13–35, 38–74, 78, 84–5, 87–9, 91, 94–6, 124, 142, 159, 161, 165–9, 172–3, 180, 190, 198, 211, 239, 241, 247, 265–6, 270, 274, 276, 278, 310–11, 327, 383, 384, 407–8, 415
revista (theatrical genre) xxxi, xxxiii, 12, 16–19, 26, 28, 33, 35, 40, 44, 48–51, 71, 76, 95, 104, 105, 116, 119–20, 126, 132, 155, 179–90, 225, 317–18, 383, 415–17, 422
revolution (of 1868) 6
Reyna Medina, Guillermo Salvador de (censor) 100, 112, 169

Riaza, Luis (playwright) 141, 295, 336, 391, 438
Rica, Carlos de la (playwright, poet) 336
Rice, Tim (playwright) 141, 430
Ridruejo, Dionisio (Director General de Propaganda, poet) xxiii, 63, 91–3, 99–100, 122, 124, 213, 338, 447
Rivas Cherif, Cipriano de (director) xxii, 16, 40, 52, 144, 265, 339
Robles Piquer, Carlos (Director General de Cultura Popular y Espectáculos) 136, 139, 236, 275, 286
Rocamora Valls, Pedro (censor) 138
Roda Pérez, Frederic (director) 446
Rodero, José María (actor) 218
Rodríguez Buded, Ricardo (playwright) 414
Rodríguez Méndez, José María (playwright) xxxiii, 208–13, 222, 229, 231–2, 236–7, 245–7, 249, 298, 326, 381, 398, 414, 428, 429, 432, 434, 436, 437, 439, 440
Roig i Llop, Tomàs (writer, amateur theatre promotor) 196
Romero Andrés, Carmelo (censor) 138, 394, 397, 399
Romeu, E. (censor) 110, 112, 199–200
Romeu, Pepe (pseudonym of José Rizo Navarro, playwright) 97, 432
Ros y Pardo, Samuel (censor) 95–6, 159
Rosillo, Ernesto (composer) 184, 196, 437, 440
Roy Hart Theatre (theatre group) 140
Ruibal, José (playwright, director) 282, 295, 297, 298–303, 381, 399, 433, 436, 438, 446
Ruiloba Palazuelos, Francisco (censor) 99
Ruiz Martínez, Vicente Amadeo (censor) 138
Rusiñol, Santiago (playwright) 194

S
'S' rating 394, 401
Sagarra, Josep Maria de (playwright, poet) 191, 194, 195
sainete (theatrical genre) 40, 44, 160–1, 207
Sainz, Tina (actor, director) 247
Sainz de Robles y Correa, Federico Carlos (censor, playwright, critic, translator) 226, 333, 335, 346, 439
Salas Pombo, Diego (Gobernador Civil de Valencia) 146–7
Salazar Ruiz, Rafael (censor) 375,
Saliquet Zumeta, Andrés (general) 157
Salom, Jaime (playwright, translator) 333, 334, 363, 383
Salvat, Ricard (director) 246, 277–8, 310, 313, 314, 334–5, 365, 368
Sánchez, Emilio (playwright) 140
Sánchez Bella, Alfredo (Ministro de Información y Turismo) 136–9, 301, 345
Sánchez Barbudo, Antonio (writer, critic) 82–5
Sánchez Godínez, Julio (playwright) 57, 445
Sánchez Pedreño, Josefina (director) 228
Sánchez Ventura, José María (Alcalde de Zaragoza) 201–2

Sancho Izquierdo, Miguel (Rector de la Universidad de Zaragoza) 201–3
Sartre, Jean-Paul (playwright) xxxv, 126, 134, 208, 217, 255, 334, 336, 347, 355, 358, 364, 366–7, 433, 435, 438
Sastre, Alfonso (playwright, translator) xxxiii, 123, 125, 135, 145, 208, 210, 215–21, 222, 227, 234–6, 249, 253, 254–62, 282, 333, 347, 355, 364, 366–7, 381, 431, 432, 433, 434, 435, 436, 437, 438, 439
Segú, Pedro (Director General de Espectáculos) 139
self-censorship xxv–viii, 28, 169, 268, 290, 294, 308, 340–1, 344, 387, 414
Sender, Ramón (playwright) 29, 55, 60, 67–8, 430
Serrallonga, Carme (translator) 365, 436
Serrano Suñer, Ramón (Ministro de Gobernación) 91, 99, 124
set design, censorship of xxviii, 119, 151, 186, 187, 286, 336, 352, 359, 416
Schaffer, Peter (playwright) 361
Shakespeare, William xxxv, 191, 197, 332, 334, 336, 339–40
Shaw, George Bernard (playwright) 359, 440
silencio administrativo (administrative silence) 131, 216, 235, 237, 269, 281, 287, 303, 323, 393
Silva Aramburu, José (playwright) 32
Sindicato de la Industria del Espectáculo (SIE, CNT trade union) 22–3, 26, 27
Sindicato Español Universitario (SEU, Francoist students' union) 221, 254, 256, 257, 258, 376
Sindicato Nacional del Espectáculo (Francoist trade union) 95, 113, 143
Sindicato Único de Espectáculos Públicos (CNT trade union) 22, 25, 72
Solana Madariaga, Javier (Ministro de Cultura) 400
Solano, Luis Felipe (playwright) 158–9, 433
Soler, Frederic (playwright) 194
Soler Chamizo, Manuel (playwright) 51, 445
Soler Leal, Amparo (actor) 227, 360
Soria Heredia, Florentino (censor) 124, 127, 138, 244, 246, 285, 290, 299, 306, 308, 317, 318, 362, 365, 366, 367
Staehlin, Carlos María (censor) 127, 224
state of exception 136, 221–2, 280, 286, 303, 304–6, 412
Strindberg, August (playwright) 334
Suárez González, Adolfo (Presidente del Gobierno) 88, 141, 288, 301, 380, 384, 389–90, 397
Suevos Fernández, Carlos (censor) 128, 300
Suevos Fernández, Jesús (Director General de Cinematografía y Teatro) 115
Sunyer Roig, María Nieves (censor) 127, 138, 300
symbolism xxxiv, 210, 220, 231, 287, 295–8, 300, 312, 336, 388, 399, 423
Synge, John Millington (playwright) 353–4, 432

T

Tábano (theatre group) xxxiv, 140, 316–23, 381, 433, 435
Talía (theatre group) 278
Taller 1 (theatre group) 318
Tamayo, José (director) 231, 267–9, 337, 341–2, 346, 353, 376, 414
Tartana, La (theatre group) 315
Tarumba, La (theatre group) 55, 60
taste, as censorship criterion 50, 71, 129, 138, 140, 182, 186–7, 190, 223–5, 230, 238, 242–3, 244, 289, 353, 358–9, 409
Teatre Experimental Català (theatre group) 311
Teatro 80 (theatre group) 309
Teatro Ambulante de Campaña (theatre group) 63
Teatro ARA (theatre group) 284, 353
Teatro de Agitación Social (theatre group) 254
Teatro de Arte y Propaganda (theatre group) 62, 69
Teatro de Cámara de Madrid (theatre group) 345
Teatro de Guerrilla (theatre group) 62
Teatro Español (state-run theatre) 29, 39, 42, 53, 61, 64, 65, 69,72, 74, 143, 157, 158, 159, 267, 328, 337, 339–41, 348
Teatro Español Universitario (student theatre group, or broader network of student companies overseen by SEU) 135, 214, 224–5, 234, 258, 259, 328, 346, 364
Teatro Estudio de Madrid (theatre group) 346
Teatro María Guerrero (state-run theatre) 40, 95, 113, 127, 157, 159, 214, 236, 254, 257, 268, 292, 302, 328, 339, 341, 343–6, 360, 370, 372, 376, 341, 342
Teatro Nacional de Cámara y Ensayo (official theatre company) 118, 127, 225, 284, 287, 317, 328, 348, 359
Teatro Nacional de la Falange 157, 339
Teatro Nacional Universitario (theatre company) 370
Teatro Popular (theatre group) 58, 60, 66–7
Teatro Popular Keyzán (theatre group) 124
Teatro Popular Universitario (theatre group) 254, 257
Teixidor, Jordi (playwright, director) 322, 437
Tejedor Pérez, Luis (censor, playwright) 122, 128, 138, 244, 251, 319, 387, 389
Tertulia Teatral (theatre group) 147
Thomas de Carranza, Enrique (Director General de Cultura Popular y Espectáculos) 189
Tirso de Molina (pseudonym of Gabriel Téllez, playwright) 52
Tomás, Mariano (playwright) 159, 434
Torrado, Adolfo (playwright) 89
Torre, Claudio de la (playwright, producer, director, censor) 127, 341
Torrente Ballester, Gonzalo (censor, playwright, novelist, translator) 55, 62, 74–5, 114, 257, 333
Torres, Francisco de (playwright) 186, 437

Torres, Hilario (playwright) 56, 444
Torres López, Manuel (Delegado Nacional de Propaganda, Director General de Cinematografía y Teatro) 99, 115, 218
transition to democracy xxi, xxxii, xxxv, 1, 88, 124, 242, 249, 253, 278, 287–8, 302, 306, 338, 346, 351, 360, 361, 364, 368, 380–401, 404, 411, 412, 413, 425
translation and censorship xxxiv–v, 6, 132, 326–71, 446
Troitiño Sánchez, Carmen (director) 216, 345

U

Ugarte, Eduardo (director) 40, 66
Unamuno, Miguel de (playwright, novelist, philosopher) 53, 207, 265, 443
Unión General de Trabajadores (UGT, socialist trade union) 22–3, 64, 26, 28, 29, 33–4, 247
US influence on Spain 309, 329, 337, 342
Ustinov, Peter (playwright, actor) 338

V

Valle-Inclán, Carlos Luis del (son of Ramón María) 267
Valle-Inclán, Ramón María del (playwright) xxii, 16, 52, 53, 105, 208, 265–9, 282–3, 295, 310, 428, 435, 436, 444, 446
Valdivieso, José de (playwright) 90
Valencia (theatre in) 5, 23, 29, 32–3, 59, 71, 146, 162, 172, 178, 188, 191, 195, 196, 246, 268
Valenty, Rosa (actor) 294

Valverde, Salvador (playwright) 27–8, 75
Varela, José Enrique (general) 75–6, 158
variedades (varierty shows) 101–2, 313
Vasallo Ramos, Jesús (censor) 138, 244, 251, 288, 319
Vázquez Dodero, José Luis (censor) 127, 138, 188, 189, 222, 238, 247, 250, 251, 300, 359, 372
Vega González, Juan José (playwright) 336
Vega y Carpio, Félix Lope de (playwright) 42, 52, 158, 443
Vélez Noguera, José Julio (actor) 279–80
Vera, Victoria (actor) 278
Vichnievski, Vsevolod (playwright) 62
Villamar, Pablo de (playwright) 383–4
Villapecellín, José Martín (playwright) 56, 443
Villares Barrio, Manuel (censor) 147, 150, 271, 354
violence against theatremakers xxxiv, 48, 85, 94–5, 142, 147, 152, 166, 265, 270, 275, 311, 376, 381, 387, 400

W

Weiss, Peter (playwright) 126, 334, 346, 347–9, 433
Wellwarth, George (academic) 295, 358
Wesolowski Fernández de Heredia, Juan (censor) 394
Wilde, Oscar (playwright) 52
Wilder, Thornton (playwright) 207, 329, 339, 342–3, 442

Williams, Tennessee (playwright) 207, 329, 342, 343–4, 361
Wilson, Earl Jr 395

X
Xirgu, Margarita (actor, director) 52, 53, 64, 265, 277

Z
Zaro, Natividad (playwright, translator, actor) 359, 440

zarzuela (genre of musical theatre) 28, 32, 95, 120, 165, 189, 196
Zubiaurre Martínez, Antonio de (censor) 138, 232, 244, 246, 248, 251, 287, 288, 308, 315–16, 319, 385, 388, 394, 398, 399
Zuffoli, Eugenia (actor) 270